MOTHER LAND

BOOKS BY PAUL THEROUX

Fiction

WALDO

FONG AND THE INDIANS

GIRLS AT PLAY

MURDER IN MOUNT HOLLY

JUNGLE LOVERS

SINNING WITH ANNIE

SAINT JACK

THE BLACK HOUSE

THE FAMILY ARSENAL

THE CONSUL'S FILE

A CHRISTMAS CARD

PICTURE PALACE

LONDON SNOW

WORLD'S END

THE MOSQUITO COAST

THE LONDON EMBASSY

HALF MOON STREET

O-ZONE

MY SECRET HISTORY

CHICAGO LOOP

MILLROY THE MAGICIAN

MY OTHER LIFE

KOWLOON TONG

HOTEL HONOLULU

THE STRANGER AT
THE PALAZZO D'ORO

BLINDING LIGHT

THE ELEPHANTA SUITE

A DEAD HAND

THE LOWER RIVER

MR. BONES

MOTHER LAND

Criticism

V. S. NAIPAUL

Nonfiction

THE GREAT RAILWAY BAZAAR

THE OLD PATAGONIAN EXPRESS

THE KINGDOM BY THE SEA

SAILING THROUGH CHINA

SUNRISE WITH SEAMONSTERS

THE IMPERIAL WAY

RIDING THE IRON ROOSTER

TO THE ENDS OF THE EARTH

THE HAPPY ISLES OF OCEANIA

THE PILLARS OF HERCULES

SIR VIDIA'S SHADOW

FRESH AIR FIEND

DARK STAR SAFARI

GHOST TRAIN TO
THE EASTERN STAR

THE TAO OF TRAVEL

THE LAST TRAIN TO ZONA VERDE

DEEP SOUTH

MOTHER LAND

PAUL THEROUX

An Eamon Dolan Book
Houghton Mifflin Harcourt
Boston   New York   2017

Library of Congress-in-Publication Data is available.
ISBN 978-0-618-83932-2 (hardcover)

Book design by Greta D. Sibley

Printed in the United States of America
DOC 10 9 8 7 6 5 4 3 2 1

Mother, Mother, Mother, Mother, Mother, please. Mother, please, please, please. Don't — don't do this. Don't do this. Lay down your life with your child.

—Jim Jones, Jonestown "Death Speech," November 28, 1978

Great hatred, little room,
Maimed us at the start.
I carry from my mother's womb
A fanatic heart.

— William Butler Yeats

PART ONE

MOTHER OF THE YEAR

WEATHER IS MEMORY. Even the wind matters. The slant of rain can serve as a nudge, so can a quality of light. You don't need a calendar to remind you of personal crises. You smell them, you feel them on your skin, you taste them. If you go on living in the same place year after year the weather begins to take on meanings, it is weighted with omens, and the temperature, the sunlight, the trees and leaves, evoke emotions on every anniversary. The whole venerating world turns on this principle of weather-sniffing familiarity: all such pieties have their origin in a season, on a particular day.

That lovely morning in May we were summoned from our homes and told Father was ill. Mother — frugal even in emergencies — seldom called long-distance, so the implication of this expensive phone call was that Father was dying, that we were being gathered together for a deathwatch, but a peculiar ritual all our own.

You come from a family as from a distant land. Ours was an outlier with its own customs and cruelties. No one knew us, nor did we invite any interest, which is why I told myself that when the moment was right I would put my family — Mother Land in every sense — on the map.

There were eight of us children, and one of us was dead. Our parents were severe, from hard work and their fear of the destitution they had seen in the Great Depression. They seemed ancient to us, but as long as they were in our lives, no matter how doddering, we remained their much younger and unformed children — still children, still behaving like children, when Mother was a living fossil. In old age we embarked on our true, awful childhood — infantile fogies ruled by their triumphant mother.

The fact that two of us were writers was a nuisance to the others, and often an embarrassment, since writing had little value in the family's estimation. Being a writer seemed to this rabble a conceited form of laziness. I was blamed for what I wrote. I doubt that my writing will figure much in this family story, except incidentally when it becomes a problem for the rest of them. My concern here is the life I lived, while I was still a flight risk, before I left home, when I was about eighteen, and the continuation of it after I returned to confront death and failure and confusion, forty years later — the beginning and the end; not the books of my life, but the bookends.

When I was very young my mother, all smiles, used to tell me the story of a man who was shortly to be hanged. As a last request he said, "I want to talk to my mother." She was taken to the foot of the gallows, where her son stood handcuffed. "Come closer, Mother," he said, and when she inclined her head he made as if to speak confidentially to her and bit into her ear. As she screamed in pain, the condemned man spat out a piece of her ear and said, "You are the reason I'm here, about to die!"

Telling the story, my mother always folded her hands in her lap and nodded in satisfaction. Was she telling me that I was luckier than that man, and that she was not that kind of mother? Or did she think I was too confident and unruly. I didn't know why, though the story terrified me, because I often felt like that condemned man, someone who had to be punished, a child among unruly children, a potential ear biter.

Even sixty years later, that was how we behaved toward one another, too, childishly, with pettiness and envy. The taunting was endless, and years after, all these big stumbling teasers, bulking and bullying, late-middle-aged potbellied kids, balding, limping, belching with ailments and complaints, went on mocking each other, wagging their fat fingers. When we were older there was much more to mock.

Our childishness was so obvious that Floyd once said, "Who was that dreamy French philosopher who talked about the permanence of childhood: A motionless but enduring childhood, disguised as history. Nobody in this family has the slightest idea of his name! Is it Pecos Bill? Time is the arch-satirist! It was Gaston Bachelard."

Each of us children had the same father — he was solid, though he was often ill. He had the nervous anxiety of a compulsive saver. Frugality was his obsession. He would take a stick of gum and tear it in half, because chewing a whole stick was a needless luxury. He saved string, saved rusty nails and screws in a jar, saved planks of wood, saved everything. To the end of his life he retained a great fondness for the town dump, for the treasures it held. Going to the dump was an outing, and it made him smile as he set off, as though headed to Filene's Basement, certain to return with a bargain. He always took a barrel of trash, but he returned with half as much in possibly reusable items he'd found, scavenging on the heaps of smoking refuse surrounded by contending seagulls. The dump was also one of his meeting places — he had friends there; the other was church. A boyhood of poverty left him with something like a lingering illness he carried with him through his life and made him grateful to be alive.

Mother was unreadable and enigmatic, at times unintelligible, like a wrathful deity. Insecure in her power, she had an impatient and demanding cruelty that seemed to come from another century, another culture, and it was never satisfied. It made her a willful killjoy. Mother's contradictions, her moods, her injustice, her disloyalty, and her unshakable favoritism made her different to every one of us; we each dealt with our own version of her, we each had a different mother, or translated her, as I am doing now, into our own particular idiom. Fred might read this book and say, "Who is this woman?" Franny or Rose might object. Hubby might growl, "You ree-tard." Gilbert did not know the woman who raised me. But Floyd, the family's other writer, had more than an inkling, and when we talked he might raise a fist and say, "The Furies! The betrayals! The cannibalism! It's the House of Atreus!"

Mother's stories and confidences varied according to which child she was talking to. I should have guessed this early on, because her habit was to see us one at a time. She encouraged us to visit her separately and hinted that she loved to be surprised with presents. But the phone call was her preferred medium of communication; it allowed for secretiveness and manipulation; she liked the surprise of a ring, the waywardness of conversation, the power of hanging up. In seven phone calls — needy people are chronic phoners — she would tell a different version of her day.

It might be Fred, the eldest, the only child she deferred to and respected. He was a lawyer, with a lawyer's circumspection and the ability to hold two opposing notions in his head, neither of which he believed. She poured out her heart to him and he responded, "This is what you should do, Ma," and then the opposing view, "Or you could do this." Later he would act as her counselor, her defender, her explainer.

Or it might be Floyd, second oldest, whom she despised and feared, saying, "He never was right." He was a university professor and an acclaimed poet. Floyd used to say, "Art is the Eden where Adam and Eve eat the serpent."

Or the sisters, Franny or Rose, both of them bulky and breathless, like those anonymous startled eyewitnesses on TV who gasp, "I've lived here my whole life and I've never seen anything like it!" Both of them, teachers of small children, addressed everyone as if addressing a child.

Or Hubby, the brooding one, of whom Mother said, "He's so good with his hands." He was an ER nurse with a fund of gruesome stories.

Or Gilbert, her favorite, a diplomat, cheerfully oblique. "He's so busy, poor kid, but I'm proud of him." Mother never said no to him.

Or me, known from birth as JP. Mother was wary with me, blinking in uncertainty when I visited her and always eager for me to leave. She had wanted me to be a doctor; she had never liked my being a writer. When someone praised a book of mine she said, "Oh?" — as if someone had woken her by prodding her with a stick.

Mother spoke to Angela, too, through the power of prayer; Angela was the dead one. This infant girl had died at birth, her life snuffed out when she was hours old, yet she had a name ("She was like an angel"); she had a personality and certain lovable quirks and was part of the family. Angela was often mentioned as the perfect one, whom we should emulate.

"I'm sure you're aware that Paul Verlaine's mother kept her two stillborn children pickled in a glass jar on a parlor shelf," Floyd said. "Mother at least spared us that spectacle" — here he looked over his half-moon glasses — "of conspicuous foeti for the family to mourn."

But Angela was more obvious and present, much more available for advice and consolation — and guidance — because of her being a specter. Such ghostly ancestral presences often dominate the daily life of folk cultures and savage tribes, the dead and the living in agreement, the motif of "the grateful dead" you read about in Lévi-Strauss.

When Mother needed an ironclad excuse or a divine intervention, it came from Angela, who warned her of disloyal whispers or dangerous portents. Angela not only had a name and a personality, she also had a history. She was mourned every January 8, when Mother was paralyzed with grief and needed to be visited or phoned, in order to pour out her sorrow and the story of her difficult pregnancy during the war. Dead Angela was also necessary in helping to plump out the family, like the dead souls in the Gogol novel, making our big family even bigger, and somewhat fictional.

"We're family," people say with a confident smile, and I think, God help you.

The phrase "big happy family" does not invoke a congenial crowd to me; it suggests weird corporate disorder, treachery, greed, and cruelty, the nearest thing in civilization to a cluster of cannibals. I am generalizing here, using the words "savage tribes" and "cannibals" for emphasis and melodrama, and I know unfairly. Reading those words you are immediately put in mind of comic, half-naked, bone-in-the-nose jungle dwellers, bow-and-arrow people, beating drums and dangerous only to themselves in their recreational violence, and of course hollering and jumping on big feet and showing their teeth. Such people don't exist in the real world. I once lived in the equatorial regions where these belittled stereotypes are said to live, and I found the folk there to be anything but savage; they were subtle, chivalrous, openhearted, dignified, and generous. It was in suburban America where I encountered savagery in its nakedest form and discovered all the mythical characteristics associated with cannibals to be the simple observable facts of my own big flesh-and-blood family.

My father was the henpecked chief, my mother his consort. Dissatisfied and frustrated, we were a collection of relentless rivals, struggling for dominance, getting away with murder, with our own language and our peculiar pieties, grievances, and anniversaries, all of them incomprehensible except to the family members themselves. Also, though we were moody, merciless, and full of envy, we were always pretending to be the opposite. The solid seamless hypocrisy of religion was an asset: big families are nearly always attached to a fanatic and unforgiving faith. Ours was. You don't think happy or sad, you think of the fury of survival and of damnation and blame.

Such families hardly exist anymore in the Western world of tiny houses, limited space, and rising costs. The birthrate in Europe is recorded in negative numbers, hinting at shrinking populations and families. This is why the story of any large family is worth telling, because such families have been forgotten, yet the members of these complex and crazed clans have helped shape the world we know now, probably for the worse.

We were seen as a big happy family, and we smiled, for while we believed there was no such thing, happy was how we advertised ourselves, because we had so much to hide. Cynicism is another big-family attribute. Some of our desperation must have arisen from the fact that we knew our family was too big to survive, too clumsy to flourish, monstrous to behold, the grotesque phenomenon of another century, a furious and isolated tribe at war with itself, ruled over by an unpindownable presence — chairperson of the board, fickle queen, empress of Mother Land.

For most of my life I was encouraged to believe my mother was a saint — a little tedious and repetitive, but virtuous and loyal. Of course, she fostered this fiction, she worked at shaping it. And I was also influenced by her public image, for she was something of a local celebrity, a former schoolteacher respected by her students, active in church affairs, shrewd about money, insightful in matters of the heart, a pious busybody beloved by everyone. To the world at large my mother was a resourceful and hardworking woman who had raised seven children (and nurtured the memory of the eighth) and put them through college, the matriarch of a big happy family. She identified with wise and long-suffering mother figures in the news, especially the annual Mother of the Year, whom she never saw as a role model but always as a rival. She also compared herself

with the wise old women depicted in the comics — *Mary Worth* was one
— and the sensible gray-bunned soul in the early TV series *I Remember
Mama*. She also prayed hard to the Virgin Mary, and her piety contained
the presumption that she and the Mother of God had much in common,
except the quality of their offspring. She would have found an easy kin-
ship with Mother Hawa — Eve, of Islam — the mother of humanity.

I marvel at my naïve belief in her self-sacrificing persona, for when I
was growing up Mother was my oppressor, and I longed to escape her injustice. Dad was mild, but she goaded him to hit us with his usual means
of punishment, his razor strop. He feared her too, and so he obeyed and
became her enforcer.

"Get over here," he'd say. "You are no more than a fart in a mitten."

We could not protest. Mother always had the last word, and it was
usually untrue, based on the maxim, Why tell the truth when it is to your
advantage to lie? In her perversity, whatever she wanted you to believe
that day was the truth. She would do anything to get your attention — be
angry, upset, abusive, or gentle in a foxy way. Sick, too: she could make
herself noticeably ill so that we would listen to her. She might also offer
us presents, but they were the sorts of crudely whittled tokens that simple
folk exchanged in the jungle.

This woman was quite old before I could admit to myself who she really was. At the age when she would become an object of gratitude and
generosity, she seemed no more than a demented monarch. People used
to say to me: Your education, your reading, your travel, your long days
at a desk. No, not at all; my doing battle with mother's malign influence
made me a flight risk.

When someone mentions a mother who dotes on her children, who
works her fingers to the bone (Mother's self-regarding catchphrase), who
often invites her children to visit her or who visits them with presents — a
kindly seeming woman full of solemn, stern advice — I think, What on
earth does the sententious old woman want? She can only be wicked and
manipulative to be so persistent, and whoever trusts her has got to be a
fool. She will use you. She will eat you alive and shit you over a cliff.

Yet nothing was obvious to me about my family, the hidden tribe in
Mother Land, until Father died.

2

"THIS IS FOR THE BEST"

IN SEVEN PHONE CALLS, and a prayer to Angela, who had been dead for forty-two years, Mother said something different to each of us. "I think you should be here," she told me — I was languishing in Polynesia. To Fred: "As the eldest, it's up to you to take charge." To Floyd: "Dad's ill. I think he'd like you to be there." To Franny, "I don't think I can manage without you." To Rose: "Franny will need your help." To Hubby: "We'll need you to do the driving." To Gilbert: "Your father's been so difficult lately. I've honestly felt like hitting him."

The sterility of the hospital was like a preparation for his going — the cold place seemed like an antechamber to a tomb, his room as bleak as a sarcophagus. There was nothing in this unornamented place that I could associate with Dad, who was untidy, and like many frugal people not a minimalist but a pack rat. Dad was a hoarder and piler of junk, a collector of oddments, a rifler of dumpsters. His garage had the stacked shelves you see in a Chinese shop, and the same dense, toppling asymmetry. How happy he was to live near the sea, for he was also a beachcomber. "That'll come in handy someday."

He lay like wreckage under the complex apparatus monitoring his heart and lungs. Mother had remained in the corridor, signaling for each of us to slip in and greet Father. We had not been together this way for years, and toward evening we grouped around his bed to pray for him, looking like superstitious jungle dwellers muttering to the gods, the first intimation I had in many years that Floyd was right: we were at heart nothing but savages.

Father struggled to speak, then gasped on his ventilator, "What a lovely reunion."

We had barely recovered from the shock of seeing him so physically reduced when Mother ordered us all into the hospital corridor. Standing there, swelling with authority, she took charge and said, "We think it's best to take him off his ventilator. He's so uncomfortable."

Taking him off the ventilator meant: let him die. I started to object, but she interrupted.

"The doctor says he doesn't have long. I think it's best."

I said, "But he'll die without it!"

"We should respect her wishes," someone said, so softly I could not tell who it was.

Mother was glassy-eyed and seemed determined, not herself but a cast-iron version, so nerved for the occasion and standing so straight she seemed energized, even a bit crazed, as though defying any of us to oppose her. She was eighty-three years old, though she was so strong, so sure of herself, you would have taken her for a lot younger. I did not know her. She was a stranger, a substitute — fierce, deaf to advice. She was not the tremulous old woman who had suffered through Father's illness; she was someone else entirely, a woman I scarcely recognized.

My throat narrowed in fear. "Where there's life there's hope," I said lamely, and thought, "Uncomfortable" is better than dead.

"Don't you see this is for the best?" she said, in a peevish tone that implied I was being unreasonable. It was the tone she used when she said, "The TV is on the fritz again. Junk it."

Her implication was that I was being weak and obstructive. He ought to be allowed to die, she was saying, in a merciful way; while I was urging her to let him live, something she regarded as cruel and insensitive. And I was misinformed.

"What's the point of letting him suffer?"

She meant that by suggesting ways to let him live, I was inflicting suffering on him.

"Why don't we all go out for a meal?" Gilbert said in an easy, peace-making voice. "Soft-shell crabs are in season."

Franny and Rose stood on either side of Mother, less like daughters than like ladies-in-waiting, seeming to prop her up. Yet they were bent over, grieving in rumpled sweat-stained clothes.

"I think I'll stay with Dad," I said.

"We should keep together," Mother said.

"We could all stay with Dad."

She said, "Let's just leave him in peace," again in a tone that implied I was being uncooperative and cruel.

"Let's do what Mumma says," Franny said.

"It's not asking too much," Rose added.

Mother just smiled her challenging smile.

Fred said to Mother, "You should do what you think is right."

Floyd said, "I don't get this at all. This is like climbing Everest with Sherpas and traversing the edge of the crevasse, all roped together. Dad slips and he's dangling on a rope way down there, and we don't know whether to cut him loose or leave him or drag him down the mountain. And there's a blizzard. And we can't hear what he's saying. And where is Sherpa Tenzing? I wonder if Hallmark makes a card for an occasion like this."

Hubby said, "That's it, make a big drama."

"Oh, right, sorry, it's not dramatic. It's only Dad dying. I forgot, Hubby."

"Asshole," Hubby said.

"I'd like to kick you through that wall," Floyd said.

Franny said, "Let's not fight."

"You're all upsetting Mumma," Rose said.

"God knows I do my best," Mother said, not in her usual self-pitying singsong but defiantly.

We went to a nearby restaurant. Whipping off his glasses, Fred surveyed the menu and, as the eldest and bossiest of us, ordered the set meal for everyone. "Gilbert was right about the soft-shell crabs." We sat like mourners, though Father was four blocks away, struggling to stay alive. I looked at the faces around the table, Mother at the head of it between Gilbert and Fred, Franny and Rose close by, all of them watching Mother with fixed smiles, loyal, submissive, and squinnying at the rest of us. Hubby and Floyd sat with their heads down, looking torn.

"It's going to be all right," Franny said.

"This is for the best," Rose said.

I had heard such clichés my whole life, but I think it was there that I realized how clichés always revealed deep cynicism, rank ignorance, and a clumsy hostility.

Franny and Rose heaved themselves toward Mother and said, "Have some bread, Ma."

"Dad would have wanted it this way," Mother said. "All of us together."

I quietly excused myself, an easy thing to do, everyone at the table assuming I was going to the men's room. It was a trick I had used as a small boy in Sunday school, raising my hand. "Please, Father." And the priest in the middle of a pep talk would wave me on my way, thinking I was going to the bathroom, and I would go home.

I went back to the hospital and found Dad alone. The nurse told me that he had been taken off his ventilator and in place of the saline IV was a morphine drip. The fearful look in his eyes appalled me. He was like a terrified captive being dragged away to an unknown place against his will, which was exactly what was happening. I held his hand; it had the heated softness of someone very ill. The morphine dulled the pain, but it also weakened him and loosened his grip on life. I could feel resignation in his slack fingers.

The gauges beside his bed showed his heart rate in a jumping light, the pattern on the screen like that of a depth sounder in a boat tracing the troughs in an irregular ocean floor. The lights and beeps, too, all seemed to me indications of his life, but also his diminishing strength.

And there was his breathing. What had begun as slow exhalation became laborious and harsh, as though he was not propped up (which he was) but flat on his back, with a demon kneeling on his chest. His breathing seemed to give him no air at all. He fought to inhale, but the air stayed in his mouth, did not fill his lungs, and so he went on gasping, without relief, his staring eyes filled with tears. He was wordless with suffocation and fear.

The nurse stepped in and leaned toward the monitors.

I said, "Is he feeling any pain?"

"I can increase the morphine," she said, and I took this to mean yes, he was having a bad time.

"He seems to be struggling."

"Agonic breathing."

She said it casually, yet it seemed to me an awful phrase.

Father labored to stay alive, but I could see from the softening lines on one monitor that his strength was ebbing. Still, I held his hand. I had no sense of time passing, but at one point his breathing became shallow, and all the needles and indicators faltered and fell. Father's jaw dropped, his mouth fell open. I clutched his hand and pressed it to my face. I kissed his stubbly cheek.

Take me with you, I thought.

The nurse returned soon after. She quickly summed up what had happened.

"Are you all right?" she asked.

"No," I said.

I walked back to the restaurant and found that all of them had gone. Of course, four hours had passed. I called Mother.

She said, "Where have you been? You left the restaurant without telling anyone. You didn't even touch your meal. Fred and the girls ate your crabs. Everyone's here now. We're talking about Dad, telling stories. So many wonderful memories. Gilbert was just about to call the hospital to see how things are going."

"He's gone," I said.

3

DO YOU BELIEVE IN ROCK AND ROLL?

THE WAKE at the funeral home in Osterville was a muddle, tragedy and farce combined; all the distant relations meeting after a long time and making jokes in the form of greetings, remarking on how fat or how thin or how bald we had become. We were children again whenever we met, which was seldom—we hated and mocked all our cousins, saw them as the savages we could not admit to being ourselves. And the pieties about Dad. Then tears. Then they just hung around and leafed through the albums of snapshots that cousins had brought: children's marriages, grandchildren, vacations, pets and gardens, and pictures of prized possessions, cars and houses, the sort of ritual objects that boastful tribesmen would haul out at a clan feast. "His name is Chanler! That's Chad! She's Tyler! This is Blair!"

"Remember Jake?"

"How could I forget Jake and the cup!"

Young Jake who, as a reckless tot, had once eaten a Styrofoam cup, ran and hid.

Mother sat near the casket, enthroned as it were, receiving people, who paid their respects — and they too seemed like emissaries from other tribes, the big families who were our relations, several of them even bigger than ours. The look on Mother's face I recognized from the hospital: exalted, somewhat crazed, with a serpent's glittering stare. She sat upright, weirdly energized by the whole business.

More rituals, the funeral mass at the church, the platitudes, the handling of the shiny coffin, the sprinkling of holy water on its lid, the processions and prayers, all of it looking eerily superstitious to me, for I kept thinking of naked, gaudily painted people in New Guinea doing similar things, preparing the corpse of an elder and calling upon the gods to protect him and to hurry his soul into the next world. All this while, Mother was the single surviving dignitary, bestowing a kiss on the polished lid of the coffin and walking past the banks of flowers with a slight and smiling hauteur.

We drove to the cemetery in a long line of cars behind the hearse. Mother was in back seat of the lead car between Franny and Rose, Fred at the wheel, Gilbert next to him. Hubby and his family were in the following car, with Floyd and me, the flawed divorced sons, behind them.

I asked Floyd about the meal I had missed at the restaurant, when I had snuck out to be with Father.

"I didn't stay," he said. "I went for a walk. So did Hubby, but in a different direction. It was just Ma and the others, I guess. I wrote a poem about it."

"I think Ma was pissed off that I didn't stay. Like it was a test of loyalty."

Floyd wasn't listening. He said, "This is uncanny," and turned the radio up. It was "American Pie."

"Remember Granma's funeral?" Floyd said, and he laughed and shook his head.

One of the footnotes to our family history was that during the funeral procession to Grandma's burial, our cousin Allie, a goofball, had the radio on, and that same song was playing. He sang along with it, drumming on the steering wheel with his grease monkey's fingers, following Grandma's hearse. None of us ever remarked on it as an insult to the dead woman, only as an extemporized piece of hilarity. *Drove my Chevy to the levee . . .* At the cemetery, we plodded past gravestones to the hole of Father's freshly dug grave. What seemed like a diverse community of many mourners was a procession of mostly members of our own family — spouses, ex-spouses, children, grandchildren, great-grandchildren. The rest were distant relations. Hardly any were friends, for my parents were at the age when most of their friends were either dead or too ill to show up.

Perhaps this is the place to stress that a big family, like ours in Mother Land, does not welcome friends, and has no room for strangers; it is acutely uncomfortable when either friends or strangers penetrate the privacy of the household and become witnesses and listeners, privy to outbursts and secrets. Even outsiders who are frank admirers are kept at a distance — especially them, for there is much that must be withheld from them in order to keep their admiration intact. In the same way, a savage tribe is not just suspicious of strangers but overtly hostile. We were cruel to each other, but we were much crueler toward outsiders. Mother Land had that, and more, in common with Albania at its most Maoist, when it was closed to the world. You don't betray the tribe.

As Mother emphasized in her gossip, spouses were outsiders and all of them were mocked, always behind their backs. It could be awkward when one of them caused trouble, but it was worse for them when they tried to be generous — offered presents, cooked a meal, paid for something. "Imagine, forking out good money for this!" The present was laughable, the meal was a joke, and if they could so easily afford to pay for something, where was the sacrifice? But a dark angry spouse might inspire a measure of respect, if the person was strong, and especially so if the person was a crazy threat, because fear was all that mattered to us. At best, spouses were tolerated, but none of them inspired warmth.

At the time of Father's funeral, neither Floyd nor I was married, and our ex-spouses and my children were not present. I tried to imagine what my family whispered about my two wives, but I knew I would never succeed in capturing the malice; I would underestimate it, and no one would tell me to my face. In both cases, after we split up, they went far away from me and my big family. Perhaps they had always suspected that they were unwelcome, and maybe they also knew how they had been satirized.

The priest stood in the wind, his cloak billowing as he declaimed his lines. What he said seemed more like a formula of recited verses than sincere prayers. "Dust to dust, ashes to ashes" — we had all heard them before, and now it was Father's turn. Much of what the priest said was drowned out by the traffic beyond the cemetery wall.

Floyd wagged his head. "Remember, Grandma used to dig dandelions here?"

Not Grandma Justus, but Mother's mother, a frugal Italian, from another big, disorderly family. She dug the dandelions as if they were a delicacy that ignorant people spurned, and dignified them by calling them by their Italian name, *soffione;* she used them in salad and soup. A cemetery was a good place to gather them, because of the wall and the gates that kept dogs out.

Floyd was reminiscing, but he could easily have been trying to make me laugh. Getting someone to laugh at a funeral was one of the skills we had acquired as altar boys. Even Father's funeral was not so solemn an event that we wouldn't try to raise a laugh somehow.

Our heads were down. We were praying, or pretending to. Floyd was humming and murmuring, *This'll be the day that I die.* Yes, he was trying to get me to laugh by reminding me of "American Pie." I glanced sideways and saw that Mother's face wore an expression I had never seen before. Her pious posture, head bowed, shoulders rounded, was that of a mourner, yet her face startled me. The haughty look was gone, so were the glittering snake eyes. Hers was a look of relief, of weird jubilation, almost rapture, like someone who has survived an ordeal — weary yet triumphant, full of life and strength.

Father's coffin was not lowered. It remained covered with a velvet cloth. Dropping it into the hole while we watched was probably considered too dramatic and depressing — indelicate, anyway.

A last prayer by the priest, who I noticed kept mispronouncing Father's name — did this invalidate the prayer? — and we filed back to our cars.

Most accounts of family funerals end here — are in fact an ending. But walking away and leaving Father behind was a beginning, and it began right away, before we left the cemetery.

Mother had been walking slowly toward the parking lot between Franny and Rose, looking small and propped up by her two daughters, whose faces, exaggeratedly solemn, shook with each step, altering their expressions.

"Take your time, Mumma," they were saying.

"I got such a lot of guidance this morning talking to Angela. 'Be strong, Ma,' she said. You know how she is."

Seeing me about to join this recession from the grave, Mother turned, broke away from the girls, and looked herself again, fairly large and confident. She approached me, squeezed my hands hard.

"I want you to get married. Find someone nice. I want you to do it for me. Will you do that?"

She had that same deranged look in her eyes as when, in the hospital corridor, she had demanded that Father be taken off the ventilator and said, "Don't you see this is for the best?"

I didn't know what to say. She had power. The death of her husband — of Father — had energized her. The king was dead, and she, as queen, was absolute monarch of the realm. She was eighty-three but in every sense a new life was beginning for her — what would become a long one, too, eventful enough to fill a book.

"Maybe we should have a little get-together," Hubby said.

We were standing in the cemetery's parking lot. Spouses and children stayed a little way off, with the wincing looks of wary people expecting to be abused.

"Dad would have wanted it — something like a family dinner, like the other night," Hubby said.

"I don't think he would have wanted that," Rose said. "He hated restaurants. He always said they were a waste of money."

"You had your chance and you blew it," Franny said. "You walked out of the restaurant the other night. So did Floyd. So did JP. So what's the point?"

"It's up to Ma," Fred said.

We looked at her; for an instant she didn't look strong anymore. She made a theatrical gesture, touching her gloved hand to her forehead, and said, "I've got a splitting headache."

Franny and Rose rushed to assist her. Gilbert carried her purse. Fred fussed.

The rest of us went our separate ways. In the car, Floyd said, "Fred's such an asshole. 'It's up to Ma.'"

I called Mother that night, but she did not answer the phone, Franny did.

"She's tired," Franny said. "Rose and I are staying here a few more days to look after her. She's had an awful shock. Her nerves are shot."

Shawk . . . shawt, the accent of Mother Land. But it seemed to me that she'd had no shock at all, just a great reward, of health and strength, a renewed vigor and confidence. She had been proud at the wake, queenly at the cemetery, surrounded by her big family. Her look of power, the triumph of the survivor, had filled me with apprehension.

I called her the next day and she said she was feeling better, with Franny and Rose staying with her. Their presence seemed odd, for both of them had jobs teaching school, which they were obviously neglecting.

Some days later, when she was alone, she called me back: "I'm sending you a little something. There was money left over from Dad's funeral expenses."

Mother paid a neighbor to clean out Dad's shed, where the tools had been. The garage, too. All of Dad's accumulated possessions were junked. The paint cans, the jars of nails, the rope, the coils of wire, the rusty screwdrivers, the ball of string, the stack of folded brown grocery bags. The yellowed newspaper clippings went. They had been nailed to the wall, and some of them were very old: one said WAR IS OVER, another said PEACE AT LAST, the Boston papers from 1945. Some were newspaper pictures of us. Floyd shooting a basket in a high school gym. Fred bundled up in a hockey uniform, his stick poised, pretending to slap a puck. Me holding a trophy from the science fair. Hubby in a group of serious-faced Boy Scouts en route to a jamboree. Clipped-out mentions of events, such as band concerts and ball games. Others were snapshots. Of Franny and her terrified prom date. Of Franny when she was a nun, draped in her penguin outfit. Of Rose, a pretty child in a white dress, hands folded: first communion. Of Gilbert smiling across the bridge of his violin. Several were attempts at family photos, but they were amateurish and awkward — there were too many of us, the camera was cheap, we looked like a discontented mob.

Father's woodstove was ripped out of the living room. He had kept it burning until the night he was taken to the hospital. No one wanted the old stove. When it was moved, ashes spilled out, and the gray dust powdering the floor was a grotesque reminder of him.

"He never did clean it out thoroughly," Mother said.

I went back to the cemetery about a month later. Father's grave looked new and colorless. I planted some geraniums in front of it and a small pointed juniper on either side. I told Mother this.

She smiled in pity, as she always did when I made a blunder. She said, "He's not there, you know."

She sent me a check for five hundred dollars. I did not want it, and yet I did not know what to do with it, for the dark secret of receiving money from Mother so confused me I kept it to myself.

Franny and Rose were busier than ever. On their way to Mother's, they stopped off to see me sometimes, bringing me candy and donuts, the sorts of things they imagined everyone ate.

"We see her every Sunday," Franny said one day. Rose just smiled. They settled into the cushions of my furniture. I was fascinated by the way these chairs announced the danger of weight in the twang of their springs. "We know how busy you are. You don't have to come if you don't want."

Soon after that, each of them bought a new car.

"Mumma likes visits," Rose said. "You know how she is."

I said I did, but did I? Nothing was simple in Mother Land.

4

LOYALTY OATHS

TO THE WORLD — and our world was our small town, our neighborhood, our church, the schools we went to — we were an exemplary family. "Your folks are the salt of the earth," Father Furty said to me in a scolding way, lashing me by praising them. "Pillars of the community," he said another day. He meant that I was negligible and that my parents were loyal to him and God-fearing. His esteem for them was shared generally in our world. Ours was a bigger family than most, and the more admirable for its size. We were noted for our struggles, our uprightness, our decency, our respectability. Not prissy, not snobbish — we could be relied upon. We were good people. We were . . . yes, this is tedious in its litany of virtues, but bear with me.

Dad was hardworking, the owner of his failing business. He was a proud, fair man, devoted to his wife and children, from a large family himself, with a lineage that was both distinguished in its heritage (French Canadian and Native American) and obscure in its achievements. Yet the centuries of vagueness added to the mystique of the family name, which was originally Justice when they had lived in New France but became Justus when they percolated south to the United States. "My great-uncle Pierre spelled it J-U-S-T-I-S-S," Dad said. He loved explaining his name and, especially, saying the original in the French way, everting his lips like a fish, leaning forward, and slushily saying, "Zhoo-stees."

Dad's family had lived in North America for three centuries. They did not have an immigrant story, the romantic myth of a long sea voyage, a tale of hope and rewarded toil and transformation, that so many American families love to retell, to explain themselves. Only the name change was a clue to when Dad's family had arrived, though all birth records had been lost. On his mother's side they'd been aboriginals, squatting in the woods for thousands of years. Dad in his dumpster-diving had inherited their instinct for being hunter-gatherers.

"Grandma used to play with the Indians," Dad said, a way of hinting that she was an Indian. "She once saw Buffalo Bill!"

One of Dad's ancestors, Antoine Justice, helped found the city of Detroit, under Antoine de la Mothe Cadillac. But here I am myself romancing. The plain truth is that this ancestor, with our uncorrupted surname, was a deckhand in the French navy, recruited as a mariner because he had worked as a ferryman in his river town of Verdun-sur-Garonne, in the Pyrenees near Toulouse. He was not a native speaker of French but a provincial, speaking Gascon. During his first winter in Canada, in 1693, instead of moaning "*Le temps est très froid*" or "*Il fait froid,*" this much more effusive son of Gascony would utter something like, "*Dieu vivent! Fa pla fred a pr'aici.*" And, feeling far from home, would mutter, "*Soi pla lan d'enta ieu,*" rather than "*Je suis bien loin de chez moi.*"

Most of Antoine Justice's fellow soldiers would have been native French speakers from Normandy, so Antoine the Gascon would have been babbling to himself, on his own, establishing a family tradition, the first in a long line of odd men out. Meanwhile, he was bullying the natives and ultimately went native himself in the wilds of Canada, becoming a fur trapper and settling down to farm after he was discharged from the navy. The family inhabited their Quebec village for three hundred years. They were older than the oaks, older than the marsh grass that gave their tiny village its Iroquois name, Yamaska, place of the reeds.

Dad's family, like Dad himself, exemplified endurance and indifference. They had survival skills, but passivity had been bred into their bones. They had the aboriginal's hatred of change, fear of novelty, and suspicion of strangers. In their muddy boots they remained peasants, hearing about the French Revolution from afar, unaffected by it. When the harvests were poor they traveled from Canada to the United States and back, oblivious of the international frontier that the family had predated. They did not have a country, they had a family and a plot of land. Passports were unknown to them. They didn't read, they didn't vote. Slow, oblique, kindly, they had the virtues of vegetable growers and chicken raisers, never boasting, proud of having gone nowhere, still holding on, still mellow, still modest, with the farmers' habitual mockery of wealth, materialism, worldliness, and pretension. They did not hate the English, who had ended up defeating and colonizing them; they simply believed the English to be another species, incomprehensible, not quite human, comic in their ambition, and, when roused, the enemy. In Father's family, chickens and cows were currency; they recognized no laws but their own; they were entirely themselves, not wishing for transformation or any change. They couldn't spell. At some point, talking to a clerk in a registry office, speaking the name they couldn't write, Justice became Justus.

Mother's family was the opposite. They were turn-of-the-century arrivals from Italy, new Americans, with the immigrant tenacity of weevils: desperate, thin-skinned, active, sniping, hustling, competitive, clinging to the ladder and measuring each rung with money, cynical, crowding to prove themselves, wanting more and never having enough. They were natural jostlers and climbers and too ambitious to risk being truthful. They could easily have become a pack of criminals.

But, lacking influence and fearing the law, needing to obey convention, they were forced to believe and finally enact their own clichés, making their platitudes into deeds. They became education-minded, the newly bourgeois father nagging his kids to succeed — one as a civil engineer, another an entrepreneur, two girls as teachers, another a nurse, and the youngest fulfilling his spiritual role in the Catholic family and becoming a priest, Father Louie. Mother deferred to him, because of his vows, and she praised the memory of her father: "He was a saint." Before her marriage, Mother had been a teacher. She returned to teaching after Gilbert was of school age; he was in her first-grade class, her star pupil.

We were churchgoers. All the priests knew us and approved. "The family that prays together, stays together," Father Furty intoned from the pulpit. The good opinion of priests was like God smiling upon us, since the priests were God's envoys on earth, his agents and deputies. They had the power to absolve us of sin, they could recommend our souls to God, their intercession could save us from hell, they could get us into heaven.

Dad was in the church choir, and his sons were altar boys and acolytes. Franny and Rose spoke of becoming nuns. We were industrious and uncomplaining. I worked at the Stop and Shop bagging groceries, stocking shelves with cans. Fred worked for Dad, who hinted that Fred would take over the business. Floyd worked at a store that sold office supplies. Hubby had a paper route, and later, because he was the last child, even Gilbert took part-time jobs. The girls babysat the neighbors' kids. We were the model of harmony and industry, an ideal family.

Much of the credit for this went to Mother. She was seen as modest and thrifty, a nurturing, intelligent, practical, unflappable, and attentive homemaker. The Mother of the Year Award was not a joke. Though Mother never said so, she implied that not only could she qualify, she was much too busy being a mother to pursue it, and so deserved to win.

But wait. All of this, of course, was essentially false, either half-truths or outright lies.

What the world knew of us was untrue. We shut the door of our big, respectable-looking house and withdrew to the dilapidated interior of wobbly tables and uncomfortable chairs and dim lights, backing into it like rats protecting their nest, baring our yellow teeth, not just keeping the world out but actively engaged in the hopeless self-deception of keeping up appearances.

Our family secrets were much too horrible to reveal. Take Father Louie. To the wider world he was a figure of piety, but we knew him as a scold, a know-it-all, a foulmouthed teller of dirty stories, a braggart, and a tyrant. He was cruel, he was probably insane. We dreaded his visits. He drank bitter-tasting Moxie soda and chain-smoked Fatima cigarettes and pinched us hard, twisting his fingers in our flesh, and told us we were lazy and spiteful. He picked on Floyd, scolding him in front of all of us: "You still wet the bed. You're killing your mother! You'll never get married — you'll pee on your wife!" Floyd said he wanted to beat Uncle Louie to a pulp.

We hated our after-school jobs. Fred was ashamed of Dad's piddling shoe business. Floyd detested his boss at the stationery store and was forced to work there even on the day he won an achievement award at school, missing the ceremony. Because I worked nights at the Stop and Shop, I never engaged in after-school activities and seldom finished my homework. I usually stayed on when the store closed to help with restocking — a full carton against my chest as I jammed cans onto the shelves. I was fast; I knew how to use a labeler for multiple cans, pounding the prices in purple ink. I could slice open a crate of toilet paper with a box cutter without slashing any of the contents, round up thirty shopping carts at a go, and arrange heads of iceberg lettuce into symmetrical piles, but I could not hit a ball with a bat, nor could I catch a football.

We were not lazy, but we were spiteful. We were backbiters, sneaks, constantly quarreling. We were also ashamed of ourselves. And Mother's screeching tantrums were embarrassing. She seemed bewildered by the fact that there were so many people in the house, crowding her and wasting her time. "Kids wreck a marriage," Dad said — one of his saws, but he said it for Mother's sake; he seemed to enjoy us. The fact that Mother had given us birth was both her boast and her complaint.

Was her father — Grampa — a saint? I knew him as a mustached pontificator, seated at a sewing machine, biting thread off a spool and knotting it with his teeth, like an otter eviscerating a herring. He would lecture me on manners, all the while hacking at pinstriped cloth with a narrow slice of marking soap. Because he was a master tailor, he made his own suits, and dressed like a dandy, with a vest and a watch chain, always flourishing a big cigar.

Later, Floyd said, "Grampa looked like Alexander Woollcott," and raising his little finger, "Woollcott, the twinkie, dash of lavender, who said to Anita Loos on one memorable occasion, 'All my life, my greatest wish has been to be a mother.'"

Grampa was henpecked by his wife — moaning and moonfaced Granma, famous for her frugality, the dandelions she dug, the dented cans and day-old bread loaves she bought. She was also famous for her disapproval of her daughter's marriage to Father, whom she regarded as an innocent fool, and she made no secret that she believed his family, the Justuses, were barbarians.

Mother resented our presence; the very fact of having children seemed to her an intrusion. She complained of our noise, hated doing the laundry, and could not cook with any competence. She did not have the patience for cooking. More than that, she did not have the love. You need to love the people who eat your food; loving your diners, you are inspired and generous in your kitchen.

Mother seemed to relish her incompetence and challenge us with it. She made pea soup that was too lumpy to swallow; it was burned and scabbed on the bottom of the pot; those globs of ham fat floating on top were for flavor, she said. She made oatmeal that was too lumpy to swallow; it was burned and scabbed on the bottom and was usually served cold. I could not taste Mother's oatmeal without wanting to vomit. When she made spaghetti the pasta congealed into a sodden cable of twisted worms because Mother was too hurried to stir it. It, too, was lumpy, burned on the bottom, yellow oil slick on top from the greasy hamburger that made it Bolognese. She made kidney stew. This was for Father, whose own mother had made it. All of us dreaded kidney stew night: stringy innards reeking of cow piss, mixed with crumbly potatoes, undercooked onions, and canned peas. "You set a wonderful table, Mother," Father said.

Her money-saving, institutional, one-dish cookery was always served from a big black pot, which we ate out of fear of offending her. One night Mother took the lid off the black pot and served a sinister stew. I could not touch it. She demanded that I eat it all. Perhaps I suspected that she deliberately gave us these awful meals because she disliked us, and I refused to be a party to this hostility.

I said, "I don't like it."

Father said, "Eat it. There's plenty of things I don't like, and I eat them."

Mother glared at him: we were both damned. She never forgave him for this indiscretion.

"You can't go to school unless you finish your oatmeal," Mother would say, and I sat there as the oatmeal stiffened. Mother was stubborn, and she loomed over me until I choked down a few mouthfuls, the taste of it bringing tears to my eyes. Several of those times I was late for school, and I gave as my excuse, with more insight than I knew, "My mother's sick."

And peanut butter and jelly sandwiches on Wonder bread, marshmallows in big crinkly bags, something called Cheez Whiz on crackers, and Karo syrup spooned onto toast. All of these we prepared and ate on our own, and we told ourselves that we enjoyed them.

Our guilty secret was that Father had gone broke. His company went into liquidation, but he was not told until the day it happened. The declaration of bankruptcy is always a whisper. In financial failure secrecy is everything: the people who matter find out the worst when it's too late. American Oak was a leather company supplying cowhides to shoe manufacturers. Father had grown up in the stink of tanning hides, one of the smelliest businesses on earth. "Nothing like leather," he boasted. He was a connoisseur of shoe leather—pebble grain, top grain, cordovan, hand stitching, tooling, the tongue, the welt, the shank, the vamp. "That's where the steer rubbed against a barbed-wire fence," he told me once, showing me a scar on a thick hide. But now the company was done for, and the shoe factories of New England would soon become a thing of the past, as dead as the cotton mills, as hollow-eyed and decrepit as their decaying towns.

Father did not rise again. He was in his mid-forties, still relatively young, yet the world of ambition and achievement and fresh starts was a mystery to him. Money and profitable employment were ever-receding enigmas, partly wreathed in mystery, the rest in criminality. Dad was an innocent, and though he could be boisterous, talkative, and a resourceful storyteller with us, he was essentially a shy man. He had moments of theatricality, almost actorish behavior, often funny, sometimes bewilderingly submissive and melodramatic, as when, to placate Mother in one of her fits of anger at us, he would lift one hand for silence and say, "'How sharper than a serpent's tooth it is to have a thankless child!'"

In that period without income, he needed work, but he was not so much looking for a job as for a benefactor. He had been raised in a culture where work was scarce and a job was a favor. If he had a passion, it was to maintain his dignity, to go on looking respectable, for the sake of family pride. He scowled and went silent and obstinate when Mother suggested that a janitor's job was available at the church. Father was appalled—his natural piety made him innately anticlerical. And we were shocked at the prospect of seeing Dad in overalls, pushing a broom down the aisle, not so much because he would be suffering the indignity of it, but because we would be embarrassed at the sight of him.

He was soon saved from this ignominy. This man who knew everything about tanneries and leather and stitching got a job in a men's clothing store in the town square, selling shoes. Though he was a clerk, he had self-respect and a pardonable vanity—after all, he had fallen far—and went on dressing like a leather baron, in pinstripes, and using the word "haberdashery." I became so accustomed to his manner of speaking that I did not realize until afterward how his euphemisms arose from embarrassed concealment.

He never said he was tired; he was "bushed." And when he was bushed he said, "I'm going to hit the hay." When he saw injustice he said, "That burns me up." For emphasis he said, "to beat the band" and "for fair." His car was "the old bus," and when he sold it at a profit, "You could've knocked me down with a feather." He did not have children, he had "kid-dos." He was euphemistic in French, too, which he spoke with idiomatic fluency. When he got exasperated with one of his sons and was on the point of hitting him, he called him "*mo' psi' bonhomme*" (*mon petit bon-homme*, my fine young gentleman). He said "*clem*" the Quebecois way, for "*crème*," always "*clem à la glass*" for ice cream, and when we made a fuss or a mess he cried out with a word that exists in French Canada but not in France: "*Plaquoteurs!*" Bunglers!

When his business failed and people tried to cheer him up, he shrugged and said, with a Quebecois twang, "*Les gens heureux n'ont pas d'histoire.*"

His fall made me ashamed and frightened, and even as a child of nine —it was 1950—I pitied him for having to endure the banter and bad jokes of his colleagues, four or five ridiculous clerks, with their spurious expertise in the area of shirts and ties: "You can't beat a Hathaway shirt . . . That would look smart with a cravat . . . What you want is a weskit . . . French cuffs are a sign of class . . . That topcoat is too dressy." Father distinguished between a blucher and a brogue, spoke of wingtips and chukka boots, of foot anatomy, of the instep and the ball of the foot, and he might recommend a shoe saying, "Good arch support — it's got a steel shank. It's a ten eddie." He said that left and right feet were always slightly different sizes: "You're right-handed," he'd say, because a right-handed person's left foot was larger than his right. Though his job was menial, he brought to it insight and learning; he was as familiar with the human foot as a podiatrist. "What you need on that foot is some powder that's astringent."

"He's not an employee, he's an aesthete there," Floyd said.

Mother made him miserable with her moods. She sometimes reminded him that he was a poor provider, and he so resented her power, he took out his anger on us. He was helpless, another of Mother's desperate victims.

He was Mother's enforcer. He was a failure at business, yet as contented a clerk as Bob Cratchit. Mother knew the secret of his weakness, his pride in his natty formality of dress, his desire to please her, and so she exploited his insecurity. She moaned about us, whispered in his ear. She had the ability to rouse Father's wrath — he was irrational and violent when he was angry, and because of his passionate love for us, he became furious, nearly demented in his confusion, and hit us harder.

He knew how to console Mother, that the greatest consolation to her was for him to punish us, for it released all of her anger and demonstrated his obedience to her. Beating us was his act of loyalty. Father loved her. He had been loved himself; he knew how to love, to be merciful, forgiving, to show gratitude. He was able to calm his excitable woman — perhaps the only man, apart from her own father; he was able to make her feel secure. He knew her better than any of us.

And he was nothing like her. He was even-tempered, unselfish, he hated gossip, he told the truth, and he was fair-minded. By his example Mother often moderated her own behavior; though Mother still whispered and lied, Father kept her in check. From an early age, I could see that although Mother was by nature tyrannical, and that she dominated Father, and all of us, she feared the strength of his passivity. Her apparent power over him unnerved her. Really, she did not know what she wanted. In his submissive, beaten-down, uncomplaining way, Father was enigmatic. Mother never knew what was in his mind, so he was always the stronger one.

5

MR. BONES

AFTER HIS DEATH, whenever I got sentimental and took on a reminiscing tone and talked about how Dad used to read to me and encourage me, I realized that I was lying. Maybe it was a way of being kind to his memory, like "You look marvelous!," another thing he used to say. "Pretty as a picture" — seldom true. "Looks good enough to eat," he declared over Mother's gristly meatloaf. But then, generosity can often seem to verge on the satirical.

My father, apparently a simple cheery soul, seemed impossible to know. His smiles made him impenetrable. There he stood at a little distance, jingling coins in his pocket, waiting for someone to need him. A satisfied man, he had the sort of good humor and obliging manner I associated with an old-fashioned servant. "Glad to oblige!"

A smile is the hardest expression to fathom—you don't inquire, you don't even wonder. He must have known that. I never thought: Who is he? What does he want? He said he was happy. He would not have said otherwise, but though I believed him, there were things I didn't know. He lost his job when American Oak folded. Never mind, he found another one. Did he like it? "I'm tickled to death!"

He was so thoroughly nice it did not occur to us that we did not know him. He didn't drink, he didn't smoke. He never went out at night except to church. Bowling and the movies he abandoned after first becoming a father. He had few friends, no close ones, no confidants—he wasn't the confiding type. He wasn't a joiner. He was the insubstantial presence he wished to be, merely a voice, a man who lived in the house. Dramatic entrance, and then silence. A hush. Dramatic departure, and then silence again.

This all sounds harmonious, yet there was disorder, tension, and conflict in our household. It was crooked in the angular splinters of the woodwork, pulsing in the air, a disturbance that was deep, subtle, and without any voice, a noiseless bewilderment and uncertainty, the vibrant presence of low-pitched rivalries, and it was all masked by politeness or sometimes by hostile displays of affection. The quiet-seeming household is often more turbulent or intimidating than the household of the bully or the drunkard.

One of the unspoken conflicts in the house was the house itself, a constant reproach in the cabinets that failed to catch, in every creak of the floorboards, the peeling wallpaper, the stains on the ceiling like mocking faces, every draft that blew under the doors. All these awkward reminders. Mother's version of the story—the one that she wouldn't let him live down—was that having decided we had to move (at the time, four kids in a tiny house, with a fifth on the way), my father would go and find a bigger one. Mother was pregnant and busy, but she was also the sort of person who provoked us to make our own decisions, so that if we failed she could say, "Whose fault is that?" Deniability was a defense she mastered long before such a word was coined.

By directing Dad to look for a new house, she became the one to be propitiated: a scolding silence if it was a good choice, loud blame if it was a bad one. Dad was like hired help, the house hunter. "And it better be a good one."

Unused to spending large amounts of money, risking this big decision, Dad became more affable, more genial, than I'd ever seen him. It was sheer nervousness, a kind of helpless hilarity, like that of an almost ruined gambler at the blackjack table betting everything on the turn of a card.

He saw three or four houses. They were unsuitable. He liked all of them. Mother was vexed. This was dinner table talk: we were discouraged from speaking during mealtime, so we listened. "What's good about it?" Mother would say. "It'll be hard to heat," or "It's not on a bus line," or "That's a bad neighborhood."

One winter night Mother was in tears. Dad had seen another house he liked and was told the price. He was in the nervous, affable mood. He did not bargain or say "My wife will have to see it," or "We'll think it over."

He said, "We'll take it!" — with a sudden flourish of money that startled the seller of the house, who was a cranky old woman in a soiled apron.

That was my mother's version, in the oral tradition of the family history, the only version that was ever allowed. In a matter of an hour or so my father had seen the house and agreed to buy it. Another detail to his discredit was that he had seen it in the dark. Because it was January and he worked until five-thirty, he would have driven there after work, tramped through the snow, looked it over, and by seven or so it was a deal.

The reason for my mother's tears was that, anticipating his finding the right house, Dad had been carrying five hundred dollars in small bills around with him, and the papers he signed that very night (the old woman had them handy in the pocket of her apron) specified a deposit of that amount, nonreturnable.

"Our whole life's savings!" my mother cried, thumping the table. "How *could* you?"

Obviously, he'd liked the house and didn't want to risk losing it. He wasn't a bargainer, and he was pressed for time, house hunting after work. It was: buy the house, pay the rest of the money with a mortgage, or lose the deposit. "Our life's savings — wasted!"

Dad suffered, smiling sheepishly through a number of scenes at the dinner table and elsewhere. I heard bedroom recriminations, rare in our household. But in a short time the mortgage was granted, the house was bought, and we moved — a huge disruption in a family unused to events involving a substantial outlay of money. It was the only time we moved house, and what made it memorable were my mother's tears. After it was done, her father and mother paid a visit. Her father, sententious, pinched and pious, a self-proclaimed Italian orphan, looked at the house, surveyed the street, pronounced it a disaster, and said, "*Poverina*," poor little thing. Not the house, but Mother.

The house was large but odd-shaped, bony and tall and narrow, like a cereal box, the narrow side facing the street, the wide side a wall of windows, and all somehow unfinished: the kitchen not quite right, the thin wood cabinets darkly varnished, the doors sagging or poorly fitting or missing, the floors creaky and uneven. But it had four bedrooms. Fred and Floyd shared a room with bunk beds. "There's room for the piano," my father said in a voice of hollow enthusiasm.

"Life's savings" was probably an exaggeration, but not much of one. My father was a mere shoe clerk. He was grateful for the job, but a man selling shoes spends a great deal of time on his knees.

He never stopped smiling that winter. His smile said, All's well. Mother banged the kitchen cabinets to demonstrate the loose hinges, the broken latches. She tugged at the front door, exaggerating the effort, saying she was coming down with a cold because of the drafts, sighing loudly, all the sounds and gestures of discontent.

Dad said, "Say, I'll see to that."

He was imperturbable, not so chummy as to cause offense, but deferentially amiable. "How can I help?" A kind of submissiveness you'd see in the native of a remote colony, with the wan demeanor of a field hand or an old retainer.

Spring came. The roof began to leak, the gutters were rotted, the nailed-on storm windows proved hard to take down. Now that we were less confined by winter, we could see that the house was big and plain and needed paint.

Dad began to paint it, with a borrowed ladder and a gallon of yellow paint. A neighbor saw him and said in a shocked voice, "You're not going to paint that house yellow!"

So Dad returned the yellow and bought some cans of gray.

"That's a lot better," the neighbor said.

Mother pointed out that he'd dripped gray paint onto the white trim. He corrected it by repainting the trim.

Mother said, "Now you've gone and dripped white paint on the shingles."

Dad smiled, repainting, never quite getting it right.

Anticipating warm weather and insects, he put up screens. The screens were loose and rusted; holes had been poked in them.

"Didn't you look at the screens before?"

She was talking about January, when he'd bought the house. This was mid-March.

The stove was unreliable, the fuel oil in the heater gurgled and leaked from the pump, which had to be replaced by a plumber, Dad's fellow choir member Mel Hankey. He worked for nothing, or for very little, groaning in wordless irritation as he toiled, like giving off a smell.

My father's new job was a problem: long hours, low pay, my mother home with the small children, with a baby due in June. She was heavy and walked with a tippy, leaning-back gait, supporting her belly with one hand, seeming to balance herself as she moved.

"I lost a child four years ago. My darling Angela." As though she was threatening to lose this one.

Dad said, "It's going to be fine."

"How would you know?"

He smiled but had no reply. As a sort of penance he washed the dishes, calling out, "Who's going to dry for me?" Because of the tension, each of us said, "I'll do it!" and pushed around trying to be helpful, like terrified children in a drunken household. But there was no drunkard here, only a disappointed woman and her smiling husband.

I said he had no recreations. He had one, the choir, legitimate because it was church-related. He had a strong, confident, rather tuneless voice, with a gravelly character, and even if there were thirty other people singing, I could always discern my father's voice in the "Pange Lingua" or "O Salutaris."

"You're not going out again, are you?"

"Say, I've got choir practice."

He prays twice who sings to the Lord was printed on the hymnal. He believed that. Choir practice was more than a form of devotion, an expression of piety; it was a spiritual duty. But Dad always went alone, never taking any of us as initiates to the choir, and he always came back happy — you could tell by the tilt of his head, his movements, his breathing, the way he listened, with a different sort of smile, a relaxed posture, his walk. He seemed to weighed less.

April came.

"The house is full of flies."

"I'll take care of that."

He repaired the screens with little squares of discarded screens.

"And the paint's peeling."

Instead of priming it or waiting until the summer, he'd painted over the grime and the paint hadn't stuck.

"The faucet drips."

"Say, I'll pick up some washers on the way home from choir."

"This is the second time I've mentioned it."

Dad was putting on his hat, snapping the brim, looking raffish.

"You never listen."

All he did was listen, but there's a certain sort of nagging repetition that can deafen you, and another sort that turns you into a liar. We didn't know we'd come to the end of a chapter, that we were starting a new one. And after it was over, we knew Dad much better, or rather knew a different side of him.

The wickedest episodes of revelation can have the most innocent beginnings. This one began with a song. Dad came home carrying a large envelope with a tucked-in flap. Trying to look casual, he got his fingers inside and with a self-conscious flourish took out some pages of sheet music. The illustration on the cover showed a black man in a gleaming top hat, white gloves, mouth smilingly open in the act of singing. I could see from his features that he was a white man wearing black makeup.

"Say" — Dad was rattling the pages — "can you play this, Mother?"

Asking a favor always made him shy. Being asked a favor made Mother ponderous and powerful. *Oh, so now you want something, do you?* she seemed to reply in the upward tilt of her head and triumphant smile.

She looked with a kind of distaste at the sheet music, plucking at it with unwilling fingers, as though it was unclean — and it *was* rather grubby, rubbed at the edges, torn at the crease where it was folded on the left side. It showed all the signs of having been propped on many music stands. Much-used sheet music had a limp, cloth-like look.

After a while, Mother brought herself and her big belly to the piano. She spun the stool to the right height and, balancing herself on it, reached over her pregnancy as if across a counter. Frowning at the music, she banged out some notes — I knew from her playing that she was angry. Dad leaned into his bifocals.

Mandy,
There's a minister handy
And it sure would be dandy . . .

He gagged a little, cleared his throat, and began again, in the wrong key.

He could not read music, though he could carry a tune if he'd heard it enough times. In this first effort he struggled to find the melody.

"You're not listening," Mother said.

"Just trying to . . ." he said, and clawed at the song sheet instead of finishing the sentence.

He started to sing again, reading the words but too fast, and Mother was pounding the keys and tramping on the pedals as though she was driving a big wooden vehicle down a steep hill.

Mandy, is there a minister handy . . .

Hearing the blundering repetition of someone being taught something from scratch was unbearable to me, because, probably from exasperation,

I learned it before they did. I was usually way ahead while they were still faltering. I was always in a fury for it to be over.

I left the room, but even two rooms away, I heard,

So don't you linger
Here's a ring for your finger
Isn't it a humdinger?

Against my will I listened to the whole thing until the song was in my head, not as it was meant to be sung, but in Dad's tuneless and halting rendition.

Later, over dinner, in reply to a question I didn't hear, Dad said, "Fella gave it to me—loaned it. I'll have to give it back afterwards."

"Who loaned it?"

"John Flaherty."

"Why?"

"Mel Hankey loaned it to him."

"What's it for?"

"Minstrel show."

Mother made a face. As if to avoid further questions, Dad filled his mouth with food and went on eating, with the faraway look he assumed when he didn't want to be questioned. *I'm busy thinking,* his expression said. *You don't want to interrupt.*

Then, out of the side of his mouth, he said, "Pass the mouse turd, sonny."

We stared at him. He was chewing.

"Tell you a great meal," he said. "Lettuce. Turnip. And pea."

He winked. We had no idea.

"Minstrel show," he seemed to feel, explained everything—and perhaps it did, though not to me. Words I had never heard before had significance for him, and a private satisfaction. But "mouse turd"?

After that, he practiced the song "Mandy" every night, singing with more confidence and tunefulness, Mother playing more loudly, thumping her pedaling feet. His voice was strong, assertive rather than melodious. Within a week he grew hoarse, lost his voice, and from the next room it was as though another man was singing, not Dad but a growly stranger.

Around this time, having mastered the song, he revealed his new name. This was at the dinner table, Mother at one end, Dad at the other, Fred, Floyd, Rose, and me between them.

"Fella says to me, 'Wasn't that song just beautiful? Didn't it touch you, Mr. Bones?' I says, 'No, but the fella that sang it touched me, and he still owes me five bucks.'"

"Who's Mr. Bones?" I asked.

"Yours truly."

"No, you're not," Fred said.

"Only one thing in the world keeps you from being a barefaced liar," he said to Fred.

We were shocked at his suddenness.

"Your mustache," Dad said, and wagged his head and chuckled.

"I don't have a mustache," Fred said.

Mother got flustered when she heard anyone telling a joke. She said, "Don't be stupid."

"You think I'm stupid?" Dad said eagerly. "You should see my brother. He walks like this." He got up from the table and bent over and hopped forward.

He did have a brother, that was the confusing part.

"You're so pretty and so intelligent," he said, striking a pose with Mother, using that new snappy voice.

"I wish I could say the same for you."

Dad laughed, a kind of cackle, as though it was just what he wanted to hear. He said, "You could, if you told as big a lie as I just did." He nudged me and said, "She was too ugly to have her face lifted. They lowered her body instead."

With that, he skipped out of the room, his hands in the air, and I thought for a moment that Mother was going to cry.

He had become different, and it had happened quickly, just like that, calling himself Mr. Bones and teasing us, teasing Mother. She was bewildered and upset. The song he mastered he kept humming, and his jokes, not really jokes, were more like taunts.

"Maybe it's his new job," Fred said in the bedroom after lights out.

Floyd said, "It's this house. Ma hates it. It's Dad's fault. He's just being silly."

"What's a minstrel show?" I asked.

No one answered.

Trying to be friendly, Mother asked Dad about his job a few days later.

"They said I'd be a connoisseur, but I'm just a common sewer."

Then that gesture with the hands, waggling his fingers.

"Said I'd be a pretty good physician, but I said 'I'm not good at fishin'.'" Or a doctor of some standing. I says, 'No, I'm sitting — in the shoe department.'"

Mother said coldly, "We need new linoleum in the upstairs bathroom."

"And you need new clothes, because your clothes are like the two French cities, Toulouse and Toulon."

"Don't be a jackass."

"*Mister* Jackass to you."

"I wish John Flaherty hadn't given you that music."

"Lightning Flaherty said I needed it. Tambo gave it to him. Play it for me again, I need a good physic."

Mother began to clear the table.

"I love work," Dad said. "I could watch it all day."

Mother went to the sink and leaned over. She had turned on the water, her back was turned, and I associated the water running into the dishpan with her tears.

He was a new man, even my brothers said so, though being older than me, they were often out of the house in the evenings when Dad — Mr. Bones — was at his friskiest. He had swagger and assurance, and if I tried to get his attention or if he was asked a question, he began to sing "Mandy." He had somehow learned two other songs. "Rosie, You Are My Posie" and "Rock-a-Bye Your Baby with a Dixie Melody" — Lightning's song, and Tambo's, so he said.

I was used to my father singing, but not these songs; used to his good humor, but there was anger in these jokes. And he, who seldom went out at night except to Benediction or choir practice, was now out most nights. He stopped asking Mother to play the piano for him; he would simply break into song, drawling it out of the side of his mouth.

When you croon, croon a tune,
From the heart of Dixie . . .

He didn't look any different; he dressed the same, in a gray suit and white shirt and a blue tie, and the topcoat he disparaged as "too dressy." One day the sleeve was limp. He flapped it at Mother and said, "I know what you're thinking: World War Two," as though his arm was missing. Then he shot the arm out of the sleeve and said, "Nope. Filene's Basement. Bad fit!"

The variation that night and for nights to come was the tambourine he had somehow acquired. When he made a joke or a quip he shook it and rapped it on his knee and elbow and shook it again. *Shika-shika-shika.*

"RSVP," he said, holding up a piece of mail. "Remember Send Vedding Present," and he jingled and tapped the tambourine.

One day after school I went to the store where he worked. Instead of walking in, I kept my head down and crept to the side window to get a glimpse of Dad. He was sitting in one of the chairs in the shoe department, his chin in his hand, not looking like Mr. Bones but sad and silent, a man trying to remember something. Other clerks in shirtsleeves had gathered at the back of the store and were laughing, but not Dad. Were they ignoring him? He paid no attention. He was reading — unusual, a shoe clerk reading. I didn't know this man either.

I began to be glad that he was out most evenings. At the other, smaller house we'd moved from, he was always at home after work, and in the early days of this new one — the bigger house that Mother hated — he was often in his chair, dressed in flannel pajamas and a fuzzy bathrobe, reading the *Globe* under a lamp in the corner. But after that first night, with "Mandy" and the jokes and the tambourine, as Mr. Bones, he sometimes didn't come home for supper, or if he did, it was "Pass the mouse turd" or, holding the pepper shaker, "This is how I feel, like pulverized pepper — fine!"

"The oil burner's back on the fritz," Mother said.

Any mention of a problem with the house these days made Dad smile his Mr. Bones smile and roll his eyes.

"Heard about the king of England? He's got a *royal* burner."

"We'll have to get Mel to look at it."

"Tambo is a busy man, yes he is. Says to me, 'What is the quickest way to the emergency ward?' I says, 'Tambo, just you stand in the middle of the road.'"

Mother did not react except to say, "It's giving off a funny smell."

"Giving off a funny smell!" Dad said, and put one finger in the air, what I now recognized as a Mr. Bones gesture — he was about to say something and wanted attention. "Mr. Interlocutor, what is the difference between an elephant passing wind and a place where you might go for a drink?"

"I don't think you understand," Mother said in a strained voice. "This house hasn't been right since the day we moved in. First it was the roof, then the paint, then the plumbing. Now it's the heat. We're not going to have any hot water. Everything's *wrong*."

Dad held his chin in his hand, as I'd seen him do at the store. He thought a moment, then looked around the table and said, "Mr. Interlocutor, the difference between an elephant passing wind and the place where you might go for a drink is — one is a barroom and the other is a *bar-room!*"

He said it so loud we jumped. He didn't laugh. He drew his chair next to Mother and sang:

Rosie, you are my posie,
You are my heart's bouquet.
Come out here in the moonlight,
There's something sweet, love,
I want to say.

Mother looked awkward and sad. She wasn't angry. In a way, by clowning, Dad took her mind off the problems of the house. She could not get his attention. And who was he, anyway? He had a different voice, a playful manner.

It wasn't any kind of joking I'd heard before from him. His teasing was more like mocking and bullying. He wouldn't call Mel Hankey anything but Tambo, and John Flaherty was Lightning. They had never been close friends before — he had very few friends — but now he had Tambo and Lightning and "Mr. Interlocutor."

"Morrie Daigle said he'd help you fix the roof."

"Mr. Interlocutor is too hot to do that. He is so hot he will only read fan mail."

That was how we found out who Mr. Interlocutor was.

"Have you lost your wallet?" Dad said to Floyd.

"No," Floyd said, and clapped his hand to his pocket.

"Good. Then give me the five dollars you owe me."

Floyd made a face, looked helpless, thrashed a little. It was true that Dad had given him five dollars, but he had not brought it up before this.

Dad said, "Hear about the Indian who had a red ant?"

I didn't understand that one at all. I pictured an Indian with an insect. It made no sense.

There was something abrupt and deflecting in his humor. He made a joke and seemed to expand, pushing the house and his job aside. He'd been at the new job for six months now and never mentioned it. I had seen him in the store, not working but sitting in the chair where the shoe customers were supposed to sit, and instead of waiting on them, or talking to the other employees, he was reading.

Mother seemed to be afraid of him. Before, she had always made a remark, or nagged, or blamed. But these days she relented. She watched him. When he made a joke she became very quiet and blinked at him, as though she was thinking, What do you mean by that?

Floyd was on the basketball team, Fred played hockey, so they were out most evenings — practicing, they said. I knew it was an excuse to stay away from home and Mr. Bones. Rose was just a little kid of seven, and she actually found Mr. Bones funny, and let him tickle her.

But I had nowhere to go, and I didn't like the angry jokes or the cruel teasing. Mr. Bones was always laughing or singing, and he never listened except when he was thinking up another joke. He was a stranger to me, and for the first time I began to think, Who are you? What do you want?

Dad's change was a surprise, but when he changed again he seemed monstrous. We thought, What next? It frightened the whole family, but maybe me especially, because I went to bed thinking, Who are you?

The light went on and I had the answer.

Most of the lights in the house were bare bulbs with no shades, hanging on frayed black whips from the ceiling — another source of Mother's complaints — and the brightness of the one dangling in my bedroom made it worse. I had been woken up, so the light blazed and half blinded me. Yet I saw enough to be terrified.

A disfigured villain from a horror comic was bending over my bed — I only realized later it was Dad — his whole face sticky black, a white oval outline around his lips. He wore a cap that even afterward I could not imagine was a wig, and a red floppy bow tie, a yellow speckled vest, and a black coat, and he was emphatically holding his hands out in white gloves. He was smiling under that blackness that shone on his face, and he leaned over me and spoke, seeming to shriek.

"Give us a kiss, sonny boy!"

Then he laughed and stood up and waved his gloved hands again and jerked the light chain, bringing down darkness.

His voice had matched his face. He was so black that I dreamed he was still in my bedroom, standing there invisible in his floppy tie: Mr. Bones. I had not heard the door shut.

I even said into the menacing gloom, "Dad, are you there?"

No answer was just the sort of thing he'd try as Mr. Bones.

I said again, "Dad?" And in a trembly voice, "Mr. Bones?"

I had not heard him leave. For all I knew he stayed there to scare me. But in the morning the room was empty.

At breakfast he was eating oatmeal as usual. He had a decorous way of holding his spoon. I looked closely at him and saw some streaks of black makeup caked in the lines on his neck. I sprinkled raisins on my oatmeal.

"Pass me the dead flies, sonny," he said in his Mr. Bones voice.

These days his remarks silenced the room. We all felt the effect of his angry humor. I didn't know how deeply Mother was upset, though I knew she was. Floyd and Fred were startled but sometimes pretended to find it funny, and occasionally they teased back. When Dad made his "Toulouse and Toulon" joke, Floyd said, "Well, you're like a town in Massachusetts — Marblehead." Instead of being insulted, Dad smiled and said, "I like that."

But he kept on worrying Fred about college, and Floyd about trumpet lessons. We didn't know what was coming next. We had not foreseen the songs or the jokes; we had not expected the black face. Maybe there was more.

His voice was hoarse from practicing, and now every night he came home in black makeup, his wig like a too-big woolly hat. He talked about Tambo and Lightning and Mr. Interlocutor, and he told the same jokes. Hearing it again and again, I came to understand the one about the Indian and the red ant — red aunt was the point of it. We never pronounced it *ant*, but always *awnt*, the New England way.

I felt embarrassed and fearful. We were afraid to ask him about his job in the shoe department these days. If Mother mentioned the house, that there were drips to be fixed, the oil burner to be mended, linoleum to be laid, painting to be done, I didn't hear it. All our attention was on him, who he was now, Mr. Bones. To almost any question he began singing.

> *A million baby kisses I'll deliver,*
> *If you will only sing the "Swanee River"*

The rhythm was there, a confident slowness and drawl, yet his voice was strained from overuse. He lifted his knees and did dance steps as he sang and he raised his white gloves. And Mother sat at the piano, looking anxious, playing the melody.

It seemed so wrong, I was always glancing at the door, scared that someone — a neighbor, the Fuller Brush man, Grampa — might come in and see him swaying and singing with a black face and that wig.

He had another song too.

> *When life seems full of clouds and rain*
> *And I am filled with naught but pain,*
> *Who soothes my thumpin' bumpin' brain?*

He would always pause after that, lower himself, put his head out, and say, "Nobody!"

His voice was gargly and cross, as though he was in pain. The weeks of rehearsals had taken away his real voice and given him this new one.

When all day long things go amiss,
And I go home to find some bliss,
Who hands to me a glowin' kiss?

He was standing over Mother at the piano with her bleak plunking notes, and smiling angrily, his wig tilted, one glove in the air.

"Nobody!"

The next time I sneaked after school to the window of the store and looked in, I saw him sitting where I'd seen him before, in the chairs reserved for customers, reading. He was not in blackface, yet his assurance, his posture, the way he sat, like the owner of the store, made him seem more than ever like Mr. Bones. He looked thoughtful, his fist against his mouth, a knuckle against his nose. The other clerks and floorwalkers seemed to avoid him, talking among themselves as if they knew he was Mr. Bones.

Outside church one Sunday, Eddie Flaherty, one of the altar boys, said, "You going to the minstrel show?"

"I don't know," I said. "Are you?"

"My old man's in it. So's yours."

"I don't even know what it's supposed to be."

"It's a pisser. Just a bunch of old guys singing, like a talent show," Eddie said.

This big event was just a talent show to him, and his white-haired father, who worked on the MTA buses, was just an old guy singing. Yet in our house Mr. Bones had taken charge and intimidated us all.

He had a different complaint about each of us. These objections were clearer when he was in blackface and a wig than when he was just Mr. Bones in name. He was now a man in a mask, someone to fear, saying things he normally avoided, singing strange songs. In his minstrel show costume he could be as reckless as he wanted.

It was true that Fred told fibs and didn't want to go to college, true that Floyd owed him money and hated trumpet lessons. And it was easy to see that Mother's nagging caused him to tease her and change the subject. His jokes were more than jokes; they were ways of telling us the truth. The yellow mustard in big quart jars was cheap and tasteless; "mouse turd" was a good name for it. The stale raisins that Mother bought cheap in the dented-package aisle were like dead flies. But it was so odd hearing these things from his gleaming black face, his white-outlined mouth, his woolly wig askew, and rapping his tambourine after he spoke.

"Dad," we said, pleading.

"Dad done gone. 'That was prior to his decease, Mr. Bones.' I says, 'He had no niece.'"

Shika-shika-shika went the tambourine.

He was not just smiling but defiantly happy, powerfully happy, talking to us, teasing us in ways I'd never heard before. He had once been remote, with a kindly smile that made him hard to approach. Now he was up close and laughing at us and he wouldn't go away.

He was someone new, convincingly a real man, as though he'd been turned inside out, the true Dad showing. Swanking in the role of a comical slave, he'd become a frightening master to us, and because he was so strange we had no way of responding to his tyrannical teasing.

Something else I discovered, because I kept going to the store to lurk and spy on him, was that instead of sitting silently alone in the shoe department he'd been hired to run, he now had company: Mel Hankey, John Flaherty, Morrie Daigle, and two men I'd never seen before. All of them with their heads together, sitting in the customers' chairs, whispering, as if they were cooking something up. So odd to see this in a store where everyone else was working or shopping or being loudly busy.

That was his secret, mine too. The whole affair looked more serious than just black faces and songs and jokes. These men were like conspirators, and the sight of them impressed me, because Dad was in charge, I could see it in his posture, sitting upright like a musician holding an instrument; but the instrument was his hand. As though wearing white gloves, he was giving directions, issuing energetic commands. Mr. Bones was their leader.

We had taken him to be a man with no friends outside the family, no interests outside the house and the church. But here he was, Mr. Bones with his pals, Tambo, Lightning, Mr. Interlocutor, and the rest whose names I didn't know.

But that same night, as if to dispute all this, he came home after dinner in blackface and his floppy coat and wig, and said, "Listen to Mr. Bones."

Fred was fiddling with the radio, Mother was at the sink with Floyd, and I was looking at a comic book.

"I says, listen to Mr. Bones!"

He spoke so loud we jumped, and as we did he banged and clicked his tambourine. He was like a drunk you couldn't talk back to, yet he hadn't had a drink.

I ain't never done nothin' to nobody,
I ain't never got nothin' from nobody, no time!
And until I get somethin' from somebody, sometime,
I don't intend to do nothin' for nobody, no time!

He searched us, shaking his head, and moaned, "Nobody, no time!"

Was it a song? Was it a poem? Was it a speech? It was too furious to be entertainment. We sat horrified by the sight of Dad in blackface, rapping his tambourine on his knee and his elbow and then bonking himself on the head with it.

Even though his recitation was painful to hear, he had our full attention. We had to listen; we couldn't look away. That proved he was the opposite of the poor soul he was describing. He was stronger than we were, and I recognized the "nobody" he spoke of. It wasn't Mr. Bones, it was Dad.

After that, he went over to Fred and said, "What are you going to do for Mr. Bones?"

"College," Fred said, blinking fiercely.

"Know the difference between a college professor and a railway conductor?"

"No."

"No what?"

"No, Mr. Bones."

"One trains minds and the other minds trains. Which one do you want to be?"

"College professor, Mr. Bones."

But Mr. Bones had turned to Floyd. "What are you going to do for Mr. Bones?"

"Trumpet lessons, Mr. Bones."

"You always were good at blowing your own trumpet. Ha!" Then he had me by the chin and was lifting it, as Dad had never done. "Who was that lady you saw me with last night?"

With his white-gloved hand gripping my chin I couldn't speak.

"That was no lady. That was my wife!"

Mother muttered as he shook his tambourine.

"You'll need some Karo syrup for that throat," Mother said, and handed him a bottle and a spoon.

He took a swig straight from the bottle, then said to Fred, "Here, want to keep this bottle up your end?"

I didn't know it was a joke until he lowered his shoulders and swung his arms and shook his tambourine.

I dreaded the minstrel show, which was just a week away, and when the day came I said, "I don't want to go. I've got a wicked bad stomachache."

"Everyone's going," Mother said, trembling with a kind of nervous insistence that I recognized: if I defied her, she might start screaming.

On a wet Saturday night in May we went together to the high school auditorium in our old car, Mother driving. I could tell she was upset from the way she drove, riding the brake, stamping on the clutch, pushing the gear shift too hard. Dad had gone separately. "Tambo's stopping by for me."

I hurried into the auditorium and slid down in my seat so that no one would see me. When the music began to play and the curtain went up, I covered my face and peered through my fingers.

Dad — Mr. Bones — was sitting in a chair onstage, and the others, too, sat on chairs in a semicircle. Mr. Bones looked confident and happy; he was dressed like a clown, but he looked powerful. He was wearing his floppy suit, his shiny vest, his big bow tie, his white gloves, his tilted wig, and his face was black. All of them were in blackface except Morrie Daigle, in the center, wearing a white suit and a white top hat.

"Mr. Bones, wasn't that music just beautiful? Didn't it touch you?"

I pressed my fingers to my ears and closed my eyes and groaned so that I wouldn't hear the rest. I wanted to disappear. I was so slumped in my seat that my head wasn't showing, and even though I kept my hands to my ears I heard familiar phrases, "physician of good standing" and "that was prior to his decease."

The songs I knew by heart penetrated me as I sat there trying to deafen myself. Mr. Bones sang "Mandy." "Rosie" and "Rock-a-Bye Your Baby" were sung by others. Someone else sang "Nobody."

"You should see my brother, he walks like this," I heard, and knew it was Mr. Bones. I heard "barefaced liar." I heard "Toulouse and Toulon."

There was much more, skits and songs. People laughing, people clapping, the loud music, the shouts, the tambourines, the familiar phrases. This was silly and embarrassing, yet the same jokes and songs had intimidated us at home. And Mr. Bones had been different at home too, not this ridiculous man clowning, far off on the stage, but someone else I didn't want to think of as Dad, teasing us and making fools of us and getting us to agree with him and make decisions. That was who he was—Dad as Mr. Bones.

When the house lights were still dimmed and the people onstage were taking bows, I said, "I have to go to the bathroom," and ran out and hid in our car.

Back home afterward, no one said anything about the show. Dad was in his regular clothes, with the faint greasy streaks of black on his neck and behind his ears. He was excited, breathless, but he didn't speak. The strange episode and uproar were over. Later, I got anxious when he hummed "Mandy" or "Rosie" while he was shaving, but he didn't make any jokes, didn't tease or taunt anymore. Looking at him through the side window of the store, I saw him standing near the cash register, smiling at the front door as if to welcome a customer.

The following year there was talk of a minstrel show, but nothing happened. We had a TV set then, and the news was of trouble in Little Rock, Arkansas, integrating the schools, black children protected by National Guardsmen, white crowds shouting abuse at the frightened black students who were being liberated. The bald-headed president made a speech on TV. Dad watched with us, saying nothing, maybe thinking how Mr. Bones had been liberated too, or banished. The news was not what he had expected, the expression on his face was vacant, stunned with sorrow, but before long Dad was smiling.

No one asked him about his menial job, or mentioned the defective house, ever again.

6

MOTHER LAND

THE MEMORY of Mr. Bones was so strong that even without mentioning it, Dad was powerful and not to be disobeyed. But when he died, and the minstrel figure no longer haunted us, and Mother became herself, I was astonished at the change in her. I saw the family in a new way — revealed, in an enlarged perspective. I am looking for an image. Balance had been lost; we were out of alignment. Now the whole family began to wobble. Do I mean entropy? We behaved differently because Dad was gone, and Mother was more demanding than ever. Getting rid of all of Father's accumulated tools was one sign. She threw out all his clothes, gave them to thrift shops and charities. She purged the house of his memory except for a few photographs. She took over the house, claimed every room. And not just the house — she dominated us, made demands and, just after Father's funeral, tested our loyalty to her, fixing each of us with a raptor's beaky stare, saying, "Here is what I want you to do for me —"

Being a closely observed citizen of Mother Land had always unsettled me. From an early age, I believed my life belonged only to me, and I avoided sharing it with my family. I needed to believe this, because so many family members were prepared to interfere with me, mock my writing, or claim that they knew better than I did.

Mother would find a book I owned — it might be a Steinbeck novel with a racy cover, such as *The Wayward Bus;* or a Mickey Spillane paperback, *I, The Jury;* or Joyce's *Portrait of the Artist* — and say, "Why are you reading this? Haven't you got anything better to do?" She meant that I should be at the Stop and Shop earning money, keeping out of trouble. Reading was idleness, and just the sight of me sitting in a corner with a book in my face enraged her. Reading was an indulgence, writing was unthinkable; no wonder they became my passion.

Mother's motto was "Keep yourself busy." This meant pursuing part-time jobs and handing her half my paycheck every week.

She did not know me. This boy she bossed around was a stranger to her, who obeyed her because obedience was simpler and sneakier than rebellion. Perhaps I had learned this from Dad: follow orders, show no defiance, do not resist, and in this way no one will ever know who you are or what is in your heart. From my obedience they would invent a personality for me, one that suited them, and my soul would belong to me alone. Maybe Mother suspected this strategy in me. Maybe it made her insecure and cranky when she realized it. Whatever, I became adept at concealment.

As a child, I had thought, One day I will flee and go far away. And I did. As soon as I graduated from college I went to Africa and stayed there. I married there — no one from my family was present. I had children. I traveled more. I divorced and married again. I wrote forty books. With Father's death I returned home to Cape Cod. Mother was still there, smaller but fiercer than ever.

My struggle to assert my belief in myself helped make me a writer, against the odds — the bewilderment of Dad, the opposition of Mother, the envy and mockery of my siblings. Floyd's experience of becoming a poet was no different from mine, though he had the respectability of tenure at Harvard to shield him from philistinism. I wrote in seclusion, loving my remoteness, finding strength in my secrecy.

My life was of my own making. I regarded it as odious that any of my family, or anyone in the wider world, would presume to tell my story. Only I had the right and the qualifications; all the acts that applied to me were known only to me. Mother I knew was at the center of my story. And I knew that once I embarked on it, I would write it with such completeness that no one would be able to deny it or supplement it. There would be nothing more to say.

In any memoir, prudery or reticence (not that I have sedulously practiced either one in my writing) only encourages commentators and speculators to fill in the blanks, and candor tends to provoke the author's family into objecting that they are not shown in a more favorable light. I knew that Mother had her supporters — how could this not be the case, since from the beginning she had actively tried to recruit them to her side. She had favorites, and her favorites plumped for her canonization, and God knows what they thought of me. But I felt that if my story was exhaustive and honest it would render every other version of my life worthless. In the end, it is the *David Copperfield* version of his upbringing that displaces the speculations of any Dickens biographer: Copperfield rightly has the last word.

I knew I could not prevent anyone from taking exception to what I wrote about the family, or from publishing their own portraits of Mother. But I also knew that my being frank in my disclosures would enfeeble all those attempts to tell my story. After I finished there would be no more secrets, nothing left to say. The truth of my fiction would put everyone else out of business.

Just after Father's death, our loyalty was tested by Mother. There was first the necessity to show up and to call regularly. Mother had put herself at the center of things. She insisted on knowing what we were doing. She demanded a say in our affairs. With me, it was a question of marriage.

"I want you to find someone," Mother had said on the phone. "Do it for me."

I had been trained from childhood to submit — at least to pay lip service to a suggestion. Of course, I said, I would find a woman to love me, but even saying this, I was smiling bitterly into the receiver.

Dad was not mentioned. His memory was displaced by Mother's ailments, at first trivial, and then, as an answered prayer, she acquired a real complaint. She had craved a condition. For a period of time in this funereal atmosphere Mother was diagnosed with a sort of arthritis. Like the hypochondriac she was, Mother could talk for hours about her symptoms and her medicine. "It's called polymyalgia," she said, and told of the pain and the swelling. "I'm on prednisone," she said, and listed not the relief she got but the side effects she read in the accompanying leaflet: nausea, swollen feet, vomit that resembled coffee grounds, mood swings, puffy face, sleeplessness, sweating, blurred vision, bone pain, cramps, water retention. Medicine was never a curative but only another burden.

"Have you found anyone?" she asked me after she'd finished describing her ailments.

"Still looking," I said.

"Time is flying," she said.

What the others were asked to do for her I didn't know — didn't ask — but the renewed bustle of activity around Mother was obvious to me. Some of us were required to visit, Franny and Rose especially. Others were encouraged to phone her often. All of us were enjoined to send her presents — tokens, souvenirs, kitsch, and more serious gifts of jewelry, or ornaments, lamps, vases, small items of furniture.

"Ma likes presents."

Franny and Rose talked about Mother as though she was a small willful girl it was their mission to placate, like one of their difficult students or someone they were eternally babysitting. They rolled their eyes and smiled when they mentioned Mother's demands, yet they showed up at her house every Sunday. They brought Mother food and trinkets; they called her several times a day and talked for hours.

I was glad they were attentive. I felt spared from having to do it myself, for the fact was that Mother had become a bore on the subject of her arthritis, repetitive in her stories, and perverse in her eagerness for bad news. And the medicine's side effects were taking hold. Talking to her made me impatient and slightly ashamed of myself for enduring the pettiness she stirred in me. She loved news of people's failures or lapses. She feasted on misfortune. She would cluck at hearing of Hubby's piles, Floyd's faltering romances, or the death of Fred's dog; yet she loved this stuff and asked for more.

In her subtle way, not in words but in shrugs and whinnying noises, Mother made it apparent that I still had not proven my loyalty. It was apparent to her that I missed Dad. I mentioned Mr. Bones, I visited his grave, I tended to its flowers and shrubs. Either through whispers or her shrewd watchfulness of my dreamy inattention when I was with her, Mother suspected me of disloyalty and squinted at me in my reverie: Where are you?

Mother's stern questions from childhood on — Where are you going? What are you doing? What are you thinking? Why are you frowning? Who do you think you are? — had turned me into a sneak and a liar, made me evasive and untruthful. You never forgive people who force you to lie. So in this frame of mind, wishing to conceal my anger, I was receptive to any suggestion that would calm her and convince her — if not of my love for her than of the fact that I was not her enemy.

Soon after I returned to the Cape, or rather the province of Mother Land, Franny stopped by my rented house one day. She wheezed as though her body was something separate from her, that burdened her, and so tired her that she gasped when she spoke, mouth-breathing, always complaining, usually about Mother.

"Ma's so needy. I tried to avoid coming this weekend. Marvin's coaching Little League, but Ma insisted. She said she wanted me to do her hair. Then she wanted me to help her clean out the drawers of her end tables. She's still trying to get rid of Dad's stuff. Do you need any ties? How about socks? And she's got a huge collection of coat hangers. I said to her, 'Ma, no one wants coat hangers,' but does she listen?"

Franny went on in this vein, whinnying, working her shoulders, her elbows resting on her knees. But I knew her well enough to guess that all this talk meant she had something else on her mind. She had Mother's trick of wearing down a listener with her talk, and when you were panting for her to finish, she would come to the point, always a demand.

Finally, she said, "Ma needs a chair."

"Hasn't she got a chair?"

"I mean, a real comfortable one that she can enjoy. Leather, with cushions, good lumbar support for her arthritis. Real workmanship. She's got some issues with her spine."

"You mean we should get her one?"

"I was hoping you'd say that. Right, everyone chipping in. We'll split it seven ways. Marvin knows a guy."

Marvin, her security guard husband, with a truncheon, a can of Mace, and a walkie-talkie on his belt, and a donut in each hand. He was also the mainstay of the local Little League, although neither of his boys had ever played in it. He liked standing at home plate and howling "Safe!" and "Out!" and "Stee-rike!" Floyd referred to him as a bunk muffin.

"There's a furniture place at the mall where he works. He can get a good deal."

The price was high. Franny said, "It's made in England." It wasn't, but never mind. What struck me about the big leather chair was how different it was from the other chairs in Mother's house. Mother sat in it from the moment it arrived — sat and knitted and talked on the phone, sat and received her children. I say "received" because the leather chair was so much like Mother's throne. And one day when she patted it and said, "Franny got it for me," I didn't bother to correct her. She would have held it against me as another defiant lie. Mother hated to be contradicted, especially when she was sitting on her throne, the monarch of Mother Land.

7

HOME LIFE

AFTER THAT — and it was years — I rarely saw Mother away from her chair, with its wrinkly leather and its creamy color and its buttons, its swollen arms and upholstered shoulders and brass foot claws, the chair (so it seemed to me) a bit like Mother herself in her younger and just-as-fierce days. She sat, she knitted, she listened, she stirred and dished, and though she was unforthcoming and canny, even at her most evasive she had perfected an I-have-nothing-to-hide face and solemnly truthful tone that became indistinguishable to me from a lying one.

I began to think that history had to be full of queens who were idle or sulky until, at the death of the king, they ascended to the throne and became queenly, as a dowager regent, gripping the scepter in skinny fingers, enigmatic, single-minded, exalted, impossible — having given no indication beforehand of what power would do to them. Robed and crowned, the tiara fitted on the frizz of hair and the yellow skull, and towering on the throne, they were absolute and unknowable in their arrogant authority.

Mother was like that. I marveled at her transformation. She claimed to be old and achy, yet she could also twinkle with affection in her goggling mock innocence and call attention to a bargain she'd landed, or a loon she had carved, or a scarf she'd knitted. But in spite of all of these trifles, she was no less a queen.

One of the conventions of the family — and, who knows, it may have been a convention of a medieval court — was our needing to observe a habit of disloyalty. We were required to satirize each other, but slyly. Any mention of another family member, with a few exceptions, always involved a backhanded remark; it was all belittling, all whispers, all betrayal. To defend anyone was unacceptable, worse than impolite, because it meant putting the mocker in the wrong. And we were most loyal to Mother when we were being disloyal to each other. Though we begged each other or angled for secrets, no confidences were respected. If anyone was incautious enough to disclose a secret, adding the warning "But don't tell anyone," then everyone was told, one person at a time. Of course, this also became a form of discourse: pretending to have a secret, you muttered the very thing you knew would excite the hearer, so it would be repeated, broadcast to your appalled rivals. Without a doubt, this stratagem of ours had to be another conspiratorial feature of a dark castle.

Keeping secrets didn't make us strong; only disclosing them was an empowerment. Telling secrets was the way we conversed, but we had to be careful. The object was to tease, to fascinate, to befriend a sibling with an apparent confidence. If the entire secret was divulged wholesale, we lost all our power. The trick was to reveal it bit by bit while seeming to tell it all, to keep something back, never to come completely clean.

It was no good claiming to know a secret; we needed to demonstrate our knowledge. We believed that the manipulation of secrets was the ultimate exercise in power. In our self-deception, we did not understand Dad's lesson, that the silent person is always the least knowable, the most masked, and the strongest.

We did nothing but talk, encouraged by Mother. Some of the talk was of course a cover, a distraction, just hollow boasting or the spinning of our wheels, but most of it was gossip. It was vicious, aggressive, beyond satire in its heartlessness — and Mother loved it.

Mother feasted on failure, had always done so; and now, with Dad gone, so did we. As children we had been merely unkind or obtuse, and now we were competitive and cruel — amazingly, in an attempt to please the old woman who was quietly knitting in her big leather chair, who pretended to be ignorant and slow, feeble and arthritic.

"Hubby needs a colonoscopy," she said to me, pretending to distract me with a bird carving she'd done. "I thought it was an old person's thing, but no, apparently if you don't take good care of yourself you need it pretty bad. Know what this is? A puffin."

Another day she said with a smile, "I guess Marvin needs a root canal. I've never needed one of those. I have every single one of my teeth."

"It seems Fred had quite a time getting back home the other day, poor kid," Mother said, clicking her knitting needles. "Those dogs, for one thing. One was pretty sick, but I imagine he'll survive." Fred was mauled by his German shepherd. "He's been asking for that."

She disliked most animals, but now and then a dog might provide entertainment. She smiled at me one morning and said, "I've just had an earful from Franny. Her precious Max was bitten by Fred's big dog. I'm sure she's making a fuss about nothing. 'Stitches in his hand, Ma!' I told her I know all about stitches, I've had a few in my time, and she said — get this — 'But this means Max will never be able to be a hand model.' God forgive me, I had to laugh. Him, a hand model!"

In Mother's Boston accent the word had two syllables, *hee-and*, which made it greater mockery.

Unless they were biting her grandchildren or being a nuisance to someone she disdained, she hated animals. She could not see the point of pets. They represented nuisance and needless expense, they were dirty, just hairballs on dirty paws, little better than vermin — cats, dogs, canaries. Fred had a pair of hounds that in Mother's eyes were an example of Fred's weakness and disobedience. Had he listened to Mother, he would never have kept them, but instead the result was two slavering mutts that had to be transported in the back of the Volvo, wreaking havoc.

These animals chewed the seats, shat on the floor mats, chased other dogs at the service areas on the turnpike, and, unless tethered, often ran away, later to be found and cited for not being licensed, no collar, no proper ID, and the consequence was, "God forgive me, I have to laugh — a fifty-dollar fine!" All this time, Fred's kids sat, cranky in the car while the dogs ran riot. Mother reported that one of Fred's children — Jake — had eaten a Styrofoam cup. It was sometimes hard to tell whether she was criticizing Fred or quietly rejoicing in the disorder of it all, finding pleasure in the tyranny of the dogs. The eating of the cup became the whole of Jake's history, like original sin, overwhelming all his achievements as an adult.

"Floyd was here," Mother said to me one day, knitting a woolen square for an afghan. She had skinny hands with knuckles like acorns and yellow nails, and her knitting looked ghoulish and efficient, the clicking of the needles like the cracking of her finger bones.

She had implored me to visit, saying that she was alone all the time. No one dropped in anymore.

"He had a long face," she said.

"I thought he had a girlfriend and that all was well. From New Jersey? Very pretty? Works for a pharmaceutical company — something like that?"

Mother smiled and worked her tongue through her thin lips as if enjoying the taste of Floyd's troubles.

"Apparently she sent him back his ring," and she smiled, "in a Jiffy bag," and smiled again, and said, "I shouldn't laugh," and laughed, "it's not funny," and laughed again. "This is — what? — his sixth or seventh true love." She lowered her face into the yarn, clicked the needles, and said, "Maybe he can write another poem about it."

To her poetry was laughable, in the same category as pets and expensive clothes and sports events and Christian Science and going to the movies. Where was the profit? And yet Mother had boasted and snipped out the news item in the *Globe* when Floyd had won a Guggenheim.

"What about Hubby?"

She smiled again. "He keeps busy. Like Dad. Puttering around. He fixed my kitchen cabinets. The only thing is, the doors don't shut properly now. I think he put the hinges on wrong." She poked and stabbed with her needles, gathering and knotting the yarn. "Still, I gave him a little something."

Hubby was a figure of fun. Because he was dependable and a trauma nurse and could fix things that baffled everyone else, he needed to be satirized. Instead of being Mister Fixit, he was portrayed as the opposite, as a klutz, all thumbs, memorable only for what he had broken, not what he had fixed.

"Hubby took me over to his house so I could admire his new sink. He says to me, 'Look, Ma.' I didn't know what to look at. I am standing in his bathroom and you know how big he is — just crowding me against the shower stall. 'Look.' And finally, 'New faucet.' I didn't dare tell him it looked exactly like the old faucet except that this one cost seventy-five dollars. Imagine! And he was so proud of it. I said, 'It's dripping.' He hadn't even noticed." She had begun her hard merciless laugh, and still laughing, half covering her mouth, she screeched, "God forgive me!"

I was staring.

She said, "He still doesn't eat right."

This remark had a history. Long after adolescence, Hubby still had a bad complexion, his nose inflamed, corrugations of infected boils on his forehead. So his face was larger than other children's, and fiercer-seeming. How he must have suffered, for there are faces that can make even the young and innocent seem dangerous.

Mother said, "If only he ate more sensibly. He never would listen. It's all the chocolate."

Yet as a schoolboy Hubby had a pimply face, and it was Mother who fed him and went on blaming him, complaining of his gluttony.

He was miserable. He grew fat and more miserable. He was miserable because he was fat, and his misery made him eat more and grow fatter.

"His stomach is distended," Mother said. After fifty years Hubby's stomach was still a topic of conversation. "You know when you eat too much your stomach gets stretched" — she dropped her knitting needles and clawed the air apart with her hands — "and you have to keep filling it."

As she was talking about his belly, Hubby — as he grumbled later to me — was at the hardware store buying galvanized brackets for her window boxes and a plunger to unstop her toilet and some neat's-foot oil for her throne.

Hubby's misery was not only the result of his acne and his girth. There was a family reason. When Gilbert learned the violin, Hubby was encouraged, as an afterthought, to play an instrument, and how about the cello? Mother said that her brother, the sadistic priest Uncle Louie, had played the cello and had liked it, and Hubby would like it too. Hubby objected, and when he was angry he quacked and flailed and made himself villainous.

"I want to learn the guitar!"

"Phonies play the guitar," Mother said. She believed that the guitar hardly qualified as a musical instrument. It was a foolish object that uneducated men slung around their neck when they sang, now and then strumming it, pretending to make music.

"The cello or nothing," Dad said, goaded by Mother.

And so, against his will, Hubby took cello lessons from a heavy-drinking music teacher two streets away, who called him "Bubby" and sometimes fell asleep in his chair, snoring loudly as Hubby played. Hubby cursed because he was no good and because he was forced to play for us all, scraping away at the only song he knew — all this because, as Mother said, Hubby had low self-esteem.

The song was "My Grandfather's Clock." The way he played it sounded, as Floyd said in a stage whisper, like a kid with a cold playing a kazoo. Hubby hunched over his cello and wheezed, dragging his bow across the strings, not sounding like a kazoo at all but like someone ripping old rags. Hubby scowled, daring us to laugh, holding his bow in his fist like a weapon.

Mother sang:

Ninety years without slumbering
Tick, tock, tick, tock,
His life seconds numbering,
Tick, tock, tick, tock,
It stopped short — never to go again —
When the old man died.

After Hubby raked his bow across the strings for the last time, with a final ripsawing motion and a splintering vibrato, we applauded, we laughed. It was terrible. Hubby had made a jackass of himself, and he knew it. He threw down his bow, kicked his cello, and quacked at us.

A week later, while Gilbert played his violin, Hubby was nagged to play his cello. Hubby refused at first, but Mother demanded it. "These music lessons cost good money." Gilbert played well, Hubby played badly, we all laughed, and when Hubby got angry and quacked again, he was scolded.

"That wasn't bad playing," Dad said.

"You have to learn to take it," Mother said, meaning that it had been bad.

What I learned from Mother was that no one learns to take it.

We had not learned. We came, we went, we were the same children we had always been. Here was Hubby putting up the window box brackets at the age of fifty-three and still smarting from the mocking laughter he had heard at the age of ten when he had failed to coax a melody from his cello.

Hubby had his revenge. He became a creative belittler and fault-finder, mastering it, triumphing in it, a close second to Mother, not an easy victory in this belittling and fault-finding family.

Was there a nick in the lip, or a hairline crack, in one of your new set of drinking glasses? Hubby would find it and point it out to you. Was there a typo in the five-hundred-page book you had just published? Hubby could give you the page and the line. Entering your newly painted house, he would squint upward and indicate where the workmen had left a dime-sized smudge on the underside of an upper windowsill. And that same day, walking down your driveway, he would lunge and dig his fingers into the gravel, find a rusty nail, and hand it to you, reminding you about the harm it could inflict on a tire. A bald tire, a dab of mayonnaise on your cheek, a twist of raccoon scat on your deck, a blush of rust on a hubcap, the faintest lip print on a tumbler — Hubby saw it, and nothing else existed except this flaw. The maddening thing was that what he indicated as needing attention was often something that had been on your mind for months, a wound awaiting a dose of Hubby's salt.

We were a flailing family, and our subversion usually took the form of pettiness. Floyd was awarded a Guggenheim for his poetry. The presentation ceremony was held in New York City. He did not invite Mother or Father.

He said, "I guess I forgot."

But he had not forgotten. "Genius has no off switch," he used to say.

I had no idea where I fitted in. If anyone had asked me, I would have said that Mother liked me for my good humor and hard work, my willingness to help, my independence, my alertness. My good manners were a form of evasion, but they were manners nonetheless. Mother said, "I love all my children equally," but "equally" was not true, and "love" sounded ritualistic to me — all mothers had to declare it, for they couldn't very well say they didn't love their children. So the statement meant nothing to me. I never felt when she said it that I was in the presence of love. It was a wordy formula, like loving God. But God was invisible, ungraspable, and so the words were meaningless to me. Any mention of love was like a secret, seldom-used password you had to say in order to get your way. Telling me that she loved me, Mother persuaded me to clean the bathroom or cut the grass. From this I learned that if I told a girl I loved her, I could slip my hand up her blouse and fondle her breast. Though sensing it was a manipulative formula, I could not bring myself to tell Mother I loved her.

But, "We love you, Mumma," Franny and Rose said. They looked after her, sighing at the burden of it, rolling their eyes, moaning about Mother's frugality, how she didn't have much money left.

"She's slowing down an awful lot," Franny said. "I goes, 'This bottle of tonic is flat.' She goes, 'I just bought it.' The cap was off. It was about a month old. She's so forgetful. She leaves the stove on. Things boil over. It's a wonder she hasn't burned the house down."

"She's so careful about her money," Rose said. "It's a good thing we visit her. If we didn't, she'd probably starve herself to death. As it is, she doesn't have much time left."

"Slowing down," "frugal," "forgetful," "doesn't have much time": I was to hear these words for the next twenty years. Mother was not slowing down at all; her memory was almost perfect, except when she pretended to forget or to be deliberately vague, in order to test us, to get more information, or to seem blameless for one of her peculiar cruelties. Cured of her arthritis, ridding herself of the medicine's side effects, she took no more pills and grew stronger.

To Franny and Rose, Mother was a feeble old thing who was lost without their dutiful attention. To Mother, Franny and Rose were figures of fun — needlessly nannying, forever in the way — whom she tolerated, doing them the favor of accepting their fussing. Mother implied that she humored them; they winked and wanted the rest of us to know they were humoring her. To each, the other was a bore and a burden.

In her oddly fluttering pretense of confusion, Mother claimed to know very little. So we said, "Oh, didn't you know that?" and each of us gave her our version of a story, usually one that reflected badly on the subject of the gossip.

Hubby ("impatient"), in his haste to put up his storm windows, smashed his thumb and needed four stitches. Franny ("careless"), not looking, backed her car into a fire hydrant. Floyd ("gullible") lost his new girlfriend to a complete stranger, who had vanished with Floyd's credit cards. Fred's neighbors had called the police ("wouldn't you know?") for his big slavering dogs. Rose ("spendthrift") was overcharged for an oil change.

Hearing such stories, Mother widened her eyes and said, "Oh?" and asked for more.

But she knew more than we did. She feasted on it, she retailed it, and was so animated by gossip, alert and bright-eyed and calculating, that she became a slightly different person, and could not disguise her excitement.

"Notice how she looks younger when she's just heard some bad news?" Floyd said. "It's uncanny, like a swamp thing tasting blood."

I had no idea what she said about me. I should have guessed, because apart from Gilbert, she did not have a kind word for anyone. If I had only reflected a little on how the others were treated, I would have known how viciously I, too, had been mocked. The fatal delusion in many families is that you are special, treated differently from all the others. If only we had considered the fact that what we said about all the others was being said about us. None of us, not even Gilbert, escaped the family fate of being the butt of a joke.

Yet I made a point of never arguing. I never contradicted, never raised my voice, and never complained. This restraint was not fortitude on my part; it was cunning evasion. Any of us who argued or complained revealed what was in his heart. I needed my secrets — I had so little else, and even then I knew that to keep a secret was necessary to self-preservation, for my secrets were the only power I had.

And where would complaining have gotten me? Mention to Mother that you needed a tooth pulled, and she would respond with one of her dental horrors, such as the molar extraction of 1925 during which part of the tooth broke off and the roots had to be drilled and dug out of her bleeding gums. Hurt your arm? So did Mother, in the winter of 1937, when she was pregnant with Fred and slipped on the ice and developed an abscess in her elbow. Lost your wallet with cash and driver's license and credit cards, did you? What's the problem? Mother lost Angela in 1946, and a baby was far more precious. A wallet and money could be replaced, but you could never replace a dead child. The reply to any misery you had to endure was that Mother had had it much worse — count your blessings.

As for being overweight or pimply or covered with a poison ivy rash or sick — whose fault was that? The weakest, most shameful thing you could do was cry or moan in pain.

Mother smiled and said, "The louder you cry, the more it proves that you're not really sick. People in severe pain don't cry at all. Doctors will tell you that. Sick people just lie there. They don't make a sound."

So, moaning showed you were actually much better, perhaps in the pink. Whatever trouble you had would be flung back in your face.

You lost something?

"It didn't just walk away!"

You spent all your money?

"A fool and his money are soon parted."

You gave Fred your sweater and you want it back?

"Maybe you should have thought about that before you gave it away."

You feel sick to your stomach?

"You should have been more careful about what you put in your mouth."

You were sad because you scored badly on a math test?

"You should have studied harder."

Mother took pleasure in blaming us for our failings, tormenting us because we were weak. She gloried in it; our imperfections exalted her.

She was never happier than when she straightened on her throne and said, "It's your own goddamned fault."

8

WEDDING BALLS

MOTHER LOVED PRESIDING over dismissals. She was bucked up by them, got throatier and more confident, turning her back and saying, "Who does she think she is?" We all suffered in various degrees, but the person who excited all of Mother's contempt was Franny's son Jonty. Above all she hated his name, which was a contraction (he had lisped it himself as a two-year-old) of John T.

"The nerve of him," Mother would say, tightening her jaw.

Franny was a fool for catering to her ungrateful children, two boys, Jonty and Max.

"Remember when Jonty kicked the windshield out of the Dodge Dart by bracing himself on the front seat?"

Mother had a peculiar posture when she was indignant. She stiffened, straightening her back like a judge at his bench, her hands like an eagle's claws gripping the arms of her leather chair. As she spoke she started forward, spitting, her eyes huge behind her glasses.

"Can you imagine the gall," she would go on.

Someone outside the family might have concluded that Jonty was an adversary Mother's own age rather than her teenage grandson. Someone in the family would know that Jonty was Mother's rival and therefore someone to destroy.

"The little prince has to have a brand-new tuxedo for the prom. Oh, no, he can't rent one from Mr. Tux. He has to have a brand-spanking-new one."

So that was the issue — the tuxedo, the exorbitant cost, the unworthy wearer who from his earliest years would pose, twinkling and wagging his head, and say, "Do you like Jonty's new pants?"

The sarcasm of her tirades against the "little prince" matched my image of Mother as a furious old queen.

She would excoriate any bright extravagance bestowed on Jonty — new shoes, a watch, fashionable sneakers, gym equipment, a new Walkman. Mother hated the attention that Jonty got from Franny, and she said how sweet-natured and generous Franny was, how awful the son, how iniquitous that this greedy sneak was taking advantage of Franny.

While Mother might have sometimes felt a lingering sentiment for her children, even the most wayward of us, she had an unqualified resentment for her grandchildren, except those who showed abject submission. Rose's twins, Bingo and Benno, learned that "I brought you a beautiful present, Grammy" was the only way to this woman's heart.

Her zestful hatred for Jonty was undisguised. As with most of Mother's prejudices, it was the cruel grain of truth in them that seized your attention, and when Mother cried, "Do you see what I mean?" you would grudgingly concede some fundamental justification, and reply, "You're

right, Ma." If she mocked Hubby for being a klutz, or Floyd for being volatile, it was because they had verifiable spells of this behavior. Mother was
not creative enough to invent, but she was so possessed by a paranoiac's
resourcefulness, her exaggerations went beyond satire into surrealism.

She had a predator's eye and nose for a person's weakness and was
remorseless in exploiting it. We were shocked at Mother's sudden denun-
ciations, and not just the vividness of them but the basis in fact, followed
by the serious question: Who's next?

Mother's contempt spoke to what we had thought was secret in our
heart. She knew that on some level we agreed with her. Jonty was a perfect victim. With the best will in the world it was hard to take to Jonty.
Even Rose, who was the closest to Franny, said, "Jonty is a pill. He can be
a sneak, too."

Jonty was casually disliked, ridiculed for his greed, his oafishness,
his timidity, his fear of insects (he would scream when he saw one) and
of strange dogs (he cowered and called for his mother), and sometimes
when he was especially frantic he gasped and worked himself into a choking fit, seeming to swoon. Whomever he was quarreling with—and it was
usually his father, Marvin, the security guard at the mall, who was timid
himself, even at 240 pounds, with his can of Mace and shiny truncheon
and walkie-talkie hooked to his belt—would become alarmed, hovering
and calling out, "Are you all right, Jonty? Take a deep breath." But seeming
to suffocate, gagging on his misery, Jonty was victorious in the quarrel,
arousing sympathy.

"Asthma," Franny said, pleading for sympathy. "Just like Dad."

Family illnesses were convenient excuses, never needing to be explained but only mentioned, like Mother's headaches or any of us with a
cold or a sprained ankle. And no one really believed them. Mother's defiant cynicism determined that anyone claiming to be sick had to be faking
or somehow at fault.

We laughed at Jonty in secret, and in secret he laughed back at us. We
were on our worst behavior when we were with him, yet we felt justified
because not only did we regard him as rude, whiny, vain, and sneaky;
Mother thought so too.

"Guess what? The little prince doesn't eat hot dogs," Mother said. "I
put some out for him. 'They have horse lips in them. And pigs' ears. And

scraps from cows' tails.'" Then Mother peered closer and said, "A lot of hungry people in the world would be damned glad to get those hot dogs. And he turned up his nose at them."

"Turned up his nose" made us think only of Jonty's nose, which was so broad all you saw were slanted staring nostrils, each one the width of a fingertip. "That lisp," we said, but it wasn't a lisp, it was a way of speaking that had no name. Jonty had such a lazy tongue that instead of being uttered as endearing lisps, words like "chicken" or "church" snagged and rolled his tongue and involved his whole mouth in a slushy chuckle. "Jordache jeans" or "jagged edge" came out in a rush of chewed lips and spittle. Just saying his own name gave him monkey cheeks.

"The little prince wants to go into radio," Mother said.

"Perfect!" Floyd said. "It is a demonstrable fact that some of the most successful people on the radio have speech defects. They lisp, they chuck their teeth, they wa-wa, they yim-yam, they spit, they're whopper-jawed!"

Another day she said, "The little prince has a girlfriend. Apparently he sees her almost every day. But does he see his poor old grandmother? Oh, no, he's much too busy for that."

It surprised me that Mother cared, but her contradictions helped keep us on our toes. She said Jonty was selfish not for visiting, but if Jonty had visited, Mother would have sneered at him for pretending to care, for patronizing her, for saying "Do you like Jonty's new pants?" as he had been saying, egged on by Franny, since he'd been able to talk. "They're Daks slacks."

"We give thanks to the Lord for this twenty-five-pound turkey," Floyd prayed at Thanksgiving, saying grace. "Which, oddly enough, is the same size as Jonty's ass."

The cruel pleasure of ganging up on one weak person was something I had known in my childhood — trading mockery, sharing contempt, freezing out the person, confusing them, jeering at them, but never quite excluding them, because we needed them near us in order to persecute them. The weird stimulation of this bullying was all the more intense for being verbal, never physical, passing the time in poisonous monologues, and strangely enjoyable because it made us feel superior and strong. If someone said that it was mean-spirited, we would have laughed and said, "That's the point!" Sometimes when we were swapping vicious stories about Jonty, I saw Mother hunch her shoulders and cover her face with her hands, weeping tears of joy.

"You won't believe this," Mother said one day, speaking with the flourish, the whoop that she saved for her choicest gossip. "The little prince is getting married."

She needed me to join in her gloating; she could not mock someone alone. She wanted an accomplice, someone to justify her contempt and to magnify it. Having an ally proved her right and made her blameless.

I seem to be suggesting that Mother corrupted us, but that's only how it looks to me from this distance. At the time I joined her willingly, and for me this cruelty was an occasion of satisfying hilarity, even of closeness and warmth, with Mother by my side. It seemed the greatest pleasure in the world to pick on someone, especially a member of our own family. As children, when wrestling in the house or throwing ourselves against each other, we called it a pig pile.

Jonty's announcing that he was getting married we saw as a way of his singling himself out as a victim. We heard that and thought, Pig pile! Mother's thinking was that Jonty took advantage of Franny, and that Mother was deprived of Franny's attention because of this demanding child. Mother was a rival, with all of a rival's sneers.

The theme of our gossip was Jonty's unworthiness, his pretentiousness. Franny would be forced to pay for this whole thing, because Jonty was lazy and wore too much hair gel, and where was this fancy job as a radio announcer for someone who sprayed you with spittle when saying "chicken chow mein"?

Mother provided little prince updates. Franny hosted an engagement dinner. There was talk about a bachelor party. He solicited gifts, he had wagged his fiancée's hand to flaunt the ring (Floyd howled, "Is she slow?" when he heard the fiancée's name was Loris), he was measured for another tuxedo — "Why didn't he wear the one he wore to the prom?" Mother said. The wedding would include a high mass, brother Max the best man, a little troupe of flower girls and boys, a reception at Cherry Hill Country Club.

I've got something special to ask, Franny wrote me in her large childish hand. *I want you and Floyd to be ushers, and I'm hoping you might recite something from a book and Floyd will write a poem.*

"What planet is she living on?" Floyd said. "She should up her meds."

And yet I could see that he was tempted, for the opportunity to ridicule the whole affair from a front-row seat, in a denunciation he would write and declaim in heroic couplets.

"I can just see him in his new tux," Floyd said, "and Loris with that snout of hers poking through her veil like an Arab peeking out of a tent, the flower girls, the overdressed munchkins, the grotesque charade of it. 'If anyone has reason to object to the union of these two people, speak now.' And I will rise from my seat and howl at them, 'Poseur! He's rotten to the core. Stop this unholy travesty!'"

But he said he had other plans.

Though we had met Loris, the fiancée, we hardly knew her. That did not stop us from mocking her for her size. Mother said, "She works in an office. Something to do with insurance."

"She'll need it!" we said, which was just the reply Mother was looking for.

The wedding preparations were whispered about and jeered at: expensive, unnecessary, pretentious, meaningless — "Just like Jonty to put on the dog." And with this, everyone began to pity Franny, who was paying for most of it — Loris's parents were Estonian immigrants. Yet when we pretended to commiserate with Franny, she deflected it and said it was a labor of love, she wouldn't have it any other way, she was so proud. It was easy to forget in our mockery that Franny was his mother, different from Mother, and might not find any satisfaction in jeering at her own son.

Franny was stern with me. "And by the way, you haven't replied to the invitation."

She had a wobbly second chin that had an expression all its own that sometimes fiercely contradicted the sentimental one above it. As she implored me with her earnest face, her chin shook with sarcasm.

I said, "I didn't realize we were expected to reply."

"It said RSVP."

Referring to a line from his Mr. Bones routine, I parried, "Dad said that meant 'Remember Send Vedding Present.'"

Honking in sudden grief, Franny said, "I wish Dad were alive, so he could come." Overwhelmed, she sat down on my sofa, her arms and knees rising as her body sank into the cushion. "We need names! It's a sit-down dinner at Cherry Hill. It's catered. Waiters. Place settings. Linen napkins. Floral arrangements."

"This must be costing a small fortune."

"You only get married once," Franny said, and then, as an afterthought, glanced at me slyly.

"You're smiling because I took the plunge twice."

"I was not smiling. I would never smile at something like that."

But another family member had an unerring ability to detect a smile, especially a gloating one, no matter how slight a pinch in the lips, no matter how small a flicker in the eye.

"I don't think I can make it."

"You have to. You're an usher."

Even if the smile had not deterred me, "You have to" was all the reason I needed to refuse. I did not *have* to do anything, especially to please someone in this family. Franny scowled, looking severe, looking — as Floyd sometimes said — like Houdon's bust of Voltaire.

"You can find another usher."

"Floyd's backing out too," Franny said. I expected her to whine, to complain, to accuse me of failing her and undermining the wedding. But all she said was "Okay. If you really can't make it. You're right. I can find someone else."

Then she leaned forward, rocked from side to side, and hitched herself out of the sofa, smiling.

"Gotta go."

She simply accepted it, or appeared to. But that was the family way, to pretend there was no pressure, to be casual — "Hey, whatever you want." But behind this easygoing pretense was a humorless determination to take offense. There was never acceptance, there was always hell to pay. Franny's silence meant she was furious, her cheery smile meant she was hurt.

"Franny was screaming about you," Hubby told me the next day. "You should have heard her. You and Floyd let her down. She's already ordered the tuxedoes. Where is she getting the money is what I want to know."

"She never mentioned tuxedoes."

"She'll never forgive you for this."

It was true. She never did. Years later, she still mentioned my absence at Jonty's wedding as a slap in her face. She had the family's long merciless memory.

Hubby went to the wedding and was ridiculed for looking silly in his ill-fitting tuxedo. (It was Floyd's.) He was an usher. Gilbert was the other usher — he was not ridiculed. Fred went too, but he was mocked for bringing one of his small children, who cried so loudly that Fred had to leave the church just as the bride and groom were exchanging vows. Rose went and said, "It was hard to keep a straight face. I kept thinking of Jonty kicking out the windshield of the Dodge Dart."

Mother presided in the front pew, looking enigmatic. She wore her favorite lavender dress and her aquamarine necklace, white gloves and a white hat. She was demure, she accepted praise, and Father Furty's sermon mentioned Mother, her standing in the community, her years of teaching, her large and successful family, how big happy families were the repository of God's grace.

And when it was over (so Gilbert reported; he found her hilarious in her spite), Mother said under her breath, "This is a farce. He's a horrible little monster. I pity his wife," and smiling, "I give this marriage a year."

9

SELF-DENIAL

WHAT HAD SURPRISED ME MOST about the wedding was Franny's written request: *I'm hoping you might recite something from a book and that Floyd will write a poem.*

It was rare for any of us to ask a favor, especially something we cared about, because doing so would expose us. The request gave you away, betrayed your need, and a need was a weakness that could be exploited and held against you. Better not to ask.

We had refused and stayed away from the wedding, couldn't be bothered, and Floyd said, "I'm going to read a poem to those philistines?"

Had it been a simpler request we might have relented. A family characteristic was never to give what was asked, but rather to give half or less, or to complain to everyone else about how much we had been imposed upon. And the little that had been granted was never acknowledged, for an acknowledgment was a conspicuous display of gratitude, and all thanks implied the weakness of indebtedness.

Yes, all this showed extreme pettiness, but pettiness animated the family and made it work. Pettiness — these trivialities — made us a mob, and we reacted because of slights or hurts or imaginings, Mother most of all. When one of us exposed a weakness to Mother, we belonged to her. She pretended not to notice at first; then, appearing to sympathize, she pumped us for enough details to turn into gossip, and she used her knowledge of this weakness to control us. At last, she owned us.

With this in mind, early in my life I developed one of my most enduring personality traits, a reluctance to seek help or favors. I learned never to ask anything of Mother. Dad was easygoing enough and helpful at times; Mother was impossible. She did not know how to give, or rather, her way of giving was instead a genius for withholding, in ways that were not obvious yet complex, as though she was the goddess with eighteen arms, each one twisted in a peculiar gesture — one giving, one taking, one hesitating, one bobbling, one fondling, one holding a weapon or a piece of fruit, and so forth. Durga needs that many arms to deal with hostile cosmic forces, and in her incarnation as a wrathful deity, Mother had adopted a similar strategy. On a sentimental and superstitious level, the way I recited prayers, I told myself that I loved her. I even prayed for her. I gave her presents — she was propitiated with presents. On a practical level she was the enemy, but an ignorant and destructive enemy, selfish and sinister, greedy for power, attentive only when she felt her power diminished.

"What's wrong with you?" she'd ask.

"Nothing. I'm all right."

"Are you sure?"

She did not want to help me; she only wanted to know whether I was in need of help. She was not evil; in fact, Mother's example convinced me that evil as unexplainable darkness might not exist. Beyond good and evil, she was weak and vain, and these qualities were more real, more human, more widespread than what people denounced as wickedness. To me a devil was just a joke, but a woman with the face of a mother and an appetite for power was dangerous. Mother did not know any better, she did not have a thought-out program, she wasn't on a campaign to ruin us; some ancient instinct that Floyd identified as tribal was at work in her.

All of this was in my mind, for after the wedding I mentioned the extravagant expense of it to Mother — what I had heard of the elaborate arrangements through the family whispers.

"How could Franny afford this big bash?"

Mother did not reply. She gave me one of her knowing, ask-me-another-question looks, a smugness, a certain slyness, a cunning display of both denying and possessing a secret, implying a deep wish to prolong the pettiness of questioning the expense.

"So, um, where did she get it?" I asked again, because Mother had made it clear that she harbored secrets.

"All I know is, they don't have an awful lot," Mother said. "Marvin doesn't make much at the mall, but he's a scrapper, you know, and Franny's been a brick. I know she thinks the world of you. She's so proud of you all."

Most of this was platitude: you had to praise someone before damning them, followed by the usual cant that we were a big happy family.

I said, with a directness I seldom used on Mother, "Did you give them any money for the wedding?"

"Who wants to know?"

"I was just wondering."

She giggled and said, "I helped them out a little bit."

This floored me. Mother, who had done nothing but mock Franny for indulging Jonty, and jeer at Jonty for being selfish and lazy, who had ridiculed the whole notion of a grand wedding and a high mass, who had, loudly at times, threatened to stay away from the whole affair ("I could sit at home and watch *All My Children*"; she seldom missed that soap opera) — Mother had actually given Franny money for Jonty's wedding.

"Helped them out a little bit" could mean two things in Mother-speak: a pittance she was boasting about, or a large amount she was concealing. She wouldn't tell me how much, though she implied, by deflecting the question, wincing slightly, that it was quite a lot. At the time, I thought, What a generous and forgiving soul to contribute to her grandson's wedding.

Unexpected news always seems to create a series of aftershocks, which we experience in successive gulps of elaboration. When "I helped them out a little bit" sank in, I realized that this news was also an indication that Mother, who claimed to be poor, had money. "I'd love to help you," she would say, "but where would I get the money? I have nothing." But she did have some. I wondered how much but didn't ask for details. Her story had always been that she had so little she still bought day-old bread and dented cans at the supermarket, using coupons. Money was not something you spent; it was a life force, something you saved.

One of Mother's essential traits was frugality, withholding praise, money, even simple attention. She would look away when I mentioned something exceptional I had done — wrote a story, won a merit badge. "What was that you said? Oh, really?" And she had a special way of refusing to help, trumpeting nostrils and the jeer, "You're not man enough to do that?" or "What you need is good old-fashioned elbow grease," or "God helps those who help themselves."

Saying so, she took a step backward, as if to dismiss me or give herself a better view of my failure.

Had she turned her back on me I could have managed, but she lingered to watch me falter. Her attitude did not make me strong; it made me insecure and resentful. Her lack of support argued a lack of interest. In time, this distance did its work, with the result — curious and sad to my young mind — that she ceased to know me.

Asking for money was out of the question and could be risky, for I knew that she would not just refuse the money — for a bike, a tent, a Boy Scout uniform, or a jackknife — she would take pleasure in belittling such useless things. Why did I think I needed a bike? I could walk just as easily. And where would I put a bike? There was no room in the garage. And if I had a bike, what would I do when I needed a new chain or a tire or a tube? A bike was just the beginning of more expenses. "Bikes cost money!" And spending money in this way was pure vanity. Take a bus.

A Saturday matinee cost ten cents. At the age of nine I did not have ten cents, and Mother refused to give it to me.

"But it's not the money," she said—although I knew it was. "You want to sit in a movie theater on a glorious day like this?" She scoffed at the self-indulgent waste of such time. "You should stay outside in God's sunshine."

God made the day for a purpose, for work and profit, and so good weather was a blessing, a cause for rejoicing. It was sinful to refuse to rejoice in it and be thankful.

Even as she hectored me, I suspected that Mother did not believe this. At bottom she was not spiritual at all. Saving money was both an art and a science; it was a way of life. This was reason enough to keep us from the movies, from any spending at all. But along with it was Mother's need for control.

It was fatal to ask why.

"Because I said so!"

Disobedience was severely punished, but the odd thing about our obedience was that, once we had submitted, we foundered and so did she: Mother did not know what to do with us. We were, like lifers in a reformatory, to be controlled for the sake of control. We needed to learn the virtues: get up early, work hard, obey your teacher, impress your boss, don't get out of line, and never complain. Kids who sold newspapers Mother respected more than kids who buried themselves in books or who excelled in a sport.

Mother's ideals terrified me. One was the pale boy in a threadbare coat and a bad haircut standing before a stack of newspapers at a street corner, clanking change in the pocket of his filthy apron. Another was the girl scuffing along a snowy street with her aged mother on one arm and a shopping bag on the other. The teenager in white overalls pushing a trolley of dirty dishes in a café and busing tables. The grinning boy with slicked-down hair in an old suit going door-to-door selling ointment or greeting cards he'd received as catalog mail orders under the promise *Earn $$$ in Your Spare Time!* These were the people Mother admired, the paragons she held up to us. The joyless, overworked, unimaginative youths, seeming so dull and luckless and unambitious to me, were embodiments of virtue to Mother, who believed that time spent with a book was time wasted, that there was something unrewarding, even effete, in study. Where was the elbow grease in scholarship? Roll up your sleeves and get your hands dirty!

Once, foolishly, on a Saturday afternoon, I let slip the fact that I was going to a matinee with a girl I longed to be alone with. I was perhaps twelve or thirteen. The movie was one I wanted to see, and the day was rainy. How was it that I was so unwise as to mention this to Mother? Perhaps I was so happy with this plan that I had let my guard down.

Mother stared at me, smiling in pity, casting her shadow over me. I had begun to gnaw my fingers.

"Why?" she asked.

I had no answer. I didn't go, and when I broke it to the girl, saying, "My mother won't let me," the girl laughed at me for being a simpleton.

The next year I pleased Mother by getting a job at the Stop and Shop. At first I was too young to stock shelves but just the right age to round up shopping carts in the parking lot. This was how I spent every Saturday for the next four years, ascending the supermarket ladder from the parking lot, to bagging groceries at the checkout stand, to stocking shelves at night, and at last to the after-hours weekend cleanup, the sweeping and mopping. As I was telling a harassed woman, "Ritz crackers? Aisle five," or "Velveeta? Dairy case," my school friends were at the football game or the library. I was neither a jock nor a scholar. My coworkers were the feebs, the failures, the wiseguys, the sturdy louts who saw such jobs as their whole future.

Work hard, be humble, be anonymous, be grateful, be self-effacing and save. Mother never said why. Mortify your flesh — that's what saints did, such as Tarcisius, the boy martyr who allowed himself to be stomped to death by a mob rather than let them desecrate the host. It was not clear to me how Tarcisius's example in Rome applied to me in Mother Land, but I took the message to be martyrdom and self-denial.

Mother set us in competition with each other. Fred worked for Father, Floyd for a stationer, I was at the supermarket. Hubby and Gilbert were too small to compete, and already Franny and Rose were Mother's handmaidens, learning housework. Being the eldest, Fred worked longer hours and earned the most money. The idea was that, in time, Fred would learn the business and eventually take over — as a shoe clerk. No one asked if this was what Fred wanted.

Floyd's part-time job at the stationer's was odd. The owner of the business was afraid of the rats that had nested in the basement and the stockroom and penetrated the rest of the building, so he kept Floyd with him at all times, to scare the rats. Floyd's fundamental task was to stamp his feet and drive them into hiding. Floyd was poorly paid, he threatened to quit, but Mother said to him, "What will you do then?" for she could not imagine his existing without a job. Being a full-time high school student, doing homework, using the library, playing basketball — which he excelled at — and relaxing with his friends was an absurdity, out of the question.

I knew this was unfair — wrong — but as Mother said, with Dad backing her up, "As long as you live in this house, you follow our rules," and so I did.

Because I was overworked and mediocre and miserable, I found school dreary, and any memory of it was inevitably an embarrassment. I was, simply, not a scholar, not a participant. I endured it, without any distinction.

On graduation, I enrolled in a university and left home, paying my own way, using my supermarket savings. "You're on your own," Mother said with her customary shrug. But I liked it: at last, away from Mother, I felt less careworn, less troubled; I felt energized, more optimistic. I began to get a notion of who I was and what I wanted, and when I had a difficult year — it came suddenly, soon after I left home — it served as such a useful gauge for all the rest of them, I regarded it as my best year.

10

THE BEST YEAR OF MY LIFE

THIS, the best year of my life, began in the worst way, more proof of the sadism of fate, convincing me that, somewhere, someone was enjoying my pain — a merciless plotter, perhaps one of Mother's wickeder allies, if not Mother herself. I got the appalling news while the whole family watched me, all of them chewing and gabbling at the kitchen table, near where the phone hung on the wall. This was a few days before Christmas, so everyone was at home, the entire cast assembled at the front of the stage for this — not tragedy, tragedy seldom visits the young — this cruel farce. I was eighteen.

"It's for you," Mother said, handing me the receiver.

My whole life was to change. I was about to step into a hole and spend a year in the dark. Typical, I thought, for my life as I lived it then — in bewilderment, frowning at the futility, and resenting the squandered time as it unrolled and flapped around me, slapping my head and making me lose the thread of whatever I was trying to do — seemed ragged and plotless: random, rancorous, out of my control, meandering from disorder to chaos, in the general direction of oblivion.

In retrospect, from the vantage point of late middle age — the helpful heights and clear air that are part of aging's greatest consolations — I see (as I wander through memories of Mother Land) that my life was closely plotted and consequential, with the structural elaboration and subtle motifs of a Victorian novel, interwoven with grace notes, subplots, and byways, coincidences that stretched credulity, and surprises so unexpected and yet inevitable. This life of mine — perhaps all lives — suffered from an excess of design: nothing random, nothing wasted, no longueurs, everything hinged and tight. Everything mattered, and the hole I'd stepped into was a magical thoroughfare that carried me to the future.

Though, as I say, at the time it all appeared to be an aimless monochrome, regret and shame and wrong turnings and wasted effort. And worse, humiliation and one specific disgrace.

Whatever befell me, my mother's shrill isolating cry was always "It's your own goddamned fault!" That blame rang in my head for years. But decades later, when other troubles came my way, I was able to say, "I've seen worse," and really mean it. Much worse than being thirty, with a wife and two small children and no money, and recently fired from my teaching job in Singapore and having to save myself, and struggling to find a house to live in. Worse than being fucked up and far from home in India, lost in China, and hard up and buried alive in London. Worse than being cuckolded. Worse than hearing "I'm leaving you" in a stifling and pissy phone booth on a crackling receiver stinking of cigarettes, "and I've found someone else," and the miserable litigation of (so it seemed) the death sentence of divorce, and the half-life of splitting up and losing that house I had struggled to find earlier in this paragraph. Worse than decades of "You're not going to like what I'm about to tell you." Worse than the loss of my father, for an old man's dying is a natural process, even if it had been hastened by a nagging wife and a quarreling family. That singular disgrace was worse than anything I was ever to know. It was entirely a young man's stupidity, as Mother was to remind me again and again: all my own goddamned fault.

That year, my first year of college, I was away most of the time, but back home for vacations, still one of the family, working to pay my way, with obligations burdening me — school bills, travel bills, food and room bills.

"It's for you," Mother was saying, now very cross, because in my angry reverie I had not taken the phone from her.

Even if you were nearer the phone, Mother answered it. All calls were routed through her, so she was in the know. Mother had insisted on the short cord: we were all visible and audible on the phone.

"A girl," Mother explained to the rest of the table.

Father answered his cue. He bit the meat off his fork and said, "Some dizzy blonde."

"Jay?"

Mona's voice was flattened, drained of vitality, but with an insinuating weight to it, just a desperate muscle of sound, clutching at me to listen. All that nuance in the way she said it, condemning me, making my name into a fault.

"Hi there," I said cheerily to throw my family off, because all eight of them were listening, holding their knives and forks upright, no longer chewing, so they could hear better.

"I missed my period. It's been three weeks. I don't know what to do. I'm a wreck" — her voice began to falter and break — "and you don't even care!"

"Yes," I said, my voice high and insincere, "I do," and I could see Mother turning her head to hear better, "as a matter of fact." All I heard was blame, that it was my period, my delay, my problem. But I kept smiling for the sake of the table. "I'll see you in a few days."

"No! Tomorrow! It has to be tomorrow. This is serious." Mona began to cry, snorting and croaking in a way that stung my ear and rang against the fragile skull box of my brain.

Eight people were staring at my head and raising a hot blister of guilt on my neck.

As I hung up, cutting Mona off in a yell of complaint, I prepared a smile for the table and turned to their silent faces. Even four-year-old Gilbert had stopped yammering. My eyes were glazed. I was shrugging, looking fatuous.

"Who was that?" Mother asked.

"Nobody you know," I said. "Nobody special."

Floyd said, "Oh, sure. I believe that. Indubitably."

"Jay's got a girlfriend," Hubby said in the slow, wheezy voice of a husky boy with a throat full of food. "And I know why."

Franny, who often asked Mother's questions for her, said, "Why?"

"So he can look at her panties."

Rose said, "Don't be fresh."

Mother smiled grimly at Father. "Are you going to let him get away with that insolence?"

Father set down his fork with a click, and swung — and both Fred and Floyd leaned back so as to spare themselves, as Father caught Hubby's head with the meat of his hand, knocking him sideways off his chair. As the blow connected, Father, overtaken by pity, reached for Hubby's arm to break his fall, but in his frantic clumsiness crushed him against the radiator instead, so that Hubby scorched his arm and howled.

"Kids wreck a marriage," Father said, for Mother's sake.

"Eat," Mother said to me, because I was goggling at Hubby's reddened arm. "Your dinner's getting cold."

In the moralizing voice of the eldest, Fred said, "I always tell people not to call me at mealtime."

"That's the way it should be," Mother said.

I had the sense that they suspected something, that all the panic and shame showed on my face. But really, it was all too dreadful for even my family to guess.

"Nobody special," I had said, and in fact Mona had become nobody special. Until that moment of my hearing her voice she had almost faded from my mind. A month or so before, I had seen her for what I had thought would be the last time. She was two years ahead of me and rented a room in a big frame house at the far edge of the campus, across the road from the Homestead, where Emily Dickinson once lived. I had visited Mona to say goodbye. We made love as if in a joyless ceremony of farewell. I was so inept a lover I never feared the worst. Pregnancies were the result of passion and experience; I was too tentative and unconfident to accomplish such a thing. I always felt off-target and impatient, as Mona squirmed in frustration, barely penetrated, as though I were merely chafing at her, approximating the act.

I had noticed her first in the cafeteria, walking fast, dressed like a scullery maid in a brown uniform and a brown cap and an apron. Later I saw her behind the counter, working with both hands, serving mashed potatoes with her right, ladling gravy with her left. The diners were all dormitory students, of whom I was one, a freshman. I loved her simple scowling good looks, a loose lock of blond hair at the rim of her cap, a neat narrow nose and skeptical lips, skinny shoulders, thin fingers. She was beautiful. I took her to be an unimpressed townie. Such a worker could seem to me aloof and unapproachable; even a scrubber could seem haughty. I had no idea she was a junior, two years older than me and an honor student. I watched her for a month or more. She never smiled. Her sulks aroused me.

I saw her in a bar one night — she was drinking with friends — and spoke to her. Her friends left us. Drinking seemed to make us equals. She said, "You think you're so smart," when I expressed an opinion. I was reading and quoting *Les Fleurs du Mal* — Baudelaire was my hero then. But she liked the fact that I worked on weekends at the university chicken farm, scraping and hosing down the cages. "Everyone else is at the football game," she said, sharing her contempt with me. Drink made her sullen and resentful, yet I could see that for all her severity she was on my side, a fellow worker.

A week or so later she sneaked me into her room. We lay on her bed, looking at Emily Dickinson's house, and I recited "Wild Nights — Wild Nights!" We made love. She could tell I was new to this. When she found out that I was so much younger she berated me — she had been drinking

— and said I had deceived her. Still, we met a few more times in her room ("Wild Nights should be / Our luxury!") before deciding not to see each other again. That was before Thanksgiving. Now it was almost Christmas, which was why her phone call had been so unexpected.

She lived in a suburb of Boston, a long bus ride and then a meander through streets of dirty ice and soot-crusted snow. I had thought seeing her might improve matters, but no. She said, "I haven't told anyone. I can't tell my parents — they'd kill me. You're the only person who knows. You have to help me."

This desperate little speech became an unwelcome refrain. Each time I saw her after that, I expected a reprieve, but the news was always bad, and got worse. When she called, which was almost every day ("It's her again," Mother said), I hoped for her to say, "At last!" But she never did. Her frequent letters ("Another one for you," Mother said. "Is it her?") were long and gloomy and blaming and self-lacerating. *Why did I ever let myself get involved with an upstart like you?* My precociousness was like a devious fault. I was still technically a teenager. Baudelaire's boasts mocked me with their cynical worldliness. I burned Mona's letters.

More weeks passed. It was January. Mona was two months along. Every phone call and letter raised my hopes and in the same instant sank them. In my dormitory room I woke up each morning dazed and sometimes happy until I remembered that my predicament was not a bad dream but a fact. I prayed for good news and found out, always after a suspenseful delay, that nothing had changed. And it was worse by far for Mona, though only I knew that. I was her solitary confidant, burdened by her misery.

Fred was at law school in New York City. New York was the wider world; people had the solutions to pregnancies there. I visited him in February. I did not tell him why I had come. I stayed in his apartment and haunted doctors' offices — just dropped in. *Do you have an appointment?* I had no idea how these things worked; I knew that abortion was illegal. Without an appointment I never saw a doctor, which was probably for the best, because how would I ask the crucial question?

"Oh, God," Fred said, "oh, Jesus," when I told him. He held his head. His haircut looked frivolous in his whitened fingers. He said, "You'll have to tell Dad and Ma."

"No," I said.

Fred's helpless panic frightened me.

"They won't be able to help," I said. "They won't know what to do. They'll go nuts."

Mother would blame me, Father would rage. I knew that. I could hear them. I knew every word of accusation they would utter.

Inert, scandalized, terrified by what he knew—feeling complicit, because he knew everything—Fred suggested that I leave New York. Though I was hurt, I was not surprised. This was my problem. And it was painful being in New York, where I envied and hated the rich, who were easily able to solve these problems with a wink and an envelope of money.

Sometime in March I moved in with Mona, her little room off campus at the top of the big frame house.

She was kinder to me when we were together. She said, "I need you now. Please help me. I can't depend on anyone else. See me through this and I'll never ask anything more of you. Do you understand? I don't want to marry you. I just want to have the baby."

"And then what?"

"Give it away," she said, blinking at her tears. "Put it up for adoption. There are agencies."

I was not shocked. This was simple desperation, like crime. The main challenge was that you had to get away with it.

Mona pushed her fists against her eyes and became stern. "If my family finds out, I'm dead."

And so am I, I thought.

Mona stopped going to classes. She got a job in a greenhouse, where they grew roses, in the countryside beyond the campus. In this way she kept out of sight. I studied, I did my work. I hated Baudelaire and developed a mind of my own, based on our predicament, and I worried all day. Mona and I lived as a serious couple in her small room.

Though I still attended lectures and wrote papers and read the required books, I did so in a detached and almost disembodied way, as another person, younger, much simpler than the fellow who woke appalled each day and comforted Mona. Writing home, repeating platitudes about the weather and my studies, I was someone else again, very guarded, and yet an earnest member of the family.

That was three people. But I was another man, too: the asparagus picker. Studying was unproductive, and Mona was working at the greenhouse, so I got a job on a work crew harvesting asparagus. I heard about this from another hard-up student and was welcomed by the farmer, who needed men. The crop was early, and it looked strange to me. Eight-to-ten-inch spears had begun to appear in clusters all over the wide bare fields; no foliage, just these slender, sharp pointed shoots. I crouched with a dozen fieldworkers, poking my cutter into the earth, severing the spears a few inches below ground level. I thought: This is real and raw. Someday I will put this odd work into a book.

All the workers were Spanish-speaking men, most of them young. They cut the asparagus, muttering among themselves, sometimes laughing, as they loaded the boxes and swung them onto the flat bed of the trailer. They did not talk to me except when we were riding in the back of the truck, being taken to a new field.

They said they were from Puerto Rico and spent eight months doing this, as migrants moving north from Florida and Georgia, where they harvested whatever was ripe — oranges, peaches, blueberries, sweet corn, tomatoes. They bantered with each other and were polite and pleasant to me when they found out I could speak some Spanish.

Puerto Rico seemed remote, exotic, sunny. They cut cane and picked pineapples there. They missed their wives and girlfriends, they said. In September or October they would go back with the money they'd earned.

"*Isla bonita*," I said.

"*Isla barata!*" one man replied. And the others joined in, giving me examples of how cheap it was to live in Puerto Rico.

I picked asparagus every morning for three weeks until, in late May, Mona, who was swollen and obviously pregnant, said, "My parents are asking when I'm coming home. They might visit. We have to get out of here."

We took a bus to New York, where I phoned Fred. I had not dared to call ahead, fearing that he would have time to think of an excuse and might rebuff us. We had nowhere else to go. Two days there proved to me that Fred didn't want us. He did not want to know this much. He was fretting again, worrying me with his fear.

He said, "Sec, what you need is a plan."

I saw an airfare on a store window: *San Juan $49*. That seemed simple. I had the money. I remembered all the shouts of *Isla barata, muy barata!* We flew there and felt safe, living in a cheap hotel for the first few nights, then got a room with a balcony in a tall house in Old San Juan. It had been a rash decision, but it was workable, as though we had dreamed it.

Away from Fred and our families in the United States we felt like people with a plan — older, independent, unobserved. It was my first experience of the way travel turns you into a new person. I understood, too, that by going far away we had removed ourselves from a dreary reality of intrusions into our private world. When people ask you questions you can't answer, I thought, it's time to leave and find new people who don't ask. On this distant island of Spanish speakers we were secure. We had enough money to last a month. In the meantime I would look for work. We felt safer, almost happy in our remoteness, among people who seemed worse off than we were, in a disorderly place that matched my mood.

I'm working on a freighter, I wrote home. *We've just docked in San Juan.*

That was another person, the deckhand. And Mother accepted this lame explanation. Because I was not asking her for anything, she was complacent, or perhaps preoccupied — all those children. She had no curiosity about me. She was probably reassured that I was taken care of and didn't need anything.

I'll be home in August or September.

The Caribe Hilton in Puerta de Tierra was fairly new and looking for employees. I applied for a job as a lifeguard, but hearing me speak English, the personnel manager suggested that I work in the newly opened restaurant. The customers were mostly English-speaking tourists. I got the job. I worked from six in the evening until midnight, when I took the bus back to Old San Juan. Now I had a salary. Mona signed up for Spanish classes. She was too big, too hot, too uncomfortable to attempt more than that.

The Puerto Ricans were kind to us. They had two faces: a dutiful, solemn, and submissive one they presented to gringos — *Anything you say, boss!* I recognized this from the asparagus fields. The other, a noisy, mischievous, teasing, helpful face, they saved for each other. They treated Mona and me as members of the family. Accustomed to messy problems, they were people who did not ask for explanations. I was grateful, though it took me a while to understand that the reason they were kind was be-cause they saw a young, pale, pregnant woman and her even younger man — probably not her husband — riding the buses, sitting in the plaza, eating ice cream, entering the stairway in the old building near the expensive Zaragozana restaurant, where we never ate. They sympathized.

Still, every day I woke up from the peacefulness of deep sleep and remembered our predicament. Contemplating it numbed me like a drug.

My family believed I was working on a ship. Mona had told her family she was teaching school in New York City. No one would find out the truth. We were too far away. Mona's mail went care of Fred in New York; he forwarded it to her in weekly bundles.

And so two months passed.

I was fine, helping Mona through this, yet whenever I remembered my family — Mother, Father, inquisitive siblings — I grew worried, because there was so much to tell, all of it hidden, all of it incriminating. I knew what everyone would say; I winced, seeing Mother's face. I had no response other than agreeing that it was all my own goddamned fault.

The strangeness of San Juan consoled me and seemed an effective form of concealment. The rough kindness of Puerto Ricans was a reassurance, because they were taking us on faith; not a single soul knew us here. I loved that anonymity, which was also a sort of innocence. I was blameless, just a skinny boy who lived in a room on Calle San Francisco with a pregnant young woman, and who set off at five from the plaza each evening on the bus to Puerta de Tierra and the Caribe Hilton. We had canned soup almost every meal. At night, when we switched on the light, glossy purplish cockroaches scuttled on the floor. Dust and noise filled the air, the street seemed to pass through the tall windows of our upper room, even the sea brimmed at our windows. But no one knew us, so there was no shame, only the tedious struggle we shared with everyone else.

Now and then it rained hard, the brief summer downpours. I carried an umbrella and wore a Panama hat. These were affectations; I was pretending to be seedy. I was off Baudelaire and reading Graham Greene and Lawrence Durrell. I learned enough Spanish so that I seldom needed to speak English. I practiced the Puerto Rican accent, *meemo* for *mismo, Joe* for *Yo,* and called the bus the *guagua* and money *chavo.* I felt that no one saw me until I got to the restaurant, and I discovered that, working there,

I was almost invisible too: I was just my uniform jacket and shirt and bow tie. My job was to take reservations over the phone, to show diners to their tables, to distribute menus, to wish them a pleasant evening. For this I was paid enough to cover rent and food for Mona and me, and to put a little extra away for our return. Now I understood how a rash decision could become a whole irreversible life.

Mona grew weak and unsteady, as though her pregnancy was an illness, and she looked at our little room with homesick eyes. She woke in the middle of the night and sobbed. Her ankles swelled. She developed heat rash. Now and then she raged at me: "How did I ever get involved with you!" Or she said, "You are all I have. Please don't leave me. Just see me through to the end."

They were like lines in a play I had wandered into, one of those anxious dreams of the deep end. I seemed to be leading someone else's life, as in that same dream when everything that occurs is unexpected yet absurdly logical.

One day I was late for work. I said to the restaurant manager, "I'm sorry I'm late. My wife is sick — she's pregnant."

He was from Peru, and his beaky nose, hard jaw, and hooded eyes gave him the look of an Inca chief. He stared at me with a seriousness that made me uncomfortable. Then he tapped my shoulder.

"Don't say 'I'm sorry.' Never say 'sorry.'" He wagged his finger. "A man doesn't say 'sorry.'" A few days later he said, "How is your wife? Better, I hope."

I gave him an answer but did not know what I was saying or who was speaking. I thought: I am whoever you take me to be. I am living five lives at once, and in one of them, of course, I am also working on a freighter. None of these lives represented the person I knew myself to be.

Mona and I saved whatever we could, and so we had no spare money. We were like everyone else we saw in San Juan: strollers, bus riders, eating the deep-fried meat pies they called *pastelillos,* treating ourselves to the slushy cones they called *piraguas,* sitting in the plaza, going to bed early. We had no telephone, no radio. The TV in the bar on the corner was tuned to soccer and news and boxing matches. We never read the newspaper, though I sometimes glanced at the headline in the daily *El Imparcial.* We had no idea what was happening in the world beyond Puerto

Rico, but one day the landlady said that the dictator Trujillo had been assassinated in Santo Domingo, and the drama of this news made our nearby plaza festive with the laughter of chattering men.

I grew fond of the disorder that concealed us, the friendly crowds, the narrow sidewalks, the heat and sunshine that seemed to soothe people and soften their mood.

One day I saw a man I recognized from a provocative lecture he had given in Amherst, at the time when Mona and I were sharing a room. He was the Reverend William Sloane Coffin, a well-known political radical, walking with two other men. They pushed past us, talking, and entered the Zaragozana, and because that was a restaurant we couldn't afford, I stopped seeing him as a radical. He was a privileged, prosperous man from the other world.

Our only way of communicating with people back home was by letter. I wrote a few more, explaining that my ship, the freighter, was in port. I fictionalized myself as a seaman, all of the details secondhand from my reading of Jack Kerouac. Mona wrote regularly to her family. Her story was that she was still working in New York as a teacher, living at Fred's address. Fred stamped and forwarded her letters home; he sent her the letters from her family.

And every morning I woke with a film of damp sweat on my face and remembered that I was living with Mona, who was pregnant, in a room in Old San Juan, and due at work at the Hilton restaurant at five-thirty. And I went numb, thinking: Hold on, stay calm, the days are passing, no one knows. There was a baby in Mona; there was a darkness inside me and a woeful weight on my soul. My thoughts were for Mona and myself, but the woe was: my family must not find out about this shameful wicked business.

Mona was obsessed by the same need for concealment. This need made us quieter, gentler with each other, like a pair of felons, moving with stealth, keeping close to avoid detection: fugitives from justice. We never ceased to think of ourselves as sneaks, and though we talked about the pregnancy, we seldom spoke of the baby except as a problem we were solving.

I was at home in San Juan's disorder: hot, littered, poor, the cracked yellow stucco, the scrawled-on walls, the slum beyond the battlements of the city wall called La Perla — the Pearl — where people were much worse off than we were: barefoot children, ragged women, drunken men.

One day in August Mona got a letter from an agency in Boston with the pitiful name The Home for Little Wanderers. The message was that they would accept Mona, see her through the birth of the baby, and then take the child. Hopeful families were waiting for such children. *Please rest assured that we will find a loving home for your child.*

Mona cried at the letter but admitted that it was what she wanted: a relief, a solution.

She woke that night and sobbed, saying that because we both wore glasses, the child would have bad eyes. She wept at the thought of sending this myopic child groping into the world.

We bought tickets to Boston. I told the Peruvian manager I would be leaving. He said, "Just as I was getting used to you."

"Lo siento," I said, as a joke. Sorry.

A few days before we left San Juan, the landlady handed us a letter with an American stamp and the Calle San Francisco address — not a letter forwarded from Fred. It was from Mona's mother. *We know everything,* it began. Mona's father had gone to New York, to Fred's apartment. He had asked to see his daughter. Fred told him the whole story and then had given him our address. *Dad's on the warpath,* Mona's mother wrote, *and so is JP's family. I had a long talk with them.*

The next days were tense. We expected Mona's father to descend on us. But of course we were too far away. Choosing San Juan had been a leap in the dark, but it had saved us. No one came. We left for Boston one hot night. We had brought all our extras — pots, towels, sheets — to La Perla and put them in the arms of a grateful woman.

Mona sat awkwardly on the plane, eight months pregnant, and we arrived in Boston at dawn. We had breakfast in a diner on Boylston Street near the Public Garden, and afterward walked into the garden. I had gotten used to walking very slowly with Mona at my side. Mona said she felt ill. She sat down on a bench and vomited onto the grass. I held her as she wiped her mouth on my shoulder. As she lay against me, heavy with trust and resignation, we were like lovers on that hot August morning. At nine o'clock we walked to the street and hailed a cab.

"Don't come with me," she said. She was sparing me. She got in and told the driver to take her to The Home for Little Wanderers.

"Joy Street," she added.

The names snatched at my heart. I called home from a phone booth at Sullivan Square and took the bus to the Cape, walking up the long hill to my house, feeling dizzy from the heat and my sleepless night on the plane.

I was returning from all my lives to the one life that I hated, and I dreaded what was to come.

On heavy feet I scuffed up the front stairs to the porch, announcing myself on the wood planks. The front door was open. No one met me. The screen door slapped shut on its spring, the coil lashing the door-frame. I was aware of wooden steps, wooden porch, wooden door, like the splintery portals to the Day of Judgment.

"In here," Mother called from the kitchen. She had heard me.

She was seated grimly with her arms on the kitchen table. Floyd sat in a chair at the far wall, trying not to smile, though he did so, horribly, half gloating, half in pity. Then he crept out of the room, and his eyes said, *Oh, boy, you're in for it.*

Mother's face was fierce and hawk-like, her nose pinched, her lips com-pressed. "Well!" She seemed to be staring me down, and at last she said with a screech of triumphant sarcasm, "I hope you're proud of yourself."

I hung my head, defeated by what I had done, as she berated me. "You should be ashamed," and "How could you do this to us?"

"And look at your jacket." She was scowling at the fresh stain of vomit on my shoulder.

The next days and weeks were easier, because Mona and I had man-aged to conceal our crime — we thought of it as a crime, a misdeed at any rate, much worse than an error. No one knew that she was living with a foster family. Only I knew where she was. I visited her secretly. She was impatient, we held hands, she said, "I think it'll be soon." That family took her to the hospital for the birth, a boy. I visited her and held the baby — he had a reddened and contented face. No one but us ever saw the child.

The second time I went to the hospital, Mona said, "The other moth-ers were laughing after you left. They said, 'How old is he? He's just a kid.'"

That was the last time I saw the baby. And I did not see Mona until after she left the hospital. Then it was late September, and we were in Amherst. We were two students again, back in the world, feeling helpless, altered, burdened with a sad story of a lost boy that we could not tell anyone. I was sad but relieved; Mona was simply sad and looked small. Some nights she begged me to come to her room, just to hold her while she sobbed. We lay clothed in her narrow bed. I turned nineteen. Mona graduated early, in January, and went away to teach. She wrote a few times, then stopped writing altogether.

I somehow knew that I would never again feel so desperate, so despised, so weak and blamed, as I did that year. And I was right. The experience of the year did not make me strong, but it gave me a vivid memory of helplessness that I carried with me through my life. I could always compare this example with whatever hardships I faced. Sometimes, in a dilemma, I smiled. Someone would say to me, "You're not going to like what I'm about to tell you." I didn't smile, but I knew even before I heard it that I had known much worse. I was prepared, remembering that year.

As for the child, wherever he was, he was better off. Now and then I dreamed that he had found me, and cornered me, and was screaming at me for the fate I had assigned him.

Sometimes people talk about an illness or a terrible accident they had in childhood when, bedridden, confined to a room, they read a great deal or learned a language or gained a skill. It was like that. I had learned to live by my wits, how to survive, to trust my instincts, to be secretive. I knew that my life was elsewhere. I had suspected, long before Mona's first phone call, that I could not rely on my family, that whatever they knew of me they would use against me, to undermine me. I had been right.

Afterward, I never went into the details with anyone. I could not bear to. That hard year, though, made the rest of my life easier, and its awful episodes were mild by comparison. I knew what desperate passages were: a whole year of them that had left their mark on me. "The worst year of my life," I used to moan, but as time passed I grew to know it, for all its struggle, as a good year, with a beginning, a middle, an end; a whole plot that had been lived before by other people, but had to be lived by me to understand it; my best year.

11

SECRETS

FORTY YEARS PASSED, my writing years, my years on the move, away from Mother Land. That pivotal episode of fatherhood tempered me, prepared me for the worst, and made me a man. Nothing so hard was ever to test me again.

Those four decades were the years of my active life, as a traveler, borne by the currents of the world, a wanderer in distant cities, a resident in dusty republics and happy islands, a husband, a father of two more boys, twice divorced. And, after a slow start, a successful writer with faithful readers, though none of them members of my family.

After all this—the struggle in words to describe the struggle in my life that became my obsessive subject, my life depicted in the tangles and thickets of my prose—I had thought that was it, that my life was over, time to . . . not fade, but to grow more compact, with the economy of a small trembling animal that wrinkles its wet nose and hugs itself into a ball, warming its limbs, to await the end, having left behind wives, children, property, books, a mountain of paper, savings, and, at last, hope abandoned. So when I was summoned to the Cape for Father's death watch, I went without hesitation. I had nowhere else to go.

Going home to live was a sure sign of personal loss. Failures ended up back where they started. I had always felt this to be true. "He lives with his mother"—you couldn't be worse off than that. But I told myself that it was temporary. I wasn't desperate, I wasn't living in Mother's house, just in the general vicinity, in Mother Land. I would be fine. So it seemed at the time.

Soon after I got back, Father's health declined, we were called to the hospital to witness him die, Mother became queen, and we were all children again, returned to our long-ago roles and rivalries. I was at first startled. I had forgotten how dangerous we were, how angry, how vicious we could be.

"He's a nonce, he's a numpty," Floyd said of Fred, and when Gilbert's name came up, "He's an exile."

"Ma says Floyd's poems are porno," Hubby said. And of Franny, "She's a moose."

"Ma finds Floyd upsetting," Franny said. "It's his attitude. 'Gimme, gimme.' He has bad energy and he yells at traffic. She hates driving anywhere with him."

"All she does is worry about her two spoiled brats," Rose said of Franny and her kids, Jonty and Max.

"I dread Angela's birthday," Fred said. "Ma's mourning gets darker every year."

"Hubby eats too much," Franny said. "It's always the wrong food. I know he's good with his hands, but have you seen the size of him? Floyd calls him a parade float."

"I've memorized most of Floyd's poems," Gilbert said, and without a flicker of irony, "One of their characteristics is that they're very easy to memorize."

What did they say of me?

As a child I had been watchful, secretive, suspicious of all interest in me, such questions as "What are you doing?" and "Where have you been?" I usually answered with lies. The terror I felt when Mother said, "I've got a bone to pick with you!" made me defiantly untruthful. But I seldom told Mother the truth, or revealed anything personal to her. She would betray me; she would use the disclosure against me; she would entrap me. And Mother must have known that I habitually lied to her. She always looked sideways at me in annoyance, wondering what I really felt, and perhaps fearful of finding out, for it had to be obvious to her that I was a lonely fantasizing child, yearning for a life elsewhere.

My childhood dilemma was easy to explain, if anyone cared to hear it, though no one did. I was not adrift, I was stuck. Being fifteen years old was like living on the lower floor of a house where, on the floor above, a man was speaking to a woman in a different room, who couldn't hear him but was talking back to him, though he couldn't hear her. To a shout, which might be tedious or revealing or shocking, life-altering or wise, each yelled, "What?" Other people, too, were calling to one another in the rooms above me, each deaf to the other.

I could hear every word. But they didn't know I was listening, or even that I existed. That was not my dilemma. My dilemma was: What do I do with all the things I am hearing?

It was my first intimation, not that I would be a writer in any important way, but that writing what I heard, or imagined, might help ease my mind.

After I left home the first time, struck with the trauma of my best year, I found it simple to invent a life for myself. I was a student, so schoolwork prevented me from going home often, and the need to work meant I had to travel and save. The scholar-traveler was the person I described in letters home, though this earnest and prudent young man did not in the least resemble me. These were the waning years of letter writing, of three or four inked sheets of notepaper folded in half and stuffed in an envelope, or two double-spaced typed pages beginning, *Dear Family.*

The late 1980s and email ended that with forgettable, untraceable, disposable, disputable cyber-messages and telegraphic memos, more like garbled conversations shouted into the wind than the stacks of letters I sent home, amounting almost to an epistolary novel. My letters were so substantial I could conceal myself in them and create a new man. I hid in my inventions, and my ardent fictionalizing in these letters home helped make me a novelist: sharpened my imagination, gave me a plausible fluency in whoppers.

The memory of my intrusive family made me choose to live off the map. I have said I was a teacher in Africa. This was partly true. "Teacher" was a heroic euphemism, for my residence in Africa seemed a laborious sacrifice, if not a martyrdom. I was learning the local language, I lived in the bush, I got my news from the shortwave radio, the mail was always late. In my letters, Africa was work. I suppressed in them the details of my real life, which, besides students and grading homework, involved writing and village beauties and beer drinking and long rides on bad roads — the riotous excesses and mythomania of an expatriate in the African bush, indulged and forgiven by a system that usually failed and expected little except poor results and phenomenal delays.

I was lazier than anyone I knew in Africa, and I laughed with shame when expatriates claimed Africans were idle. I was so appalled at how I did my job that I knew I must succeed as a writer, because I would fail at teaching or anything else. And when I published poems and stories, I felt vindicated and reassured, yet I still knew that I had cheated the Uganda Ministry of Education, my employer. I had written my stories on government time, and when this became obvious, I used the excuse of student riots in Kampala to leave for Southeast Asia, to cheat the Singapore Ministry of Education. By then I was married. My children, born in musty, smelly equatorial hospitals, where lizards flicked their tongues on white stucco windowsills, grew up pink and cranky with heat rash.

Why would any woman put up with a tiny, non-air-conditioned house abutting an open storm drain on a back street of Singapore and a selfish, single-minded husband upstairs writing stories at a desk under the croaking fan? Well, she wouldn't. My wife left me. I married again. The second time was impulsive and it lasted less than two years — no children. I lost more of what I owned, yet I had usable skills. As a teacher I could work anywhere, but teaching interfered with my writing day. I abandoned teaching, settled in England, and continued to write.

And it must have seemed that I was writing stories, book reviews, novels, travel books, magazine articles, essays, newspaper columns, more novels, more stories, another travel book. But it was not an unsorted stack of vagrant scribbles; it was in words a sort of edifice. What I was doing was giving form to a continuous account of my existence, my disappointments and obsessions, my reading, my secrets, writing every day. All these books and pieces could be laid end to end as a long linking account of who I was, bringing order to my living and publishing it, in thousands of pages of print, bound on three shelves of a bookcase, which represented my attempt to make sense of my life.

But I had never written about my family. I couldn't bear to, even obliquely. In those millions of words there is no description of a big rivalrous family. Until I returned home for Dad's death, I had not realized that the greatest subject for me was not couched in the pretensions of poetry or the imaginative vagaries of a novel or the exploration of a landscape, but would be a truthful account of my family, my long experience as a traveler in Mother Land.

All the time I'd been away, I must have seemed to Mother sober and studious. She had no idea what I was doing, but when I published my first book, a novel, she wrote me a stern letter telling me how much she disliked it. The powder-blue, tissue-thin aerogram (*No Enclosures Permitted*), with its narrow border of red and navy-blue chevrons and an eleven-cent John F. Kennedy stamp, was dated May 6, 1967.

> *Dear Jay,*
>
> *I read your book. Your publisher gave me a 25¢ discount then charged me a dollar for mailing it, in addition to the price of the book! It grieves me to tell you I did not like your book at all. I found it extremely unfunny, sordid, cheap and vulgar. Had you thought about the people who would read this creation of yours? Would you want me to hand it to Hubby or Rose and let them "enjoy" it? Could you in all honesty hand this to someone like Mr. Becker across the street and say, "This is my first novel! Hope you enjoy it!" I wonder if he would? Jay, why waste your time on trash? You will have to answer someday, even if only to your conscience, for the printed word, which will last forever. I could say much more, but I know I have inflicted enough hurt on you. I am hurt even as I write this. No one will gain from this book.*
>
> *Love, Mother*

I kept the letter those forty years as a talisman, as a goad, and as a rare example of the severe honesty of someone who seldom told the truth.

At last, everything came to an end for me. I thought: Two wives — done. Two children — done. Houses and property acquired and lost, ditto every article of furniture, everything I had accumulated since leaving home was gone, or almost. I had kept many of my books — no one fights over books. Books are burdens; they get heavier, smellier, dustier; they swell, the pages fatten, the bindings crack, the dust jackets tear and slip away. Yet I needed something to hold on to. It seemed odd to be returning home after so many years, but I had been everywhere else and, I repeat, I had nowhere else to go.

Father's failing health meant that I had to hang around and be useful, and it had allowed me to reacquaint myself with my brothers and sisters. Father's death created, if not a bond, then a family feeling, and my new nearness to Mother reminded me of why I had left all those years ago.

In this period, just after Father's death, when Mother was queening over us, I grew close to Floyd. Floyd was a satirist, had been so from child-hood. Older than me by two years, he had always loomed large, and was both funnier and more serious than anyone else in the family, marked with the satirist's traits: comedy, severity, cruelty. He was the most tor-mented, the one with natural talent. When I wrote well, I was sometimes forced to admit that I was unconsciously mimicking Floyd at his most fluent. He was too good a writer not to be a bad influence. Maybe he was another reason I had gone away and stayed: I needed to be myself.

As a satirist, Floyd was useful, perhaps essential, to understanding the quirks of the family — mocking Fred's earnestness, Franny's fussing, Rose's stubborn streak, Hubby's clumsiness, Gilbert's love of opera, his own irrationality; and he frankly mimicked my self-dramatizing tenden-cies.

In his role as mocker, Floyd was a figure of power. Growing up, I had been shocked and exhilarated by his fearless satires of Mother: he did her voice, her equivocation, her tantrums, her shallow cough, her distinctive manner of swallowing (goose-necked, gulping, with popping eyes). I had to admit that watching him in this vein had liberated me and given voice to emotions I felt.

Floyd had grown up angry and sad. He had felt passed over, and his childhood had been overshadowed by Fred, darkened by judgments against him. He used to say, "How long did Charles Dickens work in the blacking factory?" and would quickly answer, "Not long," as a way of ex-plaining how, as a child — Dickens had been twelve — even a short time could be purgatorial, unendurable, and that sometimes the merest hint of criticism left a wound that failed to heal.

A whisper never went unheard in our family; the fact of it being a whisper made it serious and inescapable. "He wets the bed" might have been spoken as little more than a breath, but we all heard. Floyd could do nothing to stop it. Years later, he still spoke of it with bitterness and shame, first appalled at waking in the morning — he might have been nine or ten — and realizing he was lying in a puddle of his own chilled pee, the soaked sheets under him, and with a sense of woe that his error could not be lied away or hidden; then terrified in anticipation of Mother's screech.

"Again! You've done it again!"

Floyd hid his face as he wept in fear and humiliation. "My fallen-angel face, filthy with tears" is a line in one of his poems. What he remembered in the poems he wrote as a Guggenheim fellow was his bedwetting, how when he was an anxious boy Mother had howled at him, "I'm going to hang that rubber sheet around your neck if you wet your bed one more time. I'll send you to school wearing the rubber sheet. Everyone will know what you do!" And, "I wash your pissy sheets!"

She told her brother Louie, the priest, who rushed to our house in his purple Studebaker and demanded that Floyd come downstairs to go for a walk. "Get down here, sonny."

When they were alone, Uncle Louie put down his glass of Moxie and ordered Floyd to stand at attention. He took Floyd's chin, lifted it, and said, "If you keep this up you'll never get married. Know why? Because you'll pee on your wife. Is that what you want?"

And of course Floyd wet the bed more than ever. He was angry, anxious, confused. In such misery, he probably did have a secret wish to piss on everyone.

"I hope you're proud of yourself," Mother said, advancing on Floyd, who was backing away on skinny legs, his wet flannel pajamas stuck to his thighs, his hair spiky from sleep. "I really am going to do it. You think I'm kidding, but I'm not. I'm going to hang that rubber sheet around your neck and you're going to wear it to school."

Mother had stripped the sheets from his bed and thrown them on the floor. The rubber sheet was black and slippery. It had a peculiar inhuman smell, a sharpness of rubber, a sour stink that, no matter how often it was washed, would linger in its fabric. It was smaller than a normal sheet and so heavy it rumbled when it was shaken.

I had a clear image of what wearing it would be like, because Audie Jackson, the coal man who delivered ice in the summer, holding a crystal block of it with a pair of tongs, wore just such a sheet like a filthy cape on his back. That was how Floyd would look, draped in the black rubber sheet, a humiliated beggar boy dressed like the limping ice man.

Even in adulthood, the rubber sheet was Floyd's defining image, like Fred's slavering dogs, Gilbert's melodious violin and shelves of Proust in French, Hubby's tuneless cello and his ball-peen hammer, Franny's tub of three-bean salad, Rose's Mixmaster ("Ma loves fudge"), Angela's halo, and the pup tent I bought for ten dollars, so that I could make camp in the backyard and sleep there on warm nights, pretending I was in the Africa of wild animals and jungles that I read about in Frank Buck's *Bring 'Em Back Alive* and Fenworth Moore's *Wrecked on Cannibal Island; or, Jerry Ford's Adventures Among Savages.*

Floyd was miserable. He could not seem to go a night without wetting the bed, and it got so bad that there was a permanent resentment against him for making more work for Mother. Whenever Floyd did something wrong—and it might be as trivial as spilling milk on the counter or muddying his knees or failing to mop the floor after he'd promised to—he was reminded of his bedwetting.

Egged on by Mother, Father would say, "Look what you've done, and after all that, this is what your mother gets for it—more of your pissy sheets!"

At the age of eleven, Floyd saw a psychiatrist, Dr. Younger, on Harrison Avenue in Boston.

I asked Floyd, "What does he do?"

"Just talks and stuff."

"What about?"

"Asks me to draw pictures and stuff."

I imagined that the doctor was being kind to him, encouraging his artwork, to make him feel better. I was envious, because a stranger's sympathy would have made me happy.

But the visits made no difference, for Mother was still so enraged that she printed Floyd's name on the rubber sheet. And she went on provoking Dad to scold Floyd, which he did, but now in a whisper: "You're killing your mother."

Floyd was well into his teenage years before he was entirely cured of his bedwetting. Leaving home had a great deal to do with the improvement, as leaving home would help me. Yet he always spoke of his misery with a fresh sense of hurt, as if it were yesterday.

Like me, he had stayed away. When he earned his doctorate, when he won the poetry prize, the Guggenheim, the Fulbright, he was alone. He never invited Mother or Dad—nor, indeed, any of us.

Like me, his marriage ended. Like me, in late middle age he found himself living in Mother Land, where we were more familiar with the weather and the seasons and the routines. Like me, he had told himself that it was temporary, and yet the years were passing and we remained ten minutes from Mother.

We resumed our friendship, Floyd and I, in a bristling, wary way, like a pair of mismatched hedgehogs. We were both passionate readers and mediocre golfers, and both single again. He was still the family satirist. "Who's this?" he would say, and screw up his face and launch into an imitation of Fred or Hubby, Franny or Rose, Hubby or Gilbert, and me, too, in a defiant way. But I was flattered, because teasing me to my face was a gesture of affection.

He was regularly visited by Franny and Rose. They brought him tribute, to disarm and obligate him — fruit, candy, T-shirts, cakes and cookies they had baked. Always on their return journey after seeing Mother, they stopped off to see him and tell him in detail how Mother was failing. "She's real feeble, she's forgetful. She leaves things on the stove with the burner on." They rolled their eyes and moaned about what a trial Mother was, how frail, how hard up, so confused.

Less often, they stopped at my place, saying the same things.

"She's really slowing down a lot," Franny said to me. She was slumped, one shoulder higher than the other, and her dress glowing heavily with sweat, sitting with her knees apart as she gasped for breath. "Plus, she repeats herself all the time."

"What's this about Ma being hard up?"

Franny narrowed her eyes and said, "Some weeks she's real short."

Saying it *shawt*, the Cape Cod way, made Mother's financial state sound dire.

Instead of mentioning what Mother had said about helping her with Jonty's wedding expenses, I merely remarked on how generous it was that she and Rose stopped in and made sure the old woman was okay.

"I know how busy you are," Franny said, though in fact this was not my point — I saw Mother fairly often, at Mother's bidding. Franny screwed up one side of her face. "You know, Jay, Ma really doesn't have a lot of money."

This seemed as odd a remark as "Some weeks she's real shawt," since Mother had always been a saver, thrifty, not to say fanatically frugal: day-old bread, dented cans, most of the clothes she gave as presents labeled *Second* and *Irreg*.

Floyd laughed at Franny for her lugubrious stories, at Rose for her nervous anger, at Mother for her sanctimony, at Fred ("he's a castrato"), at Hubby ("the village explainer"), at Gilbert ("our virtuoso on the strings"). And of course everyone else, the children, the grandchildren, their friends, their pets, "the human zoo!"

Mother was shrinking, Floyd said. "She's turning into a Q-tip." It seemed true — she was growing paler, with thin wispy hair, like cobwebs twirled on a twig, her sallow scalp showing through. Her skin was tissuey, her eyes watery, with yellow, claw-like nails on ashen hands that were almost reptilian, as though in her old age she was devolving. Yet given her physical decline, she still seemed strong, and most of the time put me in mind of a Chinese empress.

"She's all about indirection," Floyd said. "She doesn't hear you when you have something on your mind. And when you ask her how she is, she never replies at once. Instead, she looks a little croaky and coughs" — Floyd gave two dry barks, the practiced cough of a hypochondriac. Then he groaned in Mother's voice, "Oh, I'm all right. I'll be fine. *Croop-croop!*"

But for all his mockery, he indulged her, brought her books, gave her rides to the supermarket on senior citizen discount day and to the Big Scoop for an ice cream. He marveled that she was bright and busy, always knitting or reading or monologuing on the phone. "She still goes for walks!" She usually went alone, shuffling in her crepe-soled nurse's shoes, sometimes walking as far as the beach, where, her white hair blown by the wind, her big cloak lifted in an updraft, her face tightened by the cold, Floyd said, "She looks like Queen Lear!"

"Your father hated walking, but I love to be outdoors — it does you so much good," she said, implying that Dad was a drag until he died, and that he probably shortened his life by sitting indoors with a glass of Wild Turkey in one hand and doing the crossword.

"Look, Ma," Floyd would say on one of his Sunday visits, "here come your favorites."

Out the window, Franny and Rose were advancing from their cars to the front door, filling the path, smiling in anticipation.

Mother rolled her eyes to signal, *Oh, Lord, those two, back again!*

Seeing her alone, I often thought how kindly she could be, how she would hold my hand and ask me to sit down beside her and speak to me with a sympathy that, in spite of my skepticism, touched my heart.

"I want you to find someone nice. I want you to be happy. That would please me so much."

What Mother did not know—what no one knew—was that I had found someone. I was happy. But as always, I didn't know how much of this affair to tell Mother, or whether I should say anything at all.

12

DISCLOSURE

MOTHER KNEW I WAS HAPPY. I could tell by the way she blinked, bringing me into focus with each blink. I was a fifty-six-year-old child, crouched on the footstool before her leather chair. She sensed my happiness the way a predator senses crippled prey, as it crouches at the edge of a wadi and discerns a lame buck dragging its hind leg at the rear of an advancing herd, marking the animal out and preparing for the pounce. My happiness must have been as obvious as a gimpy leg, or my conspicuous grin.

I was in love. That gave me my glow, relaxed my natural suspicion, and made me vulnerable to assault—a happy person is a potential mugging victim. Another man's mother might have been relieved and delighted, but my mother became dark and watchful. For her, all happiness concealed a secret, all smiles suggested submission. I was her prey.

"I can tell you're well relaxed," Mother said. "A good night's sleep is so important"—something you would say to a small child as you stalled and scrutinized their features for a tic of self-consciousness. *What are you smiling about?* she would demand angrily when we were very young, and often, *Wipe that smile off your face.*

"I've been a night owl my whole life," she went on. Her attention always wandered back to her own habits, her ego like a powerful magnet. "But if I get six good hours I'm as good as gold." Then she shook her head. "What was I saying before that?"

"That I looked rested."

"And that makes me so happy. To see you happy."

But she did not look happy, and because she was eyeing me closely, I warned myself not to say anything more. Yet on another level, in a blissful way, in my dreamy doze, I was joyous at having a woman in my life. I was at that early, overcertain stage of desire, feeling rejuvenated and hopeful. I had a future after all, I was not going to be alone, I had someone I wanted to please, someone who wanted to please me. And there was the romantic physical side, the yearning to stroke her, and the erotic cannibal side, someone for me to eat. Her name was Melissa Gearhart. She called herself Missy and had a teenage daughter named Madison. Missy worked in a bank on the Cape. She too was divorced. I loved her.

"A mother needs to see that her children are happy," Mother said.

I had dropped in because Gilbert had called from Washington to say, "Ma's lonely. No one calls her. No one visits."

Was this so? It seemed to me that Mother had plenty of company — the phone ringing, the usual visits and inquiries and drop-ins.

"People promise but no one comes through," Gilbert said. "I'd drive up myself but I'm on an assignment, leaving tonight, wheels up at eight. Ma said, 'What if you crash? What will I do?' She's definitely low."

Fred had said something similar. "It's just Ma and that big house, all alone. I can't make it — one of the dogs has colic and the other one a suspected hernia. Poor Ma. Most of her old friends are dead. And she's lost her mate."

"She's lost her mate" made Mother sound like a grieving zoo animal, off her feed, swishing her tail at flies. But there was a distinct note of Mother's own complaints in these comments, just the language she would use. But I went all the same, and she said, "I've lost my pep."

She had often praised people, saying, "He has lots of pep." Pep was better than money. Pep was positive. Someone with lots of pep would do what you asked them to do, saying, Sure thing! Glad to oblige!

I had brought Mother a basket of fruit, which still sat at my feet, the way one might try to please a shut-in, or in Mother's case, a way of trying to propitiate her. The basket, wrapped in heavy cellophane bunched at the top and tied with a red ribbon, was still in the supermarket bag. I was so dazed in my complacency I had not handed it over.

"Oh, yes, I'm feeling fine," I said, remembering her comment — or was it a question?

She was alone and looked small, cornered, solitary — which, no doubt, was how she wished to be perceived. But this role-playing did not convince me, for behind her gaze was the narrow penetrating gleam that you see in the eyes of a night stalker.

She said, "I was thinking how much Dad loved you," and added, "You were his favorite."

The mention of Dad called up his face, and I was moved by the memory. Yes, he was generous and had indulged me, treated me as a friend, was proud of me, and made few demands. He was restful to be with because he was so openhearted. He had vanity, as we all did, but he had no guile. His inner life was a mystery that had been briefly revealed by Mr. Bones, but he did not invite anyone to look further into it. He was that rare individual, the helpful stranger who asks nothing in return.

"I see you brought something."

Only then did I remember the fruit basket. Mother was smiling. She knew it was a present and had probably been eyeing the bag from the moment I stepped into her house.

"Some fruit," I said, lifting the basket out of the shopping bag.

"I like a nice piece of fruit," Mother said, breathless at the prospect of a present. "I eat fresh fruit every morning." She smiled wanly now. "I haven't been well. Gilbert and Fred are worried about me."

She held the basket by its handles, seeming to admire the apples, the oranges, the plums, the tangerines, the bunch of grapes, the cluster of dates, the roll of figs, two small boxes of raisins, all of these snug in the deep green flutter of nesting shreds.

Looking alarmed, Mother said, "So where's the grapefruit?"

That woke me. A big basket of fruit was not good enough, not full enough. The grapefruit was missing.

"I thought there was a grapefruit in it," I said.

"Oh, no," Mother said. "If there had been, you'd see it." She poked and crunched the cellophane. "I have one every morning for breakfast."

The basket was on her lap, but it was so large that she had to put her arms around it.

"Apples, though," I said.

"They must have made a mistake," she said, still thinking about the grapefruit.

"I'll bring you a couple of them next time."

"Oh, please don't, that's too much trouble. I don't want you worrying about a little thing like that."

But it had been big enough for her to mention in the first place. She was now being brave, though there was a slight pain in her voice.

"I'll definitely remember to bring some next time."

"You're so thoughtful, Jay," Mother said. "Dad always said that."

I had failed, Mother's present was imperfect, and I was someone else's favorite, not hers.

"Was there something you wanted to say?" she asked me.

By now I was on my guard. Her selfishness had turned into a warning, and a kind of rescue, but I was not as happy as I had been when I had first entered the house.

"No," I said. "Nothing."

Of course I went on visiting Mother, and I kept my love a secret. To share it as news, or to reveal it to anyone, would alter it. I wanted it unchanged. Being loved was like a spell of great health, it was strength and optimism, an irrational sense of being right, and of loving someone else's life unselfishly. I could not wait to see Missy again. I soon forgot the fruit basket episode and wanted Mother to be as joyful as I was. But she was too watchful ever to be happy.

Each time, Mother sensed my good humor, my bliss, as weakness or distraction. And when she did not look upon me as a distinct opportunity, a wounded animal, she glanced at me in a sidelong way as a possibility, the way a mugger sees a drunk and knows how easily he can be rolled, wondering merely, Is he worth it?

All this is retrospective. At the time, I was smiling, holding a bulging bag full of grapefruit.

"You shouldn't have," Mother said, gloating over the rustling bag of fruit shifting in the crepey tissue.

She began to eye me narrowly, having noticed I was more restless than usual. I had arranged to meet Missy at the bank where she worked, to take her to a restaurant in Woods Hole that overlooked Buzzards Bay. Then, while the full moon rose and dragged the tide out and showed us the way, we would walk down the pebbly beach to the wet sandbank. There, in the bubbling clam flats, I would present her with a ring.

A commitment ring—something new to me. The name made me smile, but it was Missy who first used it, speaking the words with a solemn trust. One of her coworkers, given a commitment ring by her boyfriend, was reassured and happy. My ring would serve to show Missy I was serious while allowing me time to assess our situation. The ring was not a date-setter; it was a solemn pledge shaped in gold. I knew Missy —and I hoped Madison—would be pleased.

Still eyeing me, Mother said, "Do you have somewhere to go?"

The woman's prescience was uncanny. It was also provocative. Whenever Mother had guessed correctly what was in my mind, I instantly denied it in a high, unconvincing voice.

"Someone to see?"

"No one," I said, and because my denial was so prompt, and in its way so absurd, I laughed.

Laughter is often a case of nerves that means its opposite. Mother said, "I hope she's nice."

She saw it all, knew it before I opened my mouth. I could keep a secret from her if I stayed five thousand miles away, but up close, as she sat with her serious square face of concentration, I was helpless. Also, I was lovestruck; I wished the world well; I needed the world to wish me well.

"Very nice."

"Someone special?"

"Very special."

"Would I ever be allowed to meet her?"

"I'm sure she'd love to meet you."

"Does she live on the Cape?"

This was all going faster than my brain was working. I found myself tumbling forward, saying more than I had planned — much more, for I had planned to say nothing, and already Mother knew this woman was important to me, that I was in love.

"I want to see you happy."

"I'm happy."

"I mean, for the long term."

I smiled again. I did not dare to speak.

"Something tells me you're planning to pop the question."

I hesitated, believing that I was equivocating effectively, and said, "I've got something for her."

"Is it a ring?"

All this in the space of a minute or two, Mother's questions coming one after the other, her sharp eyes a pair of pincers on me.

"Not really a ring the way you're thinking," I said.

"Oh?"

As casually as my trembling throat would allow, I added, "It's called a commitment ring."

"Oh?"

She was hungry for more, her eyes darting, her thin lips flattened in concentration. She wanted me to explain — and I did, wondering with a sense of woe how I had gotten to this point of actually uttering the words "commitment ring" when all I had intended to do was drop off a bag of grapefruit. But Mother had complained of a loss of pep — pep was so important, pep was the world's life force — and in the presence of someone unwell I became complacent and inattentive, because the ill are themselves inattentive.

Before I knew what was happening, I was explaining the difference between a commitment ring and an engagement ring.

Mother said, "I must be getting old and muddle-headed" — she smiled — "because I don't see the difference." She leaned over, crushing the grape-fruit in her lap. "I think you're going to surprise me. And that makes me very happy."

At the door, seeing me off, she kissed me. She felt fragile, like a bunch of slender twigs in the warm bag of her dress.

"I feel better," she said.

Strangely, so did I, as if I had first come upon her and seen her as ailing, and had healed her. Yet as soon as I was in my car driving away, I felt I had made a terrible mistake.

After two courtships and two marriages and two children and two divorces, it was hard for me not to think of a third attempt as hoisting myself back on the same long swaying tightrope where I had toppled before. It was not the fall that dismayed me; it was the missing safety net. And where my heart was concerned it was always a balancing act on a high wire. Instead of looking at the far end and trying to generate a glow of contentment at the sight of the platform, I was forever gazing down to make sure the net was in place. But the thing was always too far down to see, and so it was only when I fell that I realized it was not there, and went smash.

That was what the ring meant to me — a way out. If for Missy it was a dream, the promise of a future, for me it was a visible token of indecision, a stalling strategy. Much as I loved her, happy as I was, I was weary. I had set out on this high wire before, put one foot in front of the other, dancing back and forth, looking foolish, and I had fallen badly, twice.

I loved Missy but I did not want to fail again. And after the first months of passion, wordless desire consuming us in the dark, Missy had begun to talk about all those necessary, sensible, but passion-numbing subjects: work, money, a condo, the future. And the first time she saw my house she did an odd thing, something that obscurely bothered me. She walked quickly to the porch, then stopped before a geranium in a pot and began grooming it, plucking the yellowing leaves, pinching off the blackened blossoms, taking charge of my plant, slapping at it, and flicking the withered bits to the ground.

"I've taught Madison to do this."

Madison was not an easy name for me to use without a smile. The name was genderless, a college town, a famous avenue, an American president, a kind of brand. It did not announce a big-for-her-age girl, tugging at her hip-hop clothes and yelling into her cell phone or poking messages into it. Madison had just turned fourteen and was physically a woman, though emotionally a child, and not a reader. She was rebellious, a lazy student, and like many another lazy child, a fabricator, an excuse maker, an alibi artist. But "lazy" and "excuse maker" were not words I was able to use with her mother. I suggested "indolent" and "oblique."

"I can't believe how judgmental you are," Missy said. "Instead of talking to her all the time, why don't you listen?"

Two solid reasons kept me from listening. One, Madison sulked and seldom said anything at all, and two, when she did speak, grunting, using what linguists call verbal indicators or phatic speech — "Like, so what? Like, you're like, trying to bust me" — she had nothing to say. There were tantrums, boys, unexplained nights out, mood swings, low grades, a sleepiness and arrogance. Often, out of calculated rudeness or sheer indifference, she yawned in my face.

"Don't you see she needs a father figure?" Missy said.

"She needs to cover her mouth when she yawns."

Over dinner, Madison's problems intruded, all the speculation. Missy said, "I'm worried that she's dabbling with drugs, or maybe sex."

"Isn't that what you and I are doing?"

"I hate you for saying that."

A new stage in any relationship is the uttering, however casually, in a fit of irrational temper, of the unforgettable words "I hate you."

I wanted to say that once, in Africa, I went home with a woman. There was a child sleeping in her room. She woke him, he squawked and stumbled away, and after that I couldn't perform. But I kept this from Missy. I also wanted to say that in three American states the age of consent was fourteen. But it seemed tactless to mention to a teenage girl's mother, "In South Carolina she could be married, or getting laid every night."

"She never had a real father. Buzz Gearhart left me when she was six."

"Ever think sometimes it might be better to have no father than a bad one? Or mother?"

She didn't agree. Talking about money and work and the future and her child, Missy lost all her allure, became stressed and stringy, all urgency, a timekeeper, needing immediate answers. Well, she was naturally concerned about the child she loved, someone I hardly knew.

But this evening in Woods Hole, after dinner, an hour or so after having seen Mother, I realized how deeply Mother had shaped my fears, had turned me into an excuse maker; how, when a certain mood was upon me, all women became like Mother — and I wanted to run. What Mother was all the time, my women friends were some of the time, and it terrified me.

"Poor thing's all alone, no siblings," Missy said. She was talking about the hardship of being an only child.

"That's such crap," I said, almost beside myself, but amazed at my rage. "I grew up in a family of seven children. Have you any idea what hell that is? We hated each other. We fought constantly over nothing, because we had nothing. I was always in the wrong, always teased, never rewarded or praised. I could never please my mother — and I tried. I worked. I raked the leaves. You ask Madison to rake leaves and she sighs, 'Oh, Ma,' and doesn't do it. She's manipulative the way children can be, instilling fear in you. I would have been slapped for behaving like that, but I never resisted, I never said, 'Oh, Ma.' I obeyed. I was a mediocre student because my mother demanded I get a job. My mother had favorites and I was not one of them. I was expected to share everything I had — to negotiate, always asking permission. It was crabs in a basket. There were too many of us. And you sit there telling me that it's hard to be an only child? Are you kidding? It's heaven!"

"You're shouting," Missy said. She had stopped listening. She was wincing, glancing at the other tables in the restaurant in shame.

"I'm being emphatic."

I was breathless with anger and indignation. I had the sense that in this outburst, intending to discuss her daughter, I had instead told her for the first time who I was and where I'd been.

"You've never shouted at me before."

"Just taking it to the next level, as Madison says."

She smiled at me in pity, and with a hint of triumph, saying, "Once you say things, they can't be unsaid."

So everything I had said was indelibly scratched into the ledger, un-erasable, never to be forgotten.

She continued, "It is not crap. Madison is troubled. She's not manipulative. She has issues. Her father was a drinker. I'm afraid she may have inherited that addictive personality. She's showing signs of it. Plus, she's got a body-image problem."

While Missy was talking, while I was not listening, I was thinking: Who ever thought about me in this way? Who ever worried that I might not be happy or that I might have a body-image problem? Who ever took the trouble to please me? At fourteen I was already a hardened savage, convinced that no one cared and that I needed to keep secrets, needed to make my own life as a hunter-gatherer.

"I agree with everything you say," I said, because I hadn't been listening. That was enough of a response. Missy was moved. Another lesson I had learned in childhood: you submit and then all is well.

"It's still early," Missy said.

"That's part of the plan." I had picked her up after work and rushed her here as the tide was ebbing. I called for the check. "There's something I want to show you."

We left the restaurant and strolled past the harbor to the walkway above the beach, where a flight of stairs led to the shore. The moon just risen across Vineyard Sound lighted the foreshore, the tangled mass of kelp at the tidemark, the broken shells, the shiny bearded mussels in clumps on the mounds of pitted rock.

"Where are you leading me?" But she wasn't objecting. She was pleased that I had taken charge.

"Over there." I pointed to the end of the jetty, its pillars studded with barnacles and periwinkles, jewel-like in the bluish moonlight.

"I don't see anything."

When we got there, our shoes sucking in the sandy mud of the clam flats, I took out the little box, and the ring, and slipped it on her finger.

The women I had known before had been stern believers in symbolism, votaries in a religion of the heart. I was trusting in that knowledge, how symbols had been real to them, how the symbol of a promise or an emotion was the thing itself.

Missy began to cry. Just as I thought her tears were subsiding, she wept onward, and I had to hold her. I had been happy at her first tears, but now as her sobs came harder I was troubled.

I did not say, "This is a commitment ring." She knew what it was. She knew what it meant. But she was so moved, I suspected I might have misled her.

"For Madison's sake — and work-related situations too — this has got to be a secret," she said. "I mean, for now. Later, I want everyone to know how happy you've made me. But at the moment, I need you to go on loving me and to be real patient with Maddy."

Except for a nod, I did not react. I concealed what I felt. That obvious concealment always fooled someone who was straight; a truthful person had no reason not to believe this demeanor. But in my first indication that Missy had been lied to in her life, like the members of my family, she became alert, suspecting my bland assurance to be evasive.

"Did you tell anyone?" she asked quickly, summing up the empty smile I gave in response.

"Only my mother."

She hugged me. She was a mother. She understood: a mother was a friend.

13

VISITS

EVEN AS A SMALL, CHALKY-FACED BOY with bitten fingernails and muddy knees, crouching in my pup tent on the back lawn on a summer night, aching to know what would become of me, and fearing that it would be all wrong, I used to think: I will be swallowed by this family.

To save myself, I had a habit of taking two mental steps to the right, placing myself outside the force field of Mother's power and the clamor of my brothers and sisters, at the far edge of the jungle of Mother Land. Usually I was able to see them more clearly at a safe distance. I saw myself too, the pretender, the daydreamer, the fantasist, as though in a role of my own devising, in an amateur theatrical, looking exposed and faintly ridiculous, going through the motions, guided by my reverie.

That was how I was able to verify what I had done in the misty days and weeks of October that followed the clumsily improvised ceremony of my handing over the ring to Missy in the moonlit mud of the shore of Buzzards Bay. I breathed more easily. Her trust had freed me. Happier, more relaxed, she allowed me some peace. And one day she offered me the hearty encouragement, "Madison says she likes your blue shirt." It seemed we had a future, so we had more time. I had solitude again too, a good thing, for the pressure she had exerted before getting the ring was subtle but steady, like a screw tightening in my soul. Now there was less urgency. She had what she wanted, for the time being.

That was convenient, because I had begun to be interrupted in a random way by family drop-ins, almost weekly visits by Franny and Rose, usually on Sundays, always on their way home after seeing Mother.

These visits, which I took to be partly hostile — hostility was always a component in their gift giving — I thought of as station identification: *Here we are — remember us?* Gilbert didn't drop by, but he phoned, often from an airport when his flight was delayed. He was off to London. Or he was being called unexpectedly to Venezuela. Was there anything I wanted? And he called again, just back, with a Liberty print blouse or the pound of coffee I had requested (though I didn't mention Missy). And Hubby dropped in as well, to ask if I needed help fixing anything. Yes, a leaky faucet; a slider off its rails; a circuit breaker to be replaced; a heavy sofa to be shifted. I had never known Hubby so cheerful, so conversational, such a good listener, so solicitous.

"So, what were you saying?"

"Nothing. You were telling me about your wedding anniversary."

It was the day of the pesky circuit breaker. Salt air had corroded the points, so Hubby had said. He tended to lose the thread of conversation whenever he was engaged in a task. When he held a special tool, the right-sized pliers, and was gripping something in his working hands, his mind wandered and he went deaf.

"Right." He yanked out the circuit breaker like a dentist on a molar and held it up in the beak of the pliers, examining it dentist-fashion, the contacts that had gone green.

"Marrying Moneen was one of the smartest things I've ever done. That, and insulating my basement from this sea air, which is something you did not do. Look at the verdigris," and he tossed the circuit breaker into his toolbox.

"You seem to forget I don't own this house," I said, reminding myself of my penury and, even in middle age, how lightly tethered I was to the Cape.

"Maybe you should think about moving."

Fred came over with his three kids and his two dogs, and all of them, children and dogs, ranged like fox hounds, chasing one another, dodging around the trees and the yard as though on the scent.

"I love this place," Fred said. "It's so great to have a perimeter fence."

"It's a rental."

"You should buy it. Get into the housing spiral again. Make the owner an offer — cash. It's a great place for kids. Terrific ambience. Those trees."

With his feet up on the porch rail, listening to the shouting children, the barking dogs — the loud sounds of raucous contentment — he told me how lucky I had been in my life: two wonderful children, a number of books in print, lots of foreign travel. People asked him all the time, he said, whether he was related to me.

"I've wasted my life," he said, and in his reckless candor he made it sound like a boast.

Feeling that I was the butt of another joke or perhaps being patronized, I looked closely at Fred. He seemed to be serious. Yet my life, as I saw it, was a failure. If I had keeled over on the porch at that moment, I would have been the subject of pitying eulogies, how I had not realized my full potential — all the things I might have done had I lived. *He was in his prime,* my family would have said.

"You're the only one who's made anything of himself," Fred said. "You've had the guts to take chances. I wish I'd had your optimism."

"It was desperation. I never saw myself as having made any choices in my life. I only saw one thing to do, one way, no alternative. And quite often — a lot of the time — it was the wrong thing."

"You don't ever see your strengths," Fred said. "Maybe that's your virtue. Floyd's irrational, Hubby's a complainer, Gilbert's a mystery — why is he in Kuwait this week? Franny and Rose are a pair of hamburgers. But on any given day, you know exactly what you're doing."

Praise always made me suspicious. It put me on guard as an obvious technique — "indirection" was Floyd's word for it. I was watching Fred closely, looking for Mother's influence.

People sort of brace themselves when they lie. Mother had a peculiar posture and wide-eyed gaze when she fibbed. She angled her body and moved her head in a certain way. She had a liar's hand gestures, a liar's finger movements, the way she might press her cheek or touch her eye or tap her foot, emphatic, percussive, as if demanding that you believe her.

Fred had none of these traits. He stared at me, not blinking, giving me the plain truth — or was it?

"I should have followed my instincts and become a painter," he said. "I had some talent — you remember. Edward Hopper — I could have gone that route. Lighthouses, dunes, porches like this. You took the leap, and the thing is" — he took me by the shoulders — "you still have a lot to offer."

As he whistled for his kids and rounded up his dogs, I thought: Why is he telling me this?

And each Sunday, when Franny and Rose dropped in, Franny tramped up my walkway, a shopping bag in each hand, Rose and Rose's twins in tow — all carrying presents, like tribute, sometimes cheap hostile gifts, other times the sort of presents I imagined they wanted themselves.

"Remember these? Bull's-eyes. Tootsie Rolls. Jelly beans!"

Franny brought me candy and sweets. "Penny candy!" Pounds of chocolate, Almond Roca, bonbons wrapped in tissue and foil like baubles, peanut butter treats, tubs of caramel-coated popcorn. "Moose Munch."

"Do you like it?"

Franny had a kindergarten teacher's habit — a technique, perhaps — of treating everyone like an infant. She helped me eat, unwrapping Tootsie Rolls for me as she talked. And though Rose seldom brought a gift, she helped herself to the Tootsie Rolls and talked too.

"Aren't my twins getting big?"

They were big, but they were silent, and always mentioned in the third person, as though they weren't there.

Franny and Rose traveled like peasant wives, always with their younger children, always carrying food, never with their husbands. The men kept themselves apart, exercising their silent power as authority figures. Franny's Marvin and Rose's Walter were enigmatic men who seemed to insist that you had to guess what was in their minds. I knew it was baseball and computers and beer, though they suggested by their absence and silence that it was bigger things. I understood the burdened wives, the aloof husbands: it was the family pattern of folk societies in rural Uganda, which I had known well, the sort of thing I had seen on the Congo border, in distant Bundibugyo.

Even when they were in their teens, Rose's twins accompanied her to Grammy's, and to my house on their way home. They sat saying nothing unless they were needled, their heads sunk into their tiny shoulders, knees together, mouths shut, eyes glazed.

"They have a really great relationship with Ma," Rose said. "Benno, show Uncle Jay your report card."

"It'th in the car." Lisping made Benno seem much younger than fourteen. Or perhaps I was measuring him against Madison Gearhart, who would have loomed over him as she shouted him down. Madison would also have loomed over his twin sister, Bingo, also small for her age — boyish, skinny, shy, but good to Grammy. Bing and Ben.

"Ma couldn't believe it. All A's. Bing, play something for Uncle Jay on your harmonica."

Bingo yawned in terror and seemed to gather herself into compactness as she shortened and shrank into the chair.

"Aren't they adorable?" Franny said.

I smiled, thinking: I have two children of my own — when are you going to inquire about them? Out of pride, I said nothing. Had I mentioned my kids, Franny and Rose would have patronized me.

Rose said, "But Ma started to talk about her own report card — back in 1921! 'I had wonderful handwriting. And I could play the piano.' Ma's so competitive."

"She doesn't miss Dad at all," Franny said. "It's amazing. Maybe it's because we've been so supportive. She's like a little girl."

Laughing gently at Mother, as they were doing today, was another feature of these visits, for they had always just come from a large Sunday lunch at her house and needed to ventilate their feelings.

Franny tended to nod when she told me something she wanted me to agree with, or wagged her head at something sad. She was nodding now.

"Jonty and Loris have been trying to have a baby," she said. Her scatty mind led her to non sequiturs. Her neediness meant that the non sequitur was always something related to her. I tried not to smile at "trying to have a baby." "They've been trying for about three months."

And then I really did smile at the notion of two people naked in a bed, kicking and grunting in the procreative position, "trying." But I said, "I think that's wonderful," with too much seriousness, mawkish solemnity, because I wanted to cover my smile.

Franny stared at me, as though comparing the brightness of my smile with the force of my protest, assessing the degree of contradiction. Was I mocking her? She seemed to think so. We were all highly sensitive to belittlement. Our family history was a series of slights and gibes. I was sure that Franny knew I was smiling at "trying to have a baby," but she was not subtle-minded enough to see that it was the phrase that I found funny, not the notion.

Instead of saying more, she nodded and took a piece of wrapped candy and plucked at the waxed paper, her impatient fingers clawing at the tight folds and twists, pinching it off and squeezing it into a ball as she masticated the candy at the side of her jaw. She looked at me with a big, bug-eyed face. I could see from the way she chewed that she had something on her mind.

"What a beautiful wedding they had," Rose said. "Benno was the ring bearer, weren't you, Ben?"

They were taking a dangerous tack, I felt. I had refused to attend the wedding, had made a lame excuse, and Franny had denounced me to the rest of the family.

"But it was wicked expensive," she said, smacking her lips on the chocolate and ungumming her tongue. "The tux alone cost a fortune. Then there was the rehearsal dinner, the reception, the limo, the photographer, the floral decorations, the centerpieces. The gratuities. Father Furty looks at me, like, 'And where's my tip?' We gave him a hundred bucks. I thought priests took a vow of poverty."

It was hard to tell whether Franny was boasting or complaining. It sounded like both, the groaning boast, the smug complaint. "This car's such a gas guzzler," Gilbert said of his stylish SUV, and "You wouldn't believe what it costs to heat this house," Fred said of his mansion in Osterville, and of course, "I've wasted my life" — as a highly paid lawyer. You sympathized until it dawned on you that they wanted to appear superior for having something you didn't.

Yet Franny's nodding in front of me about the wedding made me remember how I had avoided it, how I had gone to a bar with Floyd and spent the entire time mocking Jonty, recalling his bratty behavior, the farce of a big wedding and a high mass. According to Mother, Franny had said, "I'll never forgive them." And Mother had smiled and added, "I think Franny was a little miffed."

Certainly Franny had not forgiven me, for we were a family that never forgave anything. And we usually exaggerated a lapse, so the smallest hurt became unpardonable.

Yet here she was, nodding, smiling, reminiscing about Jonty — the proud mother recalling her son's glorious wedding without any undertone of resentment for her uncooperative brothers.

"He looked like a movie star in his tux. Ma said, 'He looks like my brother Louie.'"

Franny had a way of whispering, as if to emphasize that she had singled me out for this secret.

"Jonty's a man. He's a husband. Someday he'll be a father. He'll have a family. Ma couldn't believe it. Ma teared up."

I had rarely seen Mother cry except when she was defied or did not get her way. An ineluctable or effulgent vision of Jonty's potential fatherhood was unlikely to bring tears to Mother's eyes, but would only make her envious and angry. She cried as a child would cry, out of frustration or pure spite.

In my own unforgiving way, I remembered Mother's satire, and how she had let slip with a calculated smile that she had helped pay for the wedding, to help Franny, who had never acknowledged the fact.

"What we found out — the hard way," Franny said, sounding clownish in her pedantry, "you have to plan ahead."

All this talk of Jonty's wedding annoyed me, but when I remembered that they had brought me chocolate and fruit and a tin of cookies, I was ashamed of myself and fell silent.

"Get your harmonica, Bing," Rose said.

As Bingo dug her toe into the carpet and mewed like a cat, Franny said, "She played for Ma. 'The hills are alive with the sound of music.'"

"Ma identified with Maria von Trapp," I said, remembering how Mother had once wanted to go to the Trapp family chalet in Vermont and introduce herself to this other matriarch, to see if the Austrian measured up.

"You should see her on the harmonica—it's amazing," Franny said. She had not heard me. She seldom listened, another family trait of steamrolling with a story. "And Benno juggled, didn't you, Ben? Ma was amazed."

I easily pictured the kids performing, Franny and Rose calling out, "Ga-head, juggle for Grammy." "Play Grammy a tune! Ga-head! Ga-head!"

And I knew that if another of us got Mother at the right moment, she would cackle like a witch and say how horrible it had been. *But what could I say? I couldn't stop them. And the poor little thing wanted to juggle for me.*

"We've always been a musical family," I said.

"Except for Hubby's cello!" Franny laughed. "'My Grandfather's Clock.' That was harsh."

"Hubby is such a dickhead," Rose said. I wanted to tell her that she was sitting on the sofa that Hubby had helped me move.

"Fred was pretty good on the trombone," Franny said.

"He blew," Rose said.

I said, "Isn't that what you're supposed to do on a trombone?"

But, ranting, Rose didn't hear. "And Floyd. Ma used to say how embarrassed she was when he tried to play the trumpet. He tried, and went red in the face, and nothing came out."

"You always had a nice voice, Jay. You should have kept up with your singing. You could have gone somewhere."

They left soon after. A typical visit: boasting, complaining, mocking, flattering, backbiting, leaving a bag of candy and some bruised fruit. It was a family suspicion that all gift giving was a form of cynical disposal, that presents were always things that the giver did not want.

They came again the following week—more candy. They moaned about Mother's neediness.

"She didn't want us to leave. I think she misses Dad." Franny nodded. "We all need a mate."

"She looks frail," Rose said.

When I next visited Mother she looked robust, fierce, alert as a fox.

"I keep busy. I have my knitting. I keep up with the news. That poor little kid that got stuck in that well in — was it Texas?" Mother said. "I go for walks. I'm reading a biography of Madame Curie. She was Polish. She discovered radium. It glows in the dark. She died from it. Cancer. Kind of ironic. If she hadn't discovered it, she'd have lived a good long time. I watch my diet. You look well. Your friend must be taking good care of you."

14

WHISPERS

FLOYD'S VISITS were sudden and swooping, as though he'd plummeted from the sky, talking fast as he landed, sweeping me up in his talk. But they were the abrupt appearances of a friend — no guile, no stratagems, and he came quickly to the point; he was usually in a flap, needing something, the family impatience blunting his request. Did I have a 26-millimeter socket wrench with a ratchet handle? Would I loan him a copy of *Religio Medici*? What was Saul Bellow's phone number? Was Loris pregnant? Had I noticed the obvious anomaly that Willie Nelson, in order to look macho, wore his hair braided into pigtails?

Floyd did not flatter me — far from it, he insulted me, but I took that as a form of comradeship and was bucked up. He teased me to my face, but in the family this sort of teasing was friendly, even flattering, sometimes stinging, yet it was strangely companionable in its cruel honesty and defiant frankness. *You're getting fat. That shirt is hideous. Your car's a toilet.* Flattery and gift giving were hard to read and harder to deconstruct, but teasing was a form of discourse based on equality. Teasing an inferior was simply cruel and in our family amounted to recreational sadism. But teasing an equal was a form of sparring; it took nerve, and in the end — if it was calibrated so as not to destroy the friendship altogether — made the friendship stronger. In our family, teasing someone to their face was unambiguously friendly.

"I hate people who do this!" Floyd said, seeing an engraved invitation propped on my mantelpiece. He snatched it down and pretended to spit on it. "What is it, some phony English habit, showing off your social life?" He clawed his thinning hair, read the card, "'A recital will be presented' — pompous!," and handed it to me. "Don't put it up there!"

It was the invitation to Madison's dance recital. Missy had sent her daughter to dance classes — tap dancing, but the rebellious child had opted for break dancing, which turned out to be part of a hip-hop curriculum that was offered.

Floyd said, "You're not actually going to this fucking rigadoon."

"A friend of mine's daughter is performing."

"The only possible friend you'd try to please that way is a woman you're trying to nail," Floyd said, growing excited as he sketched out, more or less correctly, my situation. "And that means a single mother, living with her troubled kid in a rental somewhere on the Cape, who sees you — of all preposterous people, you — as her next husband and father figure."

I slipped the invitation between the pages of a book, thinking that if Floyd couldn't see it, he was less likely to be further inflamed in his taunting.

"Wrong," I said. "All wrong. But even if you were close to being right, what's the matter with my being a father figure? I have two children of my own."

"Two marriages, both of them failures. You're a two-time loser," Floyd said. "And your children hate you. Father figure!"

"Unlike you, the ideal husband."

"I was married to a perfidious bitch," Floyd said, without rancor but with force. "She was hideous, she had no soul, she was a retromingent she-wolf, and you could have used her piss to etch glass. Your wives were wonderful. They moved on to better things, obviously. I think it's called trading up. I need a tape measure and a felt-tip marker. Make it snappy. I don't have all day."

Both the tape measure and the marker were in the same drawer under the kitchen counter. I slid the drawer open and put them into Floyd's hand.

"Not this kind," Floyd said, tossing the tape measure onto the counter.

"This is a tailor's accessory. I want a carpenter's measure, the kind that rolls out of a metal canister and extends to ten or twenty-five feet."

"You said 'tape measure.' That's a tape measure. Notice the tape."

"The other kind is also called a tape measure, dork-face."

"I think you'll find" — this catchphrase was also a key element in the teasing — "the instrument you want is a mechanical rule."

"I think you'll find it's called a tape measure," Floyd said, and as he spoke, he popped the cap off the marker and tried to scribble on his hand. "It's dead. It's dry as rat shit. You must have left the cap off." He flung it away.

"Because it won't write on your greasy skin."

"'Writes on all surfaces' — that's what it says. Epidermis — squamous tissue — is a surface!" As he spoke, he glanced quickly at my bookshelf to see if there was a title he might borrow, and saw none apparently, because he began to head out of the house, still talking. "I have to go. This was a wasted trip. You're putting on weight. You'll be as wide as Franny if you don't watch out — she's a perfect sphere. Whose middle name was Sphere? Don't embarrass yourself by trying to guess. It was Thelonious Monk. Celtics game Friday — come over, we'll get pizza and watch it."

"That's the night of the dance recital."

"Oh, sorry. I forgot you're trying to nail that single mother. Ordeal by boredom — you sit through the daughter's recital in order to get your hands on the mother. But ask yourself, is it really worth all that trouble for a piece of ass, bearing in mind — and here the sage raises a cautionary finger" — he raised the finger in my face — "that a single mother is damaged goods and you are merely bottom-feeding."

To be offended by such banter was to risk losing his friendship. The only proper response was to give it back to him in the same spirit.

"You're absolutely right. I should follow your example. I would be much better off watching TV with a can of beer in one hand and my dick in the other. Mary Palm never fails, and your fidelity to onanism has never wavered."

He laughed at the abuse. We were even — it was over. He said, "Walk me to my car."

Outside, he told me that he had seen Mother the previous day. She had reported that Fred was in Chicago on business, that Gilbert had received a commendation from the State Department for exemplary service, that Hubby had hurt his back lifting a bag of potting soil.

Floyd said, "Dad used to call it 'loom.' He said 'peltering' when it rained hard. Funnily enough, he spoke colloquial French. Amazing how he deferred to Ma. I miss him."

"He saw that she was weak. He was being tactful."

"She always had to win an argument. Do you find her irritating? Sometimes I think I'd like to hit her with an iron pipe. Just keep whacking her." He laughed again and said, "She's still communing with Angela, who is apparently in better fettle than the rest of us. That is so fucking spooky it doesn't bear thinking about. Who is the scholar who describes how primitive people are guided by the dead?"

"I think you'll find it's Bronisław Malinowski, as well as most of the field anthropologists he inspired," I said.

"The answer I want is Lévi-Strauss — not the man of the pants but the man of the people. The grateful dead. I wonder if Jerry Garcia knew that?"

"By the way, the ungrateful Franny and Rose stopped by on Sunday."

"Did they bring you candy? Did they address you as though you were six years old? Is it from talking to their kids all day? They all belong in spazz class."

"Benno juggles. Bingo plays the harmonica. Jonty kicked a windshield to smithereens when he was a mere lad. Jake ate a Styrofoam cup. Give them a little credit."

"Unique talents that will serve them in adulthood. 'Can you describe the key tactical decision of Pickett's Charge that determined the Battle of Gettysburg?' 'No, but I can juggle.' Did you ever notice . . .'"

He had slipped behind the wheel of his car, a battered Mercedes with a *Harvard* decal on the back window, a parking badge on the windshield, and a *Question Authority* bumper sticker. He frowned and looked thoughtful and blinked as if he had forgotten what he was going to say. He revved the engine, a blatting diesel, and then put his head out the window.

"Yeah. Ever notice? When you get a divorce, you look around and everyone seems happily married. And you want to sob with self-pity, seeing all those jolly families, or old couples solemnly holding hands." Floyd craned his neck and, taking his time, pursed his lips as though to begin singing but instead spat heavily onto my driveway. "Then you meet someone and you get serious and make plans. And you look around — and every married person you know is miserable."

Floyd's mockery rang in my ears the night of the recital. The event was staged at the senior center, the only hall for hire in the area — and my first time inside, a kind of initiation, for I had often gone past it on performance nights (*Alice in Wonderland, Two Nights Only* or *Contra Dance, All Welcome*). I had never been tempted to go inside, though I had wondered who might be there. Now I knew: people like me, romancing single mothers with children who played music and sang and danced. A car went past, a man inside, the man I had once been, going out for a solitary drink.

This was a new stage in my relationship with Missy, meeting other parents, being presented to Missy's women friends, all of them the single mothers of Madison's friends. The pains they took to pretend they were not sizing me up made it obvious they were doing just that, scrutinizing my shoes, my jacket, my thinning hair. What sort of prospect was I? They seemed to me a weary but trying-to-be-cheerful sisterhood of divorcées, beset by what they would have called "issues" — children, child support payments, the cost of living, school tuition, ex-spouses (like Buzz Gearhart) who'd found new love and remarried, while these sisters were burdened by work and demoralized by growing older. Lonely mothers, unwillingly single, watching their daughters attracting boyfriends.

One mother tapped a video camera and said, "I'll make a copy for you."

Seeing it all with Floyd's skeptical eyes, I got sad — sadder still as Madison sauntered onstage, dragging her feet, with her troupe of break-dancing buddies. They wore hooded sweatshirts, baggy shorts, too-big sneakers, and baseball caps on backward — the rebellious getup of street kids. They pranced and tumbled and made gang-related hand gestures and finger signs, nodding to the music — sweet-faced girls mouthing loud raw words.

Ain't listenin' to ya, ain't listenin'.

"What is this music?" I asked, wondering what Missy would say.

"Gangster rap," she whispered.

The dancing was expert, the collapsing children, the spinning legs, the angry music stirring them. But the precision, this skill, made it somehow more awful for being accurately bad, the mimicry of something so mediocre as to be dangerous. Now they were tumbling, the wildly flop-ping dancers seeming like furious urchins.

When they took a bow — swaggering, more wrist play — Missy angled herself to get a look at me, as if assessing the vigor of my clapping.

After that, sylph-like girls and pale boys wearing lipstick strutted on-stage, scissoring their legs in a ballet. One of them looked like Franny's son Max. I tried to imagine Madison in a tutu and wondered what my reaction would have been. Had she chosen rap music because she was defiant? I knew why I hated rap: it was ignorant and crude; lacking har-mony, it wasn't music at all but a succession of boorish insults. During the next act, an ensemble playing Mozart, I spotted Bingo up front at the edge of the stage, blow-sucking on her harmonica, Franny and Rose seated in the front row.

"I'm starving. How about a pizza?" I said as the recital ended. Fearing that Franny and Rose would see me, I excused myself ("I'll warm up the car") and met Missy and Madison at the side entrance of the building. Madison still had her costume on, the hoodie, the baggy shorts. She ap-peared to be sulking — still, I supposed, in the defiant mood of the rap song.

"You need to work harder to get to know her," Missy used to say. Or, "We need to work on our relationship. You have anger issues. You've got a lot of hostility — you need to work on that."

This wasn't romance, it was work. I had never imagined love in these terms, though I knew all about negotiation and adjustment. In my family no one worked at relationships. They smiled, they told lies, they gossiped, they stabbed each other in the back, they always said yes and never meant it. No one worked, no one changed. Could I?

"I hate the crust," Madison said at the pizza parlor when the waiter, a young man in a paper hat, slid the big cheesy disk across the table.

"Anything else I can get you?" the waiter asked. "Miss?"

But Madison wasn't listening. "It tastes like wood."

"Miss? Maybe get you a beverage?" He was being excessively polite, bowing to her. "We've got some delicious lemonade in the cooler."

"I hate lemonade."

"We're fine," Missy said, smiling at the waiter.

I was suddenly very angry at this fourteen-year-old waving the waiter away with a grunted dismissal, appalled at the waiter's forced smile, swallowing his exasperation in the hope of being tipped.

"You don't have to eat the crust, honey," Missy said. "Why are you smiling, Jay?"

At the horror of it all, and the memory of Mother saying, "Eat it. It's the best part. It's a sin to waste food. People in China . . ."

Missy was smoothing Madison's cheek, and I saw that she was not wearing the commitment ring. "Be an angel and go clean off that makeup, sweetie."

"Why do I hafta?"

"Do it for me, darling."

Madison's grumbling in this ghoulish makeup seemed especially menacing. But she went, complaining under her breath, scuffing her sneakers. Missy watched her, setting her lips in a smile of pride.

"She's getting so big," Missy said, and still approvingly, "She really has a mind of her own."

That was the moment to say, Maybe she should learn a little politeness. But I had something else on my mind now. I took Missy's hand and pressed it. "What happened to the ring?"

"It's in a safe place. I love that ring. Listen, I'm glad you want me and that you're committed to me and Maddy. But that still has to be our secret. I'm just not ready for other people to know it."

"What about Madison?"

"She's not ready either." She looked up and, seeing Madison coming back to the table, her face scrubbed and girlish again, whispered, "Say something positive about her recital. She danced her heart out. She needs to be validated."

"Hey, you didn't even touch it," Madison said, lifting a slice of pizza, folding it in half, and taking a bite.

I said, "I liked your ensemble a lot."

"What's an *onsomble* supposed to be?" Her mouth was full of pizza, dabs of tomato sauce on her cheeks. She chewed, wrinkling her nose at me.

"Your rap group."

"My posse?"

"Right. It was really nice."

"'Nice.'" She quoted me in my own voice and sulked.

"I mean, it had lots of rhythm. Good moves."

"Whatever." She cocked her head to the side. "I think you mean our shit was dope."

"Maddy!" But Missy seemed to be screeching with approval.

I was silent. Perhaps Maddy knew I wanted to slap her. "Children always know when you're hostile" was one of Missy's sayings. Yes, I was hostile, but I also wanted to placate Missy. I had no idea how to accomplish that. I hated the thought that I might be auditioning for another marital flop.

A family at a nearby table was contending over a half-finished pizza — mother, father, three small boys, all different sizes, a troop of humans. The mother was harassed, picking at her wild hair with one hand, snatching at it with a brush with the other. The father sulked, wolfing a piece of pizza on his own, the kids each nibbling in his own way — one licking his fingers, another chewing with his mouth open, the youngest with his face against the table, eating a slice of pizza like a dog, lapping at it, no hands.

Once again, I saw them, as I saw most people these days, no longer as simple village folk, who, though hungry, always eat slowly — I had known such people, who usually seemed the soul of politeness, with the good manners of people who know it is fatal to have bad manners. No, I saw most people these days as monkeys, eating with dirty hands and chattering. That staring husband and father, chewing and making noises with his mouth full — that would be me. I had aced my audition, I had been accepted, I was rehearsing that role as Big Monkey.

Floyd had said, "You meet someone and you get serious and make plans. And you look around — and every married person you know is miserable."

"I hate to see food go to waste," I said as we left, half the pizza uneaten on the table.

I was parroting Mother, of course, and I hated myself for it. But no one heard me, no one cared, and why should they?

"Thanks so much, sir," the waiter said, holding the door for us, grateful for the large tip I'd given him to atone for Madison's rudeness.

No sex that night. A stifled "I love you," a chaste kiss for Madison's benefit. Missy reminded me that Madison had soccer practice tomorrow and the bank was open on Saturday mornings.

The next time I saw Mother, the following week, she said, "You must be so busy making plans." When I squinted at "plans," she said, "Wedding bells."

"I'm not getting married. It's a commitment ring. I'm not engaged."

"You said you were engaged. Doesn't engaged mean engaged to be married?"

"No. I'm committed. That's different. It's like going steady."

"Committed to what? To whom?"

"To the, um, young lady."

"But doesn't committed mean committed to marry her?"

"In the end, I suppose. If all goes well."

"That's what I mean. So you must be making plans."

"No plans at the moment, Ma."

"Oh?"

When Mother said "oh?" she looked like an interrogator in a dungeon. Her "oh?" meant: Let's go through this one more time, and now I need more detail. Mother had always been prosecutorial.

But I had no more detail to give. On reflection, I had less detail than the last time Mother and I had discussed this, weeks ago. And speaking of Missy in this offhand, almost denying way made me self-conscious. I realized we had not talked since the recital—an unusual lapse of five days. I had called but had gotten her answering machine, Madison's voice asking the caller to leave a message. I had left a succession of messages, which, as the days passed, had become increasingly bumbling and apologetic.

Sunday came, a car crunching the driveway gravel—I hoped it was Missy. No, a Subaru Forester, Franny at the wheel, Rose beside her, the twins, juggler and harmonica player, in the back seat. More candy, more fruit, a wedge of muenster cheese, and more gossip. What a melancholy fate to be visited by people you dislike when you want to be visited by people you love.

"Hubby has hemorrhoids, so I guess he's not a perfect asshole after all," Rose said.

"One of Fred's dogs has a hernia," Franny said, laughing, and, "God forgive me, Floyd's talking of having his nose reshaped. He says he's having trouble breathing, but we think it's a size thing."

"I think Ma's losing it," Rose said. "You're the only sensible one in the family."

A visit meant a review of the whole tribe, with the pretense of making me feel better. But I felt worse. After they left I was uneasy, apprehensive. Something was wrong. Since knowing her, I had not gone a whole week without hearing from Missy. I called again, and this time, early on a Sunday evening, she answered.

"I've been trying to reach you," I said.

In a low tortured voice, Missy said, "I'm a wreck. Maddy's coming apart. How could you do this to us? I thought I could trust you."

I hardly recognized the voice, the tone, the accusation. It was like a demon voice in a dream, irrational, accusing.

"I don't get it. What —?"

"Don't interrupt. I'm not finished. Madison is devastated. She came home in tears. She's humiliated. She knows everything."

"About us?"

"Yes, about us," she said fiercely in her betrayed victim's voice. "About the ring. About us getting married. I told you she wasn't ready for this," she went on, drowning out my protests. "She says I'm abandoning her. I told you she had rejection issues. She's talking about taking drugs. 'Self-medicating.'"

"How did she find out?"

"Why don't you ask about her state of mind? Why do you only care how she found out? She's a mess! The kids at school know. The other mothers know. Everyone knows. It was supposed to be our secret. The other kids were teasing her about the wedding."

"Why teasing?"

"Because you're old, I guess."

"I'm not old," I said.

"Look in the mirror."

At this point in the conversation I was seeing a new Missy, a different Gearhart, as in turbulent times one encounters surprising and sometimes shocking aspects of one's lover. I had seen her overprotective side and her businesslike side. But this was a rash, insulting, unforgiving side, and I saw how, in her belief that I had betrayed her confidence, I had failed her; how, more in search of a father for her child than a companion for herself, she had concluded that I was the wrong man. As I was mulling this, she hung up on me, cutting off her own tormented voice.

The following week I received the commitment ring back in a small padded envelope, by regular mail.

I called Floyd, seeking consolation. He was not at home. I kept trying, leaving facetious messages.

One morning I found a folded note tucked under my windshield wiper. In tiny, accusatory script: *You fucking hypocrite. Stay away from me. I don't want to see you or your wife.*

15

OUTSIDER

THE ATTENTIVE READER who has gotten this far will have known for some time — long before it dawned on me — that Mother had somehow betrayed me. She had stitched me up, bent me over, shopped me to the rest of the family, blabbed my secret, probably in slurping installments, perhaps even elaborated on it, mentioned my state of mind, my physical condition, the drape of my clothes, none of her reports complimentary. This was how she was. You saw that, I didn't.

How had I been fooled? Blame my happiness. Even in my habitual stealth with the dangerous woman, I had smiled and dropped my guard. It is always fatal to share your joy with an envious malcontent. The family rule was: vigilance, never relax. But Mother, hyperalert on her throne, knew that a happy person was less watchful than a scowler, that it was simple to traduce someone who was at peace with the world.

Yet I wasn't very surprised by Mother's behavior. I had never been convinced of the sacredness of motherhood. There were plenty of heroines who'd never had a child, and they were to me more heroic as spinsters because they were always belittled by the grudging mother-worshipers, Mother among them. "I gave birth to you!" she would howl as a boast and an exit line. Beyond its obvious factuality, what exactly did that mean?

For the very reason a mother could be powerful, a mother could also be irresponsible — cold, abstracted, twisted, corrupt, manipulative, stubborn, vain, materialistic, dictatorial. A narcissist, a strangler. The worst tyrants began as oily-voiced sidling seducers, insinuating themselves into power through people's affection.

Mother's wickedness was born as a germ. She had started life as a fibber, a trimmer, a needy child with two unhappy parents, and now in her old age she had all the attributes of a mad old queen. She was sentimental in unimportant ways but ruthless in the ones that mattered. Somehow she had lost even her animal affection for me.

Why hadn't I reminded myself of this? Oh, yes, I had been in love.

Mother was dissatisfied: other people's contentment niggled at her. She most of all resented her children's happiness. If Mother had been happy, how different our lives would have been.

I visited her. The first time, Franny's Subaru was in the driveway — odd, in the middle of the week on a school day. I drove away. The second time, the coast was clear, Mother alone in her chair.

I asked, "What have you said about me?"

Her face was at once wiped clean of lines and guile. She assumed a bland expression of innocence — this was the face of Mother caught red-handed. Goggling at me in denial, she looked like a child. She had downy cheeks and hugged a shawl, drawing it around her narrow bony shoulders, becoming smaller, with a look of both innocence and defiance.

"I never said a thing." She enunciated stiffly, as though speaking a line in a play.

She was affronted, insulted, now wincing slightly, looking offended by my question. All these moods I knew well: how haughty she grew when she was found out, how indignant she became when she was in the wrong.

But I was calm. I believed I had everything in my favor—logic, truth, reason, morality. I was the victim. Her betrayal had cost me my lover, the only friend I had, my future. I needed Mother to see how she had hurt me.

"You're the only person I told," I said.

She stared at me, her eyes glittering. She did not say a word.

"And now everyone knows." A shrill note of pleading made my voice crack, yet I was struggling to sound reasonable and unruffled.

Mother had a liar's eyes, a liar's fingers, a liar's posture, all crooked. She was a lump of untruth, bulked against her big leather chair.

"Why did you tell them?" I said loudly, because she had not said anything. "Ma?"

She squinted at my pleading, partly in contempt, partly in pain, as if wounded by my accusation.

"It was a secret! I told you it was a secret!" Now I was shouting, my throat pinched from the effort.

"Do you have any idea how you're upsetting me?" she said sharply.

"What about me? Think how upset I am, knowing that everyone knows my secret. You told them everything, and they're laughing at me."

"Do you think you're that important?"

"Ma, what do you mean?"

"Why should anyone bother to laugh at you?"

Why should they not? The answer was, because I was defeated. I had been married twice before, back in the days when I believed my family wished me well—when they hoped for me to fail; and I had failed. But I couldn't say this to Mother now or else she would use it against me.

"See? Everything's going to be all right," she said.

"No," I said in a hot whisper, "and it's your fault."

Mother put her fingertips to her temples to indicate that she was suffering. "My head is ringing. I hope you're happy. I won't be able to sleep a wink tonight."

The phone rang at her elbow. She picked up the receiver with tormented fingers, exaggerating the effort to lift it, and said in a small persecuted voice, "Hello?"

It was Franny—I heard her patronizing quack from six feet away. *You okay, Ma?*

"I'm fine," Mother said in a tone intended to convey that she was not fine at all. "I'll talk to you later."

That meant I would be further betrayed. Yet while she had been on the phone I had regained my composure. Trembling to keep my anger in check, I waited for her to hang up, then said, "There is only one way the rest of the family could have known."

She drew her shawl tighter, eyed me in pity, and said, "I didn't think you'd mind."

"Remember I said, 'It's a secret'?"

"I thought you'd be proud."

She was maddening. Now, obliquely, she was admitting having revealed the secret and gossiping to the others. She was blaming me for not seeing that this was all charitable.

"Most people would be proud to be in love. Proud to be engaged. I remember when Dad proposed to me, I couldn't wait to tell the world. Just what are you ashamed of?"

How could I tell her the consequences of her betrayal, that Missy had rejected me, that it was over, that I was alone? These were my humiliating secrets now. If I told her, she would reveal them too.

The phone rang again, and as she answered it — Franny again — I left, cursing.

My anger with Mother was also anger at myself, frustration with my pitiful state, which was of my own making. What shamed me most about losing Missy was that I had been halfhearted to begin with. It was desperate for me to think I could succeed with a much younger woman, who had a teenage child I found irritating. I had failed twice; I suspected I would fail again. And Missy was the sort of woman I feared — feared for her single-mindedness, feared that she was never casual, feared her intensity. I remembered how, the first time at my house, she had stood and twitched the withered leaves off my potted geranium, snatching at them with impatient fingers, grooming the plant, believing that she was improving the poor thing, but only leaving me with the foreboding that she would pluck at me that way.

I couldn't blame her — I sort of admired her passion. She was determined to find a husband for herself and a father for her child. *Look after us!* Such women have a practical morality and no time to waste. Their sharp sense for which men are serious and which aren't reliable enough makes them quick studies, shrewd in sizing up a potential partner, and geniuses at sorting and rejection. Missy had been unsure of me, located the source of my equivocation, and seen that I simply did not have the heart — the stomach — to raise another teenager. She had been looking for an occasion to reject me, and I was waiting for the moment to withdraw gracefully. I had told her too much about Mother and me.

Missy was a mother with a mission. I had good reason to steer clear of her and spare disappointing her. She was more passionate about being a mother than a wife.

I began to doubt my innocence in sharing my news with Mother. Did I tell her my secret because I was certain that she would undo me? Perhaps.

I was stewing the next day, disgusted with the amount of spare time I had now that Floyd had ditched me — and the others seemed to be enjoying my embarrassment — when the telephone rang. I hoped it was Missy. I wanted a miracle: *Let's put all that behind us. Let's resume as though nothing has happened. I love you.*

But that was a weak man's fantasy. Real life is remorseless, random, without miracles, without shortcuts or happy accidents. After a certain age — and I had passed it — there is no good news.

It was Fred on the line, his voice stony. He had something on his mind.

"Just talked to Franny. She says you upset Ma. Why do you keep doing this?"

"What are you saying?"

"That this isn't the first time," Fred said. "Ma's an old woman. Can't you talk to her without shouting and blaming?"

He was angry with me on Mother's behalf; so was Franny, so was Rose, so was Gilbert. Hubby was in New Hampshire. Mother had told them all. Fred, as the eldest, was taking the initiative to reprimand me.

"Don't you see that she does the best she can? She deserves better than to be vilified by her children. We should be honoring her. She gave birth to us."

Mother's own motto. But I was amazed. The woman who had betrayed my secret was now spreading the story that I had abused her. She egged

them on to oppose me, to defend her. And what had I done? I had objected to her using me as gossip.

"What exactly did Franny tell you?"

"That she called Ma after you left. That Ma was so upset she couldn't
eat. She was in tears. She was a wreck. All because of what you said to her.
Franny called again today. Ma hadn't slept all night. So Franny called me.
Why did you yell at her?"

"Why don't you ask me what really happened, instead of accusing me
and putting me on the defensive?"

"Because I know what happened. Ma told Franny everything."

Hearing Mother's stubbornness and certainty in his tone, I bristled,
my anger rising again.

"Ma's lying."

"I'm not going to listen to that."

"She's trying to turn you against me."

"It's all about you, isn't it?"

"Furthermore, she's succeeding. You think I'm a shit."

"Yelling at an eighty-seven-year-old woman."

"I wasn't yelling."

"Stop denying it. Show a little concern. Call her and apologize. The
woman is seriously upset."

Instead of replying to this, I said, "Did someone tell you I'm getting
married?"

"I heard something about it."

"From whom?"

"I don't remember. It's not news. Everyone knows."

His casual assumption was imperious, but then, he was Mother's
counselor and confidant. I said, "You didn't say anything. Why didn't you
tell me you knew?"

"You didn't ask."

"You could have congratulated me."

"I wanted to discuss it with you."

"There's nothing to discuss!"

"You might be making a big mistake."

That was Fred all over — big brother, taking no interest in my life except for his intrusions into my secrets, merely collecting data, and yet presuming to give me advice. He could be as big a scold and a bother as Mother, and he was indeed often Mother's mouthpiece.

"It was supposed to be a secret. Ma swore she wouldn't tell anyone. That's why I told her. She blabbed to everyone. She betrayed me."

"Get over it. You should be happy. You should be proud."

Just what Mother had said.

"So when's the big day?"

I eliminated him by stabbing at the button in the receiver cradle and immediately called Mother.

"Ma, what did you tell Franny?"

"Nothing. Who is this?"

"It's Jay. Did you tell Franny that I upset you?"

"Of course not. I have better things to do. I made some crab-apple jelly this morning. I went for a walk. I'm baking a pie."

"Fred said that Franny told him that you claimed you couldn't eat."

"I just had my supper. Beef noodle soup. Franny brought me a big pot of it. And Jell-O for dessert."

"I mean yesterday. That's what they said."

"I can't remember. You're confusing me."

"And that you couldn't sleep."

"Today? It's four o'clock. I just watched the news. I have a pie in the oven. I normally don't go to bed until ten or eleven."

"Last night, I guess. And that you're upset. And that it's all my fault."

"Please stop shouting. You're upsetting me now."

"And that you're angry with me."

"Why should I be angry with you?"

"That's just what I was wondering. Look, Ma, what exactly did you say about me?" I was jarred by a cracking, a pleading that slanted into my voice, distorting it and making it miserable and boyish.

"You're giving me a headache. Is that why you called me? To give me a headache?"

"Ma! What did you tell Franny?"

"Does it give you pleasure to upset me? Why do you want to have an argument?"

I took deep breaths; this was not going well. It was clear that Mother would never admit to complaining about me.

I said, "I don't want to have an argument."

"Good." She snorted. "What's the weather like?"

"Cloudy." And I hung up.

I was not a man pushing sixty, with most of my life behind me. I was a ten-year-old, feeling trapped in the house on a snowy Saturday, begging to go out. Mother was blocking the door, standing before it with her arms folded.

"But why can't I go for a hike?"

"Because I said so."

"I wanted to get some exercise."

"Then clean the bathroom. That's good exercise. Get a mop and a bucket. Get the Ajax. Shine the fixtures and mop and wax the floor. Use elbow grease."

"You said I could go for a hike. You promised."

"Are you calling me a liar?"

Then Franny appears from behind Mother. "He wants to fool around with his friends. He told Fred they shoot squirrels with their BB guns. They start fires."

"Jay's a firebug," Rose calls out from the next room. "Firebug!"

"Stay out of this," Mother says, but with a smile, because they are on her side.

Franny is holding the mop and bucket. She gives them to Mother, who hands them to me.

"I want to be able to see my face in those tiles," Mother said.

This memory had me dialing again, Franny's number. I was breathing hard.

"What did you tell Fred?"

"Nothing."

"About my getting married. You told him."

"Oh, that. I was happy for you. I was bursting with pride. So was Ma. Was it the woman you took to the dance recital? She looked real nice."

"You told Fred that I upset Ma."

"He must have misunderstood."

"You told him that Ma couldn't eat or sleep because I upset her."

From the way she breathed, I could tell that Franny was squirming and swallowing air.

"You know how Ma is," she finally said. "She exaggerates every little thing. She's like a little girl. So who's the lucky woman?"

"And Floyd," I said, ignoring Franny's wheezing question — it was as though she'd blown it up a narrow organ pipe, but to no avail, for there was no woman now in my life. "Floyd's not answering the phone. He wrote me a wicked note. He's really mad at me."

"Floyd's worse than Ma!" Franny exclaimed. "Ma used to say how he was the most difficult baby, always crying. Always wanting to be picked up. And remember all his bedwetting?"

Franny went on talking. Decades had dropped away. We were in the world of diapers and demands, rubber sheets and tantrums, the cloud of blame, Mother looming over us, for if she did not have her way, she would become hysterical: *You're upsetting me!*

There was hardly any distance between the world of childhood and the confusion I felt now, berated by Fred, snubbed by Floyd, trifled with by Franny, whispered about by Hubby and Rose, betrayed by Mother, who accused me of giving her headaches. I could easily see the small girl in big Franny. I could hear a domineering boy in Fred, the unhappiness in Floyd's angry silence. We were competing children all over again, negotiating and testing our alliances. In every encounter in the family was an unspoken and desperate yearning: *Please be my friend. Stand with me against all the others.*

Hubby came back from New Hampshire. He stopped by to help me with a plumbing problem, a glitch in my pump — a flange, a bushing, a warping of a gasket. As he tinkered, he told me he had been summoned to assist in a liver transplant operation that had taken fourteen hours. He related every suture, every ligation.

"I just talked to Ma," he finally said. "She was ragging on you. She says you're really touchy." And then with perfect mimicry he spoke in Mother's voice. "'But he's always been that way, shawt-tempid. It seems I can't do anything right.'"

16

CRAZY BASTARD

FLOYD WAS NOWHERE TO BE FOUND. I took notice: in this family, being absent signified much more than being present. Floyd would not pick up the phone when I called, would not answer the door or reply to my letters and notes. One winter day of cold, dripping sea fog I thought I saw his shape as a beaky, staring shadow at an upper window in his tall old house as I turned to look again after my futile knocking. That was the strangest feeling of all, the sense of his observing my failure to find him, like a malevolent spirit gloating from another world.

I sighed, recognizing one of the most maddening of our family traits. We had a habit, a technique — a gift, really — for disappearing at critical times, vanishing in anger. The absence was obvious, the anger invisible. The object was to make one's anger a mystery. It was our roundabout way of being difficult, plotting our own disappearance. Being missed, being gone, being needed were conspicuous ways of being unhelpful, if not antagonistic.

The strong suggestion of hostility that fueled this withdrawal was un-spoken. We slipped away quietly rather than slamming the door. Vanish-ing was a statement. The statement was: I don't like you anymore. "Passive aggressive" were words I did not hear until many years later; in our case it was more like "absent aggressive." We did not flee; we dropped from view. Being away was a reply, a final answer, because no one is more maddening than the person who remains silent.

My almost forty years of traveling the world as a writer, keeping apart from Mother and the family, was an example of this behavior. They were the years of my being a householder, a creator, of my active imagination, of my making my life. Mother didn't figure in those productive years ex-cept as a negative influence, someone who disapproved. They were the years of my books, of stability and happiness. They did not in the least resemble the years of my growing up or my latter years with Mother — the family years when, no matter our ages, we were children.

Now there was a tangle of us around Mother, who broadcast incessant updates from about what each of us was doing at any particular time — what we had told her, offhand remarks, heartaches, hopes, and often disinformation. Mother had whatever breaking news there was, and she controlled the flow of information. Anyone's disappearance was sharply noticed, as in a folk society where the absent are suspected of eavesdropping from their vantage point in the twilight zone — where no one goes away and the dead are more present and more reassuring than the living, as Angela was to Mother.

Absence could also be figurative, theoretical, a cast of mind. At any given time, some of us would not be on speaking terms, yet still we would show up and pretend to be civil. But disappearing was something else. In vanishing we made ourselves invisible, enigmatic, unreadable, and yet conspicuous, like a foul odor that hung in the void where the absent person had been.

The process was seldom theoretical, seldom the vagrant mood. Mostly it was a physical act, and sometimes it was extreme. The others had their own ways of disappearing. Fred made regular trips to China and India. It was business, but also deliberate enigma. He said he wanted to help us, but he couldn't: "The thing is, I'm in China." Gilbert was often in Europe, or Yemen or Bahrain. Hubby vanished into New Hampshire on medical trips, but also to buy tax-free lumber and appliances.

As a child I absented myself by going for hikes. I joined the Boy Scouts in order to be licensed for such disappearances, the hikes becoming overnighters and finally weekend camping trips. When Mother attempted to claw me back, I protested, "I gotta go. I'm qualifying for a merit badge." And she relented, because the Boy Scouts kept you out of trouble. But in the Scouts I learned to swear, I had my first serious fistfight, and I witnessed my first instance of racial discrimination: at Camp Fellsland, a black scout from another troop, called a nigger by a white scout, punched the boy in the face, bloodying his nose, and was sent home for fighting. As a Boy Scout I carried a hunting knife, I built fires, and at the age of thirteen, I swapped my BB gun for my first lethal rifle, a Mossberg .22.

My friends owned pistols and rifles. We were the nonathletes, the book-worms, the nerds, the undersized kids, and with a scattering of effeminate boys we called percies. All of us needed to get away. We were geeks with guns.

This wish to get out of the house, a quest for privacy and anonymity, established a pattern in my life, making me a traveler. It wasn't accidental that I had lived for years in Africa, and years more in Britain. I feared being overwhelmed by my family, and if I had been successful in my choices, I would have stayed away; I would have left after Father's funeral. But I lived near Mother, and what I had always feared would happen to me was happening, for we were all at home now, children again, and I was so alone that my years of travel seemed idyllic, for being isolated at home was the severest sort of exile.

Franny's and Rose's disappearances took the form of lame excuses and complex silences. Mother knew where they were, though, and could rouse them whenever she pleased.

Mother's own silences were preceded by her pained announcement, "I have a splitting headache."

Floyd was the most efficient at absenting himself. Whenever he was present he was restlessly conspicuous, demanding to be seen, requiring answers. "I am talking to you! You heard what I said. Do I lisp?" But at the wrong word, a misjudged opinion, a hint of criticism, anything that smacked of disagreement, or a secret that had been kept from him, he was gone. And he was capable of staying away for a long time, reappearing when you least expected him. But that could be months. Years. Whenever I saw a shag or a loon near the shore, spooked by a noise and diving, not emerging for a long time and never in that same place, holding its breath and fleeing, I thought of Floyd.

No one in the family admitted to telling Floyd about my engagement, which was not an engagement — yet someone had. And Floyd was of-fended. His reasoning ran this way: if I had truly been his friend, I would have told him everything. But I hadn't. I had held crucial things back, and much worse, I had confided my love affair to others in the family. It proved I was closer to them than to him. I had rejected him. His response was to reject me.

Sometimes a family disappearance implied, *Look for me — find me — if you really care.*

Floyd's absences were seldom that sort. This one was a total eclipse. He did not want to be found or spoken to or importuned. He might not have objected to visits from the other members of the family, but it was clear that he wanted me to stay away.

From talking to him nearly every day, I now did not talk to him at all. More weeks went by. A month, two months. I persisted but got nowhere.

I wanted to tell him that I understood the problem. I had not told him about Missy, what she had meant to me. I had not mentioned the commitment ring — I knew he would have laughed at the word, for even I found it fatuous. Well, whom had I told? Only Mother. But Floyd expected me to confide in him. He felt we were close, we were allies, we mocked the others. By telling Mother — he must have known that she was the source of the story — I was being disloyal to him.

Of course I would have told him, but there was so little to tell. What Mother had reported was mostly fiction — or supposition, or embroidery. Though she must have mentioned engagement and marriage, I had no such plans.

I had lost Missy, lost Floyd, lost Mother too, who was still telling the family I had abused her. I was alone, and I strongly suspected the others would have been giddy at the news I had been rejected. Bad news was always welcome; it made their lives seem so much richer.

I needed a friend. As a smiling cynic who had shared many of my misfortunes, Floyd would have been just the friend I needed. As children, we had been the greatest allies, and so, of course, he was capable of being my worst enemy: it was a family lesson I had learned early. He could be fiercer than anyone. But I also knew that in his rejection of me he would be more dependent on the others for support.

Floyd was that pivotal figure in any big family, the fearsome unblinking child whom everyone wants to placate and befriend. He is dangerous — feared for his moods and his wicked satire, for his eccentric intelligence, for being reckless and unpredictable. He is fretful, has no loyalties. He is the most impatient, the hungriest. He will listen to your earnest plea and then turn on you. He was the one who, as a child, tore his pants swinging on a branch, screaming, "Ungawa! Tarmangani! I'm Tarzan of the Apes!" — and afterward cut his toe because he was barefoot. He sliced the flesh at the base of his thumb and said, "I'm going to get lockjaw!" The one with dirty hands, wild hair, a smudge on his cheek, a crooked smile.

"Your brother's a crazy bastard," my friends would say, and they meant it as high praise.

I earned his admiration one day when I told him that I'd gotten the gasoline for my motorbike (it was one I'd salvaged; I was fifteen) by siphoning it from the gas tank of a car parked at the Falmouth Hospital. He liked the deed for its absurdity — all that trouble and stealth and risk to save ten cents.

"Yeah," he said, imagining the clumsy villainy of my kneeling beside a stranger's car, pushing a rubber hose into the gas tank, and sucking on it. "That's wild."

We were law-abiding, with delinquent exceptions, our successes in making a zip gun (a stolen car antenna taped to a wooden handle, with rubber bands fixed to an improvised firing pin), or hot-wiring a car, or the simplest revenge of all — jamming a potato into an exhaust pipe or sugar into a fuel tank to disable a vehicle. Our mastering these wayward talents we regarded as more heroic than excelling in school, because living in Mother Land had turned us into outlaws.

Floyd was the worst tease, the cruelest mocker, sometimes shuffling behind Mother and shadowing her, hovering and aping her movements. When she turned to confront him, he would cry out, "I am Sacajawea, the Bird Woman!" He was merciless in his imitations, a comedian, with a comedian's inevitable darkness.

He had been the butt of so many jokes himself, the object of so much scorn — for his bedwetting, his temper, his academic achievements, his poems, his chair at Harvard; he was that most dangerous of men, the one with nothing to lose. He had experienced a childhood of rejection, and in adulthood he took his revenge as a rejecter. Cross him, doubt him, lecture him, take him too lightly — trifle with him in any way — and he would try to destroy you, in a poison-pen letter, in a poem written to curse you, like a form of literary voodoo, or in one of his comic turns, directing all his humor and intelligence on the object of his scorn, with the intention of encouraging the whole family to howl that person down. In a family of evaders, he was a confronter.

Many of his characterizations were from the literature he taught. He would twist his lips at Fred and say, "Let us bid welcome to Eugene Wrayburn," or lock his eyes on Franny and her husband, Marvin, and hail them as the Veneerings. Rose was Miss Piggy, Gilbert was Filbert or Gerald Emerald, Hubby was Giant Haystacks, I was Plastic Man, Mother was Queen Lear or "Addie Bundren, cursing from her catafalque!" *I will not allow a three-hundred-pound puff adder to interfere with me,* he wrote to a neighbor of his who was sensitive about her weight. *You have all the virtues of a dog except fidelity,* he snapped to Hubby's wife, Moneen, and when the poor woman sent Floyd a Christmas present as a peace offering he returned it to her unopened, with the scrawl, *You can't be a policeman and also a thief.*

Seeking his friendship, because he was such a terrible enemy, meant propitiating him. We all brought him presents of candy and fruit, books he might like, items for his various collections. He collected ice cream scoops, cast-iron mechanical banks, literature on vampires, Coca-Cola memorabilia, signed baseballs, anything related to Marilyn Monroe, antique flintlock rifles, exotic postcards, ivory netsukes — and much else. The right present might soothe him.

At times, he teased one of us when Mother was present. "I'll take the strut out of you," he sneered, pretending to flex a whip. The butt of his joke might be Hubby — his weight, his wobble, his seriousness about tools and his peculiar relish for naming them, a spokeshave, a ball-peen hammer, a socket wrench, a shim. And although Hubby might be squinting in shame, Mother would be laughing, covering her mouth, her shoulders shaking, feasting on this while screeching, "God forgive me!"

And out of the corner of his eye, Floyd knew he had succeeded, as Mother breathlessly gulped in mirth, enjoying the spectacle of the quarreling boys that gave her pleasure and power.

"He walks like this," he would say of someone well known, and would do the walk, flinging his feet out, stiff-legged, striding, pigeon-toed. He did Franny's foot-dragging and Marvin's flat-footed tramping and swiveling shoulders, throwing his weight back and forth. He did Hubby's shuffle, Gilbert's sidling, Fred's purposeful gait with working elbows. He did Mother's hunched-over round-shouldered tread, "like a constipated geisha or a bird on a beach."

After Floyd stopped speaking to me, I still got visits from Franny and Rose. They brought me the usual presents of fruit and candy, and one day a scented candle. I saw them and always thought of how Floyd satirized them: "Franny looks like Ethel Rosenberg. Rose's eyes are George Matesky's — remember him? The Mad Bomber?"

"Are you all right?" my sisters asked.

They were fishing, hoping for news of my marriage. I had decided to conceal my failure. I did not say that I had finished writing a novel and it would soon be published. I hoped for good sales, so that I would have a ticket out of here. Mentioning it, even hoping for its success, seemed unlucky, so I quietly waited for a miracle.

"Floyd won't speak to me," I said.

"You know how he is," Franny said, and made a face.

"He's nutso," Rose said. She really did have the Mad Bomber's eyes. "If Bingo came home with someone like him, I'd freak out."

They encouraged me to dismiss him as a loon and a grudge bearer. I didn't need much encouragement, for I was hurt, I was lonely, and there was no one in the family he had not offended.

"I should forget about him," I said. "At least he's not hanging around asking me for favors."

"He really depended on you a lot," Franny said.

"I used to loan him my car, my golf clubs, my shotgun. He still hasn't given me back a rake he borrowed last year — not that I care. He can have it. Does he still have three cats?"

"One died."

I laughed. "But he's had more luck with cats than women."

"Remember that girl he was going to take to the prom, and then he chickened out?" Rose said.

"He's probably afraid of women, deep down," Franny said. "He's jealous of the fact that you're getting married."

I almost gave it away, but I said, "Who knows?" as enigmatically as I could, because all this talk of Floyd's failure with women had cautioned me. Like Floyd, I'd had two wives, two divorces, a number of other rela-tionships, and a few phantom engagements.

It did my morale good to disparage Floyd's attempts at marriage, his divorces. "And no kids," I said. "All these years he's been shooting blanks."

I needed affection. I could not tell anyone that my romance with Missy was over. Disclosing that would have meant I'd have nothing. My secret was sad, but at least it was my secret; it was something to hold on to. It gave me heart and a sort of unholy glee to talk about Floyd's failure.

"The other kids always called him a crazy bastard."

Now Franny was laughing, no longer looking like Ethel Rosenberg. She was nodding at Rose, who was laughing too, widening her Mad Bomber eyes.

The inevitable happened. Again, you probably saw it coming before I did. Floyd sent me an enraged letter, attacking me for talking about him and quoting verbatim everything I had told Franny and Rose. *Loon! Dead cat! Grudge bearer! Crazy bastard!*

Franny and Rose had reported what I had said about him, because he had told them everything I'd ever said about them. And so, without another word, they vanished from my life—out of anger, out of shame, out of fear. And I stopped hearing from anyone else in the family, except Mother, who said that everything was fine. I prayed for my novel to suc-ceed. I needed to flee.

I still called Mother, but I was cautious about what I told her. Weather was the main topic, though with Mother one seldom needed to suggest a topic. As always, she talked, I listened. One day, in a good mood, she said, "I'm bushed. I've just come from the birthday party."

"Whose birthday?"

"Floyd's, and Jake's—you know they share the same birthday. It was quite a spread. Everyone was there. Fred's so extravagant. I wish he wouldn't—it's kind of a waste, really."

Jake was Fred's older boy. The one who, long ago, had become a family legend when he revealed that he had just eaten a Styrofoam cup. When he was questioned, he puked it onto the doubter's shoes.

"I wasn't invited."

"It was just cake and ice cream," Mother said, backpedaling. "I didn't eat much." She had suddenly become self-conscious, coughing in the way Floyd always mimicked, trying to swallow her mistake.

"I guess they didn't want me there."

"Of course they did."

"If Floyd was there, it would have been awkward," I said. "But didn't you wonder where I was?"

"It was just a little get-together on Fred's back porch. I'm sure you had more important things to do."

I had nothing to do.

"Your lady love," she said.

"Right. I forgot."

After I hung up with Mother, I called Fred. I told him I was hurt. How could he have a party, just a few miles from my house, and invite everyone except me.

"I didn't think you'd want to come," he said.

He was too weak to admit that he had chosen Floyd over me. The whole family had been there, and Mother had the chair of honor at the head of the table, fed by her sons and daughters, queening it.

I soon discovered why I had been left out.

17

GOOD SPORT

FLOYD HAD DROPPED OUT of my life and reappeared among them, doing his imitations and his funny walks and screaming, "Who am I?" until someone guessed. Everyone was relieved. He was showing up again, making them laugh, like old times. They needed him, needed his complex friendship, especially needed his protection, the reassurance that he would not hurt them with his vicious wit. He was a cranky cat that they had declawed. In his absences and silences there had always been a cloud of menace. Now that they had him to themselves he was mocking on their behalf, rather than mocking them.

They had begged to be his friend, had brought him propitiatory gifts, sent him invitations. They no longer had to look over their shoulder, and could open a letter from him without trembling, for that was how he communicated his withering opinions, always in closely typed letters. But their presents had not done the trick. He was on their side because he saw me as a betrayer. *Your wife!*

I hadn't told him of my fondness for Missy — indeed, had never mentioned her name, knowing how he would mock it, especially the mockable "Gearhart." And now I couldn't tell him it was over. Everything he "knew" was in the area of gossip, speculation, and creative half-truths, the family way of making news.

Because Floyd was now a frequent guest at Fred's, at Franny's, at Rose's — less so at Hubby's and Gilbert's — I was a liability. I could not be invited or I would drive him away. They could not entertain both of us without losing him, so they chose him. He was the more satirical, the funnier, the angrier, the more eminent, the greater danger.

How had this transition been so smooth, the result so successful? Mother had been the key: from that first party to which I had not been invited, Mother had been conspicuously present. She had not mentioned me; no one had. Mother had welcomed Floyd as if he was a warrior just emerged from the wilderness, into the family clearing in the jungle. In her role as matriarch, she gave Floyd her blessing, and since she dominated the parties, she was in the position of sanctioning the guest list. I heard as a mutter from Franny that Jonty had been deleted. "Ma goes, 'Maybe it would be for the best.'" Franny believed it was a sacrifice for Floyd, but in fact it was for Mother's own sake.

I did not complain. Any complaint in this family was self-revelation. I did inquire about the parties, though: "Just wondering." Obliqueness and irony were lost on Mother, and yet, canny enough to suspect that I was hurt, she was defensive.

"Be a good sport," she said.

Mother could count on me to be mild, and she welcomed it as a weakness. I was easy, Floyd was difficult, so he was chosen. These days Mother was the guest of honor, with Floyd at her right hand, tamed and attentive. Because he was usually cantankerous, because he was now loyal to her, his presence made Mother more powerful.

Desperate to know more, I called them all to find out where I stood. Gilbert was vague; he was preparing for a trip to Syria. Hubby was busy at the hospital, but he admitted that he had been to several of Fred's barbecues and also at Franny's potluck supper. He complained of the greasy food and the warm beer and the burned burgers as a way of reminding me that I hadn't missed much. "Floyd was making jokes about Franny's three-bean salad and repeating the words 'puncheon' and 'luncheon.'" When I called Franny, for her party was news to me, she complained about Floyd —"Floyd's always been high-maintenance"— so that I wouldn't feel bad about being left out.

"It wasn't much of a party," she said. "Who told you?"

"Hubby."

"Hubby had about sixty hamburgers, a whole pile of french fries, and a ton of pie," Franny said. "Fred's dogs were in the pool. Little Benno walked straight into my screen door and needed stitches. Bingo got poison ivy."

All this was meant to make me feel I had been lucky not to be there.

And why had I wanted to? Because I had been rejected by Missy. Because I had finished my novel and wanted to tell someone. Because I was low, living near Mother, and didn't know how to flee.

I called Missy. She interrupted me as soon as she heard my voice. She said, "Do you realize what you've just done?"

"No, what?"

"You dialed my number," she said. "Don't ever do it again."

"I bought some lobsters. I thought I might bring them over. I love you."

"I don't eat lobsters. See? You claim to love me and you don't even know that simple fact about me."

I hung on to the phone so long, stunned by this rejection, that the recorded voice came on saying, *If you want to make a call, please hang up and try again,* over and over.

When I got the proofs of my book, I was occupied. But in all solitude, even the most benign, there are parts of the day, the early evening especially, when a sort of sadness descends, a shadowy stillness that is a reminder one could be elsewhere, an emptiness: something is missing. The shadow asks: What are you doing?

I went out, I drove, I visited bars. I was a more conspicuous stranger in a bar, because everyone else knew each other; I was intruding. Bar patrons were a sort of family, but a rare happy one. I had no business being among them.

And didn't I have my own family? I brought Mother a shawl. "It's nice," she said, and I knew from her faint praise that she would probably give it away, one of her many recycled gifts.

"How are you, Ma?"

"I just got my electric bill. It was astronomical. And I never leave lights burning."

One of her favorite themes, the high cost of living.

"I remember when a dollar was a lot of money."

"Even I remember that," I said.

I offered to help her financially, but halfheartedly, partly because she had not been grateful enough about the shawl, but also because I had so little money myself. But maybe my book would succeed.

"Oh, I'll manage," Mother said in a martyred voice.

To change the subject, I remarked on all the books stacked on her coffee table.

"I love a good book," Mother said. "I like to improve my mind. I never waste a minute."

"I finished my novel," I said. "It's coming out pretty soon."

"Oh?"

She said it tipping her head to the side, as though eager to hear more. But I resisted. I didn't want her to spread the word about me or my new book. I knew the news would be received with mockery. And my secrets were all I had of my own.

"Are these any good?" I asked, fingering the books.

"Floyd brings them to me. He knows I'm a reader." She pushed at the books. I saw a biography of Amelia Earhart, and a novel, and a picture book, *Italians Who Made America.*

"He hates me."

"No one hates you."

"Everyone does."

"That's very unfair," she said, and to clarify it, "of you."

"When Floyd's invited to a family dinner, I'm always excluded," I said. Mother didn't react. "He won't speak to me."

"Maybe there's a reason for that."

This meant it was my own fault.

"I have no idea what the reason could be," I said. "He wrote me some vicious letters."

"That's between the two of you," Mother said.

"Maybe you could say something to him."

Mother winced and pressed her temples. "I've got a splitting headache."

Mother had what she wanted. She needed to be in regular touch with Floyd. I mattered less, because my loyalty was never in question and I was a good sport. But Floyd was volatile, Floyd was a mocker, Floyd was dangerous—he was a power figure who could sway the others with his satire. That unsettled Mother. To have him calling and visiting, supplying books, showing up at parties and paying his respects to her—that was important. He brought her food sometimes too, as Franny and Rose did: a pound of scallops, a pair of lobsters, a tin of cookies, a basket of berries, a tray of cheeses with his scribbled note: *I love an assertive cheese.*

What Floyd did with the rest of his time was of no concern to Mother. That he whispered about me and mimicked me was my problem. Mother would have been disturbed if she'd gotten wind of the fact that he mocked her, but there were no whispers of this. Floyd inspired fear in the potential gossip.

Mother was happy. Floyd was showing up, bringing presents, being a grateful son. In my distraction I was a wayward son, not a habitual gift giver or regular visitor. I was sullen, selfish, distrusting, neglectful, and —in Mother's blaming eyes—a blamer. "Stop feeling sorry for yourself," I had heard my whole life. We were not allowed to be sad, to mourn, to be doubtful or introspective, and so we had to find other ways to express our dejection.

Mother was not interested in my problems, or anyone's problems, except as gossip, because such drama took the emphasis off her own. She wouldn't listen. It had been a mistake for me to say "He hates me." She had no natural sympathy. No one could be more wounded than she was herself. Her belief that no one was as sick as they said they were must have had its origin in her own unconscious knowledge that she was a hypochondriac, her sense that she never told the truth about her health.

Mother's egotism and indifference could be maddening, but it saved her from ever fretting about us. She was never more queenly or aloof than when a crisis arose among her children. Then, her only advice was *Be a good sport,* which meant *Shut your mouth.*

Mother's chief concern was loyalty to her. It pleased her a little that we were divided among ourselves. Not that she wanted to know the messy details — she didn't — but she was comforted by the reassurance that we were more easily dominated if we were divided and somewhat in disarray and requiring her counsel.

"Machiavelli for beginners," Floyd used to say. But I would think: Machiavelli, yes; beginners, no. Mother's was an advanced course in power.

The crisis began with my receiving in the mail a literary magazine, one of those sober academic quarterlies that list the table of contents on the cover — not one I subscribed to. Opening the plain envelope, I assumed I was on a mailing list, and I was on the point of tossing it away when I saw that Floyd had a piece in it. His short story had a characteristic title, purplish and arcane, "Envenoming Junior."

Durian Staines [so the story began], who had always envied and then came fully to hate his brother, Jack, becoming even crustier and more hostile after many years, was trying to intimidate his older son, Blore, now thirty-four, to write something poisonous about his uncle, and as a sop to the project promised to give him in return his old Jaguar XK120 if he would do so. 'But, as I say, it has to be fiction,' soberly warned his father, making an estimative grimace, which he followed with a wink. 'Anything else of course would subject you to libel.' The son, who had always lived in the shadow of this enthusiastic and unending disagreeableness that had kept his famously intolerant father angry for decades, was now finally hearing hard terms that seemed, *seemed* — he lived with doubt, suffered from anxiety — to make it all worthwhile.

But the Staineses were skeptics, indirection was their method, du-plicity their style, and suggestions were taken not as instigations but orders. His father had been badgering his son for years to write this novel.

They sat sipping green drinks on a canopied veranda in the lush area of Hidden Hills, Los Angeles, short father and tall son, looking across a row of blasting water-sprinklers to the ferret kennels that the rude, often curmudgeonly director had bought with the grosses from his most recent film release — a surprisingly successful one, since gen-erally his documentaries did very small box office . . .

"Green drinks" and "ferret kennels" were nice touches. Yet I read it with my mouth open, hardly believing he could write something so ri-diculous, and frankly so purple. In his extreme anger, Floyd never wished to risk being subtle. Durian Staines was me, in a conspiracy with my older son Blore; and the victim, Jack, was undeniably Floyd. Not only was Jack a writer, "Jack also wrote like an angel, with bold original prose that cracked like sheet lightning across the page, and, while Durian got more attention and was much more widely known and recognized, Jack, to those in the know, those who had taste, had by far the more original mind."

Ambiguity was absent from this work, and so was Floyd's wild hu-mor; it was all fury and recrimination in lurid pastiche. I was an envious hack conniving with my son to besmirch — his word — the reputation of a gifted brother. I had plagiarized an unpublished poem of my brother's and gone a step further in enlisting the help of my scribbling son to finish the job. The brainwashed boy "envenomed" by me had published a story ridiculing this worthy man, the maligned brother. Jack, the Floyd charac-ter, was a solitary genius, Durian Staines was a talentless social climber, and Blore was a monkey.

Oddly, the thing I had been accused of was the very thing he had done. I had not published anything about him, but his magazine story was about me.

I spoke to Fred. He said, "Don't pay any attention to it. Who reads this stuff?"

He did not want to be involved, and I suspected he saw a grain of truth in the depiction of me.

"'Bold original prose that cracked like sheet lightning across the page'?" Gilbert shrugged. "I don't think so."

"Was that supposed to be you?" Hubby asked.

Mother smiled grimly at me when I raised the subject. She said, "What has this got to do with me?"

Floyd's elaborately wrought public rejection of me had the desired effect. I was troubled by it — by the amount of time it must have taken for him to write and publish it. He was not merely malicious, he was conscientious in his malice. But of course Fred was right when he'd said, "Who reads this stuff?" It was a literary magazine with a negligible following, and after a few weeks of fuming I realized that what he wrote would have no effect. The attack was so concentrated, so vicious in its single-mindedness, it was ultimately artless, just a howl of rage and a shallow echo. Its chief aim had been to make me feel bad. After my initial annoyance, I let go and, like a good sport, dismissed it.

Floyd, too, must have felt the story had misfired. By sending the magazine to me, he meant to hurt me, and he had; but he needed the story to be seen. He wanted me to suffer a chorus of disapproval, yet hardly anyone had heard his lone voice.

It gave me some satisfaction to know that the magazine was beneath notice. Had it worked, had it created a flutter of ridicule, had it stung me, the matter might have ended there. But as far as he knew, it missed me, I was not scathed, and there had not been a proper response. If the object of satire is to arouse contempt and ridicule, he had failed. Perhaps his plan backfired, for he was the failure, not me.

In the meantime, as all of this was unfolding in whispered installments and updates, my novel was published. I had begun the book before Father's final decline, and the trauma of his death had accelerated my writing, turned it into a dense reverie of grieving. Father's death was not in the book, but my grief was in every line. The subject was loss, a fictional rendering of the breakdown of my second marriage. Titled *The Half Life*, it was an account of the eerie sense of amputation I'd experienced after my painful divorce.

The reviews were respectful, some admiring. The book was funny, not self-pitying but self-mocking. No villain appeared in it, and the tone was impartial — these aspects were singled out.

I was on the verge of a breakthrough, I felt — in sales, in a future book contract — when Floyd reviewed the book in *Boston* magazine.

This popular monthly featured a mention of Floyd's review on the cover in a teasing headline, "New Books: Blood Feud." The piece was unprecedented. When had an author's brother reviewed his new book and — for this seemed the only motive — trashed it? It was without doubt the worst review of my publishing career, for it not only condemned my book; it also was a bitter attack on my life.

I had received unfavorable reviews before, but even in the worst ones the reviewers pulled their punches, or damned me with faint praise, or registered disappointment, or said I'd written better in the past. I had never, until Floyd's review, been dismissed as a poseur, a hack, a whore, a slob, a meretricious scribbler. "At best a beach read, a middlebrow brick just a step above Judith Krantz or Belva Plain," he wrote. And while he mockingly and inaccurately summarized the substance of the novel, he spent most of the review (which ran to eight pages) speaking about me — things he could have learned only by talking to Mother, Fred, Gilbert, Franny, Rose, and Hubby. It was all there, my irregular life, the contents of my house, the car I drove, the food I ate, my recreations, my exercise routine, and my engagement, down to the mention of my commitment ring.

Only Floyd could have described my book as "a bizarre chiasmus, a Rumpelstiltskinian prank, the solitary connecting strand in the book the venal, unkempt, complicated, name-promoting, self-absorbed, literary hydra — the author himself — all at once, penitent, sneak, bounder, oaf, coward, bully, and show-off in a novelistic dead end, a pea-and-thimble trick with a gallery of shifty shits and scoundrels, as in the paradox of 'Schrödinger's Cat,' where the same event simultaneously both does and does not happen. With guilt and guile and grumpiness he has rehearsed over and over again the details of his divorce."

There was more. "This disgraceful novel is a portrait of himself as a bum-awful writer, a brooding fuckwit with noisome habits, unclean linen, and more crotchets than crudities coming forth in his nutty, yam-in-the-mouth way to explicate by omission everything as a person he feels he is not but brutally could be, a hyperbolic creep." And last, "It is a novel of contrition, pieced out by way of the contrivance of a writer at last taking a moment to satirize himself, not subtly . . . and to come out — even if only for the space of a story—from the cruel, carious shadows which, like a crab, he has so long chosen to inhabit."

So much for the novel. What of the novelist? I turned the page.

"He is small and surly and spiteful. He has ridiculed in print everyone he has ever known, and with exaggerated vindictiveness has found half the world wanting in goodness and grace, brains and bravery, cleanliness and character. He is famously a curmudgeon in his travel books, where grumpiness becomes half the celebration of his wandering around, and when he is at rest he habitually calumniates his own first wife. Where other writers may give themselves, he seems only to lend, the way André Gide said people who smile instead of laugh hold back in order to think themselves superior."

That was just the beginning. I could see Floyd's fingers madly tapping at the keys.

"He is weak, emotionally cold, sexually guilty, hypocritical, jealous, faithless, and afraid. He writes spitefully about cats, overeaters, prep schools, the Guggenheim Committee, tour groups, Catholicism, British manners, virgins, bad shoes, New England weather, all athletes, patronage, donuts, Irish crudeness, his hometown, soldiers, importunate telephone calls, Armenians, families, and women."

Did he say "donuts"?

"We in the family," Floyd went on, seeming to settle into his new role as Mother's enforcer, "don't mind his affected gentility, his smug and self-important airs, his urgent star-fucking insistence that he's a friend of lords and ladies, and only laugh at the fame he courts. But of his famous British accent—Cape Cod meets Cheltenham—what can I say? 'Ring me up,' he'll say, or 'How's your glass?' or 'Can you fetch me those boat cushions from the boot?' It may seem harmless, although I have long felt an unstated but cringing pain and mortification in finding him always getting pulled up for it, and his behavior vindicates a person who said to me recently, 'Your brother is envious, short, womanizing, cheap, opinionated, and angry.' The whole family laughs at him."

There were several more pages, about my pathetic house, my sidelined ex-wives, my unhappy children, my snobbery. There were sentences only Floyd could write: "He is a sedulous campaigner in the self-promotion of his ontological burdens." I was also a plagiarist and a cad.

"He has bowel worries and eats prunes for breakfast and once made inquiries to me about platform shoes," he wrote, now cheerfully delusional but well into his stride. "No one I have ever met in my life is a worse, almost pathologically unsympathetic listener. He is a writer of venomous letters, an inveterate magpie, a rumpled dresser, an egotistical, unsettled eccentric, occasionally funny, and an all-time know-it-all."

Alexander Pope, Mark Twain, and Ludwig Wittgenstein were summoned to denounce my life and work, my "awful, unlawful side," and at last, on the eighth page, I was judged by Floyd to have succeeded only "in the perverse and petty triumph of self-revelation in the failure of a book."

And though it was not news to the family, it was a revelation to the world when he mentioned "his illegitimate son"—as if I'd left a limping half-wit in my wake. "'Now, gods, stand up for bastards!'" he concluded.

That was his verdict: I was a failure. "He is ignored by the academy and smiled down on by the literary establishment, for the most part. Nobody I know has written so many books with so little serious critical recognition to show for it. None of his books are taught in colleges or have cult status or have generated, I believe, a single scholarly essay, and most of them are presently out of print."

My mouth was dry, my eyes were burning, as I pushed toward the end, though I kept glancing back to "The whole family laughs at him" and to the lies—the poison in a lie gives it a bitter vividness. It was an astonishing piece of invective. I had barely finished reading it when the telephone rang. A columnist from the *Boston Globe*.

"Just wondering..." Had I seen the piece, had I read it, what did I think?

"Obviously, it's a valentine," I said, and as I put the phone down, it rang again. Another newspaper.

The questions wouldn't go away, but why should they? In the long history of literary brothers there was no precedent for this attack. Plenty of brothers scribbled and quarreled—in fact, scribbling brothers nearly always quarreled. Thomas Mann had an angry brother, Heinrich. Henry James had William. Chekhov had Nikolai. Wilde had Willie. Joyce had Stanislaus. Lawrence Durrell had Gerald. William Faulkner had John. Hemingway had Leicester, Naipaul had Shiva—all of them rivals, more or less. The nicer-seeming brother is not necessarily the better writer, nor necessarily nicer. All had made belittling remarks, yet none of these men had ever reviewed the other's work, pronouncing the book a failure and the brother a fake. Floyd was the first.

Once, writing about Vidia and Shiva Naipaul, both of whom I'd known, I had mentioned how brothers are versions of each other, a suggestion implicit in the word itself: the "other" in "brother." The unfortunate history of scribbling brothers was full of conflict. There were no intellectual equals in brotherhood, for, being writers, they were borderline nutcases. Literary brothers were often fratricidal from birth and babyish in their battling, because of the lingering infantilism in sibling rivalry. When brothers fought, family secrets were revealed, and the shaming revelations often made forgiveness irrelevant. It is the tale told by Shem and Shaun.

But the damage was done, and my book was sinking. All publicity is good publicity, people say. Every knock a boost. But no. I was a living example of someone so furiously publicized I was buried by it, for people reading the half-truths about Floyd and me meant they didn't have to read my book. It amazed me that for this period I could be so well known and so widely discussed, yet remain so insignificant.

"'The whole family laughs at him," rankled more than anything, though "his illegitimate child" was wounding too. I called Mother and urged her to respond.

"What magazine article?" she said. "I wouldn't know anything about that. I've been baking pies. I'm carving a heron. I go for walks. I don't waste a minute on magazines."

Hating myself for my helplessness, I paid Mother a visit. After I pulled into her driveway, I sat in my car trembling, astonished at my feebleness and fear.

How long had she been standing at the door? She was stifling a triumphant smile. She loved being visited by someone who needed her help. She could see I was below par. I noticed in her eye-glint and in the set of her jaw: *He's worse than I thought.*

Inside, I threw myself into a chair, while she sat on her big leather throne and clasped her hands, studying me.

"It's about the magazine article."

"Oh?"

Cruelly impassive, playing dim and preoccupied with more important things, she made me explain the whole piece that Floyd had written. With the magazine in my hand I found myself stammering over some quotations, enraged at others. Mother claimed to know nothing about it, but when I showed her the pages, she turned away and dismissed it with her skinny hand.

"Oh, you know how he is. Always trying to start trouble."

"Ma! No one has ever done this before."

"Then you've been lucky," Mother said. "Lots of people have criticized me."

"I mean in history. A guy writing that his brother's book is crap. Even Hemingway's brother didn't do it."

"Maybe he should have." Mother laughed. "I never thought much of Hemingway's work. Thought he was so important, killing all those animals. And then he killed himself."

I should not have mentioned Hemingway. He was a classic example of the sort of person Mother ridiculed, for in his roistering, his self-pity, and his death he was to blame for his own problem. *Oh, he committed suicide,* she would say. *Whose fault is that?*

"Floyd says here that I have bowel problems. That I wear platform shoes. That my kids hate me."

"I sometimes wonder what my children really think of me," Mother said.

"Listen. 'The whole family laughs at him.' That's not true — you know it's not."

"Of course not. We love you. We admire everything you've written."

Her praise, as always, filled me with gloom and eroded my confidence.

"You could say that, Ma. You could put that into a letter to the editor. About admiring me."

Mother smiled. "I ask you, what earthly good would that do?"

"It would help."

"Oh?"

She winced and touched her head, fingertips to temples, at first gently, as if she were comforting a small animal, and then as if testing a fruit for ripeness. After a moment she got a better grip and said that she had a splitting headache. She looked exactly like Floyd's imitation of her. She smiled through her pain.

"Just let it go." She winced a little, inviting me to pity her. "Be a good sport."

I glanced at the magazine in my hand and reflected that there was a stack of them on every newsstand in the state.

"Do it for me," she said.

Why was she being so unhelpful? I was sure that it was because, since his break with me, Floyd had become close to her — valuable to her — and the others had rallied around. This closeness was her victory.

"Do it for me," she said as I left. "Do it for your mother."

Floyd's article intensified the family's fear of him. They were glad the subject was me and not any of them. They were not outraged, they were relieved.

Still, I asked Fred if he might write a letter to the magazine's editor to set the record straight.

"What can I do?" he said, meaning he would do nothing.

"Floyd said, 'The whole family laughs at him.' You could say you don't."

"That would just stir things up."

"No. It would clarify them."

Fred smiled at me, at my helpless fury. He was Floyd smiling at me; Mother had been Floyd too. All my detractors looked like Floyd now, the same hair, the flinty eyes, the satirical lips. They even talked like him, adopting his tone.

"He's crazy, you know," Fred said.

"You could say that in your letter to the editor."

A flicker of uncertainty passed across Fred's face, a blink of caution, for what if I told Floyd what he had just said? He knew he had said too much.

Fred must have alerted Franny, because when I called her she was overprepared to rebuff me. Rose didn't say much, indeed seemed to imply that I was to blame for Floyd's piece. Gilbert and Hubby weren't helpful either. I had the sense that all of them believed that I deserved it, that every lie and wild assertion Floyd had written was essentially true. And so, really, the whole family *was* laughing at me.

Just as bad, sales of the book were affected. Every interview on every stop of my book tour included the question, "Why did your brother write that piece about you?"

I said, "Why don't you ask him?" and gave them Floyd's telephone number, and I went on smiling and describing the piece as a valentine.

And I realized that Mother was not strong at all. She was weak and needy. She could not handle dissension, she was a poor disciplinarian, she was too narcissistic to be in complete control. She required connivance, deference, and respect, but was never sure how best to gain that obedience. Floyd was a help. At that time she wanted me outside her orbit; she wanted Floyd in it, no matter the cost, for with Floyd she had more power, and although she was weak, she was in charge. In that way she was obeyed.

Too late I remembered that it was a family in which we had been conditioned never to ask for a favor.

18

SECOND CHILDHOOD

PLAQUOTEURS!" Father would have shouted at all this fuss, had he been alive. Bunglers! In the family turmoil that had followed his death, four full years of Mother and heading into the fifth, I had grown older, and not in years alone. I was weaker, and my decline was a shock to me. I had always imagined — don't most people? — that my life would be a long upward climb, growing in prosperity, with improving views and the clarity of sky, passing the crags, braced and vitalized by the sharp air, a series of steady achievements, more comfort, more money. Soul mate by my side.

I had never envisioned my life as a rugged descent, bumping down the glacier of neglect, this wearisome solitude, finding myself hard up, hunched over a poorly lit desk in a chilly room, writing a self-pitying sentence such as this.

My book tanked. I blamed Floyd. I blamed the whole indifferent family, who, if they took any notice at all, were secretly, smugly pleased. I had proof that they resented me. I had known years of fame and prosperity in my thirties and forties and into my fifties—what a biographer would have called my middle years. Now that I was sixty I was given a terrifying perspective of all that elapsed time, like a view from a bleak summit, the truth that it is all downhill from here. I had been doing all right until this failure, which reminded me of all my other failures. Floyd's eight-page review of my book—his assessment of my despicable life—crushed me.

So what do you think about your brother's piece?

I had an answer.

Live long enough and, from the thin air in the heights of age, you see everything. You eventually understand that you reach a point in life when there is no more for you, nothing but diminishing repetition, the dying echo of things past. The upward climb, so difficult at the time, now seems horribly brief, the satisfactions few, the intensity blunted by all the rest of the bother. I was shocked to realize that I'd had my time. What I was living now was something like a second childhood. Fortifying this impression was the looming figure of Mother, still alive, still fierce, still enigmatic, still dominant, still hard to please, and not really on anyone's side.

So, with the failure of that book, my middle years, the active part of my life, was over. Awful to contemplate with Mother looking on. I knew now there was nothing more for me. I had seen the worst, and now that events were repeating—the repetition seemed like mockery—I was frightened, for I was being told that there was nothing new for me. It was someone else's turn—for prizes, for fame, for pleasure and rewards, the windfall. I understood, as the young seldom do, that I could not make it happen again. The hardest thing for me was to disguise my disappointment as I knocked on the door of sixty-one. Impotence is one way of describing it, but it was worse than that, for I was impotent in every respect, except the one the word was supposed to describe.

I had known years of productive work and some achievement, a better score than many people. Public years, years of travel and challenge, of unexpected rewards, years that could be happily chronicled and accounted for, years of "I've got some good news for you!" Years of using time and knowing love, and also knowing failure, but failure of a kind that strengthened and improved me as a man and a writer. I was a familiar face, and because my intimate thoughts were published in my own voice, I was well known. I had few secrets in those years. I lived my life, and lived my crises, in full view of the spectators who were my readers. I turned my crises into fiction and endured them that way, ultimately learning to value them.

Those years on the record, interviewers would ask blunt questions about my marriage or divorce, my children, my money, what I'd had for breakfast, and what I was writing. Even a lazy biographer on a fellowship, with grad students doing the grunt work, could do justice to those years — could probably describe them as well as I. My successes were public, my failures were in full view, exaggerated by all that sunlight. It sometimes seemed in those years that I belonged to the public, to my readers, to the people eager for the minor scandals associated with me — the two wives, the two children, the houses, the travel, the squandered fortune, the color and buzz of my writing life. I had lived through a time when a writer was a magic figure, a person of influence and power, watched closely and admired and envied.

Perhaps the way I lived, sharing my life with the world, was the reason it all came to an end. I was popular for thirty years, and then I was out of favor, I was hidden, I became what's-his-name. Maybe I was dead. Yet I was alive and alert, wondering in my new obscurity what would come next, and all I saw was Mother.

Everything that had come before those years of public life was yearning — fantasy, pain and preparation, Mother's scorn, stocking supermarket shelves. Everything that followed those years was diminution, as I sank. Everything I did occurred with a dying fall. I began to understand the older people I had known earlier in my life, the men and women I had smiled at and not taken seriously, because they had not taken me seriously. Their mood of disappointment, their skepticism, their bitter humor, their refrain of "You'll see, I was like you once." I remembered how they had mocked my hope, jeered at my ambition. "What will you write about? Who'll publish it? Do you have anything to say? Who will care?" — the challenges that Mother had made that rang in my mind all those years.

At a certain stage of life you realize that most of what you'd hoped for will never come to you. Not gonna happen! I consoled myself with the thought that I'd been luckier than most. I'd had decades of pleasure, of dreams fulfilled. It was just that I wanted more. I had not guessed that it would all end, was not prepared for it, and the ending made those earlier years seem unreal, as though they'd happened to someone else, not anyone who resembled me, for I had nothing to show for my effort. All gone! I was back where I'd started, literally so, with Mother, Fred and Floyd, Franny and Rose, Hubby and Gilbert, and the ghost of Angela. Back in Mother Land.

I had never written about that — my family, my early years of hope and ambition and yearning. No big families appeared in any of my books; the mothers I described were blurry but benign. What I wrote about, what people mostly write about, the busy years, the noisy years in the limelight, when they are on good terms with the world, are far less important than the hidden years, of doubt and struggle, because they are so messy and shameful. Although they are severely plotted, like my "best year," they seem at the time to have no order to them. As a child, as an aspiring writer, I felt like an ant: I believed I had an ant's chance of success. I saw very little; no one could see me. I was beneath notice, insignificant.

How I survived in the family, struggling to hold my own, keeping my secrets and my dreams intact — and what happened next — were what mattered to me most. I developed such a solemn habit of concealment I was not able to write about the circumstances that made me who I was. And I knew what I was concealing was too sad to think about.

The years I had spent trying to keep my dreams intact while living with my intrusive family — those years were formative, painful, humiliating, the source of all my secrecy and my creative energy. Not romantic, not even colorful, full of hurts and embarrassments and put-downs, and Mother's cries of "It's your own goddamned fault!" and "Who do you think you are?" But those hurts drove me in my middle years, the work I am known for. What I had dreaded most had come to pass: I was back home, with Mother.

I had come from nowhere, I was going nowhere. But wait: the middle years were not half so human, so truthful in their raggedness, as where I was now. My middle years were in my books. I had published that part of my life, and I had found myself at another bookend.

Now in obscurity, back home, I saw that I had failed as I had feared, and that I was ending my life as I had started it, among my jeering brothers and sisters, with Mother enthroned at the center of her own land.

I hated what I now understood to be my life. I had been kidding myself, as many men do, about remarrying. I had misled Missy and her dim daughter. I would never have another wife, another child. And who knew whether I'd have another book?

"Are you one of these writers who gets up early and does all his work before breakfast?" a friend of mine had asked the great Chicago novelist Nelson Algren a few years before his death — a man who knew a lot about the bitter end.

"No," Algren said. "I'm one of those writers who doesn't write at all anymore."

It had been a torment to be young with Mother telling me I might never have a career; it was just as bad to be in late middle age with Mother to remind me that my career was over. Downhill, all over except the paltry remainder of my life, and Mother never looked stronger. She seemed to exist and thrive purely to show me that I had decades of disappointment ahead of me.

I visited her. She wanted presents. She needed me to tell her how well she looked. She wanted compliments.

"Guess what tomorrow is?" she asked, and looked coy. "My wedding anniversary. It would have been our sixty-sixth."

What about my two wedding anniversaries that no one remembered, not even me?

"Look what Franny brought me. Cashmere."

A shawl. She draped it across her shoulders and posed.

"This is from Fred."

A chunk of porous yellow stone, set in a cube of Lucite and labeled *Piece of the Great Wall of China*, with two flags, America's and China's. *Certified Authentic.*

"Gilbert and Rose clubbed together to get me this."

A footstool, leather-cushioned, with a margin of brass tacks and sturdy legs.

"And these are from Floyd."

More books, smelling — as old books always do — of mice droppings and sticky mold and damp decay. I had come to hate the sight of books.

"I never see him."

"Oh?"

The way she cocked her head, like a bystander at a train wreck, told me she was taking no responsibility, nor would she be giving me any information. Mother was always posturing, always playing at something, and now she was playing dumb.

"Because of what he wrote. He gave my book a stinker of a review. My own brother!"

"Oh?"

"Floyd reviewed my book!"

"Why are you shouting?"

"'The whole family laughs at him' — that's what he said."

"I don't know anything about it." She folded her hands and shrank a little inside her new cashmere shawl.

"Yes, you do. It was in the magazine."

Mother blew open her nostrils in a sneer. She said, "Are you still brooding about that?"

"People keep asking me about it."

"Oh?"

Her tone was pitying, belittling me. But she was right. I ought to have let it go. Yet I hated her tone of *It's your own goddamned fault.*

"Maybe you did something to offend him," she said.

I said, "No writer's brother has ever done this, Ma. Hemingway, Henry James, all the rest of them. Like I told you. Their brothers never did this. It's a first. I mean, this would actually be amazingly interesting if it wasn't me, Ma."

Mother had stopped listening. I could tell from the slant of her head and the look in her eyes that she was thinking about something else. Her expression indicated that she was waiting for me to stop, a look of irritated and impatient boredom. *Are you still blabbing?* When I finished — I did so abruptly, just faltering and shrugging and going silent — Mother smiled at me.

"I walked all the way down to the public beach this morning."

She wanted a compliment, *Lordy, you are one in a million — I don't know how you do it,* but feeling hostile, I instead said, "You should be careful. You could fall. Do you remember to take your cane? A lot of people your age stumble and break a hip."

She smiled, but I could tell from her pinched nose that she was affronted.

"I've always been a good walker. Miles — I've walked miles. I never complain."

"I only mentioned a hip because a replacement is so expensive. You don't want to get into a cash crunch."

It was all mutual rebuke. I had gone there hurting, looking for a listener, and now I hurt more. Mother offered no consolation. And her obstinacy made me obstinate: I refused to praise her walking.

Gilbert called me the next day. He seemed in a hurry, but he was agitated too; he hated confrontation, and one was looming. I knew this was not a friendly call.

"Aren't you supposed to be in Riyadh?"

"Next week," he said. "Listen, I just got off the phone with Franny. She was talking to Ma this morning. Ma was really upset about what you said."

"What did I say?"

"Let's not get into that, okay? What you don't seem to realize is that walking to the beach is one of Ma's recreations. She said you were determined to scare her — wait —" I had tried to interrupt. "Don't discourage her, and for God's sake stop trying to scare her. She won't fall down. She's pretty spry. She was so upset she couldn't sleep."

Hubby called and said, "I saw Ma. She was talking about you. She even mentioned your book," and in Mother's voice he added, "'More porno!'"

Fred called later. He said, "I guess you know why I'm calling. Ma's a wreck. Why do you try to worry her? Give her a break. She's old."

Mother did not seem old to me. She seemed ageless and fierce, more powerful than ever, surrounded by courtiers and ladies-in-waiting and flatterers and protectors, demanding obedience from her subjects, of whom I was one of the lowliest. She seemed to grow stronger as I grew weaker, and now I felt ant-like again, a humiliated child, reprimanded by Mother's surrogates. I was fairly miserable. Mother was very happy. She preserved her happiness by blaming me for my misery. And she was probably right to blame me. My book had failed. *Whose fault is that?*

19

THE SIDE EFFECTS OF MELANCHOLY

WHEN MY CHILDREN CALLED, as they did every month or so, another example of station identification, I tried to reassure them that I was doing fine. I had released them into the world. I wanted to avoid doing to them what Mother had done to me. I left them to themselves. I made no demands on them. I thought about them every day, yearning to see them, but I seldom did.

"I'm okay," I would repeat, yet I knew that my voice had that strangled intensity as when one is trying too hard to be convincing. They said they would visit. Though I didn't press them, they kept promising. As youngsters they had adored me. Older, they had kept their distance, so that my shadow would not fall across them, so that they could make their own lives. My early success had disturbed them; they had feared being overwhelmed by me, absorbed into my life, losing their own creative ambitions by becoming part of the family business.

Now they were embarked on their own careers, the elder, Julian, a screenwriter, the younger, Harry, a maker of TV documentaries, neither of them married. Perhaps what they had seen of marriage in their youth had made them wary of any surrender to romance. They both lived in London. Being so far gave them an excuse to stay away, but I knew that their real reason was their fear of becoming entangled in my affairs — and who could blame them?

Yet I adored their visits. Probably that was something else that put them off, my smothering attention, my eager inquiries into their lives. They needed distance, to be themselves. I did not fault them for wanting to keep apart from my success, and I strenuously urged them to steer clear of my failure. Now I was in between, in a sort of creative twilight. The season matched my mood. It was early fall. My book had failed: I pegged its decline to the week that Floyd's grotesque piece appeared. In his attack on the book and me, Floyd had cast himself in the role of spokesman for the family.

I abandoned any hope for my book, a reminder of an early intimation of mine, that although I wished to make a mark as a writer, it would never happen. As a hopeful high school scribbler, with a paperback of *On the Road,* nursing a dream of becoming a writer, I was embarrassed to tell anyone. Secretly I believed myself to be one of Kerouac's Subterraneans, yet the notion of being a writer was too extravagant. I was not worthy of it; I was talentless — Mother's message of *You're not good enough.* It was how I had felt then. It was how I felt now.

Late September days of bright sunlight and cool nights filled me with the desire to work, a project for the indoor months to come. But I had nothing to do. I was glad for a chance to pretend to be busy in what remained of this mild breezy weather. I sailed single-handed in my sprit-rigged dory out of Lewis Bay and beyond the Hyannis Port jetty, telling myself that I was lucky to be able to prolong the summer while everyone else was working, not daring to admit to myself that I would rather have been writing.

That, too, had been a feature of my childhood: solitary trips in a rowboat, lonely hikes, any excuse to get out of the house, away from Mother's fuss and blame, the family whispers. No one must know where I am and what I am doing. I protected my privacy, fearing that I would be satirized by the others. Ganders in a flock, seeing an old goose stumble and fall, attack the bird without mercy, stabbing with their beaks, pecking its head, beating it with their wings.

The same self-conscious solitude I had known as a secretive child enclosed me now, and so I was hyperalert when the phone rang. I put on a special voice of greeting, a false *I'm all right* tone when I answered the phone.

"Dad!" It was Julian, calling from the airport. "We just arrived. Harry's getting a car."

"This is a surprise."

Did they perhaps suspect that I was unable to offer a lift? They were brisk and capable.

"Anything we can bring?" Julian asked.

"Just yourselves."

"See you in a bit."

They arrived late, and coming out of the dark into the lamplit house, they seemed tall and self-assured. I guessed from their bonhomie that they were worried about me.

"You look great, Dad. You've been sailing. Your nose is sunburned."

All good parents worry about their children, but only the most irresponsible parents require their children to worry about them. I did not want them to be anxious, yet they were. Perhaps they had reason to be.

They hugged me, squeezing hard, making me feel frail. Meaning well, they asked me questions, believing the answers would buck me up. But there were no simple answers to "Is this a rental?" and "Where's all your wonderful furniture?" and "How long are you going to be here?" and "How's the book?" and "What's up with the family?"

They insisted on taking me to a Japanese restaurant in Yarmouth Port to eat sushi.

"You look fit, Dad," Harry said. "You've lost weight."

"I haven't been eating."

"Dieting?"

"Sort of."

One side effect of melancholy was a numbed palate.

Julian pushed the sushi platter over to me, saying, "Go for it, Dad," and then, when I hesitated, "What's wrong?"

It was the question they had wanted to ask since the moment they'd arrived. Everything I had lived through since Father's death was etched on my face, not sorrow or grief but the more complex mask of experience, the sort of weather-beaten face you see on a mountain climber who has survived a harrowing descent and lost some of his companions and perhaps a few toes to frostbite.

"Nothing," I said. They stared at me. "My family."

"Uncle Floyd is so weird," Harry said. "What made him write that crazy thing?"

Floyd's piece was as famous for its vitriol as for its being unexplainable. It had overshadowed my book in ways that might have surprised Floyd himself.

"I think he was annoyed because I kept him out of the loop."

My children had no idea that I had planned to marry for a third time. I had not wanted to tell them, because I had suspected that it was a bad idea, that it might fail, that there was nothing to tell.

"I think Floyd felt I was keeping secrets from him."

They were shrewd and humane boys. They asked nothing more that night. It was not until the next afternoon, helping me rake leaves, that Julian said, "What kind of secrets?"

"Nothing important. But you know how it is in my family. They have to know everything, or else."

"Or else what?" Harry asked.

"You get blackballed and excluded. No one talks to you."

"What about your friends?"

How could I tell them that I had no one, that I had lost Missy, that my family had let me down, though we were somehow all still hovering around Mother, at her insistence.

"Uncle Floyd's piece was mentioned in some of the London papers. They quoted bits of it," Julian said. "Very creepy."

"I'm glad you agree it was strange. People asked me about it, and I couldn't explain it. I wanted someone in the family to speak up for me, but none of them would."

Julian was looking on me with a tenderness and concern that was also troubled by anxiety and disbelief. "What did you want them to say?"

"Anything." I turned away, raking more leaves into a pile.

The scrape of rakes, clawing at pebbles and leaves, filled the silence.

"You sound so young saying that."

"I went to my mother. She wouldn't help."

"You sound even younger."

"She just dismissed me," I said.

"What does any of this have to do with Grandma?"

"I think she's behind it all," I said. "She never liked me."

From the way their rakes stuttered I could tell that Julian and Harry were exchanging glances behind my back.

"My mother tells Franny I'm upsetting her. Franny tells Fred and Gilbert. They call me and accuse me of starting trouble."

Harry said, "Is Fred still living around here?"

"We all are. Because my mother's so old. It's like we never left." I could not keep a catch out of my throat when I added, "They're saying terrible things about me."

They glanced at each other again, I knew. I was embarrassing them, and worse, they pitied me. Even so, I felt wronged.

"I can't convince my mother to take me seriously."

Julian said, "Why, at your age, do you care what your mother thinks?"

I had no answer to this. I was even a bit startled by the question. My befuddlement showed in the determined way I was dragging my rake.

"I've got my self-respect," I said.

"What about Aunt Franny and Aunt Rose?"

"They bring me fruit and candy. There's plenty left in the house. Cookies. Franny has the idea that I love cheese balls."

Speaking of food, I suggested we stop the raking and eat something. They were September leaves, not many of them, nothing like the November deluge. We went into the house and made coffee. I brought out Franny's tin of cookies, the candy, the cheese balls.

The boys remained tactful. I could see their concern in their posture. They were attentive, obliquely collecting information, yet trying to avoid putting me on the defensive.

"One thing you could do is call Floyd," Julian said. "Tell him how you feel."

"I tried that. He won't talk to me. He tells the others not to talk to me." The boys were staring at me. "They have parties and refuse to invite me. Then they pretend there was no party."

Now both boys were sipping coffee, keeping their heads down, not making eye contact.

"They really treat me terribly," I said. "Although Hubby still speaks to me. My mother seems to enjoy stirring them up against me."

Sounds of the coffee being sipped kept me talking.

"They can be really unkind. They're always talking about me behind my back."

When there was no response, I replayed in my mind what I had just said. Still I felt wronged.

"It's all my mother's fault!"

The boys raised their eyes to me. They looked wise and sad, not sure where to begin.

"I know what you're thinking," I said.

I was a resentful child, and they — taller than me, and polite in their pity — were adults. They had work and deadlines and girlfriends; they had pleasures and income. They were self-sufficient, reasonable, and upright, regarding me from those heights and being strong, trying to buck me up and, with the best will in the world, patronizing me.

I could see that they were surprised to find me in such humble circumstances, reduced to renting a damp bungalow, sitting among someone else's furniture, Reader's Digest Condensed Books, and yard sale accessories, and complaining about my neglectful family.

"The reason we came," Julian said, " is because we both have meetings in New York. Business stuff."

"We can't stay much longer," Harry said. "Projects."

They made a point of never telling me what things they were working on. I understood that reticence in a child. They were glad for an excuse to leave. I was also relieved that they were not staying. Their scrutiny made me self-conscious. I knew I was not in the wrong, yet they made me feel ridiculous: they were from the outside world, they had lost touch with the family, and they had never understood how it made me so miserable.

That night over dinner — they had bought lobsters and corn — Julian said, "We have to leave first thing tomorrow."

"I'll be sorry to see you go." I wondered if they heard the flat note of insincerity behind this.

Strangers had never been welcome in the family. As honest, mature, well-adjusted young men, they were strangers here. The family was all around me: in my house, in this room, at the table, in my head.

Next morning they were up early, busy in the kitchen, impatient to go, while I lay awake upstairs, waiting for the preparation noises to subside. And my fatigue was another side effect of melancholy.

They were eating breakfast, all dressed, their bags at the doorway, when I came down, yawning, still in my bathrobe, barefoot, clawing at my tangled hair.

Harry said, "We were just talking about money. I hadn't realized the exchange rate was so favorable. We changed more pounds than we needed."

"We've got all this extra wonga," Julian said.

His gentle eyes were filled with concern. Harry looked at him, perhaps wondering what would come next. Julian held a thickness of dollars, folded over like a sandwich.

I said, "Now you have to come back and help me spend it."

Too polite to press the matter, they made their excuses and left me feeling like a lost boy.

PART TWO

20

HOLIDAYS

AFTER THAT, every time I gathered fallen leaves to burn, held the
rake handle at a scraping angle, keeping my head down, feeling a
numbing lumbar tug as I dragged the rake, never trapping as many leaves
as I wished to, I remembered the visit of my two innocent adult sons.

The sick feeling and my prickling eyes made me snatch harder with
denying swipes of the rake. I saw the abashed faces of my children: the
horror they pretended was faint surprise, the disbelief they masked as
amusement, the shock they contrived to turn into a look of mild concern.
They had pitied me. They thought I hadn't noticed — and I hadn't, at first.
My shame sank in slowly. I felt it soaking me. It was still sinking in weeks
later, at Thanksgiving, another holiday I was spending alone.

What was it about dead crushed leaves and yard work that made me
remember? The menial routine humbled me, and in this mood I was reflective, resentful, solitary; no one to help me. I was no good at this work.
This drudgery — all drudgery — made me feel small.

Of course I seemed childish! I was home again, a failure among my
envious siblings. I got no pleasure settling scores, but I needed the truth
of who I really was, who I had been. *Who I Was* had been a title I had
planned to use for my autobiography. The rest of my life, the middle years
of being a husband, a father, and a hardworking writer, seemed no more
than a glimmering interlude between the confusion of my earliest years

and the castaway I was now. Next to this the fictions I had imagined were meaningless and concocted, simply yarn-spinnings, and yet the family drama was so extravagant and manipulated there was something fictive in it, which drew me in deeper.

Some weeks after the raking, I was shoveling snow, or pushing at it with a snow scoop. The snow-shoveling posture induced in me the same thoughts, the same justifications, dragged the same mood over me. Thanksgiving was a week away, and looming behind it, Christmas.

My children, those two boys, were the only adults I saw for ages. They were scandalized by what they saw of me. I wanted them to understand, yet I could not explain adequately what I felt and why I was still living here, near Mother and all my childish, contending siblings. Even though it had been an awkward few days, I had loved being with my boys.

They were out of sympathy with me, or else I would have kept them informed of what my life was like. Out of habit I sometimes tried.

"She talked constantly about how her father was a saint."

"Don't tell me."

"She wants me to bring her presents."

"Please, Dad. I don't care."

"She goes on talking about her will."

"What about it?"

"She asks how her money should be divided."

"A lot of old people do that."

"Not like she's doing."

Mother mentioned the will all the time. Before Father's death the subject had never come up. In the years since then it was a frequent topic of conversation. The first time she mentioned it to me I had been surprised.

"You should do whatever you want to with your money," I said, surprised that she had enough money to make this worth discussing.

"But I want your advice, Jay," she said. "What do you think is the best way to divide it?"

"Since you put it like that, there's only one way — seven equal shares."

This seemed to startle her, as if the obvious answer had not occurred to her, as if dividing her money equally was some great novelty.

"I'll have to think about that." She adjusted her glasses and stared at me, seeming to perform some complex mathematical calculation in her mind.

I smiled and said, "Those who don't need their share can put it back in the pot."

"But there's property," she said. "That makes it complicated."

"Property could be sold, and the money divided seven ways."

"And why do you say seven ways?"

For a moment, a flash of her eyes in the big lenses, she seemed insane.

"Because there are seven of us."

"What about Angela?"

"Where would we put her share?" And I whispered, "Ma, she's dead."

"Something nice for her grave," Mother said of her dead child, speaking like a superstitious aboriginal in a jungle clearing. "I'm sure she'd like something nice for herself."

"Divide the money eight ways, then," I said. "But equally."

"I'll have to think about that."

Again, this seemed to her a bizarre notion.

I did not tell my children about this conversation, or the others that followed it, or the events that occurred, always on low frequencies, as gossip. This was a narrative that kept building, something new every day, always something surprising, which made me think, Only in this family. And money was the theme.

We talked about generosity, even harped on it. But no one was generous. That talk was a trick, to get us to give. In the absence of generosity we had to learn how to take, to be artful thieves, to be plausible, to appear to be respectable in our snatching, yet to know how to scavenge and survive.

Money was the measure of generosity. But Mother never gave us any, for to do that would reveal to us that she had some, and her mantra was that she had none. Money did not exist in our family as a fact, only as an abstraction, something whispered about, so hard won it was almost unattainable. I might see a few dollars in a wallet or some coins in a purse, but never more than that. The wad of money, the thick roll of bills, the chunk of change, were fantastic absurdities. And because it was unseen, magic was attached to money, but black magic, a kind of curse. We did not think we deserved to have money, and if by chance we got some, we could not spend it, because spending was wasteful. Money in your pocket tripped you up. You were better off without it.

Money was a thing of darkness, always put away. Money was something that was saved — stacked up, hoarded, stashed for a rainy day, but always small amounts scraped into a pile, like Father's winding knotted lengths of string into a ball. But why? We didn't ask.

Money was whispered about because it was tainted. Other people had it — we did not; we would never have it. We had no idea where money came from. We did not know anyone who had it. The ways in which other people got money were a mystery to us. No one had money in Mother Land.

Money did not grow on trees. Money was the root of all evil. Money was filthy lucre. A fool and his money were soon parted. Most people had more money than brains. They spent money like a drunken sailor. They knew the price of everything and the value of nothing.

We were so in awe of the rich that we were forbidden to use the word. Instead of "They're rich" we had to say, "They're comfortably off." Rich families were like members of another species, but a dangerous one that needed to be propitiated with our being submissive. We saw them as a conquering tribe; the world belonged to them. They were comfortable, the rest of you were getting by, we were pinched and hard up. We were moneyless, and so powerless.

At first, when Mother claimed to have no money, we took her at her word and pitied her a little. We got part-time jobs and gave her half our weekly pay. "This will go toward the electric bill," Mother would say. "This will help pay for your food." That was her way of saying it would never be enough. We went on paying her off in a cycle of endless peonage and debt slavery.

Later, from vague hints and chance remarks, we suspected that Mother had some money, somewhere. Perhaps her bleak insistence that she was poor was the giveaway. "I'm wearing a dead woman's dress," she sometimes said, to emphasize her poverty — a morbid hand-me-down, with the coffin stink or the sickroom pong still on it. That shocked us. If one of us asked for something and she paid for it, she made such a fuss and we felt so bad we never asked again. She had no checkbook; she never used credit. She paid in cash, though she always concealed these transactions from us to maintain the fiction that she had no money. Paying for something, handing over money, was probably the most solemn and covert of her secret ceremonies.

Dad had nothing to do with money. He gave all his pay to Mother at the end of the week. It wasn't much, as Mother often said, to Dad's shame, her bony thumb upon him. He never mentioned money.

She was hard on the grandchildren for wasting money — particularly Jonty, Franny's eldest, with his history of tantrums. Not just the windshield he punted out of the Dart, but his various school fees. Franny's other son took ballet lessons. "Max is a playing card," Franny said, "in *Alice in Wonderland.*" Mother considered these lessons a foolish expense, and she, too, found humor in "Max is a playing card." Mother said, "I wonder which card?"

Since gossip was oxygen for Mother, she asked me in the canniest way what I had heard, pretending not to know anything so as to compare my version of a story with the one she had already been told, always hungry for the smallest detail of frailty or frittering away money. Her eyes glittered with pleasure at a choice tidbit, and hearing something truly disgraceful, she could not prevent herself from laughing out loud, showing her yellow teeth to their wolfish roots.

My reward for visiting her was that she confided these disgraces. And sometimes they were betrayals that took my breath away. She jeered at her children for their pretensions, and at their spouses for incompetence or greed. Her harshest remarks were aimed at members of her family, Angela excepted. Spending money was the worst stupidity and roused her greatest scorn.

Autumn had tightened around me, the early darkness enclosed me. I tried to work but felt too small, too defeated, to rise above my sadness and write well, or at all. As in that earlier time, of my first childhood, my days were full of indecision and interruption and false starts.

Unemployed, lacking the will to work, I searched for solace in my past and signed up to go to my fortieth high school reunion. I had last been to the twentieth, which had reassured me by reminding me that I had friends who'd been closer to me than family: John Brodie and other boys I'd known since grade school; old girlfriends; my high school buddy George Davis, my first black friend.

The reunion was held in a hotel ballroom in Falmouth, and to my delight George was in the portico, finishing a cigarette as I approached.

"Fortifying myself," he said in a hoarse whisper, holding his breath, pinching the cigarette in his fingers. And then I saw it was a joint, what he would have called a roach in high school. After he swallowed the smoke he hugged me and said, "Great to see you."

"I almost didn't come."

"I guess I know why," he said, and laughed — a stoner's hiccupping laugh.

"What do you mean?"

"You got a target on your back, man." He nodded, sucked on the joint again, then tossed it. "From that thing you wrote."

"What thing?"

"About the last reunion."

"That was twenty years ago."

He laughed again and took my arm. We entered the lobby and picked up our name stickers. I lingered by the table, wondering if I recognized the two gray-haired women sitting behind it.

"I'm looking for John Brodie."

"He died," one of the women said, "years ago."

I put my hand out. "Jay Justus."

The woman folded her arms and leaned away. "I know who you are."

The ballroom was noisy, jammed with elderly men and women shouting at each other, sipping at plastic cups of wine. My first thought was that I'd come to the wrong place, until I realized that I looked just like them. Only George was still dapper and, with his shaven head gleaming like a chestnut, looked younger than anyone else.

"There's that guy Tony that used to be with us in Trebino's chemistry class," he said, and indicated a stout, red-faced man in a three-piece suit who was bantering with another bulky man, tapping the man's lapel with a thick finger.

"Tony," I said, and stepped toward him.

He raised his arms in mock horror. "Don't know ya!"

Seeing this, the men near him laughed and, with Tony, turned their backs on me. Someone muttered approvingly, in a joke echo, "Don't know ya!"

I wandered away, taking refuge by a far wall, and remained there, feeling futile, looking at the crowd. They'd become louder, more confident, happier, and many were hugging. George slipped next to me and stood, sighing. He said nothing for a while; he was nodding at the room.

"They're all drinking," he said. "In a little while, they'll be toasted." He squeezed my arm. "You don't want to be here then, man."

I went home, heavy with sadness, slouched in my seat, not trusting myself to drive fast.

Fred called. "I just spoke to Ma. She said she's feeling alone. Will you go visit her and cheer her up?"

"Why don't you?"

"I'm in China. I'm seeing clients."

I called Franny. I had resented her being so close to Floyd, so I came straight to the point.

"Fred said Ma's lonely. You have to visit her."

"Marvin has acid reflux. He's day to day. It could be an ulcer. I can't leave him like this."

"I'll explain that to Ma."

"Someone will have to go. Don't you know what day this is?"

I had no idea. Melancholy had a way of blurring time.

"It's January fourth."

"What are you saying?"

"Angela's birthday in four days. This is a hard month for her."

So it was no longer one day of grief but rather a monthlong period of mourning, a funereal season.

"I'll go," I said.

On my way to Mother's I stopped off to see Hubby. He was shoveling out his basement — for headroom, he said. I told him where I was going and why.

"Ma's fine. I saw her yesterday."

"Fred called me today."

Talking over me, he said, "She was telling me stories about her mother. She worked in a corset factory in Boston. When she got married, guess what they gave her as a wedding present?"

"A corset," I said. "I've heard this story."

I continued on my way to Mother's. She was seated on the big leather throne. She said she was glad to see me. Mother being Mother, her forthrightness itself seemed a kind of evasion. Her eyes enlarged in her glasses followed me around her parlor.

"Fred said you were lonely."

"I'm no such thing" — more certainty that made her seem unsure.

"So he said."

"I don't know where he got that idea."

"He said you told him."

"Fred is in China." This was indirection and had no bearing on the question, but was a characteristic response from Mother when she didn't want to give a straight answer.

"I'm fine," she said. Her eyes were huge and imperious. She smiled, or rather showed her teeth, so it was not a smile but more like an animal baring its fangs before something edible. "You know how Fred exaggerates."

I suspected she was denying her loneliness because she didn't want to confide in me, didn't really want me to visit. She was disappointed that one of her favored children wasn't there, Franny or Fred or Gilbert.

"Hubby said he was here yesterday."

"All of him," Mother said, widening her eyes. "The size of him. Naturally he was hungry. He did nothing but talk about how he's fixing up his basement. I think he was hinting that he wanted some financial help. But what can I do? I don't have much — hardly anything. Is there something wrong?"

I had been holding my jaw. I'd chipped a filling, and though I hadn't intended to tell her, I explained what had happened.

Mother winced, then slowly shook her head and said, "I woke up one morning with a toothache. I was nine. It was like a knife going through my jaw. My mother said, 'If you're strong enough to cry, it can't hurt that bad. It's when you can't cry that the pain is really bad.' She gave me a clove to bite and made me go to school. A few days later the dentist drilled it, without anesthesia. We didn't have Novocain in those days. My jaw was swollen for a week."

Mother touched her jaw in the place where the dentist had done his work eighty years before. As she grimaced at the memory, my tooth ached more than ever.

"Angela was spared sore teeth," Mother said. "She was spared a lot of heartaches."

True, a newborn who'd died almost at birth had managed to elude a great deal of life's pain.

"You know what next Monday is?" Mother asked.

"Angela's birthday." I was glad that Franny had reminded me of this holy day on the family calendar.

"She would have been fifty-four."

In my mind's eye I saw a big potbellied angel with gray hair, a fat face, and a gown a bit like Franny's loose shapeless dress, beating her tattered wings, trying to keep aloft.

That night Rose called me. "Franny's been on the phone with Ma ever since you left. Will you please stop talking about your tooth problems when you talk to Ma? This is a hard month. Next Monday's a dark day. Ma's right, all you think about is yourself."

Holidays in a big fragmented family are nightmarish, tests of loyalty and will, occasions of interaction — and in this narrative of family interaction, every gesture seemed provoked by hostility. Being invited to an event was often worse than being excluded. I heard from Fred that Franny and Rose were hosting Mother at Franny's house for Thanksgiving. Floyd was there, and because he was present, I had to be absent. Fred was invited but he had made other arrangements. Gilbert was in Kuwait that week. Hubby fled to New Hampshire with his wife and daughter because he found holiday dinners stressful. I spent the day, like most days, alone, and ate a solitary meal of microwaved chili and a few beers, Thanksgiving being one of those days when you remember what you ate, especially if it isn't turkey. Holidays may be hell for families, but they are purgatorial for people on their own.

Christmas loomed, another reminder of my solitude. Hubby stopped by to ask what my plans were. He also mentioned that he had passed by Mother's and seen Franny and Rose shoveling slush from her walkway.

"'Somebody's got to do it,' Rose said." Hubby's impersonation of her nagging nasal voice was dead accurate: no one was a better mimic than an angry sibling. "It was her way of telling us we're lazy. That she and Franny always look after Ma. But I just took all Ma's trash to the dump. And who fixed the ball cock in her terlet?"

Terlet was more family mimicry, Mother's locution.

"What are you doing for Christmas?" I asked Hubby.

"Ma and Gil are coming over Christmas Eve. Fred's having her Christmas day."

"What about Floyd?"

"He'll be playing pocket pool, as usual."

But at the last moment, in what I took to be a deftly timed hostile move, Fred canceled and took his family to Florida. Mother spent Christmas at Franny's house, and Rose joined them with the twins, Bingo and Benno. Rose's husband Walter, whom Floyd called "a creature of phenomenal dullness," remained at his computer; Marvin watched the football game, sipping medicine for his acid reflux. Gilbert took Mother to Franny's, and to get there the pair of them would have ridden past Hubby's house, Floyd's house, and my house. I did not know whether Floyd was invited. No one would tell me, because telling me would have indicated his or her complicity in Floyd's campaign against me.

While Dad had been alive, Christmas would have been spent in one of our houses, one of us playing host and everyone pitching in to help, bringing dessert, fruit, or wine. Dad and Mother would have sat in the place of honor while we talked happily, or sang, or served food. We opened presents. A stranger peering through the window would have seen a day of joy and remarked, "What a happy family. This is the meaning of Christmas."

But if this stranger had looked closer, he would have seen a room full of rancor — whiners, complainers, and backbiters: the host feeling put-upon by having to buy all the food and accommodate all the people; the host's spouse ill tempered at the sight of this fractious family and the thought of having to clean up after them; Fred muttering that he could have taken his family to Florida and made business deals at the same time; Franny passing out Swedish meatballs, offended that no one was eating them; Jonty boasting, Bingo grasping her harmonica but not playing it, Benno holding three bean bags but not juggling; Hubby complaining about Floyd, Rose rolling her eyes at Franny, Gilbert sighing that he had to leave for Istanbul early the next morning; and the whispers going round and round, one child belittling another, and at last Floyd proposing a loud and abusive toast to whoever was hosting, saying, "Charge your glasses, and raise them to Fezziwig . . ."

All of us in the room jostling, wishing each other Merry Christmas and laughing up our sleeves. Hubby was the butt of jokes about overeating, Fred was the butt of jokes about pomposity, and as for Floyd's wild hair, Gilbert's fussiness, Franny's cooking, Rose's temper, and all the badly behaved children — everything was noticed. I was mocked, of course, but did not know how. That was the torment of the big unruly family: you were never quite sure how you failed to measure up, or what was taken to be your salient weakness.

Presiding over it all was grateful sentimental Dad and grasping sentimental Mother.

"Your family!" my first wife, Diana, would say afterward. And later, when she left me and I remarried, my second wife, Heather, would say the same thing, "Your family!" This was the reason why, apart from holidays, I spent my middle years, my productive years, far away from Mother Land.

For a few years after Father died we tried to keep these Christmases going, but they were failures. We could not all be in one room at the same time. There were too many of us, and we were far too angry. Christmas was something else now. It was Mother and Gilbert at Franny's, with Rose and her kids. Perhaps Floyd dropped by. I had no way of knowing. No one mentioned Floyd to me anymore.

21

TRAITORS

I SAW CLEARLY NOW what I had suspected all my life. But I was almost an old man before I was able to put into words what I had felt in my guts since childhood. We were traitors. We were dizzy with the vertigo of unprincipled paranoiacs, knowing that we were betrayers. I had known it without having the precise word for it. In the past when Floyd had hooted, "We're savages!" I took it as his usual hyperbole. He meant lawless, ruthless, amoral, opportunistic, simple creatures of the mud hut and the bow and arrow; and of course all this was true. But we had been taught a thousand ways to be unfaithful, as well as having drummed into us its underlying reason: give yourself to someone completely, and she or he will let you down, hurt you, disappoint you, destroy you. That's what came of surrender, of generosity, of love. Far better to hold off and practice treachery. The act of betrayal, the Judas gift, was a sure way of finding an ally.

As for withholding, not trusting, not committing completely, this was the guarantee that our love affairs never worked and our friendships were failures.

None of this was put into words. In our oral tradition, we were subtler in our actions than we had ways to describe them — like jungle illiterates, elaborate in the nuance of gestures and facial expressions. As a result we were close observers of human nature, not bookish but intensely social, highly sensitive to other people's moods, to the quality of their responses, to modes of gratitude and sorts of apologies and the many kinds of laughter, especially the telling tonalities of insincerity. From birth we had been needy — Mother had regaled us for years about how we had screamed as infants — yet we were also untrusting, hard to console, impossible to soothe. These qualities, this powerful recipe for unhappiness, is also, in the right person, a recipe for intense creativity — rebellious vision, boldness of expression, risk taking, artful foolery. The long memory and the violent imagination were the good things — the great things — that were scorched into us by the family, and that made us, each of us in our own way, fanatical.

Mother's first lesson, implied rather than spoken plainly, was that our affection for each other was a sign of weakness. Loyalty was dangerous, like an obscure form of cheating. Our love for one another would make us unreliable, for it interfered with our first, our most important, duty: obedience to Mother.

At her most cunning, using her indirection to confuse us, Mother preached against unkindness. She convinced us of the virtues of disloyalty by telling us the opposite. She taught us betrayal in unusual ways, in a system of pious mottoes. "I want my children to love each other." "I want harmony in the family." "You must help each other." "How I hate it when my children fight." "You have to learn to get along." "Remember the Golden Rule."

But, to rule us, she needed disharmony, and she recognized that, by mastering duplicity, she could exercise control. She made us fight, incited us to quarrel. After speaking with her, Fred called me up and screamed at me. He wept in pleading phone calls to Floyd: "Can't you see she's old and frail?" Floyd howled at Hubby: "You greedy bastard, stuffing your face with Ma's muffins."

While maintaining that she wanted peace, and making us listen to her platitudes, she whispered against us, each in turn, until we were so furious with one another that we went to her in the infantile and whining spirit of "He hit me!" and "He started it!"

Mother blamed us for being hostile to each other while at the same time creating the hostility. And why? Stalin would have known the answer, so would Chairman Mao or Pol Pot — Brother Number One — or Comrade Hoxha of Albania: so that we would obey only her.

"Don't fight" meant fight. "Help each other" meant hurt each other. Harmony and peace meant their opposites. And if any one of us took her at her word and helped a brother or sister unselfishly — following Mother's advice literally — the result was unexpectedly horrible, for we quickly learned that the person we had helped was laughing at us, egged on by Mother, as we labored in vain. You were a sucker for helping. And, Mother reasoned, why were you spending time and money helping one another when your duty was to help her? Effort spent on each other was effort denied to her.

Were you home dusting shelves?

Mother said, "I've got some shelves that could use a good dusting."

Were you making a meal for Hubby?

Mother said, "He's got a hollow leg. Where does all that food go? One of these days he's going to explode."

Were you going to Boston with Floyd?

Mother said, "I haven't been to Boston for years."

Were you giving Gilbert a lift to the Hyannis Airport?

Mother said, "I don't know how I'm going to get to my dental appointment next week."

Were you serving Franny and Marvin scallops for dinner?

Mother said, "I love scallops. I don't remember the last time I had any."

All this was in the early days, when we were much younger, when we had just set off to make our lives. It was before I had a clear idea of what we were, before I understood the word "traitor."

After Father's death and my return, Mother tightened her grip. And now, after all those intervening years, I saw what we had become: savages, sneaks, spies, rats.

Out of habit, for the sake of peace, I tried to please her. In the years after Father died, living on the Cape and single, I frequently visited Mother. The leaf raking and snow shoveling: I performed those chores for Mother too. After Floyd had become my enemy, I realized I could not fight him. I had no allies; it was something I would have to swallow. I had already tried to elicit Mother's sympathy, or a bit of support for Floyd's public attack on me. Mother said, "I hate it when my children quarrel," and the next day she would be at Floyd's for dinner. Floyd might have been vicious toward me, but he was dutiful where Mother was concerned, even if she seldom acknowledged his generosity.

But, then, she seldom acknowledged anyone's generosity. To your face she would equivocate — she might even be profuse in her thanks. But she had no memory for gifts, or the gift grew smaller and smaller, until it was a pathetic shrunken thing that had been forced upon her, that she had never really needed in the first place.

For Mother to be grateful meant that you mattered, that what you had done was important. She withheld praise. So you had done very little after all, and you would have to keep trying, because you had failed. She did not come out and tell us we had failed. In fact, she might say that she was pleased, but she conveyed the message with a contrived irony that suggested that she was not pleased at all.

"Are you sure you like it?" I might ask.

"Of course I am," Mother would reply, and I knew from her hollow tone that this meant, "No, I am not."

In time, we all became adept at translating the looking-glass language of her petty tyranny, so when she alluded to the Golden Rule, or more likely recited it, one skinny finger upraised, we knew in our hearts that what she meant was the opposite.

As a child I had been bamboozled by Mother. I fumbled and failed until, at last, after high school, I had gone away and more or less stayed away. Years passed. Now I knew exactly what was happening, and though the process appalled me, I was impressed by its complex dynamics and its effectiveness.

It was not easy to roil a whole family — Mother was constantly stirring — but in her earnest plotting she had managed to divide us. We bickered and whispered: it was her triumph, for all our attention was directed toward her — gifts, flowers, fruit, sympathy, support. Her lessons in the tactics of disloyalty and hypocrisy had been heeded by us. We children disliked each other, we associated selectively, because there were cliques among us. But we all told Mother we loved her.

Winter passed. Spring came. Easter was an event — another meal at someone's house, with significant exclusions. Floyd was, in this period, never excluded. He was invited first and it was hoped he would show up, because if he stayed away, he was probably mocking you, as he was relentlessly mocking me.

Now, five years after Dad's death, Mother and Floyd were close. Their closeness meant Mother had plenty of information about him. She jeered at him to Fred and Gilbert, though she had nothing to say to Franny or Rose on the subject of Floyd. Fred was the most fearful of Floyd: he patronized him, but he laughed at Floyd to me. Hubby hated Floyd and disliked Fred for being hospitable to him, but Hubby liked hospitality and could not resist Fred's barbecues. Gilbert, circumspect with Floyd, stayed with Mother when he was on the Cape, so he was able to remain elusive to the rest of us. Hubby badmouthed Fred to me while at the same time eating with him. Franny and Rose disliked Hubby because he was helpful to Mother and to Franny and Rose, though they resented their need of him.

Fred appeared to be friendly toward me, yet he delighted in my downfall. Gilbert was solicitous, at times genuinely friendly, but far too busy to look closely at anyone's life. Franny had once seen me as useful, because my name was known. But she had not forgiven me for staying away from Jonty's wedding. In the spirit of Mother's indirection, Franny showed her hostility by bringing me masses of inexpensive yet encumbering presents — cheap chocolates, bags of bruised apples, T-shirts from outlet stores, mismatched socks. Rose showed her hostility more directly by not giving me anything, indeed by avoiding me, because she and her children had become close to Floyd.

"Uncle Floyd put us in his will," little Benno had said to me on one of their rare visits. Little Bingo agreed: "We're getting his stuff when he dies."

Using your last will and testament to get someone's attention meant you would command fidelity until your death. This strategy was a page from Mother's playbook.

Franny and Rose were careful with me, usually disguising the fact that they were friendly with Floyd. "We don't see much of him." I knew differently, and that anything I told them would be used as little gifts: they would report anything they saw or heard at my house to Floyd, to ingratiate themselves. Such gossip was a sort of present, as much to prove their loyalty to him as to prove their disloyalty to me. To throw me off they ridiculed Floyd when they were with me, but gently, subtly, so that I would not have something to hold against them. It is tricky to be a traitor if you also want to have some allies.

When we were in her presence, Mother, in her judicious way, told us she loved us and was grateful for our attention. But when we were out of sight, she told whoever would listen that we were not very reliable, nor generous, nor helpful. She always praised me when I visited. And afterward Fred or Franny or someone else would report that she said, "Jay upsets me. I don't know what I've done to deserve it."

Floyd's attack-dog hatred was now so long-standing that it inspired fear in the others. There was no way I could think of to make peace with Floyd, but as time passed I began to see that I was more fortunate than the others. Because of Floyd's peculiar disposition and his demands, it was far more oppressive to be Floyd's friend than his enemy. As his enemy, I had long stretches of time to myself, while his friends and the rest of the family had to deal with him every day. He had done his worst: written his malicious review of my book. But though my book had failed, the review was so bizarre, unhinged, and incoherent, Floyd had attracted attention by making a fool of himself, and unwelcome inquiries and baffled questions began to haunt him.

As his enemy, I did not have to please him. I was detached and did not have to propitiate him, as the others did, with presents and tribute, something for his collections — Coca-Cola memorabilia, vintage ice cream scoops, and all the rest of it. The others lived in terror of offending him. I was luckier in living beneath his notice.

I pitied Fred, who would drop off an ivory netsuke at Floyd's and then visit me and mock Floyd's acquisitiveness. "He's compulsive!" It was the twisted loyalty Mother had instilled in us — Fred believing that by mocking Floyd he was pleasing me, when I knew well that after he left my house he got on the phone and mocked me to another sibling. And Fred was not the only one who behaved this way. We all did. I mocked them all behind their backs.

We were traitors on Mother's behalf. And, strange to say, it was a success. We were not happy, but Mother was, and that was all that mattered.

22

TEN MINUTES FROM MOTHER

S O THIS IS HOW YOU GROW OLD, I sometimes thought, wondering at my passivity, which induced in me an anguish of suffocation, living near the sea in a rented house on a street of blowing sand and misshapen, arthritic-limbed pitch pines shedding their needles. No miracles would befall me now. I lived in a vegetative state of semiretirement, with diminishing funds, and so did most of the family. I feared complete retirement because I needed somewhere to go every morning. But that was only part of the problem: having retired from active employment, we had also retired our dreams and ambitions. We had more time on our hands than ever, and plenty of solitude to recall all our old resentments. We had outgrown our yearnings and our hopes. Whatever had been meant for us, whatever success or happiness, had either already occurred or never would. Destiny was behind me. Fate was irrelevant. Only death was certain. You think: This is it.

I had known a modest sort of fame, and now it was gone except for an ambiguous afterglow, as when I was cashing a check and my name was recognized by a bewildered stranger who was not quite sure why he knew it.

"Didn't you write something once?"

It was a clerk in a hardware store in Osterville, putting his blunt fingertip on my printed name on the check.

I was entering that gray and uneventful desert-like region of late middle age. I thought of stretches of sand dunes, like the ones in Truro — low and infertile, no clear path, not much vegetation, little comfort, only emptiness beyond them. All this is hidden from the young, the barren region where all striving seems futile and any enthusiasm or serious effort appears foolish. Nothing happens except unfortunate accidents, and ill luck is a condition of this stage of life. But I was no cynic; I was almost serene. Strangers did not see me, or if they did, their gaze did not linger.

But when I thought of Mother, or visited her and was in the presence of her fury or cunning or the energy of her evasion, I knew I was wrong about myself. I looked at her and thought: I'm not old at all. I am her much younger child, her third son, still a swimmer and a cyclist, a capable drinker, a sometime cook, and if Mother's age is any indication of longevity, I have another thirty-something years left. Thirty more years of this!

The notion of all that time, like a jail sentence, cast a spell on me and made me brood. What to do with those years? It made me deeply melancholy to think that I was headed for a life like Mother's: alone in her home with her telephone, stirring up her children, and receiving visitors, dropping hints to excite their envy or whispering in their ears to remind them of their duties.

Mother had lost weight, an amount that made an older person seem satisfied and settled, somewhat immobilized, and good-humored. Mother was now pared down to her essence: skeletal, pale, with the sort of loose yellowish skin you find on the carcasses of warm plucked poultry. She wore a shawl she had knitted herself, or a sweater, even in summer, and always her nurse's shoes that Hubby got her wholesale from the hospital supplier.

"Hear what Floyd said about Ma?" Hubby asked one day, calling me out of the blue.

"I never talk to him." I hated hearing his name. "How would I know?"

"The usual way."

It was true: the grapevine was alive with whispers, even from people we hadn't seen in years.

"He says she looks like Bertrand Russell."

In spite of myself, I laughed.

"You think that's funny?" Hubby was indignant.

"No," I said, though it was perfect: the skull on the scrawny neck, the white tufts of hair, the androgyny. Bertrand Russell looked like a lot of grandmothers.

"Floyd's a clown. What are you doing?"

"A little work."

I was doing nothing. I did not have the heart to begin another book. I wrote pieces instead, magazine hackwork that got me out of the house and paid my rent — a thousand words on Cape Cod cycle paths, fifteen hundred on Martha's Vineyard in the off-season, the text for a photo essay on lighthouses, a reminiscence of a traveler I had known, vignettes on scrimshaw, on lobstering, on sailing, on bass fishing, the Cape Cod clichés repeated for a new readership, filling space in magazines aiming to make money for pages of advertising.

Measured against Mother, I was a young man. In her presence I felt like a boy. I stopped brooding about being old. I had changed my mind and decided to live. I visited her to renew my sense of my youthfulness.

Perhaps the reminder of my relative youth helped keep me on the Cape, living ten minutes from Mother. When I tried to work it out, I became self-conscious and confused and thought: Never mind. Doesn't matter. It's only for the time being.

And besides, in the weirdly tribal way I have already described, this was my world — my family, my culture. I spoke the special language of this tiny band of people whose lives were part of my own, and though I protested, their habits and beliefs were mine, even the diet, even the secrets.

In time — this was the unspoken taboo — Mother would die, and then I would be old. Her death would make me old.

Mother had stopped talking about her passing, had stopped talking about her will. She had solicited everyone's opinion about it, how her estate should be apportioned. There wasn't much, I was sure, but Mother was still vigorously alive, still needing our attention, and so each of us served some purpose for her. My life of ambition, my career as a serious writer, was over. My life of striving was over. I was no longer an aspirant. Knowing this calmed me and kept me in one place.

Alive, alert, Mother kept me young. No matter how feeble or forgetful or ill she was, her very existence made me a boy. We were Mother and son, Madonna and child, the contrast in us the visible proof of my youth. When this sank in I took a greater interest in seeing her. Like a peasant on a hillside in a foreign land, regarding his queen-empress in her distant castle, I had learned to live with her tyranny and see some advantages in it. And like that peasant, I was beneath her notice most of the time. It had ceased to matter whether she was on my side or not, sowing confusion, stirring up trouble, telling lies about me, whispering, mocking. All I cared about was her endurance, the everlastingness of her, her value as a symbol, a totem, the head of our family. I hoped she would live forever. I wanted her to be eternal. I did not want to contemplate her death, for as long as she lived I would never die. More than that, I would remain a boy.

That bracing thought (it seemed logical despite being untrue) was another reason to live ten minutes from Mother.

Mother seemed her usual sly and evasive self, perhaps more pronounced now because she was skinnier, her profile in sharper relief, when I brought her a present. She often said, tapping a box of chocolates with her bony hands, "Franny likes these. She and Rose are coming down tomorrow." And, with a dig at them, "I don't know why they bother. I can manage perfectly well on my own." An expression of disgusted pity flickered on her face, making her seem like a coquette with a sour stomach. "But if it makes them feel better" — and she sighed.

That was Mother all over, belittling someone for doing the very thing she wanted them to do.

I imagined, though, that Franny and Rose were visiting Mother for the same reason I was — venerating the old woman as a pagan idol, glorying in her life, propitiating her vanity, flattering themselves that they were young, rejuvenated by being in the same room with an eighty-eight-year-old mother.

I liked hearing Mother boast, "I went for a walk today," or "I've been weeding the garden," or "I've been to the beach."

When I called and the phone rang a few times more than I expected, her house seeming emptier, growing hollower with each ring, I feared she might be lying face-down, dying, clawing the carpet. My heart gave a little jump when the ringing was cut off and she said hello in her usual way, a two-tone "Hull-oh?"

She always spoke in an uncertain tone, as though intruded upon in a dark room. Her note of dumb wonder and inquiry was the result of her not knowing who was at the other end, and she did not have a true voice until she knew who it was. She had a different voice for each of us, a different quality of greeting, all of them true, all of them false.

"It's me."

"Gilbert?" she said brightly, going giddy.

"No, it's me." Now, of course, I was teasing.

"Hubby?" she said in a discouraged way.

"He's at the hospital."

"Freddy?" she said with hope in her voice.

"JP," I said, putting her out of her misery.

"Oh?" Her incurious sigh was one of disappointment, but I didn't mind. I was glad she was alive.

As soon as I established that fact, I wanted to put the phone down. But I stayed on the line and listened to her aches, her recent purchases ("peaches are sixty-nine cents a pound"), birthday updates ("Bingo has a birthday this month"), the weather report (though I lived nearby and the same rain fell on me), and reminiscences — how a teacher had praised her handwriting in 1927, and what her father had always said. She quoted this man constantly, his struggles, his dreams, his sensitivity, how much he had loved her. She did not seem to realize that as a child I had known this sententious old patriarch who demanded to examine my school report card. Often Mother quoted Angela, with whom she regularly communed, channeling the dead child's wisdom. "I can feel her looking down on me from above," as though she was in an earthly pew, and her father and

Angela stood in a golden gallery, clutching the ornate rail, puffy Tiepolo clouds floating by, while they nodded in approval.

Often in a phone call she made belittling compliments, backhanders of a kind that Mother had turned into a fine art. "I see Hubby has a nice new car. I don't know where he gets the money," "Gilbert just got a promotion. That means he'll be traveling more, poor kid. I worry about his health," and "Franny and Rose swept out the garage. I guess they think their old mother is too weak or too lazy to do it," and "I haven't heard from you lately. You must be so busy with your fiancée."

I didn't take the bait. I said, "I'm never too busy to call you. We spoke yesterday."

"I don't think so." She did not say it as if she was unsure but as if I was telling a lie.

"You mentioned that you walked down to the beach."

"That wasn't yesterday."

She had me on the witness stand, poking holes in my testimony while I stammered to be believed.

"It doesn't matter," I said.

"It matters if it's not true," she said, refusing to concede.

"I guess I didn't call you yesterday," I said, knowing that I could not win.

"Ah," she said, at last triumphant, and then, in her flat, news-giving voice, "Floyd was over here today."

The name was like a lash. Strangers hearing my name often brightened as they mentioned his attack on me and my book, and some could quote the more savagely memorable parts of it to me. Sometimes sentences that Floyd had written purely to annoy me turned up in judgments on me in essays about my work: "obsessed with his bowels," "fact fetishist," "phony English accent," "solipsistic in his monstrous pomposity," "family finds him ridiculous."

"Hello?" Mother said, as though from the bottom of a silent well.

"I'm still here."

"I thought we were cut off. I was talking about Floyd."

"Ma, he won't speak to me."

"I don't know anything about that."

"I haven't heard from Floyd for two years. He seems to hate me."

"No one hates you. Don't commit the sin of pride. Do you really think you're important enough for anyone to hate?"

No sooner had she said this than various faces swam before me with hatred in their eyes, Melissa Gearhart among them, and more haters massing behind them like a bank of storm clouds.

"Floyd wrote that horrible review. You saw it."

Mother became haughty with flamboyant piety, protesting her innocence. "I haven't seen a solitary thing."

"Never mind."

That mention of Floyd, as in "Floyd was over here today," was intended to make me squirm, to feel small, to remind me that I was a victim with a ruthless enemy. Her malice was clearer to me and came over the phone more distinctly than if I had been in her presence, since she affected a fluttering saintliness, a sort of resolute suffering, an intense sanctimony, especially when she was being malicious.

She was gossiping. They all were. Hubby often stopped by my house, always with a grievance, sometimes with a hospital story. Defeat had turned me into a good listener. Besides, Hubby lived in the real world of life and death, of order, of regular hours, clocking in, clocking out, collecting his check every week. He had colleagues, he had bosses, he had employees and assistants. He had patients. Responsibility was shared; so were jokes. He had paid vacations and holidays off. I knew nothing about any of this in my improvisational life of disorder, and I often envied him, not for his work but for the sociability of his day, the friendships, his being in the world of illness, which was also the world of healing.

Hubby had been a medic in Vietnam, and after his discharge he made a smooth entry into nursing. Wide-bodied, with powerful shoulders, a thick neck, and big pink hands, he seemed to enjoy growling, "I'm a nurse," for the way the announcement made people's faces twitch with disbelief.

"We had a woman in the ER today," Hubby said to me one night around this time — starting a story was a form of hello in our family. "Early this morning. I was having my coffee. She'd OD'd on Vicodin. I ran her name through the records and got the headline that this was the third time she'd tried to kill herself. We hooked her up, pumped her out, and all this time she's barfing and complaining. I says to her, 'Hey, lady. Instead of wasting our time, why don't you do it right? I'd be happy to tell you how to off yourself so that you stay offed.'"

"How did she take that?"

"She hauled off and slapped me in the face. 'Fuck you!'" Hubby laughed at the memory of it. "I was in shock. I wanted to hit her back. The other nurse yells, 'Clean up your act, lady.' Then she lashed out at him. More f-bombs, and puke all over her lips."

I envied Hubby his drama. That's what I was missing—real life. I guessed that Hubby seldom felt, as I did, superfluous.

"Had a guy in last week. 'I've got a wicked pain in my stomach.' He said it in a girlish way. X-ray showed a foreign object. We removed a six-inch vibrator that had somehow disappeared up his ass. I mean, he could have said something to us about it beforehand, maybe? All he said was 'That thing does not belong to me. I have no idea where it came from.'"

This was his usual warm-up. After a few more stories like this, I was sure Hubby would return to our obsessive subject, the other members of the family. Lately, his grievances had been sharper than mine.

He squeezed his face between his thick hands, distorting it, in what seemed a gesture of friendliness, but also indicating that he was changing the subject.

"Ma's acting weird these days."

"There's a headline."

"No, really. 'Do this, do that.' Very demanding."

I almost said, *Franny and Rose said the same thing,* because just a week before, on a Sunday, they had dropped in to complain about Mother. They moaned and flapped for a full hour about her tyranny.

Hubby narrowed his eyes at me: What did I know? But I just shrugged. It was always a mistake in this family to offer information. If someone did, the listener—Hubby was deft at this—pretended not to hear or interrupted at times, talking over it in his outraged voice. But every detail of the indiscretion was noted and remembered, to be repeated later, with embellishments.

I offered him nothing in return, so he yawned, complained about the chores Mother gave him, and said he had to go.

Franny and Rose had in the past often sighed over Mother's meddling and neediness ("like a little girl"), her infantile glee at receiving presents. But never before, as they did these days, had they sounded bitter or oppressed.

Franny had said, "I can't take much more of this," which was extreme for her, since she was vain about her ability to endure suffering.

Rose blamed Fred. "He said he was coming to visit Ma. He never keeps his word. He sent her a fruit basket out of guilt."

"Ma's not comfortable with Hubby," Franny said.

They knew better than to mention Floyd to me. Hubby had said that he was doing all the maintenance on Mother's house — cleaned the gutters, replaced fallen shingles, resprung the screen doors, put new clamps on the hoses. Mother, he'd said, was unreasonable, never satisfied, as cheap as they come.

I visited Mother that week. She said she could not remember whether Hubby had visited.

"Didn't he do some chores around the house?"

"A few little things," Mother said dismissively. "I could have done them myself. I should have — it would have been quicker."

"How are you feeling?"

"Oh, fine," she said, sounding wounded and unconvincing.

"Isn't there anything I can do to help?"

"You're busy," Mother said, putting me in the wrong, wincing in self-pity. Then, goggling at me through her big lenses, she added with feeling, "My bags are packed."

The expression was new with her. Where had she learned it? Only from someone her age, perhaps someone in the waiting room at the doctor's office, or one of the aged whittlers at her bird-carving class. I would not have known what it meant if Franny had not warned me. It was Mother's way of saying, I am ready to die.

Hubby had heard her say that too. So had Floyd, Hubby said.

"What did Floyd say?"

"He quoted Winston Churchill. What a pisser he is."

"What was the quote?"

"Something about, 'If I got a telegram saying that Stalin was dead, I would ask myself, What does he mean by that?'"

23

THE ACRE

O NE HOT SUMMER DAY of high blue sky, the light breeze off the ocean fragrant with wild roses and beach plums and the tang of the sea, the noon heat cooking and concentrating the aromas, I drove over to bring Mother a carton of blueberries. She was sitting under her maple tree at the back of the house, sipping iced tea. As I approached her, she angled her shoulders and knees at me, and still sipping her tea, holding the tumbler like a measuring device, assessing me as I drew nearer to her. Even outside, Mother looked imperious. Whatever she sat on was a throne, including this old chair. Exposed to her penetrating gaze and inquisitive smile, I felt clumsy, and faltered. To compensate I walked with exaggerated care, hen-like, an altar boy observed by a congregation. The dull tap and fidget of ice in Mother's tumbler told me that she was still eyeing me.

"You're limping," she said.

She remained watchful as I corrected my step, turning to align my aching foot, trying to deny it. Mother's unsympathetic alertness was that of an unblinking lioness observing a distant antelope for signs of weakness. How had she seen? But I was prey: she saw everything. Her watchfulness was also that of a tyrant, and it struck me again that a tyrant is often a paranoiac.

"Nothing serious."

"If it's not serious, why are you doing it?" The illogical always made her smile in pity.

"My foot's sore."

"Did you break something?" She seemed hopeful, saying this.

"Gout," I said.

"My father had gout, rest his soul. He suffered terribly. He took pills."

"I'm taking pills."

Mother smiled, and when she did, I knew from her look of contentment that she was thinking of herself.

"I don't take anything," she said. "I was at my carving class the other
day. All the rest of them were talking about their medications. Jim Gaffey
is on blood thinner. Irene is on prednisone. Walter takes Vioxx. Who
takes stool softeners? Someone. Zyloprim. They looked at me, because
I hadn't said anything. 'What are you on?' I just smiled" — saying this,
she enjoyed the same smile now, smug and tight under her raptor's nose.
"Then I said, 'I'm not on anything.'"

She sipped some more tea. The tumbler was no longer a measuring
beaker; it was just a glass again. Drinking, she became self-absorbed. Her
way of swallowing and going glassy-eyed was a kind of selfishness.

And, for effect, she repeated the answer: "I'm not *awn* anything."

I said, "The trouble is having to remember to take the pills three times
a day with food. It's so boring."

"I'm never bored," Mother said.

That morning I had felt better, over the worst, the first indication that
the indomethacin was taking hold, a subsiding of the soreness in my big-
toe joint. In Mother's presence, it was sore again. I felt much worse —
sicker, sorer, more demoralized and unconsoled — having visited Mother.

"Not that it matters that I'm never bored," she said, still swallowing. "I
won't be around much longer."

"Don't be silly, Ma. You're looking great. I brought you these blueberries."

She eyed them as I placed them on her side table.

"My bags are packed."

She said it as though she would be leaving the blueberries behind.

"Have you heard from anyone?" she asked.

I said, "On my way over I took the scenic route, to get these berries at
the farm stand. I saw a backhoe on the Acre."

"I have no idea what that is."

"A digger. For making a foundation."

"Oh?"

Mother and Dad had bought the vacant lot they called the Acre years
before, from a man so desperate for money he sold it way below the market

price. Some days Mother walked the quarter mile from her house to stare at it, as if she expected fruit trees to start from the ground, and springs to bubble up, and flowers to blossom. Her gaze was just so absorbing and demanding and hopeful.

"Are you planning to build on it?"

"No," she said, and the implication of her tone in this simple word was that my question was stupid and intrusive, like a bratty child's nagging.

And so we talked about the weather, and she wanted to know why the carton of blueberries had leaves and twigs in it. Then I left her, limping badly, my foot much sorer than when I'd arrived.

A few days later, Franny called me. Her voice was agitated and tearful.

"Have you heard? Hubby's got the Acre." She started to cry, snorting into the phone. "He's already broken ground!"

"The Acre? How did he get it?"

"Three guesses." She was still struggling to speak through her sobs. "I don't know why I'm so upset. He doesn't deserve it. What has he ever done?"

"Ma must have sold it to him."

"He tricked her. You know how he is." She was snuffling snot and tears, like someone being tumbled in surf. "Dad never meant the Acre to be sold!"

But I was thinking of Mother. She hadn't said a word of this to me, nor had she told me a single lie.

Soon, everyone in the family knew, and everyone, even Hubby, was angry.

I said to him, "How much did you pay for it?"

"Everyone's asking me the same stupid question!"

"So what's the answer?"

In a growly voice he said, "The price was right."

I was surprised by how indignant the rest of them were. It was as if the Acre had been taken from them. I reasoned that the land was Mother's to dispose of as she wished. Odd, though, that she would sell it to Hubby, whom she so often mocked behind his back.

"He's got more than me," we used to say at the dinner table. "She's got a bigger piece." Or: "He's having seconds." Years of that. And Hubby's ending up owning the Acre was just another version of it.

Mother was excited by the angry interplay, vitalized by the contro-
versy. Her fascination was vivid and palpable and seemed to strengthen
her. She seemed years younger in her indignation.

"The nerve of them, asking me about the Acre," she said to me.

"I suppose it's natural curiosity," I said, to see what she would reply.

"It's unnatural. I'll do as I goddamn please!"

She only pretended to be angry. She loved the helpless fury of our ignorant questioning, so that she could be defiant. She wanted the arrangement with Hubby to be noticed, whatever arrangement it was — the more
shadowy and covert-seeming the better, because it was all a provocation
to us. She wanted to say, *Do I ask you what you do with your money and
property?* She was delighted that we were confounded with unanswered
questions. She exploited our confusion.

The attention she got so energized her that she stopped saying "My
bags are packed." The flurry of curiosity, the backbiting and envy, restored
her will to live.

And our objections showed her how weak we were, how easily manipulated.

I was also thinking, Hubby — of all people! Because he made an effort
to help and was never thanked, he was the fault-finder, the complainer,
the begrudger, at least in the eyes of the others, who disparaged his effort.
He offered medical advice, drug samples, and bandages, and I saw him as
the handyman, the essential person in a big, breakable household, Nurse
Fixit. He was jeered at, but when someone had an ache or a swelling, had
a drain to unclog or a gutter to clear or a mower to mend, had something
to be bandaged or glued, Hubby had the answer.

He was expert in his own profession, as a practical nurse, usually in
triage at the ER in Hyannis, but no one spoke of him as a medical man.
He was the family menial, expert in niggling repairs.

One of the family's cruelest characteristics was its cynicism in giving
no credit to those who helped. By minimizing someone's generosity, you
owed nothing. The greater the favor you did, the more you were mocked
for your folly in offering it, or worse, you were ignored. I would be asked
for a loan. It might be ten thousand dollars. I would agree — too read-
ily — and so the amount would be doubled, and soon the figure might
be twenty-six thousand. The borrower had just suffered a crisis and was

facing financial ruin. I was enjoying literary success — the good years. I found it more poignant than flattering that a sibling should come to me, hat in hand, begging for a loan, and so I would say yes.

An ominous quality of frenzied joy, a giddy relief, takes hold of people who have gotten what they wanted from you. This joy raises the suspicion that they will never repay you. They are a bit too happy, too relieved, all at once carefree, the burden lifted. Infused with an almost indefinable and irrational hysteria.

"I'll pay you back," said with such insistence, made me suspicious. Why wouldn't I be paid back?

"I insist on paying interest. A bank would make me do it. It's only fair."

In some cases a document would be drawn up and the borrower would smile at our parallel signatures. Alarmed by this ritual, I'd repeat that at some point I'd have to be repaid.

Years went by, my fortunes flagged, I was going through a divorce, and now our positions were reversed, the borrower now flush with success. I needed the money.

"What money?"

I'd mention the amount and I'd be stared at, as though I might be off my head, not just delusional but something of a nuisance. I'd repeat the amount in a tremulous voice.

"Are you sure?"

Smiling at my confusion, looking like Mother, the borrower regarded my request as absurd, a shakedown of my own. I was the trickster now. So it often happens with a loan: the loaner becomes the villain, the recipient of the loan the victim.

All memory of the loan had been wiped clean, and the borrower's casual geniality made me anxious.

"We had a contract," I'd say.

"Nothing like that in my files."

Years of living abroad had made me a paper saver: an expatriate exists in documents. In time I'd find the contract, which would put the borrower in the wrong. The loan, now an established fact, was a great nuisance, not something to thank me for, but something to negotiate.

"I just don't have that kind of money."

Then I was the beggar, and after a while I'd be sent a check, with a graceless memo. It was bad manners on my part to have raised this awkward matter, and I'd be whispered about in the family as a nuisance and a time waster. A nobler person than I would never have asked for the money back. I was a cheapskate for asking to be repaid.

Some happiness came from these experiences. After the first flush of bitterness subsided, I felt a throb of enlightened satisfaction, from the liberating sense that someone else in the family had been revealed as never to be trusted again. Such a revelation of disloyalty and ingratitude made me oddly joyous, relieving me of any further obligation to care.

I was to feel this moral certainty whenever I was cheated, whenever I discovered someone had lied to me, when a woman was unfaithful to me, when I'd been swindled. After my first rush of indignation, I was possessed by an exalted sense of rightness, a kind of cynical bliss. Knowing that I'd been let down freed me from any responsibility to the offender. Though I took a ghastly pleasure in smiling at such cheaters, I never took them seriously again. I was spared the effort of expending another ounce of sympathy on them.

But the family was pitiless with Hubby. He deserved nothing—certainly not the Acre. And, true to the family tradition, Hubby denied that he had gotten anything substantial from Mother.

"The Acre was just sitting there," he said to me on one of his drive-bys. "Just a bunch of weeds, poison ivy, sumac trees, and tangled-up grapevines. Any of you could have had it. No one did a thing for years. Ma sells it to me and everyone goes nuts. People are yelling at me."

He was indignant rather than grateful, and he implied that he'd had to pay quite a bit for it.

Our speculation over the Acre made us yell at each other, and for a time, the yelling brought us together.

"Can you believe his gall?" Fred said to me. "He's sitting on an acre of prime land—water view—and pretends he has a God-given right to it. How about, 'Thanks, Ma'?"

I was reminded of one of the loans I'd made to a family member, who'd paid it back only because I'd found the contract. But I said, "Hubby's been useful around the house."

"Idiot jobs. Replacing a lightbulb. That land is worth eighty K!"

This figure was repeated. The supposition was that Hubby had paid

Mother nowhere near the market price. He'd secretly acquired it, taken it from us — so to speak — and had conned Mother. No one suggested that Mother had conspired with him. In our scenarios, she was the injured party.

Franny and Rose wailed the loudest.

"Look at you," Franny said to me. "You don't have a house. You're in a rental. You could have used that land."

"But I couldn't have bought it. Franny, I don't have any money."

"Your fiancée might have chipped in."

This was how out of touch she was — they all were. It had been years since Missy had dumped me, and I'd found no one else. But I had at last understood the wisdom that a secret is something you don't tell.

"Hubby is such a sneak," Rose said. "He's a bully, too. Ma's afraid of him. That's why she agreed to it. If I'd known, I would have done something about it."

Franny said, "He doesn't deserve that land. He's going to build a nice house there while the rest of us are in hovels."

"I hope he has trouble getting a building permit," Rose said.

Hubby did have trouble getting the permit. The perc test failed. He had to get an engineer to create a hillock on the land for the septic system, and then he underwent the ordeal of a public hearing. Because the hearing was held in the winter, when his neighbors on the Cape had nothing to do but attend such meetings and frustrate building permits, this one attracted attention. Franny and Rose went on that cold night, and so did Fred. It seemed the greatest opposition to the permit came from their corner of the room. It was pointed out that they were not abutters, and the permit was granted over their objections.

For a while there was no construction, but when the land thawed in the early spring, the hillock began to swell on the Acre.

"I paid good money for this," Hubby said when he drove by to complain that the others had attended the hearing to vote down his permit.

"Floyd's angry with me," Mother said. "'You gave the Acre to Hubby!' What right does he have to question me?"

Her way of putting me in my place was loudly to put someone else in his place. But I had no serious complaint. I didn't have the money; I didn't care. And besides, Hubby took on all the unpleasant jobs I could not do.

I recalled him fixing a clogged drain, reaching in and yanking out a dripping clump of Mother's hair as sleek as a ferret from the pipe.

Franny said, "If Dad were alive he'd never have agreed to this."

Dead Dad was the missing sense of fairness.

"How could she?" Franny said over the phone, between sobs. Rose was simply furious — no tears. Gilbert took Mother's side. "Maybe she did what made her happy." Fred raged at Hubby for all the faults I'd found in Fred — arrogance, meanness, amnesia.

We were talking, we were arguing, and Mother had never been happier. She would not say why she had sold the Acre, or how much it had cost. She rebuffed all questions, and yet she welcomed questions, because she enjoyed rebuffing them, creating greater confusion, more questions. From Mother's standpoint this was perfect. We had no idea what she was thinking, while she knew exactly what was on our minds.

This confusion persisted into the spring and summer, during which Hubby dug a foundation, put in a septic system, poured a slab, and began framing a modest house. And this might have been the end of it, as one of the many family enigmas, a quiet deal that extended Mother's power and her greater air of mystery, leaving us with a sense of injustice. But, buffeted by the criticism and feeling wronged, Hubby began again to complain about all the jobs Mother asked him to do — the summer chores, of window boxes, gutters, shingles.

"I have people dying at the hospital, I'm trying to finish my house, and I have to run over there and patch Ma's screen door," Hubby said. "I'm doing triage, I've got a motorcycle victim with massive head trauma, I can see his cortex is compromised, and I get a call from Ma. 'The sink's blocked. Could you ever come over and fix it?'"

Dramatizing his job, Hubby often transformed himself into a neurosurgeon.

Mother went on being evasive, defending Hubby, until she heard from Franny that Hubby had been telling the rest of us, "I've worked for this. I've earned this."

Unexpectedly, Mother said, "He did no such thing."

This assertion went around the family. We asked her to repeat it. She did so, her eyes dancing in anger. And she stopped defending Hubby. She began attacking his ingratitude. Everything he said seemed calculated to undermine Mother and prove her wrong. She had said the terms of the sale were secret. But Hubby kept blabbing.

When the truth came out, it was hard to know who had been told first, because one day everyone knew.

"Guess what he paid for the Acre?" Mother asked.

Perhaps she told each of us in turn. If so, it all happened fast. On the day she told me, I had begun the conversation by saying how hard Hubby worked, springing to his defense. He was useful, he was helpful, and we owed him so much for being a handyman when he was also so busy in his job at the hospital. Mother fixed me with a hard stare and asked me the question.

"No idea," I said.

"One dollar," she said. "One measly dollar."

Mother's way of saying it made it even more negligible, a *dawlah*. That was the smallest possible amount allowed by law for conveying the land to him.

Then we all knew, and Hubby was cursed for taking advantage. But if this was the truth, then Mother emerged as being more unreadable than ever.

24

THE COTTAGE

MOTHER WAS STRENGTHENED, because she had kept from us her real motive in handing over a valuable piece of land; the mention of one dollar only made her more enigmatic. Hubby getting the land from this obsessively frugal woman for a buck was much more serious than his getting it for nothing. We dangled a dollar next to an acre and were angry and resentful and confused. It had to be a trick, surely.

If Mother would do that, what might she do next? This extravagant and uncharacteristic deed said: Do not presume. I am capable of anything.

So she had succeeded—there was brilliance in her behavior. She was revealed as mysterious, unfriendly, aloof, disloyal, even to Hubby, who had gotten the land, because of course she had betrayed him. "Ma promised she wouldn't tell anyone," he said, quacking.

In one stroke she had demonstrated her irrationality, her fickleness, and because of this, her power. Because we could not fathom her motive, we were bewildered and weakened, and so she had more power.

Land and power and money were the issues, and yet when I visited Mother after that, and she said, "I've got something special for you," I smiled hopefully.

She kicked and scuffed into the kitchen and fumbled with a tin tray, took up a knife, and began stabbing at something in the tray. Mother with a knife in her hand looked dangerous.

"Hermits," she said. "I baked them especially for you."

In my mind, I set a paper plate of crumbling, knifed-apart hermits next to an acre of land with an ocean view.

Perhaps she guessed I was comparing them, because she said, "I put a whole cup of raisins in them."

Franny stopped by my house a week or so later. When she sat, the sofa spoke, sounds of stressed wood and metal from within it that I'd never heard before. A brown bag rested on the hammock formed by Franny's two flung-apart knees. She untwisted the top of the bag and began to cry.

"Banana bread," she sobbed. "Ma gave it to me!"

Fred, she said, had gotten a carved loon, Rose a pair of knitted mittens, Gilbert a jar of crab-apple jelly, and Floyd, if he got anything at all, did not get much more than this.

"I got some hermits," I said.

Everything Mother made looked like cat food, including the mittens she knitted, so her gifts were all a form of mockery. We had to be grateful, to say how it was just what we wanted, to tuck the thing under one arm and head home, with the thought that Hubby had received eighty thousand dollars' worth of ocean-view acreage that was appreciating at twelve percent a year.

"I forgive her," Franny said. She screwed up one eye in pity. "She's like a little girl." Then she looked squarely at me. "But we should do something."

I said, "What about Floyd. Have you seen him?"

She made a face of shocked indignation.

"I never see him," she said, and when I went on staring, she added, "I think Rose sees him now and then. Bingo and Benno adore him. Apparently he put them in his will."

Whenever I saw them, Franny and Rose complained about Hubby, how he had hoodwinked Mother. And Hubby complained about the land. "It was an unbuildable lot. I had to get a special permit. It failed the perc test. I have to put in a septic system that'll cost me an arm and a leg." He suggested that he had been swindled. The land was just a headache, and here he was the victim of a whisper campaign.

I said, "The others are whispering because you got the land for a dollar."

"I told you the price was fair. I didn't lie."

"A dollar, Hubby."

"Ma said that no one else was interested in it."

"For a dollar?"

"That's what she said."

"I'll give you two dollars for it and you can double your investment."

"You think it's funny."

No, I didn't. I was confused and angry and envious, like everyone else in the family, except Mother, who, far from being hoodwinked, had made her point.

Fred called me to complain. He said, "If Ma had asked me, I would have advised her to sell the land and divide the proceeds seven ways. I can't understand why she didn't ask me."

"Obviously, because she didn't want to."

"It's her land," Gilbert said. "She can do whatever she wants with it."

Gilbert's consistently defending Mother convinced the others that he had been secretly rewarded by her. But that struck me as too straightforward. Something so simple and logical could not have been true. With Mother, only the most complex and irrational transactions were real.

Soon I had proof of this. Franny and Rose went from blaming Hubby to blaming Mother, and Mother herself—when I visited, to be given more crumbly hermits — began mocking Franny and Rose again, all this delivered in the most cordial way.

"Franny was out of breath from just a little mincing walk from her car to the front door. And I had to reglue the chair leg after she sat on it. But I didn't mind her wolfing down four hermits. I was flattered! I do wish Rose would tell me what's on her mind. I ought to consult Angela, who is always a ray of sunshine, bless her soul. Franny and Rose say they want to help me, but heaven knows I'm perfectly capable of helping myself. Frankly, I think the only reason they come over here is because they like a little fresh air, and the ride does them a world of good. I mean, what must it be like to be married to men who just watch TV? Dad was never that way. I think it shows in the children — lazy people have lazy kids. Not that I'm calling anyone lazy. I know they mean well . . ."

Droning on like this, she ran them all down, and after I had listened for an hour or more she had made me an accomplice, if not a co-conspirator, so I could not object. Objecting to such disdain was, paradoxically enough, considered the height of bad manners.

But this talk was a dodge in any case, for a day or two later, Hubby came over to my house crowing that at roughly the time Mother was disparaging Franny and Rose, and blessing Angela's soul, she had signed an entire house over to the two daughters, the cottage on Weathervane Lane. This lovely little place had always been Mother's rental property, a source of income and pride.

"Are you sure she gave it to them?"

Hubby said, "Do bears shit in the woods?"

This was another occasion when I wanted to call my own children and cry, Look what she's doing to me!

So Franny and Rose's obsession with Hubby's land, their mockery of Mother, and Mother's mockery of them had one clear source: they had been given a house. Why did I not see this? I ought to have known much earlier that Hubby's badmouthing Mother meant that he had gotten something substantial from her, and the onset of Franny and Rose's bitchery and envy was a sly, ungrateful way of dealing with their having been given a cottage.

A gift was always an occasion for indirection, and the best form of indirection was complaint. In our family, the most effective way of hiding

generosity was not merely pretending nothing had been given, but asserting that the giver was a skinflint.

Rose said, "Dad always wanted me to have it."

So it was not a present at all, but a piece of property to which she had
long been entitled.

"We're planning to fix it up and rent it," Franny said.

Rose simply stared at this suggestion, though she said, "It needs an
awful lot of work."

"It's a mess," Franny said.

The cottage was in poor shape, so it could not be considered a generous gift. Like Hubby's ocean-view acre that needed a septic system and
permits, it was a burden.

"It's incredible," Fred said. "It's not that they're getting something they
earned. They're taking this away from the rest of us. I thought this cottage
belonged to all of us."

"Ma was really upset," Gilbert told me. He was speaking from Yemen,
but he kept in close touch with Mother. "Floyd went over there and said,
'Hah! You've really done it now. Franny and Rose's husbands are going to
be sleeping in those beds and farting on the sofa. You made it possible for
them to sit on the porch and drink beer. I hope you're proud of yourself.
Two lazy slobs in the house, and they don't even like you!' Can you believe
this?"

I said yes, I could now believe it. For although Mother winced under
Floyd's sarcasm, she had carefully created this situation. We were bewildered and angry again — a whole house had been handed over without
any explanation or justification. Hubby said that he had been stuck with
a piece of land; Franny and Rose said that the cottage was a wreck; Floyd
and Fred were howling with rage. Gilbert was annoyed by the fuss. No
one was satisfied, except Mother, who was delighted.

Mother said, "What's everyone so upset about?" Yet she knew exactly
what the problem was. "I'm glad I have Angela on my side at least."

The dead were always available to offer consolation that the living denied her. Mother wore a martyred look, but of course by means of her
tactical gifts, she had become even more enigmatic and powerful. Mother
at her most dominant was unreadable. The truly powerful are always un-

predictable. You could not second-guess her or calculate what she would do next, and nothing was more of a sign of danger than the smile that floated on her lips these days.

The cottage on Weathervane Lane was a low wooden cedar-shingle structure with the proportions of a cigar box, its lid ajar and slightly raised, which gave its roof a modest slant. A bedroom in each corner allowed it to accommodate enough people to assure its value as a profitable summer rental — eight twin beds and a couple of cots, a tiny kitchen, a porch hammered to the back by Dad in one of his fits of renovation, a rusty grill blowtorched from an oil drum, a picnic table in the yard. It had, early on, been the family's seaside retreat, and each of us had contributed something to its purchase. I had used part of my first book's advance, almost forty years before, to help with the down payment. We all took turns keeping it in shape, painting it, shingling the roof, fixing the fences, planting hydrangeas. The cottage was surrounded by stunted pitch pines and bluish junipers and brambly *Rosa rugosa* — the indestructible plants of the Cape.

In this simple cottage, with its sour stink of damp clothes and the sea — the odors trapped in the house — I had spent some of my happiest days as a young man, a husband, and a father; as a son and a brother. Harry and Julian could have said the same, for it was the scene of many of our summer vacations, the barefoot days of hot sand and picnics on the outside table.

Its weathered boards, peeling paint, threadbare carpets, and faded curtains made it lovable. You had the sense that thousands of people had enjoyed it over the years, and they probably had, because as a rental property — self-supporting, a source of income — it had always been occupied.

Newly married, overeager, and naïve, I had gone there with my first wife, and later with her and the children, wishing to reclaim the happiness of my summer days on the Cape and to give these foreigners, my wife and children, a sense of Cape Cod and America. I rejoiced in their experiencing the seaside warmth that I had known: the sun cooking the thickened odors of tall grass and wildflowers into the air, the dazzling light on the ocean, the breath of summer scented with white oak and pine, and the dustiness and brine of the dunes, on which the wind whipped the long tufts of sword grass so hard they scraped a circle around themselves from the swirl of their blades. The cold water of Cape Cod Bay sloshed and smoothed the stones on the beach into perfect shapes for us to skip them, or to play the stone-tossing game my father had taught me on a Cape beach, Duck on a Rock.

After their early childhood in Africa and Singapore, my own boys found the simplest American pleasures a sunlit fantasy of bliss — not just the lapping waves, the hot days, the lounging on hammocks, and the ease of a Cape summer, but the food, too, lobsters and steamed clams, hamburgers, platters of spaghetti, pitchers of lemonade, ice cream, apple pie, treats from the corner shop — Twinkies and moon pies. The abundance of it all.

At night the sound of crickets calmed us as we sat drinking and joking. Everyone was welcome. These were the family's happiest days, perhaps — only Fred and I were married then. The first year Fred had rented a large house, with his wife and three children, near Weathervane Lane, and we had the cottage. Hubby was still in school, so was Gilbert. Rose was unmarried, Franny had a boyfriend. So they filled up the cottage and yakked on the phone and we all went to South Village Beach and sat in the sunshine and talked and swam. In the evening we had a cookout, a clambake, or a tureen of spaghetti and meatballs.

Our incessant teasing disturbed my English wife. She could not understand Floyd doing imitations of Hubby when his back was turned. Hubby mocked Floyd's girlfriend, and all of us rolled our eyes behind Fred's back for the way he submitted to his wife's nagging — Fred, the eldest, whom we thought of as an authority figure, being bossed by this snobbish woman, Erma, from out of state. My wife said, "It's a bit off. Maybe someday I'll understand." Some evenings Mother and Dad drove over from their house, half a mile away, for a family dinner. When they left, we all laughed at things Mother had said, her catchphrases — "My father was a saint," "I'll bet you dollars to donuts," "Laugh and the world laughs with you — weep, and you weep alone," "Every dog has his day." Or we'd remark on how Father might stare out the cottage window at the sea, a fixed smile of disapproval on his face, and say with some drama, "Nevah!"

Happy days, and happiest that first summer after I had been away so long. On the last day, Mother came alone, I thought to thank me for hosting the extended family for a month at the cottage, or to say how pleased she was to see me on this visit after my years abroad.

But she said, "I've got a bone to pick with you. Next time you come — if you do come next year — could you come after Labor Day?"

I smiled at her because I didn't understand. "The water's cold then," I said. "The kids will be in school."

"Then maybe you should make other arrangements."

"I don't get it," I said, smiling more. I was sad to be leaving the Cape and hated to let go, for the long drive to Boston, then the cramped flight to our life in clammy south London.

"You've been here a whole month," Mother said. And now she was smiling back at me, one of her angry toothy smiles. "We could have rented the cottage for that time. We've lost a lot of money by your staying so long."

I stared at her, still smiling.

"Remember I helped with the down payment for this place?"

Mother smiled back at me, squinting in defiance. She said, "It's high season."

I had not spent a summer vacation at home for years. I had a wife and two small children. Mother and Father had spent time with them on this vacation for the first time. This was my wife's second visit to the United States. She had been reluctant; she had wanted a vacation in France — it was nearer to London, with better weather and better food, and for the English, life was sweet in France. Someone had told her about the Dordogne. She spoke French. But feeling homesick, I had badgered her. I promised good weather and lobsters and hospitality. "The cottage near the ocean," I said. "I'm part owner of it. And my family's looking forward to our coming." They had, they filled the house, they were around most mealtimes. But now they were gone, we were packed, loading our rental car, hovered over by Mother, who was smiling in stern disappointment as she set out the rules for next year's visit.

To get her to stop, and to call her bluff, I said, "I'd be happy to pay you something."

Her smile slipped away. She pressed her hands together and said, "That would be only fair."

"Say a hundred a week? I'll give you four hundred."

Now Mother looked wounded and pitying. "That's half the usual rent."

Seeking sympathy, I said, "That's all the money I have."

A slight puff of air from one of her nostrils, a fugitive murmur, suggested that she didn't believe me. She was of the opinion that people always lied in matters of money, because she did. But I had told her the awful truth.

I wrote her a check, there in the driveway, leaning on the hood of my rental car. Mother folded it and said, "I could have gotten twice this from the Marrottas."

Mother was younger then, and though fleshier she still had the look of a raptor, beaky, with long claws, and a way of standing when she was holding a check that made it seem as if she was protecting a kill. I wasn't her son. I was just a renter.

Though I was mortified and angry, in a small corner of my soul I felt the satisfaction of a saving cynicism, the knowledge that I was seeing Mother at her meanest, drained of all sympathy. It was another family lesson I took into the world, and my satisfaction rose from the sense that I was liberated from all future responsibility. Having treated me badly, she had incurred a debt from me, and I was free to do as I liked. I believed that Mother's meanness was self-defeating, for though she had asked for all she wanted, in her small-mindedness she had not asked for very much. She had lost me for four hundred dollars.

"Your family!" my wife said. "Good God, you swore they wanted to see us."

"That's what they said."

"And you believed them," she said. "The more fool you."

Hearing this, Harry said, "I liked the hermit crabs. The way they crept along with their little shells for houses."

The word "houses" made my wife remember. She said, "You told me you owned a share in that cottage."

No one had remembered my contribution to the down payment. That was another hurt that freed me. I vowed never to stay in the cottage again. We probably would not have been welcome in any case. The high-season rent was now up to one thousand a month.

Good times came, successful books, large advances, in dollars I could bank in the States. When I had the money, a few years after that first visit, I bought a house about twenty miles away, on the upper Cape, and this became our summer destination. In the months that we were there it was filled with my family, Mother and Dad too, who enjoyed our hospitality and especially the fact that we weren't in the cottage. Strangers rented it, and Mother pocketed the money. When it needed to be painted we all pitched in. We fixed the roof, we cleaned the gutters, we planted more trees, we put flowers in the window boxes, Hubby rewired it, and when we were helping in this way Mother reminded us that the cottage belonged to us all; it was part of the family legacy, to be shared. Even in the real estate boom of the '80s, when it could have been sold for an enormous profit, Mother said, "Dad won't part with it," though it was clear that she was holding on to it as a rental.

This was the cottage that, one day, Mother gave to Franny and Rose. Further proof that they had gotten the house was that these close, intimately involved sisters began to quarrel with each other. They went on criticizing Mother, and they appealed to the rest of us to take sides.

So Mother had succeeded in creating a family feud that put her in the middle, a guarantee that she would be paramount. Others joined the fray, for the issue was not between Franny and Rose but their husbands — whom we never saw — each one disputing the other's right to use the house. Months of this, another sideshow, which we regarded the way sweaty ragged people in jungle clearings watch a cockfight and cheer the feathered shrieks and the frantic pecking, the blood, the struggle, as Mother looked on, with the sort of indefinable half-smile that I had seen in only one other place, floating across the lips of the monumental heads of gods and kings at Angkor Wat, representing defiance one moment, sadness the next, then sadism, contempt, pity, power — everything but pleasure.

25

STRUGGLES

IN OUR STRUGGLES and our ill-humored teasing we were unlike any other family I knew. Contention thumped in our blood — no
peace, no victory; ours was a war of minor skirmishes, a rising tide of
rancor. Yet Mother was the first to deplore, or solemnly pity, the families
that broke apart, the messy divorces, the whimpering runaways, the es-
tranged children, the families that didn't go to church, or the ones that sat
in different pews, the split-ups, the broken homes.

"Say a little prayer for them," Mother would say. Or: "Imagine a mother
leaving her children like that." "God help them," she'd remark of the family
with an adulterous father or a delinquent child. "You're so lucky," she said
to us. "Count your blessings."

Locked in battle, we were kept together. We were enmeshed in perpetual contention. What seemed a truce at the hectic dinner table, among
the few of us who were still on speaking terms, was false and forced, the
pretense purely for Mother's sake, to prove she was benign. She beamed at
the thought of presiding over this meal attended by some of her children,
but never all of them at once. They might be Fred and Gilbert, or Hubby
and me, or the girls — but probably not the girls these days, because they
were trying to conceal the fact that they had been given a whole house.
Floyd kept to himself, though everyone but me saw him.

I raged against him, against the family, and now and then I would
shout and slam down the phone with such force I felt blinded by my anger. And the day after one of these tantrums I would feel the nausea and
self-disgust, from my bad night and my fury, which, like a hangover, but
worse, left me raw.

Floyd's vicious profile of me, which interviewers still used to challenge me, was a reminder that I had to be careful what I wrote and said
— or shouted at the others. Floyd had made a fool of himself in having
published his abuse, yet his gibes about "his illegitimate son" still stung.

That lost boy was my shameful secret. I had abandoned him, and I was so appalled by what I had done, I had not disclosed his existence to my ex-wives or my children. They found out the secret in the worst way, but a way that was characteristic of my family's whispers. Fred, who of course knew, had told his wife, and she had told her three children, to belittle me. Two of Fred's kids were the same age as Julian and Harry, and one day, Jake, the bigger of the two, had said, "You got a brother somewhere. Your dad gave him away when he was little. The whole thing's a secret."

My boys came to me indignant, angry that they had been insulted by a wicked lie. They were eight and ten. And they listened, breathing hard in a sorrowful silence, while I told them the truth. And after they knew, they looked — not older but sadder, bent over and burdened. They never lost the sense that I had deceived them by keeping the secret from them until their ten-year-old cousin had revealed it. They struggled to contain their disappointment, and yet they knew they had been betrayed, that I had another family somewhere, a shadow wife, an older ghost-child, a cluttered wayward past. And here I was, a taskmaster, expecting them to be perfect.

Was it any wonder I never confided in Mother, or in any of them, ever again?

"It wasn't me," Fred said. "Erma did it. I don't know why."

I knew why. Revealed secrets and teasing, mimicry and gibes, gifts to some but not to others, a bizarre system of rewards and punishments, the low level of quarreling that was a dueling drone that never let up. You always knew that as soon as you left the room you were gloatingly mocked for what you had just said, or what you were wearing, or for your children's failings, or your spouse's idle remark. And if you had given Mother a present, the present was jeered at, because it was never enough, and Mother herself might initiate the jeering by rolling her eyes or using her ambiguous smile while weighing the thing in her skinny hands.

Yet it all appeared normal to me. This battling seemed somehow truer, more real, than the submissive happiness of the other families I knew. I never quite accepted their contentment: they had to be hiding something. I was certain of this as an adult, but even as a child I did not believe and did not trust the platitudes of the happy family. There was no such thing.

Most families (I thought) were probably as hateful as ours, but the difference was that we admitted it and they didn't. I was glad I knew the depth of disloyalty in our family, the capacity we had to mock one another, how this knowledge liberated me and strengthened me in my cynicism. Otherwise, I would have felt defenseless. But as I write this, I realize I am deluding myself, because despite knowing how disloyal we were, I was continually surprised by the greater and greater betrayals. Even the deepest cynicism does not prepare you for the worst that a family can do to you.

I visited Mother for news.

"Oh, God," she said. "You don't want to know."

Her putting it in this tantalizing way convinced me that I did want to know.

"Franny and Rose, at each other's throats."

Mother was almost jubilant. Her gift of the cottage had created envy, anger, and resentment among us, and serious conflict between Franny and Rose. The gift was a kind of thunderbolt, splitting us up, scattering us. Mother was at the center of it, at peace, surveying the dissension, its only true beneficiary.

"I've written them a letter," Mother said. "It's very brief, just two words. 'Make peace.'"

Any fool knew that two families, and especially Franny's and Rose's, would never be able to share one house. You could not contemplate such a letter, such an order, without seeing that it would only make these daughters angrier.

She reached to the table beside her throne and passed me the letter, the two words in block capitals in the center, and under them, *Love, Mother.*

At a loss for something to say about such an insincere and provocative message, I said, "You have lovely handwriting, Ma."

"I was first in my penmanship class at Lowell Normal," Mother said. "Mr. Stoner singled me out. He asked me to stand up. He praised my cursive. Palmer method. And he mentioned how I had joined the college in the second semester. I had missed months of work, but I caught up by working my fingers to the bone."

The penmanship story I had heard before, but her late arrival was news.

"How come you missed the first semester? Were you sick?"

"Oh, no. I was working."

"Working where?"

"Gilchrist's."

"When was this?"

"After I graduated from high school."

Gilchrist's was a department store on Main Street in Medford, where Mother had been raised and had gone to high school. I tried not to show my shock.

"What sort of work at Gilchrist's?"

"Ladies' department. Foundation garments," Mother said. "Corsets. Girdles. Bras."

"Selling them?"

"That was my counter, yes."

I said, "But you had just graduated from high school. You were a good student. Why didn't you go to college?"

"I did, but not then."

"How did it happen that you went to college?"

Even asking the question, I saw Mother amid a big pile of pink satin bloomers.

"I was going home one October day and saw one of my friends. She was just leaving the train station. She was at the college, she said. She commuted to Lowell. I hadn't seen her since graduation. She told me a little bit about it. 'You should apply,' she said. So I did. But I couldn't start until the second semester."

"Your friend told you, I get it. But what I don't understand is why your family didn't encourage you to go to college."

Mother became a small bewildered girl, looking lost, compressing her lips and slightly bowing her head, so that her neck looked skinny and frail, wisps of hair trailing onto it, her hands clasped.

"I don't know."

"They sent you out to work?"

"They didn't send me. I really didn't know what to do. A job is a good thing."

"But this friend of yours encouraged you to go to college."

"Agnes Doherty," Mother said.

"Why didn't you ask your family about going to college?"

"I didn't want to cause trouble," she said. "And they didn't know any better."

All the stories I had heard before this were about her nurturing family, her saintly father, her loyal mother, her well-educated brothers. This was the first I had heard that she, the only daughter, had been sent into the world to find her own way, to sell women's underwear at Gilchrist's. It hinted at turbulence in her family, and neglect or indifference. She had been rescued from the girdle department by a pitying school friend. In that accidental way she had received an education and gotten a teaching job worthy of her intelligence. I had not known this. It saddened me to think of Mother, after her high school graduation, toiling in a department store.

"I caught up on every bit of the work. Mr. Stoner praised me. He asked me to stand up."

This was a struggle parable too. Mother turned the story of her family's indifference into a story of overcoming the odds, studying late at night, hitting the books, improving her penmanship — a moral tale of hard work rewarded.

How little I knew of Mother's past. But that was her habit of concealment, because she wanted us to believe in her virtue, the articles of her faith, the holiness of her family, all the fictional details that gave her authority and strengthened her. In every sense, Mother was self-made. That seemed to me a characteristic of tyrants, and being her own creation was enigmatic, if not unknowable.

Pedestrian facts of the private lives of tyrants diminish them, or so they think. The striving is epic and a little vague. They need to be glorified, they require an element of mystery. Like Mother they come from nowhere and are subjected to a series of ordeals. There is always an official version of the struggle. I had heard of Mother's early poverty, her helping her father in his work, being laughed at by other students for her old-fashioned clothes. She never went on dates. She excelled in school, saved money, adored her parents. But the details of her late application to college contradicted the official version.

Mother's early life had been random. Her family had obviously taken little notice of her. She graduated from high school in May and had begun to work as a salesgirl. Months later, in October, she was still laying out girdles and tapping the cash register. The notion of going to college did not occur to her until one of her friends bumped into her and, seeing the absurdity of this intelligent woman wasting her life in a department store, suggested she go to college. Mother's family had been passive the whole time.

"What did your parents say when you told them you were going to college?"

"They were very proud of me. They knew the importance of a good education."

A lie, of course — the received version. But what lingered in my mind was Mother's acceptance, and her own passivity. Her brothers had gone to college, but she had not believed she was good enough for a college education until her friend told her.

I was fascinated by how casual Mother's education had come about, for later she defined herself as an educator, the mother as teacher. But it had all happened as a result of a chance meeting.

Usually when I visited Mother I felt worse afterward — smaller, weaker, unworthy, defeated, resentful, trifled with, and sometimes I wished I were dead. Not today. With this glimpse of the past I felt sorry for Mother. And so I decided to stay a little longer.

"What were you going to tell me about Franny and Rose?"

"I guess the fur is flying," Mother said. She pursed her lips and swallowed in pleasure, as though she'd downed a gulp of something delicious.

"Is it the cottage?"

Mother smiled and swallowed again. She said, "All I wanted was for them to be happy."

She explained that the fuss had begun with her handing over the key. Who would get the one key? There was an argument about having duplicate keys cut. "But why does Walter need one if you have one?" Franny had said. "Walter is my husband," Rose replied. That seemed ominous in the way superfluous statements often did.

Walter was a plodding and unforthcoming person, pleasant enough, but with the trembling lip and cold stare of a godly man resisting the pull of evil. His jutting jaw and bony chin and empty, deep-set eyes gave him the beaten look of someone searching for a fellow sufferer.

And soon Franny found a fellow teacher to rent the cottage for the whole month of July at the high-season rate. Rose had equivocated, and when Franny chased her for a reply — this was in late April, when summer plans had to be made — Walter called Franny.

"We decided not to go with renting. Renters will just trash the place."

"These are very dear friends of mine. They'd respect the cottage," Franny said, and getting no response, she added, "Plus, I promised them."

"Sorry," Walter said.

The toneless way he said it frightened Franny. She wanted to reply — as she said to Mother — "Don't I have a say in this?" But she said, "Okay," and tried to think how she might break the news to her friends.

Mother said to me, "I'm keeping out of it," but she could barely hide her pleasure.

We decided not to go with renting!

Franny was humiliated and cast down. Any hope that the cottage would be an earner was dashed, and not by Rose — whom Franny now saw in a new light, wondering, Who is she? — but by Walter, a son-in-law whom Mother disliked. Walter never showed up. He didn't send presents or birthday cards. He could have offered to fix the screens or mow the lawn, but never did. The oddest aspect of Walter, perhaps his triumph, was that he seemed in his selfishness and his silence more passive aggressive than any of us.

"We could have rented it the whole summer," Franny wailed to Mother.

"I don't want to get involved," Mother told Fred, who said Walter was being unreasonable — and what sort of joint-ownership agreement did they have? Gilbert assured Mother that there was worse to come. Hubby satirized them for the crisis they had created. Floyd berated Mother for handing over the cottage in the first place. According to Fred, Floyd had screamed, "It's our legacy."

Gilbert was right. A greater struggle started.

For a month they took turns using the cottage, Rose and her family for a week or so, then Franny and her family. At the end of the month, Franny called Rose to say that Jonty and his wife Loris wanted to use it for a few weeks.

Rose said, "I'll have to ask Walter if that's okay."

Franny was made to wait for three days while the request was discussed. In the end the answer was no, Jonty's family visit would not be convenient. The cottage interior was being painted.

Franny said to Rose, "I don't understand why it's being painted. It's just a rental."

Rose said, "You can't put a new carpet in a house until it's been painted or you risk getting drips and stains on the new carpet."

"What new carpet?"

"Walter wants a berber for the lounge."

"Is this berber one of the renters?"

To Franny, Mother said, "It's a sensible idea to take good care of the place. Think of it as an asset."

Rose had complained to Mother about Franny's not wanting to renovate the cottage. But "lounge"? It had never had a lounge before.

Franny said to Mother, "I just got a bill for the new carpet and the paint job. More than twelve hundred dollars! We could have made more than that by renting it. I don't even like the carpet. What's a berber? Marvin's a wreck."

No one in the family was interested in Franny's tale of woe. The cottage had been given to her for nothing, after all.

"Walter wanted a new icebox," Mother said. She retained these old turns of speech — icebox for fridge, piazza for porch, tonic for soda, scrod for fish, dinner for lunch. "An Amana. Nothing but the best for him. He didn't discuss it first. Just went out and bought it."

And Walter sent Franny her share of the bill. He did the same with a new microwave and a toaster — bought expensive ones and sent Franny the bills. And a new vacuum cleaner for the new carpet.

"What did Rose say?" I asked Mother.

"That Franny doesn't appreciate all the work that Walter's doing to upgrade the cottage."

As a tactic to make Franny submit, it was ingenious. I could see from far off what Rose and Walter had planned. They wanted the cottage for themselves, that was obvious — Rose repeated, "Dad always wanted me to have the cottage" — but how to dislodge Franny and Marvin as joint owners? The answer was to make ownership so expensive and burdensome that Franny would beg to have her name removed from the deed.

New plumbing, new lights, a paved driveway, and what Rose called "plantings." Franny was upset, but what could she do?

Mother told me all this in a sorrowful tone, but I knew by that very tone that she was delighted. She regarded it as a victory that she had, by a calculated act of generosity, managed to divide her daughters and set their husbands against one another. Had there been harmony, Mother would have felt threatened. Had they been close and conciliatory, Mother would have imagined them whispering against her, staying away, perhaps conspiring. Disunity among Mother's children strengthened her grip.

Before Mother handed over the cottage, Franny and Rose had begun to visit her in the same car. This was too cozy, providing too many opportunities to whisper and compare. Mother wanted them in separate cars.

What seemed like Mother's dark policy, something worked out by a plotting queen, was an instinctive response made up of her natural deviousness. She proved to me that tyrants were not shaped by dogma or scholarship or carefully laid plans, but by circumstantial and nervous improvisation at crises and the impulses of their weak and anxious hearts.

"What would you have done?" Mother asked me.

I said, "I would have sold the cottage and divided the money seven ways and, by being scrupulously fair, would have made seven children happy."

She began to laugh in a mocking way, and I expected her to jeer at me, saying, "Stop making sense," but she stopped laughing and said, "I hate it when my children don't get along."

I said, "I guess Franny will be forced to give her share to Rose."

"Do you really think so?"

Mother was wide-eyed, her big bland blameless face disbelieving what seemed obvious to me. But of course she knew, she was prepared for it, had perhaps hoped for it from the start.

And that was what happened. It had already taken place some days before, and Mother still said she knew nothing about it. Pretending she was in the dark was Mother's way of angling for more.

Franny said to me, "Let Rose and Walter have the cottage. They're welcome to it."

This sounded generous, but it was just a way of concealing what really happened. Soon afterward, Mother put Franny's name on the deed to her own house, the family house, site of her throne and her knitting and her shelf of hand-carved birds. She claimed she'd done it out of pity for Franny, but all of us knew that her intention was to foment conflict.

This seemed to be how it always worked in the family. A gift by Mother to any of us produced one ungrateful child and six malcontents.

26

REMINDERS

IN LATE MIDDLE AGE, living at the ragged edges of all this family strife, I was continually reminded why I had left home as a youth. I was reminded of much else besides. Father's death had drawn me back, and in the shadow of his passing, and Mother's ascendancy, my career had faltered. I had lingered too long, and in that hesitation I was caught, even as I knew it was a mistake to stay.

Travel had always been my salvation, though perhaps I was less a traveler than a refugee. I set off in the same spirit that another person might have felt burrowing into the bedclothes and hugging himself into a ball. I needed the physical relief of going into the wider world, to lose myself, in every respect to vanish without a trace.

Leaving home, as I saw it, was also a hostile act. I am outta here, I thought. On every trip I took, no matter how attractive the destination, my fundamental motivation was to turn my back on home, travel as refutation. Everywhere I went I found strangers kinder and more civilized than my family.

I was still traveling from my rented house on the Cape, still seeking relief from the family. I had just returned from Uganda, where I had been gathering material for the sort of magazine article I was asked for these days. But I had been on other trips, some for months, choosing a lengthy but specific itinerary. The previous year, during the handing out of Mother's properties, I'd traveled the shores of the Mediterranean, and on my return, I'd written a book about it, and repaid most of my debts.

In the week before I'd left for Uganda, Gilbert had visited. He had called me from the airport: Would I pick him up? I did so gladly, because as the youngest, and unmarried, he was the most rational sibling. I relished the hour-and-a-half drive from Boston, going slowly in the rain, hearing about his recent post as a political officer in Yemen — his trips to Mocha, to Rimbaud's house in Aden, the rhino horn handles of tribal daggers being hawked in the bazaar, the disaffected fanatics of the cities, the sententious mullahs, the culture of khat chewers and stewed coffee husks.

He was still talking as we arrived at Mother's. She was waiting at the door, looking out, and from the end of the driveway I could see her eager eyes, enlarged by her glasses.

"Gil-bert," she cried, singing his two-note name, embracing him, wrapping her skinny arms around him, clutching his neck, leading him inside. "Are you hungry? I made some fish chowder, your favorite. What about some juice. How about a nice piece of fruit."

I was still standing on the walkway in the rain.

"I'll be going," I said.

"Bye." I could not tell which one had spoken.

A few days later, Fred visited. He had something to tell me, he said. It seemed that Floyd had wanted to see Gilbert, so Fred had not invited me to the family reunion at his house, and his message to me was, "It wasn't much. I didn't think you'd want to come."

Franny stopped by to complain about this party to which I had not been invited. "I'm eating some mashed potatoes," she said, the historical present being her usual tense for such stories, "and Floyd makes a face at me and screams, 'That's death on a fork!' Fred's kids are uncontrollable. Somehow they managed to leave footprints on the walls. I feel so sorry for them. They have no boundaries. Hubby's getting awful heavy. But I'm glad Rose is happy with her house. It's kind of funny. She keeps saying how Dad wanted her to have it, but what about Walter, who never does anything for Ma and who now has a house? Good — they can choke on it. I don't think Ma had a very good time at the party. I could see that she wanted to be alone with Gilbert."

"So I guess I didn't miss much," I said, waiting for her reaction.

"You were lucky you didn't go," Franny said. "I don't even want to think about Ma's birthday."

She gave me a Tupperware tray of Swedish meatballs, a box of peppermint patties, a jar of Marshmallow Fluff, two brownies, and a half-gallon of Coke. Treats for her she thought would be a treat for me.

After such events as the party to which I was not invited, I traveled happily. Distant travel was my way of asserting that I had no family, that I recognized no obligations, that I wanted to be out of touch. Travel can serve as the unambiguous gesture of giving the finger to people you've left at home — it was in my case. Homesickness was an ailment I never suffered. Travel for me, as I had written, was flight and pursuit in equal parts. When I was away from them, I forgot them and their malice. In a new place, among strangers, I was who I wanted to be: a solitary soul on the move.

I told myself that in travel I was looking for material, in search of new experiences. In retrospect, I realized that I was looking for innocence — a simpler world, perhaps the contented childhood I'd been denied through overcrowding. And I often succeeded in this. I was nearly always helped on my way, lucky in the people I met. I put up with nuisances, and sometimes endured hardships, but I never came to any serious harm.

Large friendly families still existed in these remote places: extended families in Africa, in rural India, in South America, and on Pacific islands. The one-child family of China was just weird: two harassed parents and a brat in a vertiginous tenement room. But I never saw — in the rain forest, the jungle, the savanna, the obscure river systems of the bush, or the deserts of the outback — any group of people as tangled, as rancorous, as my own family. I marveled at the serenity of these coherent clans. This discovery encouraged my wider travel and the realization that I would have been a traveler even if I had never been a writer: going for the fresh air, the freedom of the open road, to remind myself that my family was not the world.

I wrote about these trips. The books must speak for themselves. I can make no claim except to say that they stand as an accurate record of what happened to me every day — all the things I said and did, everything I saw and heard — for the duration of the journey. Five or six months' experience, sometimes a year or more, between covers. This was the reason my trip did not in the least resemble anyone else's trip, a cause for annoyance among some critics.

Fiction was something else for me, a conviction, a passion, and it worried me a little when I looked closely at what I created, for though I was depicting aspects of my life or my fantasies in my novels and stories, I was not providing any context. Rather than write about big families, I took the ambiguity of distant places as my subject. I wrote about restless and discontented men much like myself, but these men were nearly always solitary. And here I was, a member of a savage tribe that practiced endocannibalism, feeding on ourselves. I wanted to write about my family, but I didn't dare to, couldn't bear to, didn't know how.

Moving back home, into a family atmosphere of death and greed and failure, had clarified my position by reacquainting me with rancor, but it also created problems. This homecoming was an extreme mode of travel, my first experience, as a traveler, of severe hardship, corrosive solitude, danger, risk, frustration, and harassment—worse than anything I had ever known on the road. My life of travel, long and difficult though it had been, had not prepared me for any of it, but all of it was a reminder of my earlier life, my childhood, the torn and flapping narrative of my family.

So, again, I fled. It was always a joy to flee Mother Land. The relief of it made even the worst places bearable. In the average hellhole I smiled, reflecting: It could be worse, I could be home! I was a patient and grateful alien. I chose itineraries that offered the most vivid encounters, and I watched closely, confronting these new surroundings, noting my reactions and impressions, thinking: I am recording what this place is like in this particular moment—I alone am seeing it now in this strange and seismic way, and because I am an unsparing witness, perhaps what I write will have value in times to come, as part of a historical record. But at the very least I have provided myself with some diversion and have succeeded in being away from home. I have been happy.

Yet always I had to return home. Home might be grim, a struggle, the everlastingness of Mother, but I had nowhere else to go.

On that return from Uganda, in the stack of accumulated mail—unpaid bills, threats to cut off the electricity, stern reminders from the landlord about trivialities, the odd poignant letter from a reader, junk mail and circulars — in that unsorted pile was a letter I had been dreading almost my whole life.

The letters we fear most are the ones we hold in our hands unopened, the flap glued shut; letters that we can recite by heart before we've taken a knife to the envelope; the ones we've been blindly mumbling the words of for years, verbatim, with the prescient anxiety of anticipation.

This was one. I saw *Mona* in the name on the return address. I did not know the surname, but I knew it was she, and that she had unwelcome news, because for years I had rehearsed this moment in my head. True fear is not unexpected; it is the occurrence of something painful one has imagined in every particular. And then it happens, and it is just as awful as one had guessed. What other reason would Mona have had for writing me? After that terrible year that I called the best year of my life, for the way it had prepared me, steeling me for the horrors to come, Mona and I had hardly spoken — the obvious subject was too awful for talk. It was the stuff of nightmares. We weren't friends, we were unhappy memories. I had not received a letter from her for almost forty years. And so, with a trembling hand, I used the knife on it.

Guess what?

But I had already guessed. The letter fluttered in my hand.

I found our son! It was the most amazing thing — I can barely write I'm so excited —

My heart sank. I had foreseen all those words, and what was coming next, painful reminders of what I already knew.

My mind raced ahead of the letter. I looked up and saw it all, not in consecutive words but a jumping montage of fearsome images. The boy had been raised in a small house, not the big ramshackle houses I had lived in, but a mean narrow place where he knew he did not belong, a house that was always both confining him and pressing him to the door. He was bursting with anger. He blamed me for rejecting him; he hated me; he wanted something from me that I could never give him — his childhood back. For years he had lived with this fury, helpless because he was a stranger and I was unknown to him. We were lost to each other, and a good thing, too: we would never know the extent of each other's misery. The danger was that he might one day discover that I existed, and where

I lived. Until then, there was no one on whom he could honestly vent his rage. I was to blame; but where was I?

All this I saw in torn, scrambled dismemberment — faces, hands, blowing clothes, vague shapes. Yet he was real and pink — he was flesh, he had a name. In my self-lacerating imagery he was busy, manic, as vengeful people usually seem; his adoptive parents were pale-faced, small, unlike him; perhaps he had siblings like stick figures, in that flimsy house like a cardboard box you could kick apart.

But that was what I imagined; it was not what the letter said. It was what I saw, with the paranoia of a haunted man. I sat down and summoned the strength to read the letter.

27

THE LETTER

IT WAS NOTEPAPER, a thickness of it, folded in half and crammed into the envelope. I smoothed the many small sheets. I could see Mona's face, her lips, her fingers, in her impatient handwriting; the loops and shapes of her words, all the reminders of how she looked in the way her ballpoint pen pressed into the paper, deforming it like Braille, the sloping script I associated with the mournfulness and desperation of forty years before. So much was revealed in the ink. People these days seldom went to the trouble of writing a letter on light squares of pinched-over notepaper, but it helped me remember, and all the scribbles scared me.

The peculiar slant of her writing was like the anxious tone of voice that I easily recalled, and her untidiness showed in the hurried and jumbled way it was formed. Everything was revealed in her handwriting — her fear, her pleas, her knotted clothes at the foot of her unmade bed, the blond wisps of hair beside her face. Yes, still blond — she had not aged in this familiar penmanship. I had to remind myself that she was older than me.

Nothing seemed to be going right in my life. My daughter was getting married. I somehow needed to know for sure if our son could be found. I was prepared to fail but I figured why not give it a shot? So I did. I did a little homework. I found that both sides have to approve — the birth parent and the child. I would not be able to find him if he wasn't willing. Luckily he put his name forward. He had signed the Search Form because his sister (also adopted) wanted to find her birth parents and he was kind of encouraging her. There was a lot of paperwork but believe me it was worth it. As soon as I started my search his name came right up and we were put in touch.

I called him up and we talked for over an hour. We've talked a few times since then. He's a great kid! He's married with a little boy (2). I think the birth of his son was one of the reasons for his getting interested in who his birth parents were, plus his sister's plan. He's real smart. He reads. He's got a successful business. He's happily married — and he had a wonderful upbringing, way beyond anything we could have done for him. I'm hoping to meet him soon. I knew you'd be excited and I wanted you to have this incredible news.

At first glance, an amazing letter. On further examination, it was full of gaps and hurried simplifications and a kind of breathlessness that left me with questions. There was only her name at the bottom — Mona — no explanation of her married name or her circumstances. She had a daughter? The return address in New Hampshire sounded rural, flinty, strewn with pine needles. I saw a long, rutted driveway and smoke rising from the chimney of a wood-frame house on a back road, tire tracks through a meadow, the house dwarfed by trees, a lawn that needed mowing. Through the window (dusty ivy trailing from a pot) I saw the trestle table where she'd written the letter, a pile of bills, an address book, a telephone, some pencils, a yellow-eyed lamp.

I wanted to weep. This letter was my first experience of the words "birth parents." Of all the stones to turn over, this one was the biggest, the mossiest, hiding the most sorrow. Finding our son was one thing, but what came next? And consider what I didn't know: Where was he? What were his circumstances? What was his mood? What did he know of me?

He hated me, I was sure of that. And, by the way, what had Mona told him of me? Nothing of this was in the letter. Detail was lacking. Where did he live? What was his business? The writer in me was irked by this hasty letter. The father in me was apprehensive.

Using her married name and the town on the envelope, I called information, got Mona's number, and called it.

The voice I heard, answering, seemed to be backing away in suspicion. "Mona?"

"Yes" — though the word was uncertain.

"It's Jay."

She said, "This isn't a good time."

Her prompt, adenoidal voice had an intimidated tone. I guessed that someone was listening.

"It's nice to hear your voice after all these years," I said, to test her.

"Me too," she said, failing the test. The correct reply would have been, Nice to hear your voice too. A disapproving man was scowling at her in the drafty New Hampshire kitchen, which smelled of stew and brown bread and kerosene.

"I guess you know why I'm calling."

She said, "I'm sorry, I really can't talk," and hung up before I could leave her with another thought.

So I was stuck holding the leaves of notepaper, knowing something but not knowing enough, left with questions. I reread the letter and thought of more questions.

I let two days pass. I had recently returned from a long African trip and had a travel piece to write. In this time I reflected on what had happened, the almost unthinkable emergence of our lost, handed-over son, whose name I did not know, about whom I knew nothing but his age, which had to be forty-one. This was maddening. In her impulsive way, Mona had told me just enough to worry me, not enough to give me any hope or peace, and yet she was excited.

What I imagined was a big angry man shaking his finger at me, demanding — what? Compensation for having been abandoned?

In my misery and apprehension I remembered the anxious year long ago when I'd had to hide Mona and our error from our families; the shame I'd felt; and after we'd endured months of seclusion, the spell in Puerto Rico, my job at the restaurant, the sense of being despised and poor and in the wrong, what I still felt had been the defining year of my life, how arriving home that September day, Mother had said, "I hope you're proud of yourself." And after a sullen pause, her fists on the kitchen table like two tormenting weapons, "You should be ashamed," and "How could you do this to us?"

I could not tell her then, or later, that I had been proud, that I'd seen Mona through it all. I'd only been ashamed that we'd been found out, after we'd succeeded in solving the problem, when there was only blame left to apportion. And years later I could see Floyd sitting in the kitchen on that hot day with Mother, making a face at me that said, *Oh, boy, you're in for it.*

I had called Mona that first time on a Saturday afternoon. She had not been alone. I guessed afterward that her working husband was home. I let Sunday and Monday pass — and I remembered everything. I called again on Tuesday. This time her voice was guarded, but when I greeted her she brightened.

I said, "Are you alone?"

"Yes. Jay, I'm so glad you called back."

"I almost didn't."

"It's a little complicated here at the moment," she said, and that might have meant anything.

Just then there was a knock at my front door. I looked out and saw the big bearish form of Hubby, in green scrubs, waving his arms, indicating that the door was locked and gesturing for me to open it, though it was plain for him to see that I was on the telephone. He made a clownish face, poking his scummy tongue at me.

"Mona, someone's at the door. I'll have to call you later."

"Please, don't," she said. "Give me your number. I'll call you from school."

So we were still hiding, sneaking, concealing, whispering, after almost forty years, living in the narrow corners and shadows of other people's lives. She was hiding from — whom? Probably her husband. I was hiding from Hubby, and everyone else, with this news. I gave her my number and hung up and answered the door.

"What are you doing, dipshit?" Hubby asked. "Who are you talking to?"

"No one," I said.

"Sure." He was annoyed at my evasion. He had the wounded gruffness of someone who suspects he's being whispered about, who knows he will never find out what people are saying. This perpetual suspicion in Hubby made him more of a whisperer. "Like there was no one on the phone."

In Hubby's mind — I knew this, because I knew my family — I was probably on the phone with Fred or Gilbert, and I was disparaging Hubby for his size, or his wearing scrubs under his wool jacket, or his bamboozling Mother out of the Acre. These were the topics that loomed in his mind. It would never have occurred to him that I was talking to the mother of my long-ago abandoned son, about the boy's reappearance. This was family history so old and so shameful it was buried, along with the worst failures we had endured — the liquidation of Dad's company, Dad's year of unemployment, the Christmas we got no presents, our divorces.

"No one important."

I hated his forcing me to say this, and my resentment rekindled the memory of no one helping me or Mona, of the sorry episode being a succession of intrusions, crowned with blame.

"So what's new?"

"Nothing."

He was fishing. He wanted to chat. Something was afoot or else he would not have been so circumspect. He glanced at the phone, perhaps hoping it would ring, so that he would catch me in a lie.

Using his thumb and forefinger, he plucked a burdock ball from the wool of his sleeve. He held it up, squinted at it, then neatly dropped it onto the side table beside the phone, where it lay like a withered shuttlecock.

"Don't say I never gave you nothing."

The backhanded expression was like a family greeting, always said of off-loaded trivia.

"Got anything to drink?"

"Just water. I've been away." He stared at me with the merest suggestion of a smile. I said, "In Turkana Land, Lodwar to be specific. I haven't had time to do any shopping."

I was fascinated by how he put me on the defensive, and at the same time resented it.

"Okay, water."

"In the kitchen."

I followed him in.

"What would you like to know about Lodwar, or the Turkana?"

"Nothing," he said. "Hear about Weathervane Lane? Rose's got the cottage all to herself. She and Walter fixed it up. Berber carpet. Any idea what that stuff costs? It's got to be a couple of hundred a square foot." He put his hands on his hips. "So where are the glasses?"

I took a tumbler from the cupboard and handed it to him.

"Which one is the cold water?" he asked, balking at the three faucets, as though I was trapping him.

Irritated, I turned one on. He filled his glass, but didn't drink. He made a ceremony of holding the glass in front of him and walking back to the living room. His tramping around reminded me of how much I hated this rented house. Hubby's size-eleven crepe-soled hospital shoes made the floor shudder and house feel small and temporary.

"There's nowhere to sit!"

I had sat down. There were books and papers on two of the other chairs.

"You can put those books on the floor."

He sighed and made a business of placing the glass on a bookshelf, then clearing the books from the chair. This was Hubby's way of telling me that I was inconveniencing him, which put me on the defensive again. It was, most of all, Mother's manner of making you wrong. Whenever a sibling was with me, Mother was also in the room.

He winced as he sat down — Mother's wince — and squirmed in his seat, thrashing a little, and said, "Ever heard of cushions?"

Now I just stared, to remind him that he had gone too far.

"What's that supposed to be?"

Mona's letter lay on the table next to the phone and the dried burdock pod.

"Nothing."

"Looks like a note. Do people still write notes?"

"Ma does."

"That's not Ma's handwriting. Ma has beautiful handwriting, as you know. That's a hasty scrawl."

He was watchful in the way suspicious and needy people are watchful, something animal, too, in his noticing, so alert, so skilled at crowding me. Yet, like an overfed pet, he was merely instinctive, not witty. His reactions rose from greed, hunger, habit, anxiety.

"So what do you think?"

"About what?"

My mind was on Mona's letter, our resurrected child.

"Rose and the cottage."

"She can have it," I said. "Franny's probably apeshit."

"Not what I heard."

"What did you hear?"

He sipped the water and peered at me over the rim of the glass.

"Ma took care of her."

"Put her name on the house. So I heard."

"*Gave* her the friggin' house, more like it."

"So what?"

"So what about us?"

As we both knew, he had been given an acre of prime land by Mother, for a dollar.

"Are you complaining, Hubby?"

"No, and you know why? Because Ma can't give Marvin anything to cure his ulcers. We get ulcer people in the ER some nights, wailing. Bleeding ulcers. That's what Floyd needs." He gave me a sly, moist grin and said, "I was at Floyd's the other day. I walk into his yard. He's on the porch. He starts yelling at me, 'Apologize or leave! Apologize or leave!'"

"Apologize for what?"

"Beats the hell out of me. He's a whack job."

"I have not spoken to Floyd for almost four years."

"He's nuts — he's worse than Franny and Rose. Are you mad about something?"

"No. Why do you ask?"

"You look pissed off."

Another family rejoinder: the angry ones among us accused the others of anger. Mother, when she was harassed, would say crossly, "Stop sulking or I'll give you something to sulk about."

"Just busy."

"What, that phone call?"

He knew he had interrupted me, knew that I'd hung up quickly, guessed that it was important, perhaps linked to the sheets of notepaper by the phone. He wasn't Sherlock, but he was cunning.

"I've just gotten back from Kenya."

"Tarzan of the Apes," Hubby said. "Guess whose birthday is coming up?"

"Ma," I said.

"Her ninetieth," Hubby said. "That's a big one. We have to do something."

"I've been dreading it."

"It'll be great — everyone in the same room, the whole happy family."

"Fred will arrange something. Gilbert will help."

"Will you go?"

"I guess."

He looked away. "It'll be a friggin' zoo. Think about it."

But all I could think of was Mona's letter and the interrupted phone calls.

28

CHARLIE

IN HER SLACK, rag-like voice, like a slow child confounded by a cold-eyed stranger — even over the phone she seemed to twist her head at me and squint — Mona said, "I can't talk long. I'm at work. I'm expecting someone. Where are you?"

"Home."

Home in the world of my fiction was unusual — no one was ever home. Home in the world of my travel was a far-off destination, a place I had fled. Yet here I was in Mother Land, where I'd been born, among the sand dunes and scrub cherry trees and pin oaks and pitch pines, the lumped-up terminal moraine of the Cape, where I'd started out, where I'd returned.

"Oh," Mona said, because of all the places you could be, home needed the least explanation.

I had the impression of Mona as someone like Mother: "difficult," a wisp of a woman, ectoplasmic, with a steel core, ungraspable, complaining of frailty, the receiver jammed against her thin skull. If I raised my voice she'd fall silent, she'd be spooked, she'd flutter away, just a pair of furiously fanning wings, trailing the glitter of dust and scales, before vanishing out the window. Now dark trees loomed over her where she stood in New Hampshire, the earth there dense with pine needles.

Her small sidling voice reminded me of her pale body and staring breasts and how in that year of the child we had seldom laughed. Our time together, all those anxious months, had been enforced by her pregnancy. I had been captured and held prisoner with her as she'd grown bigger, slower, sadder. But of course we'd been each other's prisoner, and on the run, and she had suffered far more than I.

"Jay?"

Because I'd been lost in this memory, I said, "I'm here."

I imagined her in a schoolroom — that sort of echo, cold walls, no carpet or curtains. Or a shared office. *I'm making a personal call. I won't be long.*

"I thought you'd hung up." That was the old Mona, imagining the worst.

"Are you a teacher? What do you teach?"

"This isn't about me. This is about our son."

She sounded upset. "Mona, what's the matter?"

"My husband." She hesitated. I heard her teeth in her breath. "He's not comfortable with me talking to you."

I kept myself from yelling in frustration, a monkey howl that would ream the telephone wire. But Mona was fragile, bewildered, glancing sideways, brushing her hair away from her eyes with the back of her slender fingers.

"He's kind of intimidated by your being a famous writer. What did you just say?"

"I was laughing," I said, but I had started to howl. "I'm broke," and the hideous finality of the word, its nakedness, made me angry. "My last book tanked. I live alone in a rented house. My wife — second wife — left me eight years ago. My kids feel sorry for me, but they hardly talk to me. I've just come back from a remote part of Kenya. I'm trying to save up some money to finance a book about Africa. I microwaved some canned chili for lunch. I'm not famous."

As I talked, hearing myself, it seemed like a success story, of survival against the odds.

"Most people think I'm dead or that I've stopped writing."

"Quit complaining," Mona said in a hot whisper, almost hissing at me. I instantly knew this desperate tearful voice, the *Please don't leave me* of almost forty years ago, beseeching me, but now she seemed to be saying, *Get out of my life.*

"I'm not complaining," I said, and calmed myself with three deep breaths, remembering why she had called me. Her helpless fear aroused my pity. "You must be so glad to have found the boy."

"Overjoyed," she said sadly, her anger subsiding. "I can't tell you how happy I am. He's so smart. He was captain of the cross-country team. He owns a big company. He skis. He runs marathons."

I was smiling in disbelief. Who was this boy? I knew no one like him. My own sons resembled me: loners, readers, puzzle solvers, studious, tending to concealment, freelancers, natural-born travelers. But I had raised them to be that way.

"What's his name?"

"Charlie," she said. "He's named after his father."

"I thought I was his father."

"Is that supposed to be funny?"

"Funny? I'm terrified."

"That's right. It's all about you."

"I don't know what to say."

"Try listening. I just realized why I'm so happy. Because he's normal."

"And I'm not?"

"I don't know you anymore. I can't read your books. Just seeing your name on a book makes me sad."

"Please tell me about Charlie."

"Listen," she said.

She began to talk, and as she did, the image of Charlie formed in my mind. He came alive, one detail after another. He swelled and smiled, grew taller, acquired a sense of humor and a bank account and a swift pair of legs, had a Dartmouth degree and two adoring parents who had devoted the best years of their lives to him. As Charlie came into focus, upbeat, confident, well bred, a shrewd businessman and tenacious competitor, an athlete, a doting husband, a cultured man — reader, moviegoer, music lover — he grew less and less familiar to me, and at last I realized I did not know him at all.

"He looks just like you," Mona said at last. "He has your eyes and nose, even the way you stand, your odd posture."

"So you've seen him?"

"We had lunch at his house. I invited myself — I was dying to see him. He was very sweet about it. His wife is lovely. His son is beautiful."

"That would be our grandson."

"We have no rights," Mona said. "We gave him away."

She began to cry, and it sounded strange over the phone, like coughing, with long pauses between coughs. That was all I heard, a skirl of disturbed air, sudden halts, a scratchy throat, not grief.

"I have to go," she said in a small stifled voice.

"I'd like to know more about Charlie. Please?"

"He wants to meet you."

"What did you tell him about me?"

"Everything I knew."

"He'll want something. I don't blame him. We gave him nothing."

"No, Jay. You don't get it. He's well-off — rich — really rich. I saw his house."

"You told him I'm a writer?"

"He knew that right away. He knew your name. His mother's got a lot of your books."

"And that I'm from the Cape?"

"Yes, all that. It's all on your book jackets."

"What did you tell them about my family?" I said, already resenting her presumption, because no one outside our family knew anything about us, this tribe of hectoring misfits.

"That it's a big family, and — I don't know — that it's interesting."

"Mona, it's not interesting. It's big, yes, but it's a monstrosity. Don't you remember how they blamed us? That they didn't help us? How awful it was?"

"That doesn't matter now."

"It does!"

"Please keep your voice down."

Floyd's saying "his illegitimate son" in his widely quoted magazine piece had never left my mind. No one in the big interesting family had taken exception to this objectionable phrase, not even Mother, whose own father had been an orphan, and who burst into tears when the subject of his being a bastard came up.

"Yes, it does matter," I said. "My family hasn't changed a bit. They're exactly the same, or maybe worse. I remember how my mother reacted when I got home from Puerto Rico — when you went into that home. She was horrible to me. 'You should be ashamed of yourself.'"

"You remember that?"

"I remember everything."

"At least you have a family. I have no one. That's why I'm so glad that Charlie's in my life now."

"This assumption that everyone needs a family — I don't get it. Mine is destructive, selfish, mean, competitive, disloyal. They gloated over my misfortunes, even Charlie. He's their flesh and blood, but all they see is a huge mistake."

In a whisper of bewilderment, Mona said, "I thought your family was so close."

"My family is a nightmare."

"Then look at it this way. Maybe this is a good thing. I mean, Charlie. Maybe you'll get involved. He's a great guy."

"What am I supposed to do?"

"He's waiting to hear from you. I'll give you his address. Now I have to go. But one more thing. Are you listening?"

"I'm here."

"I think it might be best if we don't talk again."

So, as she was dictating Charlie's address to me, and urging me to be in touch with him, she was forbidding me to call her.

In all farewells I have a glimpse of the past, of an earlier page in the relationship, a time when things were different. Saying goodbye to Mona now in this loveless and perfunctory way, as she dismissed me, I saw her clearly, a slim, straight-haired blonde returning from the ladies' room to a table in a bar where we sat with some friends. As she sat beside me, she slid close and discreetly put something into my jacket pocket. I reached in and felt the warm damp silk of her panties, then looked into her bright wicked eyes. She stuck her tongue out at me like a teasing child. Now, on the phone, she was saying coldly, "Okay, bye."

This was like inhabiting a fiction, events and coincidences and surprises — Mona's unexpected letter, and then Charlie, a new character popping up out of nowhere, but wholly logical, because he was mentioned as a minor character in an earlier subplot. Charlie seemed unreal, yet here was his full name and address. He was a fact. And he knew all about me.

I could not think of Charlie without reflecting on my family's lack of support for Mona and me all those years ago, that I had been blamed as wayward, that this birth had been a horrible secret, the family's shame. How would I break this news to them?

Some twisted people love bad news. They yearn to know that someone has been robbed, or lost a valuable thing, or been through a divorce. For a person who feels rejected it is a way of feeling better — and I suppose, given that pathology, a miserable person who lacks a regular stream of such bad news eventually turns to crime, because causing mayhem, bringing violence upon a stable world, can be a way of creating bad news and feeling better. Perhaps murder is the ultimate form of rejection.

Any biography of Stalin or Mao Zedong was helpful in understanding Mother's mind. I learned more about Mother from *The Private Life of Chairman Mao,* by Mao's personal physician, Dr. Li Zhisui, than from Dr. Spock. I knew from such books how, through banishments and manipulation, the tyrant rewrites history; how inconvenient are the ghosts of the past.

But this ghost, this lost boy, had been found. *He wants to see you.* What else did he want? I had no money. I was merely clinging to this rented house in the hope of raising enough cash for another African trip and a possible book.

All my writing and book publishing existed in another dimension, unrelated to my family. It was "work" — as obscure, unknowable, and negligible as Marvin in his uniform doing security detail at the Cape Cod Mall, or Hubby in his green scrubs at the Hyannis Hospital, or Fred's "I'm doing some business in China," or Gilbert in the Emirates, or Franny's and Rose's teaching, or Floyd's professorship in poetry. I had no idea what their work entailed. As for mine, no one knew what I did; no one inquired. I had no idea whether anyone in the family apart from Floyd had read anything I'd written. And so much time had passed in their ignoring it that I really didn't want any of them to read it, and was annoyed when the subject of my writing came up, usually in the form of, "There's this guy where I work who asked if I was related to you. He says he reads your stuff."

And now there was a new member of the family. Why should he care?

Instead of calling Charlie, I wrote him a letter. I needed a written record of our exchanges; I also wanted to see his penmanship, which tells so much. In my letter, I explained that I was writing him with trepidation, that I had never expected to know him, that I was frankly confused. I felt that I must somehow apologize to him for having conspired to abandon him all those years ago — that Mona and I had set him adrift, and I saw him in a little bobbing bassinet, floating on the current, like Moses in the bulrushes.

On a day of low, dark, rain-loaded clouds, with a sinking heart I slipped the letter into a mailbox and thought, Let it come down.

Great to hear from you, he wrote back. *That's exactly what my mother used to tell me.* "We found you, just like Moses. You were our Christmas present." He went on to say, *You don't have to apologize. I've got an awesome family. I've had a wonderful upbringing. My life couldn't have been better.* He listed his pleasures as fishing, music, reading, and "family time." As Mona had surmised, he'd gotten interested in who his birth parents might be — their disposition and health — after the birth of his own child. *And look,* he wrote in his enthusiastic way, *is this amazing or what? After my great upbringing, and all the good things that have happened to me, my father turns out to be you. See how lucky I am? How awesome is that?*

I was not entirely reassured. Anyone's high spirits always put me on guard; they made me cautious — another family trait. I assumed that enthusiasm was forced or exaggerated, if not faked, the enthusiast trying to pull a fast one by selling me his bright mood. In a family of inward and self-regarding cynics, no one's elation was altruistic, or even healthy; no one was straight. Happiness was a ploy to distract your attention from their essential ill will. Good cheer did not exist in the family, any more than it existed in a bucket of crabs.

Yet I trusted Charlie. He'd been raised elsewhere. He'd been spared the struggle that I had endured. He even seemed to speak differently, judging from the tone of his letter — a clear, untroubled voice, eager to be heard. He was a patient listener, too. This simplicity, this promptness, and this gratitude were strange to me.

I wrote again. I was thankful for his directness. Being close to him meant that Mona, from long ago, would remain no more than a spectral presence. I now feared all families, and did not want her to be part of this discourse, or a probable friendship. I could not imagine the three of us reconstituted as a family. I was wary of Mona's possible intrusion, for gentle-seeming people could also be unexpectedly fierce. And all I knew of family life was wreckage — a shipwreck that cast forth scavengers and wounded, frightened people, potential cannibals, fighting to survive on the barren shore of Boon Island.

In his next letter, Charlie answered more of my questions. Yes, he had a sister, also adopted. No, he had not traveled much. His degree from Dartmouth had been in history, not economics or business. *I still read a lot of history and biography — anything about Teddy Roosevelt, Civil War battles, the Lewis and Clark Expedition.* He enclosed some snapshots of his wife, Julie, his son, Patrick, of himself. In one he was holding up a silvery fish, a plump-bellied striped bass, its wide mouth gaping.

That last snapshot held my attention. As Mona had said, he did resemble me — the nose, the eyes, the shape of his face, his alertness, the set of his mouth. But that was detail I saw in passing. What I noticed more clearly was that he was standing at the edge of a marsh, by a creek, a bridge behind him, where the creek passed under a country road.

I knew the marsh, the creek, the bridge, the road. I wrote back: *The fish is a beauty, and I know where you caught it — in Scorton Creek, by the bridge on Route 6A at half-tide, when the marsh is clear. The reason I know this is that until ten or so years ago I lived fifty yards away, up that road.*

Too impatient to wait for his reply, I gave him my telephone number. He called a few days later, midmorning, from his office. His voice was as friendly as his letters had been, the tone of excitement and pleasure, the easy good humor I was so unused to in my family.

"That's incredible. You actually lived there at the time I was fishing. I used to park on that road all the time!"

"Maybe you saw me on the creek. I had a wooden rowboat, a kind of dory. It was the only one there."

"I saw you! Long sculling oars — spoon blades. I loved that boat. I did some rowing at Dartmouth."

"That was me."

"I'd be casting from the bank, wishing I could troll from that boat."

"Not knowing that the guy rowing the boat was your father."

"That's so awesome."

He had been raised about ten miles up the road, in a big house in Barnstable that I knew by sight — that most people knew, because of its elegance and its conspicuous site on a bend of the main road just before the county courthouse. He'd gone to school there, and then to a nearby prep school. His father was a well-known philanthropist who had made his fortune in importing plywood from the Soviet Union at a time when few people did business behind the Iron Curtain. A self-made man who'd devoted himself to his children, Charlie's father had been suspicious of Mona's approach, the birth mother seeking her child.

"When I told my father I was meeting her, he said" — and here Charlie became gruff — "'Don't give her any money.'"

I said, "When can we meet?"

"I'm coming down to the Cape next week. How about lunch?"

Seeing Charlie entering Friendly's Grille in Sagamore, I had the impression of seeing myself as a young man. He was just my height, with a brisk way of moving, looking around, prepared to smile, and when he recognized me, he beamed. I shook his hand, he hugged me, we sat in the booth, and I could not stop smiling.

He looked like me — he looked like one of the family. But what delighted me was that he had been raised by complete strangers, who had obviously adored him and had withheld nothing from him. In that earlier telephone conversation Charlie said that his father's sole ambition in life had been to make him happy, and he had repaid this by pleasing his father, studying hard, excelling at sports, making the old man proud. "And my mother is a fabulous woman — she's good at everything."

"Julie wanted to come today, but she has to take Patrick to nursery school. She's dying to meet you. What about your boys — are they on the Cape?"

"London — England. I haven't told them about you. I know they'll be happy."

"I've got brothers! I always wanted brothers. Mona said you had a big family."

"Very big," I said, wondering whether to elaborate. "You have no idea."

We ordered sandwiches. I let him talk, so that I could look at him, and I realized that I was happier than I'd been in years. He was asking questions, eager for answers.

"I have a grandmother," he said. "I bet she's awesome. What a trip."

29

BIRTHDAY CARDS

THE BIRTHDAY CARD that expressed my true feelings for Mother did not exist, because my feelings were wolfish. I glanced at the cards on the rack at Centerville Pharmacy, to torment myself with the nagging doggerel. *A Mother is someone we keep very near, In our hearts and our thoughts each day of the year* probably contained a grain of truth, but the next idiot couplet ran, *Because we cherish her, Because she's so dear.* "Cherish" was a verb that repelled me. Another card, bound with pink ribbon, had the pretensions of a cocktail menu, listing Mother's assets: *A smile when you're sad, A hand when you're down, A word when you're blue,* and ten more, ending with, *A friend like no other, Thanks for being that kind of Mother.*

A woman near me jerked her jowly face at my sudden hacking cough of dissent.

The message I wanted was

Mother, in your twisted will,
Greedy for attention still,
Bitter woman, incomplete,
Who taught me how to lie and cheat . . .

When I quoted that to Hubby, he choked in a convulsion of genuine mirth. Then, with unconvincing piety, he said, "Give Ma a break, Jay. She's going to be ninety. Statute of limitations for being a witch ran out."

"Happy birthday, Mother, you maimed me from the start. I carry from your womb a fanatic heart," I said. "Apologies to W. B. Yeats."

"I'm squealing on you!" he said, giggling and scratching his hairy forearm in excitement. *I'm squeelun!*

"All the cards have the word 'cherish' in them. I'd replace that word with 'fear.'"

"Poor old Ma."

"Healthier than you, Hubby." But I was also thinking: birthday cards were not messages, they were merely token gestures — phatic, so to speak.

"Fuck you, homo."

"Eat me."

"She's a living fossil!"

But Mother did not seem any older than when, on the morning of my return from Mona's abandoning the child, she had sat stony-faced at the kitchen table and rapped her skinny hand on the surface and said, "I hope you're proud of yourself."

She seemed old then, but no older now. And I had not aged at all.

I *had* been proud of myself in helping to see Mona through the crisis. But I sat sorrowing for the months of struggle, and for the day I had parted from lonely Mona, who had never stopped grieving for the child.

I was then a child myself, an angry, humiliated child, and Mother was a fierce, unsatisfied woman. The worst of it was that in the family time had stopped. I was still that boy, and she was still that scolding woman.

Franny called, about Mother's ninetieth. I tried one of my satirical poems on her. She said, "I know how you feel," which was a lie. The calls were constant because of the approaching day. A seemingly impossible event was being planned: a birthday lunch that was supposed to include all of us, including Fred, who was usually in China; Gilbert, who might be in Bahrain; the two working daughters, who'd have to take the day off — it was a weekday; all the spouses, who never felt welcome; and, hardest of all, Floyd, who hated me.

The last time we'd all been together as a family was seven years earlier, around Father's deathbed, and then at his funeral.

We think it's best to take him off his ventilator.

But he'll die without it!

We should respect her wishes.

To test Mother, I went to see her and said that I might be traveling on her birthday. "Work-related travel," I said. She sat leaning slightly forward, her bird-woman profile backlit by the last of the daylight that emphasized her smallness and her ferocity.

"Oh?"

I said, "I need to raise some money for a book I want to write."

The mention of money always made her pause, like a bird stiffening at the snap of a twig.

She said, "I remember when I was a lot younger, having to work my fingers to the bone to make ends meet."

I had half expected her to offer me a pittance, but not even that.

"I always managed to set a little time aside for my parents, though," she said. "In spite of everything."

"I'm kind of strapped for cash."

I was describing how hard up I was, and how busy, as a way of dramatizing the sacrifice I would be making by attending her birthday party. I was trying to see if she cared. She was not moved by my mention of my dilemma. With a half-smile of serenity that could also have been sadism, she watched me teetering.

"But I'll do my best."

"That's all I expect." She folded her arms and in this compact posture seemed like one of her own little carvings.

"There's a lot of animosity going around, though," I said. "Bad feelings."

She tightened her features, pointing her beaky face at me, losing the faint traces of her color, and I thought how a plucked bird can look reptilian.

She said, "What do you mean by that?"

"Your children."

"My children?" This uprush of indignation was pure theater.

"Some of them hate each other."

Using her shoulders to convey shock, she said, "That's not true. You know damn well that's not true. Are you trying to upset me?"

"Floyd hates me."

"No one hates you." She regarded me with contempt, her nose lengthening and lizard-like. "Do you really think you're so damned important?"

That "damned" meant she was genuinely angry, and that she was in the wrong. Just as she was about to speak, the phone rang. She picked up the receiver, exaggerating its heaviness with the gesture. The thing squawked.

"Hello . . . Oh, fine . . . Yes, of course I am." She sounded unconvincing and wounded. "I'll have to call you back later."

When she hung up I stared at the phone in puzzlement.

"Franny," Mother said. She rolled her eyes. "She thinks I'm an invalid."

She had not told Franny I was there. But I had known for many years how she kept her children separate. And this dig at Franny meant that when she spoke to Franny she would disparage me.

"And Fred hates Floyd," I said, picking up the thread of the conversation.

"Fred is a kind and generous boy," she said, narrowing her eyes at me in sympathy. "Poor kid, he's always working. He hardly gets a wink of sleep. All that traveling."

"I travel."

"To China?" She smiled, playing this trump card. "And he has school-age children."

I left Mother that afternoon, as so many times before, feeling defeated, undercut, belittled, doubted. And I knew from the way she had answered the phone that all she'd remember of my visit was that I had upset her, not the news that I had canceled my plans to be at her birthday party.

The call came that night from Rose, harsh, hectoring, not to be interrupted.

"What the fuck is your problem? It's Ma's birthday in two weeks and you go all the way over there to upset her. You are such an asshole."

I allowed a pause. I said, "She told you that?"

"She told Franny, who told Fred."

"I thought you were on the outs with Fred."

"We're supposed to be planning a family party, you dork."

"Whisper, whisper."

"We're lucky that Ma is still with us."

"You're lucky she gave you a house. I helped pay for that house. And your ass and your husband's ass are parked in it."

But the drone on the line told me that Rose had hung up.

Hubby called too, and left a message on my answering machine. "Ass-hat."

"I don't think you realize how sensitive Ma is," Gilbert told me, on a crackling line from Qatar. "She was really hurt by what you said."

"What did I say?"

"You accused her of being an inattentive mother," he said, as I listened, astonished at the woman's mendacity. "And you know how hard she tries."

In this outpouring of good feeling for Mother as her birthday approached, I was the only holdout, it seemed. I loved her less than anyone. I perhaps did not love her at all. I saw her as cruel and selfish — and how was it possible that I was the only one of her children who felt this way? In this sprawling family I was the single skeptic. I wondered why, yet I did not doubt my feelings. I suspected the motives of the others, the ones whom Mother corrupted with her gifts and compromised with her gossip. I had no allies.

Or perhaps I had one.

It was one of the perversities of the family to see an occasion such as this, a birthday, a wedding, any celebration, as a chance to settle old scores. Because it was superficially benign and included everyone, a family gathering was an opportunity to inflict pain, to get even with the maximum number of people at one time. A family meal, everyone with his guard down, I remembered as raised voices, vicious words, unforgiving whispers, kicks under the table, sudden departures, floods of tears, and slammed doors.

"I'm not angry!" someone would scream.

In the endless, inward, contained war, the family like a bag of ferrets, a birthday or a wedding was a separate pitched battle. I dreaded the skirmish to come.

Fred invited me to his house in Barnstable for a drink. This sort of hospitality I saw as hostile.

He poured me a small glass of clear viscous liquor and said, "This is Chinese gin. *Baijiu.* I hand-carried it back from Shanghai. Go on, chug it."

"Razor blades," I said.

"Best quality — Maotai," he said, clinking his glass. "*Ganbei!*" and he drank. "Listen, I want you to come to the party."

This gratuitous prologue meant one thing, and we both knew it: he didn't want me to come to the party. An italicized *but* loomed.

"But Ma said you were traveling, that you had some kind of assignment. So, I'm just saying — and look, I really want you to be there — that you don't have to be there. We understand."

He looked fussed, he took another drink, he hated holding this conversation. He wanted me to say that I had other plans so he would be off the hook.

I said, "I want to be there."

He tried to conceal his look of disappointment with another drink, wincing as the liquor went down.

"It's just a lunch at the Happy Clam. Not really a party. An hour at most. No one'll be missed. My kids have soccer. If you had plans, you could take Ma out another day. She'd love that."

"Fred, you sound like you don't want me to go."

"Did I say that?" He sighed. He made a business of pouring another drink and slowly screwing the cap on the bottle so that he could turn his back on me. "I said I want you to come to the party."

"I don't have other plans. Turning ninety is a big deal for Ma. I'm going."

Fred smiled at me, a version of the pitying smile that Mother had perfected — and talking to Fred, I often had the feeling I was talking to Mother.

"Floyd's going to be there," he said with moistened lips.

"So?"

"I'm just saying. Floyd's signed on."

Floyd's name was a weapon in the family, and for years this weapon had been used against me, waved in my face, flourished, glinting in the sun like a hammered blade.

"Ma said she wanted everyone there."

"Right, right," and now Fred looked alarmed. "That's why Floyd's going."

"And that's why I'm going."

Now Fred began to smile, and I knew worse was to come. "He can be difficult." He went on smiling. "He's crazy, you know."

"You can handle him," I said, smiling back.

But his smile was meant to threaten me. Fred said, "He can be violent. What if he freaks?"

I realized that I enjoyed confounding Fred, seeing him squirm, and now I knew that he feared trouble — Floyd ranting at me, my hollering back at him, Mother covering her eyes ("You're killing me!"), the girls sobbing, "Mumma! Mumma!" Unfinished meals, untasted drinks, bruised shins, hurt feelings, slammed doors.

"I'm going," I said.

Fred's face shone with insincerity, a feeble expression of fear as he clucked and wrung his hands. "Like I said, I want you to be there. And Ma wants everyone to be there. It's a big day."

30

UPSIDE-DOWN CAKE

BIRTHDAY CAN BE a kind of funeral. But I saw it as an opportunity, and made my arrangements, and looked forward to the event. The private function room at the Happy Clam *was* funereal, with the bouquets and the long faces — Rose with her back turned, Gilbert and Fred conferring, Franny fussing over her son Jonty, Jonty nagging his daughter Jilly. No one wanted to sit next to me. We all stood gaping, glassy-eyed, as though we were about to bury someone.

I had arrived early, resolving to see it through. The spouses were rattled — Marvin ill at ease out of his security guard uniform, Fred's wife Erma sighing and snatching at her hair, Walter monkeying with a camera as a way of snubbing everyone else. Jilly was the center of attention, the adults shouting at her as she ran back and forth.

"Run to Granma! Run to Granma!" Jonty called out. "Jilly, listen to me!"

Mother winced at the approaching child. Mother had a way of recoiling as she was being attacked. She smiled slightly as Jilly tripped and fell and began bawling. Mother squinted at the sobbing girl. Jonty swept up Jilly.

"I had a child named Angela," Mother said. "She died. She's in heaven."

"Granma is, I believe, the name of the Cuban press agency," someone said very loudly. It was Floyd, in a black fedora, leaning on his tightly rolled umbrella. "I always found that terribly ironic. It was named after the yacht that brought the guerrillas to fight in the Cuban Revolution in 1956."

"But why was it called *Granma*?" Rose asked.

"Funnily enough, because the man who owned it, a gringo, had named it after his granma. But you knew that, of course."

"Jilly, tell me where it hurts, honey," Jonty pleaded with the howling child.

"Who was it who said, 'If you're strong enough to scream, it can't hurt very much'?" Floyd asked, winking at Mother and stepping past me to give her a kiss. "Was it you, Mother?"

This was the Floyd I remembered from happier days, the man who burned up the air in the room and left people gasping in the vacuum.

"We're waiting for Hubby — oh, there he is," Fred said as Hubby and Moneen appeared at the door.

"Puffing like a grampus," Floyd said. He tilted his wide-brimmed hat and made a face. "That is, a cetacean of the northern seas. But you knew that, didn't you?"

Hubby scowled — the first cut of the day — and ignored Floyd. Moneen hurried to the other spouses, the second tier of relations, in the cheap seats.

The triumph at such a family gathering lay in concealing your real feelings. But already this was unraveling. Hubby was stung, Rose hunched her shoulders and refused to greet me, Mother was still wincing at Jilly. Everyone but Jonty and Loris had left their small children at home. Franny handed Floyd a shopping bag. "Your favorites," she said. Floyd picked through the bag, sorting fruit and packages of candy, and he held up a pink metal drum of Almond Roca.

"The trouble with them is I can't open them fast enough," Franny said.

"One would never have known that," Floyd said, "to look at you." He found something else, a cellophane bag. "Mixed nuts. That is so appropriate to this day of days."

"Maybe we could sit down," Fred said, raising his arms. "Everyone's here."

Floyd began shaking nuts into his hand. "Why is it," he said as he rattled the nuts like dice in his fist and shot them into his mouth, "that people always do this when they're eating nuts?"

"I'm not sitting next to him," Hubby said, and moved his place card down the table, away from Floyd's.

Floyd saw this and said, "Nice shirt, Hubby. I've always said those are going to come back in style someday."

"Butthole," Hubby said.

"Gilbert's just come back from, I think, Kuwait," Fred said as Gilbert greeted everyone. "And won't be going back, *inshallah*."

"The *placement*," Floyd said, a French accent on the word, *plassmon*, fluttering his fingers at the place cards. "It's worthy of the court of Versailles. 'I know my place.' 'Who's in, who's out?' 'I won't sit next to you.'"

"But there's an extra place," Marvin said.

Mother stared at him. He stammered and clutched his belt, as no doubt he did at the mall, one hand on his billy club, one on his Mace can.

"Mah-vin," Franny said. Still an outsider, not one of us, after all these years, Marvin did not realize his mistake even when it was pointed out to him: this seemingly extra place was of course for Angela, who had been with us, guiding Mother, for fifty years after dying at birth.

Fred and Gilbert sat on either side of Mother, Franny and Rose next to the brothers, then Hubby, Jonty (Jilly on his lap), and the spouses, Marvin, Moneen, Erma, Loris, and the others — Walter snapping pictures. Floyd took his seat, and I sat next to him on the only remaining chair.

Floyd started to tug at my shirt. "This is—what?—shirred silk? Chiffon? I like its epicene *in-soo-shuntz*. Its drape. Its hand." He twisted it and dropped it. "I hope you're clad in clean linen. I can't abide any other. Mother, to you!" he said, snatching my water glass and raising it to Mother. "I love a fruity vintage. I need an assertive cheese."

Mother beamed over the motley crowd at the table. Seven years on from Father's funeral, we looked bigger but droopier, the same people but wearing odder, older masks, all of us like large, misshapen children.

"How wonderful to have all my family here," Mother said. "I'm so lucky."

"We're the lucky ones, Mumma," Franny said.

"Ma, we've been looking forward to this," Rose said.

Hubby said, "Will someone pass the bread?"

Floyd juggled a bread stick and said, "Are you saying you'd like one of these up your end?"

Breathing hard in impatience, Hubby scowled. He said, "So, do we get menus?"

"Menu is, of course, the grandson of Brahma, and his law must be observed," Floyd said. "I think you knew that. One apposite law regarding temperance is 'He must eat without distraction of mind.'"

"No menus. Fred chose the meal," Mother said. "It's simpler. We thought you'd prefer it that way."

Mother said she was happy, and for once she seemed to be telling the truth. But her happiness was possible only because the rest of us were miserable. Looking around the room, I saw how shamefaced we seemed. We had betrayed each other too many times to sit comfortably around the same table together. We were there because we were failures—still lived in Mother Land, ten minutes from Mother, had lost money and families, needed Mother, and that other distortion, that only when we were together did we see how different we were, how unlike a real family.

None of us had really wanted to show up. We disliked each other so much that the notion of peacemaking implied in sharing a meal only made us angrier. The very fact that we were there proved that we were failures. We needed to be separate to function properly; we had to be secretive to survive. But Mother had prevailed. She had insisted on our being there, and had implied—as she often did—that if we cooperated, there would be a reward for us in her will. She held out the prospect of her death always, yet she was the only happy person at the table, the only one who, small and sinewy, looked healthy. So Mother had her wish and was fulfilled in all the important ways — having her birthday party, getting presents, and in this large get-together dividing us by creating more confusion.

"May I request a beverage?" Floyd said.

"Take your hat off," Fred said.

"If you say the magic word," Floyd said, squinting at him, removing his hat and spinning it on his finger. "'O for a beaker full of the warm South!'" He was leaning toward Jonty. "'The blushful Hippocrene, with beaded bubbles winking at the brim.' Source?"

Jonty turned away. Hubby set his face at Floyd. Franny and Rose shrugged.

"You want Johnny Keats," Floyd said, and raised a finger, reciting, "'The dunces flutterblasting, with food-splashed faces.' A citation, if you please."

Hubby said "Diet Coke" to the waiter.

"I think you'll find that it was I who penned those words," Floyd said, swinging himself sideways toward Hubby and crossing his legs. "Why is it that your so-called diet drinks are the preference of the chubbies and the chunkies, as if some arcane magic attached —"

"Shut up," Hubby said.

The drinks were handed out, we toasted Mother again, and the first course was served, clam chowder and soda crackers.

"Careful, hon," Franny said to Marvin, "don't season it," and explained to the table, "He's got acid reflux wicked bad. He's on Zantac."

"For the PPI," Marvin said with the pedantry of a chronic sufferer. "Proton pump inhibitors."

"I seem to recall it was stool softeners," Floyd said, "a bewitching pair of words. Like panty shields."

When Marvin looked up, his chin thrust out like a claw hammer, Rose said, "It's not funny. I've got OIC, opioid-induced constipation, Ma."

Mother smiled like a cat and licked the rim of milky chowder from the bristles above her lips.

"Has anyone here tried Ambien?" Gilbert said. "I've finally gotten a night's sleep with them. Call it my drug of choice."

"Walter's on Paxil," Rose said. "It seems to calm him down — doesn't it, honey? — and helps him sleep."

"I take like a ton of potassium," Jonty said. "I've got a problem with electrolytes."

"I love the gallant names," Floyd said. "Ceedrex, for my liver and lights. I eat them like candy."

"All I take is blood thinner," Hubby said.

"What about that stuff to lower your cholesterol?" Moneen said.

"And that — Lipitor."

"What are you on, Ma?" Franny said, raising her voice, as we all did when addressing Mother.

"These people who take nitroglycerin for their heart," Floyd said. "Why don't they explode? And by the way, in which novel does a character self-combust?"

"*Bleak House,*" I said. "The rag-and-bone man Krook. 'Inborn, inbred, engendered in the corrupted humors of the vicious body itself.'"

"Isn't education a wonderful thing?" Floyd said.

"What am I *awn?*" Mother said, but did not speak again until all eyes shifted to her, as she sat glaring at Rose. When we had fallen silent, she said again, "What am I *awn?*" She spoke loudly and became indignant. Her girlish shudder was studied and stagy, shoulders twisting under her shawl. "I'm not *awn* anything."

Though we marveled at Mother for taking no medication, it seemed to me that she was calling attention to her hypochondria. Abstinence was her way of outdoing us in our maladies.

"There is no medicine for what I have," Mother said, her fingers stroking the skin flaps of her scrawny throat.

"Mumma!" Franny cried, as if summoning her.

"Old age is incurable." Mother half closed her eyes. "My bags are packed."

"Please, don't, Mumma," Rose said, whinnying a little.

Franny vomited up a sob as Gilbert placed a reassuring arm around Mother, who wore an expression of quiet suffering, tragic and serene.

Marvin whispered to his son Jonty, "You gonna finish the rest of that chowda?"

The spouses were flustered. In his confusion, Walter was walking around the long table, his head bowed over his viewfinder, snapping pictures of us.

"Why don't we all take turns telling our happy memories," Fred said. "Of Ma. Way back when."

Mother closed her eyes completely. She seemed to be lying in state as the meal became a proper funeral, with valedictions and reminiscences, Mother in the place of honor with her embalmed expression, looking thwarted and doll-like, as the dead do, her skinny fingers twisted in her green shawl.

"Like when we had that creamy oatmeal," Hubby said, "that was never lumpy. Yum-yum."

"My favorite was the al dente pasta," Rose said. "With the bolo sauce."

"Both were thewy and farinaceous," Floyd said, tearing at a piece of bread. "And what was that witches' brew we had on Saturday nights, with the crunchy undercooked onion. And the fatty meat — 'That was the best part!'"

"Bruised fruit is what I remember," I said. "Meatloaf sandwiches that fell apart because of all the ketchup."

"Pea soup," Franny said. "Kidney stew."

"Dad's favorite," Mother said. She was deaf to irony. Believing that her cooking was being praised, her eyes puddled and she began to cry. She dabbed at her eyes. "I tried so hard to please you."

Floyd said, "Pot roast. Baked chicken. Fork-tender."

"The way you put crunched-up potato chips on your fish casserole is what I used to like," Rose said. "I do that for my Walter."

Mother was smiling through her tears, feeling venerated, but also looking like a dead child.

"Ma made her own rolls," Hubby said. "No one does that anymore. Home-baked and fluffy."

"I do," Moneen said.

"Not like Ma's."

"Parker House rolls," Mother said.

"Your chocolate cake," Gilbert said, giving Mother a hug.

"And boeuf en daube," Floyd said. "A splash of brandy and a lovely Côtes du Rhone in the pot, served with baby carrots, lightly sautéed morel mushrooms, the pancetta, the bouquet garni, the white truffles, just a hint of tarragon."

"Don't be a jerk," Fred said. He had been squirming as we'd satirized Mother's cooking.

"I have all Ma's recipes," Franny said.

"Sure you do," Hubby said. The flecks of chowder in the corners of his mouth made him seem more menacing.

The sarcasm about Mother's food thickened the air with frank hostility. We disapproved of the way we were behaving; we were childish and insincere. None of us wanted to be there, so we were spoiling it, and as we did the main course was served. Broiled scallops, mashed potatoes, coleslaw, and an ear of corn for each person lay in its own trough-shaped dish.

"I can't eat," Mother said. She looked limp, her face slack and corpselike.

"Are you upset, Ma?" Franny said.

Jonty said "Just take a bite for Daddy" to his daughter, poking at her face with a spoonful of potato.

"Bay scallops," Marvin said, pronouncing it the off-Cape way, instead of rhyming it with *wallop,* and we all stared at him.

"You always wonder, which bay?" Floyd said. "But I happen to know. It is of course a species and not any specific bay." He whipped around and said to Jonty, "I feel certain you could have told me that."

Behind us, Walter kept scraping his feet around the table, taking pictures, his camera making a sucking sound. He was one of those people who is determined to impress you by exaggerating the motion and noise of his job.

"Your anthropologists will tell you that communal eating is a grand gesture of harmony," Floyd said. "We are partaking, therefore we are in accord, and all our ill will is behind us, our — dare I say? — motiveless malignity."

Mother's eyes were shut, her expression meditative, slightly sunken, as though in a coffin. No one had responded to Floyd. We went on eating. None of us wanted to be there, and as this feeling penetrated us, the conversation became milder, brittle with forced politeness. The more correct we were, the more obviously hostile.

"May I have a piece of bread?"

"You *may* have a piece of bread."

That sort of thing went on for a while, and then the table was cleared, the cake brought in and placed before Mother. The waitresses seemed harassed and incompetent, teenage girls with untidy hair. "Enjoy," one of them said.

"An expression I deplore for its being a grammatical goofball," Floyd said. And to Jonty, "A solecism, as you might put it."

Mother smiled at the slumping soggy cake, topped with eight lurid pineapple slices, most of them with a cherry in the middle, two with candles, and on the sloping front side, MOTHER spelled out in shaky piping, with scrolls and roses around it.

"Make a wish, Ma," Franny said. "Pineapple upside-down cake. Your favorite."

But Mother had begun to look past us. "Hello?" she said, as though answering the telephone.

I followed Mother's line of sight and saw at the door of the room, just entering, Charlie and Julie, and little Patrick asleep in Julie's arms. The moment they entered, the temperature in the room went down, the silence and the stillness shadowing forth a chill.

I stood up and said, "Let me introduce everyone." When I turned back to the table I saw puzzled, unwelcoming faces — savages, staring at outsiders who had invaded their feast. "This is Charlie, his wife Julie. And Patrick."

"Dead to the world," Charlie said. "Long ride!"

No one spoke. Mother straightened in her chair and looked resentful, for the attention had been taken from her. Hubby and the others shifted in their seats. As though sensing the bewilderment, and taking advantage of the uncertainty, Jonty's daughter Jilly began to bawl. Little Patrick's eyes fluttered at the squawk, seeming to recognize the child's complaint, like a common language.

"Let me get you a chair," I said.

"How about this one?" Charlie seized a chair back.

Someone snorted. "No, no," I said. "That's Angela's."

"She in the john?" Charlie said.

"She's in heaven," Mother said.

I found some folding chairs stacked in the corner. Charlie helped me set them up, a second row behind me. No one else moved, or spoke.

"Blow out your candles, Mumma," Rose said.

The candles had melted and dripped and charred the flesh of the pine-apples on the upside-down cake, but still the orange flames swayed.

"Here goes," Mother said.

"Her ninetieth," Marvin explained to Charlie, who had drawn his chair nearer the table so that he could see better. Julie held their sleepy child. Their presence was a derangement that delighted me.

Everyone at the table had gone silent, not knowing how to handle the abrupt entrance of these strangers. And because I had introduced them, the hostility was directed at me. The family was naturally suspicious, but the unexpected arrival of these three smiling people at Mother's birthday party made them seem intruders. They had stumbled upon our secret ritual and might have overheard us in our mumblings and chants. To a disorderly and angry family, all outsiders were enemies, even the spouses. I was somehow responsible, so I was glared at more than Charlie.

"Take a group picture, Walter," I said.

"What about Angela?" Charlie said, gesturing to the empty chair.

Mother shut her eyes and suffered a little, as Franny and Rose gave Charlie dark looks. But he must have misheard when Mother had said that Angela was in heaven, perhaps thinking that she was in another room.

After the cake had been cut and apportioned, Walter obliged with a family portrait. Floyd stood at the rear of the group, and just before Walter snapped, Floyd said, "The House of Atreus!"

"Jay is something of a fop, but we forgive him his pretensions," Floyd said to Charlie. "He's the objective correlative by which we assess our plausibility. Let's face it" — were still posing, Walter still snapping — "he has made some questionable choices. But in his mind, he is the sane one. We are unfathomable grotesques."

"Give it a rest," Fred said. "Ma has a headache."

But family teasing was the test of friendship, and Floyd was being friendly. I took his fooling as a peacemaking gesture. Needling was a form of dialogue.

"Floyd's choices have been irreproachable," I said, and Floyd laughed.

"It's nice of you to have us," Charlie said, glancing at Mother, who stared at him, "especially on this big day."

"Ya welcome," Rose said out of the corner of her mouth.

As though dismissing Charlie and Julie, Fred said, "Want seconds on the cake?"

Coffee was served by the harassed waitresses, but by then the family members had gotten to their feet, yawning, making grunts of farewell, mutters of apology, shufflings of departure. With the arrival of Charlie, the birthday had come apart, and only a residue, a faint echo of the meal, remained. The family had been intruded upon, but the hostility had leaked away, leaving—what? Confusion, collapse, for ill will had held us together and now there was simply indifference.

"Stick around," I said to the table. "We can talk."

But no one lingered, no one gave Charlie a second glance.

"Charlie owns a software company in Boston," I said. "Ma, Charlie was looking forward to meeting you."

But Mother was being helped out of the room by Gilbert, and Fred turned to me, pointed his finger at his head, and made a face, meaning "headache."

When we were alone in the room, Charlie said, "Sorry, did we break up the party?"

"No, of course not," I said. He had, more suddenly than I had expected, but as I spoke he gave me a hug, and little Patrick said, "Who's that man?"

31

MY NATURE IS TO STING

EVERYONE IN THE BIG, porous, leaky family complained about Mother's birthday party afterward, whispering heavily into the phone, including Mother—guest of honor, recipient of presents—who'd had a good time. But Mother had a motive.

"I can't believe that Jonty had the nerve to bring that daughter of his," Mother said to me when I visited her with more chocolates. "Who ever gave her permission to do that? And where was Loris?"

I was surprised by Mother's fierceness, excessive even for her. She stood and stamped her tiny feet when she was angry, cords were drawn tight in her neck, she grew hoarse in her indignation and choked slightly —*hlook! hlook!*—bone-in-the-throat gasping that always got my attention, though I despaired of the naggy emphasis of her amateur acting.

"Jonty should have known better. I specifically said, *no children.*"

Her child hating was not a pose, the weary exasperation of a sentimental mother who spoke of them as rug rats and burdens. Mother genuinely disliked them, but I did not realize this until I had children myself. She had already raised eight of them, including the ghost of Angela—why more? Children bored her, they irritated her, they were always in the way; most of all they took attention away from her. When there was a child in the same room with her, she knew that at least two people were not listening—the child and the child's parent—and perhaps many more.

"And only the immediate family," she added.

Then I knew what this was about. In this outburst of criticism Mother was of course reprimanding me for inviting Charlie, Julie, and little Patrick to the family event. This was how she stirred: criticism was always oblique. By blaming Jonty for precisely the same liberty that I had taken, I was being told that I was myself at fault. After almost forty years, Charlie was still unwelcome, and his child—my grandson, Mother's other great-grandchild—was no more than an irritant.

At one point in the cake cutting I had wanted to say, "Can I have everyone's attention?"—and I was going to proclaim him. I resisted, but loved the fantasy of apostrophizing, and even now, listening to Mother complain, I had the urge to say, "That was my son!"

Mother said, "Who did Jonty think was paying for that party?"

"I forgot to ask—aren't we sharing it?"

"I paid for it with my own money," Mother said, screeching like a child shaking an empty piggy bank.

I watched her for a while and then said, "Maybe I shouldn't have brought my friends."

The noncommittal way Mother rolled the bones in her shoulders told me more than she said. The bones said, *Why are you putting me through this by saying that?* Mother said, "They seemed very nice. I didn't mind their being there. I'm sorry I didn't get a chance to talk with them." One of her bony shoulders snapped back and seemed to say, *Don't care!*

"No one said much to them."

Seizing this with a jeering laugh, Mother said, "We're busy, Jay. Everyone is. You can't just show up and expect people to be at your beck and call."

"But they had a good time. They liked meeting the family."

Mother smiled unpleasantly. "The little one came back for another piece of cake."

She had noticed everything. She saw them as gate-crashers, leeching and gobbling.

A day or so later, Franny confirmed my suspicions of what Mother had said — and by suspicions I mean what I had translated of her words, the family-speak that was always inverted, when "I didn't mind their being there" meant that she did mind.

"Ma was kinda put out by your friends," Franny said.

"They didn't eat much."

"They had an awful lot of cake. Seconds."

"So what?"

"It's kinda the principle of the thing."

Bemoaning a three-year-old for eating a small wet piece of upside-down cake was so preposterous I could not think of a reply. I hoped my silence would shame Franny. But she persisted.

"And Hubby had seconds of chowder. And three big slices of cake."

"Is that a problem?"

"I'm just saying. I'm kinda worried about his health. He has issues. And he's always been heavy."

Another family irony was that the target of one person's criticism was the critic of his accuser, and the blame was usually identical. Franny said that Hubby was fat and greedy, then covered it with this insincerity about his health; and Hubby returned the compliment. We seemed to know by instinct who was watching us, and why.

"Franny really stuffed herself," Hubby said to me the next day. "And she's a blimp."

When, a few days later, Rose found fault with Fred — "wicked bossy bastard, playing God with the menu" — I knew that Fred would have a reply, and he did: "Her husband sticking his camera in my face. And she's getting so manipulative."

My phone kept ringing, and always it was a sibling carping about another sibling.

"At least Ma had a good time," I said.

"She was upset by all the little children," Fred said.

Two children, one of them my guest. No one dared criticize me to my face, which meant that behind my back they were buzzing, all of them angry with me. And I knew why. Charlie dropping in with his wife and child, the strangers presuming on a family gathering, violated a family rule, probably an ancient taboo in the world of savages: no outsider must be allowed to observe us in our private rituals. The taboo had been transgressed. But this postscript of whispers was also an example of the family love of moaning as a way of testing affinities and finding allies.

"I know Ma's angry with me," I said to Franny, who spoke to Mother four times a day on the phone.

"She *was* kinda miffed."

In the lingua franca of Mother Land, "kinda miffed" meant furious.

"What did she say?"

Franny would certainly tell me, because it was her blameless way of putting me in my place.

"She said you had kind of a nerve bringing those friends of yours."

Perhaps I had expected that all along. Perhaps it was worse than mere presumption on my part. I suspected that my motive for inviting my long-lost son to a family gathering — a family that had taken no interest in him — was a distinct form of aggression. I had challenged them, knowing they would object, knowing that I would be hurt. Charlie had become an expression of my defiance. And what they didn't know, in seeing him as an intruder, was that he was a member of the family.

All he said afterward was, "Thanks for having us. What an amazing family, even if it's a little scary. But I'm so happy to have a grandmother."

In all this rancor, a voice that was generous.

The biggest surprise to me at Mother's ninetieth birthday party was Floyd — that he showed up was something of a miracle, but that was not all. His bearishness and pedantry were immutable aspects of his personality. What I had not expected were the energy and inventiveness of his incessant teasing.

Teasing in the family, as I have said, was always meaningful, but it needed to be deconstructed. It could be mocking, it could be casually cruel, it could be an expression of boredom — something like turning a hose on a puppy — and at its most sadistic it could be a way of amusing bystanders by ridiculing the weakest person in the room. It could be affectionate, a form of sparring, taking a shot at someone and allowing him to hit back. That was Floyd's manner in the function room at the Happy Clam. His teasing had been friendly, with an acerbic geniality. Mostly, he had been performing, throwing elbows at the others and digs at me. I had teased him back. Though you had to have grown up in the family to appreciate the nuances of it, his teasing had been a compliment, the nearest thing there was in this family to a hug.

I could tell from his teasing that Floyd wished to forget the past. He was elaborate in covering his embarrassment. And he was so subtle in it that I was sure that no one at the table had seen this. Amazing that this secret, this tentative proposal of a détente, had been enacted in front of the whole family, and yet only he and I understood his true intent. He wanted to be my friend.

The details of his printed attack on me still angered me, and so I had avoided him. And it puzzled me that no one had taken my side in the affair. All along, people had said to me, "How could he say those terrible things about you?"

I had said, "He's a piece of work, actually. Someone said it looks like Cain and Abel. I said, 'No. It's like Tom and Jerry.'"

I always thought of Floyd in terms of the Sufi story about the helpful tortoise and the stranded scorpion. After the tortoise carries the scorpion across the river, the scorpion stings him. The tortoise says, "My nature is to be helpful. I have helped you, and now you sting me." The scorpion replies, "But my nature is to sting. Why do you seek to transform your nature into a virtue and mine into a villainy?"

Floyd's nature was to sting. What I could not tell anyone was how his attack had served to expose the family's hostility toward me.

At the birthday lunch I saw him as the older brother I had once loved.

He was funny and ironic, evasive, cranky, unexpected, forever chattering and mimicking, except when he was sulking.

He was a reader. No one else in the family read books. He respected me for my reading, and he saw the rest of the family as either ignorant or intellectually lazy.

People who read widely and with fervor learn a language and inhabit a world that is different from the world of the nonreader. I don't mean illiterates, many of whom I knew in Africa, who develop special skills of observation. Nonreaders are merely idle and arrogant and obtuse. And by "readers" I don't mean the chasers of the latest books but rather wanderers in the whole realm of literature, all its thickets and caverns, the seldom-trodden pathways among the wayward geniuses. The famous names, of course — Shakespeare, Dickens (the Shakespeare of the novel), Flaubert, Joyce, Twain, and Melville. Even nonreaders know those names, and if they never open a book, they know "To be or not to be" and "Please, sir, I want some more," and that Captain Ahab had a peg leg and that the whale was white. But they have never heard the names Baron Corvo, Mervyn Peake, Trollope, Turgenev, George Gissing, Zora Neale Hurston, or Ford Madox Ford. Floyd was an authority on his Cape neighbor Edward Gorey — and a friend of his, too. He had translated Celine's *Mort à Crédit* into English, and Collier's *His Monkey Wife* into French. He knew Edward Dahlberg's *Bottom Dogs* almost by heart; he had read the whole of Samuel Beckett, and all of Yeats and Faulkner.

Floyd had made literary pilgrimages to Pola and Tirana and Burwash, "for obvious reasons." He boasted of owning a rare set of the New York Edition of Henry James, he had met and ranted at Beckett in Paris, he could read Greek, he knew sign language from his years as a Trappist monk, and as a result of a subsequent spell in a Franciscan monastery, he was fluent in conversational Latin. This learning was part of his language, his set of references, his jokes. When he talked he often mocked bystanders who had no idea what he was saying, exactly like those new immigrants who feel safe in a crowd of English speakers, talking to each other and jeering at people within earshot, who have no idea that they are the butt of the joke.

In seeming to yak at Jonty and Franny, Floyd had been talking to me. What had seemed like random teasing and byplay at the lunch was a conversation, Floyd and I settling into an old form of discourse. We understood each other; no one else did. And this was a great relief, the pleasure of being able to talk to someone in one's own language without needing to edit or simplify or explain.

I knew that when Floyd had scowled and said, "The House of Atreus!" he was in his *Oresteia* rant, identifying Mother as Clytemnestra. In his day, Father had been Agamemnon. But Mother was also Queen Lear, and when she spoke about her will, she was Volpone. He called Fred's wife Rappaccini's daughter; he made a joke about being Peer Gynt and Mother being Åse; he called Franny's husband Claggart, Fred he called Pecksniff, and Rose's family the Veneerings.

I was the only one present who understood him, who could reply, and so I knew he looked upon me with respect, a little relieved that his learning was appreciated.

"I've been puzzling for a means to take the strut out of you, you posturing snob," he said, quoting Charles Laughton as Captain Bligh and pretending to brandish a whip, and to Walter's picture-taking he had said, "It can't be true — it ain't complicated enough," quoting Flem Snopes.

His reading was a reflection of how much he hated Harvard and his fellow professors with narrow interests. "Fact fetishists! Fanatical explicators!" Floyd was obsessive, addicted to books, print-hungry, more partial to the glissade of an elaborate metaphor than to its function, because its use was to dazzle, not to advance a narrative. He hated a pithy declarative sentence like this one. His definition of a savage was a nonreader, not an illiterate but someone who knew how and didn't do it. At the lunch I was reminded that he was a kindred soul, sharing my language, a brother in a profound sense. I was sorry for all the years of silence and recriminations, but I knew there was hope for something better, for — sadly — we didn't have anyone else.

Mother's birthday lunch had been one of the important events of the family, a way-marker, like Father's funeral (which everyone went to), Jonty's wedding (which some of us had snubbed), my failed romance with Missy, and Floyd's crazy, accusatory essay about me — pivotal, awkward, revelatory.

Walter sent everyone a set of pictures. Most of them were generic snapshots of us eating — jumbled faces, busy arms — or of Mother posing with Fred and Gilbert, then with Franny and Rose. Hubby was shown sneaking a second helping of cake; Jonty's daughter Jilly looked like a furious dwarf in a folktale, her face splashed with chocolate. One of Mother — amazing how the camera doesn't lie — made her seem like a Roman matriarch, one of those poisoners and plotters. From the snapshots it was clearly a heavy family, with sour mouths, greedy eyes, food-smeared cheeks, sitting in rigid postures that told how they resented having to be together at the same table, hunched joylessly with fixed expressions, only Mother exulting.

The frowning faces and the eyes reddened by Walter's flash attachment made the whole group grimmer. We looked like grumpy and misshapen orphans, crowding their demonic housemother.

The best picture, one I had hoped for, and treasured, showed us all, with Charlie and Julie in front, little Patrick on Charlie's knee. I was crouched next to them. Mother was right behind them, recoiling slightly, but affecting a pose of superiority in the way she leaned back, the better to be seen.

This was my prize. I made a number of copies of that group picture, enlarged so as to give the photograph the formality of a portrait. Then I sat down and wrote a little note, and made multiple copies of it:

> I am enclosing a picture taken at Mother's birthday party, which shows my son Charlie, his wife Julia, and my grandson Patrick. You may remember that he was born in 1961. He has come into my life and is a part of my family. I omitted to mention this on the day.

This I sent, with a picture, to everyone. It was a dig, of course. They had not deserved to be introduced to them. They had blamed me when Charlie was born, had never inquired about him, had forgotten about him. At the party, as an anonymous stranger — but a cheery soul — he had been ignored. Yet here he was with a name, my flesh and blood, prosperous and happy, with obvious family features. I wondered what they would say.

Mother was the first to call. She was at once combative, cross that she had been upstaged, and, "Why didn't you tell me?"

It was an indictment. As a stranger, Charlie had excited no interest; as my long-lost son, he was sought after.

"No one talked to him," I said.

"We didn't know him."

"You were angry because I brought him."

"How was I to know he was your son?"

"That's the point. He was a guest, someone close to me. You thought he ate too much. Afterward, when I mentioned him, you said to me, 'You can't just show up and expect people to be at your beck and call.'"

"I never said that."

"Those very words."

"I am a warm and hospitable woman who would never send a helpless person from my door."

"Charlie has a lovely house. He owns a big company."

"Where does he live?"

"I'd rather not say."

"I want to write to him."

"He's forty-two years old. Isn't it a bit late for a letter?"

"I am his grandmother!" I could tell, even on the phone, that Mother rapped these words with her fist on the arm of her chair as she spoke them.

"You were angry when he was born. You said I should be ashamed. You never went to see him at the Mass. General."

Snorts on the phone indicated that Mother had begun to cry.

"Want to hear the funny part?" I said.

Mother's sobbing sounded to me like she was swallowing soup, gulping it, all the snufflings and throat noises of a meal she seemed to be enjoying.

"I want to send him a little something," Mother said, smacking her lips.

"That's the funny part," I said. "He's a multimillionaire."

"Jay," Mother said, moaning my name with regret. "You can be so cruel."

Fred called. He said, "You made me feel like a fool. You didn't say anything about him."

"I left it up to you. It was a test of initiative. You failed, Freddy. Everyone failed. Ma failed."

"She called me. She told me you insulted her. She's a wreck."

I had no sooner banged the phone down than Franny called.

"I had a feeling," Franny said. "I thought he looked like you. I knew all along. I didn't want to say anything."

Rose didn't call. Gilbert sent me a postcard from Bahrain. Hubby said, "I was just a little kid when he was born. As Dad would say, it's ancient history."

Floyd sent me a postcard with an enigmatic image on it, a painting by Goya, titled *Perro Semihundido en la Arena — Dog Half-Submerged —* a dark study of a little mutt buried up to its ears in sand, its snout upturned, its eyes imploring, under a big, smoky-yellow sky. Floyd's message: *I think this just about sums it up.*

Not wishing to let him have the last word, I replied with a postcard of my own, a more hopeful one, Poussin's painting of Moses discovered in the bulrushes, and wrote, *Or this.*

That was the only way of dealing with it — obliquely, for I had been oblique. But everyone got the message — that I was angry over something that had happened almost forty years ago (in our family this was yesterday), and that inviting Charlie to Mother's party and not introducing him was pure hostility, an act of rejection.

32

STATION IDENTIFICATION

FOR YEARS, nothing happened. Then, in a matter of days, everything happened. The long, steady slog toward a large family gathering — funeral, wedding, birthday — was always followed by a period of surprises, sudden and sometimes shocking. We crested that event and were tipped over, sped rapidly downward in all the foolish postures of tumbled clowns, glimpsed in our weakness, one revelation after another, bump, bump, bump.

Mother begged me for Charlie's address. I refused to hand it over; too late, I said. Rose accused me of persecuting Mother. "Jonty was wondering if you could put him in touch with Charlie," Franny asked. "Jilly could play with Patrick." Jonty had heard that Charlie was wealthy; this was a networking move—his wife was an insurance agent, always looking for a new client and cash flow. I said, "Please leave him alone." Hubby wondered if Charlie fished—Hubby was a fisherman.

I said, "He's busy."

Rebuffing them invigorated me and made me as confident as a traffic cop. I loved especially turning down Mother's request. Her response was to spread the word that I was cruel.

Charlie kept in touch, met me at Baxter's on Hyannis Harbor for lunch, and told me the story of his upbringing. This sunny narrative convinced me that Mona had done the right thing in handing him over to people better able to take care of him: they had been grateful, they loved him, they raised him in a small, uncomplicated family, without rivalries.

"I'd like to meet your adoptive parents," I said.

"They're not ready for that."

Now I knew what it was like to be rebuffed. I was reminded that I had no rights.

"It must have been tough for you and Mona," he said another day, another lunch, Centerville Pizza.

"The worst year of my life," I said. "It was also the best year. Do you understand that? How it made me?"

"I guess so." But how could he? He had grown up in a generous household. He did not need to learn anything about struggle and savagery, about the bitching and counterbitching that was a dialogue of Mother Land.

"What did your father think about your finding your birth parents?"

"Like I said, 'Don't give them any money!'" And Charlie laughed at the thought of it.

Being with Charlie, this unsuspicious and appreciative soul, so positive, so polite, was a tonic to me. He did not draw off my energy, as my family did. He lifted my spirits, and I always felt stronger after I was with him. I knew this because afterward, when I was with someone in my family, I felt diminished, exhausted by their deviousness.

Fred came by. He, too, wanted to get in touch with Charlie. "We're opening a Boston office. We could throw some money his way—our computer installation is still out for bids. He might like the business."

"He seems to be doing fine. I don't think he needs you."

No one in the family ever said what they meant. I had to translate. Mother had said, "I can't give him money—you know I don't have much —but I can knit a sweater for little Patrick." Yet what she really needed was to atone, to be forgiven for ignoring him from birth. Franny wanted to patronize him, Jonty wanted a wealthy friend, everyone wanted something from him. None of us had anything to offer him; he didn't need us. He had grown up fulfilled, while we had been raised like wolves.

I said to Fred, "He's got plenty of business."

"I'm just trying to help."

In Mother Land this meant the opposite: he wanted Charlie to help him, perhaps find him clients. Was it possible to be a lawyer and not behave like a predator?

We were in my yard, Fred and I. I had been sweeping sand off my driveway. I kept sweeping—passive aggressive. Years ago I would have invited Fred into the house for a beer. No longer.

"Excuse me?" I bumped the broom on his shoes.

"Sorry."

He stepped aside, and I swept where his feet had been, a technique Mother had taught me. This broom-bumping meant: *You are idle and in the way.*

"I just came from Ma's," he said. He took out a piece of paper and unfolded it—a used envelope scribbled in blue ink. "She says to me, 'Freddy, will you check and see if I paid my water bill? Those damn people sent me a reminder notice, charging me fifty cents interest for nonpayment.'"

"Don't laugh. Half a buck is a lot of money for Ma."

"That's what I used to think."

He gave me a sly look.

"You mean half a buck is not a lot of money to Ma?" I asked.

"Sixteen thousand is probably a more reliable figure. That's what she gave Franny."

I put down my broom, crossed my arms, and gave him my full attention. He was holding the creased envelope in his cupped palm, referring to it like a speechmaker glancing at his notes.

"Gave her sixteen grand, did you say?"

"To renovate her kitchen. I saw the check stub. And" — he glanced down again — "eleven thousand to Rose, to put in a new septic system at the cottage. And you remember that the cottage was a gift." He lifted his hand to his face, examined the paper, and went on. "Eight thousand toward a new car for Franny. Five thousand for Bingo's college tuition. Two thousand for something called 'dental work' for Franny. Oh, and Hubby got a few thousand for a paint job."

"But all of them got land or houses," I said.

"Right. And money. These are rough figures." Seeing that I had dropped my broom and was craning my neck for a look at the scribbled envelope, he folded it smaller and crammed it into his pocket. "I was looking through Ma's accounts, as I said." He was smiling because he had caught my interest. "These are the figures that stuck out. About forty grand over the past year or so."

"That's unfair."

"But, look, it's Ma's money," he said, trifling with me.

"Ma handed over forty grand?"

"Probably more. I didn't have much time to examine the books." Fred was casual, and he could afford to be, because I was riveted by this disclosure.

"They're shaking Ma down!"

"Not really. She can do what she wants. It's her money." Now, having seized my full attention, Fred said, "Gotta go."

So his revenge on me for not putting me in touch with Charlie was to drop this scandal into my lap and then vanish. It was Mother's method: a wicked word in your ear and then she would withdraw, and might deny ever having said the wicked word.

"Almost forgot," Fred said. "Walter got fifty dollars for taking pictures at the birthday party."

"They weren't even good pictures."

Fred was still walking to his car, as I followed, picking up my broom on the way. He got in, started the engine, and rolled down the window.

"What I just told you?" he said. "It's confidential. Don't tell anyone."

That, too, meant the opposite. Tell everyone, he was saying. But I was not sure whom to tell.

· · ·

Fred's showing up with that news unsettled me, which had been his intention. It was a family of droppers-in. *Remember me?* they seemed to say. They looked for gossip, they left some gossip behind. *Where do I stand?* they wondered. The whole process of showing up and nudging me, leaving me stirred. Station identification.

Even my sons did it, but benignly, making sure I was all right, for as they had indicated a few years before, they were the adults and we were the children.

They had phoned from London to say how sorry they were to have missed Mother's ninetieth. They had not known they weren't invited. I didn't tell them that Jonty was criticized for bringing Jilly, that I had been jeered at for inviting Charlie — that is, until they realized he was my millionaire son. But I had broken the news to them of Charlie's existence, and told them that I'd invited him and his family to the party. Each mention of Charlie to them, I felt, was a way of easing him into their consciousness.

Julian arrived first, having called from Boston. "I had some business in New York."

He didn't have business in New York. He was trying not to condescend, or obligate me, with his sudden worried visit.

"I haven't heard from you for ages," he said. "Also, I wanted to bring Grandma a birthday present. Amazing that she's ninety."

"What did you bring her?"

"Green bananas. And a long book," he said. "She's going to last forever."

I loved his visits, despite knowing that it was a form of station identification. I liked the glare of his intelligent scrutiny. I could not hide anything from him. I felt even better when Harry showed up a few days later. Together they were more relaxed, their gaze less intense. They enjoyed each other's company, and mine. Because they were among the few people I spoke with who had a genuine interest in my work, I told them about my Africa book.

"I spent a lot of time in buses and beat-up trucks."

"Trust Dad to find the slowest way of crossing Africa," Julian said.

Harry said with mock seriousness, "You must have met a lot of English kids, traveling on their gap year. That's what they do, take buses in banana republics."

We were having lunch in the sushi bar in Yarmouth Port. I had declared a holiday because of their visit and put my work aside.

"I'm sorry I missed Grandma's birthday," Julian said. "She said I would have loved it."

Now that the party was over, it was safe for Grandma to lament their absence.

I said, "Grandma had a good time. No one else did."

"Charlie said he liked it," Harry said. "He emailed me. He sent some pictures."

"I mailed that group photo to everyone with a note," I said, and told them how I had worded it.

"That is pure hostility," Harry said.

"Where is your sense of fun?"

"This family never changes," Julian said.

"Yes, it does," I said. "It gets worse."

"I'm glad I wasn't there. You and Uncle Floyd in the same room," Julian said. He shuddered. "Dr. Mongoose and Mr. Cobra."

I said, "He was fine — in good form. We fooled around."

They exchanged glances. I didn't blame them. It was impossible to think of Floyd and me without imagining loud abuse, or else embarrassed silence.

Knowing that I had their attention, I said, "We could stop by his house after lunch. It's on the way."

"No, no," Harry said.

"I want to. I have something to tell him." I wanted most of all to prove to them that I was an adult, that I'd finally overcome the childishness of the years of feuding.

My sons were worried, they were anxious, but they were fascinated. Uncle Floyd was to them an almost mythical figure, famous for his rages, celebrated for his learning, a well-known poet, a cantankerous Harvard prof, widely published, a man in a black cape who had known Samuel Beckett, and in a sense had been anointed by him, as Joyce had anointed Beckett, extending a literary tradition. Floyd was part of this lineage.

Driving down Route 6A from the sushi bar, I slowed the car at Willow Street. Julian said, "I don't want to do this." But I knew that what I intended was another form of station identification.

As I drew up to Floyd's driveway, Floyd was snipping with hedge clippers at a squatting, vaguely human-shaped bush. He wore a Panama hat, a white linen suit, and espadrilles.

"I have such a weakness for topiary," he said.

"Is it a monkey?" Harry asked.

"Not even close," Floyd said, still snipping. "The Ape of Thoth. Notice its prognathic visage. Question — which second-rate diabolist called his mistress the Ape of Thoth?"

"You want Aleister Crowley," I said.

"As every schoolboy knows," Floyd said. "Consecrated the Scarlet Woman by Crowley, and thus she was the initiatrix of his becoming Ipsissimus. Bride of Chaos, as she was known to him. But what was she known as to the world at large? You want simple, screwy Leah Hirsig, she of the turdish tastes in a world of cack, and I might add, not only American but one of nine children, so I think we can safely say she was one of us."

"Nice to see you, Uncle Floyd," Julian said.

Floyd put down his hedge clippers and adjusted his Panama hat at a more foppish angle. He squinted at my sons and said, "Now tell me about England, which is ever so ducky, and that muffin-faced queen who is head of the church, God help her."

"She can cure scrofula by just touching a person," Harry said. "The English monarch has magical powers."

"I'll rub-a-dub," Floyd said. "What a credulous, class-ridden kingdom. But of course I miss Fitzrovia and 'the taking of a toast and tea.' Whom am I quoting?"

"Henry James?" Julian said.

"Toilets, which is an anagram of T. S. Eliot," Floyd said. "What have you brought me? Nothing. What have you brought your aged grandmother? Nothing."

We were now following him across the grass where, under a tree, a table was scattered with scribbled-on paper, a human skull serving as a paperweight.

"This is a masterpiece," Floyd said, tapping the paper, "and this is of course an ancestor skull, used by the Asmat people of New Guinea as a headrest or a pillow. Note the patina and the shell inlay and the overmodeling. Did you want something? Am I wearing something of yours? Do I owe you money?"

"Mum sent her regards," Julian said.

"A good woman. Her sensibly shod feet squarely on the ground," Floyd said. "Your father took her very much for granted and paid dearly for it, if I'm not mistaken." He was glancing at the paper he'd written on. "Oh, most assuredly this is a *capolavoro.*"

The boys were laughing. They had relaxed, recognizing the old Floyd, teasing and good-tempered and overacting. They were reassured, and so was I. It had been more than ten years since I'd been here at his house. Instead of commenting on that directly, he welcomed us with a burst of family abuse, which was his oblique form of welcome.

"The birthday party was a fiasco," he said. "Why was Hubby sulking? Was he having a fit of the vapors? Franny's husband looks like a penguin. Walter is pan-headed, Jonty's daughter is a monkey, but then, what five-year-old isn't the very image of a bonobo chimp? And, *entre nous,* did you know that bonobos are ardent masturbators? The food was terrible. Places like that should provide a vomitorium. Did you see Fred? I want to give the eulogy at his funeral. I'll stand over his casket and say, 'I never really knew this man.'"

"Grandma said she enjoyed herself," Julian said.

"Because it's the House of Atreus. It feeds on chaos," Floyd said. "Sit down. Have a drink."

"We're fine," I said.

"That's it, take charge," Floyd said. "Do you want orange squash? Ribena? Lucozade? Stone's ginger wine? A lemon shandy? Where do the English get these drinks, out of a kiddie's book? They love nursery food, the English, especially the upper classes. 'I want bikkies, I want pudding!'"

The boys knew better than to challenge him. Julian said, "You're right. They're pathetic."

"Did I say that? Never mind. Have some lemonade. It's a man's drink." Still speaking, he walked to his house and returned a few minutes later with a jug of lemonade and four glasses.

"You want that skull, but you can't have it," he said, patting the cranium. "Which poet saw the skull beneath the skin?" he asked, and in the hesitation said, "The answer is Webster, but the judgment is Toilets, a wicked anti-Semite and I believe no stranger to sodomy. His wife was a martyr to dysmenorrhea, poor thing. She turned to Bertrand Russell for consolation, which sent her barmy. Drink up."

I said, "Fred dropped in the other day."

"The human doormat," Floyd said. "Mister M'Choakumchild. What is it with lawyers? They have no souls."

"He had just come from Ma's," I said. "Somehow he got a look at her accounts. She's been giving money to Franny and Rose. Big money."

"Looking in Ma's accounts for clues," Floyd said to Julian and Harry. He flapped his fingers at me as though casting a spell, and made a face. "Step forth, Auguste Dupin."

"Sixteen thousand, ten thousand, new kitchen, new car."

"I'm not surprised," Floyd said.

But he was surprised. He rattled the ice in his glass and looked into the distance, across his lawn to his limestone gazebo.

"I asked her for a loan a few years ago," he said in a new, reflective voice, his own. "She said, 'Money doesn't grow on trees.' Funnily enough, I knew that." He turned to me. "Why did Fred tell you about the money?"

"To wind me up, obviously," I said. "He says he doesn't care. That means he does care. The thing is, all he wrote down were the big figures. Apparently, she's given quite a lot away."

"Queen Lear," Floyd said. "Two adoring daughters. 'We love you, Mumma!' I wonder how much she gave them altogether?"

"We can find out. Look at the accounts. But I'm not sure how."

Though he said nothing at first, I could see from his face that Floyd was becoming even more animated. He was mentally hurrying to Mother's house, casing the joint, slipping on a pair of gloves, and tiptoeing around it in his espadrilles.

"Cat-burgle it," he said. "Creepy-crawl it. Find out the truth. This is treachery." He raised one eyebrow and fixed me with his gaze. "More lemonade, Watson?"

33

CAT BURGLARY

THERE WE WERE, Floyd and I, in my old Jeep Renegade, once stylish, then a banger, later vintage, now a classic, setting off to burgle Mother's house. Floyd said, "I hate cars like this. What is it that you lack in your life that makes you need something of this sort?"

"It's sturdy."

"For all those cross-country drives! For all those treks in the Mato Grosso!"

As he spoke, he was trying to adjust the seat, biting air in frustration, jerking his body back and forth, snatching at the lever on the side, as though humping down a hill of wet snow on an old sled.

"It's a gas hog. How often do you put it in four-wheel drive, eh, Indy?"

"When I drive across your lumpy ass."

"The trend toward survivalism in consumer goods. Titanium sunglasses. Indestructible mountain bikes. Big fat knobby tires. Hunting knives. Cargo pants. I wrote a poem about it. Effeminate executives are wearing waterproof divers' watches that can still tick at two hundred meters under the sea. Hummers — you could invade Somalia with them, but yuppies use them to pick up sushi."

"This isn't a Hummer."

"Same thing. It's overkill."

"I want a car like yours," I said. "A twenty-year-old Mercedes with peeling paint and a Harvard sticker on the back window saying *Veritas*."

"You wish you had one so wicked bad, instead of this piece of dated yuppie frivolity."

"But yours is a toilet."

Floyd bucked in his seat with hilarity and cackled, "I love that expression."

It was as if no time had passed. The day was sunny, Father was still alive, we were in high school. We were cruising around, shouting at each other, yelling at traffic. Floyd had a habit of waving at pretty girls — in cars, on the sidewalk — encouraging them to wave back. The world was big and strange, therefore we mocked it and re-created it as our own fiction. We had no money, but we had secrets, we had hopes, we were outlaws, we gloried in self-dramatization.

"There's pecker tracks on the rear seat," Floyd said.

Seeing a yellow light ahead, I stomped on the gas pedal and ran the red.

"Fuck a duck," Floyd said.

We were alone. My two sons had returned to London, shaking their heads over the family. And Floyd was affectionately jeering at me, as he'd done long ago. He did not allude to the fact that we had been at odds for the past eight years. He had not said a word on the subject, that he had disparaged me in a set of extravagant lies and rubbished my book in his bilious review. The matter did not arise. I guessed his teasing to be a way of moving on.

As two happy boys in the car, speeding down the Cape, the prospect of this act of villainy filled us with joy, like teenagers swaggering toward a petty crime. I remembered the old thrill of smashing streetlights and running to hide, siphoning gas from cars, making zip guns, and jamming potatoes into exhaust pipes.

"I brought a screwdriver and a crowbar."

"And a jimmy!" Floyd said. "He's getting into the mind of a criminal. He's a walking time bomb. He's Raskolnikov, ambiguous guilt all over his face. See, he really *wants* someone to catch him stealing from his mother."

"And you're on an emotional roller coaster."

Nothing made Floyd happier than a cliché. "You've got issues," he said. "And Fred is a sentimentalist. He's Edward Ashburnham in *The Good Soldier*, looking for his Flory Hurlbird. 'Shuttlecocks!' He looks at Ma's accounts and scribbles down a few figures on the back of an envelope. Would you hire this guy — never mind as a lawyer. Would you hire him to replace the refill in your ballpoint pen? He's not serious. He's pettifogging with us, and so he has left us no option. Ha!"

"We are going to the scene of the crime."

"And if it turns out that Ma has been giving Franny and Rose money, I'm going to write them a note. Just a few words on a postcard. 'Someone should shoot you.'" He jerked his body impatiently in the seat again. "She might have locked the whole place."

"Look at this." I held up the screwdriver.

"Listen, Arthur Flegenheimer, aka Dutch Schultz," Floyd said. "Do me the courtesy of not boasting in advance. It would pain me ever so much to see you chopfallen."

"Fred wouldn't have mentioned it if there hadn't been any truth in it."

"Franny and Rose, the Wobbling Weird Sisters. How could Ma favor them like that?" Floyd said. "What about me? I can handle things. I'm smart" — his imitation of Fredo in *The Godfather*.

"We'll see."

"Ma is such a fox," he said. He sat back, remembering. "It's just before graduation, 1957. I have won the American Legion Award. We are asked to appear for a group photo taken by Dwight Davis — he of the gimpy leg — all the prizewinners, all the scholarship students. But I am not in the photograph. Where am I? Look in the basement of Murray's Stationery on Riverside Ave. and you will find me stacking reams of paper, because Ma wants me to work. Because money doesn't grow on trees." He straightened and shouted, "I will break down her door and ransack her files!"

His voice cracked like a teenager's. This was fun, like old times. The only pleasures I knew in this family were the rebellious deceptions of my boyhood, which today Floyd and I were reliving — outsmarting Mother, betraying Franny and Rose, mocking Fred, ranting against the injustices of the family: "It's a study in jealousy and begrudgery!"

Rolling down Route 28 toward Mother's house, Floyd was saying, "Ma's perfidious brother Louie, that sanctimonious bastard, used to take me aside and say, 'You're killing your mother. By wetting your bed. Do you realize how that hurts your mother? When are you going to stop? When you get married you're going to pee on your wife.' And he was a priest, so we couldn't answer back. He's straight out of Boccaccio. He's as bad as the pervert priests buggering altar boys in Dorchester. I was ten years old! No, no, take a right here —"

I turned off the main road, followed the side street for half a mile, then, at Floyd's insistent pointing, I took a back road to Mother's.

"It's her day for carving class at the senior center. I know these things," Floyd said. "But you can never tell — she might not have gone. Or she might have come back early. She might have finished her great crested grebe. Oh, shit."

We had reached the intersection of Mother's street. Her house was the fourth one down, and we could see that a large SUV was parked in her driveway.

"Who's that?"

"It's Fred's car."

"Oh, Jesus, wouldn't you know."

Floyd sighed as he peered out the window.

"Maybe he's visiting."

"Of course he's visiting. Ma decided to cancel her carving class so that she could spend some quality time with Fred." He laughed a little at this: the day we decide to burgle Mother, Fred is there to spoil our plan. The nerve of him.

"I'll go in," I said.

"I don't want him to see me," Floyd said. "I'll wait here. No, I'll walk around the block. I'll meet you at the end of the street."

He got out of the car, cursing. I drove up the street to Mother's and parked near Fred's big Land Cruiser.

"Hello," I called through the screen door.

"In here." A woman's voice — Erma, Fred's wife. "Hi, Jay. Are you looking for your mother?"

"Yes. Where is she?"

"At carving class. She let me in. I'm just waiting for a phone call from Fred."

"Where is he?"

"On his way to Hong Kong."

"And he's calling you here?"

"Our phone's not working. Maybe it's the batteries."

She stared at me. You would have thought she was smiling, but it was a smile-like expression of bewilderment. She was foxed by anything mechanical. She unplugged all the appliances when she went away, in the belief that, left hooked up, one of them would start a fire.

"Did you unplug the phone?"

This question made her wary. She didn't answer. She behaved as though I was criticizing her, and I suppose I was.

"What time is Fred going to call?"

"Eleven."

"It's half past."

"I'm wondering if I should wait."

I wanted her to say "I'm going." I wanted the phone to ring. But she sat, a huge, baffled obstruction, frustrating our plan.

"I'll tell your mom you were here. She'll be back around one."

"I forgot about the carving class."

"Every Friday," Erma said.

"Okay. See you later."

"I'll tell Fred you were asking for him."

"Do that."

I found Floyd standing under a maple tree, looking like an escaped felon. He said, "Does the word 'dentifrice' bother you as much as it bothers me?"

He had been vexed with this problem under the tree, probably grinding his teeth. I told him what I had found at Mother's, and Erma's explanation.

"Waiting for a phone call?" he said. "The woman is a ree-tard. What a waste of time this is. All this driving and waiting, and that foolish bitch parks her ass on Ma's sofa. She has nothing to do. I have a poem to finish. I've got grass to cut. I'm correcting page proofs. I'd like to go back there and toss her out of the house."

He was furious again, blaming Erma for thwarting our plans.

"This is the most wasted day of my life!"

But the attempted burglary (perhaps like all burglaries) was a bonding experience. Floyd and I were reconciled. And after that everyone avoided us. They were afraid of Floyd, and of course they knew — or guessed — that Floyd would tell me all the disparaging things they told him behind my back, in the days when they were close to Floyd and avoided me.

So, the worst of all things that can befall a big polarized family occurred in ours — the two bitterest enemies became friends, or at least allies. The children's factions were forced into new alliances: they were exposed, they were fearful, they hardly trusted one another, and they knew that their old allies, and in a sense their protectors, the two former enemies, were comparing notes on them.

But I could not let my guard down with Floyd. He was funny and intelligent and could be charming, but he could also be lethal. Say the wrong word and he could turn in seconds from a charmer to a demon. I was always cautioned in my behavior with him by the story of the tortoise and the scorpion. *My nature is to sting . . .*

We met again the following week, on the day of Mother's carving class, her only morning out of the house. Floyd was somewhat subdued. He did not satirize my Jeep (I had thought of some rejoinders). He said he'd spent the week in Cambridge, teaching his seminar on Milton.

Floyd had the odd smoky voice of someone who's seen something. He had a tendency to "see" things. "I saw that," he would say, remarking on his prescience.

"This Jewish guy's doing a graduate degree in literature," Floyd said. "He thinks it'll help him in his psychiatric work — he's a shrink in Newton. He wants to be the next Harry Stack Sullivan. As you probably don't know, Sullivan used classical literature to illustrate certain psychological traits and tendencies."

"Unlike Freud, of course, who never wrote about Oedipus or Dostoyevsky and who generally avoided pathologies in literature."

"Noted," Floyd said. "And now, will you shut your arse while I make my point? This guy Silverstone — observe the ingenious nomenclature — was in my office discussing some passages in *Paradise Lost,* and he says, 'I have real difficulty treating Jewish patients, because they don't forgive. They refuse to let go.' Just to keep him going — because, I mean, where's the headline? — I said, 'How do you know?' 'Take me, for example,' he says. 'I hate my mother.' This seized my attention, needless to say. I grilled him a little. He said that he and his brother wanted warm coats in the winter — he grew up in Brooklyn. His mother refused to buy them warm coats. Her excuse? 'You'd just lose them, or leave them somewhere.'"

"That's nice."

"Take this left," Floyd said. "Pequod Lane. Do you think that anyone on this benighted fucking street has any idea of the literary origin of this name? Anyway, in the evening this domineering harpy heated them a bowl of noodle soup from a can. Or thawed out a kosher hot dog. Later, when her husband came home — their father — she cooked up a London broil or a fricassee of fish cheeks. You get the picture. Little Silverstone complains that this is unfair, and his mother says, 'I'd do it for you, but you wouldn't appreciate it.'"

"I like that," I said.

"He says to me, 'She was the most selfish person I've ever known in my life.' This is a doctor speaking, and I think we're aware that sick people are not only a pain in the arse but unbelievably narcissistic."

"So maybe Ma is not so bad after all? Some kids have it worse?"

"We shall see," he said, holding up the screwdriver.

We continued on our way to Mother's. I slowed down at the junction of her street. No cars were parked near her house. The coast was clear, Floyd said, leaning forward, looking hard.

"Park near the house. If anyone comes in, our story is that we're visiting her. See? I brought her a present."

He showed me a bag of apples.

I parked. We got out, went to the back of the house, and stepped onto the porch, Floyd walking ahead. He twisted the doorknob.

"Unlocked," he said, waving the screwdriver. "We shall enter by the postern rather than jimmying the portcullis."

We went through the house — the whole place with its peculiar odors of Mother: toast and coffee, talcum, several struggling house plants, including a wilted narcissus, a scorched smell as of baked-on grease, the itch of unvacuumed carpets, book dust, a tang of urine.

"There is nothing worth stealing in this house," he said.

"Except this," I said, and slipped a porcelain duck into my pocket, something I had been looking at my whole life, a present from the uncle whom Floyd hated.

"You crazy bastard," Floyd said in an admiring way. He sniffed the air. "Some old ladies' houses, you know immediately they're incontinent."

"Spare me that thought."

Floyd was in the study, rifling her desk, pulling out folders.

"Fred was here. Fred saw these. Ah," Floyd said, "here's the check register."

He heaved open a black spiral binder and began flipping pages.

"Good God, look at this," he said. "Five thousand for Franny, three thousand for Rose, fifty bucks for her son-in-law. This is — look, there's more."

He was pushing pages aside, moving quickly through the accounts. Then he looked up and clawed his hair. "This is unreal. It's a shakedown."

I looked at the check register and saw in Mother's neat handwriting the lists of payments — small sums for food and electricity, large sums for Franny and Rose, many of them recent.

"Fred wrote down a few numbers on an envelope and he thinks he's cracked the case," Floyd said. "He's a fucking lawyer!"

"We should make copies of them," I said.

"There's a Kinko's in Dennis Port. We have time to photocopy them and still put them back."

"How much should we copy?"

"All — everything since Dad died. Every page."

He weighed the check register, then handed it to me.

"You do it — hurry up. I'll wait here."

"What if Ma comes back early?"

He smiled. "I've got my present. The apples. Now go."

The Kinko's store was not far, and the photocopier was available. The trouble was that I had to do each page separately, flopping the binder this way and that because the register was spiral-bound. Altogether, about eighty pages of closely spaced check descriptions. Mother was meticulous: number of check, payee, purpose, and amount. Tens of thousands to the daughters, very little to anyone else — a few dollars on a birthday or anniversary, a bill payment, here and there a pittance to a charity. Certain entries stood out, the ones that Fred had flagged: *Rose — new septic system, $11,000,* or *Franny — toward new car — $8,000.*

It took me almost an hour to make the copies and sort them. Then I shoved them into my bag with the check register and headed back to Mother's. The return journey was slower. I was caught in Hyannis-bound traffic and realized, inching along, that it was eleven-thirty. Mother was due home at noon. I fumed, got sweaty, growled at the creeping line of cars ahead of me. And, at last, when I turned into Mother's street, I thought I had just made it.

I was wrong. Floyd and Mother were in the front yard, Floyd seeming to query her, Mother pointing to her flower bed.

"There you are," Mother said. "What a nice surprise. And look what Floyd brought me."

She showed me a bitten apple. "I like a nice piece of fruit."

Floyd said, "Jay, do me a favor. I left my keys in the house. Will you get them for me?"

Mother said, "The house is locked."

"No," Floyd said. "You must have left it unlocked. That's why I was out here — guarding it."

I went inside, restored the check register to the desk drawer where Floyd had found it. I saw Floyd's keys on the coffee table. He had worked out this chess move.

"Thanks," Floyd said when I tossed him the keys.

Mother said, "Don't go. I've got some Swedish meatballs that Franny brought me yesterday. I can heat them up for you."

"We're fine," Floyd said. "We have to go."

"I'm glad you two are on friendly terms again," Mother said.

But she sounded disappointed. Floyd and I together, apparently friends, were a liability. We would compare notes, we might conspire. She gave us a wan smile and said, "There's so many things you can do to-gether."

"We'll think of a few," Floyd said.

"Life's so short," Mother said.

In the car, Floyd said, "Ninety years old and she's saying life's so short? What does she mean? And look" — he was riffling pages — "Franny was there yesterday, bringing her meatballs. That was the fifteenth. Here it is, July fifteenth. Check four-oh-six. 'Franny — toward her vacation, fifteen hundred dollars.' This is appalling. It is thievish — the sisters, the glib and oily art of them!"

He continued to go through the copies of the check register as we crossed the Cape, and he went on raging.

"Who the fuck is this woman?" he said, slapping the pages. "Who is she?"

34

REWARDS

WITH FLOYD'S QUESTION ringing in my ears as I examined Mother's accounts, I saw who she really was. It was all much worse than I had guessed, worse than Fred had suggested, worse than Floyd's rants and screams. In her own code, the check number, the payee, the date, the stated reason — even at her most secretive, Mother remained literal-minded — and the amount, I saw in actual numbers the reality of Mother's affection.

The numbers were also a glimpse into her inner life. Seeing these dollar amounts, I knew her and I was saddened — disappointed, angry, puzzled. That buried sense of rejection that bulged at the bottom of my consciousness — now I had a reason for feeling it.

On any single page of the ledger I could see how Mother, for whom money was emotion, expressed her love, her inclination, her dislike; every shade of feeling was registered in dollars and cents. And here was a revelation: in these terms I was not the least loved — that position was Floyd's. I came somewhere near the bottom. Franny was first. A rough total of her take so far was in the many thousands, and add the house to it — the house that Mother still lived in — and the total was nearer half a million. Rose came second, with thousands in cash, plus the cottage, for a total of about three hundred large. Fred's and Hubby's gifts took the payout to almost a million dollars. No wonder Floyd had sat beside me in the car thumping the pages, screaming and quoting *King Lear.* I'd gotten under a thousand, Floyd slightly less.

He called Franny and howled.

Franny said, "I haven't taken a penny from Ma."

He called Rose, who said, "After all I've done for you," and hung up.

Raging, he wrote to Fred, one of his lapidary letters, like a papal bull, denouncing him for allowing this to happen. He believed that Fred was Mother's executor, that he ought to have protected Mother's money.

"They took that money from me!"

But Fred had been in the dark. Mother was at her most secretive when it came to money; not trusting anyone to be her executor, she remained in full control of her banking, keeping her checkbook in her claw, using it to win allies.

The payments had begun soon after Father's funeral, at the time when I'd noticed Mother's odd alteration of mood, Maoist in an expansive and megalomaniacal way, even more domineering and needy, telling me to get married, retailing gossip, whispering against us, one against the other, isolating those of us who sounded disloyal, which meant in her mind not sufficiently flattering.

That period had also coincided with Franny and Rose's regular visits to Mother, weekly drop-ins, usually on Sundays, and now we knew why. They had come with tales of woe, to leave some food, to moan about their fate; slurpingly, to tell Mother how much they loved her, and to collect a check. They had been regular in their collection, ingenious in their reasons (teeth, house repairs, children's tuition, groceries), and always covert. While Mother was giving me a plate of hermits, or Fred a loon she had carved, Franny was pocketing a check for six thousand dollars, scribbled, *Toward new kitchen*.

We children were not impecunious people. We were reasonably well-off, most of us house owners. I was the only renter, but I had hopes. The heaviest recipients of Mother's gifts were double-income families.

Floyd called me. "It's all in *King Lear*. They go to Ma's and say, '"I love you more than words can wield the matter; dearer than eyesight, space, and liberty" — and help yourself to a Swedish meatball.'"

"But on the other hand," I said, "'Better to go down dignified with boughten friendship at your side than none at all.'"

"'Provide, Provide,'" Floyd said. "The cynical poem of a damaged man who was also an old fart."

I called Fred. I said that I'd seen the accounts, though I didn't say how, or that I'd photocopied them.

"She's given away much more than you said."

"That's her right," Fred said. "She can do what she wants."

"Tens of thousands."

"It's her money, Jay."

"I haven't seen any."

"Do you need money?"

"Does anyone really need it?" I said, my shrill voice going childish. "No one does. Fred, this is just greed and opportunism."

"We should rejoice that Ma is still alive. She's over ninety. She's healthy. She's been through a lot. She's our mother."

He said more, and as he did, he slipped into Mother's mode, her imagery, her logic, her tone of voice.

When he was done, I said, "I see what you mean."

But I didn't. Floyd was right: Fred was on Mother's side, with Gilbert. They implied that it was unfair to criticize Mother for writing checks, even if she was doing so with a shaky hand and a forgetful mind. So Franny and Rose were in the clear, and as the check register showed, they were still collecting.

I lost all of what remained of my loyalty to her, my sympathy evaporated. I had known she was canny; I did not realize how treacherous she was. Not maternal at all but rather an unusual and deceitful old woman, who obviously did not like me very much, who was afraid of Floyd, who was ingenious in her many deceptions.

I had known she was a habitual liar, but I had thought she was impartial in her lies. I hadn't guessed that she was truthful with her daughters, to whom she confided, whom she trusted and enriched. She was more complicated than I'd thought. It had never crossed my mind that she could be generous. Yet she was abundantly philanthropic to her girls, even kind to them, giving them her time. All this meant that she was not the tricky soul I had taken her to be, with lapses into kindness, but tortured and elliptical, even more of a scheming old queen.

In the turbulence and mutual recrimination that followed the discovery of Mother's accounts, I tried to be calm. I asked myself why I cared about her writing checks to my sisters. Murmuring "It's her money," I decided that I had no grounds for objection, I had no right to expect a payout, but — never mind me — she was handing over her nest egg.

What if she needed money for medical bills, assisted care, nursing, an old folks' home? Who would pay for that? This played in my head, my concern for her security, but when I examined my feelings I knew that, after all, I was insulted by having been passed over. I resented Mother's secrecy, and I hated the thought that when they had stopped by my sad little house with apples and hermits and wedges of cheese, Franny and Rose had checks for thousands in their pockets.

PART
THREE

35

THE ALGEBRA OF LOVE

NOW I KNEW THE TRUTH, and the truth made me snarl with bitter joy. It was a family cynicism that I shared — a sour trait — glee at seeing the worst in people, the confirmation that all of us were dogs. I complained to Floyd. I encouraged him to rant, I said that I was outraged, I shook the photocopies of Mother's check register — a great flapping sheaf of betrayal — and I went on howling. But I was happy in a grim and deeply satisfying way, taking a morbid pleasure in having the truth in my hand.

How often in life are you certain of the unvarnished truth, have laid out before you the meticulously kept balance sheet of affection, the algebra of love? Here it was, all those columns of figures, and explanations too. *Franny's kitchen $16,000* and *Rose's septic system $11,000* and *Hubby, repayment for groceries $80* and *Jay birthday $10* and *Gilbert birthday $500* and *Franny car $6,000* and *People in Africa $20* and *Fred children's tuition $1,500.* Fred was a multimillionaire.

Money was love. On the basis of Mother's financial records I had the heptagram of her love, also her indifference, her favorites, her weaknesses, her dislikes, and more. Her disposition in every sense. She had drawn up this balance sheet and in doing so had reconfigured the family, arranged the real family into a set of numbers. Franny came out on top with sums of five figures, Rose was second, Hubby and Fred next, and Gilbert had gotten a smallish amount.

Floyd and I came at the bottom, behind Angela, who was dead but who had been lavished with candles and flowers and memorial masses and contributions to charities — missions in India and Africa and South America — in her name: a hospital in Angola, her representation as a cherub in a stained-glass window in Peru, a gift of goats to a village in Ethiopia. What was beautiful was the linking of Floyd and me at the bottom of the balance sheet, for after all the years of backstabbing and recriminations and *Look what he did to me!* and *He hit me first!*, Floyd and I became allies — more than that, the best of friends, as in our earliest childhood, when he had protected me and comforted me with stories at bedtime. "Tell me about the circus," I had pleaded with him in the suffocating darkness of our attic bedroom.

In the real family, which these accounts revealed, Father did not matter much, apart from *Geraniums $2.99* and *Memorial Mass $25.* And Floyd and I were negligible, seemingly punished, though God knows for what. We did not figure in Mother's accounts, and so did not occupy much space in her mind or her memory. We had gotten nothing, so we were at the margin, and in the center the rewarded ones were arrayed: Gilbert, who had received a few checks; Fred, who'd been given tuition money for his kids; Hubby, who'd gotten a large piece of land for a dollar. Franny and Rose had, between them, reaped a fortune in money and property.

The abusive phone calls that Floyd had made had put them all on notice. Mother had no idea what we knew. All the children still visited her, brought her presents of plants and fruit and trinkets. We took turns driving her to church and invited her for meals. But we did this separately. Apart from Floyd and me, our paths did not cross. There were no more family dinners, cookouts, or birthday parties, none of the old family routines. We knew too much of Mother now to see each other in the same way.

The real family consisted of lobbyists and gossips, of which Franny and Rose were the most active. We now knew they were Mother's handmaidens and heiresses, and as in all such opportunistic relationships, it was hard to tell whether she owned them through her patronage or they possessed her by their flattery.

As recipients, they were not calmed. They were, if anything, more competitive. Had Mother intended this? The sisters especially hated Hubby and saw him as undeserving.

Floyd said, "Remember the shit fit Franny threw when Ma gave Hubby the Acre?"

It was true. She had been tearful, appealing to us for support.

"She wanted it for herself."

Hubby did not mention the gift of land or the various sums of money Mother had sent his way—the check register told it all—yet he swore and yelled about his sisters' greed, their gall, and when he was challenged, claimed that the land he'd been given had been worthless, unbuildable, until he'd put in an expensive septic system.

Fred, the eldest, and Gilbert, the youngest, were allies. Floyd hated them both. "Vacillators! They ratted us out!"

After some months, Mother noticed the hostility, and she asked to be visited more often. The alliances altered, at her direction, Floyd reported to me. In Floyd's eyes the greatest crime of Fred and Gilbert was that they now spoke to Franny and Rose, and joined Mother and them for Sunday lunch, the potluck meals that included potato salad, salami, Swedish meatballs, coleslaw, and Mother's nutty hermits.

"They actually eat this stuff," Floyd said. "It's not a meal, it's more like a hazing ritual. A tribal initiation. Consuming the unnamable. And for what? For more money."

Could this be so?

We waited for another Friday, another bird-carving class. We drove to Mother's and cautiously approached the house, parking two streets away, as we had before, thinking of ourselves, in our juvenile way, as commandos. The back door was unlocked, though the front door was bolted.

Floyd said, "Look, Ma still saves jelly jars."

We hurried to her desk and flipped open the spiral-bound check register.

"What did I tell you?"

Franny—Happy Anniversary $500. Rose car insurance—$700. Benno—good report card—$50. Franny Air Fare to visit Max $1,200. Fred—tuition $1,500. Hubby—for window boxes $200.

"This thing is hemorrhaging money," Floyd said, pounding the binder shut. "And nothing for me. What about me? I'm smart and I want respect."

He was clowning, stamping his feet, flinging himself from room to room. He finally alighted on the cabinet of knickknacks.

"I want this!" He flung open the cabinet door and took out a porcelain Hummel figure. "Goose girl, you're mine." And then he put it back. "This is rat shit. By the way, are you aware that these tchotchkes are the brain-child of a materialistic German nun?"

I was seated on Mother's throne, watching him fuss.

"The real problem in this house is that there's nothing left to steal. That must happen in a lot of families." He went to the bookshelf and poked at the spines of some books. "Worthless. But what about these albums?"

A stack of fat albums were crammed onto one shelf. We pulled them out, looked over the old photos, and found snapshots from the 1920s — Mother's family, Father's family. Then the 1930s — their marriage. And the 1940s — our baby pictures, photos of us growing up. Various houses we'd occupied. Mother's father, looking like a tycoon, a heavy watch chain draped on his vest front, a cigar in his chubby hand.

"Family history," Floyd said. "This is gold. These are priceless."

"Should we take them?"

"Why not?"

We made a pile of the albums with the rarest photos and left the rest. Floyd returned to Mother's desk, lifted the glass on it, slipped out the smiling photo of Franny, wrote *Fatso* on the back, and then replaced it.

"Someday Franny will be dusting and she'll find that."

We ate an apple and half a ham sandwich from the refrigerator.

Floyd said, "Remember that guy who raped and murdered a woman in her trailer? She had been eating a hamburger. After he strangled her, he finished her hamburger."

He was chewing, holding the sandwich in one hand and the family albums under his arm.

"They fried him. It wasn't just the murder. That was bad. It was the hamburger. That was somehow worse." He made a face, then wiped his mouth. "Why does Ma use so much mayo?"

We crept out of Mother's house and, looking left and right, sneaked through the backyards to my Jeep.

We complained, we objected, Floyd howled, but we were happy. The pleasure this gave us was almost indescribable. Why did it outweigh most of the pleasures I had known in my life?

Burgling Mother's house was childish fun at its most intense, savored in adulthood. The joy in being young, scattering in the neighborhood or the nearby woods, was in breaking the rules and being unobserved, somehow upsetting the natural order — shattering windows, stealing trifles, scribbling swear words on a wall, slashing someone's tires, snapping off a car antenna and using a length of it to make a zip gun. Part of the thrill of this mischief was that while we were invisible, the misdeed was noticed — we were making someone angry. We were always so near the scene of the crime that no one suspected us.

Our satisfaction now was in the secrecy, in the teamwork — we were a little gang — in the risk and the foolery and the reward of finding out (in our case) where we stood in the family. That it was petty crime — break-in and larceny — made it all the more pleasurable.

The excitement of driving with Floyd to Mother's to sneak in made me giddy. It was the happiest of outings. Floyd was in high spirits, joking as I drove, doing imitations of Mother ("Has anyone seen my albums?") and Franny ("Want some meatballs, Ma? They'll cost you ten grand.") and Rose (waiting for a handout).

"At this moment, as we are casing the joint," Floyd had said, pushing his way through Mother's hydrangeas, "someone is playing golf, believing he is having fun. But really, you can't beat this for a good time."

"I agree, burgling is better than golf."

"I asked her for a loan a few years ago. She said she didn't have any money," Floyd said. "And look."

The week he had been turned down for a loan, Mother had given Rose a check, itemized under *Window treatments.*

We should have been dismayed, yet we were happy. Among the papers we found was one in Mother's handwriting specifying that, upon her death, the entire contents of the house would be conveyed to Franny. This was obviously one of Franny's ruses, since she had already been given the house.

"Ma, can I have the grandfather clock?" Floyd said in Franny's oinking voice. "Ma, what about the sofa and the desk? And could I ever have the carpet?"

I said, "Do you really want that stuff?"

"No, but why should she have it?"

Irrationality was another of our joys, the pleasurable perversity of pure spite, being a meaningless nuisance. Because in all of this — the intrusion, our anger, the teasing, the indignation — we were children; we were boys again.

And I laughed hard at the end of that day when Floyd handed me the stolen albums, looked at his watch, and said, "I've got to hit the road. I have to be at Harvard at seven for my seminar on Wallace Stevens's *Opus Posthumous*."

Floyd wrote a letter to Franny and Rose, condemning them. It was an indictment, berating them in his characteristic way. *Your shameless opportunism, your naked greed, everything you lit upon you snatched and then you hurried away on your busy hocks and trotters.*

He made Mother the victim. *Your poor unassuming mother, whose pocket you pick.*

The other children were also implicated: *While your spineless brothers looked indifferently upon this heinous act of betrayal . . .*

Famous for his denouncing letters, Floyd taught another course at Harvard called The Epistolary Tradition in Literature, from Richardson to Bellow. This family letter was two pages of accusation, closely printed, and like the letters he'd sent in the past to each of us, it was fierce and so abusive it was unanswerable in its invective.

His letter was unusual in that it portrayed Mother as the victim of their plotting. Mother was feeble, helpless, infantilized. I did not remark on this, but it seemed strange, since I had always seen Mother as the manipulator, and the check register seemed to bear this out. Yet for Floyd, Franny and Rose were the chief villains.

In the letter, Mother was not Queen Lear, as Floyd had sometimes called her. She was instead an elderly and unsuspecting woman who had been bamboozled by her daughters.

Declaiming the letter to me on my porch in Centerville, Floyd strode up and down, slapping the pages, stabbing the air with his finger. I thought, as I had many times, how he would have made a marvelous actor, although much of this was melodrama, if not parody.

"We have been cozened!" he cried. "We are the poor dupes of a pea-and-thimble trick. And who is left? A bewildered crone, gibbering in her chair, her shoulders shaking under her thin shawl, whimpering, 'Why me? Why me?'"

He finished, clearly pleased with himself, folding the pages and tucking them into the breast pocket of his seersucker jacket.

"Are you sending a copy to Ma?"

"Everyone gets one," he said. "That way, there is no misunderstanding."

"What do you think she'll say?"

"Ma? She'll see we're on her side. That she's been conned. That's what this is all about. We're the only ones who see the truth. Ma is the victim."

36

CHECKS AND BALANCES

I DID NOT SEE MOTHER in the way Floyd did, and perhaps this was another of her triumphs. With her timely gifts, Mother had reconfigured the family to suit her needs. Some of us were trusted, and rewarded for being trustworthy; others were less reliable. Floyd and I were beyond the pale. I objected to this until I saw Mother's crystalline logic — she was right not to trust me.

Floyd's orotund document was both a warning and an accusation. He tended toward the lapidary, but among "inasmuch" and "vouchsafe" and "money-grubbing harridans and moralizing mountebanks in muumuus," the message was clear: *We are watching you.*

Mother was now ninety-one. Nearly all her old friends had died. She was making new ones. They loved her wisdom and her twinkle, they admired her health and strength. "I do the best I can," she said, and lowered her eyes — Mother's pose of modesty was effective. She knew she was healthier than any of the others in her carving class, the doddering octogenarians, the seventy-odds with early-onset Alzheimer's. She was thin as a stick but with the same fierce face I had known all my life, the hawk nose, the flinty eyes, the sharp tongue. Her hearing was perfect: "No need to shout" became one of her catchphrases. Marvin had high blood pressure, now worsened by his having retired from his job as a mall cop. Mother said, "It's his own goddamned fault." Fred's wife Erma had fallen and bruised her arm. Mother said, "When I was carrying Gilbert I slipped on the ice and chipped my elbow. They expected me to miscarry. Did I complain?" Loris was pregnant again. "She's as big as a house," Mother said, hooting, "God forgive me."

She seemed more malicious than ever, more willful, and would not be corrected. Talking to her, I forgot her age. She was quicker-witted than me, two moves ahead of me usually, all her faculties intact. Her accounts were complex but revealing — one could understand the state of her mind from the movements of her money, the handouts big and small, and the melancholy fact that now she had a lot less money in the bank and no property left to dispose of. Apart from that money, she had left herself with few assets. Each item in the house had someone's name on it, and the house itself was Franny's. She was eating off crockery that was legally Rose's, wearing jewelry that she'd willed to Fred.

But Mother's gifts were only part of my concern. The bigger question was how would she go on living, supporting herself, if her health failed? She wouldn't be able to live on her own much longer. Soon she'd be the resident of an old folks' home. Assisted living was expensive, and at some point she'd need twenty-four-hour nursing, money for rent, for medicine, for care. A hundred grand was not enough to cover this. The next time I visited her, I brought the subject up.

With a rocking motion of her body that signaled her impatience, Mother said, "I'm insured."

"Do you have long-term-care insurance?"

"I'm covered. I was a teacher, you know. I have a good policy."

"They don't cover old folks' homes."

"I'm not in an old folks' home, in case you didn't notice."

"You might need money sometime," I said.

This anxiety also lay behind Floyd's letter. It was why he had said to me, "Ma will end up thanking us for this."

"I have money," Mother said.

"You might need more."

"I have enough."

Because I knew so much, I had to tread carefully. I did not want to reveal the extent of my knowledge, for fear she would ask how I'd come by it. I said, "But if you give any away, you might find yourself short."

Mother sat back and smiled at my stupidity. "Give it away?" And she laughed, an unconvincing whickering. "To whom?"

"Say, to your children."

"I haven't given anyone a penny," she said, and when she delivered this line — the blanket denial that was never true — she fixed her gaze on me, arranging herself in her mendacious posture.

As though to a lying child I said lightly, "You might have given them something."

"Nothing," she said, reminding me how defiant she got when caught in a lie. That, too, like a child.

"Maybe a little?"

"Did you hear me? I said nothing."

I had nowhere to go with this, and yet, leaning forward on her throne, stamping out the words on the carpet with her tiny foot, she was not through with me.

"Are you calling me a liar?"

"I would never do that."

"You're trying to upset me again."

Staring at me, she made it plain that my time was up. After I left, she called Franny and Rose and Fred. She said that I'd accused her of lying, a cruel accusation for a child to make to his mother. The three of them called me and berated me for my wickedness.

Mother denied everything. She would not take responsibility for anything she'd said or done. Still, I was so stung by being told I was wicked that I called her up.

"I didn't accuse you of lying," I said.

"I never said you did."

"Fred told me."

"Oh, Fred. What has that got to do with me?"

Putting me in the wrong, Fred had said, "It's her money." He was right. I had no business questioning her. I told this to Floyd.

"Fred let it happen. He's like Ariel Sharon letting the Christian falangists into Shatila to kill those Palestinian prisoners!"

This shout made me wary. Floyd was enraged by the accounts, and for a few moments he was inarticulate in his anger, wetting his lips, trying to swallow, nodding to get his bearings.

"Fred's not the executor," I said. "Don't you see, Ma is Ariel Sharon."

"Two points," he said, trying to calm himself. "The first is that the daughters have her money. The second is that when she needs assisted living in a so-called facility we'll have to pay for it. This is monstrous."

What I did not tell him about Mother's denial was that in facing me and defying me, in the way she set her jaw and stamped her foot, she became a petulant child, insolent and unforgiving, as she told me obvious lies.

"She's like a little girl," Franny had said to me many times. She knew Mother well, and that little girl in Mother was susceptible to Franny's mothering and Rose's flattery. Mother wanted praise, needed attention, craved to be noticed and marveled at, and like a tantrum-prone two-year-old, she wanted independence. I was not good at this sort of manipulation, and Floyd was even worse than me.

I began to understand all tyrants in the world as willful, twisted children. The evil king was a little boy on a throne, the wicked queen was a little girl, the dictator was a peculiar brat, obsessive and single-minded as all brats are — vindictive, too. The history of tyranny was the history of a damaged childhood — the child with power, of idiotic excesses and spite, which accounted for the irrationality and the violence. Political outrages and purges began as tantrums and ended as edicts. The vanity and greed of a tyrant was essentially infantile, but enacted on a grand scale.

The telephone was Mother's natural weapon. Each of us was encouraged to call her once a day. Franny and Rose called her two or three times a day. That amounted to almost a hundred phone calls a week. None of the calls were sincere, none of them truthful, yet all were necessary to reassure Mother that she was still our mother and in sole charge of the family — and that we loved her, though the word "love" in this context was meaningless.

"Franny said she got a hateful letter," Mother said to me during one of these calls.

"It might have been the letter that Floyd sent," I said.

Shrewd woman that she was, Mother did not admit that she'd received one too.

"Why would he ever do a thing like that?"

I said, "I think he had the idea that you were giving Franny and Rose money."

"I have never given them a penny."

"And that they were taking advantage of you."

"Franny and Rose are two of my dearest children, loving and kind. Franny calls me every night at bedtime, to say good night."

I hadn't known that it was important to Mother to be bidden good night. Calling Mother at bedtime was something I had never thought of doing, because she had never done so with me. Bedtime had always been a screech of "Turn off that goddamn light!" Franny knew better.

"I cherish them. I wish I could say the same for some of my other children."

"Some of your other children are concerned that you might need your money. Maybe for health care."

"My health is perfect. I take no medicine. Of course I have the usual aches and pains." She paused and, reflecting on this, gave one of her shallow coughs.

"I'm thinking about the future."

"I have what I need. Don't worry about me. I worry about those poor people in Africa. I send them a little something now and then."

"The unexpected — that's the concern."

"I have made provisions," Mother said.

What did this mean? I guessed that Franny and Rose's infantilizing of Mother was complete: having taken most of her fortune, they had left her with the impression that they would see her through any medical emergency. Maybe this meant they would invite her into their homes when she was no longer able to care for herself.

To get off the phone gracefully, I said, "You know, I never gave you my last book. I'm going to bring you a copy."

"Don't bother. It would just be wasted on me," Mother said. "I can only read large-print books these days, and I don't think any of your books is in large print. They only do it for the big bestsellers."

I reported Mother's saying "I have made provisions" to Floyd, who said, "What will they do if she's gibbering and incontinent like this old guy I know in Chatham? He needs round-the-clock nursing. He needs diapers. He's on a feeding tube."

"Ma doesn't want to think of that."

"She'll be put in a hospital. We'll get the bill."

"I guess it'll be shared."

He screamed, not a word but a howl of defiance: "The fatties spent all the money she gave them!"

I spoke to Gilbert. He said, "Obviously we should do something, but we shouldn't upset her."

I spoke to Hubby. He said, "I ain't paying."

I spoke to Fred. "There are three ways of looking at this," he said in his lawyerly way. But what his convoluted reply really meant was: Please don't bring this up. And in a smiling voice, he said, "Jay, what you don't seem to accept is that Ma can do whatever she wants with her money."

"Even divide us."

"That's a little harsh."

"We hate each other, Fred. How many of us are on speaking terms?"

"I spoke to Gilbert just yesterday. I spoke to Ma today."

"As usual, you're just fencing with me."

"Look, don't you see that the person who matters most is Ma? We're lucky she's still alive — we still have her. She's healthy. We have no right to upset her."

He went in this vein. This was Mother speaking, as usual.

That was another characteristic of tyrants. They created other, smaller tyrants, operatives and surrogates who spoke for them, who perpetrated the lies, and who kept them powerful.

Behind all this confusion I sensed Mother's defiance. She now suspected that some of her children were questioning her judgment. Floyd's letter had stung her. I was vilified for speaking about it. She had told

Franny and Rose that she loved them. She had told everyone that I was upsetting her.

The tyrant's nightmare was to have all his agents of unrest in one room. Mother feared having us all together, facing her. She needed us apart, because she treated each of us differently, and it helped her that we were at odds with one another. United, we might oppose her; separate, quarreling, uncertain, and unequal, we needed her. This had been the case for years. But she was more secretive and fickle now than in the past — colder, harder to fathom, and contradictory.

I could tell that Mother was angry. She believed that Floyd and I were questioning her. She hated that; even the simplest question was a challenge.

"The facts are on our side," Floyd said. "We've got to do something."

"What are we actually trying to accomplish?" I asked. "You don't want money. I don't either."

"Strange as it might seem, given her hostility to us, we have to protect her."

"From what?"

"From predators. From her handing out the last of her money."

He proposed sending photocopies, bound booklets of the hundred or so pages of the check register, to every member of the family.

"In the spirit of transparency, of openness." But Floyd was laughing — he was like Mother too. He saw turmoil in such a move.

"What about sending a sample page?" I said. "That will shut them up."

"We have to do more than that. I'm sick of hearing all the denials."

We compromised. We photocopied the choicest pages, on which the largest payments were listed — payments to Franny and Rose, mostly the four- and five-figure sums. The pages were a selective history of a woman buying favors from some of her children, while excluding others altogether, seven distinct versions of mothering, a chronicle of favoritism.

"I know a guy in Dayton, Ohio," Floyd said. "I'll make up the envelopes and send them to him to mail."

"What's the point of that?"

"No one will have the slightest idea of who sent them."

This was cleverness of a sort that Mother might have approved.

"But they'll know it's one of us," I said. "We can send the letters from Boston. They won't know which one."

We did this, and the effect was immediate. Franny hurried to Mother's with a scrapbook of Mother's thank-you notes. Leafing through them, Franny wept, saying, "Am I a thief? Did I steal from you, Ma?"

Rose did the same, on a different day.

Mother told these stories to each of us when we called, not to mock her daughters but to defend them. She defended the presents to Fred, to Hubby, to Gilbert—how dare we question those?

Fred called me. He told me that we had made a big mistake in sending the copies. I said I had no idea who'd done it, but that I'd found them interesting.

"And how is Ma?" I asked.

I had assumed that revealing the payments would be a cautionary move, that Mother would see the injustice of it, that she might be contrite.

"She's on the warpath," he said.

The next time I visited her, she was. She'd been reading a book, but she put it down beside her chair to give me her full attention. In our last conversation, when I'd mentioned bringing her one of my books, she told me not to bother; she could read only large-print books. Given that she had recently refused my offer, I was curious to know what the book was, but as it was on the far side of her big chair, I could not see the cover. Anyway, she had other matters on her mind.

She did not mention the fact that one of her children had broken into her house and made copies of her check register. This seemed to be a predictable crime, one that was to be expected in a tyranny. Since she was underhanded herself, she was not shocked.

She had seen the photocopies. Franny had shown her in an attempt to vindicate herself. But the manner of Mother's being questioned was unimportant. What angered her was that she was questioned at all.

"Do you know anything about this?" she asked me, fixing me with a rocking motion that was meant to corner me.

I said that I had seen the accounts. Some mysterious person had mailed them to me. She continued to stare at me. I said, "It was news to me. I didn't know that you handed out half a million bucks."

Her fingers clutched the ends of the chair arms. She tightened her grip and pulled herself forward. "Whose money is it?"

Her gargle of rage made me wince. I said, "Yours, of course."

"Do I ask you what you do with your money?"

"I don't have any."

"Whose fault is that?"

"It's my own goddamned fault," I said, in Mother's voice.

"If I want to help someone with a little gift, that's my business," she said.

"Is a house a little gift?" I said. "Is thirty grand a little gift?"

"That's for me to judge," Mother said.

"Do you remember, some time ago, you asked me how your will should be construed? 'How shall I divide it?' you asked. I said that it should be apportioned equally."

Logic infuriated her. But instead of raging at me, she smiled at my simplicity of mind. She said, "People are not equal. Some of them are nicer and more loving than others. Some of them have needs. Some of them love me."

Only when she used the word "love" did she display any anger, and she showed it by setting her jaw at me.

I said, "Some of us might be wondering why you chose to give most of your money and property away to just a few of your children."

She sat straight in her chair, and although she was small and thin, she bristled in such a way as to suggest ferocity. "Who are you to question me? I can do whatever I want with my money. Now look what you've done." She clutched her head and massaged it. "You've given me a splitting headache."

As a courtesy, I lifted the book from the floor beside her chair and placed it on her lap. It was very heavy, and not a large-print book. *Eleanor: The Years Alone,* by Joseph P. Lash, about Mrs. Roosevelt.

Within hours, in her usual sequence of phone calls she told the others that I had attacked her.

"You're a fool," Fred said to me. "I was afraid of this."

"What's there to be afraid of?"

"She still has money," he said. "And she's mad. And she knows who her friends are."

"By the way," I said, "did you know that Franny calls her every night at bedtime to say good night?"

"No. God bless her."

37

DEFIANCE

FRED, the lawyer son, was a confident man. He had been a confident boy. He had learned as an infant how to be a model citizen of Mother Land. Fred was unlike the rest of us, a different child. He was the closest to Mother, and because of this proximity he saw Mother in his own way.

As the eldest, he was regarded as singular. For his first years, the formative ones, he had been an only child, two years alone with Mother, until Floyd came along and found himself unwelcome. With that second birth a lifelong rivalry began, yet Fred never altered his belief in his own power, the one child who never felt the need to negotiate or ingratiate himself. Ingratiation was one of the most common modes of behavior of our big family — perhaps of all big families, a pretense of submission to please and placate another sibling when a favor is needed. It was the art of insincere cringing, a form of cynical satire, a sort of dance. He was anything but straightforward, and yet Fred didn't do it. Fred was special.

Mother had told him so. An intelligence test arranged by his proud parents when he was ten revealed his IQ as 140, beyond superior. "Borderline genius," Mother said. We all knew Fred's number. It was a winning score — none of us could beat it. No point in testing us. Mother confided in Fred; he was her counselor, her defender, her go-between. He saw us through Mother's eyes. He told Hubby that he was ungrateful, told me I was difficult, said that Floyd was crazy. He thanked Franny and Rose for visiting Mother, because it spared him from having to. He was always elsewhere, busy with being a lawyer, spending months at a time in China, negotiating contracts. "Poor kid," Mother said. "He works so hard." I once asked him why, if there were so many lawyers in China, none of them ever defended the poor bastards who were put in jail for disagreeing with the government. Fred said, "Do you realize how prosperous China is?" A Fred answer was never an answer, only a form of indirection.

"Franny and Rose are going down to Ma's to get more stuff out of her," I said.

"It's a long drive for them," Fred said.

"For money!"

"Ma appreciates it," he said. "What are we doing for her?"

"I visit her, I bring her books," I said. "Not ones I've written. She's not a fan."

"She loves your work," he said. "We all do."

"You didn't say anything about my last book."

"I prefer your nonfiction to your fiction," Fred said. I smiled at the answer, so Fred-like. "Ma's proud of you," he went on. "You know how much she loves to read, how we were raised on the written word."

I was still smiling. This was the family myth, that we had been brought up bookish: Father reading us *Treasure Island*, Ma reciting poems—no TV, no movies. We lived in a cultural hothouse, thrilled by adventure stories. And then as readers ourselves we had created our own intellectual lives, Fred to law school, Floyd to his PhD in literature and a career as a poet, me to the life of a novelist-traveler, like Melville, whom Father had read us, declaiming Father Mapple's sermon in the seamen's bethel.

No. Not at all, apart from some snippets of Long John Silver late at night that caused us to name our attic dorm the Benbow Inn. The truth of it all was part-time jobs after school and the *Saturday Evening Post, Life* magazine and *Reader's Digest*, Frances Parkinson Keyes and *The Little World of Don Camillo*. One year it was *I'll Cry Tomorrow*, about actress Lillian Roth's drinking, but what drew me to the book were the descriptions of her domineering mother, who drove her to the booze. Floyd read Thomas Merton on his monastic life, and Mother's copy of an Ethel Mannin novel about an atheist who becomes a priest. I read books about camping, survival in the jungle, and going far away. One summer I read *Generation of Vipers* and delighted in the term "momism." The next summer it was Dante's *Inferno*. Then it was *Peyton Place* and Henry Miller. We got a TV set finally, and Dad discovered that he enjoyed *Bonanza, The Jackie Gleason Show*, and the quiz shows that turned out to be rigged. That was our cultural hothouse — that, and the church: hymns, sermons, outings, fasts, penances, and confessions. For we were sinners, mostly venial sins, some mortal, the ones that sent you to hell, which was why I read the *Inferno*, regarding it as a guidebook to the afterlife.

"What are you thinking?" Fred said.

But he would not have wanted to hear what I was thinking, so I said, "Ma's still giving them money."

"Of course she is," Fred said. "She's trying to teach us a lesson. That she can do whatever she wants. We deserve that."

Floyd's angry letter and the photocopies of the financial records had precipitated this. By accusing Mother of handing out money and property to her daughters, Floyd had insulted her. In her defiance, she would (Fred said) give much more to them — perhaps ridiculous amounts — to prove she could do as she pleased. A spoiled child reprimanded for poking the frosting of a cake responds to the rebuke by poking it again and insolently licking her finger. A tyrant criticized for killing innocent people reacts by ordering a fresh massacre that includes the critic. You can't tell me what to do!

After this talk with Fred, I drove over to Mother's to bring her a pie. I saw two new cars in the driveway, and so I drove on, believing that people I didn't know were visiting her.

A day or two later, Fred called and, in a disgusted, accusatory voice, said, "She gave Franny and Rose new cars. See what you made her do?"

His prediction had been correct. "Where does she get this money?"

"She's got more than you think," Fred said.

To test this, Hubby asked her for a loan. She said she couldn't afford to give him any money, but that she'd knit him a pillow cover.

I relayed all this information to Floyd. Because he would not speak to anyone else, I was his sole source of family information. "I'm going back," he said, and slipped into Mother's once again to examine the accounts. Not much was missing, he said. The hundred grand was intact. The only amounts missing were checks to Fred and Gilbert, a birthday present to Jonty, and a memorial mass for Angela. "But I knew she had to have a stash somewhere," he said. "A slush fund." That was when he found, at the back of one of the drawers, hidden the way a child would hide a candy bar, the Merrill-Lynch account, a ring binder of monthly statements.

"How much is in that account?" I asked.

"Telephone numbers," Floyd said. "And there are big withdrawals every month. If you had come with me, we could have photocopied the pages. But no, you had agenbite of inwit and stayed home, you wimp. This is family silver being boosted!"

I asked Fred whether he knew of Mother's Merrill-Lynch portfolio.

"Sure, but I didn't know how it was performing."

Apparently it was performing well, because the gifts were lavish.

Around this time, Bingo was admitted to Smith College. Rose brought the great news, along with Bingo, to Mother and mentioned that the first year's tuition would be forty grand.

"Play something for Grammy," Rose said.

Bingo played "Climb Every Mountain" on her harmonica, and went home with a check.

How did I know this? Because Mother told Fred how badly Bingo played the harmonica, that she — Mother — had to force herself not to laugh at the farce of it all, and how proud Rose was of the tuneless blowing. Mother mocked Bingo's seriousness and jeered at the high cost of Smith College. And in a stage whisper she intended everyone to hear, Mother mentioned that she'd given Bingo "a little something," which she muttered was a few thousand dollars. Take that!

So, even in her generosity, in her role as matriarch, Mother was disloyal. This disloyalty extended even to herself, for she was by nature frugal, not to say miserly. She still clipped coupons, and had never lost the habit of buying day-old bread and bruised fruit and dented cans, or the ten-cent mystery cans that sat shining in the bargain basket, their labels torn off. She pounced on the cereal boxes with the cut-open ends, the taped-up packages of pasta, the tray of pork chops that was past its sell-by date. It was in her nature to look for a bargain, despite the risk of eating spoiled food. Handing over money was contrary to her nature, for it was her settled belief that it was wrong to give someone something for nothing.

She was a canny and secretive woman, much of whose life as a mother was lived in solitary consultation with one child and then another; she was a full-time study. And it sometimes seemed — it must seem so in this

narrative — that I did nothing else but watch the movements, the stratagems, the passive aggression of my antagonistic family.

But no, I was also living my life, the productive part that had nothing
to do with my family: books, boats, travel, and being a father to my own
children, including Charlie. If I was more than usually attentive to Mother,
it was because I thought that at any minute she would die. In any given
visit I might be seeing her for the last time. But she would have laughed if
I'd said that to her. Though she never explicitly conveyed the impression
to me, always assuming that I'd be back soon, and even speaking with that
valedictory sigh of her bags being packed ("I'm ready to go"), she seemed
to insist that she would be here long after everyone else had gone.

At intervals I fled Mother Land. I needed to insert myself in the world
of reasonable people and vitalizing work. To get away from the family I
had traveled in Africa for ten months, from north to south.

I made this travel into a book. When the book appeared, I was seen
as a contrarian because of my skeptical view of the aid business and the
charities, the virtue industry — not altruistic at all, but self-serving, and
many of them doing harm. A contrarian is useful in the spectacle of me-
dia head-butting. The book sold well, and I was asked to write another —
more travel. This removed me again from the furious buzz of the family. I
saw my boys in London and discovered the pleasure of being their house-
guest, their dinner companion, a fourth at Scrabble or whist.

In a library, a bookstore, a restaurant, or a distant land — Zambia or
South Africa, or even the London of my first marriage — I was reminded
of why I left home. I was happy in those places. I had no past. People
spoke with affection about parents or children, they talked politics, they
discussed books or plays or music.

I had forgotten how clearheaded I could be, how there were other people in the world besides my narcissistic mother and predatory siblings.
Now and then I came across a problematical family. An African would
complain that he had to marry his brother's wife, because his brother
had died, and his brother had no cattle. Or a familiar tale of daughters-
turned-handmaidens who picked their mothers' pockets — quite a common pattern. But no matter where on earth I roamed I never came across
any mother resembling Mother in her ferocity, her vulnerability, her meg-

alomania, or in her calculated partiality, her deliberate injustices. "Ma's disloyalty makes her unique, outside the pages of the *Oresteia*," Floyd often said, and it seemed true.

I had a relationship for a time with a woman I loved, though I knew it was doomed. She was still of childbearing years, and I told her frankly that my days of fathering more children were over. But just as important, I could not imagine bringing a woman so innocent into my family. And so we parted, and she found a father for the child she wanted, and I never heard from her again. She had become a mother.

Long ago, I had discovered that in travel I became another person, someone I knew well and liked best — the person I really was. Among strangers, under another sky, in a distant land, I was myself: travel brought me to adulthood, the joy of traveling alone. In these years of family oppression, I fled and wrote about the remote Oriente province of Ecuador, I paddled a kayak down the Zambezi, I cycled through Scotland, I researched Ayurvedic India, I planned a second long journey for a book. And all this time in lecture halls and in bookstores I met my readers.

On one of those trips I found myself talking to a lawyer. This was in Ohio. He told me he was from a large family. "Eight children, actually," he said, almost in apology, feeling that he'd have to justify the number of kids, defend them, give them some color. I knew the feeling. It was saying you were from another country, another culture, one that needed a little explaining, because it was Mother Land. Usually on these trips my family was far away and forgotten, but this man interested me.

"How many of you are on speaking terms?" I asked.

"I see one of my younger brothers," he said. "The rest of them . . ." His voice trailed off, though I could have finished his sentence.

"I know," I said, and told him a little about my family.

"It's terrible when there's money involved," he said. "We had quite a lot of that conflict."

I told him about Mother, but holding back, just hinting at her contradictions, her manipulations, the milder examples of her treachery.

"That's very Mediterranean," he said. "My mother was just the same. Impossible."

"My mother still writes checks."

"She *what?*" He threw his head back and howled.

I wanted to tell him more, because he was a stranger, because he came from a similar family, because he recognized Mother and didn't judge her, or me. But there wasn't time to get into it.

"This can't be a conversation," he said, sizing up the situation and my state of mind. He was, after all, a lawyer. "There's too much for idle talk."

"Maybe it's a book."

"It's a book," he said. "And you may think you're having a hard time now. But your mother is still alive. You're still her children. You can't imagine what life will be like without her."

That was the event I could not contemplate, because it filled me with confusion. A normal reaction would have been, *How awful,* and yet I sometimes dreamed of it as a release. He seemed to guess at my thoughts.

"When your mother dies you won't feel like a child anymore. Your siblings won't be children. You'll be bewildered. You'll have to put the whole family back together. But you won't have her. You'll suddenly be orphans. Your mother can't be replaced."

Maybe he saw me smiling. To cover myself I said, "And then what?"

"You'll look for allies within the family. Or maybe there'll be no one. Families go to pieces. Mine did."

"I have children. That's my family."

Before an assignment in Scotland, I stopped in London. I invited my two boys to dinner at Rules restaurant in Maiden Lane. I associated the restaurant with happiness, with celebrations, times when I was feeling flush. Over steak and grouse pie and a bottle of Merlot, we talked of their projects — Julian was writing a book, Harry was making a documentary. And what was I doing?

"Going biking through the Highlands," I said. "Starting at Inverness."

"I remember doing that when we were at school," Julian said. "Fun."

I was abashed hearing this: reduced to that, a big man on a bike, pedaling up and down the Scottish hills, looking for something to write about.

Harry said, "You see more from a bike, actually," making a case for me.

"It wasn't my idea. A magazine wanted it. They get advertising from the Scottish Tourist Board. That's how these things work."

"You should write another novel," Julian said.

"I haven't got the heart," I said. "It takes courage. Anyway, all the good stories I know are true."

"Pretty soon it'll be time for your autobiography. You always said you'd write one like Rousseau's *Confessions,* putting everything in — the whole truth."

Harry said, "The only autobiography you can trust is the one that reveals something that's disgraceful. Orwell said that."

"I agree. But I've changed my mind. No autobiography."

"Why, Dad?" Harry said, seeming genuinely disappointed. "You've had such an adventurous life. You've seen so much. The sixties — you were there! You were the fifth Beatle."

"I think I'll keep it to myself. I'm not sure I want my life to be reviewed."

Julian said, "So you don't have any ideas?"

"I might do something with my family — find a way of fictionalizing them somehow. I've never written about them."

"That's a book I'd read," Harry said.

"But I don't have the time. I'm trying to finish another travel book. And I'm too close to my family at the moment." I thought about the events of the past year and smiled. "It's funny, I never thought I'd be friends with Floyd, or conspiring with him in petty burglaries."

The boys looked up from their meal, rather hesitant, still holding on to their knives and forks, in the way of people thinking they might have just heard some bad news — but not too sure, hoping they hadn't, squinting a little at the possibility of further disclosures.

"Burglaries?" Julian asked at the unexpected word. "What kind?"

"Break-ins."

"That's serious."

"No," I said, and laughed. "It was just Grandma's house. Last year. And most of the time there was no break-in at all. We just walked in."

"You did it more than once?"

"A couple of times. Uncle Floyd went back a few more times," I said. "What's wrong?"

They had lowered their faces at me, looking shocked, embarrassed — none of the smiles I had expected, no encouragement. I felt I had told them a great joke and they were outside it, disapproving, as though the joke was in bad taste.

"We didn't take anything," I said. "We just creepy-crawled her house when she was at her weekly woodcarving class."

"What was the point of breaking in?" Harry asked.

"To find her check register. See whom she'd been giving money to. I broke in one day and took them all to Kinko's and photocopied them. A hundred pages! We nicked a few things for the hell of it." They looked even gloomier. "What's wrong? We're in there padding around like cat burglars, whispering. It was a great feeling, intruding on my mother's privacy for a change, looking at her lies and deceptions. She's given a ton of money away, mostly to Franny and Rose. I've got all the proof, the little rationalizations, in her own handwriting. We know everything now."

I saw myself and Floyd squeezing through the back door, unscrewing the hasp, lifting off the chain, and tiptoeing into the still house. A childhood caper, and a childish thrill, certainly, but what was more intense and satisfying than a childish thrill? The aromas of Mother's awful food and yellow soap and dusty curtains; Floyd talking about fingerprints, slipping on gloves, hoisting a flower as he passed a vase, walking in a self-conscious, spidery way, all the while suppressing giggles — the excitement and absurdity of it, Floyd finally saying, "Look what she's making us do. It's all her fault!"

Julian looked irritable. He shook his head. "I don't want to hear any more."

"You actually sneaked into her house?" Harry said.

"We had to," I said. "We wanted to find out where the money was going."

"What's the point?"

"She might need it in the future. She's being scammed. We're looking out for her interests."

"That's not the reason," Julian said. "You're doing it because it's fun."

"Of course." But they were adamant in their disapproval. "You don't understand."

"I don't want to understand," Harry said.

It was impossible to explain to them why this was so important to me, why at the age of sixty I had taken the greatest pleasure in breaking into my mother's house, why I had considered it a victory—how close I'd felt to Floyd, how happy I'd been on those days of the break-ins.

"It's so childish," Julian said.

"Yes," I said. "That's why it's such a pleasure. And I found out the truth of my mother's feelings, looking at where the checks had gone."

"What's the truth, then?"

"That she doesn't like me. I have the proof."

"Why do you need it?"

"Maybe it absolves me for disliking her."

They didn't want to know any more. It was a mistake to have told them so much, but I found the whole subject irresistible.

"We love you, Dad," Harry said. "Can we leave it at that?"

After my Scottish trip and the writing of the piece, I went back to the Cape and descended into childhood again. Floyd had left a message on my answering machine. *Call me. I've got news.*

He had gone to Mother's while I was away and found money missing from all the accounts, had even found a new account, a money market fund that could be used for checking. He had found envelopes with jewelry tucked inside, one with Franny's name on it, the other Rose's.

"The ultimate break-in," Floyd said when I saw him. "We boost something valuable, maybe some jewelry."

It was as though he was now so used to coming and going in the house that he felt he could claim anything, because he'd seen what others had done.

We went back, this time wearing coats with big pockets, looking to carry away something of value. The house was locked. The door had a second chain on it, another bolt.

"She must suspect something," Floyd said.

But we were undeterred. We got in through an upper window, using the ladder from Dad's shed. Then, creeping from room to room, we went through her desk, her chest of drawers, her jewelry box. And we found nothing. The envelopes were gone. The check register and the other financial records were in new hiding places.

"Bitches!" Floyd said. "They've taken it all. There's nothing left to steal."

38

HOT DINNERS

DRIVING DOWN THE EMPTY ROAD toward Mother's — she had called, with an ambiguous summons, saying, "Of course, if you'd rather not come . . ." — I was marveling at the nakedness of the Cape in February. My tires hissed, licking at the grit and slime of winter. Tree branches were so crooked when they were stripped bare, the trees themselves so witch-like. Freezing weather made me feel aged and fragile; the winter creature, confined, shrunken by the cold.

Summer on the Cape, by contrast, was a green world of sunlit privacies, the density of speckled and shadowy woods, the leafy trees giving the impression of largeness and health, protecting the house, hiding the neighbors. The Cape foliage was its real beauty, more beautiful even than its sloping dunes and beaches of smooth stones. The Cape trees looked indestructible: seedlings with their fans of shapely oak leaves sprang up between the hydrangeas and needed to be yanked like weeds. Infant pitch pines and cedars bristled at the margin of the lawn and were sometimes mowed. Never mind that the soil was bad. Dig down six inches and there was sour sand, but the native trees were suited to it; they seemed big and powerful, and so were the local roses, small floppy blossoms on a tangle of brambles.

On winter days like this the real size of the trees was obvious. Without leaves, the oaks and locusts and pepperidge trees were spindly, round-shouldered, starved, hollow-eyed, and knobby. The pitch pines were revealed as frail—the sea winds killed them with salt, they shedded half their needles. Only the cedars and junipers stood straight, but were not thick enough to hide the neighbors. The roses were over, the geraniums had blackened in the first frost, and, in this soil, none of the trees grew tall.

I had known the Cape summers as a small boy. I had gloried in those sunny months, loving the whine of insects, the hot tang of tar bubbles on the sun-softened roads, the marsh hawks hovering. As an older man, working through the seasons, I saw the truth of the Cape: it was lovely only in the summer. Locals hated tourists, so they longed for cold months, but the cold months were bleak and there were often nine of them. The fall colors were too brief to be an event — the russet and gold leaves were beaten down by the rain; and the winter was stark, the Cape a corpse in the sickly light, gray grass, black trees, gangrenous leaf mold, and too many houses. Far fewer people to support the stores and the restaurants, giving the towns a look of abandonment. The roads were always wet and peculiarly dirty in winter, the roadsides thick with ropes and twists of accumulated sand and grit. Blown leaves were bunched against stone walls and rusty fences and pasted onto the broken roads, for in winter the frost heaved the roads apart, and the scrape of snow plows deepened the potholes. The rain was brown, falling from the brown sky, or else it shot hard out of the northeast, thrashing, whips of it against the shingles. *I like it when it's bleak,* some Capies dishonestly boasted. They meant: *We have no other place to go. We are dying here.*

The Cape in winter made me feel morbid. I resented the conceit of Mother's ancient vanity. I hated old age.

No matter how resourceful an adult I could be in the world at large — the solitary traveler in the African bush — when I was on the Cape I was a boy, a son, something of a burden, an annoying brother. This also meant that, on the Cape, I found it hard to relate to my own children, who were not boys at all but men — Charlie in Boston, Julian and Harry in London. I heard from them all the time; their lives were busy, busier than mine. But I seldom saw them. The pull of Mother, the gravity of accumulated distress, was strong.

My Africa book was published. This account of my overland trip from Cairo to Cape Town — trains, trucks, buses, boats, bush taxies, and on foot — got the usual reviews, some praise for being truthful and felicitous, some abuse for being critical. Mother's example had convinced me that most praise sounded like belittlement. I dedicated the book to her. And on this cold day I was visiting her with a copy of the book lying gift-wrapped on the passenger seat.

"I want you to look at something," Mother said as a way of greeting me, seizing my wrist and guiding me across the front lawn, which was stubbly this late winter afternoon, the grass decaying in the dampness, the soil as soft as cake. Mother had a remarkable grip. I could feel her finger bones pinching me hard like salad tongs, that same cold tug, that same snap.

I saw nothing. I said so. Mother said, "Because you're not looking!"

Mother always spoke as if someone else was listening — many people, in fact.

The thing she wanted me to see was a birdbath, a cement saucer propped on a fluted cement stand, a crust of frost-rimmed ice in its declivity.

"Nice," I said. From where I stood it looked like a crude toadstool, lifeless in the early dusk.

"Look closer."

Lettering carved around the rim, or rather cast in the cement (you bought these things at Wally's Garden Center in South Yarmouth), read, *To the Dearest Mother on Earth.* A bird had shat on it, making the crucial word read *Direst.*

"It's lovely, Ma."

"Rose's idea," she said. "What's that?"

She was looking at the wrapped parcel under my arm.

"A book."

"Oh?"

"One of mine."

"Oh." She sounded disappointed.

"About Africa."

"Those poor people," she said. "I give them a little something every Christmas."

"It's for you. Look." I unwrapped it and turned to the dedication page. *To my Mother, on her 92nd birthday.*

Tucking it under her arm, she said, "I'd like to give it to Rose. She's so generous. Isn't that the most beautiful birdbath you've ever seen? She knows how much I love birds."

In that moment, with hardly any effort, she managed to insult me, anger Rose — who would be getting the book secondhand — and maintain control over us. What annoyed me even more was that I resented giving Mother a copy of the book in the first place.

"I always knew you were going to be a writer," Mother said, leading the way into the house. "You used to lie on the living room floor with a pencil and a piece of paper."

I sat and Mother began to talk about how proud she was of the family. She was triumphant. We were at war with each other. The coils of complexity, the old whispers and jealousies, the sedition and sniping, the combustible memories in the family, and the ancient sadism — all of it made it impossible for me to tell when the war had started. At birth, probably: we had never known peace.

There wasn't much love, but somehow Mother had taught us that love and money were equal, that money was a measure of love. She was brilliant in her partiality, keeping every amount she gave unequal, She had a competitive and resentful person's instinct for measuring, for teaching us the subtleties of shortfall, the scourge of scarcity. Father had been a moderating influence — his gentle persuasion made Mother aware of her unfairness. "Measure, measure," was one of his taunts. Later, I learned how, with a compulsive measurer, you always fail.

This was running through my head as we sat in Mother's house on this cold day, Mother talking about Rose's gift of the birdbath and Franny's attentiveness to her.

"Would you do me a favor? I would be so grateful," Mother said, still in the voice that suggested she believed she was being overheard by many people.

"Gladly."

"There's a towel on the clothesline," Mother said. "Would you ever go out and get it for me? It should be dry by now. I hung it out to dry this morning. The ground was so slippery! I thought I might fall and break my hip. But I had no choice. The towel was soaking wet."

This seemed an extravagant explanation for a wet towel. I guessed there was a story behind it, or else I would not have heard all this prologue. Mother never spoke of effort without following it up with blame.

I got the towel. It was still damp and gray on this damp gray day. Mother, too frugal for a clothes dryer, was perhaps the last person on the Cape to use wooden clothespins.

"That's Floyd's," she said.

"Floyd's towel?"

"The one he used." She cocked her head. "He was here yesterday."

She spoke in a weary way, as though characterizing Floyd's visit as an ordeal.

"Really — he was here?"

"At the crack of dawn," Mother said. "I was still in my bathrobe, making coffee." By her tone I could see that she was the victim of an early-morning siege, Floyd hammering on her door. She made a martyred face. "He brought me a pizza," she said, "that he made himself. 'You can eat it for dinner with a bottle of wine'"— her mimicry of Floyd's glottal stop on "bottle" — *baw-oo* — was accurate.

She went on telling me what was to be a story that typified the triumphant phase of her motherhood.

But even so, I was surprised, because I knew the story that lay behind it. Another Christmas had come and gone, another set of separations. Six weeks before, around New Year's, Floyd had complained to me of Mother's generosity toward Franny and Rose over the holidays: large checks — Floyd was still monitoring the outflow. He had received a pillow, I had gotten a jar of grape jelly ("Made by Trappist Monks"). We had all chipped in at Fred's suggestion and bought Mother a rocker. This angered Floyd.

"Great, we just bought Franny and Marvin a new chair."

He reminded me of the letter among Mother's papers specifying that all the furniture in the house belonged to the inheritor — Franny.

Floyd was particularly aggrieved because the winter's low temperatures had frozen his water pipes. His oil burner was broken. Apart from a kerosene stove that gave off noxious fumes, Floyd had no heat or water.

"I'm living like a rodent! I'm nibbling cheese! My nose is running. And Franny has a new rocker. She owns Ma's house!"

Floyd did not communicate with Mother for six weeks. Normally he called her, as I did, once or twice a week to ask whether she needed anything — and of course, as we all did, to find out if she was still alive.

On one of my calls, Mother said, "Is Floyd mad at me?"

"I don't know."

It was a family trait to avoid being anyone's advocate, because it seemed to demonstrate an alliance.

"Are you sure he's not mad at me? I haven't heard a word from him for some time."

Mother was still sharp enough at ninety-two to evaluate the separate attentions of her children. Her alertness was in keeping with her need to control: no one was safe from her gaze, and even the despised children were scrutinized — perhaps given more scrutiny.

I said, "Why don't you call him? See what's on his mind."

She seemed doubtful, a long silence on the phone, a familiar sigh, vibrato from the roof of her mouth.

I said, "I mean, you're his mother."

This remark came back to me the next day, Hubby in a bantering call telling me that Mother had mocked my saying (and she improved it a little), *After all, you are his mother, aren't you?* — turning it into an accusation.

Yet, seeming to act on what I'd said, she called Floyd. She invited him over. And, overcoming all his Christmas fury, Floyd had visited. I now knew that he'd brought her a pizza he'd made. He had also — the towel was proof — taken a shower there, because his pipes had frozen.

Mother got what she'd asked for, a visit from her son. And afterward she sat jeering at him, laughing at his pizza, lamenting his early arrival.

"And he left me a little present — his wet towel to launder."

He'd given her what she wanted more than anything, a grievance.

Two more cold Cape Cod months drizzled by. Easter came. Floyd was in Pennsylvania — a new girlfriend and also an escape from the holiday. Few of us still went to church. It seemed that Franny and Rose had other plans. Only Hubby and I were on the Cape. I kept my head down. Hubby was not Mother's favorite, but he wanted to make some improvements to his house on the Acre, and he had a plan to soften Mother up for a loan. He called it a loan, but when the lender is ninety-two years old, all loans can be comfortably regarded as gifts.

Realizing that she would be spending Easter on her own, Mother encouraged Hubby to visit. If she couldn't have one of her favorites, she would settle for him. And before he made the visit final, Hubby said he needed a little money: "Just a loan. I'll pay you back." Eager for his company and his bringing food, relieved that she wouldn't be alone, Mother agreed in principle to the loan.

"I'll bring scallops," Hubby said.

Mother said, "I love scallops," yet as soon as she hung up, Fred called unexpectedly to say that he'd just arrived excitedly from China. He was on the Cape. Could he host her for Easter dinner?

"Hubby insisted he wanted to come over," Mother said to Fred. "You know how he is. He doesn't seem to realize that I can look after myself."

Hubby's visit was now a burden, and particularly annoying because it meant she'd have to turn down Fred's invitation to dinner.

Hubby and Moneen made their Easter visit to Mother. They sat with her to watch the Easter service on TV. They brought flowers. Moneen sautéed the scallops and served them on angel hair pasta. Hubby presented Mother with a chocolate cake. Then he scraped his chair back and clutched his face and told her his tale of woe. Mother sent him away with a check.

"But remember, it's a loan," Hubby said. "I'm paying you back."

So powerful was Mother's conceit that she was indestructible, she said, "I can give you a few years, Hubbard, but no more than that."

That night she called Franny and Rose, she called Fred and Gilbert, she prayed to Angela, she even called me. In a towering rage she denounced Hubby to everyone. He and Moneen had shown up late, with a pound of scallops ("I know for a fact that they were on sale") and "a store-bought cake." He'd then demanded money. "How could I refuse?" She'd given him a check, and instead of thanking her he'd made a big show of saying he'd pay her back. What a bore it had all been. And on Easter, the holiest day of the year.

"They took home the leftovers," she said. "They left me dishes to wash."

To please Mother, we joined her in disparaging Hubby and pitied her for the unsatisfactory dinner, the wasted day, the ingratitude.

We entertained her after that, early dinners at nearby restaurants, but because each of us children were on bad terms with each other, we took her out separately.

"Franny and Rose would have loved to be here," Mother said to me at her favorite restaurant, the Happy Clam — my night to host her for dinner. She knew they would not have come for anything, but it was another way of putting me in the wrong and justifying her role as a benign dictator.

"They hate me," I said.

"No one hates you," she said.

"It's true. But I'm all right with it."

Mother was chewing as she said, "It's so sad when people can't learn to get along."

The dinners continued. Mother was the only one of us who was truly happy. Because of this, she concealed her happiness, so that we would not be complacent. In her oblique, not to say perverse, pathology, she became even more secretive. She said the opposite of what she felt, or else was noncommittal. She was soon famous for her silences.

"Read my mind," she seemed to say, and she smiled whenever we attempted this impossible feat. We were always wrong. No matter how hard we tried, we could not get her to admit she was happy. She refused to be satisfied, because admitting this would also be to admit that we had succeeded. She saw her mother role as that of someone who had to insist that we had failed her. Only that way could she triumph. Every dinner was a celebration of our failure. Angela was perfect, but Angela was dead, only useful as a spiritual guide. Angela could not pay the bill at the Happy Clam.

I apologized to her at one of these dinners, just to see what she would say.

"You'll just have to try harder," she said.

I came to understand that each of us was alone. Each of us pretended to have Mother, but it was not so. Nor did we have anyone else. Mother had us all. Mother had everything.

39

A NEST OF VIPERS

AFTER YEARS OF STEADY WORK, a daily routine, writing all morning, a walk after lunch, more work in the late afternoon until wine o'clock, at six or seven, I had begun to slow down. And, in my solitude, I began to observe the family with a fascinated gaze. I saw what

I had missed before. The battles had wearied me, yet had not repelled me. I had become absorbed in the bickering; the fighting in the family was like a sulfurous form of vitality. I even turned it into work, making notes as I had done as a young man in central Africa, in a district of warring clans or a peculiarly feud-prone village. I saw that what I had taken to be quarrelsome siblings and a vain and manipulative mother was much more poisonous, disruptive, and dangerous — a nest of vipers. The dreary family now seemed extraordinary in its cruelty and selfishness. This revelation liberated me and made me patient in my fascination.

My new habit of doing nothing, or very little, seemed natural, a period of rest after labor. I wrote less, I read more. I noticed that the memoirs I was rereading, Greene's *A Sort of Life,* Conrad's *A Personal Record,* and Kipling's *Something of Myself,* were all published by writers in their sixties. Waugh wrote *A Little Learning* in his late fifties. These evasive books convinced me that I would never do this myself. I had been pondering this subject ever since the lunch at Rules in London when Julian had said, "Pretty soon it'll be time for your autobiography." I would never write an autobiography, with all the misleading facts, half-truths, and evasions of an irregular life. A memoir with big gaps seemed worse than an exhaustive self-examination.

I imagined the book's appearance. My life would be reviewed by envious hacks, bitter academics, and ambitious young writers. I knew — I had been all of these people in my career. The summation of my life: "Some good parts, lots of boring parts, wasted time — on the whole, a mediocre life. Not recommended."

It must occur as a grim foreboding to many writers that when the autobiography is written, it is handed to a reviewer to be graded on readability as well as veracity and fundamental worth. With this notion of my life being given a C-minus, I began to understand the omissions in autobiography and the many writers who refused to write one.

Besides, I had at times bared my soul. What is more autobiographical than the sort of travel book, a dozen tomes, that I had been writing for the past forty years? In every sense that candor goes with the territory. And the setting down of personal detail can be a devastating emotional experience. The assumption that the autobiography signals the end of a writing career also made me pause. Here it is, with a drum roll, the final volume before the writer is overshadowed by silence and death, a sort of farewell and an unmistakable signal that one is "written out."

And what is there to write? In the second volume of his autobiography, V. S. Pritchett speaks of how "the professional writer who spends his time becoming other people and places, real or imaginary, finds he has written his life away and has become almost nothing." Pritchett goes on, "The true autobiography of this egotist is exposed in all its intimate foliage in his work."

The more I reflected on my life, the greater the appeal of the auto-biographical novel. The immediate family is typically the first subject an American writer contemplates. I never felt that my life was substantial enough to qualify for the anecdotal narrative that enriches autobiography. I had never thought of writing about the sort of big, talkative family I grew up in, and early on I developed the fiction writer's useful habit of taking liberties — exaggeration, embroidery, reticence, invention, heroics, mythomania, compulsive revisionism, and all the rest that are so valuable to fiction.

I thought of a line in Anthony Powell's novel *Books Do Furnish a Room,* where the narrator, Nicholas Jenkins, reflecting on a slew of memoirs he is reviewing, writes, "Every individual's story has its enthralling aspect, though the essential pivot was usually omitted or obscured by most autobiographers."

My essential pivot, was it Mother?

This decision not to write an account of my life made me happy. It was a reprieve from a chore I'd dreaded, and it gave me more leisure to think about my family — a different sort of chronicle, nothing about writing but rather a reflection on power, a study of malice.

I was watchful. I seemed to slip into idleness, as though I had sustained a bad injury — cracked my spine, maybe — and in the process of healing grew fat and, most of my passion spent, never regained the desire for effort. "I don't have the fire in my belly anymore," older men used to say to me, to explain why they'd retired from their work. They were usually bureaucrats, foreign service officers, competitive men, and when they said it I always involuntarily glanced down and saw a broad complacent paunch.

That was my condition now, living in Mother Land, my family of greater interest to me than any people I had traveled among in a life of roaming the world of hungry people struggling to survive. The family now seemed to me just like those strugglers and scavengers, except that they wore shoes. And in the meantime, in my leisure, I found other things to like. I learned, as one does in idleness, to avoid occasions when people were laboring, toiling for a fair day's pay. I needed to be around other idle people, stragglers like myself. I did not have to look farther than my family.

I found a horrid enjoyment in the bickering, took a bystander's glee in the fighting of the siblings — the ones who'd gotten a bit of Mother's money battling the ones who'd gotten a lot of it. "It's so depressing," Floyd said. "Didi doesn't understand it at all." Didi was his new woman, just a name so far; I hadn't seen her. But the struggle seemed to me like a process of life, like the oldest story in the world, the queen setting her subjects at odds, animating them with unequal handouts to test them and to guarantee her dominance. It was at once like the origin of war and the key to power, for the more the subjects fought among themselves, the less the queen was threatened.

Had Mother guessed how violent a process she had kicked into motion? I don't think so. Mother was vain but she wasn't evil, and on a fundamental level she needed us. She would not have wanted us to destroy each other. She would have been shocked if she had known how fierce we fought — the insults, the gibes — how close we came to wrecking one another's lives, and how miserable it made us all.

And yet that was what happened. What made this antagonism so bad was that, as older adults, we behaved more like children than ever before. We seemed intent on devouring each other, the endo-cannibalism that existed in the most self-destructive rituals of remote peoples. We had the time for it. Our careers were over, or we were part-timers. Not much else to do but fight; not ambitious but still greedy, still angry.

Mother was more alive, more active than I could remember, more acute and demanding, on the phone all day and half the night, wanting to be visited, eager for presents, the center of our world.

Mother's health was good, so she mocked other people's illnesses — Marvin's hypochondria, Jonty's whining, Franny's worrying. Of Walter's back problems Mother said, "I've never had anything wrong with my back." Of Rose's reduced hours at school, Mother said, "She only works two days a week," always comparing others to herself and to her life of toil.

Mocking the daughters was a dodge. I knew that now. It was Mother's way of disguising the fact that she was still regularly writing checks to them, for small and big amounts. Mother's reasoning — transparent to me — was: *If I'm rude about them, no one will suspect that I'm giving them money for attending to me.* I knew that Franny and Rose's position was secure as Mother's favorite visitors.

But here was a further subtlety: I really did not know whether Mother was actually concealing her gifts or whether she was only pretending to conceal them. She was so shrewd that either could have been the case. She had me fooled — Floyd, too. He had kept current with her handouts, but in his romantic bliss with Didi, whoever she might be, he'd stopped caring about the outflow of money.

Sunday belonged to Franny and Rose. None of us wanted to bump into them, so we stayed away. Hubby visited on Saturday. Gilbert stayed for a few days at a time when he was back in the States. Fred made a point of taking Mother out to eat, the sort of dinner date that Mother loved. These outings were less for the dinners than for the doggy bags that Mother appealed for. Floyd visited now and then — a few times a month. I dropped in on the days I visited Father's grave — Oak Grove was not far from Mother's house. I say "Mother's house," but of course the house had been deeded to Franny and Marvin.

I was reminded that the house was Franny's on the occasions when Mother pointed out that she had ordered new carpets, a new stove, a skylight in the living room, a new brick walkway — all the improvements that Franny egged her on to make, so that she could enjoy them when Mother herself was in Oak Grove.

I, who had prided myself on my clear-sightedness, was confused. It was never completely clear to me if Mother was manipulating those of us she was giving money to, or were these people manipulating her? I looked for a villain. But it was Mother's genius that she could seem both tyrant and victim, oppressor and oppressed.

This was the confusion, the tang of blood in the air, that made us vipers. In the past we had been covert, resorting to casual abuse and whispering, happy that what we said would be reported back, as in the times when I'd heard, "Fred thinks you're pompous," "Franny said you're so cheap all you eat are Japanese noodles," "Hubby says you put him to work every time you see him — he's sick of being your handyman," "Floyd says you're competitive," "Rose says you're angry," that sort of thing (these were aimed at me), all of it secondhand and specious, and deniable.

"I never said that," Franny would protest to me. "You're the most generous one in the family" — compounding her lies.

But we changed. We were older. We had nothing to gain by pretending to be polite. We turned from a whispering hypocritical family into an openly abusive one.

"Why am I not entering this house?" Floyd called through the door, seeing that Fred was seated in a chair next to Mother. "Because I deprecate you. I have no fondness at all for you. Because you are a sententious bore."

"What was that?" Mother said. Her hearing was at last failing.

Hubby went out of his way to remind Rose's kids that their dog had been run over by a FedEx truck.

"Where's Wags?" he asked, and their eyes filled with tears. "Oh, that's right. Wags is roadkill."

This was at the Stop and Shop. Rose turned on him and cried, "You asshole!"

We became those people you sometimes see embarrassing themselves in public places: the sudden yell, the clash of supermarket carts, the red faces on the sidewalk, the slammed door. Our public displays were more common these days because it was only in public that we met — at the movies, at the beach, at the dump, or at Father's grave.

"What are you doing here?" I asked Franny at Oak Grove, and I ridiculed her for her pathetic pot of wilted, sour-smelling marigolds.

Rose saw me crossing the main street of Osterville as she was driving by. She speeded past me, saying, "What the fuck is your problem?"

"Up yours," I said when I saw who it was.

"Watch it, fella," an old man said, frowning at me.

"She almost ran me down," I said to him. "I've got the right of way."

But how could that nice old man have known that the two foulmouthed people were not an impatient motorist and a jaywalker, but a brother and sister. And a bigger shock was that I had not recognized her at first. The person I saw was a gray-haired old lady, her head sunk into her shoulders, screaming at me, showing her discolored teeth. Rose!

Franny wrote me a message on the back of a greeting card with the salutation, *Thinking of You.* The big loopy letters of her first-grade teacher's handwriting said, *I pray for you because your soul is black. If you died right now in your state of Mortal Sin you'd go to Hell.*

Both sisters hounded Hubby and, as takers often do, complained of his greed.

Fred had a cookout for some clients. He invited Mother. In what seemed a new ploy, to encumber him, Mother said, "Is Rose welcome? She was going to visit me today."

So Fred invited Rose, and midway through the meal Rose accused Fred of being bossy and abusive. She was an ill-tempered person whose way of expressing it was to put her furious face into someone else's and say, "You're really angry."

This was calculated to enrage whomever she said it to, and getting this reaction she'd say, "See? Listen to yourself."

The cookout at Fred's ended with Rose sitting in her car, in tears, her terrified children beside her — and they were much older now, Bingo in college, Benno a senior in high school. When Fred tried to console her, she screamed, "There's something wrong with you!"

Mother was sitting beside Fred's pool, out of earshot, sipping water and saying to one of Fred's guests, "I don't take any medication at all. 'What are you *awn?*' people ask me. I'm not *awn* anything."

We tormented each other's children and made a point of mentioning their lapses — shoplifting, vandalism, failures at school. Jake would never live down the fact that he had once eaten a Styrofoam cup, and the defining episode in Jonty's life was his kicking out the windshield of the Dodge Dart. Floyd said to me in passing, "Do your kids still have those phony British accents?" and he sent Fred a postcard, a view of Woods Hole, with the message, *Your children hate you.*

And yet, when I dropped in on Mother, she'd say, "Have you seen Rose?" or "Franny was asking about you," or "Hubby made some new window boxes for me," as though this was a big happy family, the harmonious fiction that Mother always maintained as fact.

I was at her house one afternoon. The phone rang. Mother answered it, said "Yes," then hung up.

"Who was that?" I asked.

"Franny. She always calls at this time."

"What did she say?"

"She asked me if I had company."

She moved us around like chess pieces, and we allowed ourselves to be moved. We did the same, moved each other around.

Floyd said to me, "Fred once took me to Mexico. He used his frequent flyer miles, though he led me to believe he was paying. At the end of the trip I thanked him and said I'd love to repay him. Without missing a beat he asked me for my Harper's Ferry flintlock. Fool that I am, I gave it to him. He's a pea-and-thimble man! I was blindsided."

Hubby remembered slights from years back, as when he was a twelve-year-old playing "My Grandfather's Clock" on his cello and hitting the wrong notes, and we watched and listened, trying to contain our laughter, with shaking shoulders.

Franny and Rose claimed that someone in the family ("And we know who he is") had vandalized their houses — tipped over garden statuary, stolen flowers, swiped important letters from the mail cans.

After that, Floyd, who trolled for rare books on the Internet, sent me a printout listing ten books by me that Rose and Walter had sold to a book dealer in New York. They were described as "highly collectible association copies." All were first editions, all inscribed *To Rose and Walter, with love, Jay* — tokens of Christmas, birthdays, family gatherings. They were priced in the thousands. When someone is selling a book you've inscribed to them, a message is being sent. It may seem a small matter, just a book after all, but it cuts deep — the book more valuable because of the fond or loving inscription, the recipient a sister and brother-in-law, the reminder of the circumstances. The books were not memories of happy days, only part of the pretense of them, and the inscription was proof of the pretense, for the fact was that I was no more sincere in giving the book than they were in receiving it. Now it was an expensive artifact, surviving from an earlier time, representing a false emotion.

"Treachery," Floyd said, and because he mentioned it to Mother, the next time I saw her she told me, with characteristic guile, how much Rose loved me and my work.

"But she sold my books, the ones I gave to her and Walter."

"I would never do a thing like that," Mother said.

"I didn't say you would. But Rose did."

"I'm sure you're mistaken."

"They're in a catalogue. Floyd showed me."

"You know how Floyd is."

"I saw the books listed. My name was there."

Mother went vague. She adjusted her glasses, rocked her body a little. She said, "I don't know anything about it."

"That's why I'm telling you," I said.

"Why are you shouting?"

"I'm annoyed because they sold my books for a lot of money."

It was a mistake to solicit sympathy: Mother had none. But the word "money" got Mother's attention.

"How much?" she asked.

"Thousands."

That made her laugh. She knew I was exaggerating, if not lying. No book was worth that, none had ever been sold for that amount. For all her knowingness, she was, like many queens, isolated and innocent of much of the world, especially the world of modern first editions.

"I'm sure it's all a misunderstanding," she said. "They're coming over tomorrow. Do you want to join us for a little bite?"

Mother claimed to be forgetful. She really did seem forgetful. Or was she purposely leaving the gas on and the faucet running? She was so completely credible in her vagueness that I was almost sure it was an act. I say "almost." I had no idea what was lurking in her mind.

"I won't be there," I said.

"Rose will be so disappointed."

This left me gaping at her. I said, "She sold my books. She calls me names. She hates me."

"Don't be silly," Mother said. "The first lesson I taught my children was that they must love each other. That's the most important lesson of all. 'Love one another as I have loved you,' Jesus said. If there's no love in a family, why, where would we be?"

40

MOTTLE SIN

Tнат was when i learned that weather is memory. That even the wind matters. That you don't need a calendar to remind you of anniversaries. You smell them, you feel them on your skin, you taste them. If you go on living in the same place year after year the weather begins to take on meanings; it is weighted with omens, and the temperature, the light, the trees and leaves, evoke emotions. The whole venerating world turns on this principle of weather-sniffing familiarity: all such pieties have their origin in a season, on a particular day. It had been a warm fragrant morning in May when Father was buried.

So there was something primitive in the way we stood in the parking lot of St. Joe's Catholic Church on Station Avenue — all of us, heavier, older, none of us making eye contact. It was the month, it was the day, it was the morning, it was the very weather of ten years before, when we had gathered for Father's funeral: the same heat, the same light, the same smells of damp earth and fresh leaves. May thirtieth — the pungency of new warmth on the rain-sodden turf of spring, the rising sourness of sun-cooked and crumbled dirt, the whiff of pine duff and the sting of leaf mold ripening into mulch, the suggestion of wet roots and swelling bulbs pricking through the wet earth, the earliest flowers — daffodils, jonquils, azaleas, the big rosy buds of rhododendrons, heavy yellow forsythia, the sweetness of white viburnum.

Even Mother felt it. "My favorite flower." And she added to test us, "Do you remember my favorite?" Before anyone could supply the right answer, she said, "Magnolia."

We all agreed in a reluctant murmur, a chorus of muffled moos. The grudging tone of this owed much to the fact that while each of us wanted to be at the church, for Father's sake, to honor his memory, we did not want to be together.

"I'd like all of us to be there," Mother said when she told us individually of her plan. "As a family."

At the lowest, most savage mood of this family, the nastiest and most corrosive I had known — "You asshole," "You shithead," "You fat greedy fuck," all that — Mother announced that she had paid for a memorial high mass to be said for Father and that we were expected to be there on our knees.

"It's for the repose of his soul," Mother said, using the church's formula.

Floyd remarked on the medieval practice of buying a church service, paying for prayers.

"Selling indulgences," he said. "Paying money to get redemption — it's what Luther objected to. 'The Pardoner's Tale.' And here it is again, coin to gain advancement. Look!"

He turned me around to face the sidewalk where two people were carrying signs, jerking them up and down to call attention to the messages. One sign said, *Reclaim Our Church,* the other, *Punish the Pedophile Priests.* Near them on the lawn some other people were kneeling, saying the rosary.

"It's kinda bad taste," Franny said to no one in particular. "That's what I think."

"Would you say that if a priest had sodomized Jonty when he was twelve?" Hubby said. " 'Cause that's what they were doing, nailing twelve-year-old boys on camping trips."

Fred rolled his eyes and put his arm around Mother.

The scandal had been reported in the *Cape Cod Times* — disturbed, wild-haired men coming forward to claim they had been fondled and raped by homosexual priests in Boston twenty and thirty years ago. The lawsuits and accusations had divided the church; the Boston cardinal had protected the priests — indeed, had sent them to new parishes, where they abused more boys. Some priests had recently been sent to prison, others were soon to stand trial. The lawsuits demanded millions — so much money that the diocese had begun to close churches, anticipating the huge payout.

"Shanley's in Provincetown," Floyd said. "In our very midst."

The recently arrested Father Shanley was one of the accused pedophile priests, out on bail, awaiting trial, living in the gay enclave on the lower Cape. While still a priest, he had been a charter member of the North American Man/Boy Love Association.

"Maybe he's saying mass today," Hubby said.

"He's been defrocked," I said.

"After defrocking all those little boys."

"I think he was frocking them," Hubby said.

"Keep it down," Rose said.

"You're disgusting," Franny said.

"That's right, criticize me. Don't say anything about the pervert priests."

Our shrillness exaggerated our frailty and our age. Arguing, growing wheezy with anger, we seemed older and crueler, and our ill temper suggested weakness.

And we did look old. I had been shocked by the sight of the crone in the car in Osterville, screaming out the window at me — Rose. But Franny was a crone too, Fred was an old coot, Floyd was almost wholly bald, and Hubby had a tonsure. Gilbert had a paunch. I was balding and fatter. No one was more undignified than a foulmouthed oldster.

Only Mother was unchanged. She was a stick figure but seemed indestructible. At ninety-three, she looked no older than she had ten years before at the funeral. She was standing with her arms folded, her big Sunday handbag hanging from one arm, at the center of our family group. We were still shuffling like penguins in the parking lot.

"I think we should go in," she said. "I've reserved a special pew for us up front. Who's that?"

It was Charlie, hurrying toward us from his car.

"Charlie," I said.

Mother said, "Who's Charlie?"

"My son — one of them."

"Oh, that's right, I remember," Mother said.

"Hope I'm not late," Charlie said.

"I can feel Angela here," Mother said. "Her presence. She's speaking to me. She's grieving for Dad. Would anyone like to say anything to her? I can pass on the message."

Mother, assuming the role of sibyl and go-between, was speaking loudly, attracting the attention of other people who'd already taken their seats. It struck me that Mother intended to make a spectacle of our entrance into the church, our procession down the main aisle, Mother and her seven children, like Snow White and the dwarfs.

"She says she's happy that we're all together, in harmony," Mother said, looking left and right. "As a family."

Fred walked on one side of her, turtle-headed, looking ill. Franny and Rose jostled on the other side. Hubby was behind them, walking alone, next came Gilbert and me, and finally Floyd. Charlie and the grandchildren and the spouses were far to the rear. Perhaps the people in the church saw us as the exemplary family Mother wished them to see—the many offspring supporting their aged, widowed mother in her mourning. Perhaps they did not see what I felt profoundly, that we were old and mean, ugly children with their aged mother, committing sacrilege by pretending to pray.

Father would have been uncomfortable with the charade, the paid-for mass, the expensive flowers, the procession, the pomp, the show of fake solidarity, the appeal to Angela. He would have crept through a side door, sat in the back, and expressed himself with full-throated singing, his favorite hymns, or kneeling with closed eyes, in prayer.

At the front of the altar rail Mother genuflected before the tabernacle, in conspicuous piety, and then directed us into the first pew. We sidled in and sat compactly. Was it obvious that we hated to be together, that we were sitting separately, that only Floyd and I were conversing, the rest of them sitting stony-faced?

"Has it occurred to you that Ma might be the poorest one of us?" Floyd said in a whisper. "Think of all the money and property she's given away. She doesn't even own the house she's living in."

I lowered my head and said, "She might have another bank account or investments we don't know about."

"Look at them," Floyd said. "Queen Lear with Regan and Goneril."

The three of them were kneeling, Mother between the two daughters, all of them praying with folded hands, their bums against the pew. Mother blessed herself, made the sign of the cross. The daughters did the same. And they sat.

Then they stood—we all did. The priest had entered, followed by two gray-haired women, one very thin, the other one potbellied, both purse-lipped and ostentatiously pious, like busybodies.

"What happened to altar boys?" I asked Floyd.

"When's the last time you were in church?"

The day of Father's funeral was the correct answer, a decade ago, and before that I could not remember. The whole service seemed strange to me now, the altar positioned like a dining table, the priest standing behind it, facing the churchgoers, flanked by the two biddies. It was all unfamiliar, not like any other mass I had ever attended.

The priest was a big, pink-faced man with a crown of white hair, handling the items on the altar with chubby fingers, pushing at the pages of the thick missal lying in its cradle, then clasping his hands and praying loudly — more ostentatious piety. The two women jostled on either side of him, seeming to compete for attention, while the priest carried himself back and forth, his big belly draped in brocaded vestments, gold tassels, his surplice trimmed in fine lace.

"Nullifidian," Floyd said under his breath. "Father Corkery, heretic and blasphemer. I miss Father Furty."

We stood, we knelt, we sat, we muttered responses. A man with a guitar strummed and sang "The Impossible Dream" while some people hummed. Then one of the women jingled a set of bells, and the priest, looking like a chef in drag, fussed with the chalice as if he was seasoning a soufflé.

Adjusting his lace cuffs, tugging his sleeves, Father Corkery ascended the pulpit. He was a glowing, well-fed priest, plump under his swelling vestments. Now that he was lit by the blaze from above him, I could study him. It was obvious that he was vain about his thick white hair. His pink face set it off, his eyes were pale blue, his head seemed oversized and babyish because of his short neck, lost in the frills of his collar, and when he gripped the edge of the pulpit I could see the sparkle of his rings on those thick fingers.

As Father Corkery frowned and inhaled and began, Floyd said, "He is the reason the Mormons call the Catholic Church the Great Whore of Babylon."

I heard Boston Irish in his voice as Father Corkery intoned the formulas of the mass. His *hee-yah* for here, his *hee-yands* for hands, his *onnaments* for ornaments, and his nasal squeak marked him as a Southie native. He announced as his subject "Mottle Sin."

"In the reading today" — and clipping the *r*, the word came out *veeding*

— "Paul mentions fy-ah. He means hell fy-ah, as a penalty for mottle sin."
He tapped the open Bible. "So it says right hee-yah . . ."

I was not following his argument. I was listening to the peculiarities
of his speech, imagining how to write them phonetically, and reflecting
on how people spoke blithely of the Boston accent. But there was no such
thing. There were fifty ways of speaking, and his was the lower-middle-
class Irish accent of South Boston — "the lace-curtain Irish," Father called
them, as opposed to "the shanty Irish." Someone from Southie could
probably identify the priest's precise neighborhood. Such men became
the priests, the policemen, the politicians, roughly equivalent roles in the
status-minded city.

He was speaking about the sanctity of life, how "all living creetchahs
belawng to Gawd." As this was Father's memorial mass, I listened for any
mention of him.

"Here it comes," Floyd murmured.

"Yet there are people who give this idea shawt shriff," Father Corkery
said. "Who are bent on destroying life. Believe me, that takes its toll."

He said this word as *thole*, using his emphatic tongue. That was true to
his part of Boston, for in his next sentence he used the expression "square
deal" — *squa-yah theel* — and how there were people who "vipped living
children from the wombs of their mothers, Gawd love them, and then
flushed them down the terlet. And dint cay-yah! Went to a function!
Fixed themselves something to eat. Took and made themselves a drink.
Had a bee-yah. Had a time!"

"See what he's doing? What he's not talking about?" Floyd said. "No
buggery. It's what magicians call indirection."

Though Father Corkery was railing against abortion, speaking of the
abortionists as murderers, the clinics as slaughterhouses and Nazi death
camps "like Os-wich" (making it sound like a town on the Cape near
Hah-wich), and that things had to change, I continued to be fascinated by
his accent. Why did no one ever put this sort of local speech into a book?

The heckling sermon went on, but I was thinking how local accents in
America were being lost and absorbed into the more homogenized speech
of TV and radio. That was a shame, because there was something in a local accent that helped you to verify the truth of what someone was saying.
I could tell from the way Father Corkery spoke that he was posturing. He

was talking about "doctors drinking a bottle of tonic" — *bawtell of tawnic* — "on their piazzas without a cay-ah in the world, and yet they're in a state of mottle sin."

We could do something about it, he said. There was an election coming this fall.

"If you're fed up to hee-yah, go over they-ah to that polling booth and take your ballot and mahk it. Vote for the candidate who promises to overturn the mottle sin of abortion. Tell your friends and nay-biz. Tell them Father Cokkery wants to know. Demand to know where the candidates stee-yand on the issue."

"Ayatollah," Floyd said.

Mother's head was bent in prayer.

"Notice how much time he's spending on the pervert priests," Floyd murmured again.

What I had noticed was that Father Corkery had been raising his voice throughout the sermon, along with a contrary wail, a sort of chanting, coming from outside the church but piercing the stained-glass windows with its shrillness.

And when at last Father Corkery said, "Let us join ourselves in pray-yah," I heard the rhythmic shouts again, not clear but loud and discordant with emotion.

In this prayer that followed the sermon, Father Corkery mentioned the souls that had departed from this church, and lifted his eyes as if they had been launched through the roof of St. Joe's. Among the three or four deceased, he spoke Father's name, mispronouncing it as *Joo-stiss*.

Making the sign of the cross, Floyd murmured, "In the name of the former and of the latter and of their holocaust. All men."

With muffled voices that became shouts, the doors of the church burst open and red-faced people appeared in the aisle, crying "Hypocrites!" in cracked nervous voices.

They were protesting the cover-up of the pedophile priests, but we shrank — everyone did — taking the word personally.

The mass fell apart at this point — it was almost over anyway. The priest busied himself, clutched at his skirts, said some hurried prayers, and fled. The churchgoers got up and pressed toward the door, driving out the protesters, who without their signs mingled with everyone else and were indistinguishable. Because we were in the long pew at the front of the church, we stood and shuffled and were the last to leave.

We gathered again in the parking lot. Charlie said he had to go back to work.

"I think it would be appropriate to visit Dad's grave," Mother said.

"I'll be there," Charlie said. "Work can wait."

We drove separately to Oak Grove and met again in a group before Father's rough-textured stone — two names on it, Father's with his dates, and Mother's with a birth date.

In her primary school teacher's voice, Mother said, "I'd like you all to form a circle."

We stepped forward, frowning, hating to be together.

"Shall we join hands?" Mother asked.

"No way," Hubby said.

"Is it necessary?" Rose asked.

"I think it might be a nice idea," Mother said.

No one looked up. Fred said, "I agree." He was Mother's enforcer now, as Father had sometimes been. I reached to the left and right, and my hands were caught, I did not want to know by whom. Dry scaly fingers and soft palms, almost reptilian, damp in the May warmth, held mine in an unwilling grip, as Mother intoned, "Let us pray."

41

"WHAT ARE YOU DOING HERE?"

PEOPLE DO NOT do us all the harm they are capable of, an obscure Frenchman once said. He did not know the abuses in Mother Land. Still, seeing the whole bad-tempered bunch mumbling insincere prayers at Father's grave made me feel so rebellious, the next chance I had, I broke into Mother's house — blindly, idly, on an insolent impulse.

But the break-in did not go as planned. I had told myself that I wanted to sneak another look at the revealing check register, and a defiant thought urged me to steal something of value that might easily fit into my pocket —a ring, a keepsake, one of Mother's rarer, uglier porcelain Hummels from the china cabinet. I did not want a souvenir or a trophy but a sort of token hostage, even better if it happened to be one of the lumpy baubles Mother had earmarked as heirlooms for Franny and Rose.

I knocked, to give myself an excuse in case she might be home, though it was her morning for bird carving at the senior center. Hearing no reply —she had to be at the class—I crept to the back door and shoved it open as far as the security chain would allow, about three inches. I was insulted that she had locked it, indignant that she was so untrusting as to think someone might try to break in.

Annoyed by the brass chain, which was evidence of her suspicion, I jammed my shoulder against it and reached through the crack to un- screw the plate that secured the chain fastener. My nimble fingers, my tiny screwdriver — Floyd had marveled at my diabolical dexterity the first time I had accomplished this. I stepped inside and screwed the plate back in place, then entered the kitchen, flipping open cupboard doors and glancing at the objects on the shelves, thinking, Anything I want . . .

Passing a mirror, I got a glimpse at my face, dog-like and grim, and kept walking. A few glittering items on a saucer or a shelf had me raising my hand, but I became angry with myself for being distracted by them —a cheap thimble, a worthless salt shaker, an old bobbin, some Canadian coins. Past a narcissus blooming on a plant stand was a clock, loudly tick- ing, displaying the wrong time.

I made for Mother's desk and the check register, quickly scanning it for payments. I made a note of the larger amounts, then opened the china cabinet. The Hummels included a fat friar, a goose girl, an urchin, a cho- rister, a Madonna — pieces of hideous kitsch, yet I knew they had some value. I picked up some of them, checking for their authenticity — the bee inside the V on the base — and I saw a crystal Swarovski owl I had bought Mother at a duty-free shop many years before. Why not take that? It was mine anyway. Or what about those two Russian icons that Fred had brought from Moscow? The smaller of the two was resting against a mirror, and in the mirror I saw Mother on the sofa, her head to one side, her slack mouth half-open.

My first thought was that Mother was dead. She had been sitting, probably reading, with a book at her feet, as if it had slipped from her knees. But she was canted sideways, her shoulders tipped, her slumped head resting on the back of the sofa, her hands in her lap, her face gray. She lay askew in the collapsed posture of someone who'd been assaulted.

Behind her, a big, slow horsefly bumped the windowpane. Mother's angle was not the repose of sleep but the collapsed-looking awkwardness of death, in extreme discomfort. I heard the fly, but I did not hear Mother breathing, though I knew that old people sleep with their mouths open. She was motionless, fragile, as if made of ashes, crumple-faced, with bluish fingers, twisted on the sofa.

I was still holding the small crystal owl that had caught my eye. Mother was dead, so it didn't matter. I was relieved that she couldn't blame me — no, this cruel satisfaction was unworthy of me. I was so ashamed of the thought, I put the owl back into the china cabinet and latched the glass door. I accepted Mother's death, thinking, I didn't do it! and What now?

"Hello?"

The click of the door latch had awakened Mother. She twitched. She did not open her eyes, but she drew her mouth shut, blew out her thin lips and breathed, then sank back into stifled sleep, her mouth falling open again, her greenish tongue floating behind her teeth.

Seeing her this way, back from the dead, exposed to any intruder — I could have been that stranger, standing six feet away, about to plunder her house — I wanted to protect her. I had never seen her so vulnerable, like a pale child discovered alone in an empty house.

She had seemed stronger, stiffer, when I'd taken her to be dead. Now, knowing she was sleeping, she seemed more breakable than any of the porcelain objects in front of me.

I was moved by the thought of her so small, so shrunken on the sofa that was like another throne, and I felt something like love for her — not the love I'd ever felt for anyone else, but the word as shorthand for a rapture of gratitude that she had not been lying there dead, that she was only sleeping. I had a second chance to redeem myself.

Sometimes you see a child throwing a tantrum and your immediate impulse is hatred. But then you notice how skinny and helpless the child is, peculiarly grotesque in the tantrum, tear-smeared cheeks, snot on her chin, and you realize that she is not angry but afraid. Then your hatred is overtaken by sympathy. The poor thing feels trapped and terrified, feels weak, and you are strong. Why not try to help, or at least not judge the kid? That was the feeling I had for Mother, a kind of resolve, not love but pity, a shallow reflex of mercy for her frailty.

"What are you doing here?" Mother said. "How did you get in?"

"Through the back door," I said, stammering, because she was fully awake.

"It was locked," she said with a flash of malice.

"I thought something was wrong. I knocked. You didn't answer. I was worried." I gulped in my lie.

"I was just resting my eyes," Mother said, another lie.

I hated myself for my lie; I hated Mother's lie. After all the purifying wash of emotion, my sympathy became hostility again.

"I was trying to make sure you were all right."

More lies, falsehood as conversation. I resented her putting me through this.

"Carving class was canceled. I was reading. I like a good book. I don't need TV." She smacked her lips in this sanctimony.

"I thought something might have happened."

She pulled herself upright. "What were you doing in my china cabinet?"

"Nothing."

"You were going to take something."

Mother, the interrogator, was expert at bluffing, and was successful at this informed sort of game playing, because her instincts were uncanny, especially in assessing the basest motives. She was prescient when it came to criminality, but this was another way of saying that she believed no one was reliable, no one loyal, everyone a potential intruder and felon; no one could be trusted. Anyone who offered her a helping hand she suspected was intending to pick her pocket. She woke from a nap and, startled by her own child in her house, saw a thief.

"I wouldn't take anything from you, Ma."

"Oh, no, not you," she said, her cynicism making her jolly. She was wide awake now. She clearly saw my lie, and it made her happy.

"Want a drink of something?"

"Just water."

She drank loudly, lapping and swallowing, sucking at the lip of the tumbler, her forehead and scalp contracting with the effort. I felt sorry for her again, hearing the gurgle-gulp in her throat. She never looked older than when she was eating or drinking.

"Guess what?" she said, handing me the glass.

I knew it had to be bad news: she was trying not to smile.

"Walter didn't get his promotion."

Mother seldom hid her contempt for the in-laws. She began to laugh at Rose's husband.

"God forgive me" — her mirth was genuine, another sign of life — "but what difference will it make?"

The most reassuring sound in the world, the Chinese say, is the thump of your neighbor falling off his roof. This was the sort of cruel folk wisdom that appealed to our family, and especially to Mother, for the best news, the news that traveled fastest, always concerned someone's misfortune.

A flooded basement, a downed tree on a car, frozen pipes, a painful ailment (better still if the ailment had a ridiculous name like shingles or hives or mono) — these brought joy to us, to all but the victim. "Guess what?" Hubby might say — Mother's voice, Mother's question. Someone had piles. Or someone's teenager totaled the family car. The fact that the wrecked car was expensive made the news even sweeter. My first divorce and the penury that followed had been followed by whispers of derision — Jay's been taken down a peg. Floyd had told me this in detail, and he had a great deal to tell, because we'd been on the outs when I'd split up with Diana. The rest of the family had descended on Floyd, knowing that he would welcome news of my failure and disgrace. When this turned into my deep unhappiness and bankruptcy they all pitched in and told him what they thought of me — and of course, in this way, ingratiated themselves with him. *Have we got some wicked news for you!* I had, so to speak, fallen off my roof. But after Floyd and I became friends again he was able to tell me all these stories of betrayal, of the other family members laughing behind my back.

The source of most of the pitiless whispers was Mother. Crashing a BMW was what happened when you had money to burn. It was your own goddamned fault. If you broke your ankle skiing, it was something you'd asked for — after all, the rest of us were working while you were on the slopes. Hubby's dog died, sending Mother into giggles of glee as she mimicked his grief. Like most pet haters, Mother was a penny pincher. What on earth are they for? "Do you think he'll cry like that when I die? I doubt it. A dog!"

Mother was at the center of all this bad news, because she competed with these misfortunes for attention. By spinning the news, turning tragedy into farce, she could stay in control. Her attitude had been established a decade back when, after Dad died, our grieving for him implied we were being disloyal to her. More than anything, a misfortune proved our weakness, our moral faults, our inferiority; misfortune put us in our place. Mother's was a primitive, fatalistic view of life: bad things happened to bad people.

I did not need a psychiatrist to explain to me that there were dark reasons for Mother to stew in this ill will. She was weak, her self-esteem was low, she needed attention. But that was a determination on a cerebral level — Mother as a Case, Mother as a Study in Tyranny, Mother's power politics in the dynamics of the family. Living in the misery of Mother Land, I was seldom able to summon the rationality that would allow me to be objective about this unhappy woman. Crowded and mocked by all these conspirators, I reacted in passionate and petty ways, always competing, and often delighting like Mother in someone's downfall. We embodied the spirit of the rabble, a mob instinct, destructive and envious in a world where no one was to be trusted or praised, where the dominant craving was the desire to get even.

"Every dog has his day," Mother used to say, one of her favorite proverbs. She often said it while looking out the window — raindrops spattering the glass, the sky brown, the trees black, a smell of decay raised by the rain. The saying had once summarized for me a spirit of hope. But as the years passed and Mother repeated it, I saw it as a sinister promise, a piece of brutish wisdom, something like revenge, in a wilderness of baying hounds.

"I guess Rose is going to have to work a little bit harder," Mother was saying to me. She had risen from the sofa and was rattling plastic bags and prying open the tops of Tupperware containers in the kitchen. "Maybe I can fix you something for lunch. Here's some ravioli Rose brought me when she told me the news."

Because this was just a few weeks after Father's memorial mass, the bad news was welcome, a little gift to remind Mother of someone else's misery, meant to revive her and make her feel better.

Widening her eyes, pretending innocence, Mother said, "I understand Walter's going to be a consultant." She ridiculed the word by pausing and uttering it in a tone of disbelief. All new words sounded like lame excuses to her. "Does that mean he's been fired?"

Walter's becoming a consultant meant that Rose was even more dependent on her for support. She would need to be more loyal, more grateful, more careful. A messiah loves a broken family — Jesus and Mao and Jim Jones were family-haters. Follow me, they said. Leave your family behind, they said. It was all in Matthew: I have come to set a man against his father, a daughter against her mother, a son's wife against her mother-in-law; and a man will find enemies under his own roof. And so did Mother.

I left with a bag of Mother's hermits and three "church window" cookies. With a younger brother's glee, like a sweaty boy, panting and simple, with the wicked satisfaction of having a juicy piece of news, I hurried to Floyd's house. I wanted to tell him I'd seen another big payment to Rose. The news was my gift to him. Mother was buying favors — that was the pretext. But in my heart the pettiness of this fuss made me feel young. The return to childhood had its annoyances but also its pleasures. Even the story of my embarrassment was entertaining.

"Guess what?"

"The second-story man," Floyd said blandly, motioning me to a rocker on his porch.

"What do you mean?"

"The cat burglar," he said. "Mr. Sneaky. Light-fingered Larry. Raffles, the amateur cracksman."

I was smiling. How could he possibly know this? He read the question on my face and leaned against the porch railing with his arms folded.

"Creepy-crawling your poor old ma. She just called and told me. She said everyone is scandalized."

A ten-minute drive from Mother's to Floyd's: in that time she'd apparently called the other children to denounce me for snooping in her house, suggesting I'd taken some of her valuables.

"Ripping off your mother!" Floyd laughed. "She caught you red-handed. You've lost your touch, buddy-boy."

"You could have come along."

"To purloin Ma's property?" he said. "Excuse me, I have more important things to do than mugging an old lady."

I was grinning, rocking on my heels like a teenager. What was more enjoyable than spending a sunny day in the supreme violation of breaking into your mother's house and robbing her — sifting through her records, weighing her artifacts and mementos, and lolling on her throne-like chair with your muddy feet on her coffee table. It was never too late to be a juvenile delinquent.

"It was fun," I said.

"Some of us are adults," he said, affecting haughtiness. "Did you get anything good?"

"As you once acerbically pointed out, there's nothing left in the house to steal."

42

BAD NEWS

PROBABLY IN ALL FAMILIES — certainly in the doomed clans of Mother Land — there comes a point when no more good news is possible. It is all ill tidings. People get older, they fail, they get fired, they go broke, they stop aspiring, they cheat. Time passing means that things get worse (one of Mother's notions, which we all came to believe): people fall ill, they weaken, they stink, they die.

So a family crumbles, but in stages, falling like a stand of trees in a forest with its roots in thin soil, like the pitch pines on the Cape rooted in loose sand. The trees don't go all at once. They fall one by one, from rot, from infestation by bore beetles, from wind, from the undermining of the rising sea, from being too tall or the wrong shape. They snap, they topple, they sometimes knock each other down, and finally they're all gone. You might discern seedlings, delicate as houseplants, sprouting in the mess of needles and decayed splinters, but it will be decades before they will climb to a stand, and it is a certainty that they will fall too, for even as they rise, they are weakening.

No one gets healthier, no one grows stronger. Our mortality pursues us, our vices overtake us — smoking and drinking and telling lies. Time itself pulls us apart. The family crumbles slowly. It crumbles in installments, but it crumbles.

Hubby was diagnosed with high blood pressure and was put on sick leave. Mother hooted at the irony of a hospital worker, toiling among the healers and pills, becoming ill. "He eats too much," she said. "He eats the wrong food." It had to be his own fault.

"One in twenty people who check into a hospital catch a hospital-related illness," Hubby said. "Hospitals are unhealthy places — everyone knows that."

"Did you catch high blood pressure?" I asked.

"Very funny," Hubby said. "Ma says it's a blessing in disguise. I need to slow down and put my house in order. It's kind of a wake-up call. I think she's right."

As though competing in these illness stakes, and craving attention, Marvin developed a tummy ache he claimed was a bleeding ulcer.

"Stress," Mother said, cackling at the word — for her one of the new bogus ones — and laughing at the contradiction, for how was it possible to have been stressed in such a simple job as mall cop, circling the benches between Mrs. Fields cookies and Dunkin' Donuts? Mother reminded us that she was ninety-four years old, was taking no medicine at all, walked up and down her street every afternoon, and was healthy — "No complaints."

She called me one evening to report that Fred had had a stroke. She sounded certain of the fact, yet somewhat bewildered about the reasons for it. "Apparently, he'd been traveling. China. He got home and was reading the paper. Erma heard him say, 'I feel funny.' One whole side of his body was seizing up and he went all feverish. He was rushed to Emergency. They're doing tests."

Her story was precise. By the time she called me, she had probably called five or six others, so she sounded practiced. But what did it all mean? You could not be ill without somehow asking for it — sickness in the family indicated a moral fault. What had Fred done to deserve it?

Lately Fred had been a nag, blaming Floyd and me for stirring up trouble by demanding to know which of the children were getting payouts from Mother, and how much, and why.

"Can't you just let the matter rest?" he'd said in an email, repeating, "Ma can do whatever she wants with her money."

Really? Here was a woman in her mid-nineties who might very well need the money to pay for round-the-clock nursing or assisted living. She would not be living alone and reading books and making phone calls and going for walks much longer.

"It upsets her to know that her judgment is being questioned," Fred went on — same email. "She's frail, she's forgetful. She gets confused. You should show some compassion."

I replied saying that someone who was frail and confused at ninety-four should not be handing out checks willy-nilly. There was a contradiction here: either she was feeble and needed guidance, or she was hearty and could do what she wanted. But Fred was no help. This was another example of his lawyer's ability to hold two opposite views in his head at the same time, and argue them convincingly without believing in either of them.

Now he was in Cape Cod Hospital's intensive care unit, attached to plastic tubes, one of his hands (so Mother said) "like a dead paw."

Mother was angry. She could not rationalize the illness of a favored son, her eldest. She blamed his work, his travel, his diet, his wife, his children, his dogs.

"It's just not fair," she said to me. I took this to mean that she felt he'd abandoned her: his sickness was a form of disloyalty. Bad things happened to bad people, and also, if he'd really loved Mother, he would not have had the stroke.

Floyd said, "The big explainer! The big moralizer! Look at him now, drooling into his pillow, snatching at the air, crying 'More light!' Where is his indirection now? Stroke! I like that. He has been struck down."

Hubby said, "I heard he's having trouble swallowing, and they might have to put a grommet in his abdominal wall and do a gastrostomy — hook him up to a feeding tube."

His tone was horrified satisfaction, gloating at the prospect of the eldest brother kept alive and immobile by a set of pipes feeding him goop. As a nurse, Hubby became important as an interpreter of the science behind the feeding tube.

"I visited Fred today," Mother said. "He was a wreck."

She was not moved to pity by the sight of her son lying in intensive care; she felt superior and stronger. She was prepared to release him, for, in a way, he was being sacrificed. He had been Mother's ally and counselor, and so the stroke was perhaps the result of his effort at being tenaciously loyal. Enduring the stroke was something he'd done for Mother.

"He was lying there," she said. "He just looked at me with those glassy eyes. He couldn't speak, but I knew what he wanted to say. 'Thank you, Mother. Thank you.' He was letting go."

We all visited Fred, for the novelty of seeing this once-powerful deputy of Mother's in his sickbed. We went separately, in the family fashion, and insincerely paid our respects. Fred was rigid, looked broken and beat up. He was wordless apart from a few protesting groans. I listened with satisfaction to the bubbling in his tubes, which resembled the sound of the aerator in a fish tank.

His doctor visited while I was seated, watching. I asked the doctor the obvious question.

"These things are to be expected at his age," the doctor said.

"He's only seventy-something," I said.

"He's getting on."

Mother visited Fred often and always returned home revitalized — more phone calls, more baked hermits, more walks up and down the street. His sickness made Mother healthier, boastfully so.

"Hubby explained what an angioplasty is," she said to me, "but what is a stent? Hubby just confuses me."

I explained the little I knew of the procedure.

"They did that to Fred yesterday," she said and, sounding rueful, added, "It seems to be working."

Eventually, Fred recovered much of his strength, though one arm remained slack. He learned to walk, but he tended to shuffle. He was soon disparaging me again, and ridiculing Hubby for his explanations and for conferring with Mother. He'd had a near-death experience, always revealing, for it is only at such times that you find out what people really think of you. He'd discovered that we were joking about his condition in whispers — no sympathy at all.

"We almost had another saint in the family," Floyd said.

I told him what the doctor had said about Fred's age, a little over seventy and susceptible. "He's getting on." It was a reminder — we seldom had them — of how old Mother was, and not just old but, it seemed, everlasting.

43

BEST MAN

I WAS NAGGED BY A MEMORY of something that had happened earlier at Floyd's. It was the day of my break-in at Mother's when I had discovered her corpse twisted on her sofa, and then she had awakened from the dead. ("What are you doing here?") I had hurried to Floyd's, but Mother had already called him to report that she had caught me in her house, that I was a burglar.

Two things interested me about the visit to Floyd's, though they did not come to mind until much later. They were powerful afterthoughts.

Floyd was clean-shaven, his wild hair had been combed, he was wearing a seersucker suit. Normally he was scruffy, unshaven, wearing a Red Sox shirt, sometimes with a hat on in his house. Absorbed in his work, if he didn't have a class to teach, he might not bathe or change his clothes for days—weeks, even. His tidiness was always a sign of happiness or at least contentment.

And I sensed he was not alone. It was not knowledge on my part, just an impression, a clutch of details, a vagrant surmise. The seersucker suit was not unusual. But with the suit he was wearing zoris—Japanese sandals. An extended residence in Japan, teaching English, researching the life of Lafcadio Hearn, and learning to compose haiku verses, had given Floyd some Japanese habits he'd never shed. Eating sushi and collecting ukiyo-e woodblock prints and netsuke were some of his loves, and a sign at his door instructed visitors to remove their shoes before entering.

On that visit, when he had said, "Creepy-crawling your poor old ma," we had been standing on the porch by his back door, where I had casually recorded in my mind as a contrasting image, next to Floyd's big muddy boots, a tiny pair of shoes and an almost toy-sized pair of sky-blue boots, like a child's fanciful footwear. Afterward, remembering these diminutive shoes and boots, I concluded that their owner was in the house. That was why—though I failed to question it at the time—Floyd didn't invite me inside, as he normally did. In hindsight, I was sure of it. Who was she?

I had not seen much of Floyd during Fred's health crisis. This was odd, and unlike him. We were not close friends now, but we were allies, and in this family being an ally mattered more than being a brother. I enjoyed hearing Floyd's rants about the other siblings—he could howl for hours on the subject of duplicitous greed. "Double-dipping! Fawning over Ma! Trollops!" He had briefly gloated over Fred's stroke. He'd done a cruelly accurate imitation of hemiplegia, limping, drooling, gargling when he tried to speak, one arm swinging loosely, one side of his mouth drawn down. Floyd could be hilarious in his cruelty, but this time he was more perfunctory.

I had wanted more, because his merciless satire was cathartic. But Floyd was elsewhere—or rather, as I now realized, he was home, but keeping to himself. And he was not alone.

Floyd had a history with women. Like me, he had been married and divorced twice, but neither wife had produced a child. His divorces figured in his poems; he saw his poetry as both a scourge and an expiation,

even as a kind of voodoo that would destroy the women. He was infuriated when that did not happen, when the women became well known and
somewhat in demand as minor celebrities for nothing more than being
Floyd's ex-wives. That was to be expected about women whom he'd depicted with such venomous brilliance. "I've been cozened!" he'd cry.

Yet women went on adoring him. He was charming, he could be
funny. He had a succession of girlfriends. But with wives and girlfriends
always the spell was eventually broken. Floyd blamed the woman. "She
has a vocabulary of fifty words!" Women were necessities who became
superfluous and ultimately obstacles.

"Sonny Barger was right. He of the Hells Angels. Women — can't live
with 'em, can't use their bones for soup." But the reality was that Floyd
needed privacy to write, and he wrote all the time.

Privacy was a theme in the family. Perhaps it is a theme in all big families. Mother's gruesome relief at Father's death could be ascribed to her
selfish satisfaction in having the whole house to herself. She hated house-
guests; she disliked staying with any of us.

She wouldn't share — none of us shared. Nothing was more infuriat-
ing than the rap at the bathroom door. "Hurry up!" Our need for privacy
had made us solitary people — at last, after a childhood of bunk beds and
hand-me-downs, we had a place of our own, so any visitor was a potential
violation.

Floyd's new woman friend living under his roof was a departure from
his need for solitude. Maybe in such a turbulent family he needed an ally.
But an ally was not a fiancée. *You married a woman to stop her getting
away,* he'd recite. *Now she's there all day.* He claimed that he had written
those lines. Was he testing me? The women inevitably left. He claimed
they'd abandoned him, but the truth was that he had driven them out
with his moods, his silences, his speeches, his absences. He always wailed
that he was alone, but in his heart he was relieved that they'd gone.

Men like Floyd who entertained general theories about women always
seemed to be justifying a dislike of them. Subscribing to such theories is
usually fatal to a relationship. "Women leak" was one, and "Women constantly look at the clock, yet they always know the time" was another. "If a
woman stands listening to you without moving, it's a sign she has sex on

her mind," and "They are always looking for a man to help them live their lives." He had written a poem on the theme, "Women Extend the Cheek — Men Kiss It." But his generalizations about women made me think that he feared them.

As he had grown older, the successive women had become younger and the relationships shorter. That was the pattern. How would this one be any different? From past experience, I guessed that at some point he would show up howling, "Perfidious bitch!" and claim that he'd been abandoned. But not this time.

He invited me for a meal. The table was set with plates and chopsticks, little dishes of soy sauce and wasabi paste; bigger platters of sushi, sashimi, tempura, and dumplings; bowls of miso soup.

"I have been thoroughly Nipponized," Floyd said. "In here, honey."

She entered from behind a pile of books stacked in a column taller than she was, treading in small, pawing steps. She was beaming, head cocked somewhat submissively, hands together.

"Gloria Fujii, but we call her Didi," Floyd said. "East meets West."

She took my hands in hers and smiled, nodding with gratitude. Her father had been Japanese, her mother Italian, and the result was a sort of exotic Mexican, with a strong hint of Asia. An aquiline nose, hooded eyes, thick black hair — pretty, in her mid-thirties. Floyd was sixty-six.

"Floyd's told me all about you."

She pronounced his name *Freud,* which made me smile, because Floyd was such a hater of psychoanalysis and its jargon. Floyd seemed not to notice. He was pouring out little glasses of sake.

"Let's say I warned her about your waywardness." He lifted one of the glasses. "Take a glass. I am making an announcement. I will be brief. In a word, Didi and I are getting married. To each other."

He downed the sake and made a face, deliberately comic, blowing out his cheeks, and looked at Gloria. She was smiling adoringly at him, her lips glistening with the sake she'd just drunk.

"A tad more, don't mind if I do." Floyd poured and drank again. He said, "We've selected you to be best man. Don't look so puzzled."

"I'm delighted." The sake had burned my throat, but it didn't matter — Floyd was still talking.

The date was six weeks away. The ceremony would be held in the local Catholic church, a chapel by the roadside on the Cranberry Highway near his house.

"Secrecy is the watchword."

Apart from Mother and me, no one else in the family would be invited, though it was essential that they should know about it, because what was the point of excluding people unless they were sharply reminded of their exclusion? They had to know that they were not wanted.

It could be said that in this period of Mother's dominance, we looked for ways ostentatiously to exclude each other from our lives. No pleasure was complete unless we made sure the others felt unwelcome. It was difficult to have a good time unless we were certain that our siblings were having a bad time. Their misery became part of our pleasure, perhaps the best part.

"Ma's coming?" I asked.

"Ma's coming."

"We want her to be there," Gloria said. "She is so old and so wise. Amazing woman. She doesn't take any medicine."

Floyd frowned at this with a fiancé's indulgence. He said, "But Ma doesn't know it yet."

The idea was that Mother would be invited for brunch on the day, around seven. Before she was picked up — this was one of my jobs — she would be told it was Floyd's wedding. She'd have two hours to get ready. In that time, she'd make her family calls. Everyone would be told and they would know they weren't invited.

Laughing and joking over the meal, seeing Floyd and Gloria conversing in Japanese — I assumed they were endearments — I felt that at last something positive was happening in the family.

"The rest of them will be sulking at home!" Floyd said. The very thought of this lifted his spirits.

Floyd and Gloria made all the preparations. It would be a small affair: a few of his friends, Mother and me, Gloria's mother — her father was dead — and some of her friends; fifteen of us in all. The reception afterward would be on Floyd's lawn, a buffet. They would honeymoon in Maine.

We met the day before the wedding for the rehearsal, Floyd self-conscious and clowning. The morning of the wedding he called me.

"She knows. I just told her. You're picking her up at nine."

Mother was sitting on her throne when I arrived.

"I never thought this day would ever come," Mother said. She blinked and goggled at me, holding her mouth open in what seemed a calculated look of astonishment. "Do you know that Floyd is getting married today?"

"That's where we're going," I said.

I could never tell whether she was pretending to be confused, in order to elicit more information, or that she was really and truly bewildered.

"To the church," I said.

"You know about it?"

"Ma, I'm driving you. That's why I'm here. I'm the best man."

Even Mother saw the irony in this, my old family enemy asking me to prop him up and be part of the ceremony.

"No one else knows," Mother said in a tone of wonderment, which struck me as possibly genuine. "No one else was invited."

So she had made her calls already. Floyd had succeeded in tormenting them.

I helped her into my old Jeep, not easy because the seat was high, and her shoe was unsteady on the metal step. She seemed so shrunken and brittle, so frail when she was out of the house, off her throne, just a basket of bones, her arm like a chicken wing, her hand like a claw. Yet she had carefully dressed up in her favorite color, pale purple, a lavender dress, a lilac-colored hat with a small veil. She wore a string of South Sea black pearls I had bought for her in Tahiti, and seeing them on her neck, I gave a thought to stealing them from her before she gave them away. I clicked her seat belt in. She sat compactly, very watchful and a little nervous in her passenger seat, like a small girl in a stranger's car.

"Floyd," she said. She was still marveling. "Getting married again."

"It's a happy day."

"At his age."

"Big news."

"No one tells me anything." She was more relaxed now, and with confidence she became resentful. By the time we got to the church parking lot she was scowling. "Hardly any cars," she said.

I counted four cars, and though there were not many people the church was festive inside, the front three pews occupied by wedding guests, about a dozen. Mother took her seat in the front pew and made the sign of the cross, like a semaphore, as she knelt to pray.

Floyd was standing at the side of the altar in a morning suit, striped trousers and tails, a white carnation in his lapel. I walked over and stood with him as the organ sounded. We watched Gloria being led down the aisle by her uncle, a severe man taking studied steps, as though in formal reluctance. He was Japanese and unreadable.

The priest looked harassed, his vestments untidy, and his sandals contrasted oddly with Floyd's elegant shoes. During the ceremony I glanced at Mother. In the exchange of vows her eyes brimmed with tears. I was touched by her emotion, softened by her reaction, and began to regret every grudge I'd held against her. I had judged her too harshly; I did not really know this woman; I had never known her.

And then in a rumble of organ notes the bride and groom smiled and were saluted by the priest. They headed down the aisle, man and wife.

The reception at Floyd's house was a joyful lunch party with the dozen friends and family. I discovered through them that Gloria was a painter. Her friends were painters and art students, easygoing, sociable in the way of art students, finding much to praise in Floyd's house of books and prints and artifacts.

"He's got a collection of human skulls," I heard one of the students say. "They've got scrimshaw on them. Some are Tibetan bowls. It's far-out."

Floyd must have heard them. He brought out a skull — shells in its eyes, feather ornaments hanging from its jaw.

"My last duchess," he said.

Mother had found a throne on Floyd's porch and was soon in her element, smiling through the comments from the wedding guests who praised her great age and her good health.

Mother told her medicine story, which began "What are you *awn?*" and ended "I am not *awn* anything."

"What a lovely day this is," she said. "I'm so lucky to be here to enjoy it. I'll be ninety-five in a few months."

"Teddy Roosevelt was president when you were born," someone said.

"Of course I was just a toddler then," Mother said. "My father was a very strong Roosevelt supporter. Not Franklin but Teddy. My father was a saint, rest his soul."

In the meantime, Floyd and Gloria had changed clothes. They appeared on the lawn, holding hands.

"And now Didi and I are going to Maine," Floyd said. "Don't feel you have to leave. Finish the food, and there's more wine in the refrigerator. The last person please shut off the lights and lock the door."

Then they were gone. Seeing them drive off, I knew I had lost an ally. Floyd had another life now, a real life with someone outside the family. He had no need of us, no need of Mother anymore. It was like watching a prisoner plucked from captivity by the timely intervention of a heroine. I felt sheepish and superfluous driving Mother home.

"What did you think?" I asked her.

"I got lots of compliments."

That night, Hubby called me, quacking, talking over me. "What a sideshow. Who's the unlucky girl? I'm not surprised the church was empty. I give that marriage two months. Floyd's a maniac."

Over the next two days, I got more calls, and heard Mother's version of the wedding, the one she told her other children.

She had not known (so these versions went) that Floyd was getting married until she'd arrived at the church and saw the flowers and Floyd wearing an old-fashioned tuxedo. She had said to me, "Why are we here?" No one was in the church — no one had been invited.

There might have been some people, but she didn't see them. Imagine, no wedding guests. She had sat there not knowing what to do. She'd been embarrassed to look. Floyd seemed so old and ridiculous in his tuxedo. His bride was young. Mother could not remember her name; she looked strange, foreign, maybe Chinese. Her dress didn't fit very well.

And (Mother went on) she had no idea what was happening. No one had told her anything. The food at the reception was also very odd: uncooked scrod and noodles and tiny vegetables and brown soup. Some of the people were trying to use chopsticks. She felt a bit sorry for Floyd and his new wife. She was thinking of giving them a little something.

I heard this from Hubby, from Fred, from Gilbert, all of whom confirmed that Franny and Rose had been told the same tale. I knew that I would hear variations of the wedding from everyone, including strangers and friends of the family, for years; what a farce it had been, how small and unsatisfactory. No one would believe me when I tried to tell them what had actually happened, because Mother's story was so different from mine.

With Floyd's marriage came the prospect that I would lose my only ally. He had grown up and gone away, and here I was still, in short pants.

44

WINNERS

I T MAY SEEM as if I had no other life, no other sphere of interest, no pleasures or distractions. Yet I had all of these. As a writer, I had always lived a double life: the obsessive mythomaniac at his desk was one, the passive and dreamy civilian the other. A wiser writer than I had once spoken of how in the inner history of any writer's mind there is a break at a crucial point, the moment when the writer rejects the people who surround him and discovers the necessity of talking to himself, and not to them. The "them" in this case was my family.

I was a writer still, and when luck came my way in the form of a windfall—I had sold the movie rights to one of my novels—I was more noticed as a writer. Movies aren't escapist entertainment; on the contrary, the hyperreality of the money and glamour compels us to take life more seriously. I published another novel and a collection of stories; I wrote for magazines. And I had some friendship in my life, with a hope it would sweeten into romance.

A woman as busy as I was, as preoccupied with her work and her aged parents, relieved some of my weekends when she was not on call. She was a doctor. I saw her for intellectual companionship, for friendship, to share meals, for sex. She had the unsentimental practicality bordering on selfishness of her profession. Was there time? Okay, let's do it. I think I can fit you in.

We were intimate friends. And since she had another life at the hospital — no one was busier: she was at the mercy of her pager — she welcomed our irregular meetings. We lived for those days and nights, infrequent though they were. I loved her scientific mind, her efficiency, her unspiritual sense, her confidence and skepticism — her factuality — her casual familiarity with death and dying. We made no plans for the future, we asked very little of each other; we had little to give. She had lank blond hair, she never wore makeup, her skin was pale and warm. She had an older woman's generosity in bed. She was not a conventional beauty, but her intelligence and humor made her desirable to me. And she was tough, unbreakable, always smiling, as if to say, Try me. She was a fully rational adult of a kind that did not exist in my family. Her name was Alex.

I did not mention my family to her or anyone. I did not write about Mother or anyone resembling her. My fictional characters were usually parentless, and for a reason. Where would I begin? In my writer's mind I was an orphan, a changeling, someone rejected to make my own life. Far from being self-pitying, I boasted of my sense of abandonment; and it was better that way, for this conceit, my struggle, had been the making of me as a writer.

And as a further provocation I had that nagging but effective goad, Mother, rubbishing my work and somehow setting others against me. How much worse my life would have been if she had been breathing down my neck, praising my writing, pushing me in my ambition, dragging me to publishers, puffing me up — one of those pushy stage mothers who live through their talented children. Was it that Mother wanted to go on being superior to me — perhaps to all of us? I didn't know. I only knew that I was inferior and inadequate. She laughed at me behind my back. She mocked my writing to my siblings. She was wholly philistine in saying, "He never got his hands dirty," and "He calls that work!," and in her look of disgust (so it was reported) when she said, "Jay writes porno." In her mid-nineties, she was fiercer than ever.

I was astonished that she was still alive. Her endurance compelled my admiration. But she was not merely everlasting — there were plenty of zombies on the Cape, more dead than alive, driving slowly or clomping along, clutching the handlebars of aluminum walkers. Mother was healthy, healthier than her two panting daughters, burdened by bags of groceries. Mother was sturdier than her stroke-victim son, or portly Floyd, who was plagued by indigestion. She was nimbler than Hubby, whose green scrubs grew tighter by the month. She was quicker-witted than me. When I mentioned any of this to her, she began to boast, for she was vain about her daily shuffle-walk to the corner, her command of woodcarving, and within the past year she had started to attend a weekly class on Cape Cod history at the community college.

Mother attended the class as a living legend, an eyewitness to the entire twentieth century. Franny or Rose drove her and basked in the reflected glory of her appearance. Her role was not to study history but to display her knowledge of it, as interrupter and commentator. She became famous for her interruptions, piping up in the middle of a lecture and correcting the teacher on a date or a name or a pronunciation. She was a living native fossil.

Funerals were her other pastime, more frequent now. She called me or Floyd, or whoever happened to be around, and asked to be driven to a wake or a funeral mass for one of her recently deceased friends or acquaintances — always someone much younger than she, as she invariably pointed out in the midst of her grieving.

"She was on medication," Mother would say on the way to the service.

Even when she was kneeling and praying, her posture seemed to gloat: *I won. You lost.*

In Mother's mind, medication was the commonest cause of death. Medicine made you ill. Pills were poison. Hospitals were infectious. Doctors were dangerous — they were bullying and invasive and much too young. Doctors violated you.

My friend Alex at Cape Cod Hospital would have been amused. I liked her unshockable doctor's manner, though without a medico's smugness. She was an ob-gyn and often talked about mothering. She delivered babies at all hours. She was observant, and when she generalized she sometimes had the smiling detachment of a veterinarian talking about cows.

"When a woman becomes a mother, she changes," Alex said. We were at Baxter's in Hyannis, eating fish and chips, waiting for her pager to go off — she had a patient in labor in the hospital up the street. "I see these submissive women get pregnant and become strong. They turn into confident mothers, much tougher and self-reliant. Something kicks in. It seems like a law of nature."

"And what if she has a lot of children?" As I said, I had not mentioned my family to Dr. Alex.

"You can't imagine how her character would change," she said. "How stubborn she'd become, how empowered, how different from what she was before. How tough."

"How difficult. A pill."

"But for a reason." She regarded me with a diagnostic half-smile. "Men have no idea."

Beyond the periphery of my tribal existence, life went on. Work saved me; work was my sanity. Though I seldom heard from my sons, I took this as a sign that they were fulfilled, preoccupied with their own work, and in any case did not need me to be interested. I called to inquire: How were they? Did they have love in their lives? What was new?

"I'd rather not say," Julian told me in his guarded way. From whom had he gotten this caution? Not from me. "I don't want to jinx it."

I took this as a promising response. I did not press him or ask for more. A month or so later he called to say that he had good news: he was engaged and wanted to be married soon. Would I come to the wedding in England? And Harry called to say that he, too, had fallen in love and could now tell me he was living with a wonderful woman. Might I be inclined to visit?

I flew to London, feeling like a tourist in a city where I'd lived for seventeen years. I was a stranger once more. A whole cycle had passed, and I was stepping into a new phase: different names in the newspapers, different people in publishing, new books, new critics, new products on the billboards of the tidier and more prosperous city, with its much younger pedestrians and more youthful police.

In a rented car I drove to Shropshire, to the hotel where Julian had reserved me a room. And on the hotel stairs, just moments after I arrived, I met my ex-wife Diana, Julian's mother, an older, fragile version of the woman I'd married almost forty years before.

"Isn't it exciting?"

She hugged me and gave me a kiss. I was so unused to such uncompli-cated affection I almost resisted, but then I returned it and was happy to be held like this.

"And this is my partner, Piers," she said. "Piers, meet Jay."

"Partner" made me smile. The man had been hovering just behind her, a balding fellow in a tight suit with a meaningful handshake and an assertive manner, as though to reinforce the fact that he had usurped me and was in charge now.

"Pleasure," he said, and tucked the thumb of his free hand into his waistcoat pocket.

Julian welcomed me, introduced me to Marion, his fiancée. He was happy, so was she, the smile making her radiant. She was a beauty, with the face of a wise child, thick curly hair, and dark eyes — part Welsh, Julian had told me.

"Dad, this is Sophie," Harry said, and a slender woman in a fluttering dress stepped forward to shake my hand. Her hand, so pale and pretty, was rough to the touch, a roughness that was in surprising contrast to her feline face, her piercing eyes, her look of robust health.

"Sophie's a landscape architect," Harry said, and then I understood the hands and her lovely color.

Harry showed me the way to the village church, for the wedding rehearsal. There, I met Marion's parents and those of Julian's friends who were part of the ceremony. Later, we gathered for dinner, and I sat listening to the loud talk and laughter, besotted with the sweetness of it all.

"Why are you smiling, Dad?" Harry asked. "What are you thinking?"

"I'm happy. This is what a family should be."

The wedding itself was a small, intense, and joyful affair, just family and friends in the old stone village church. Diana's "partner" was the official photographer.

Posing with her beforehand, I said, "I like this arrangement. That Piers is the photographer."

"Why?"

"Because he won't be in any of the pictures."

"Now isn't that just typical of you," she said, smiling sternly.

"This conversation is going downhill, Dad. Please," Harry said.

Julian put me into the service. I read from Whitman's "Song of the Open Road." Someone sang with guitar accompaniment. The small boys who assisted looked nervous and normal. Afterward, at the wedding dinner, Harry gave a speech — needling, praising, funny. He invited others to speak. Diana rose and recounted a memory of Julian's boyhood. Julian's old school friend Gavin told a complimentary story, a memory of Julian conjugating an irregular Latin verb. How poised they all were. They gave me strength. Marion spoke, mentioning cautions she'd been given about living with a restless creative person, for Julian was a writer, a filmmaker, a traveler.

When it was my turn, I stood and took in the blurred spinning room and all the hot faces. I felt slow and unsteady. I addressed the centerpiece of flowers, saying how happy I was, but saying so I sounded tearful, and my weepy voice quieted the room. I saw Marion's anxious eyes. I spoke to her.

"When Julian goes away, don't think he's feeling liberated and free," I said. "He is suffering. Travel is dreadfully lonely. Keep him in your heart, because that's where you are — in his heart. Being on his own doesn't mean a lack of love. Love is what he needs to travel. Love is necessary to his privacy. He needs love to work, to think, to be productive and happy."

A mass of tin trays clattering to a tiled floor in the adjacent kitchen made me pause, but the noise also had the effect of hushing the silent table even more.

"Don't feel that, in his travel, Julian has run off. Or that you need to run yourself, to find another friend to spend time with — someone else to love." Here I paused, and then I pleaded, tears on my face. "Wait for him. In traveling he is waiting for you. He doesn't love you less because he's away. You are his family. When he's away from you his love is, if anything, deeper, with a longing to see you again. He needs you to wait, for you to hold him in your heart."

The table of festive wedding guests was very somber now. I raised a glass to the bridal couple and, to everyone's relief, I sat down.

I had embarrassed myself. It didn't do to cry in England. "American men cry," Diana's mother had said to me once, in derision. "And they wear hats in the house." Afterward, Julian said, "You said what was on your mind. That's not bad. I'm glad you felt relaxed enough to say it."

Not relaxed, perhaps drunk. But the moment passed, happiness returned with chatter and the clinking of glasses. Finally, as the meal dissolved into smaller groups, Julian and Marion made their exit.

Diana came over to me and said, "Are you angry with me?"

"No," I said, and wondered if I were. But it was too late to be angry. All my anger had been buried by time. Smiling to reassure her, I remembered her pretty face at our own wedding, our innocence, before everything happened, everything unexpected and strange. Yet here we were.

"This is a joyous occasion," she said. "It's like a scene in a Shakespeare play, one of the late ones, where the younger generation redeems the older one. And there's peace — music and merrymaking, even wedding bells. Am I thinking of *The Winter's Tale*?"

"No weddings at the end of that," I said, "but I know what you mean."

"No, no. After Hermione appears, Leontes says to Paulina, 'Thou shouldst a husband take by my consent,' and he tells Camillo to take her by the hand. They get married," Diana said, giving me an Oxford wink. "Anyway, we made a mess of things, but they're doing it right. We have a lot to learn from them."

I said, "I apologize for making that remark about your friend Piers. About taking the pictures. Not being in any of them."

"Thank you. On his behalf, I accept your apology. I meant to ask, how is your mother? Why are you making that face?"

"Because I had forgotten all about her."

"But tell me, how is she?"

"I don't want to think about her on this happy day."

"Then why not tell me what's happened to you in this wide gap of time since first we were dissevered?"

I stood gaping at her like a dog that's just heard music.

"Last line of *The Winter's Tale*," she said. "'Hastily lead away.'"

I did not want that day to end. But I woke the following morning to find that everyone had dispersed, and I was alone again, and had to go home.

· · ·

Mother had left a message on my answering machine, not inquiring about the wedding but asking where I was. I had not called her for the week I'd been in Britain. As soon as I was settled, I returned her call and told her about the festivities.

"Do English people take pictures at weddings?" she said.

I visited her, bringing my small camera, with the photos I'd taken. Diana had said that Piers would be sending a disk with all his pictures. I sat with Mother on the sofa and clicked through the sequence of ceremonial snapshots, of Julian and Marion, of the cake-cutting, and some group shots of everyone who'd attended.

Mother said, "The cake is nice."

She meant, The cake is small and unappetizing.

I said, "In England they don't go in for big, tall layer cakes. It's more a kind of rectangular fruitcake that's traditional. Some people take home pieces in little boxes."

But Mother had stopped listening. "What kind of church is that?"

She meant, It looks Protestant.

"St. Mary's," I said. "Eleventh century. Imagine — it's a thousand years old."

Mother said, "Who are those people?"

"Those are the people who came to the wedding."

"Is that all of them?"

She meant, Just a few people.

"Is that an umbrella?" Mother said, putting her yellow nail on the camera panel. How had she seen that tightly rolled brolly?

She meant, And it rained.

"There was a sprinkle just as we left the church."

I knew what she would report to the family about Julian's wedding: tiny cake, Protestant church, handful of people, a rainy day. I didn't mind that she saw it through the darkness of her fault-finding. It had been a happy day. I was undeserving. I had done nothing to make it happy — I'd made no arrangements. They had done it all, yet I felt like a winner.

"Is that all the pictures you have?" Mother said.

I took this to mean, A whole wedding but just six snapshots — how sad.

"I'd love to have some."

She picked up my tiny digital camera. Mother had a way of handling something that made it seem negligible. She squinted at it, then gave it to me. She seemed dismissive and abrupt. She stood up and busied herself tidying the coffee table — yarn, knitting basket, books, a carved bird, yesterday's newspaper, a holy missal, a postcard of Sharm el-Sheik, some papers.

"You must be tired," she said.

"Not at all. I'm fine. I slept well last night. I just have to return my rental car."

"You look a little drawn." She was still twitching the papers on the table. "A little peaky."

"Peaky?"

What was she saying? I tried to translate this Mother-speak but failed to make sense of it. Did "tired" mean I had wasted my time in flying to Britain for the wedding? Or did it mean it was pointless for me to have visited with just a few wedding pictures? Normally, at this point in a visit to Mother she would offer me a nice piece of fruit, or a nice piece of candy, or a nice drink of juice. But she wasn't offering me anything.

Before I could protest any more I heard the sound of a car, and I understood. Mother had been hinting for me to leave. I was tired and ill-looking; I belonged at home, right now. She had been expecting someone, obviously the person who had driven up in front. I heard the ratchet and crunch of an emergency brake.

"My goodness," Mother said, trying to sound surprised. But she had been expecting this all along. "I wonder who that can be?"

Mother seemed disapproving as she looked out the front window.

"I wonder what she wants?"

I joined her and saw a woman laboring on the brick pathway. She was tipped sideways with a bag and walked heavily, humping and bumping in a big unbuttoned coat that drooped and shook with each step. Something about the shaking of the coat enlarged what it covered, the impression of the woman being even bigger. Her cheeks were tugged down by each footfall. She seemed like someone at the end of a long journey or an unfair foot race, gasping to finish.

The coat was new, and so was the car and the broad red handbag, yet the woman herself was careworn, with streaky gray hair frizzed out at the sides of an absurd beret, and her face was gray too. Her thick ankles swelled over her brown shoes. Some people's shoes can look so punished.

Franny. I had not seen her since the long-ago memorial mass. She was unsteady, she seemed weary, she was grayer. In her nervous agitation that I was watching this arrival with her, Mother was nimble, touching her chair, jerking the curtain, tapping her fingers on her face.

"I'd better go," I said.

"At least say hello."

She had badly wanted me to go before Franny arrived. Mother hated the awkwardness of two or more of her ill-assorted children in her presence. Now, in her quandary, Mother was not sure who she was supposed to be at this moment, caught between two of her hostile children. She quivered, shape-shifting, yet her expression was so uncertain it made her seem almost ectoplasmic.

"Ma, whose car is that?" Franny said, heaving herself through the door and dropping her bag, a thud on the floorboards beneath the carpet.

Franny stepped back and shook a little when she caught sight of me, like someone recoiling from a loud noise. I was no less shocked. I recognized the voice — *whose cah?* — but the body seemed to belong to someone I didn't know. Perhaps she felt the same about me.

I said, "Hi."

At the word, the light dimmed in her eyes and she repeated with no interest, "Hi."

Working her arms like flippers, as though to propel herself, she shuffled forward and kissed Mother.

"Ma, you okay?"

Two old ladies, one big, one tiny, clutching each other like grieving widows.

"I'm fine," Mother said. She coughed, two shallow dust-hacks, as she usually did when saying *I'm fine.*

I stood, leaning, eyeing the door, awaiting my chance to leave.

"How's Rose?" I asked.

"I wouldn't know." Franny was wearing white ankle socks.

Mother winced and became tense again. Obviously I had raised an unwelcome subject. Maybe the daughters were in the midst of one of their tiffs.

"What about Fred?"

"Why don't you ask him?"

Mother sighed. This was everything she feared, her feuding children meeting before her, compromising her feelings.

Seeing my camera on the coffee table, a wedding picture still displayed on its panel, I stepped toward it. I did not want Mother to show the pictures to Franny or anyone else — did not really want them to know about the wedding. Like Floyd, I hoped to exclude them. We were a family frantic to protect our secrets; we needed our secrets for strength. And most of all I wanted to keep this bitter family away from my happiness.

I snatched the camera and palmed it, pressing my thumb on the power button to blacken the screen.

"Gotta go return my rental car."

Franny was staring at me with narrowed eyes, as though I was an intrusive stranger who'd wandered into her house. She had screwed up one side of her face with the expression of someone staring into sunlight. She looked like a big soft monument, and Mother beaky and white, like a plucked bird.

A certain noxious smell rises from people who hate you. I had a whiff of it now that stung my nostrils.

Outside, before I got to the driveway, Franny was squinting at the gutters, the eaves, the roof, with a scrutinizing grin of anger. The house was hers. She was not visiting her aged mother, she was paying a call at her own house — like an agitated landlord, appalled at the sight of her sitting tenant who was still alive and inhabiting the property, her clutter all spread out — thinking, Why aren't you dead?

Franny was a winner, yet Mother's shrewdness had obligated and encumbered her. Yes, she could have the house, but Mother came with it, and all Mother's needs. This early bequest had come as a burden. Mother had been right not to trust me, and right in holding back with some of the others. In Franny she saw the perfect caregiver, hypocritical and hungry, and Mother had trapped her in her greed.

Mother had endured, had prevailed. In that time, Franny had grown old. She had expected Mother to have died years ago. All this time, Franny had been waiting, and now she was ever more burdened by the weekly visits. She seemed feebler than Mother. She might never get to enjoy the property and money she'd pocketed. She had spent more than half her life as Mother's handmaiden, realizing only now, late in the game, that in making her seem special, Mother had conned her.

Franny, in being a winner, was defeated. She wore that defeat on her lined face.

Fred, too, was ailing, his heart ticking more erratically than Mother's. Hubby was on beta-blockers. Rose was angry — a kind of stewing rage of gasping and choking that was like a sickness. Gilbert was away — I guessed in Sharm el-Sheikh, judging from the postcard on the table. Floyd, with Didi, was elsewhere.

The other great irony of Franny's having to suffer the burden of the house, while Mother refused to die and allow her to live there, was that Rose had misread the gifts. Rose hated Franny for her seeming victory. They had quarreled over the inheritance and the presents. At last, Mother had broken them, split them apart and soured the friendship, isolated them, so that now she had two caregivers competing for her attention.

45

ALIENS

CROSS THE RECEDING IMAGE in my rearview mirror was a lettered stripe, cautioning, *Objects in mirror are closer than they appear,* and the image was of Mother and Franny standing side by side, like a big girl and her doll, the larger kind of doll that you might win at a country fair after successfully knocking over six objects from a shelf. Mother was skeletal and upright and beaky, as though her very bones had shrunk inside her, the features of her skull distinct in the tissuey skin of her tiny head. Her neck was stringy, her skinny hands clenched at her sides. Her clothes were loose and faded, reminding me that most old people don't buy new clothes. *These duds will see me out.*

Franny loomed over her, her drooping dress like a dustcloth draped over a chair. And she was breathing hard, working her jaw in wordless honks. A similarity in posture, a way of leaning, a way of holding their arms, the family feet. But there was a difference. Mother's old malevolence and grandeur were gone. She was diminished to half her original size, hardly recognizable as the mother I had known and feared. And just like a fragile discount doll, she was modeled after the other woman. Franny was so much bigger, as if, along with everything else, the daughter had drawn off all her mother's wind and bulk, taken over Mother's size and strength, and stood there in the driveway like a wheezy version of the woman who'd made her. I believed strongly in inherited characteristics now. Franny was like Mother used to be.

Yet even dwarfed and desiccated—bird bones and sparse white hair on a pink scalp, in the threadbare sack of a dress—Mother looked as indestructible as she had been my whole life. And now she seemed saurian, the way oldsters sometimes do, blinking in my rearview mirror, closer than she appeared.

Next to this pale, petrified old woman, Franny was unsteady and lopsided, tottering in tortured shoes. Soon they were out of sight, and I was on my way home. But it was hard to rid my mind of them.

Mother was healthier than ever, but in a passive and prune-like way. She often remarked with satisfaction that she had to go for walks alone —"Franny doesn't feel up to it"; that she wanted to learn Spanish at night school, and to register for Advanced Woodcarving, where they fashioned larger birds—raptors and pelicans—and used power tools and an array of expensive knives. Mother still attended the weekly history class and, at least once a month, someone's funeral.

Mother went to the funerals as a living reproach, a flesh-and-blood I-told-you-so specter in a black hat and black veil, hanging like a fruit bat, a frowning power figure commanding fear and veneration. The funerals, like many other outings that Mother made, were public appearances for a reason: Mother left the house to solicit praise, to inspire awe, to shame people with her great age and healthy habits.

Franny still drove over on Sundays, as always, big and wheezy from Mother's bounty. Rose showed up on Saturdays.

"They want to find out if I'm dead," Mother said spitefully. But that spite did not have the corrosive effect it had on other people: it kept Mother alive.

The rotisserie chicken, the ham sandwich, the meatballs, the takeout trays that Franny bought on the way as meals, she'd microwave. Then they'd eat, Franny silently lamenting that she could not take up residence in the house, that she'd have to find someone to cut the grass, rake the leaves, and shovel the walk. That's what Mother told me, and others probably heard more colorful versions.

"I don't know why she always brings me food," Mother said. "I have Meals on Wheels from Hubby."

Fred, too, once so vital — the multitasking lawyer with twenty arms — was useless. The stroke had broken him in half. He was spiritless, even more lopsided than Franny, with one loose arm and a drawn-down mouth. He couldn't drive his own car, and on the rare days when he came to my house, dragging one foot, one arm swinging as though made of cloth — his wife was like his keeper — he said, "I've wasted my life. I should have been a painter. I could have done it. I had talent. But what good is it now? You made the right choice. I could have had yours or Floyd's life."

"He's a hypocrite," Floyd said. "He's done exactly what he's wanted his whole life. It's insulting to be told that."

That was a flash of the old Floyd. As a married man he'd become circumspect and kept to himself. He never mentioned his wife. He was preoccupied, a bit sensitive, still writing, more interested in the future than he'd ever been. He was embarked on one of his miscellanies, a volume he called *Anomalies*. It was, he said, his big book.

"Give me an example."

"George H. W. Bush said, 'Read my lips: No new taxes.' But look closely. He has no lips."

Hubby told me he was thinking of taking early retirement from the hospital. He had high blood pressure, acid reflux, and flat feet. Even with her shuffle, Mother walked faster when she was with him. "I'm burned out," Hubby said. Like the rest of us, he saw himself as being at the end of his working life. "I've been offered a buyout. Maybe I'll be a consultant."

Rose was content now that Bingo and Benno were in college, and she too talked of retirement. Rose had nothing to do except regret their absence and rage at Franny, who, it was now clear, had most of Mother's money.

Gilbert, the brightest, the kindest, the most forgiving, the most elusive, was in Afghanistan, on assignment at the embassy in Kabul. Whenever I asked him about the war, he deflected the question by complaining about the quality of Afghan carpets. "Lurid chemical dyes. Inferior knots." And he might add, "The Panjshir Valley has been pacified, and the good news is that agriculture has returned to many provinces. The bad news is that their cash crop is opium poppies."

Angela was now fifty-five, and though she had been dead for nearly that whole time, she was seen as triumphant by Mother, who said, "She's had the best life of any of us."

And I was trying to make sense of it all. How had it happened that after all these years, this big, gray-haired bunch were still children? Yet we were aging, each of us frail in our own way, without the possibility of any successes ahead of us, only the repetition of small failures that would lead us to the grave.

In each of our minds was the question of what to do with Mother. We were old ourselves and at the end of our working lives, Fred lame, Floyd on the verge of retirement, Gilbert talking about leaving the foreign service to write a book, Franny and Rose about to abandon teaching. My writing was no more than a few fidgety and speculative hours now — note-taking, but the notes were pessimistic, like those of a traveler who'd gone too far and was stuck and saw there was no turning back, like Captain Robert Falcon Scott starving in his tent, writing messages to a world he hoped would not forget him.

As for the family, we had entered that scrubby twilit landscape where the wide road stuttered into a path, and that path into a slender track, going nowhere, squeezing toward the end of ambition. The young didn't know this, could hardly guess at it. But there was a point on the living road where there were no signposts, no way-markers, no ambition, and not many other people. All happy surprises were in the past. No more miracles, nothing to be expected, no hope even, only those rocky heights and the barren hills, and oblivion behind them in unreadable shadow, pushing on, every turnoff looking treacherous, the whole way forward tending toward darkness.

That's life, we said, meaning, That's death.

We resembled Mother in the way we easily forgot things, and were repetitious and set in our ways. What a relief it would have been — or a diversion, anyway — to take control, as Mother had done, and enjoy some importance, however brief; a degree of power or respect. But no, we were incapable of that.

We had Mother's life without any of Mother's satisfactions. Our lives were growing thinner and emptying out. We were traveling in that harsh hinterland of aging, on that narrowing path where no one willingly accompanies you. Old love is an illusion. My affair with Dr. Alex had ended, amicably, as mature affairs between sensible adults tended to — we were too independent to find a way of living together, and too advanced in years. And perhaps she suspected how much in thrall I was to Mother and my family. We were largely ignored, unremarkable, all aspiration gone, and in our helplessness were still subservient, still attending to Mother. As her aged children, we were her limping servants, her graying subjects; we did not dare dislike her, but we had never disliked each other more.

"I'd like to shoot Franny in the thighs," Floyd said to me.

Hubby said, "We have lots of wackos just like Floyd at the hospital. We sedate them."

"Have you ever noticed that Hubby's head is shaped like a jezail bullet," Floyd said. "And he's got webbed feet. Why is that?"

We were retired or semiretired, with plenty of time for this. There was no common ground, we had no shared interests, nothing to talk about, except the subject that wouldn't go away — Mother.

We were all fairly fat and shaggy, but we looked different and our personalities were distinct. We were so unlike each other it was as though we belonged to separate families — or not family members at all, but rather orphans of the storm.

"How's your brother?" strangers might say of Fred or Floyd. "Is she related to you?" they'd remark of Franny or Rose. Or "What do you talk about when you're together?" It seemed an enigma that we could be so different, and the result, of course, was that we found it impossible to talk reasonably to one another. As a traveler, I knew that strangers could be unpredictable. But strangers in the same family are dangerous.

As Franny had discovered — I'd seen it on her face, the look she had at the table when all the food was gone, while she sat with a fork in her fist — there was no money left. Mother's gifts these days were her knitted throw rugs and her carved birds. "This is a loon . . . This is a nuthatch," Floyd mocked. "And these are vultures, so gorged on their thievishness they're too fat to fly."

"Maybe we should make another foray through the back door," I said.

"There's nothing left to steal," he said. "There hasn't been anything for years."

"Just for fun."

"You always did have a perverse notion of fun. Why is that? Are you insane? Stop gabbling. The treasure has been plundered."

We were at his house, on his porch, the sounds of Gloria inside rattling pans in the kitchen. She brought us coffee. She was the woman Floyd had waited for his whole life. Now, nearing seventy, he had found Mrs. Right, who adored him. She lingered, because he was still talking.

"And to think that Ma's fortune at Dad's death still had its maidenhead, 'never sacked, turned, nor wrought . . . ,'" he said. "'The mines not broken with sledges, nor their images pulled down out of their temples.' Source?" He took Gloria's hand. "Look at him squirm."

I said, "It sounds familiar. John Donne?"

"Raleigh. You didn't know that?" And Gloria kissed him. He said, "I am cursed with total recall, my darling."

On one of my visits to Mother around this time, she said to me, "Do you think I belong in a home?"

I gave her the answer she wanted.

She said, "Some people think I do."

She mentioned it as a power play, being forced into exile; and again, saying this, she sounded more than ever like a despot losing her grip, fighting a rearguard action against potential usurpers.

"Some people want to ship me out of here."

"Which people?"

"I'd rather not say." In her great age, Mother's head had grown smaller, yet her nose was still beak-like and inquisitive. "But you'd be surprised."

That meant Franny and Rose. "Horrible," I said, spotting an opportunity to appear sympathetic and ingratiate myself. "You're independent. You've got friends and interests. You can cook for yourself."

"I got myself to the dentist the other day without anyone's help."

"Sure you did." Did she? "Why would you want to go to an old folks' home?"

"I'd die in one of those places."

"Right. Whoever made that suggestion would be sending you to your death."

"I'd have no privacy at all," she said.

"It would be like a prison," I said.

Staring, Mother became reflective, her fingertips tracing the waxen contours of her face.

"I know I haven't been perfect," she finally said.

"You've done fine, Ma."

"I'm sure I've made a lot of mistakes."

I peered closely at her, and as though speaking to an oversensitive child, I said, "Don't think about it, Ma."

This was the wrong answer. Mother's face tightened, her mouth became grim. "So you think I have?"

"Of course not."

"Why didn't you say so?"

"I did." But I hadn't, and now it was too late.

"There may come a time for me to go into a home," Mother said. She turned away from me, her jaw set against the possibility of ever leaving her chair.

"Not soon," I said.

"When I'm old," she said.

She was ninety-six, twig-like, but so hardened she seemed to exist in a state of ossification, the bony essence of what she had been.

Rose called me that night. "You asshole. Ma said she didn't get a wink of sleep after you upset her. Okay, maybe she did make a few bad decisions, but why do you insist on telling her about all the mistakes she's made?"

It was not really a question. It was an accusation. Without another word, Rose banged the phone down.

After I'd left, in a maneuver I'd lived through a hundred times, Mother had called around and maligned me. Mother did not think of herself as old. We were the ones who were aging, not she. Her mention of the dentist: I kept thinking about it, how even at her age she had most of her teeth and went on getting them fixed, tinkering with them, having them scaled and filled. She saw a podiatrist for her bunions, the internist for her shallow cough. After ninety-six years she was keeping her time-battered body in repair. She still had usable teeth! Her feet and legs still worked! Even that reaction to my visit, that old reflex of malice that kept her whispering against me, inventing stories, making trouble ("Jay upset me!"), even that still animated her.

Fred stopped by after calling me from his car. He happened to be passing. Might he drop in? Nothing was casual with Fred. I knew that he was headed my way and wanted to talk, and that I would not be able to dissuade him.

He looked older, much thinner, limp-armed still. It was not just that he seemed feebler than Mother. He looked as if he didn't have long to live. After the effort of climbing the four stairs to my porch, he sat, got his breath, and said he'd made a tour of the retirement homes on the Cape. It was time to come up with a plan.

I said, "Ma says you're putting her into a prison."

"We have to think ahead."

"Who's going to pay for it?"

"I'm sure that everyone will be willing to chip in," he said.

Putting Mother in a home meant that Franny would get to move into the house that Mother had given her but not vacated yet. And, since Mother had handed out all her money, we'd each be assessed for the cost of Mother's care at the assisted living facility. Those of us who had received nothing or very little from Mother would still have to assume a share of the cost.

Instead of mentioning these petty objections, I said to Fred, "Ma will be demoralized if we bring this up."

"We won't bring it up, then."

"So you're not giving her a choice in the matter?"

"As you say, it'll hurt her if we go on talking about putting her into assisted care."

"Then you're treating her like a child."

"I have her best interests at heart," Fred said.

"She told me she doesn't want to be put into a home," I said. "And I don't blame her."

But coughing and canted over on a chair in my living room, Fred looked like the one who should have been thinking of assisted living, not Mother. He looked more like her husband than her son.

"At least I take her out to eat. I visit her. I call her almost every day."

"And you've gotten money from her," I said.

"Not as much as Franny or Rose."

"More than Floyd," I said. "More than me."

"Floyd's done all right."

The discussion ended that way, as most family discussions did, running down the balance sheet.

We were still at war, but being too tired for all-out battle, we engaged in the occasional skirmish. Our ill will did not seem so surprising to me. What bewildered me were happy families. All those loud, jolly people in the backyard, standing around the charcoal grill, bantering and drinking beer and wolfing the potluck they'd brought in big platters — pasta salad, guacamole dip, tuna casserole, bubble biscuits, coleslaw. What was wrong with them? Why weren't they fighting, or at least sulking? How could twenty or more of them be gathered together without half of them howling abuse?

The scholarship winners, the athletes, the survivors of sickness or catastrophes, who spoke of their families as supportive — they seemed delusional, or brainwashed, or sufferers of Stockholm syndrome. "My mom was always there for me," one might say, or "I couldn't have done it without my family." Runners, cyclists, winners of talent contests, teenage golf champs and tennis oafs and swimmers, all of them stood on podiums and thanked their mothers. I did not doubt their sincerity, but where had these mothers come from, and how had they got that way? I felt these children had been more manipulated than we'd been, and that all these ostentatious mom-thankers were not to be admired but pitied. They were pathetic in their gratitude, like members of a cult.

I understood the family feud that ended in a stabbing or a drive-by shooting or a massacre, the daughter who'd swindled her mom out of her pension, the mother who sued her son for breach of promise, the barbecue that became a brawl. This waywardness no longer dismayed me but seemed like a sign of health. The saintly, salt-of-the-earth mother was more of an enigma and seemed dangerous in her apparent unselfishness. Such a softhearted being was capable of anything, especially of making you believe in her and twisting you to her will. But our mother was someone I would never trust. She was a much truer reflection of the world I knew, and now, as she headed toward the century mark, it seemed she would outlive us all.

46

MY MUSE

IN DAD'S TIME, we had often met at the town dump — Fred dropping off his tenants' rubbish; Floyd looking through the books at the swap shop, where he'd once found a first edition of *The Naked and the Dead,* slightly foxed but with a dust jacket; Franny leaving refundable bottles at the Little League shed; Dad himself scavenging and perhaps disinterring a pair of hinges or a sheet of plywood. "Might come in handy," or "I know just what I'm going to do with that." Once it had been a big smoking hill of trash — stinks and seagulls rising above a swamp of poison, green with leachate. Then it was a landfill. Finally, a transfer station. But it had never ceased to be called a dump, and for Dad something like a men's club, where he met his friends and they talked about the Red Sox or the weather — kibitzed, in Father's word; chewed the fat.

Although now we could not stand the sight of each other, we still met at the dump and the post office, not for deliberate assignations but chance encounters, usually unwelcome.

Not long after the futile discussions about putting Mother into a home — the quarrels over who would pay for it, whether the home would be near Franny or one of the others, whether it would be a retirement community or the more expensive assisted living facility — after all this effort, which Mother saw, with reason, as a plot against her, a power grab to dislodge her from her house, I was driving into the dump and saw Franny just behind me. Instead of getting rid of my trash in her presence, I drove off without disposing of it. I did not want to see her. More than that, I did not want her to see what I was chucking away — did not want her to know anything of me.

When I headed back about an hour later, I saw Erma pitching trash bags off the back of her pickup truck. I circled the dump and did not drop my trash until I saw that she had driven away — Fred sitting in the passenger seat, his useless arm in his lap.

Leaving the dump another day, I saw Rose driving in. I pretended not to see her, yet she unambiguously gave me the finger when I looked up.

None of us went to church, for fear of meeting one another. Mother had her own reasons for seeing each of us alone. We welcomed these solitary audiences now, but did not go into the house if we spotted anyone else's car in the driveway. If we passed each other on the street, at the Cape Cod Mall, or anywhere else, we did not say hello.

We hid from each other for a reason. No one knows more about you than your family. No one can inflict more pain on you than a family member. So it was not surprising that we hid and, picking our way through the dangers, chose our allies carefully. We were more fearful of each other than of anyone outside the family. The very word "family" filled us with a dread of violation that was expressed as mockery or satire, as a general cynicism of the world at large, as a deep distrust of anyone's motives.

We were not believers, not (as I said earlier) cultists who smiled at Mother's manipulation and turned cartwheels for her, or won races, and thanked her when we got awards. We were the subjects in Mother Land of her dictatorial rule, each of us a sullen dissident. She had taught us all the subtleties of betrayal.

Lesson one was that attachment was always a mistake; lesson two, that sentiment was a weakness; lesson three, that trust was foolish and fatal, and the key to power was the knowledge of the other siblings' secrets. Even something as simple as their movements was essential to knowing them. A trip to the dump was revealing, for what you discarded was a key to your life, and in knowing their secrets you possessed them, their essence, their strength. You might have to pump their friends or children for information; you did what you had to do, and needed to be as conscienceless as Mother, and as ruthless. Your knowledge neutralized them.

None of these lessons came from a book, some dense study in the elements of power, or a leadership manual for CEOs, or a medieval treatise on kingship. Mother had never read Machiavelli's *The Prince* or Castiglione's *The Book of the Courtier* or Sun Tzu's *The Art of War*. Yet her whole life, and especially her motherhood, was a vernacular paraphrase of these classics. For example, in Mother Land, as in Sun Tzu's China, there were five classes of spies: local spies, inward spies, converted spies, doomed spies, and surviving spies. And she would have agreed with the Master that when these five spies were all at work, no one could discover the secret system. "This is called 'divine manipulation of the threads.' It is the sovereign's most precious faculty."

Mother's version of this was homegrown, refined in her family throughout generations of sniping and survival, in the same way that, after successive reigns of absolute monarchs, a diabolical tyrant is produced, the result of all those bad families, the years of whispering and backstabbing and discreet poisonings and espionage.

Mother was a fox. Even at her advanced age, she read a great deal, but narrowly — romantic fiction and hagiography — always books that helped her to perfect her role as a wise old thing. The sententious crone whom everyone admires — "Lordy, I don't know how she does it" — more common in fiction than in real life, was Mother's persona. She was so far from the mainstream of human contact, she had to read books to find out how people lived and what they wanted. We all had to look outside the family for instances of kindness, generosity, and unselfishness. We had none, though even if we had, we would have kept them hidden, for fear we'd have been exploited for our sentiment.

We knew all this through Mother, not merely because she was a liar, but because she was a terrible liar, inept and obvious. The special language that every unhappy family creates, the dialect of deception, was Mother's native tongue. Because she was habitually mean in her giving, she assumed everyone else was too. What you gave her had to be second rate — why else were you handing it over? — and so she was never satisfied. In the same way, whatever you said to her had to be a lie — why else would you speak to her with passion? Only a liar would make such an effort.

Knowing we would never find encouragement within the family — knowing in advance we would always be undermined — we sought it elsewhere. This need sent us into the world. Except for Franny and Rose, who had tied themselves to Mother, all of us had looked for a welcome we never found at home. So some of us became travelers.

I say "we," but I mean "I." I was no better than any of them. I had everything in common, but I was peculiar. Early on, I had resisted Mother's influence. That resistance, the sense that I was being watched and whispered about, gave me the motivation to slip away, to vanish and find my own path.

I can only speak for myself when I say that all the negative aspects of growing up had some positive results. I learned this early in my best year with Mona, the year that set me free. I discovered that freedom is painful and lonely. I kept going. My history of coping in this family, negotiating with the others, hiding from Mother, made me adaptable. Mother was the queen of subversion. The fear that I might be subverted by her helped me in the scrutiny necessary to the writing life, the urgent feeling that everything matters: the tone of voice, the shading of vowels, the slightest gesture, the unexpected laughter, the touch of an anxious hand, the quality of light and shadow of a person. I had been both sensitized and hardened. My writing ability and my desire for solitude were intensified by my spells in Mother Land.

Edmund Wilson's mother said she'd never read a word of his. D. H. Lawrence's father mocked his son's writing and called it a kind of slacking. Joyce's wife famously jeered at his verbal ingenuity (and was bewildered hearing him laughing in the next room as he worked on *Finnegans Wake*), and Joyce pointedly did not attend his mother's funeral. Hemingway's mother hated *The Sun Also Rises* and called it "one of the filthiest books of the year." "Every page fills me with sick loathing," she wrote to him. At the end of his memoir *Family History,* John Lanchester comments, "Once my mother wasn't able to read my books, I finally began writing them."

Toward the end of her life, Edith Wharton wrote in a letter, "My literary success puzzled and embarrassed my old friends far more than it impressed them, and in my family it created a kind of constraint which increased with the years. None of my relations ever spoke to me of my books."

Late in his life, F. Scott Fitzgerald wrote a short story called "An Author's Mother." Based on his own mother, it is the portrait of a philistine and an unappreciative parent. "Her son was a successful author. She had by no means abetted him in the choice of that profession but had wanted him to be an army officer, or else go into business like his brother. An author was something distinctly peculiar." And later, "But the books by her son were not vivid to her, and while she was proud of him in a way, and was always glad when a librarian mentioned him or when someone asked her if she was his mother, her secret opinion was that such a profession was risky and eccentric." Fitzgerald wrote the story in 1937, publishing it in *Esquire.* His mother was still alive, and though on her last legs — she died a year later — she undoubtedly read it.

Floyd left a piece of paper under the windshield wiper of my Jeep one day, a quotation written in ballpoint, headed "I've been reading *The Rambler* — it seems Dr. Johnson knew Ma." And under it: "Equally dangerous and equally detestable are the cruelties often exercised in private families, under the venerable sanction of parental authority; the power which we are taught to honour from the first moments of reason; which is guarded from insult and violation by all that can impress awe upon the mind of man; and which therefore may wanton in cruelty without control, and trample the bounds of right with innumerable transgressions, before duty or piety will dare to seek redress . . ."

"Shaw hugely disliked his mother. His family never helped him as a writer," Floyd said one day, flipping open Stephen Winsten's *Days with Bernard Shaw* and reading from it. "'Fostered! Every conceivable difficulty was put in my way. I never saw my father with a book in his hand, and my mother ignored my existence completely.'"

Floyd licked his finger and slashed at the pages.

"He goes on, 'My mother never had a friend and never made the least effort to win my affection, and I certainly made no effort to win hers. When my manuscripts were returned she wasn't in the least interested. I don't think she read a single one of them. She accepted me as a burdensome good-for-nothing, just what she would expect from the son of her husband. My father at least had satisfaction in seeing my work in print and actually praised, but never referred to it.'" Floyd shut the book and said, "Shaw was a great friend of T. E. Lawrence."

"I think I knew that."

"It was Lawrence's exasperation with his domineering mother that made him want to go far away. You could say that his mother was the main reason for his becoming Lawrence of Arabia. And she hated his writing."

I wasn't alone. So, when Mother told people that she had always known I was going to be a writer — or took credit for one book or another — smiling, with my unread book in her lap — implying that she had made me a writer, the statement was true, though in the opposite way she'd meant. She'd driven me to it. But then most of what Mother said was the opposite of what she meant.

"Who is she?" Floyd had once demanded, back in the days when we'd discovered that Mother was secretly handing out money to the others and getting favors for it. I was not sure who she was, though I had some facts.

This was the woman who had raised me. I had always suspected that in some profoundly negative sense she had made me a writer, even if it was as basic as having hounded me out of the house, forcing me to make my own life. The mathematical proof, in payouts, of the degrees of her sympathy, spanning the spectrum from generous to stingy, convinced me that she had kept me as an outsider, always insufficient. I had never been able to please her — that, I'd known long ago; I had stopped trying. Yet she figured in my life. I was sixty-four, she was ninety-seven; we were still linked. I had burgled her house and rifled her desk, and now I knew where I stood.

You grow up thinking that a life of writing is made possible by someone serving you lunch and praising your work, an affectionate and sympathetic person to whom you read your novel in progress in the evening, the beloved name on the dedication page and beside it the affectionate words "who lived it with me, who made this book possible."

"It's really rather wonderful," says this — appalling word — helpmeet. "It's one of the best things you've done."

"I couldn't have written it without you" is the simpering reply.

In that cozy household of loyalty, you labor in the slanted light of your gooseneck lamp, white paper, black ink, the aroma of thick soup or of roasted tarragon chicken from the kitchen, the grateful muse — mother or spouse — stirring the rich broth of the fragrant stew. Everything solid, everything positive, nothing but praise in the steady climb from the obscurity of the study to the sunshine of the wider world.

But, no, it was not that way with me at all.

The turbulence in the family, the very size of it, had made me seek the solitude of reading, the orderliness of writing. I had sometimes produced results. Instead of a big warm embrace or any affirmation, Mother — from my earliest years of reading and writing — had frowned at me and said, "You're doing *what?*"

She had rolled her eyes, sighed in impatience when she saw me typing on my old Remington, one finger at a time. The effort seemed a peculiar form of idleness, a waste of paper, a kind of ugliness even, something unnatural and unproductive. I was selfish, indulging myself; I was a dissident. And it enraged her that I would not let her see what I was typing. Far from encouraging me, she demanded that I not write — that writing was worse than a waste of time. Writing was misleading, wrong, and vain, revealing your foolishness to the whole world and disgracing the family.

"What are you going to *do* with it?" She would stand in the doorway of the back room where I had hidden myself to write. "What will you do when you need money?"

Mother was literal-minded. Proof was something she needed to hold in her hand, and not just hold but weigh. Only one thing had weight in her world.

Money was the measure of everything: it represented work and honor, value and reward. Money was strength, money was goodness, money was praise, money was love. Money was a form of grace, even sanctifying grace. Though she had been stingy with it while we were growing up, Mother had dispensed it after Father's death: it became an expression of her power, and perhaps of her insecurity. She bought Franny, she bought Rose, and they whinnied around her, to make themselves worthy of more. She owned them while making them believe that they possessed her. They were all sisters, with their hands in one another's pockets. The ledger, the check register, was a sort of history, a secret chronicle of Mother's true feelings.

Money had always mattered. Early on, with the first sign of my love of writing, my pleasure in reading, she had thwarted me by insisting I get a job. I happened to be copying a paragraph from a novel into my notebook.

"You can't just moon around the house like this."

Mother Land was hostile to the intellect. So, as a high school student, I spent all my weekends and many of my weekdays stocking shelves at the Stop and Shop, working alongside smutty-minded men who taught me wisecracks and whist.

Work is social. I learned a little about the lives of these cynical, foul-mouthed men in white aprons, and I put this superficial experience into a worldly poem, which Mother found. I had typed it and accidentally left it in the roller of my Remington.

"This is filth!" she said, making a disgusted face. She tore it up.

She had found my fat green Olympia Press copy, in the Traveller's Companion series, of *Tropic of Cancer* by Henry Miller, and burned it. I had borrowed it from a guy at the Stop and Shop. There was something final and fanatical about her burning it rather than throwing it away. The man screamed at me for (as I claimed) losing it. "I'll never get another one! It's forbidden!" Books like that, being contraband, were treasured.

Mother had never heard of Henry Miller, but she saw the word "fuck" in the text. She had never heard of James Joyce or Baudelaire. She sneered at my copy of *Les Fleurs du Mal,* my high school macabre period, reading the poems with a dictionary, along with *Black Spring* and Faulkner's *Sanctuary* and the hard-core porno of Akbar del Piombo. I had copied out and hidden the E. E. Cummings poem "the way to hump a cow," so that I could memorize it.

> *the way to hump a cow is not*
> *to get yourself a stool*
> *but draw a line around the spot*
> *and call it beautifool*

All of this for Mother was kindling for a bonfire. She was a book banner, the latest in a long tradition of tyrants who feared and hated the unsparing word. Books were burned in Mother Land.

Although she did not disparage reading, she said that work took precedence, because work represented ready money. Writing was destructive. "Who'll publish it?" and "If you can't make money from it, what's the point of doing it?"

She read Frances Parkinson Keyes's *Dinner at Antoine's, The Little World of Don Camillo,* and *I'll Cry Tomorrow.* She read the *Pilot,* Boston's Catholic weekly, and the *Maryknoll Magazine.* She quoted Edgar Guest and twinkled on the lines "It takes a heap o' livin' in a house t' make it home." That was writing to her. So what on earth was I doing?

She had no interest in my writing apart from a wish to sabotage it. She would have stolen my pen or snipped off my typewriter ribbon if I'd let her. The arrogant thought that I might publish something did not anger her; it aroused her pity. I was making a fool of myself by revealing my ambition, as though I was saying, "I'm going to buy a Rolls-Royce and drive it to the ends of the earth." The desire to write meant I was getting above myself, and it would reflect badly on her. All writing was setting her up for humiliation. But working in a donut shop, stamping prices on cans of soup, or selling newspapers — that was ambition, and purpose, and it showed grit and virtue. It was money.

"She wanted me to join the navy," Floyd said after he'd published his first book.

Dad was no different, but instead of being hostile he was quietly embarrassed by our bookishness. He had never read a word I wrote, or if he did, never mentioned the fact. It was like an embarrassing secret we shared, of a creepy proclivity I had, something that we couldn't discuss without awkwardness.

It was not that he didn't read. He enjoyed history, especially local history — of Boston, New England, his ancestral province of Quebec. The Lewis and Clark Expedition fascinated him to the point where he would declaim the hardships the team faced, with the stout-hearted Sacagawea, the bad weather, the plagues of wasps. ("They were taw-men-ted!" Floyd would cry, wagging his finger, imitating Dad's characteristic way of speaking.) He read everything he could find on the assassination of Lincoln and had a detailed knowledge of the conspirators. He got the newspaper every day and read his holy missal the way a Muslim reads the Koran — and his missal had the thickened and thumbed look of a Wahhabi's Koran. He read about whaling and could tell you what flensing was and the composition of baleen, about Gloucester fishermen, the Battle of Lexington, the works of Edward Rowe Snow — all of that, but no work of mine.

At first I was bewildered, then relieved, and finally I was indifferent. Father did not read novels — anyone's novels, at least not modern ones. And I had not become a writer to please my parents, only myself. A writer is rarely able to do both, and I know that, far from wishing to please them, I wrote as an act of rebellion.

It took me years to understand how hostile a family could be to a writer in their midst. Mother was the most vocal. Appalled, she could sound like a Soviet censor in the way she denounced me. She tore at my writing, her fingers working like scissors when she found it. She bleated when she heard the clack and rattle of the Remington. "Stop making all that noise!" she had cried. "My nerves are shot!" She stood hovering where I sat, disapproving of my very posture, my back hunched, seeming to cower submissively. So I stopped pounding the Remington and used a pencil, silently scratching on paper, but doing that, a few lines at a time, seemed to Mother like even greater idleness than typing.

"You're going to ruin your eyes," Dad said.

"Would you show this to Father Furty?" Mother said as she tore up a poem or a page from a story, a secret agony committed to paper.

Years later, I understood the secret scribblers in the gulags, the dissident hiding his diary, the smuggled stub of a pencil.

Mother wanted to send me out of the house to a real job with a weekly salary, to a man who would pay me and thank her for handing me over to him. She did not really know the world of employment. In that world she was a confused peasant, twisting her shawl in her fingers, in the way she magnified the big unseen outer world of business and the powerful people who ran it. You could not impress these people of power with any writing; you had to respect them. If you did, they'd treat you right. They laughed at books, they worshiped money, they demanded work. You had to sweat for them, stocking shelves or mopping floors. You didn't need imagination, you needed gumption, and no jokes. "Elbow grease! Don't be afraid to get your hands dirty! Roll up your sleeves!" All this time I was reading Henry Miller. Writing about Rimbaud, Miller said, "My natural temperament was that of a kind, joyous, open-hearted individual — as a youngster I was often referred to as 'an angel.' But the demon of revolt had taken possession of me at a very early age. It was my mother who implanted it in me. It was against her, against all that she represented, that I directed my uncontrollable energy."

Somewhere Miller had written that his mother told his third wife, Lepska, that she had never read anything he'd published, yet still she disparaged his writing. He often dreamed about an ideal mother. "It occurred to me that if my mother had been like the mother I dreamed about, perhaps I wouldn't have become a writer after all," Miller said. "I might have become a tailor like my father."

As for my mother, the rule was: Be small, work hard, shut your mouth, learn the value of a dollar, show some respect, get a haircut, don't waste your time with poems, don't be a sissy, hustle while you wait. Reading might be fine for some, but it was a luxury. Reading didn't put food on the table.

Who was Mother? In all this, Mother was my muse.

PART FOUR

47

PASTORAL

A SMALL VOICE fluttering like a moth trapped in the wall was calling "Mama" with each push of its papery wings. I woke and lay listening for the cry to be answered and the frail-sounding thing to be stilled. I was in darkness, in a small room in an unfamiliar bed, a sweet-sour smell in the warm air of damp dirt and woodsmoke, of a smothered fire, of crushed flowers. A window shape squeezed to a trapezoid of sharp-edged moonlight flat on the floor lit the room, so I didn't need to switch on my phone, as I usually did to illuminate my way. I got up, unbolted the wooden plank door, and went outside, barefoot, in my pajama bottoms, the gasp "Mama" still pulsing behind the plaster. I knew I wasn't home.

The whole steep river valley and the bulge of mountains clawed by erosion behind it were silvered by the moon. Even the pebbles and smooth boulders near my feet were gem-like, carbuncular in moonglow, the forest in the middle distance a puddle of blue from the milky lunar drip of moon over its bunches of leaves and dense foliage. All of it stillness and silence except for a distant and bewildered dog yap. I seemed to lie against the bosom of the world, the tickle of dust, the softness of light, the tender earth underfoot.

The call "Mama" came pattering again, hoarsely now like the scrape of dead leaves, and then the mother's murmur of consolation, a whispered reassurance that moved me — the mother so patient and responsive, sur-rendering, clucking to the child. A sigh of satisfaction became a soft coo-ing, and then silence.

I'd been woken in my dream, a recurring one, pleasurable in its harm-less oddity. I'd just been released from prison and been given a brown paper bag of my possessions and an envelope of money. I was waiting at a bus stop alone on a hot street. Not an anxiety dream, but a dream of pu-rity and simplicity: an outlaw reborn as a citizen — exhilarated, solitary, and anonymous, the bus slowing down, its brakes snorting, to take me away, to begin again in a distant place, with a new name. My B. Traven dream of escape.

Another whiff in the night air, of roasted meat and burned beans, kerosene fumes and damp plaster. And a sharp chalky odor suggested by what I'd seen the day before on the valley floor, the scattered bones, the sun-bleached cow skull, the toothy jawbone, the splintered ribs — maybe goats, maybe mules — white bones crumbled in the dry soil like broken coral on a tropical beach.

My job — my unfinished magazine article — rattled in my head. Usu-ally it was only when I finished a piece that I was calmed, but I was calm now, even with my work incomplete.

Then I remembered I was in a village in Mexico, and recalled the stages by which I'd gotten here, tumbling through the country to come to rest in this hut, feeling at peace.

In the early, searching part of my life, as a teacher in Africa and South-east Asia, when I read everything, including the small print on the labels of ketchup bottles, I'd happened upon *The Death Ship* and discovered a writer to my taste. B. Traven was a rebel, a wanderer, a bitter satirist, an underdogger — and a mystery. After that book, *The Treasure of the Sierra Madre, The Cotton Pickers,* short stories, and the sequence of six novels of rebellion, the "Jungle Novels," about turmoil in the southern state of Chiapas. The mystery was that though they were written by B. Traven, no one knew who he was; no one had ever seen him. He seemed to be a man with at least four other names and no final identity, who had re-jected his family and his birth name and exiled himself to Mexico, where he lived with a much younger Mexican woman, who guarded his privacy.

But I felt I knew him. Read enough of the same writer and you develop an intimacy with the person on the page—his moods, his preferences, his tastes in politics and romance, his views on family and friendship, his pleasure in weather and food and the use of certain words. I came to know aspects of B. Traven—the important ones—and formed the portrait of a traveler, an outsider in Mexico, a revolutionary, a bit of an outlaw. As a younger writer I had found him a compelling figure who'd lived a life I aspired to, as a fulfilled loner.

No one had ever knowingly interviewed him. To the people who believed they'd met him, he claimed to be Traven's literary agent, Hal Croves. And he was two or three other shadowy people, each with a distinct name, none with a verifiable past. But this crowd of aliases was a dodge. His books were the work of one man, and as he wrote in one of them, "The creative person should have no other biography than his work."

Amen, Mother.

Hidden, productive, loved; living in Mexico, a restless man, a linguist, a photographer, an occasional explorer in the jungle—sought out but never found—he had always been a hero to me, especially now, as I reflected that I was living at home near my mother and among my contentious family, deeply in debt, pitied by my children, unregarded, unproductive, unloved.

So when a magazine editor asked me to write a travel piece—the sort of thing I did to pay bills—I suggested as a subject "B. Traven's Mexico." Much of the mystery of Traven's identity had been solved by a British writer in the 1980s, yet that book, and the man himself, were no longer news.

"Name rings a bell," my editor said, as people do when they haven't the slightest idea and don't want to seem stupid. I explained, with a few titles, and he said, "Oh, I adore that movie. I'm a total Bogart freak. 'We don't need no stinkin' badges'"—and bought the concept. It had everything: coastal Tampico, upscale Mexico City, distant Chiapas, quotes from the books, a then-and-now angle, an atmosphere of the bygone and the boutique, with a glow of nostalgia.

"Maybe work 'Sierra Madre' into the title—what's that, 'Mountains of Mother'? I love it."

"Could refer to Mother of God in this case."

"Good point. And Jay?"

"Yes?"

"Find some great little restaurants and some shopping tips for the sidebar. Bijoux hotels, maybe a spa experience."

Now I was near remote Ocosingo, watched by three young boys as I crouched by the bank of the Río Jataté in midafternoon heat and long black shadows, an odor of marsh blossoms and stagnation like an old foul stew, in the hot silence and a buzzing of sawflies. And the memory of "maybe a spa experience" made me smile.

The plop of footsteps in the mud of the foreshore. I looked behind me — a young woman, black hair, white blouse, long skirt, bare feet.

"*Comida para Usted, señor,*" she said. Her skirt reached to her ankles, her blouse was untucked, her breasts filling it. This was only the second time I'd seen her — I'd arrived the day before — and she was shy but curious in the country way, averting her gaze as she added, "*De mi madre.*"

"*Que es eso?*"

"*Tamale.*" She spoke in a soft querying voice, presenting the parcel wrapped in banana leaves, using both her hands, out of respect.

"*Tamale chiapaneca,*" a squatting boy said.

"*Cual es su nombre, señorita?*"

She lowered her eyes, because I had gotten to my feet and walked up to her to accept the tamale, perhaps too close. Her hands flew to her face. She peered at me between her slender fingers.

"Luma," she whispered, holding the word in her mouth out of shyness.

"Thank you, Luma," I said in English, and she laughed in confusion, then tugged at her skirt and stepped away, taking the path through the marsh grass to the slope that led to the house.

After she'd gone, the three boys I'd been talking to began to laugh. The one who called himself Nelson was standing on the flat sloping stone that served as a boat slipway. Álvaro was sitting in the boat that was tilted against the stone, ready to be launched. And Jorge, the smallest, was scrubbing the gunwales with a rag. They were her younger brothers.

"Ciguena likes you," Nelson said in Spanish.

"Why do you call her that?" It was the word for stork.

"Her legs. Her way of standing and—" He broke off and laughed with the others.

"How do you know she likes me?"

"Because you have what she wants."

"Money," I said.

"And also money," Álvaro said.

The others hooted, believing he'd made a subtle joke.

"You are a man," Nelson said.

"So are you."

"She is our sister!" Nelson pretended to be shocked.

I leaned toward him and said, *"Soy un hombre viejo."*

"Un gringo viejo es bueno," Nelson said. *"Lo tienes todo."*

"I don't have everything."

"Sí, todo — pero no Ciguena," Álvaro said.

"Take her and live with us here," Nelson said. "Mother will make food. Ciguena will have your children. We will be happy."

"Aren't you happy now?"

"Yes. But we will be more happy with the gringo in the house."

Idle village talk from teasing boys, so I said, *"Su marido."*

Nelson, the shrewdest one, shook his head. Even he could see that "husband" was absurd. Making a fine distinction in what my status would be, he said, *"Nuestro padrino."*

Not her husband, but their godfather. I unwrapped the banana leaf and offered pieces of the tamale to them. They accepted a small piece each and ate, nibbling, as hungry people did in those parts, making it last, chewing slowly.

"Will you read to us tonight again?"

"Yes. Of course."

"About the bones?"

"Why not?" Then I remembered. "I heard a baby crying early this morning. A little baby."

"Ciguena's boy — a few months old."

Now I knew why they called her the stork, but why were they teasing me about wooing her?

• • •

My travel for the B. Traven magazine piece had brought me here. Tampico had been a bust — an ugly harbor city of oil depots; Mexico City was vast, polluted, chaotic, and traffic-ridden. I did what Traven would have done, fled south to Chiapas in a rental car, first to the old mountain town of San Cristóbal de las Casas, then more easterly still to Ocosingo, and finally here to the edge of the Lacandon Jungle, which Traven explored in the 1920s and used as the setting for his novels of rebellion. Traven's funeral had been held in Ocosingo, his ashes scattered in the Río Jataté, where I was now living with the Trinidad family: the grandmother, Abuela; her daughter, Rosa, the *madre;* and Luma, apparently unmarried but with a small baby. A house of mothers.

I had found them by chance, near the village of La Soledad, as I'd driven on the road that ran parallel to the river. Seeing a well-built house and a woman in the yard hanging clothes on a line, I'd stopped to ask for directions the day before. "Directions" was my ploy to engage the woman and talk in general about security on this country road. Some people in Ocosingo had warned me of the rebel group who called themselves Zapatistas and were active in parts of the state and generally hostile to foreigners. Traven would have loved them for their anticapitalism, their indigenous roots, and their subversion.

Seeing me parking my car, the woman approached, a wet towel draped on her arm. She greeted me, we spoke for a while — pleasantries — and then she said, "What is it you are looking for on this road?"

"For a place to stay. For food. For people to talk to." As I spoke, she began to smile. I added, *"Tranquilidad."*

She straightened and threw her head back, a haughty and assured gesture that seemed consciously theatrical. "Then you have arrived. You can find a bed here. And food, and people who will tell you what you want to know."

Plucking at the towel on her arm, she stared at me with kindly eyes for a response. She was an older woman, looking sixty or so, but probably much younger, in a blue smock. Her black hair was tightened on her skull, drawn back in a single braid. Her neatness and self-assurance gave me confidence. Behind her a very old woman sat rigid, knees together, in a chair on the veranda. The house was also reassuring, one story high, of plaster and brick, with a flat roof bordered by a low parapet of fanciful crenellations, very solid and plump, like a little citadel between the road and the river. The river valley beyond was the backdrop; there were no other houses nearby.

"I will think about it," I said.

"While you are thinking, please sit down," and she indicated a chair near the old woman. "I will bring you some food." She called out "I am Rosa" as she entered the house.

I was taken by her directness and familiarity. I said hello to the old woman and sat down. The old woman mumbled a greeting but seemed distracted, and when she turned to me she did not look at my face but rather to the side of me and beyond. Her eyes were clouded — wide open and glistening — and I realized that she might be blind. For a long while she was silent, taking no notice of me. Was she blind? What threw me was that at her elbow there was a book. I tilted my head and saw on the spine that it was a Bible.

"*La Santa Biblia,*" I said.

She nodded and gave a little grunt.

"I am an American. United States. I am a stranger."

The old woman smiled and tapped her fingers on the arm of her chair, her hand very slender with yellow fingernails. She seemed to repeat what I had said and added more, just as Rosa returned with a tin tray, a thick white plate of food on it — a tamale, some corn on the cob, a tumbler of milky coffee — and placed it on the table next to me.

"My mother is saying you are not a stranger. You are with our family."

"Thank you," I said. "This food" — I chewed and swallowed — "very tasty!"

"To help you think," Rosa said, and sat below me on the veranda steps while I ate.

"My mother is alive," I said, wondering at my boasting. "She is over one hundred years old."

"*Dios la bendiga,*" Rosa said. "You are very lucky. You will live a long time."

"So will you. Your mother is also old."

"She is more than seventy years."

I did not say, Not much older than me. I said, "*Dios la bendiga.* She has a beautiful face."

"She is not healthy, and she is blind."

All this time I was eating the tamale, which was filled with raisins and nuts, mixed with the meat and tomatoes and an herb flavor I couldn't name. As I finished, Rosa stood up and said she would get me some more. I thanked her and said no, then reached for the Bible.

"We read to her," Rosa said.

The Bible was worn, the leather cover bumped and scuffed, the tissuey pages thickened and smudged from being pushed by licked fingers. The stringy threadbare ribbon marked the book of Ezekiel. To show my thanks, to be agreeable, the harmless gringo, I read, *"La mano del Señor vino sobre mí"* — the hand of the Lord was on me — and continued, *"Hijo de hombre, vivirán estos huesos?"* — Son of Man, how can these bones live?

The old woman was nodding in recognition as I spoke. She said, *"Señor Dios, tu la sabes."*

"I like this," I said.

"Aquí es el valle de los huesos secos," Rosa said. "And these bones are alive."

Now, with the clap of the screen door, a young woman appeared at the doorway from inside the house, but she stopped when she saw me. Some boys peered at me from the corner of the house. That it was a house of women and children somehow relaxed and encouraged me.

Perhaps it was for their benefit that Rosa said, like a command, *"Puedes estarte con nosotros unos días,"* and as I seemed to weaken, she added, "Or a week, or more, *si quieres"* — if you wish. Still in Spanish, she said, "It is cheaper than a hotel, and there are no hotels in La Soledad. There is nothing in La Soledad." She called to the young woman. "Bring a basin of water so that our guest can wash his hands."

The young woman obeyed, hurrying inside the house and then returning with the basin, bowing, holding it while I wagged my hands in the water. Rosa stood aside and watched, seeming to evaluate the encounter. The woman was perhaps twenty, with the Asiatic features of Mexicans in these parts, many of whom were Mayan: dark eyes, long black hair, and full lips, and with these delicate features, strong hands gripping the basin she held between us in a posture of submission, her heavy breasts swinging within her white blouse, bowing slightly, not looking at me, her eyes cast down out of shyness or respect, so I saw only her eyelashes, the thick wide sweep of them, black against her smooth cheeks.

"Maybe for a few days," I said.

Like that, I had a large clean room with a view of the river, a soft bed, and a table for writing. I had good food and friendly company. I had a family.

That night, after dinner of a stew they called *menudo,* of tripe and vegetables, and more corn, sitting around the trestle table in the big kitchen that looked out on the yard (pigs in a pen, chickens in a coop), one of the smaller boys, at Rosa's urging, brought the Bible to me.

"Read to us," Rosa said. "Abuela likes to hear your voice." She said my voice was *raro* — unusual.

The young woman had not joined us for dinner, and I wondered whether she was hired help — a maid, a servant of some sort. In my weird vanity I had hoped to impress her with my reading.

Opening the Bible to where the ribbon lay, I said "Ezekiel," and the old woman clasped her bony hands and rocked a little.

"*Entonces El mi dijo, profetiza.* Prophesy to these bones and say to them, 'Dry bones, hear the word of the Lord.'"

The room was still, the faces attentive, gleaming by lantern light, the table like an altar. I had a delicious hint of what it might be like to be a preacher, to have the power of conveying the word of God to believers — their solemnity, their trust, their belief in me, the messenger from the Almighty. I was bringing hope to them, and glory.

So the next day, by the river, when Nelson said, "Will you read to us tonight?" I was touched. But I also recognized that to them I was a novelty, a diversion, someone who might prove useful, a gringo with a car and money, perhaps easily tempted.

The house was well built because Rosa's husband, working in California, had for some years (*"Por algunos años"*) sent money every month. He no longer did so. "He is waiting for his papers" — another vagueness — I took to mean he was illegal. He had not come home for eight years. A visit to Mexico, I guessed, would mean that he'd be unable to return to his job at the *fabrica de procesamiento de pollo* — chicken processing plant — in Stockton; nor could Rosa visit him.

For these reasons and more, I was a welcome visitor. In the following days I ceased to be a guest and became the sole adult male of the household, giving them rides to the market at La Soledad to buy vegetables and cooking oil, and beer for me; helping to fix Álvaro's bicycle; reading to them after dinner, always the Bible.

In the morning I worked at the table in my room—and often overheard Rosa saying, *"No molestarlo—el está ocupado,"* outside my door. Most afternoons I walked along the river or joined the boys at the slipway near where they caught fish in a weir they'd made at the neck of a narrow backwater. They had a small boat they sometimes used for fishing or for ferrying firewood from the far bank. Seeing that the hull had dings and leaks, I told them that if they hauled it out, I'd help them repair it with material I'd buy in Ocosingo. And I introduced them to the simple effort of mixing chemical potions, hardener and fiberglass resin—and the magic of fiberglass patches.

"We can travel downriver in this boat," I said. "We will have an adventure."

We were sitting on the riverbank below the house, admiring my handiwork, the gleam of the patches on the old boat. Just then, Nelson looked up and saw Luma standing near the house, holding her baby.

I said, "Where is the father of that baby?"

"Se fugó," Álvaro said.

"Se escapó," Nelson said.

Gone. So Luma was abandoned and perhaps disgraced, and I saw how as a godfather I might fit into this family with the dead grandfather, the husband who'd stopped sending money, and the daughter whose lover had bolted.

"She is good. She is not spoiled, *señor,*" Nelson said. "She never went to school and picked up bad habits like others."

It was easy to see what they'd envisioned for me, the designated male adult with a steady income. It was a role that suited me even better, perhaps, than they'd imagined. I was not dismayed. I liked the straightforwardness of it. I thought, Maybe this is the answer, maybe this is my future. The irony of it was that it had been B. Traven's answer too, turning his back on his parents, his ex-wife, his child, abandoning everything he'd known for a new life as a writer in Mexico, obsessed with protecting his privacy and looking after his young Mexican wife.

Abuela was not well — *muriendo,* Rosa said. Dying. Rosa ran the house but did not see me as a potential mate, although she was younger than me. Luma was the bait. Such an arrangement was not odd here, where older men often married much younger women, nearly always as a benefit to the whole family in the role of breadwinner or patriarch. And a gringo offered the added promise of American passports.

They were not cynical manipulators; they were practical in the manner of peasants, for whom sentimentality was usually fatal. They were not so much looking for an alliance as for a father figure — *padrino* said it all, a godfather. On the first day, they'd asked me all the pointed questions: Did I have a wife? Children? Family? I assured them I was unencumbered, and from this they rightly surmised that I was adrift; they understood that I was grateful for their hospitality. They knew that I was happy, and I could tell from the way they teased me that they were comfortable around me. They must have known on some level that I was tempted by Luma, or why else after a week was I still here?

They were right. This was the fantasy I craved, life at its simplest, a house in the tropics by a river, a place to work, a pleasant climate, good food, naps in a hammock, chickens clucking beneath me; tenderness, too, perhaps even a sortie at romance. All this and the pleasure of being far away, my dream of living the fantasy of "What's become of Waring since he gave us all the slip?"

The persuasive part of the fantasy was not the romance but the contented family — large, self-sufficient, and happier for my being with them, because I had money. None of them had gone to school past a few early grades, and though they knew a handful English words, only Rosa could read. My Spanish was improving. That was another of my uses — reading to them after dinner by lamplight while they sat, bright-eyed. At some point in the past, probably from an encounter with another stranger on the road from Ocosingo, this one an evangelical, they'd converted from improvisational folk Catholicism to the salvation of fundamentalist Bible-thumping, and I was the answer to their prayers in this respect, too.

"*Mas, Tío Hay.*"

I wasn't the gringo anymore. I was Uncle Jay, and sometimes *padrino*. All they needed to do was think of a way of making me wish to stay. They'd agreed to the boat trip down the Río Jataté; they'd left me alone, undisturbed, when I was writing; they encouraged me to hold the baby, Carlos, whom they called Carlito, and talked up Luma. They could see, in my procrastination, that I was weakening.

It seemed insane, certainly improbable, yet I had found myself in a kind of Eden. I'd come on the pretext of planning to write about it. But why would I leave? They were right: I had everything here I would ever want. It seemed slightly creepy to take Luma as a junior wife, but they assured me that was the village way. What it meant was that I would have to keep my part of the bargain: stay with them, be loyal, and support them all. Even on my small budget I could do that, because I now got a monthly Social Security check, enough money to live well in the depths of Chiapas in a modest house by the river.

"The mother of Tío Hay is almost one hundred years old," Rosa said at the dinner table one evening.

"Older than our *papelillo*," Nelson said.

He meant the big tree in the yard that supported one end of the woven hammock, a vast, reddish, peeling paperbark tree that Mexicans sometimes called the gringo tree, for its sunburnt coloration.

Hearing this news of Mother's age, they looked upon me as someone of even greater value, not only for my money but for my strength and protection, my longevity. I was not marrying one woman; I was forming an alliance with an entire family.

A further advantage to my living here was that my phone didn't work. I had no Internet access. At La Soledad phone contact was intermittent; only in Ocosingo, more than forty miles away, was I able to make a call from my phone, but so far all I'd done was extend my car rental. This was a liberation. Intending to write a piece about B. Traven, I had become B. Traven, uncontactable, the vanished American. I loved the thought that I'd disappeared—from Mother, from my rancorous siblings—and to "Where's Jay?" there was no answer, only bafflement.

Whenever she saw me sitting on the veranda or lying in the hammock, Luma would bring me baby Carlito and offer him to be held. And I was happy to cuddle him, watch him gurgling, often a sweet milky breath from Luma's breasts. And she knelt, watching.

One day, holding the baby, I said, "I'm not going away. I love being here. I love your family. I want to go down the river with your brothers — to fish, to look. But I will come back. I will play with Carlito. I will take you to Ocosingo, to the shops. I will read to you. I want nothing else."

Saying it, I saw a whole life, my check deposited every month in the bank branch at La Soledad, writing in my room in the little plaster-and-brick citadel, picnics by the river, being looked after by the Trinidad family, and looking after them. I studiously avoided any mention of marriage or romance.

"We will be happy. Do you believe me?"

I was not sure what I was trying to say, yet — full of hope — I was giddy.

"*Sí, padrino.*"

Luma sat closer while I held the baby. She caressed his cheek, nuzzled him and made him laugh, and put her pretty finger on his lips. I was happy, I was the baby. I thought, This is the life I've always dreamed of.

"Will you please take me to Ocosingo?" Luma said in a low voice. "I want to see the doctor there. Just for a checkup."

Revisión médica. Sensible mother.

"Sure," I said. "Tomorrow. We will leave early."

Luma's younger brothers saw us off, and Rosa gave us food for the journey and a shopping list.

"*Hasta pronto!*" they called out.

Alone with me, Luma became talkative, telling me how she'd always wanted to go to the coast and see the Pacific Ocean, how she liked music and the fiestas at San Cristóbal, and perhaps she would travel when Carlito was bigger, maybe to the United States, just for a visit, to see all the things that people talked about. I encouraged her with questions, and I thought, I can make that happen.

Nearing Ocosingo, she said, "I hear music. What is it?"

At first I was bewildered; I hadn't heard anything. Then I remembered my phone in my bag in the back seat, with my passport and valuables. I said, "My ring tone?" and she laughed at my odd words, but softly, and shook her head, holding the sleeping baby in her arms.

I pulled over near a beer sign, *Cerveza Amnesia Nocturna,* and as I did the baby woke and smacked his lips, and Luma was clucking at him. That was what I would remember, the odd sign, the contented baby, Luma's smile, and the message glowing on my phone: *Mother ill. Come home at once, wherever you are.*

48

ANGOR ANIMI

THE FIRST hard autumn rain had beaten the brown leaves from the trees — mid-November on the Cape, the days growing bleaker with each denuded branch, and instead of the sigh of leafy boughs, the sorrowful moan against the black limbs and the knuckles of the twig ends stuttering in the gusts. Impossible to sit in this early darkness, a season of withdrawal and departure and desiccation, brittle leaves and the frizz of withered blossoms, and not think of death or the mental paralysis I'd suffered before I vanished in Chiapas. And I had traded that sunny, hopeful household in the jungly south of Mexico just a day before for this — for this.

"It's all a shock. We don't think Mumma's going to make it," Franny said when I called for an update. Her voice was the familiar one of the people in this family, which was a peculiar country with its own discouraging accent. *It's awl a shawk.* "She's wicked thin. I brought her a bottle of tonic and she wouldn't even drink it. It's like she wants to go."

"When's the last time you saw her?" And I had winced at *bawdle of tawnic.*

"Two weeks back. Marvin keeps me busy. He can't use his walker anymore. He needs a wheelchair. I have to put him in it and then take him out. Plus, he's got wicked bad digestion issues. And restless leg keeps him awake all night."

"Who's looking after Ma, then?"

"Fred was, until a week ago. But he's been diagnosed with phlebitis. They think it's all his flying catching up with him. Or maybe peripheral vascular — that's what Hubby says. That's why we sent you the message."

"I was really busy," I said, and an image of the friendly faces at the dinner table, shining by lamplight, sprang to mind. "I don't see why Floyd couldn't have stepped in."

"He's scheduled for a gallbladder operation," Franny said. "Remember he had that acid reflux? Remember Hubby told him to take Zantac for it, or was it Tums?"

"I don't remember. I don't care."

"It wasn't acid reflux. It was gallstones. He's going in for surgery. Hubby explained everything."

"Is Hubby looking after Ma, then?"

"Not really. He's pre-diabetic. It's either type one or type two. Which is the nonserious one."

"Aren't they both serious?"

"The one you don't need to take insulin for. He's in and out of the hospital."

"And what's Rose's excuse?"

"She had a bad fall. She's day to day."

"Gilbert? I guess he's in Kabul. Know what? I was once in Kabul. I went down the Khyber Pass. Did anyone in the family wonder why?"

"Gil's in DC with serious lower back issues. It's work-related."

"All he does is sit. In various far-off countries. At various desks."

"'Sitting is the new smoking.' That's what he told me."

"So no one's looking after Ma."

"You are, Jay."

"Because everyone's sick."

"Everyone's wicked sick."

"Especially Ma?"

"Like I said, we don't think she's going to make it." Franny gasped into the phone. "Jay, she's nearly a hundred!"

"What's wrong with her?"

"Everything."

"What does her doctor say?"

"You know how she feels about doctors."

Mother distrusted doctors for creating alarm and despondency, for exaggerating consequences. Look closely at doctors, she said; are they so healthy that they should be lecturing the rest of us on how to live? No, they were pale, they were fat, and many of the ones Mother had known had been smokers. This folk wisdom was shared by Roald Amundsen, who refused to take a doctor on his expedition to the South Pole, for the reasons Mother enumerated. Captain Scott had a doctor, Edward Wilson. Amundsen successfully reached the pole and returned in triumph. Scott and his doctor found Amundsen's flag and froze to death on the way back.

As for medicine, Mother preached that the side effects outweighed the benefits. All medicine was snake oil, a confidence trick, weakening you and then bringing you down. Medicine did not cure you, it deluded you, then it killed you. I had begun to think she might be right.

"You have to go see her. It's all up to you now."

"In which hospital?"

From the tone of her reply, she found my question ridiculous. "Mumma's home."

She was sitting on her throne among her shelves of knickknacks and family photographs, wrapped in a shawl. Rain lashed the front windows. I'd brought a basket of fruit, and this time remembered to include a pineapple.

"Are you all right, Ma?"

"Where have you been?"

"Mexico."

"My brother Fran went to Mexico once. His company was building a bridge in the jungle. He was a civil engineer, very well respected."

"I was in southern Mexico."

"Oh?" she said, tightening her shawl against her shoulders.

"I got a message you were ill."

Hearing this, she opened her mouth, unhinging her lower jaw in a sudden drop, like a lizard spotting a fly, and she coughed, the shallow keck-keck, to affirm that she was not well.

But she said, "Not too bad," and coughed some more, a dry choking that sounded like a stammer.

"The others are sick."

"So I hear." Her tone was mocking, or at least disbelieving, as though they were malingering.

"I mean, everyone is ill. That's the news."

"Is that a pineapple?" she asked, peering at the fruit basket, gesturing with her clump of knitting.

"Yes, all for you."

"I like a nice piece of fruit," she said. "Fred put me in the Fruit of the Month Club one year." Then she squinted and seemed to recall what I had said about the others. In a stern voice she said, "They don't know what sickness really is. Only a mother understands pain, because only a mother experiences it in childbirth. For me it was eight agonizing episodes — eight times in the valley of the shadow of death." She put her knitting on her lap. "Hubby comes to me. 'I'm diabetic, Ma.'" Her imitation of Hubby's manner of speaking was cruelly accurate, down to his wagging head. "He eats candy. He always did. He's overweight. And now he's diabetic. Whose fault is that?"

"Fred's got something wrong with his legs. Maybe bad circulation."

"Flying. Dad never had that, but then Dad never went hither and yon to China. Nor did I."

"For Floyd it's his gallbladder."

Mother gave me a twinkling smile, the lenses of her thick glasses shining in the light of her reading lamp, hiding her eyes. "I always said that Floyd had a lot of gall. Ha! Maybe it's heartburn. I wouldn't be surprised."

We were going nowhere. I said, "What are your symptoms, Ma?"

"Like Dad used to say, when you're old you never have a good day." She lifted her ball of yarn and resumed poking one needle then the other through the loops of purple wool.

"So you don't think Floyd is really sick?"

"I didn't say that." She was frowning at the wool, intent on the deft twists of her knitting. "All I'm saying is that if you have a lot of time on your hands you tend to make yourself sick. Ever notice, really busy people stay healthy. They don't have time to get sick."

"But you're ill, right?"

"I'm *old*," she said, rounding her thin lips like a grommet and drawing out the word.

"I got an urgent message saying that I was to come home right away and look after you."

"Maybe you were better off where you were."

Exasperation made me breathless. I said, "I was happy."

"Where were you?"

"Like I said, Mexico."

"Oh?"

The click of her needles in the silence that followed indicated to me an utter lack of interest. No one ever wants to hear your travel stories; perhaps that is why so many travelers become writers, because no one will listen to a verbal account. It occurred to me that the news of the others' ailments, one child after another falling ill, annoyed her and took attention away from her. She decided to develop symptoms of her own, not serious enough to warrant a doctor, or a hospital, or medicine, but serious all the same, requiring the concern of her children.

And now that she had our attention, she decided that someone as old as she was not long for this world. Perhaps it was not medical care that she needed but rather a death watch. A doctor or medicine would create the distraction of hope, inconvenient to someone who had her sights set on the grave. It was not pills she craved but morbid concern, helpless fascination, ashen faces around her bed, her children sighing and desperate. "Mumma, Mumma, what are we gonna do?"

She did not look different from the way she had when I'd left for Mexico on my magazine assignment. Perhaps she'd lost a few pounds, but that was a feature of her aging, a sort of physical shrinkage, but staying just as vital and, as I witnessed today, combative.

"What can I do for you?"

"Take care of yourself. Don't you get sick too. I don't think I could bear hearing about one more person's ailments."

Above her head, hung on the wall, was a tapestry portrait of her and Dad, side by side in the sunshine, that I'd had copied from an old photograph and commissioned in the 1980s in a needlepoint factory in Shandong. At that time, such traditional work, the so-called forbidden stitch, was made to order, before the assembling of cell phones and toasters and beach chairs displaced it.

Dad was smiling his uncomplicated, approving smile. I said, "I miss Dad."

Mother tut-tutted, clicking her knitting needles, and shook her head. She said, "I miss Angela."

Angela! Stillborn, seventy years before!

"Like Dad," I said, "she's gone to her reward."

"You don't understand," Mother said, and on her upturned face her glasses flashed, her eyes crazed and distorted and unreadable. "I feel I can reach out and touch her. She is with me every waking minute."

Mother's spooky certainty made me swallow hard, and I could not begin to frame a reply. I said I had to be going and slipped out the front door, the cold rain hitting my face. I came home from Chiapas to this.

The sole benefit to me of all the illnesses was that it was inconceivable that anyone would suggest having a family gathering, two weeks away, for Thanksgiving — always painful and often rancorous. No one was well enough to host such a meal; no one would want to attend. Everyone had a coveted doctor's excuse — mine was that I was looking after Mother. I'd bring her some turkey; I'd listen to her for an afternoon. With any luck, and some more malingering, Christmas would be canceled, the excruciating holidays put on hold, a relief from the days when the family was forced to sit in a room together, seething, hating every minute, thinking, Where did we go wrong?

Holidays meant seeing one another and the possibility of knowing more, and proximity was potentially disastrous. Any sort of revelation meant a loss in power. A family was a peculiar cluster of misfits, an arrangement whereby people who did not want their privacies to be known were trapped in a place of maddening intimacy. As a consequence, being forced to share that space, none of us told the truth about ourselves, and we had a tendency toward calculated indirection and hollow boasts.

I phoned Floyd's wife Gloria, who said, "You haven't heard? Floyd's in the hospital," and she gave me his room number. She said she'd appreciate my going to visit him, because she was commuting to Boston these days, doing some teaching.

"I've been away."

"Where to?"

"Southern Mexico."

She said, "Doing a story for a magazine?"

Out of a habit of not wishing to let anyone in the family know what I was actually doing, I said, "No, I'm thinking of investing in a mineral operation. Amber mines in Chiapas. Not well known, big opportunity."

"Oh?"

"So Floyd's got something serious?"

"It started with chest pains — gallstones. He's had the operation, laparoscopic surgery. He's much better now. He'll be in the hospital for the rest of this week, recuperating and getting tests."

She spoke slowly, with feeling, and I was touched by her tenderness toward Floyd — so unusual, since in the family, Floyd was a figure of fun or else a bogeyman, to be mocked or feared.

"Did you tell my mother?"

"Not really. We don't want her to worry. Marvin's the big worry. He thinks he's going to die."

Gloria was relatively new to the family. How was she to know that for almost the entirety of my adult life I had been hearing stories of Marvin's ailments — his flat feet, his stomach ulcers, his high blood pressure. One year it was cellulitis, some sort of infection, and there was always "he's struggling with his weight." Whenever I felt the urge to jeer at him, he would reveal that he was afflicted with something serious or life-threatening, as when he had the stroke, impossible to fake, the slack jaw, the dead arm, the shuffle, and the amputation of his left leg. And now it was "incontinence issues" and "restless leg" — his remaining leg. Mother had always belittled him for being a hypochondriac who guzzled pink pills, but there was sometimes truth in his symptoms and stark fear in his pale plump face.

As soon as I put the phone down on Gloria I hurried to the hospital. I found Floyd propped in bed, a drip in his arm, an old thick book with a flaking spine in his lap.

"Billy Hazlitt — it's a tonic. I'm force-feeding him to my students next semester. It will serve to enlarge their livers, and they will be like Christmas geese, the carcass fit for the table, the innards perfect for foie gras. Bear with me."

He adjusted the tube in his arm and tugged the sleeve of his hospital pajamas. He licked his finger, skidded it across some pages, and slapped the book. With an upraised finger for emphasis, he began to read.

"'Nature seems (the more we look into it) made up of antipathies: without something to hate, we should lose the very spring of thought and action. Life would turn to a stagnant pool, were it not ruffled by the jarring interests, the unruly passions, of men. The white streak in our own fortunes is brightened (or just rendered visible) by making all around it as dark as possible; so the rainbow paints its form upon the cloud.'" He sat up and stared at me. "'Is it pride? Is it envy? Is it the force of contrast? Is it weakness or malice?'" Then louder: "'But so it is, that there is a secret affinity, a *hankering* after, evil in the human mind, and that it takes a perverse, but a fortunate delight in mischief, since it is a never-failing source of satisfaction. Pure good soon grows insipid, wants variety and spirit. Pain is a bittersweet, which never surfeits. Love turns, with a little indulgence, to indifference or disgust: hatred alone is immortal.'" He snapped the book shut.

"William Hazlitt? I don't know that one."

"'On the Pleasure of Hating.' And here's something else you don't know. Hazlitt's father was a Unitarian preacher who brought the family, including young Billy, to Boston, at a time when it was a hotbed of sedition and whining colonists."

I had been in the room perhaps fifteen minutes, I had hardly spoken, and my head was ringing: I was exhausted from his barracking voice.

"What are you doing here?" Floyd said. "I understand you were dallying in the Limpopo, attended by buttocky tribeswomen by day, crawling on all fours to unspeakable rites at night."

"Mexico," I said.

"Even better. Our bean-eating neighbors."

"Chiapas," I said.

"Stoutly defended in the sixteenth century by the Dominican friar Bartolemé de las Casas," Floyd said. "To some, a heretic. To others, a theological extremist. To me, a paragon of virtue. Like you, he was obsessed with his bowels."

Instead of doing battle, I said, "Sorry to hear about your gallbladder."

"It's gone! I'm cured. The doctor's a genius. He made a tiny incision and plucked it out with the expertise of a fisherman twitching an eel from a boghole. When I get my bandage off I'll show you the amazing small cut, a mere nick in my abdomen."

"Everyone's sick."

"So it seems," Floyd said. "To varying degrees. Mother most of all."

"The usual competition."

"Yes. Never mind that I was at death's door. Mother gets the medal."

"I saw her yesterday. She looked fine. She said she missed Angela."

"Her guiding spirit, who will no doubt materialize one day, like the incarnation of Lono among the Hawaiians. We're savages. This is rank ancestor worship!"

"Mother seems indestructible," I said. "I think she's right that medicine is bad for you."

"Did she give you her cough?" He went *keck-keck,* mimicking the sound with cruel exactitude. "She is — what? — ninety-eight? The Ling people of Burma deal with their old and futile relatives by eating them. The Inuit send them into a winter storm to freeze solid. The Ik people, according to our friend Colin Turnbull, leave the oldies to starve to death on a distant hillside. What do we do? We're the worst of all. We allow them to decay before our very eyes."

"So what should we do about Mother?"

"The eternal question," Floyd said. "Fred's sick. Gilbert and Hubby are ailing. Rose has problems. How clever of Mother to trump us all."

"You forgot Franny and Marvin."

"Marvin is an anthology of complaints," Floyd said. "I love to hear about him, because I adore the language of illness. Chancres. Buboes. Blebs. Pustules. *Angor animi* — anguish of the soul, the sense that you're toast. The conviction you're about to die. I think Marvin was diagnosed with a gangrenous leg before they turned him into Captain Ahab. The thing about illness, the mood of affliction, is that it endows the sufferer with great predictive powers — thus, *angor animi.* Marvin knows something, he has the prescience of illness . . . Jay, for the love of God, say something."

I had been thinking about how Mother always mocked Marvin. Competing with him for Franny's affection. When they lopped his leg off at the knee she said, "It's not as though he was ever a great walker, so maybe he won't miss it."

"I was in a lovely place in Chiapas, living with a local family," I said. "I got a message to come back. I was really happy in that household."

"Don't brood. Employ your customary expedient — write about it."

That very idea had occurred to me. A man like me goes to a remote village. He is generous. He buys food and tools and pays people's bills. When he then decides to leave, they won't let him go. They keep him captive for his money, a lesson in corruption in a simple place, a parable of do-gooding and a creative way to deal with my disappointment at having been forced to return home from my idyll beside the river.

Floyd flung the curtain aside next to his bed. He said, "There was a man languishing in that bed until two days ago. He would sleep for eighteen hours, then be awake for twenty-four. He was melancholic, and his antipsychotic drugs weren't working. The diagnosis? Refractory depression. What a great pair of words! He, too, had fits of *angor animi.*"

"Looks like I'm the only one who's not sick," I said. "Just a touch of gout."

"That's right. You're the only healthy, rational one in the family. So you present yourself in your work. As for the rest of us, we are simply meat and plumbing."

It was Floyd's usual criticism, that I depicted myself in my writing as objective and sane, coolly viewing the madness of the wider world. My narcissism, he said. But he was lying in a hospital bed with tubes in his arm and a bandage on his belly and a catheter up his leg, so I resisted arguing with him.

"And when you visited Ma, did you deign to mention that she was sitting in a house that she handed over to her daughter? That, in effect, Mother is a tenant in her own house?"

"No, I didn't bring that up."

"You complain about Fred to me, but do you ever tell him that he's a perfidious weasel and a traitor, who traduced the family, allowed the coffers to be opened in a land 'that hath yet her maidenhead, never sacked, turned, nor wrought . . . the mines not broken with sledges, nor their images pulled down out of their temples'? Source?"

"Raleigh, in Guiana. You've quoted it before."

Repetition — of stories, of remarks and rejoinders — was a cultural habit in Mother Land, perhaps apparent in this narrative.

Annoyed that I remembered his quote, he shouted, "And now it has all been sacked, turned, and wrought by the Wobbling Weird Sisters in the Year of the Big Word."

He was sitting forward now. He'd taken his thumb out of the Hazlitt book and was yelling at me. The only thing that prevented him, it seemed, from leaping on me was the restraining tangle of tubes in his arm and up his leg.

"You're as bad as the rest of them," he shouted.

"I came home because I was summoned," I said. I got up and kicked the chair back, because I didn't want to hear this.

"You should have stayed where you were. It seems you were better off there."

"I promised to look after Mum."

"You hate all of us. Your delight in mischief is a never-failing source of satisfaction."

"Bull."

"She's healthier than you. She's healthier than all of us," he yelled after me.

That was not Mother's story. After a week of my visits she said she needed Franny's attention. She still talked to Franny by phone three times a day, but she wanted a visit — and Franny, who had received the house as a gift, could not refuse Mother's demand. Marvin will be fine, Mother said, believing him to be faking. And on one of those visits to Mother — a Sunday, Swedish meatballs, a tray of manicotti, ginger ale, and Hydrox cookies — the phone rang: Jonty, in tears. Marvin was dead.

49

THE SURVIVOR

MOTHER NEVER LOOKED STRONGER or more superior than at Marvin's funeral, tapping her stick down the main aisle of the church, her head high, the queen reviewing her troops. And the troops were suffering, still recovering from their various ailments: Fred limping, Gilbert in the straitjacket of a back brace, Floyd clutching his chest, Franny and Rose wheezing, dragging themselves to the family pew. We were together again, and furious, all of us in the church, as the priest reminded us what a great soul Marvin was, while everyone else saw him as the mall cop armed with a can of Mace, a martyr to donuts.

Seemingly strengthened by Marvin's death, and now with Franny to herself, Mother forgot she'd been ill and stopped coughing as a reply when we asked how she felt. She began taking afternoon constitutionals, walking up and down her neighborhood. She asked to be driven to the beach, and she started a weekly routine of going to a nearby restaurant, the Oyster Bed, and eating eighteen raw oysters, served in three waves by an admiring waitress, and finishing with a bowl of vanilla ice cream.

Floyd said, "Karen Blixen lived on oysters in her old age at Rungsted, but unlike Ma, she was inconvenienced by the tertiary syphilis she contracted from her fiendish husband."

Mother said she was saddened by Marvin's death; she sorrowed for Franny, who was grief-stricken. Mother confided to each of us individually that she had consulted Angela, who was as always a consolation. Yet in this grieving period Mother gained a lightness of spirit, she was physically nimbler, and it seemed that Marvin's death gave her a sparkle that was now a familiar mood. I realized that over the past decade or so, whenever one of her friends or neighbors died, she did not darken or brood, but instead was vitalized, more talkative, more animated and assertive, while at the same time more relaxed. I had expected something else, a foreboding, a reminder of the Big Sleep, but no — what was it?

She was a survivor. She was the fortunate traveler at the gate who missed the plane that had crashed on takeoff. At Marvin's funeral, her face upturned as if listening hard, she seemed to radiate the pronouncement, I'm here — you're not. That was her victory: she was still standing, the winner.

"It is not enough that I win," Floyd used to say. "Others must lose."

So in this short period of time, passing from ninety-eight to ninety-nine, Mother was on top again, saying that she despaired of her children, who were growing old, whose health was failing.

"We don't think Mumma's going to make it," Franny had said. But it seemed now that Mother might be the only one who *would* make it.

Having abandoned my trip to Mexico in response to the summons on my cell phone (farewell to my assignment, *adiós* to my expense report), I visited Mother most days. Watching her knit — a skill I did not have — and walking with her, she seemed determined to exhaust me, or at least outwalk me. I would try to engage her in conversation, but that was futile too. She was not a conversationalist; she was either a talker, monologuing in the role of Wise Old Thing — Mary Worth, Mother of the Year, the bun-haired crone (played by Peggy Wood) from *I Remember Mama* — or, bored with this, a competing interrogator.

"Can you name your first-grade teacher, Jay?"

"Miss Purcell."

"Mine was Mr. Watson," Mother said, and then rapidly: "Second grade, Miss Eliot. Third grade, Miss Cramer. Fourth grade —"

That became her party trick, a feat of memory that stretched back ninety years. Mother could recall every teacher she'd ever had and many of their approving remarks.

Then it was her neighbors. I was poor on neighbors — I could only remember my friends' families.

"We lived at 134 Jerome Street. The Bergins were at 136. Across the street at 137, the Duggers — Major Dugger was in World War One. He was black. They named the park after him. The Kountzes, at 139, were also black. Lovely people. On the corner, an Italian family . . ."

And so on, down one side of the street and up the other. It was impressive, but like many other virtuoso feats — high-wire acts, juggling, tap-dancing — it soon became monotony. You wanted it to stop. Enough, I'd think, and mourn again my abrupt departure from the Trinidad family in Chiapas, who had no phone and didn't write.

Mother was proud of having saved a lot of money, but proudest of all of her frugalities and folk remedies — putting mercurochrome on a bad laceration instead of going to the doctor, jamming a clove onto a bad tooth, drinking Karo syrup for a sore throat, repairing eyeglasses with Scotch tape, darning socks, patching pants, and there were those rubber soles that we glued onto shoes to make them last. Mother prided herself on her sacrifices, saving and economizing, because she'd grown up having to learn the survival skills of the Great Depression. But the habit refined itself into a game and finally a competition: the winner was the person who spent the least money, and the greatest spender was regarded as the biggest fool.

Mother's good memory, her mending and making-do—these were admirable qualities. But her gloating over them, turning everything into a contest, was annoying, for the fact was that Mother would never admit defeat in any of it. She was merciless in her need to win.

We all said now, "She'll outlast us," and it seemed so. Marvin was gone, leaving Franny oddly buoyant and renewed, as Mother had been when Dad died. Fred had what seemed a permanent limp and couldn't walk without a cane. Floyd had recovered from his surgery but had put on weight and was always short of breath after one of his rants—and more of his rants were directed at me. He became more choleric and overbearing, with a wife and a new life, while I was alone in a rented house, writing about a solitary gringo in a Mexican village, being fleeced by the people he'd befriended on a remote river, the family having become parasitical. Saddened by what I'd lost, realizing it was unattainable, I was attacking it.

Mother seemed indestructible, shrunken to her essence, more powerful than we would ever be. As I lamented the loss of my Mexican idyll, I marveled at her, sitting upright in her chair, while I crouched on a stool before her, as she knitted a scarf or squares for an afghan. She was half the size she had been at Father's funeral, and that lightness made her stronger. She moved more quickly and was alert in a bird-like way, with bird bones and a bird beak and a bird's beady eyes, even a bird-like way of jerking her head and twitching at a unexpected noise.

Someone so old seems to exist in a region beyond physicality: Mother had no fleshly essence. She was a wisp, a wraith, a vapor, almost ghostly, insubstantial and gray, as though spun from cobwebs. And I felt old and frail and cheated, taking medicine for my gout.

"Dad had gout," Mother said. "I think the medicine he took for it contributed to his poor health. It might have killed him."

I was forced to listen in silence. My days of arguing with her were over. She was above reproach and she knew it. As a survivor of so many deaths and crises, she had attained the status of an immortal—not a figurative deity but an actual goddess. She could not be criticized or contradicted, not opposed or doubted.

Yet she still lived alone and did most of her own cooking—a soft-boiled egg for breakfast, half a can of soup for lunch, wilted salad for dinner: short rations on which she thrived. She read the local newspaper every day, always had a book on the go—never one of mine—did the daily crossword. Once a week she was picked up and taken to bird-carving class by a fellow carver, whom she flirted with in a grotesque geriatric way that might have inspired a work by Samuel Beckett.

As mercurial as ever, and often irritating, maddening at times, she had outlived the criticize-by date, and so was blameless in everything she did and said. Yet she did not seem any older, cruising through her ninety-eighth year.

She was bored with me, bored with all of us. She needed more stimulation, different admirers, less skeptical listeners. But then, she was always more responsive to attention from outside the family than from any of her children, even the ones who adored her, or claimed to. She'd heard it all before; she needed something new.

The Ohlendorfs were a family from Connecticut whom Fred had known for a while, lawyer father, dentist mother, two kids, who visited the Cape and discovered Mother as they might have discovered a rare old treasure in a museum that they returned to every summer to gaze upon with rapture. They had no equivalent matriarch in their own family, and their pent-up piety they discharged on Mother, who basked in their fascination. They brought her bouquets of flowers, posed for pictures with her, as they might have with a queen or a goddess or a municipal statue, and Mother had a claim to each role. Their visits were too reverential to be termed drop-ins. For me—for the rest of us—the annual visit of the Ohlendorfs meant we could take a few days off; Mother was otherwise engaged. I had no idea of the entertainments the Ohlendorfs had planned for Mother, apart from the chocolates, the flowers, the extravagant praise, the group photographs.

"Jollification with the Ohlendorfs," Floyd said.

Mother, who was our burden, became their trophy and their boast. Fred reported that they took her out, made a day of it. They had lunch at a Brazilian restaurant in Hyannis. None of us had ever risked such a thing, but they had a Brazilian friend who'd suggested it. In and out of a car, a long drive, a huge meal — and Mother was game.

Another couple joined them, marveling at Mother's health and humor. They owned a boat, and after the Brazilian restaurant they all drove to Hyannis Harbor and took her aboard and sailed her around Lewis Bay while she sat on the poop deck like a queen on the royal barge.

"My children have never done this for me," she was reported to have told Madge Ohlendorf, who casually told it to Fred.

Mother was lame the next day. She had overdone it, but she was so eager to praise the Ohlendorfs, her hosts and benefactors — who'd done more than we ever had — that she could not complain of her aches. Yet she had seriously bruised her knee and could not walk.

"Maybe take some aspirin?" I suggested.

"I'll be fine."

But she was hobbling. Nevertheless, the blow-by-blow: "Brazilian food is delicious. There's music. Gauchos come to your table and give you pieces of meat."

Mother had other admirers from outside the family. A woman down the street, Wanda, who worked at the library, dropped in weekly, always bringing a book or two. There were weekenders from across the street, the cookie-baking wife, the husband a retired state trooper who did odd jobs. The woodcarvers from the class were always on call and, being old themselves, knew what she might need — a can of soup, a dozen eggs, and food items that had never occurred to me — it seemed that Mother loved hot chocolate and lobster bisque and the occasional jelly donut. I had no idea.

With Mother receiving so much attention from others, we slackened in our efforts, weary, demoralized, unappreciated. Her talk of the gauchos and the Brazilian meat and her tacking around the bay made her seem independent, happier elsewhere. That was no surprise to me: I had been happier in Mexico, with strangers who were grateful for my company. Gilbert still took Mother for oysters whenever he was on the Cape, but his work — whatever it was — kept him away most of the time, these days in Baghdad or Kabul. "He can't talk about it," Mother said with pride. "It's all secret."

In that period when Mother was occupied with visitors and admirers and gift-givers, we kept away, each of us for our own reasons. I was writing my novel about the outsider held captive in the village, Fred was still doing legal work, Floyd was teaching, Hubby worked at the hospital, all versions of semiretirement, everyone occupied. Each of us believed we were absorbed in our work, that someone was looking after Mother. Weeks went by without my seeing her, though I called every few days to ask how she was doing.

"No complaints."

This from a woman headed downhill toward ninety-nine.

"I'm expecting the girls this weekend," she'd add.

At that point I'd cut her off. It demoralized me to hear anything about the others, what they'd brought her to eat, what presents, the news of their spouses and children. And I was certain that when my name came up they'd change the subject too. Even the malicious pleasure of backbiting had lost its appeal. I could not tell whether she was boasting or heaping hot coals on my head when she spoke of the others. Mother had become enigmatic, less readable than ever, and though she was still a gossip, I knew that the salient element in gossip (apart from calling attention to oneself) was mendacity.

The family was now populous with grandchildren and great-grandchildren. I hardly knew their names, but Mother remembered them all and often had a discreditable word for one or another — troubled teen, loser, failure, dropout. I did not want to hear any more, so I stayed away. How was I to know that the others were themselves absent, doing the same?

Fred got a call from a neighbor of Mother's, who wished (so she said) to remain anonymous but sounded like Wanda, the librarian friend.

"I'm terribly worried about your mother. She's not eating. She's wasting away. No one ever visits her. If she was my mother . . ."

That got our attention. Mother was such an unreliable witness we suspected what the neighbor was saying might not be true. Even Fred's report seemed an exaggeration. He said he found Mother alone, thin, dehydrated, not having eaten, dirty dishes in the sink, the toilet unflushed, her clothes unwashed. Each of us then visited, verifying her condition, which was that of a hostage.

"I thought you were looking after her."

"What about you?"

"You let her starve."

"She's a skeleton. You were supposed to visit."

Round and round, accusations, recriminations, blame that we leveled at each other. But the sorry fact was that Mother was in poor health, living in a dirty house, slowly dying.

"*Que madre!*" I heard my Mexicans say, meaning, "What a mess!"

50

THE KINDLY ONES

IN MOTHER LAND no one listened and nothing was news. We never expressed honest surprise at anything we'd heard. Never "I didn't know that," but always "I know, I know," which meant "Shut up!" In a family of talkers, it seemed there were no listeners.

But this was a pretense. We were hungry for information, we had Mother's voracious appetite for bad news, and all of us were the canniest listeners.

One of the most disconcerting, exasperating habits of the family was our ability to listen keenly while talking nonstop, never betraying any interest in what was being said — and, while yakking or interrupting, remembering every word that was said to us, every interjection, especially if it could be reused as gossip or scandal.

It was never clear whether the talker actually heard what you said as he or she rambled boringly on. The talker was not impressed enough to comment. So you assumed they were deaf to what you'd told them, or uninterested, or that what you'd said had been unimportant after all.

But this very lack of comment signified interest and even fascination. The monologue was another form of indirection. You were not accorded any acknowledgment: that would have imposed a sense of obligation, or required offering you some credit. Yet afterward the story you'd told to the talker and interrupter, or the mention you'd made, or the opinion you'd expressed — seemingly to deaf ears — was the story that made the rounds, usually in an improved form, wickeder, crueler, unanswerable.

This was another trait of Mother Land, one that we'd brought to a pitch of perfection. We feigned indifference, affecting to be careless; we pretended to ignore the idle or revealing remark. But this indifference made us more insistent and sometimes more candid, often more emphatic. While turned away, seeming not to care, making important-sounding noises of our own, we were more highly tuned, the most sensitive and alert and attentive creatures, as predators always are — the motionless boomslang seeming to snooze, coiled on an overhead branch, the lion flattened on its belly in the tall grass, the hyena lurking at the periphery of a browsing herd.

It seemed a small thing, just another family quirk, kind of peculiar. But it was a subtle form of entrapment, and in the way it extracted the essence, and preserved it while seeming to reject or ignore it, was a magnification of blame, enormous in extending our quarrels.

The stark truth in all this deflecting talk was that Mother was shrunken and living in squalor.

So we talked, interrupted, held the floor, and filibustered. No one wanted to assume the responsibility for Mother sitting askew on her throne, her head cocked to the side, her mouth half-open, her tongue drooping. "Making the Q-sign," Hubby said, an indication of futility, like the patients nearest death, in the last bed on the ward, the one next to the exit door.

Our talking did not take place in a room as a sort of forum on the topic "What shall we do about Mother?" We were too unforgiving to be able to occupy a single room. These were asides, drop-ins, accusations, snarls, the Chinese whispers of sequential phone calls. Sometimes they were cries of rage, all of it was jabber, no one listening — at least no one seemed to.

We brought food, flowers, chocolates, intending to revive Mother with gifts and good cheer.

"You're going to be all right, Ma," I said.

"Everyone says that, but why? There's nothing wrong with me."

That was the most worrying assertion of all, that in her dire state — growing thinner in her dirty house, a figure of neglect — she protested that all was well with her.

When we were teenagers, Mother had devised a system for us to clean the house. Each of us was assigned a room — kitchen, living room, dining room, or one of the many bedrooms — and we were responsible for cleaning it. We could not leave the house for any reason until Mother inspected the room and said it had been done to her satisfaction. The bathroom was another story; it was punishment for the person who had performed poorly the previous week. One bathroom for all those people in the house. It was a vile job. "I want it shipshape," Mother said, echoing Dad. It meant scrubbing, not mopping, polishing, dusting. "It builds character," Dad said. He was probably right. From childhood I could never understand anyone who endured a dirty house, and if there were children in the household, why were they not mopping and vacuuming?

In the period of Mother's decline and shrinkage, we applied this system to her house, each of us responsible for a room. Hubby had the bathroom because as a hospital employee he had access to discount quantities of industrial cleaners and disinfectant, Franny and Rose tidied the kitchen, the others took the dining room and the bedrooms. I opted for Mother's study, formerly a bedroom, now a small office with bookshelves and a substantial oak desk, all the drawers kept locked since the days of the mysterious break-in and suspected thefts.

"Know what I hate?" Hubby said. "It's not Ma's house anymore. It's Franny's. We're cleaning Franny's house. She should be paying us to do this."

"But you got the Acre from Ma, so what are you complaining about?"

"I'm not asking you to mow my lawn," Hubby said. And he sulked.

Floyd made the same point. Why were we cleaning Franny's house?

Fred said, "We're doing it for Mum. Do you want her to live in squalor?"

The condition of Mother's house improved, Mother began eating again, and I found that having something practical to do on my weekly visit — dusting books, tidying the desk, waxing the end tables — made my appearance purposeful. And Mother was grateful for the attention.

She called from the next room, "Everything all right?"

"Coming along," I said, squirting the window, wiping the dirt off. "I wish my work was going better, though."

"Oh?"

"Trying to write a novel," I said, and saying it aloud, yelling it to the other room, made it sound absurd. "My landlord just raised my rent, so I have to take little assignments to pay bills. 'My favorite piece of luggage.' 'A book that influenced me.' 'A memorable meal.' Always about five hundred words." I was scrubbing the window, looking out at the road, watching a squirrel seated upright on the curb, looking baffled, its tail flicking in what seemed indecision. A wet day, no acorns apparent. I was that squirrel.

"Would you ever —" Mother cleared her throat and began again, "Would you ever write about me?"

"In what respect — kind of a memoir?" I eliminated the last smudge from the window and went to the door of the study. Mother was in her chair, leaning forward.

"Exclusively about you? Like *I Remember Mama*? You used to love that show."

Mother said, "Maybe about everything I did for you. All the sacrifices I made."

It was a gray day in late spring, exhalations of vapor from the damp earth, buds on the trees but no leaves, a season of hesitation, the daffodils and tulips past their best but nothing else in bloom except a few whips of forsythia and a blush of azaleas, the sky heavy, a dampness in the road, the lawn still soggy from the late mud season, the grass uncut and shaggy — whose job was that? The ninety-nine-year-old woman and her sixty-five-year-old son alone in the old house. Her request made me sad. I wanted to weep when I reflected on what she was asking: this severe woman who claimed I had never done anything right was requesting a hagiography.

"Like I said, I'm struggling to write something."

"Oh?"

"I just wish my Social Security payments would kick in. I won't get anything for another year. I wish I were done with this book."

Mother said, "My father always said that you had to work hard to do anything well."

I stared at her, a squirt bottle of Windex in one hand, a damp rag in the other.

"Nothing is easy in this world," she added.

"I've generally found that to be the case," I said, trying to control myself.

"If your book isn't done, whose fault is that? It means you have to get up earlier and apply yourself. Roll up your sleeves and get down to business. Burn the midnight oil."

I felt the strong urge to slap her, jerking her face sideways with the force of the blow, all the while howling at her. But it was a vagrant thought. The stronger sense I had was: she's better, she's back on form, I don't pity her, I'm not worried. She's stronger and meaner than me.

A week went by. I returned to tidy and dust the study. Mother was more watchful than usual, and I noticed that she had put on a few pounds. The house smelled of lemon wax and Hubby's industrial disinfectant and the sharpness, like varnish, of rotisserie chicken.

Sorting the papers on Mother's desk, I uncovered a thick book, stamped *Journal,* and — making sure that I was not being observed — opened it. It was a diary of sorts, in the form of a logbook, the kind a ship's captain might keep, noting the compass heading and weather conditions and occurrences in one-liners. Mother, too, recorded the weather. *Sunny* one day, *Showers* another, and *Breezy.* She kept track of visits. Franny brought food, and Fred chocolates, and Gilbert called from London. The pages were arranged in weeks. I looked at the previous Wednesday for a mention of my cleaning. *Jay showed up,* her entry began. *His usual complaints. My hard life, no money. Poor me, poor me.*

I did not take this as a slight, or as mockery, but rather as further affirmation that Mother was her old self again.

To help provide regular meals, rather than depend on food drops, Hubby renewed Mother's visits of Meals on Wheels. As with everything we did, no matter how small, this became his boast, as the cleaning of Mother's study was my boast and the kitchen was crowed over by the daughters. "See what I did?" And we knew that there is no more irritating person than the one who loudly calls attention to a minor task he or she has done. But of course we boasted of these trivialities for that very reason, because it was annoying.

Mother thanked Hubby for taking the trouble (so he reported), and she told the rest of us in turn that the food was terrible. "I leave it for the seagulls," she said—the big scavenging birds roosted on her back fence. "I keep the little carton of milk for myself." She laughed at the notion that Hubby believed he was helping with the food.

"If you call it food!"

But the soup and the rolls and the stew that we brought began to accumulate in her refrigerator. Mother sipped and nibbled at it but did not finish anything. The trips to the Oyster Bed tailed off—we were too busy, or else away, or found it a chore. We wondered whether Mother might be declining again.

"She needs a caregiver," Fred said.

Because of her age and her apparently slender means, Mother qualified for a twice-a-week visit from a home aide, deputized by the town's Senior Care Initiative, to make a simple meal and do basic cleaning.

The woman, Maureen, was middle-aged and slow, and lasted one day, not even to the end of that day. Mother couldn't bear her.

"I think she smokes. A few flicks with the duster and she's done. I don't call that cleaning. After an hour she tells me she's tired. I said, 'If you're tired, go home. But don't come back.'"

Mother mocked her as she mocked Meals on Wheels, and the woman begged to be released.

"Angela didn't like her either," Mother said.

That was another feature of Mother's mood: her more frequent allusions to Angela as an eyewitness.

Floyd, still recovering from his gallbladder surgery, sent Gloria to bring food for Mother. But it ended badly, as I discovered from a letter that Floyd sent me the following day:

Dear Jay,

"Floyd's wife Gloria is here, going through my checkbook," Mother told Rose this morning at 10 a.m. when she telephoned. Gloria had just brought Mom vegetable soup and homemade blueberry pie when

Mother, fretting, quickly dragged her into her study to show her a doctor's bill ($35) for which she claimed she had been double-billed.

Crying out that she had already paid the bill, Mother pulled out all her checks, checkbook, you name it. Always helpful, completely innocent, worried for Mother, hoping to help her out and get to the bottom of it, Gloria called the doctor's office twice, the bank twice, and found out that the bill had been paid but not yet received, was perhaps lost. Immediately, the phone rang. Rose had meanwhile notified Fred, no doubt claiming that Gloria was stealing Mother's money, and within minutes Fred telephoned the house and began to upbraid Gloria for "looking at my mother's finances." He harangued her, badgered her, and shouted at her that he had paid that bill.

"Do not look into my mother's checkbook! That is private!"

What this old grizzled fool, devious himself, fails to understand is that Gloria is the most honest human being on the planet, cannot even conceive of stealing, feels awkward about taking a food sample offered to her by a lady in a supermarket! Gloria began to cry, telephoned me, and I told Mother, when she put her on, immediately to call Fred and Rose. Gloria tried Rose, could not reach her, but she called Fred back and straightened him out.

I am very angry. Gloria is inconsolable, angry, hurt, and justifiably convinced we are all brutes. I want this hellacious story told, not only because it is true, but because it is just the kind of thing — secrecy, suspicion, gossip, cruelty, calumny, the Furies!, the Kindly Ones! — we live by in this awful family. The Oresteia replayed as farce!

— Floyd

I called him for more details, but he was too furious to listen. He began to yell, "Look at the food her children are giving her! No nutrition, just bottles of Ensure. It's sludge! The refrigerator's full of garbage. Swill! Chanklings! Dog food! They give her chew toys to eat!"

Hearing me snigger — it was the word "chanklings" — he banged the phone down.

A daily visitor was what Mother needed, a hot meal in the evening, the laundry done, the bed made. And so a Brazilian woman was found to be Mother's caregiver. Fred located her — the Cape was full of Brazilians, many of them illegal immigrants, but this one came highly recommended. She looked after an elderly woman in the same neighborhood, and a visit to Mother could be part of her schedule.

Her name was Selma. She looked Italian, dark unruly hair, hook-nosed, duck-butted, a grandmother, she said, from Cuiabá.

"What a coincidence," Floyd said. "The very town from which Lévi-Strauss set out to discover the secret history of the Nambikwara people. I long to engage Selma on this subject, and on structural anthropology, the opposition of *Le Cru et le Cui,* and what could pass for the portrait of this family, his seminal work, *La Pensée Sauvage.* Like you, when I mention Lévi-Strauss, she'll think I'm referring to the maker of blue jeans."

Selma had a friend, João — Mother called him Joe — who volunteered to cut the grass if Mother paid him twenty-five dollars an hour. Mother agreed, and — perhaps as she intended — this opened a whole new discussion: Was Joe cutting Mother's grass or Franny's grass?

Screams from Floyd, howls from Hubby, sarcasm from me, tears from Rose. Franny ended up paying, but claimed she was being overcharged.

"I think Selma steals," Mother said.

Mother shuffled to her china cabinet. She tapped the glass front and said, "The souvenir plate Dad and I got from Niagara Falls. Some Hummels. A teacup from Japan. And some pieces are missing from my jewel box, those black pearls you brought me from the Pacific."

All the items she mentioned had been taken by Floyd and me, years before.

"Maybe you mislaid them," I offered.

"They were in the china cabinet. The pearls were in the box. I didn't touch them."

To ease her mind, and mine, I brought back the hideous Hummel figures I'd taken, and the black pearls, and put them where I'd found them. A week later, I looked again in the china cabinet and the jewel box and saw they were gone. When I remarked on this to Mother, she said that the only person who had been in the house since she'd seen me last was Selma. So Selma had to go.

"I am glad you say that," Selma said. "I want to leave. You mother never happy with me. You mother never happy with no one. She talk on the telephone and complain all the day. Now give me my money and I go."

"Give me back the things you've stolen and I'll pay you."

"You call me feef? You tink I hob her?"

She was fierce, and indignant in her ferocity, and denied she'd taken anything. But I knew she had. And when she finally went away, without much protest, I realized that she must have been illegal and feared arrest and deportation. We had the locks changed and new keys cut and returned to our former routine, each child responsible for a room.

This was not the answer to "What shall we do about Mother?" It was not practical. But it was unsatisfactory in another respect. Being in Mother's house, cleaning the rooms, listening to her reminisce about Angela, or correct us, or complain, was a painful reminder of the life we thought we'd left behind long ago, inhabiting the same space, always at odds, saying "Look what I did" when we were children, as though at this late stage in our lives we were getting younger and younger, or at least more infantile.

51

MOTHER'S CENTURY

MOTHER'S BIRTHDAY, the month and the day, was a command: March fourth. "Think of it," Mother often said, and here she would square her skinny shoulders, level her long, indicating nose, and stare straight ahead. "March forth!"

We had always obeyed, marching out of step, but now with her hundredth approaching we had made no plans. What to do was only part of the problem. Christmas had just passed, and because Mother had contrived for most of her life to divide us, so as to be the focus of attention, we spent the holiday separately with her, taking turns, like patients visiting a doctor, keeping appointments, not speaking to each other, merely seeking approval, punching in, signing out. The procession of gift-givers and well-wishers put Mother in a good mood, but soured us. The division haunted us, most of us were not on speaking terms, and those who were, such as Floyd and me, were overlooking a great deal of our own combative history. Floyd was well aware that recently, to amuse Hubby, I'd told him that I suspected Floyd to be the Unabomber, Ted Kaczynski, based on his threats, his prose style, his angry letters to celebrities and politicians, his wild hair, his hermit-like existence, his ingenuity, and his rage. Hubby, who was the leakiest one of us all, told everyone, and of course my cheap shot got back to Floyd, likely in an even more twisted and abusive form.

Given that we seldom communicated, it was hard to agree on what to do about Mother's caregiver. And the hundredth birthday party seemed beyond anyone's ability to organize. At the end of December, Christmas safely out of the way, I ran into Fred at the town transfer station — the dump had closed, and this new facility did not encourage dawdling or chitchat or dumpster diving, nor was there a swap shop to trawl for treasures. Fred was carrying an armload of grease-stained pizza boxes to the paper-recycling receptacle.

"What about Mum's birthday?" I said, startling him. "Maybe the Happy Clam again?"

He did not break his stride. He returned to his car for the glass and plastic recyclables, saying, as he passed me, "Anything can happen. There's a lot of time between now and then." He kept walking. He dumped his barrel of glass and plastic. Passing me again, he said, "I don't buy her green bananas anymore," and then, "or long books."

And using his good arm and his good leg, he drove off. Mother's birthday was a little over two months away. "Anything can happen" meant she might die, relieving us of the burden of having to plan a party. Ours had never been a family of planners, but it was obvious that unless someone took action, Mother would not be celebrating her century.

There followed a typical family pattern of passivity and evasion, of a sort we'd rehearsed as children: one cookie left on the plate — who would be brazen enough to pick it up? In a big family the last cookie is never taken, never eaten. It remains on the plate as a challenge, a taunt, a problem, and there it goes stale, making everyone angry.

In the end, Gilbert — the kindest, the hardest to read, the motto on his escutcheon *Mother never says no* — made a reservation at the Oyster Bed from his bolthole in Baghdad, using the Internet, and relayed the information to us. Lunch on the fourth, the whole restaurant had been booked. "Mum's looking forward to it."

"Eighteen oysters for her and heartburn for the rest of us," I said to Julian and Harry the day before, when they arrived, flying into Boston from London.

"Park it, please, Dad," Julian said. "She's your mother, she's a hundred years old, she's an idol. If she were in Britain, she'd be getting a telegram from the queen, congratulating her."

"And she gives us hope," Harry said. "It means you'll live a long time. We'll have you for years."

They were tall—taller than me; they had their mother's coloring, my first wife's English pallor; and they were healthy—Julian from daily tai chi, Harry a dedicated cyclist. They were both in their forties, Julian with traces of gray in his hair, middle-aged from an actuarial perspective, responsible and sober, with houses and wives and children—my grandchildren, whom I seldom saw. My children were adults and I was the cranky child.

But they shamed me out of it, taking me again to Yarmouth Port for sushi and inquiring about my work. It was rare that anyone discussed writing with me, the one activity I cared about, that kept me sane and hopeful, my mission in life, my only intensity.

"'We work in the dark—we do what we can—we give what we have,'" I said. "'Our doubt is our passion and our passion is our task. The rest is the madness of art.'"

"You sound like Uncle Floyd."

"Harry's right, but I know it's Henry James," Julian said. "People ask me all the time if I'm related to you. They wonder what you're publishing next."

"A novel set in Mexico," I said, and telling them about the book, based on my brief stay with the family on the Río Jataté in Chiapas, I began to believe in the story, and saw it whole, and became happy and hopeful again. I had turned this friendly family into hostage takers, transferring the confinement I felt with Mother and my own family into the narrative: the man in the narrative held captive by a manipulative family in Mexico.

"That sounds great," Harry said. "The man comes with good intentions and they keep him prisoner. A kind of parable. *Homo homini lupus.* Man is a wolf to man."

"Who said that?"

"Lots of people. I came across it in Freud. *Civilization and Its Discontents.*"

"You know, Freud's mother lived almost as long as mine. Yet he never wrote much about mothers or motherhood."

Julian said, "How can you have an Oedipus complex without a mother?"

"Freud claimed he didn't have a clue about women," I said. "He claimed that if you want to know about women, you need to examine your own experiences of life, or read poetry. He was exasperated by women. He said he couldn't answer the question 'What does a woman want?' He knew my mother!"

"Put your chopsticks down," Harry said, "and let's join hands."

We held hands, our arms extended across the table.

Harry said, "Grandma is a hundred years old. The statute of limitations on family rancor has run out. Repeat after me. 'All is forgiven. No more rancor. Right thought, right action.'"

"Are you a Buddhist now?"

"Repeat it, please."

"All is forgiven. No more rancor," I said. "Right thought, right action."

They held on to me, tugging slightly, longer than I expected, long enough for the words to sink in, for me to be ashamed of my casual abuse and lingering resentment.

"Now, for God's sake let's talk about something else," Julian said. "One more story about Grandma and I'm getting the next plane home."

What they had said was true: she was an idol, small and shriveled and yellowish, but looking indestructible, with bright eyes, a solemn expression, and a dusty glow. She sat between Fred and Gilbert, her favorites. Freud was right about that: a mother's favorite child was usually a conqueror, triumphant in life. An empty chair next to Gilbert—Angela's, in her memory. Franny and Rose at adjacent tables, with glum Walter, and children. Jonty's two, the great-grandchildren, ran among the tables, yapping like puppies. There was Jonty's brother Max, whom I had not seen since he was a playing card in the ballet *Alice in Wonderland,* a skulking wife in tow. Four generations at the Oyster Bed, decorated today with a hundred roses and a hundred cupcakes, sent by Mother's well-wishers, the Ohlendorfs.

I sat down with Julian and Harry, and Charlie joined us, saying to Julian, "Hey, bro," and they fist-bumped, and I reminded myself that Charlie was nearing fifty.

With Harry's mantra of compassion in mind, I was less happy than detached. I looked at everyone closely and saw, not siblings or cousins and near relations, but characters, faintly fictional, as though they were strenuously auditioning for a part in something I might write.

That was how my brothers and sisters seemed to me — fixed and fictional, vaguely menacing, as comic characters often are, unpredictable, and because of that unreliable, always posing a threat, conveying through the subtlest gestures and nuances of speech and bad jokes that they were antagonists. Their claims of reassurance were never a consolation. I took them as an excess of insincerity. The most menacing sentence an isolated person could hear from someone nearby was *I'm not going to hurt you.* You think: That had not occurred to me, but now I'm worried.

Now, with this detachment, seeing them as characters, I watched them at the birthday party like puppets in a play — Gilbert on Mother's right, Fred on her left, and the rest of us at greater distances. I sat in a far-off booth jammed between Julian and the wall, Charlie and Harry opposite.

"Grandma looks happy," Julian said.

"Yes," and I thought, Not merely happy but triumphant.

My children were right — she'd outlived the whole family, she'd outlasted all her friends, and if she'd had enemies, she'd buried them too. Of her generation, only she was left standing. All the others were gone, and so she remained, like a silent emissary from the distant past.

Of the others, what could one say? Her rivalrous children didn't count, but a new generation was obvious in the room — the grandchildren, the cousins, all of them much bigger and bulkier than I remembered, Bingo with a fiancé, Benno with a beard. Jonty announced that he had a public relations company; Fred's son Jake, who had once seemed troubled and hopeless, was a successful computer programmer and had a newborn son, whom he displayed like a ham, and the child looked scalded, as infants do. I thought of them as they'd been: the juggler, the harmonica player, the screechy brat, the boy who'd left footprints on the wall of my dining room, the one who'd eaten a Styrofoam cup. But they were grown now, they had jobs, some were married, and though still wary of their weird uncles and aunts, they seemed content.

A new generation to displace the one above them. All of us were Mother's subjects, but some had suffered more than others. For these younger ones in the birthday room, knowing little of the fanatic heart of the family, there was a measure of hope. They hadn't suffered at all — to them, Mother was a noble soul who could always be relied upon, the embodiment of sympathy and generosity, baker of church-window cookies, knitter of scarves and afghans, carver of birds, head of the family, defender of the faith. Empress of Mother Land.

For the duration of Mother's hundredth an unspoken truce was observed — no wisecracks, no casual abuse, no tasteless jokes — and this made for a dullness that seemed interminable. Oh, for a bitchy remark or a low blow. I also thought, So this was the prevailing atmosphere of families who got along, a mood of tedium and forbearance and Christian charity. How awful. But I kept my vow from the night before: all is forgiven, no more rancor. The vow did not inspire any sweetness, only an alien sense of sanctimony, of slight fraudulence, and a leaden quality of patience. No matter who you are or what you say, I will retain this moronic half-smile and this heavy-lidded gaze.

An insistent tapping on a water glass silenced the room. Gilbert had risen, and as he shuffled some papers, Fred shushed Hubby, who had been giggling over a story.

"Thank you all for being here," Gilbert said. "With your permission —"

"Denied," Floyd called out.

"— I'd like to remind you of what this woman has witnessed so far in her life. When Mother was born, William Howard Taft was president. At three hundred and forty pounds, Taft was the very definition of love handles. She has seen sixteen presidents come and go since then. Fenway Park was being built that same year, and the *Titanic* sank soon after, the *Lusitania* a few years later. Orville Wright flew a plane for nine minutes, a world record, the year of her birth. Consider that feat and then consider that this woman witnessed the moon landing and rockets to Mars."

"It's one small step for a man," Hubby intoned.

"Two world wars, the Korean War, the Vietnam War, the invasions of Iraq and Afghanistan. The murder of Rasputin in Petrograd, and fifty years later Martin Luther King in Memphis."

"Is there a connection?" someone said loudly.

But Gilbert persevered, through Fatty Arbuckle, Prohibition, the St. Valentine's Day Massacre, the Crash of '29, Pearl Harbor, Elvis, the Beatles, and the Internet.

"Mother's century can be called the greatest, most meaningful in history."

"The Renaissance was a blip compared to it," Floyd said.

"It was a century of modernization and great change," Gilbert said, batting away the interjections with his free hand. "But some things did not change — Mother's humanity, her kindness, her generosity, her love for her family. Ladies and gentlemen, let us raise a toast — to Mother."

"To Mother!" came the cry.

The celebrants crowded forward to congratulate Mother, to gush, to grope for her hands, to be remembered, to ask for her blessing.

The contrast between Mother and these people was remarkable. She did not resemble anyone else in the room. We were hairy, pale, misshapen. In a strange sense most of us looked older than Mother as we shuffled among the tables, bumping shoulders, stepping on each other's toes; we were fleshy and overgrown. Mother was smaller than ever, birdboned, bright-eyed, narrow-shouldered, physically unlike the others, in many respects healthier, with the old glow of the little yellow goddess, all of us murmuring our thanks and saying goodbye as if we were doomed and departing but Mother wasn't going anywhere.

We were broken, Mother was whole — that was apparent. At least half the people in the room were strangers to me, either relatives I'd never seen or heard about, or else distant acquaintances.

"Your mother is a marvel," one of them said, a middle-aged woman whose name rang no bells.

That was the chorus: Mother is amazing! Lordy, how does she do it? What a lovely family! And with my new detachment I began to think so too. It wasn't a question of forgiving transgressions or forgetting slights and hurts. These were irrelevant now. Mother had done her work; she had formed us, and therefore did not need to exert any power over us. She had what she wanted. Mother, who had no profound capacity for happiness, who was consistent in her ritual of telling us how we'd fallen short, seemed happier that day than I had ever seen her. Her satisfaction showed in her silence. She sat wordlessly acknowledging the praise of the partygoers, accepting their presents, quite formal, looking superior to everyone — indeed, most of those who approached her for her blessing looked fumbling and inadequate, needing her attention but not quite sure how to seize it. Mother perhaps suspected this uneasiness, and it gave her greater strength — power over them, over us.

She grew ever more regal at her table, now and then whispering to Gilbert or Fred. I knew from my time spent in Africa how the most powerful chiefs never spoke, never addressed a crowd, hardly uttered a sound — such talk was beneath them. All announcements were left to the *porte-parole*, the chief's spokesman at his elbow, word carrier and confidant, who would incline his head and listen, then speak for the chief in a voice of authority. The Chinese empress dowager Ci Xi did the same, whispering to a mandarin or a noble eunuch, who would convey the command, screeching to the Qing court.

In this strange manner, Mother, who had no sense of history and knew nothing of chiefs or kings, managed to contrive, through willpower and egotism, the pretenses of an empress.

Her intense gaze and her calculated silences impressed me, because I had become so used to her remarks, sometimes shrewd, sometimes cruel, always stinging. Her talk had once made my head hurt, and now she didn't talk at all. From that day onward, Mother, whose reputation for jawing — a word from her early youth — was well established, became known for saying nothing. And I soon realized that silence could be devastating — eloquent, unsettling, capable of inflicting long-lasting harm.

Mother, reflective and serene, triumphant, seemingly at peace, the center of attention at her hundredth, flanked by Gilbert and Fred and a hundred roses and a hundred cupcakes at a table piled with presents — feared, loved, forgiven, blameless, majestic — cue the organ recital, you think — but wait.

Something in the way the conflicted elements resolved themselves into the appearance of order seemed to nag and invite disharmony. The grandchildren were in a corner of the room, out of earshot. The feeling of rebellion was much greater than the wish of a child to poke a finger onto a surface marked with the sign *Wet Paint*. That was just a lark. This was more akin to rapping on the bars of a cage where the lions were asleep, snoring on their forepaws.

What was it? The birthday serenity, unbearable bliss, unfamiliar harmony, provoked its opposite, a kind of malice, none of it directed toward Mother — she was sacred now, above criticism, revered for her great age — but aimed at each other, the siblings at war.

"Look at Franny," Hubby said. "She sold your books on the Internet, the ones you signed for her." And when he saw that I was insufficiently riled, he added, "I don't think she got much for them."

"I understand you made some unwelcome suggestions to Hubby," Floyd said to me, and with his arm around Gloria, went on, "That, um, I might be the Unabomber. That is patently untrue, since the miscreant has been caught, while you seem a living example of why travelers have bad marriages."

Gloria looked at me with confusion — she was still new to this sniping — as Floyd turned to Rose, saying, "I notice Bingo has a dusky boyfriend. Do you find that every seventh of December he has an insatiable urge to bomb Pearl Bailey?"

In reply, Rose said to Gloria, "Does Floyd still wet the bed? Seems to me you'd be the first to know."

"Don't tell Jay anything," Franny said. "He'll just put it into a book."

"It'll be safe there," Rose said. "No one ever reads his frigging books." Before I could think of a rejoinder, she said, "Why are you so angry?"

Overhearing us, Fred said, "For Pete's sake, will you give it a rest?"

"Who put you in charge?" Hubby said.

Floyd had called Benno over and was saying to him, "Put your fingers in the corners of your mouth like this and say, 'I'm a banker.'"

Benno, who was afraid of Floyd's temper, did as he was told, grunting the words "I'm a wanker."

"Grow up," Gilbert said, and obviously worried that this ill humor would worsen, he lifted Mother to her feet and guided her to the door, as her well-wishers cheered her.

"Ass hat," Hubby said to Floyd.

"Monorhine," Floyd said. "Rump swab."

"You're all unbearable," Rose said.

"This is a nightmare," Franny said, but she was wearing a crooked smile.

"I think you'll find," Floyd said, "that the word is 'homeostasis.' Back to our old ways, our need for transgression and conflict, and loving every minute of it. Hey, like the ancient Greek. Goes to a tailor to get his pants mended. Tailor says, 'Euripides?' Guy says, 'Eumenides.'"

52

MEMENTO MORI

THE BIRTHDAY CELEBRATION OVER, the hundred cupcakes apportioned and dispersed, the hundred roses withered, we returned to our lives, satisfied that we were still at odds, reassured by the conflict, stung and eager to sting back. Elevated by the ritual of her hundredth, Mother was in a state of grace, while we remained sinners, unforgiving toward each other.

For all our quarreling and confrontation, the noises off, the slammed doors and muffled sighs, the insults and sudden departures, in this family of cruel exit lines, all-out war was avoided. Violence would have ended the misery with a vanquishing, bloodstained winner, and a loser licking his wounds. We preferred the messiness of skirmishing and sniping, no death blows, only the bruising and slaps of whispers and insults. And this occupied us to such an extent these days that Mother was forgotten.

In her silence, which gave the illusion of superiority — wisdom and dignity and remoteness — Mother was above the fray, her natural element. Now her work, her mischief, was complete. She could retire from it all, watch or listen if she cared to, or more likely indulge in one of her vitalizing hobbies — knitting, reading, doing crosswords — and contemplate her next birthday.

But having achieved one hundred, her next birthday was not a certainty. It is natural to assume that someone in her late nineties will attain one hundred, but after that, any more birthdays are pure speculation, so distant as to seem unlikely. Certainly we felt that way, assuming a finality in her century; that having gasped to the finish line in this long-distance race, she would not be going much farther.

She fortified that assumption, saying with greater assurance, "My bags are packed." And after a pause, "Are yours, Jay?"

I had no bags, I had no answer, though I sometimes felt: I can start again, meet someone, tell her my stories, encourage her ambitions, move to a better climate, perhaps have more children. Why not? I'm still a child of sorts, not old, my mother is alive. I have a mother! She was like an insurance policy guaranteeing that I would stay young, or at least youthful. Having a mother was a gift of hope. No, my bags were not packed. Mother was alive and strong — why should I think of death? Her very existence rid me of morbid thoughts.

Love, wife, child, and scribble-scribble — I could do it all again, another life, of the sort I had briefly contemplated in Mexico, encouraged by the smiling Trinidad family and willing Luma. Ending my days in a hut in a village, unobtainable and reclusive, seemed perfect. Perhaps a good career move, too, since no writer was in greater demand or the object of such intense publicity as the one who chose to vanish into obscurity. I could become famous for rejecting fame, as some shrewd writers did, attracting notice. *Lives in a remote part of Mexico*, had a nice ring to it. *Refuses interviews* would create buzz. This delusion buoyed my spirits as I worked on my book.

And so, again, we visited Mother less frequently. My once-a-week became once-a-month. Franny and Rose still dropped in most weekends, but often made excuses — they had family obligations, jobs, friends, and distractions, and they were old and frail. Fred was often ill — phlebitis, his eyes, migraines that gave him cramps. Floyd was occupied with Gloria, who, in the manner of a new wife, was rearranging his house, sorting his belongings, and evaluating the loyalty of his friends. She was the subject of most of his poems these days. Hubby, who had turned down the hospital's offer of a buyout, worked longer hours to boost savings. Gilbert was in Mazar-i-Sharif. And in my resolute and solitary way, working in the dark, doing what I could, fantasizing about my future, I was writing my novel about the man held captive in the village.

Floyd, on one of his visits to borrow a book, asked me why I was still writing.

I said, "To keep the wolf from the door."

He said, "So you read your book to the wolf?"

Mother seemed to accept our absences. She no longer clamored for our company or accused us of not calling her. She had Meals on Wheels, the daily visit that kept her in food and verified that she was alive. A despised weekly cleaner still showed up and developed a bantering relationship with her — Mother feeling superior because the woman let drop that she took daily pills, cueing Mother's "I'm not *awn* anything." Mother seemed as independent as ever, looked after herself, had her hair done, and got the occasional pedicure. Still writing checks, she kept her financial affairs a secret. Did she have money? We didn't know, but she now and then complained of being hard up, and that complaint is usually a sign of solvency and often great wealth.

She spoke on the phone, she could talk for hours, but even that was a form of silence, because it was repetitive — her days of stirring us were over. She no longer seemed malicious to me, and while a certain sanctimony had always served as a cover for her cruelty, I was now convinced of a definite late-life sweetness. She seemed grateful and at peace, and often complimentary.

"Lots of leg room," she said in my Jeep when I drove her to the supermarket, her tiny legs barely reaching the floor. She told me how proud she was of Julian and Harry and, fantasizing a little, described how she'd knitted baby clothes for Charlie in the weeks before Mona and I gave him away. The baby clothes were fictional; she'd been hard on me, as I have described; but she wished to create a rosy glow from that episode, and now I was well past blaming her for making me miserable. I claimed to Floyd that I was writing for money, but money was a negligible part of it: I wrote to give order to my life, I wrote to ease my mind, I wrote to forget.

"Gloria is good to Floyd," Mother said, and, "She sews, she cooks, she's an excellent painter." No irony, no bitterness. "I miss Dad," she said. He'd been dead for more than fifteen years. "He was good to me. He loved me. He had such a kind heart." Then a glance out the window. "The magnolias are in bloom" — it was May. "My favorite flower."

"How are you?" I'd ask in a call or a visit.

"No complaints."

Always a book in her hand or a newspaper in her lap, or a ball of yarn. She was sweeter, she was quieter — more silences. She was smaller, half the size she'd been at the time of Dad's death. These days — baffling to me — I was consoled by seeing her.

After a visit, I might get a call from Floyd or Rose: "I saw your Jeep at Ma's. Did she give you anything? Did you take anything?"

"Someone's sneaking food out of Ma's fridge," Hubby said to me. "Is it you?"

"Don't even think about getting Mumma's diamond engagement ring," Franny said. "She promised it to me."

"I paid for that grandfather clock," Floyd said. "It's a Seth Thomas chimer. I know my antique timepieces. I should winch it out of there before it gets stolen by the daughters."

Still the family growling, but in all this Mother was serene, growing ever smaller, her dusty glow deepening with sunset touches. I had trouble fitting this woman to the image of the fierce empress who had created such turbulence in the family.

On one of my visits I looked into her refrigerator to see whether any of it seemed plundered. Far from any diminishment, the thing was full, every shelf jammed with food and bottles and plastic containers. "Dog food, chanklings," Floyd had once said of the contents of the refrigerator. It was an accumulation of leftovers, graying meat and aging vegetables and softening fruit, cheese whiskery with mold, sour clotted milk, tubs of soup with stagnation on the surface in scummy disks.

"Are you eating all right, Ma?"

"When I'm hungry."

She spoke in a feeble whisper from her chair. And with only her reading lamp on, the rest of the parlor was in darkness.

"I could microwave you something — maybe heat up a can of soup."

"I had crackers for lunch."

"Crackers? Is that all?"

"With peanut butter."

"Ma, you've got to do better than that."

She smiled at me for nagging her. "You sound just like my mother."

That night I called Floyd. I told him I was worried about Mother.

"Worried!" He laughed so hard in a mirthless mocking way I had to lift the phone from my ear. "So you visited the holy of holies. What did you boost off the shelves?"

"Nothing. Look, she's skinny, she looks weak, she doesn't eat."

"It's me you're talking to, sonny!" he shouted. "Do you think for a minute that I've forgotten the sight of your prehensile fingers trawling through her gewgaws? What is this note of concern I hear that sounds so much like the braying of an ass?"

And he hung up.

Jeered at and abused by the others for visiting her, suspected of rifling her drawers or of soliciting favors — and the ones who'd gotten money from Mother in the past were the most suspicious — I now drove to Mother's in secret and, self-conscious, went less often. What did the others do? We had never shared confidences unless it was gossip, so I had no idea when they visited or whether they went at all.

My novel of the captive, a book about confinement and misguided intentions, began to catch fire. I worked on my kitchen table, among the breakfast breadcrumbs and the patches of sticky marmalade, –and I was exhilarated, because my writing lifted my spirits and dignified this simple place. It was no longer a shingled bungalow set on a slab in sand on a side road in Centerville, with a narrow bed, a creaking floor, a gummed-up microwave, and a screen door that slapped shut on the twang of its rusty spring. It was an abode of bliss where I sat with a pen in my hand, forming sentences in black ink on good paper, making something new, all my own, my secret, my hope, my joy. Absorbed in this, I took little notice of the small house or the cluttered table, except at the end of the workday, when I pushed my papers aside and thought, I am happy, feeling that the room, the whole house, was hallowed by this writing.

Without realizing it, in my contentment, I stayed away from Mother. We children took pride in believing we were different from one another — serious Fred, apostrophizing Floyd, practical Hubby, and the others, each distinct, even as a physical type — fat, thin, tall, short, bald, shaggy. But in Mother's post-century, her hundred and first year, we were alike in our thinking. I wasn't the only one who stayed away; the others did too, discovering as I had a measure of contentment in their solitude.

So it was a shock when I, and then the others, did visit her, seeing her afresh after many weeks, perhaps a month or more. It was like visiting a dying animal.

"Ma, are you all right?"

She lay canted sideways in her chair, her mouth half-open, her eyes glazed, her skinny hands in her lap, her fingers crooked and intertwined, as though she was clutching a dead bird or the fragment of an ossuary. I could not understand her whisper. I asked her to repeat it.

"No complaints."

But she was weak, she hardly moved, her tongue was green and gummy, she was dehydrated.

"I'll get you a drink of water."

The kitchen was tidy. Too clean; no one had cooked for days.

Mother lapped at the water like a spaniel while I held the glass, and she drank with difficulty, as if she was losing her swallowing reflex, as starving people do. I sat with her, making sure she finished the water, though she resisted.

"I'm fine," she said, but without conviction.

She wasn't fine. She seemed near death.

I called Hubby from her study, out of her hearing. I told him what I'd seen and asked him when he'd last visited Mother.

"I've been drywalling my basement," he said. "It looks fabulous." Like me, he'd discovered contentment in his own work. "And I've been working nights at the hospital. I figured you've been looking after Ma."

"I'm with her. She looks terrible. I don't think anyone's been visiting. Please come over, Hub. She needs help."

"Then help her, dick-wad."

"You have medical training. I don't."

"Probably needs electrolytes. No fried food, nothing heavy. There's Ensure in the fridge."

"You don't get it — she looks like she might be dying. Do something."

"What about Floyd?"

"I'll call him. I'm calling everyone. She needs attention. Jesus!"

I hung up. Approaching Mother from the study, I had the feeling, from her slack posture, that she had died. She lay against her chair, her head to one side, her greenish tongue slightly protruding.

"Ma?"

"What is it now?"

"I'm worried about you."

She did not say anything. She smiled a familiar lopsided smile of contempt.

"If you're so worried about me, why did you just show up today?" She hacked out one of her dry coughs, raising her hand as though to cover her mouth but not succeeding, only coughing onto the tips of her bony fingers. "How many weeks has it been?" And she coughed again, or maybe it was a bitter laugh. "So I bet dollars to donuts you're not all that worried."

I had no excuse. I did not try to think of one. I said, "I want to help."

"That's what everyone says. But they don't do anything."

"What can I do?"

"Leave me in peace."

"I'm afraid" — and here I chose my words carefully, I didn't want to mention death — "you'll get sick."

"It doesn't matter. No one cares."

"I care. We all care."

Her indignation seemed to give her strength, because in a mocking voice she said, "Then where has everyone been?" And she laughed, a choking noise that she spat out, nodding, "Remember? Everyone dies. I'm not special."

She had decided to die.

"What happened to that woman who was helping you?"

"Helping me? That's a laugh. I fired her. She was a dizzy blonde."

In the way that Mother had once decided to defy us with her sickness, and then rose again as a survivor, now, out of spite, she had set her mind on dying. In some folk societies people willed themselves to death. Followers of the Jain religion of India (those people who don't kill flies), hundreds of them every year, killed themselves, refusing all food in a ritual of starvation that helped them attain *moksha,* ultimate soul freedom. And it was just as common everywhere on earth for melancholics to expire in the same way, curling up in a ball, as Mother seemed to be doing.

Mother was alone, and from her resentful voice it was easy enough for her to take herself to the other side. It occurred to me that she was planning to starve herself, so that one of us would find her dead in her chair. It was not the bid for attention of some suicides, but a spiteful decision.

Seeing me sizing her up, frantic in my way, seemed to give her a little joy. *See what your neglect has done to me?* On the brink, slipping away, she seemed gladdened by my alarm.

A clattering at the door, the clump of work boots — Hubby, his arms whitened with plaster dust.

"You clown," he said. "Hi, Ma!"

"Another one," Mother said. "Which one are you?"

Hubby took her pulse, shone a small flashlight in her eyes, roved with his stethoscope. "She needs a drip. I'll set up an IV," he said. "You're going to be all right, Ma," he called out as he left the house, heading home for his equipment.

"What difference does it make?" Mother said with a grim smile, powerful even in this extreme moment.

She was our luck and our longevity. It was essential that she survive. She had to live, for our sake.

53

THE UNKNOWN

CRISES had always brought out the worst in us: Fred's stroke, Marvin's death, Floyd's gallbladder, Hubby's diabetes, any mention of hemorrhoids — jokes, gibes, wisecracks, whispers.

Were we softening? In the weeks after Mother's near-death experience, we clamored to visit her, taking turns, never meeting, often delivering food or flowers, a potted narcissus or the chocolate she loved, anything to keep her alive, to rekindle her interest in living. We feared losing her; we realized how close we'd come to her slipping away forever. Our greatest fear was contemplating life without her. Just as acute was the awful thought that we, her children, would have to deal with one another. Who were we without Mother as referee? We didn't know. We were reluctant to find out, and so we clung to Mother.

She knew this and, as usual, seemed way ahead of us. Extreme as her self-starvation was — shrinking to a wisp, apparently conscious that she was at death's door — it occurred to me that it was calculated. Mortifying her flesh in a devout fast, the famished Saint Thérèse (one of Mother's favorites), whose self-denial sent her into ecstasies, prayed before a ripe peach. In the following weeks, Mother received us individually, keeping the needle of Hubby's IV drip in her arm long after it was needed, as though impressing us with the wound it left, a sort of stigmata.

"They might have to put a gusset in my body," she said, "for me to be fed with a tube."

"Who told you that?"

"Hubby. It's a normal procedure in intensive care."

"Ma, you're not in intensive care."

"I almost was."

She said this with a stern smile of reproach.

Hubby said, "I never told her she needed a gusset. I said 'grommet.'

She asked me for the worst-case scenario. I hooked her to an IV. I got her rehydrated. And for this I get flak!"

To replace the cleaning woman who had been glad to go, we hired a Thai woman, Poon — mild, hardworking, two children. Mother took to her and treated her like a pet. Poon discovered Mother's fondness for jelly donuts, hot chocolate, and lobster bisque. For any favor of this kind, Mother gave Poon a dollar. The arrangement seemed perfect.

Poon had worked as a cleaner in a nursing home on the lower Cape, Arcadia, in Chatham. The experience had given her a hatred of such places.

"No send Mummy to a home," she said. "The people so roney. They say to me, 'Pease he'p me.' They faw down. They cry, 'I want to go home.'"

"Of course Poon's going to say that," Fred said. "She's protecting her job. She wants to keep this gig with Ma."

"Ma likes her."

"We need a backup plan. Arcadia could be part of it."

Fred sent one of his lawyerly memos to the rest of us with the subject heading "Options." In it he outlined the various courses of action: keep Poon as a helper, find a professional caregiver, put Mother in a place such as Arcadia, and more. It was a severe edict, set out in his usual long-winded way, with a section about doing nothing followed by a subsection suggesting action; a section acknowledging that Mother was unwilling to move to an old folks' home was followed by paragraphs describing how, by subterfuge, she might be persuaded. A "What if she falls?" section, undercut by a "What if she outlasts us?" section. A whole page was devoted to possible schedules for visits by us, by nurses, by dietitians, by the local police for their "Reassurance Program" — a once-a-day call from a concerned cop, to ask, "You okay?"

Mother was not okay, but would not admit it. A place like Arcadia was the answer — preliminary visits by her might ease her into agreeing to a room with a view — but Fred's memo, the dancing around Mother's stubbornness, indicated the futility of its options, because Mother, wasting away, with as yet no intention of moving, would continue to be an unsolvable problem.

Pages of this, and at the end Fred asked for our thoughts, but before anyone replied, he fired off a second memo, briefer than the first, explaining at length that he had several interactions with Arcadia's director. The place was clean, well run, not far away, and had a medical wing for residents who were ill, demented, or incapacitated. He urged us to see it for ourselves.

"They have," he wrote, "a weekly 'Chowder Day' for prospective clients."

Put off by the name, busy with my book, I avoided Chowder Day — free soup — and the get-acquainted tour of Arcadia. Let the others decide, I thought. I'd go on visiting Mother as often as I could at her house, where she seemed content with Poon, healthier than before, knitting and reading again, doing the daily crossword, and no longer hooked up to a drip.

"Have you heard what they want to do with me?" she said one day.

"I'm not sure what you mean."

She leaned forward and, with her teeth clenched for the emphasis of a dramatic hiss, said, "They want to stick me in a home."

"That place, Arcadia?"

"You know about it!"

"Fred mentioned it. I haven't seen it."

"But I have. Chowder Day." Mother made a face. But she was so small it was undefinable.

"Were they nice to you?"

"Of course they were. They want my money — although, God knows, I have very little," she added quickly. "They want me to sign up and move in." She called out "Poon!" and then coughed from the effort.

The Thai woman appeared at the bedroom door. "Yah?"

"Arcadia. Good or not good?"

"Not good," the woman said.

Mother said, "See?" And then, "All they did was smile."

Mother's suspicion of anyone who was overly pleasant verged on paranoia. Snakes might smile, but snakes were cruel too. Most people were snakes, which was why it was wise to stay in the security of your own home.

"They want me to leave all this!"

"All this" didn't look like much. The furniture was worn, the carpets were threadbare, the clutter on the coffee table dated from when Dad was alive. Mother refused to improve the house because she no longer owned it, and Franny did nothing because she didn't live there. The filled bookshelves may have given the illusion of scholarship and seriousness, but many were our old school textbooks or library discards, with stained covers and brittle pages mildewed by the Cape's humidity — sunned, as book dealers said; foxed, hinges loose, jackets torn, spines cocked. Nor had they ever been removed from the shelves and dusted, so, sitting in the red armchair near the shelves, I always found myself gagging, my skin prickling with the peculiarly irritating dust that accumulates on unread and browning books.

The kitchen was small, and it had its own family smell of Mother and stale bread — the same odor, really — the counters sticky to the touch. Mother in her frugality washed her own dishes in a plastic basin in the sink, though Poon might have been doing it these days. In the center of the kitchen table, in one of Dad's souvenir saucers (*The Old North Church, One if by land, two if by sea*), were the salt and pepper shakers, a jar of mustard, a bottle of ketchup, a jar of jam all bearded and crusted with residue, a small quiver of toothpicks, a button, and some paperclips.

And cushions, comforters, shawls, tissues: Mother's nest, penetrated by Mother's odor – the odor that met you like cobwebs draping your face as soon as you opened the front door.

"Don't let them do it to me, Jay," Mother said. "I'm happy here. Don't make me leave."

One family argument for putting Mother in a nursing home was that a fog of senility might be clouding her brain. Hubby found a list of standard questions in the files of the geriatric ward at the hospital and urged me to test Mother's clarity. When I visited, Mother was canted forward in her chair, absorbed in the crossword puzzle.

"Ma, what day of the week is it?"

"Monday," she said promptly, not looking up.

"You're sure?"

"Do you think they'd print the wrong day in the newspaper?" she said, tapping her finger on the page.

"What year is it?"

Now she raised her head and straightened her glasses to see me better. "Nineteen forty-nine," she said with solemnity she held whirring in her nose.

"Who is the president?"

"Harry Truman, who else?"

"Are you sure it's nineteen forty-nine?"

"It is always nineteen forty-nine in my heart. The year I was pregnant with Angela. I was young and hopeful. Not like now."

"By 'now' do you mean a different year?"

"Of course." She rapped her pen against the crossword puzzle in annoyance. "Are you trying to confuse me?"

"One more question. You have $100 and you go to the store to buy a dozen apples for $3 and a tricycle for $20."

She stared at me, tilting her head, with a crooked smile, and flattened the newspaper on her lap.

"How much did you spend? How much do you have left?"

I had leaned toward her to dramatize my sympathy. She laughed in my face, her first real mirth in ages. "Show me a store where I can get apples for three dollars and a bike for twenty and I'm doing my Christmas shopping there."

I sat back and watched her resume the puzzle.

"Hawaiian goose," she said, reading a clue. "Nene. Everyone knows that."

Mother's fear of the unknown—of darkness, of strangers, of foreign travel, of odd food, of the uncertainty that lay outside the family—all this had its counterpart in the mud villages where I'd lived in the Malawi bush, in the hearts of the people I'd met in Borneo and upper Burma, and elsewhere: among the frizzy-haired Trobrianders, the Big Nambas on the island of Malekula in Vanuatu, the Asaro Mudmen of Goroka, and the tobacco-chewing peckerwoods of the Ozarks, for whom the unknown was a fearful void and a darkness, like stepping into a deep hole.

We're savages, Floyd continually said of us, swearing that every trait of the family had its origin in peasant misery and folk superstition, our ancestors' brutishness. We were near to the soil and the blood feuds of our barbarian relatives.

He proved this assertion with details from our daily lives, describing how any of us could easily fit into a painting of peasant life by a Dutch realist who specialized in wooden clogs and codpieces. We were potato eaters, we were dumb bumpkins dazzled by natural phenomena, we were clumsy, unlettered, natural-born menials, indecisive, doomed to peonage and passivity. "Think of the feral child raised by a wolfhound," Floyd said. "He's doggy and drooly but somehow manages to get into Harvard, where he excels. But on graduation day his attention is seized by a passing car, and he dies chasing it."

It seemed to me that Mother's fear was justified. Never mind Floyd's flights of fancy and his mockery. Humankind is united in its fear of the unknown.

This fear had made her the matriarch of Mother Land, kept her home, motivated her to gather her children around her, created (you might say) the stable conditions for what passed for a common culture in the family — our characteristic sayings, our soapy food, our improvisational rules and reactions. No guests, no friends, ever felt at home in Mother Land: as soon as they entered they were bewildered, as though having stumbled into barbarism. They did not understand us, nor did they sense any familiarity with anything they saw or heard. I remember the look of astonished fear on the face of my friend John Brodie being served a bowl of Mother's pea soup, so thick a mouse could have trotted across it. He stuck his spoon into it and lifted a dollop but did not taste it; he did not recognize it as food. I was embarrassed: he had glimpsed one of our secrets. Yet Brodie and these other strangers, too, probably feared the unknown themselves and might not have been different from us in that respect. As for Mother, she would have needed a tribal purgation to overcome the fear.

I did not share this dread. To me, the unknown held helpful possibilities and offered hope. I believed this from an early age when I read the books I loved most, of African travel and polar exploration — Clyde Beatty, Admiral Byrd, Allan Quatermain, Frank Buck (*Bring 'Em Back Alive*) — up the Amazon, down the Nile, across the Sahara, climbers of Everest, bushwhackers in the outback. I did not know the word at the time, but what I was seeking, and what I imagined the unknown might grant me, was transformation. From my earliest years I wanted to go away. I equated travel with salvation. Darkness was not to be feared: it offered a second chance.

What had made Mother a shut-in had made me a traveler.

Don't let them do it to me, rang in my head. *Don't let them send me away.*

The plea of the Choctaw in Mississippi just before the Trail of Tears, the lament of the Jew in the shtetl hearing the train whistle and the clatter of jackboots, the whisper of a dissident in Stalin's Russia, dreading a possible fate in the frozen prison settlement in Siberian Magadan.

So I became Mother's protector. I visited her more often. Relations with my brothers and sisters were chilly, but we were happier not seeing each other, and I was too absorbed in my novel to have any time for them. Being midway through a novel was like treading along a high wire, a balancing act that would end in a fall if I was disturbed. I phoned Mother, I dropped in with food, and I noticed—from crumbs, from scraps, from left-behind hats and gloves—that the others did the same.

But more and more, Mother neglected to pick up the phone. And when, out of concern, I went over to make sure she was not dead, I found she was gone, the house locked. I smiled to think she locked a house she'd given away, from which everything valuable except the grandfather clock had been either handed out or stolen. But, anyway, where was she?

And then, one Tuesday, unable to raise her by phone, I remembered that the same had been true the previous Tuesday.

"I couldn't find you yesterday," I said the next day.

"I was out."

"Anywhere special?"

"With Fred."

"As long as you're being looked after—that's the main thing," I said, taking her hand, clutching the bird claw. "I won't let them send you away."

"I often consult Angela," Mother said. "Have you brought me a present?"

And that was that. The following Tuesday I called, got no answer, and went to the house. Maybe she was ill? Maybe out? Maybe dead? Maybe she'd gone somewhere with Fred, and if so, where?

Waiting on Mother's front steps on this damp late afternoon, the clouds thickening in the mottled sky, idly grinding sand against the brick walkway with my foot soles, my forearms resting on my knees, I felt like a latchkey child, killing time, humming tunelessly, wondering where his mother might be—a sad, anxious, neglected child on a gray day. How long will he have to wait? What will become of him? Where is his mother? Shouldn't we do something about him?

I was not a sixty-something author who'd left his desk and the scattered pages of his manuscript. I was a little boy crouched by his mother's front door. I enjoyed wallowing in the self-pity for a while, feeling small and forlorn. And then I heard a car.

It was a new Prius, one I didn't recognize. Gliding up behind my old Jeep, it looked like a boast.

"Candy-ass." Floyd, in a leather bomber jacket and a Red Sox cap, climbed from the car, still talking.

I regretted having lingered. I didn't want to see anyone, and certainly not my siblings. I hated looking idle. But if I bolted now, Floyd would jeer even more.

"Where's your mother?" he said.

"No idea. I called her but she didn't answer, so I got worried and came over."

"*'Hypocrite lecteur, mon semblable, mon frère!'*"

"You took the words out of my mouth."

"I see you failed to bring her a present." Saying this, he plucked a box of chocolates out of his jacket and wagged it at me as a taunt. He could see I was empty-handed.

"Will those bonbons make up for all you've stolen from her?"

"Hah! Look who's talking — Autolycus, the snapper-up of unconsidered trifles." He kicked a wet clump of dead leaves.

"Let's talk about the weather."

"The weather?" he said, putting his face close to mine.

"Why not? It's a gray day, a lowering sky."

"I hate it when people tell me what sort of a day it is."

"What would you say?"

"I would say" — and he straightened and sniffed the air — "obnubilate."

For all his faults, Floyd was capable of spontaneous comic turns. I did not love him, I did not even like him, and yet I admired his nimble brain. He was still able to amuse me — certainly the only one in the family who could do it, and one of the few people I knew, tailoring his wit to order, for me alone, either a gesture or a single word.

There is no reply to "obnubilate." Floyd knew that, smacking his lips, savoring his victory.

Just then, a car — this I recognized as Fred's, a Chevy Blazer, his license plate SUE EM — and Mother in the front seat, looking like a small girl. Floyd and I watched as Fred hurried to the passenger side and helped her out. He guided the small, pale, shuffling woman up the brick walkway.

Mother looked furtive and oppressed, the effect of being in the presence of her three eldest children. She was our mother, but she was a different mother to each of us, and this gathering provoked confusion of the kind experienced by someone with multiple identities surprised by three witnesses. It was as though she'd been caught in a lie.

"What a nice surprise," Mother said, and I was convinced of her dismay.

"I was worried about you," I said.

"Don't be silly," she said.

She lifted her shoes and kicked with them, a clockwork way of walking that involved toppling forward and jerking upright just in time.

"Cute hat," Fred said to Floyd.

"The only known cure for baldness," Floyd said. "Such a simple expedient would surely benefit you."

Mother said, "Be nice."

The hundred-year-old woman, her three aged boys, her shadowy house, the dark day of tumbling furry clouds, the twisted pitch pines — all the elements of a folktale, including the sinister command *Be nice*.

This wolfish woman saying that to her three snarling cubs made me laugh out loud. Mother took this to be friendly mirth and smiled, extending her bird claw. I helped her up her front stairs.

"Where have you been?"

"For a ride," Mother said coyly, and poked at the keyhole with her latchkey. Then, with a half-turn toward us, she made a face.

There was a century of family history in that face. An essay could have been written about the subtlety of its meanings, like the ambiguous smile floating on the lips of a Khmer goddess at Angkor Wat. It was mockery, it was interrogation, it was doubt, it was defiance.

"Chowder Day," Fred said.

54

ARCADIA

MOTHER'S WAY OF KEEPING A SECRET was to tell it to one person at a time; disclosing a confidence sequentially was to her the utmost in tact. That's what we believed. Mother talked, she often gossiped, we thought she was the soul of indiscretion. Distracted by her whispers and disclosures, we did not imagine that there was anything she kept to herself. But there was much we didn't know, that she didn't tell, that no one would ever fathom.

For weeks she had been visiting Arcadia covertly, always on Chowder Day — free food, a grateful welcome, the staff beseeching her to move in. She usually went there with Fred, who practiced Mother's habit of selective disclosure.

"Why didn't you tell me you've been spending so much time with Mum at Arcadia?"

"You didn't ask."

A lawyer's reply, because in the world of lawyers you volunteer nothing. You say, "I wasn't home." You avoided saying, "I wasn't home because I was getting free chowder at Arcadia in Chatham." Fred himself had taught me that.

Though Mother had said nothing to anyone else about these visits — we had the impression she was isolated and slowly starving herself to death — it seemed she enjoyed the outings well enough to repeat them week after week. Her fears of the unknown were allayed by her eagerness for complimentary meals, as the Ohlendorfs had found by taking Mother to the Brazilian restaurant and setting the "gauchos" in motion.

"They wanted to hear all about my father," she said of Arcadia. "They couldn't believe my memory, that I was able to recite all my teachers' names. They were so sorry to hear about Angela. I did the crossword after lunch. They watched me with their mouths open."

Mother had discovered what many of us find by leaving the house: the joys of meeting new people, to whom you can relate your fund of stories — fascinating tales when told the first time. You think you've cast a spell. But in such a courtship, the strong person, the dominant one, the charmer, is not the teller but the listener.

"They loved my shawl. I said, 'Oh, that old thing. I knitted it myself.' 'You still remember cable stitch?' they said. They were bowled over."

Mother was fingering a small wooden carving as she told me this, a gray and yellow bird with a longish tail and some white markings.

"Next time I'll be sure to bring this along. When I tell them I carved it myself they'll be astonished." She held it for me to examine. "A phoebe, also called a flycatcher. I read up on them. They're seasonal here. They migrate from faraway south to lay their eggs and hatch their young on the Cape. Go on, hold it. I sanded and painted it myself. When the little birds can fly, they all move on."

I held the beaky bird. It stared at me with the glowing pellets of its eyes.

"I should move on," Mother said.

"You mean to Arcadia?"

"I don't know," she said, startled — she knew she'd given away too much.

"Won't you miss your house?"

"This is Franny's house."

"What about your friends?"

"All my friends are dead." She became thoughtful, her face puzzled and pinched in reflection, that same expression she wore when she smelled something she could not name. Then, in solemn bewilderment, she remembered. "A man at Arcadia said he'd read a book by you."

"Which one?"

"He was in a wheelchair. He coughed a lot."

"Which book, I mean?"

"How would I know?"

"Anyway, that's nice."

She wasn't so sure. She said, "He asked me if I was your mother."

"What did you tell him?"

She stared at me. She said, "I can't remember."

· · ·

Mother's Chowder Day visits continued through the summer, but with fall and the first sign of leaves turning, a nip in the air at evening, the foretaste of cold days and early darkness, Mother moved into Arcadia.

In the stark simplicity of her small apartment — bedroom, sitting room, bathroom, kitchenette — Mother acquired a dignity that she had lost in the gloom and ambiguous odors of her house. She was released from everything she'd given away, the place she no longer owned. She brought some clothes, her knitting in a basket, family photographs, a picture she'd painted — sand dune, sailboat in the distance, gull in the blue sky — some religious paraphernalia, not much else. Oh, yes, a loud clock. She'd whittled her possessions down to what she'd brought with her, but the defining piece of furniture was her throne-like chair of old — well worn but impressively so, the leather distressed and rubbed to softness, the brass tack-heads with a reddish patina, the wood darkened with age. Shuffling to the chair, Mother was elderly and uncertain; seated in it, she was an intimidating figure, someone to whom you told the truth.

Seeing her in her small suite for the first time, I expected to find her disoriented and homesick. *Take me home, Jay.* But she was calmer than I'd seen her in years, in her big wing chair with a newspaper open to the puzzle page — the crossword, the Jumble, the quiz — and on the table before her the loud clock reminding her that her time was running out. There was a contemplative narcissus blossom in a flute-like vase, a jar of peanut butter, and a calendar where Mother wrote in her careful block letters the names of her visitors, Arcadia events (CONCERT, MOVIE), meals she'd had, the weather she could see from her window, her usual sort of sea captain's logbook.

"It's like a hotel."

But Mother had seen few hotels. Arcadia was more like a ship — a cruise ship on a peaceful sea where all the crew wore white uniforms and white shoes. The staterooms gave onto a long corridor, the galley below; a gong was rung to signal mealtimes; the whole of it seeming to plow through rain and wind and sunshine, though that was the illusion of the weather moving past it. Mealtime was like mealtime on a cruise ship, the diners obeying the gong and taking up their places at familiar tables, greeted by waiters who knew their tastes. Then the talk of "There's a movie in the lounge tonight," "There's a party this weekend," and when the van pulled up in the morning to take the few energetic ones into Chatham for shopping, it was like they were going ashore.

I discovered this because I joined Mother for dinner on my first visit. She approved of the food: fruit cup, Salisbury steak with mashed potatoes and green beans, Jell-O for dessert.

Two women sat with us — neither as old as Mother, probably mid-eighties — and introduced themselves as Mrs. Nickerson and Mrs. Wragby.

"This is my son Jay."

"What work did you used to do, Jay?"

"I used to be a writer."

They accepted this without further question. They told their stories: both from Boston originally, moved to the Cape when their husbands retired, then their husbands died, now Arcadia.

"You'll be joining us at some point in the not-too-distant future, I imagine," Mrs. Nickerson said.

"I don't think so," I said. "I have other plans."

"It's like a hotel," Mrs. Wragby said.

"No offense, but I'm not that fond of hotels," I said.

In the silence that followed, Mother said with a certain pride, "I was born here on the Cape."

"It must have been so different then."

"The train went to Truro," Mother said. "When World War One ended they rang the bell at my school."

Now the women stared. Mrs. Wragby said, "That would make you —?"

"One hundred and one," Mother said, and shivered with pleasure, then looked for a reaction.

"Mae Kibby is a hundred and one," Mrs. Nickerson said.

"I think Grace Almond is a hundred and two."

Mother moved her mouth slowly, in silence, chewing her disappointment, looking determined.

Back at her apartment, I said, "You've adjusted so well and so quickly. Good for you."

"Angela has been a great help," Mother said in a confiding voice.

Of course, the long-dead child a greater source of comfort than the seven surviving children. I said, "That's great," but no more. Why amplify her delusion with further questions?

Leaving that day, I bumped into Floyd at the front door. Like me, he was making his first visit, accompanied by Gloria.

"*Et in Arcadia Ego,*" he said as a greeting. "Source?"

"I think you're looking for Waugh. *Brideshead.*"

"The obvious middlebrow reply. What I had in mind was the ambiguous painting by Nicolas Poussin in which the enigmatic *ego* might — who knows? — refer to death speaking."

Gloria said, "Guercino did one as well. Baroque."

"Clever girl," Floyd said. "Jay is overwhelmed, punching above his weight with that reference to Waugh."

I said, "Mum thinks that Angela is here. That's why she likes it."

"Leave her to her delusions. They can be life-enhancing for some of us."

"Not me, thanks very much."

"You have Jell-O in the corners of your mouth. Two demerits."

And with Gloria on his arm he pushed past me.

Arcadia's main building, baronial by the standards of Cape Cod, lay behind a high perimeter wall, so all you could see from the road was its rooftops and its parapet. Approaching it by Pleasant Bay Road from the Mid-Cape Highway, you passed stands of pitch pine and scrub oak and twisted cherry trees stunted by the sandy hillock and salt wind. The winding road was bleak, here and there a cottage of weather-whitened shingles, a broken fence, a cranberry bog looking drowned, scraped flat by the recent harvest. Mother must have seen all this with a sinking heart.

But once past the spiked swinging gate of Arcadia the season seemed to turn. The ingenious gardeners had planted evergreens — holly trees, yews, blue spruce — and laid a formal driveway to the front door that was a boulevard, lined by a colonnade of tall, wide-hipped arborvitae, the whole green garden looking hopeful and edible. Rhododendrons are never without buds; a whole wall of them lined the walkway and ivy had jumped to the façade of Arcadia's main building. The grass was ankle-deep and dark green — well fertilized, neatly cut, no sign of grubs. The box hedge and the feathery junipers were thick, every shrub dense with sprays of needles. So the whole effect, even on a cold day in late fall, was of lushness and abundance, a great verdant salad swelling against the red brick walls, a garden all the more welcoming for looking like a healthy meal, no suggestion of death or decline.

This vitality was an illusion on the withered autumnal Cape, a trick of landscaping, but it worked. Healthy evergreens and fat bushes were an encouragement. When I visited, I felt Mother was in good hands. She seemed strengthened by the greenery too, and the attention she was getting. She sat straighter, she was more active, she had a dignity and self-possession I'd rarely seen in her before. Away from the mouse-nibbled carpets and dusty shelves and the glum, sticky kitchen of her old house, she looked haughty in Arcadia, regaining the dusty glow of immortality I'd noticed when she turned one hundred, the goddess aura, like a gold mist behind her head.

The third time I visited, a woman blocked my way.

"Can I help you?" she said, placing her pear shape and sloping stomach between the entrance and me, as though I was a tramp, sneaking in to get warm.

"No thanks," I said. "I know where I'm going."

"Do you have an appointment?"

"An appointment? To see my mother?"

"You'll need to sign in," she said. "The receptionist's on break."

"And you are — who?"

"I'm the life enrichment director. There's an event in progress. You'll have to wait."

In the lounge, which smelled of human decrepitude, I read a copy of *Modern Maturity*, listened to the tick of a clock and the muffled sounds of the event, which (I saw from a poster propped on an easel) was a slide-show lecture on the shore birds of Cape Cod.

"I told them all about the flycatcher," Mother said afterward. "I showed them the one I carved. They said, 'Did you do this all yourself?'"

She seemed uncommonly chipper. I said, "Do they have these afternoon events very often?"

We were now in the elevator. Even so, Mother whispered, her hand to her face, a bird claw against her cheek.

"They hold them to take our minds off things." She made a knowing face, widening her eyes and nodding slowly.

"What things?"

With a pained expression, Mother said, "Mae Kibby passed away yesterday, God rest her soul. It's a blow. We all feel it."

But at once she lost her look of anguish and became serene, stood straighter, blinked at the pinger signaling that we'd come to her floor, and faced the doors grinding open.

"That makes you the oldest resident," I said.

"Not yet. Grace Almond is a hundred and two," she said. She turned and squinted at me. "But she's not at all well."

Within a month Grace Almond had passed away. Another event (barbershop quartet) was held to cheer up the residents, and Mother took her place as the oldest person at Arcadia, a position she held with pride, enjoying the attention, affecting quiet humility and restraint that was overwhelmed by her vanity.

On my next visit, the fourth in four weeks, I was entering the elevator when I was summoned back by a woman leaning out of the sliding glass partition at the reception counter. Pinching her glasses to get a better look at me, she seemed vigilant and rather stern.

"Are you making a delivery?"

That's how I looked on this December day in my old coat and fedora and muddy shoes, like a deliveryman.

"Yes, I am," and showed her the bunch of flowers I'd brought Mother.

"We were expecting some paper products."

"I'm visiting someone."

"You need to sign in." She tapped the open visitors' book.

"Really?"

"Everyone who sets foot on the campus needs to sign in. It's the rule."

The campus? And the protocol, the suggestion that seeing Mother was in the nature of an appointment — Name, Destination, Make of Car, Plate Number, Time In, Time Out. At Mother's house we'd dropped in at all hours, seldom knocking, kicking the sand off our shoes at the threshold. *Hi, Ma!*

"What suite?" the woman said, seeing I'd left that column blank.

"Two-two-eight."

"Is she expecting you?"

"She's my mother." And when the woman continued to stare, I added, "She's always expecting me."

I remarked on the signing-in ritual to Mother, who said, "You can't be too careful."

"How are you?"

"No complaints."

Mother looked more brittle and bird-boned than ever, yet she glowed with certainty and, even bird-boned, looked unbreakable. Was it an effect of the passing of the other centenarians, Mae Kibby and Grace Almond, that Mother was now the oldest resident, at almost one hundred and two? The eldest, as a tribe would assess her, and therefore the wisest, the most privileged, the *mkazi wamkulu,* as we said long ago in Nyasaland, the Senior Woman. It seemed tactless to ask.

"Health and Wellness," I said, reading from the day's schedule of events.

"I never go to those things."

Still reading, I said, "Stress Management, and Coping and Relaxation Strategies."

"I've never been stressed. The Wall Street crash was hard for some, but I had a job, unlike other people — Harvard graduates selling apples on the street. I was a schoolteacher." She thought a moment. "Pearl Harbor. The Cocoanut Grove fire in Boston. The year I slipped on the ice and got an abscess on my elbow. I cope all right. I go to sleep as soon as my head hits the pillow."

"Maybe sometimes, some relaxation strategies?"

"Maybe when I'm older."

"So what do you do all day?"

"This," Mother said, and indicated the folded-over *Cape Cod Times* and the crossword puzzle she had mostly filled in, "and my knitting. And my reading. Once a week I do memoir writing."

"That's wonderful, Ma."

"Look to your laurels."

"What are you writing about?"

"All the things I've seen."

I stayed awhile, sitting on a straight-backed chair, facing her, as though I was being interviewed. Yet even physically close to me, Mother seemed distant, secure in this new setting, looked after by the efficient and good-natured staff. She was proof that Arcadia was a life enhancer, a life extender. The staff valued her as the eldest, someone special, and put her in a mood that bordered on the majestic, but neutralized, in exile from Mother Land.

I tried to see Mother as the people at Arcadia saw her. They were somewhat at a disadvantage, having missed her first hundred years — the years that had tested her, the years of struggle and rivalry, of secrecy, of turbulent children, of her widowhood and queenship, her battling plotters and choosing sides, of whispers, the years of court intrigues, a century of rehearsal for this.

She'd been whittled small and quieted, and in the glare of sunlight from the window next to her desk she was sometimes almost translucent — spare, reduced, skeletal, her head hardly a head, more a skull with tufts of hair on its tightened scalp. Her fingers were narrow bones and slow to grasp, but they were sure, in the block letters she habitually formed. Only her handwriting — bold, clear — was unchanged; everything else about her was new.

All these old selves burned away! That history was over, and Mother the battler was overtaken by this sweet aged woman. I had inwardly raged at how she had treated me long ago, but this was a mild and saintly being who meant it when she said, "No complaints," strangely grateful yet self-possessed enough not to cling when I said I had to go.

She'd always hovered at the periphery of my life, as part of my routine, a thought bubble over her head: *What are you going to do with me?*

That was no longer the case. She had removed herself to Arcadia. The question of how Mother was paying for it had yet to arise. Fred had told Hubby, in confidence, that Mother had plenty of money socked away in money market accounts and mutual funds — and Hubby told everyone. Mother was still writing checks. She didn't need us any longer except for the occasional visit as a diversion. But we needed her more than ever, because we, her children, were fearful of each other, afraid of what would become of us.

At Arcadia we were subjected to the scrutiny of the jowly woman at the reception desk, who one day took pleasure in telling me, "Your mother says she's not to be disturbed."

"I'll just be a minute."

"She says that she's busy with Angela."

Even the staff, groveling to please their senior resident, were conniving with Mother in her delusion.

Mother's mentions of Angela became more frequent.

"Angela just left."

"Angela is so good to me."

"What would I do without my angel?"

Leave her to her delusions, Floyd had said. *They can be life-enhancing for some of us.*

And soon she turned one hundred and two, and became like a saint with a serene face, like the plaster Madonnas that were carried in festivals in Boston through adoring crowds. In my youth we mocked the Italians in the North End who howled and blessed themselves and pinned dollar bills and gold bangles and necklaces to the images of the Madonna delle Grazie or Saint Rocco or Saint Joe that were paraded through the streets until these big painted dolls were cloaked in money and tinkling jewelry. All the while the brass band played, and the Italians wept and prayed. Now it had come to that: Mother was the idol, we were the venerators.

We took turns pushing her from her apartment to the elevator, down one floor to the lobby, and out the French doors into the garden, and all that way like a royal progress Mother was greeted by everyone she passed, their faces brightening when they saw her, because now, as the oldest person in the place, her survival and continued good health gave them hope.

Despite her poor eyesight and deafness, exiled in a contracted world of sight and sound, she was aware of their fascination, and she lifted her skinny hand like a regent in a sedan chair, acknowledging the salutations of her loyal subjects, giving her an air both pompous and aloof that enlarged her presence.

Yet she was still shrinking, very tiny now. Her small size gave her a greater glow, and that, too, added to her look of divinity, as if she'd been successfully transformed into a life-size image of herself, carved out of old ivory.

On other days, in poor light, she looked mummified, like an upright feature of a catacomb. Or, beaky and bony, like a prehistoric bird, a giant moa, a vast, flesh-colored sparrow.

Now and then, she asked for a meal at the Oyster Bed, and she was wheeled through the restaurant like a patron saint. She could still manage a dozen oysters, sometimes more. But except for that, and the wheelchair rides at Arcadia, there were no events for her. She preferred to sit at the table in her room, poking at papers. And we visited, always in a spirit of veneration, the more so because she seldom moved, was always upright in her customary chair, not the fierce empress on the throne that had disparaged me and made mischief and divided her children, but a solemn skeletal relic, awaiting her anxious visitors, often with a crooked smile that seemed to gloat, *Still here, still here,* as though to imply, *I will outlast you.*

"I don't know anyone my age," Mother said, partly in wonderment, partly as a boast.

She seemed to suggest that she was the oldest woman in the world, a belief that gave her immense power and commanded respect — the witness to more than a century of human folly and achievement, as though she had personally influenced events: war, progress, death.

We were her aged children, too preoccupied with looking after her to quarrel anymore, sometimes jostling for her attention, but usually taking turns, baffled that on her way to one hundred and three she was still alive, still at the center of everything, allowing us to cling to our childhood.

A believer in the significance of milestones, superstitious, guided by omens and signs — though always thanking God for granting them to her — she was convinced that, having passed the century mark, she would continue, liberated by this big number. And so it happened: one hundred and one had been unremarkable — a small cake; one hundred and two was expected — balloons, ice cream; and each new death at Arcadia seemed to suffuse Mother with a new vitality. She was once again the survivor and seemed to draw strength from the other oldies, all of them younger than she. Someone had to live, and it seemed the lucky person was Mother.

55

CLAMBAKE

EVERY VISIT to an aged parent is in the nature of a farewell. When I got the invitation to the clambake at Arcadia, I thought: Is this a good idea? In the meantime, I looked for solace by the sea near my house. Another winter, alone again, early darkness and cold like a wet hand on my face; wind gusts against the dark ocean smacking clumps of whiteness on its greasy surface and flattening the feathers of the gulls squatting beak-first into the wind with shortened necks. Yellow bubbles in the fluffy ribs of speckled sea foam by the dumping waves.

My hands jammed into my pockets, I kicked through the tide wrack of tangled rope and slimy kelp, looking for a sign. Was there a message here for me? What are the waves saying? I searched for omens everywhere. Maybe I'd find a note in a bottle, a tumbled box of treasure, or a waterproof package of cocaine—street value immense—tossed from a passing drug boat.

I saw decay and death: broken clamshells, crushed crabs, shards of quahogs, bleached fish bones, bitten corncobs and lobster claws, salty withered tissue that was once oyster bellies, and masses of ugly indestructible plastic, all of it like the remnants of a long-ago clambake. The beach in winter seems to tell a story out of scattered objects: you don't matter, you're not missed, you've been marooned, no one's looking for you—a vision of ruins, the blighted coast of Mother Land.

We were old, Mother was ageless. She might last forever, I thought. She was past one hundred and two. She might go at any moment. She might have just died.

My solitary walks were a melancholy foretaste of Mother's passing. What to do? Whom to call? I drifted back to my old stabilizer, my only sanity—my desk, which was the kitchen table, and my writing. Mother's hen-like face now and then appeared before me, to utter the subtext to every family failing. *It's your own goddamned fault.* And what had been a squawk was now a hiss.

Often I circled back to Arcadia, less for Mother's sake than my own. Each time I approached her apartment I wondered, Is she still here?

She always was, in her chair, crouched over a puzzle or a book, a pen pinched in her fingers — alive, alert, motionless, then seeing me and asking, "Who is it?"

"Just me."

"Angela, is that you?"

I let it pass.

"What is your greatest regret?" I wanted to ask her, but could not bring myself to say the words. It was too intimate a question, and when in my life had I been on intimate terms with Mother? I had never known the back-and-forth of easy talk and slow disclosure, never had a conversation — spiky dialogues didn't count. Talk with Mother had always been a battle to be heard, as it was with the rest of the family, expostulation, not listening and replying, but incessant shouts and whispers.

More and more on my visits to Arcadia I saw the same young woman attending to Mother, delivering a dinner tray — Mother preferred room service — or emptying a wastebasket, sometimes on her haunches, massaging Mother's feet or snipping her yellow toenails, always smiling at me when I said hello, and then she would withdraw, perhaps out of tact, to allow mother and son their privacy. I would have liked to talk to the young woman for the novelty of an actual chat. Feeling thwarted, the young woman slipping away, I thought with horror, God help me, am I that lonely?

"This is Angela," Mother said one day. The young woman was making the bed and couldn't drop it and go. "Angela, this is my son Jay."

I said, "Really?" And to the woman, "Are you Angela?"

She looked at me shyly. "Yes. Thank you. I finish now."

So there was such a person.

"*Buenos días, señorita.*"

She glowed with the greeting, smiling in relief.

"*Gracias por ayudar a mi madre,*" I said. "*Usted es realmente un ángel de la misericordia.*"

"*Su madre es un ángel. Mi querida.*"

"*Dónde está su madre ahora?*"

"*A su casa, en México, en mi pueblo.*"

"What are you saying?" Mother said, sounding peevish. "I don't understand."

"I tell him my mother in Mexico," Angela said.

Mother laughed. "I'm your mother."

"Yes," Angela said, tucking in the sheets, plumping Mother's pillows. "You my mother now."

Angela was small, smooth-faced, with dark, Asiatic eyes above her high cheekbones, full lips, beautiful teeth, and thick black hair drawn tight with a red headband. Even in her loose green uniform I could see she had a good figure, but a slight one, and in all her movements there was willingness and grace. I loved her slender legs and small feet, her subtle, simian way of pawing from one side of the bed to the other when she was straightening the sheets.

"Okay — madam," she said to Mother. "You need anything, please call."

"I need a kiss, Angela," Mother said.

"Of course," and she bent toward Mother, hugged her, kissed her head, an act of such extraordinary affection, almost unprecedented in our family, I watched with rapt attention.

Don't go, I thought.

"You coming to the clambake?" she asked me.

"*Tal vez,*" I said. Perhaps.

"It make you mother so happy," she said, and with a little bow she was gone.

Nothing for years, and then, like that, a flicker of desire, a reminder that you're a man, and the further reminder that with desire and a glow of hope there is always struggle and sadness, the complication of someone else.

"She's good as gold," Mother said. "I hope you didn't bring me anything. I don't need anything."

We talked for perhaps five minutes. These days, Mother had no memory of time passing. I said, "I think I should go."

I had seen Angela pushing a food cart past Mother's door.

"Be good," Mother said.

Angela was waiting by the elevator, another smile. "I like you mother so much."

"I worry about her," I said. "Can I have your cell phone number? That way, you can tell me how she is when I'm not able to be here, and then I won't worry."

Peering down at her face, I saw the length of her eyelashes, silken, up-swept, a smear of lipstick on her cheek, a freshness in her face, her small fingers manipulating the buttons on the phone. It was not just desire; it was the obvious thought that she was a better person than me, nor was she that young — mid-thirties, maybe more, not a youthful raver but a sensible woman.

"She talk about the clambake. She like the *ostras.* You say *ostras*?"

"Oysters," I said, loving the wetness of her lips and tongue.

I returned the next day, less to see Mother than to get a glimpse of Angela again. Mother's door was closed — usually it was open. I hesitated, then opened it slowly, saying hello.

"Wait, please." Angela was at Mother's bedside with a basin and a sponge. "Oh, Señor Jay" — she pronounced it *Shay* — and seemed relieved.

Mother had not moved; her deafness spared her the shock of my in-trusion. She was propped up on the bed, Angela holding her skinny arm and dabbing at it with the sponge.

I had never seen Mother naked. She was not naked now, but she was nakeder than normal. The ritual of her bath in bed, and Angela with the sponge, revealed more of Mother's body than I'd ever seen, more than I wanted to see. I closed the door behind me but stayed in the doorway, so as not to interrupt Angela in this intimate task. The small dark beauty worked the sponge gently across Mother's arm, and in a tender reflex of concern lifted a stray wisp of hair, twirling it away from Mother's cheek.

"Who's that?" Mother asked, now aware of me.

"You leetle boy," Angela said.

I was staring at Angela's boyish buttocks, the way they tightened in the green scrubs when she leaned toward Mother, how they shifted, slipping against each other, like melons in a sling, when Angela moved from foot to foot.

"It's me — Jay," I called out.

"I leave you now. I come back later," Angela said.

Mother protested, first a squawk, then clinging to Angela, clutching her now, digging her claws into Angela's arm, saying, "No, stay. He can come back."

I signaled that it was okay—a little wave—and withdrew. Mother knew she was in good hands. In my Jeep, driving away, I remembered how, in one of my favorite stories, Tolstoy's "The Death of Ivan Ilyich," it is the earthy peasant boy Gerasim who gives Ivan solace and spiritual sweetness in the pain of his death throes, not any member of Ivan's family, the fractious Golovins.

The formality of Arcadia meant that we visited in relays, signing in, signing out. Mother didn't need us; we didn't need each other. Yet we went on visiting, superstitiously pretending it was not a goodbye.

Mother was not sick. Even now, she took no medicine. One day she surprised me by saying, "I have a dental appointment. Fred's taking me." One-hundred-and-two-year-old molars in for a tune-up. She still had most of her teeth.

She was smaller still, glassy-eyed, shrunken, desiccated, with a twitchy way of reacting, but fully alert, a book open on her table, a half-completed crossword in her lap.

"The print's so small I can hardly read it."

"Maybe you need new glasses?"

"No—it's them. They use less ink these days, so it's gray instead of black," Mother said. "Think they're so smart, saving money on ink!"

Some of the other people in Arcadia tried to attract attention with their ailments—limping, sighing, moaning, complaining how the weather swelled their joints. Mother was conspicuous for her health, boasting of her sound sleep and her energy.

"I'm looking forward to the clambake," she told me.

The jowly woman at the front desk, whose glasses were always propped on top of her head, told me I'd have to register for the clambake and pay in advance. I did so, wondering who else in the family would show up, and speculating on what I'd say to them if they did.

I heard a brass band on the day of the clambake, audible in the lobby as I entered and signed in. A jazz combo— four older men in checkered vests, derby hats, bow ties—was playing "On the Sunny Side of the Street."

And around a table, my brothers and sisters, all of them, I saw with a sinking heart.

"Look who's here."

"It's doo-doo head."

"Jaybird."

"Where's Ma?" I asked.

"On her way," Fred said.

Fred, Floyd, Hubby, Gilbert, Franny, and Rose – the heptad, no spouses — the men gray-haired or bald, the women careworn and misshapen, all of them with their thick forearms braced on the table, as though impatient.

Floyd said, "You're just in time for the pop quiz."

"Sit down, take a load off," Gilbert said.

"Aren't you supposed to be in Wadi Halfa?" I said.

"Wadi El Natrun," Gilbert said promptly. "Natrun for the salt."

"Pipe down," Floyd said. "What was the name of the man who delivered coal to our house for the furnace?"

Just then, Mother appeared in her wheelchair, pushed by Angela, who steered her to the head of the table, then stood behind her, steadying the chair, in attendance.

"The music's too loud," Hubby said.

"Yes, you seem disinhibited as a result," Floyd said. "Ma, we're having a quiz."

A tactful move. In a contentious group, better to create a harmless game, because conversation is dangerous, and games, even wicked ones, were from childhood our mode of interaction.

"His name was Audie Jackson," Mother said to the first question. "He carried the coal in bags on his back and dumped them into the iron chute that led to the coal cellar. He brought us ice in the summer."

"What was Dad's name in the minstrel show, and what song did he sing?"

"He called himself Mr. Bones," Mother said. "He sang 'Mandy, is there a minister handy.' I played the piano. All his practice gave him a sore throat."

"I wasn't alive then," Gilbert said.

"I was," Hubby said. "But I don't remember it."

"What was the one thing I yearned for all through childhood but never got?" Floyd said. "Cowboy boots. What was Dad's business?"

Mother said, "Shoes."

"Dad had the front page of two Boston newspapers nailed to the wall of his workshop," Floyd said. "What did the headlines say?"

"'War Is Over,'" Mother said. "'Peace at Last.' The *Globe* and the *Traveler.*"

"Mum wins the quiz," Floyd said, as Mother beamed, turning to look at Angela.

In the few minutes of Floyd's quiz the table was harmonious, or at least calm and attentive, but with Floyd announcing Mother as the winner, a restlessness overtook it — the table itself rocked a little, and Rose grunted.

"Quit kicking me," Rose said to Hubby. "Are you doing that on purpose?"

"If I was doing it on purpose you'd be crippled."

"I'm wicked hungry," Franny said.

"Yeah, you look like you're wasting away," Floyd said.

"It's a buffet," Gilbert said. "Kind of a walking thing."

Fred said, "For Mum's sake, let's be civil."

"Where's the fun in that?" Floyd said and, pointing to me, "Jay carried from his mother's womb a fanatic heart."

The band still played, absurdly, old songs that resonated more for being out of tune: "On Moonlight Bay," "Alexander's Ragtime Band," "If You Knew Susie."

"Someone please get me some oysters," Mother said.

Fred stood up, so did Gilbert and Rose, a scramble, competing to get the oysters, and then Hubby pushed past them.

"He's such an asshole," Rose said.

All this while I was glancing at Angela, who held the handles of Mother's wheelchair, standing with a patient smile on her Mayan face. She took no notice of the table, Mother's children, all of us old, most retired, and Mother herself, ancient, indestructible, now tipping raw oysters into her mouth.

"I don't know why I bothered to come," Rose said.

"Maybe it was the irresistible prospect of the buffet," Floyd said.

With a hiss, Rose mouthed an obscenity.

"That's a sibilant fricative," Floyd said. "But of course you knew that."

"We're doing it for Mumma," Franny said.

"I want some buddah for my lobstah," Hubby said, waving a lobster tail he'd speared on his fork. "Buddah, buddah."

Hubby had shaved his head since the last time I'd seen him, and with this cue ball and his plastic lobster bib he looked like a fat baby with a rattle in his fist.

"This music blows," Gilbert said, buttering an ear of corn with swiping motions of his knife.

"Arcadia reminds me of a cruise ship," I said. "The staterooms, the meals, the activities and events. No one goes ashore for any length of time. The ship never arrives."

"A sinking ship," Floyd said. "*Das Narrenschiff.* Allegorical. My beloved Gloria could explicate the Bosch triptych of the same name."

"And you on the poop deck," Hubby said.

"Watch your mouth," Franny said.

"From the Latin *puppis,* as you know," Floyd said. "Meaning 'stern.'" And he raised his glass to Hubby. "Silence was his stern reply."

"Up yours," Hubby said, tracing his fingers lightly over his baldness, as shaven men often do.

"We should be ashamed," Fred said in a low voice, so that Mother couldn't hear — and his whisper caused us to glance at Mother, who had turned to smile at Angela behind her. "Behaving like children."

"Which we are," Floyd said. "Which we will ever be."

This remark, too, provoked us to look at Mother again, perhaps out of self-consciousness. But Mother did not react. Except when she was using her frantic twisted fingers to grip an oyster shell and slip its innards into her upraised mouth, Mother sat like an apparition. She was spectral.

The clambake itself was a clatter of plastic plates and croaking voices, a shuffling scrum to the buffet, and the loud music, a shouting from table to table of old coots. Floyd said it was like being in a well-lighted catacomb of people who'd been mummified in their summer clothes. Hubby told him to shut up. "You think that's the tamale of the lobster," Floyd said, a clot of green paste on his thumb. "But it's snot." And we glanced at Mother again, expecting a reprimand.

But there was nothing, not a flutter, from this delicate and doll-like figure, shrunken to the size of a household god in a corner shrine, and with the same smoky aura. Mother was so insubstantial she was more like a thought, a fugitive idea, a wisp of motherhood, as though woven from cobwebs. That aura was a small flame reduced to a pale glow that was to be venerated, and she was all the more powerful for making no sound.

"Sorry, Ma," someone muttered.

Mother moved her lips—wordless—perhaps she was chewing. But being so dry and withered and odorless, she was an unreadable petrifaction.

We her children were raw meat, big and gray, fat shoulders and crazy hair, or no hair, thick, fleshy, porcine, ursine, sweaty from the effort of cramming lobster claws and corncobs and dripping littleneck clams into our mouths, our lips flecked with wet bits of chewed and bitten clambake.

"I'm tired," Mother said with a blank stare, to no one in particular.

Was she aware of our gluttony and dissension and foolery? If so, she didn't indicate it. She was very deaf, her eyesight was poor, her voice a whisper, but these traits made her statuesque and idol-like. She drew her shawl tighter and said, "Angela?"

"Yes, Mama," Angela said, and wheeled her away.

"Ma ate eighteen oysters," Hubby said.

"I'm never going to do this again," Gilbert said, untying his bib.

"I think we're unanimous on that point," Floyd said. "But what about her next birthday?"

"It's six months off," I said.

"I have to go to a funeral that day," Hubby said. He lifted the front of his shirt, wiped his sweaty face, and mopped his head.

"That's funny," Rose said.

"No, it's not," Franny said.

Floyd unfolded his stained napkin and shook it open, intoning, "The Shroud of Turin, fully authenticated. You came to mock—you will stay to pray."

Rose was about to curse when Fred, looking beyond us, raised his hand in a cautioning way, his face reddening.

A young man and woman had approached our table. The man wore a blue blazer and white slacks, his sunglasses propped on his head, expensive loafers, no socks—stylish. The woman, in a wide-brimmed straw hat and a floral print dress, was fresh-faced and smiling in a submissive and grateful way, probably from nervousness.

"Sorry to interrupt. Hey, we've been checking you out and it looks like you're having an awesome time," the man said. "I'm Chase, this is Laura." He nodded with exaggerated approval, surveying our impudent faces, our splashed clothes, the wreckage of our meal—shells and bones and the garbage of our leavings.

"What can we do for you?" Fred said.

"We're with my parents, just here for the day, getting acquainted. They're looking for a senior option. Great clambake, nice place. Ate my head off..."

"But we were wondering," the woman said.

"Yeah," the man said with this cue. "How do you guys like living here at Arcadia?"

56

ANGELA

WHAT STAYED IN MY MIND: Mother, the skeletal idol, like a starved Madonna, and Angela, the Mexican beauty, upright behind her, steadying her wheelchair—Angela especially.

Using the clambake and my concern for Mother as a pretext, I called Angela on her cell phone and asked for news. Had Mother found it tiring, and did she have enough to eat, and by the way, there was a restaurant in Hyannis, Cholo's Cantina, and was she, Angela, interested in going out for a drink or a meal?

The hum on the line was like the whirr of her suspicion, processing my questions.

Then, "What you want, Shay?"

I want relief from being immobilized by Mother. I need a lift after the humiliation of the clambake, especially being mistaken for a resident of an old folks' home. A night out, a bit of human warmth, a break from my routine of writing, propped on my left hand, scribbling slowly with my right, amid the crumbs of my kitchen table. A smile, a word, anything, please.

"Just to see you," I said as casually as I could. The hum came again, the whirr of suspicion, prompting me. "Maybe talk about my mother."

"You mother very nice."

"She likes you so much."

Still, Angela hesitated, but I pressed harder — Mother, Mother — and she relented, saying okay without much encouragement.

"I'll pick you up."

Angela's house was the sort of small, brown-shingled box that was numerous on the back roads of the Cape, where the seasonal workers, the menials, and the poorer vacationers stayed — pine needles thick on the roof and clogging the gutters, the tin downspout askew, the paving stone walkway overgrown, the split-rail fence that fronted the road in need of repair, the stunted shrubs and scrawny trees and dead hydrangeas proof that it was a place built on sand. All this was obvious, and I saw it with sympathy, because it was a house much like my own.

"Hello." She was at the door, dressed up and ready, blocking the entrance, as though not wishing me to linger and see who else was inside, or the sorry condition of the interior.

Looking past her, I could see the backs of three heads, two women and a man laughing, watching a rerun of *The Golden Girls,* too absorbed to notice me. Kitchen help from Arcadia, Angela explained, whispering their Brazilian names.

"I don't want them to know that I see you." She sighed. "I don't want to make a problem."

"I understand."

"Nice *coche,*" she said, buckling herself into my old Jeep. "Good for where I live — good for bad roads." She meant her home in Mexico.

This was what I wanted to hear. I saw myself driving down a rutted country road in a sunny valley, Angela by my side, clinging to the handle on the dashboard, leaving a cloud of dust behind.

"Where is your village?"

"In Chiapas — so far away."

"Not far," I said. "I was there not long ago, in a place near Ocosingo."

"That's nice. You went to San Cristóbal? You see the churches?"

"I loved the churches. I loved the mountains and the Río Jataté." She smiled hearing the familiar name. "We can drive there, four or five days to Texas, then the *frontera*."

"Ha," she said, like a throat-clearing, without mirth, staring straight ahead.

"I'm serious. We could go anytime."

Angela said, "And who take care you mother?"

My giddiness abated. Angela was young, but she was practical. Perhaps if the other Angela, Mother's adored child, had not died but had grown and matured, she would have been the same: sensible, devoted to Mother, not susceptible to a man's idle promises. I knew from traveling in hungry, hard-up countries that the poor grew up fast, were burdened early in their lives, had children when they were young, saw starvation in laziness, pounced on opportunities. Frivolity was a trap. Hungry, like prey animals —and who could blame them?—they never ceased to be alert.

"I never see this road before."

I had taken a detour from the Mid-Cape Highway, through Yarmouth and by back roads to Hyannis.

"It's the quick way."

"I have no *coche*."

And then we were at Cholo's Cantina, quiet on a weekday evening, and walking up the ramp under the awning, I met the gaze of a woman smoking, her arms crossed. After rapid scrutiny of Angela she frowned at me, having decided that I was an old pig. What was I doing with this young attractive woman? I had to be exploiting her. The woman kept looking with scorn as we entered the restaurant, and my nerve failed me: perhaps I was the pig she took me to be.

"What this place?" Angela was compact and watchful after we were shown to a booth.

"Mexican food."

Angela smiled at the illustrated menu. "Maybe this is food. But this not Mexican."

"No *tamales chiapaneca*," I said, and she smiled. "We can leave."

She shrugged. Her shrug said, "It doesn't matter," and now I concluded, from her hesitation on the phone, from her talk, from these twitches in her posture, that she was a skeptic, the natural reaction of someone who is used to being cheated, underpaid, lied to, and used.

She was right to be on her guard. She didn't know what I wanted. *I* didn't know what I wanted. But I thought, there and then: Do I want to be here with her? Yes.

With distaste, she opened her napkin and scrubbed the tines of her fork, then polished the knife and spoon, saying "*Sucio.*"

After the waitress's "Get you guys a beverage?," after the complimentary chips and salsa, after the ritual of ordering and eating, after my *mariscos* and Angela's *pollo,* after she repeated "This not Mexican," I said, "Tell me about your village."

"You no want to hear about you mother?"

"Yes, I do," I said in a panic, as if she'd caught me in a ruse. "Tell me, how is she?"

"She very nice," Angela said, dabbing sauce from her lips. "She like creamy soup. She no want crunchy—hard to eat. She always smile to me, and say thank you, and I do nothing, just my work."

"My mother used to be so fierce," I said. "*Fuerte.*"

"*Feroz,*" Angela said, lightly correcting me.

"Very tough. Very hard." With facial expressions and gestures I described Mother as she had been for so long: a tyrant, a dragon, an intimidator. But Angela simply stared at me, said nothing, scowled. "She was impatient and unpredictable—you understand?"

At last Angela shook her head, not in disagreement but in a pained wince of sympathy, as though witnessing my obvious mistake, or worse, my stupidity.

"You mother," she said. "Seven children, big and small. Maybe sometimes little money. Always tired, from work, from making food."

Angela's certainty annoyed me. I said, "You know that?"

"Yes, I know that," she said. "I know when I see her." Angela used her fingers to dramatize the way she'd seen Mother, like a sorceress gesturing to her flashing eyes.

"What else do you know?" I asked.

If this meal had started with the promise, however slight, of romance or any flirtation, that promise had faded. I resented the turn this discussion had taken, the knowingness of someone whose experience of Mother was limited to a matter of months. But Angela was undaunted.

"I know you mother had a hard life," she said softly, nodding again.

I had no answer to that: she was right. I had never spent any time reflecting on Mother's upbringing, thinking only of my own. In her straightforward declaration, Angela explained Mother — who she was, who she'd been, why she was the person she'd become. A hard life was part of it.

"That's true."

And Angela didn't know the rest. Two world wars, the Great Depression, Dad's business failures, the disruptions of moving from the small, overcrowded bungalow to the large, drafty house that resembled a cereal box. The strange season of Mr. Bones, the frugality and false economy, a scrimping life of hand-me-downs and dented cans, the precarious belief in a life based on faith: that we'd be safe, that things would work out, all the time law-abiding, tax-paying, churchgoing, determined to be respectable and decent. Mother's century, as Gilbert had described it at Mother's hundredth.

Without knowing any of the details, Angela divined this, as if her own hard upbringing had given her insights and an enlarged awareness of motherhood.

"How old are you?"

She smiled. "Not a good question."

I took this to mean older than I guessed. I said, "It's a compliment. You're young but you are wise. You know? *Intelligente — sabia.*"

"*Sabia* — no. But I have a mother also."

"And father?"

"He is dead, from making an accident."

"I'm sorry to hear that."

"So long ago, when I was a small girl," she said. "My mother has three children. I have to help. That is why I come here — to send money."

"Your mother, is she in Chiapas?"

"Yes. In a small village in the countryside."

"I like those words. A small village in the countryside."

Angela smiled at last. "Yes. I miss my home. I want to be there sometimes. But is necessary to be here, for work. For money."

"You have chickens?"

"You are funny. Yes, chickens. Ducks in the pool by the river. Pigs also. Gardens. A maize field. A bean field."

And I saw it, the small village in the river valley, perhaps not far from where I'd spent a happy week near La Soledad, a cluster of houses in a grove of trees, at the end of a rutted road, chickens pecking in the door-yard, ducks gliding in the pool, a pig tottering in the distance. The deep green foliage on the slope of the sierra beyond the field of corn, the high Mexican sky, a vagrant mariachi sound—guitar, accordion, violin, the plonking accompaniment to this pastoral vision.

I easily found a place for myself in it, from what I'd discovered on my Mexican journey, the abandoned B. Traven piece—on a chair on the veranda or in a hammock strung between trees. I had idealized the ano-nymity of Traven, the solitary wanderings of Ambrose Bierce, the mule rides of Graham Greene.

"Your village, is it near San Cristóbal?"

"No, far from the city. But there is a bus from Las Angostura."

Malcolm Lowry drinking himself silly in Veracruz, Trotsky the refu-gee in Coyoacán. D. H. Lawrence griping in Oaxaca.

Mexico, a country that was kind to exiles, had a place for me, some-thing secure and remote, where I could support myself on my monthly Social Security check, eating the food I loved, living in the bosom of a little family, a real family.

"It is a poor village," Angela said. She was shrewd: she knew from my silence that I was lost in a pastoral reverie.

"How poor?"

"Water from the river—not a clean river. No electric. The road very bad. The bus only go to Las Angostura."

"What's the name of your village?"

"Villaflores."

"A village called Villaflores cannot be bad. And it's home."

She said, "Where is your mother, is always home."

Perhaps she thought she was deflating my vision by calling the village poor. But no, after what I'd seen of the wealthy world, a poor village was where I wished to be.

Where's Jay? I imagined people saying — editors, other writers, readers, people to whom I owed money. *He's gone to Mexico. He's in some village — no one knows where.*

My magazine assignment had been a rehearsal for this. Did I really want to vanish, or was it a bid for attention? It didn't matter. It was a cure for my rancorous family, and Angela might be part of the plan. And I thought, If no one knew where I was, I would remain myself, intact.

"Now we go," she said.

In the Jeep, I drove up-Cape, toward Centerville, on back roads.

"This is different," Angela said, leaning forward, straining against her seat belt to see better. "This is not the same way."

"It's quicker," I said. But she shook her head. She'd remembered the route we'd taken, and this was not it. "Don't worry."

She said, "When people say 'Don't worry,' that is when I worry."

I liked that. Even her doubt, her harsh and humorless scrutiny, her unforgiving memory, impressed me, because they were clear signs of intelligence and her experience of the world. She's right, I thought, why didn't it occur to me? Mother had a hard life.

Out of the blue, just before the Centerville turnoff, she said, "You brothers and you sisters visit the mother. They stay for some few minutes, then they leave. And for hours and hours mother is alone, calling 'Angela.'"

"Why don't they stay longer?" I asked, to test her.

"They just want to see, 'Is she alive?' 'Yes, she is alive. Now we go.'"

I had come to a stop, deliberately parking under a streetlight so she wouldn't feel threatened.

"What is this place?"

"My house."

She sighed. "No. Please. Take me to my house."

I almost said, Don't worry, but thought better of it, fearing it would frighten her. I said, "I want to show you where I live. If you see this, you will know me better." I took her by the hand. "I want you to know me better. I want to know you. Maybe we can be friends. Maybe I'll call you Angelita."

"Angelita," she said quietly. "It is the name we give to the dead child."

"I'll remember that."

I slipped out of the Jeep and went to my front door, reached in, and switched on the lights, including the lantern on the post by the sidewalk. And then I waited.

At last Angela followed, looking from side to side, her animal alertness giving her an intense gaze and an efficient way of walking, slightly crouched, seeming smaller in her watchfulness, prepared to flee.

She hesitated by the front door, then stepped aside. I saw it all with her eyes: the big worn sofa and the footstool piled with old newspapers, the cream-colored lampshade, brown in spots from the scorch marks of hot bulbs, the stacks of books on the floor, some of them open, and the kitchen table — my notebooks, my pens, my laptop on the side — it all looked messy, secondhand, temporary, and the house a brown-shingled box.

"What do you see?" I asked.

She shook her head, then shrugged.

"I'm a writer," I said. "This is what a writer's house looks like."

"Like my house," she said.

"We can go now," I said, but the front door was still open.

I wanted to show her that I had no money, I was not a rich American, my Jeep was old, I lived in a nest of papers and books. It was no good telling her that I was hard up; she needed to see it. This messy house, this table of notebooks and pens — this is who I am.

My mention of leaving seemed to give her confidence. She moved away from me, entered the house, took a turn around the living room, peered into the kitchen, glanced at the bedroom. I liked her courage, her curiosity, her scrutiny.

Back in the Jeep I said, "What do you think?"

She considered the question, sighed a little in a way that I was now used to, and then, "You have no picture of mother in your house."

Now I evaluated everything I did and said from Angela's point of view. In the past, for years, I saw my actions from the perspective of my brothers and sisters, and I felt I was no worse than they were — often I felt superior. With Angela's scrutiny things were different. I saw how little I gave to

Mother, how I was without sentiment, how it was all a competition with my siblings, my reacting to them. I recalled how, after the clambake, Angela wheeled Mother back to her apartment while the siblings quarreled and were easily mistaken for senile residents of Arcadia.

In the following days and weeks I saw Mother more often. I saw Angela too, both at Arcadia and on the nights when she was free. After the first few nights she seemed to feel safe with me, and she grew bold enough to poke me in the chest to make a point. Now and then I held her hand or took her by the waist. We did not go back to Cholo's Cantina, but we found other congenial places — a sushi restaurant, a bar overlooking Hyannis's inner harbor, a pizza joint in Centerville.

On one of my visits to Arcadia Mother said, as Angela was leaving the room, "You should find someone like her." This was the old assertive Mother, issuing a directive, tapping an insistent finger.

I said, "I've already found her."

When I mentioned this to Angela later, she said, "You want me?"

I said, "Yes."

She said, "You know me?"

This was by the back door at Arcadia, where I'd found her, in her green scrubs, holding a heart-rate monitor, a stethoscope, a Velcro sleeve, a gauge, and I was impressed that she had some nursing skills.

I did not crowd her. She had said that she didn't want the people at Arcadia to know we were seeing each other. Anyone happening by would have concluded that here was the son of a resident inquiring about his mother from one of the staff. All this was conducted in whispers.

"I don't know you," I said.

She smiled. She had made her point.

"But I want to know you," I said quickly as she hurried away. It had been a hot whisper; I was not sure that she heard me.

All that in about three weeks — winter weeks of early darkness, of fat white snowflakes, of dirty snow and yellow ice by the roadside. No wonder when we met that I fantasized about the green sunlit valleys of Chiapas, the wheel tracks through the dusty woods, and me swinging in a hammock, the life I had imagined on my previous visit, improbably with Luma.

Angela's work at Arcadia — her busy days and few free evenings — reminded me of how idle I was. I had not retired; if you didn't have a job in the first place, how could you retire? But the day was mine to use as I wished. I wrote every morning, but if I had a productive morning, I spent the rest of the day reading, running errands, or walking along Dowses Beach, anything, provided there was no chance of running into my brothers or sisters. That also meant studying the parking lot at Arcadia, to make sure I was alone with Mother.

I told this to Angela, the part about her being busy and my being free to do as I wished.

She had a way of sizing me up. I knew she was thinking hard, not about what I'd told her, but the implications of it, weighing them with her skeptical mind.

She said, "If you have so much time, why you no visit you mother?"

"Yes, I should go more often."

"Yes."

I saw what she wanted from me — proof of my virtue, evidence of my loyalty, making an effort to see Mother. It was the only way she could know who I was. Angela had never mentioned my age, or the difference in our ages. She had a single imperative: she wanted someone who was true. It was no good my making promises or telling her who I was. She needed to see me in action, being a loving son to this old woman.

I went there the next day. I brought a bouquet of flowers and a box of chocolates.

"What's that?"

"Flowers."

"Put them over there," she said, not looking at them.

"How are you, Ma?"

"No complaints."

Then she stared past me, her eyes clouded. I wanted to leave this stillness, Mother's hands folded on her lap on the open newspaper, on the table the jar of peanut butter, the alarm clock, a bird carving, the day's menu printed on a sheet of paper, a check mark next to *Meatloaf.*

I forced myself to stay and hoped somehow that Angela would notice. I would do this every day if need be; I wanted to convince her of my worth. And, sitting before Mother — who said nothing, who seemed to see nothing, who was like a masterpiece of human taxidermy — I saw a loveliness in her, all her furious selves burned away. What remained was the essence of the woman, the essential Mother. The fight had left her, and the residue was sweetness, fragility, and grace — and acceptance; she wanted nothing. There was nothing I could do for her, nothing she needed, nothing I could bring, except myself.

I studied her lined face. I could see her skull. Now, almost one hundred and three, she sat, glowing softly, saying nothing. Why had I needed Angela to tell me the simple truth? She'd had a hard life, she had suffered. Why had it been necessary for someone to tell me that?

What was the worst part of growing old? I pondered this in Mother's room, a place that more and more resembled a chapel, and Mother a graven image in it, an example of what it meant to be ancient. The knowledge that at some point you must see that you can't do it all again, with babies and risk and hope. No lover to rescue you, no more lives to live, only the one you're living, which is growing smaller and simpler, more and more like Mother, motionless in a chair, in a still room, the only sound a ticking clock, waiting for the end.

57

BULLETINS

O N EVERY VISIT I made these days Mother would pinch my hand for emphasis and say, with relief and pride, "This is Angela," forgetting that she'd already told me. Whether Mother thought this was her long-ago dead daughter returned to ease her into the afterlife, or simply stating that Angela was a capable caregiver at Arcadia, I did not know.

Then I would see them together, Mother in her chair, Angela beside her, and I was struck — as I had never been, seeing Franny or Rose or any of us with Mother — by the quality of attention, the tender sympathy, Angela giving, Mother accepting, the ideal in piety of Mother and daughter, the roles reversed in Mother's old age. Angela fed her, dabbed her lips, sang to her, tidied her hair, adjusted her shawl, and often bathed her. No wonder Mother was so content, and might well have believed that the much-mourned Angela had reappeared to comfort her. No point trying to argue her out of this, if indeed she believed it; she was too deaf, too slow, too old to reason with. There must have been days when she felt she'd been reunited in heaven with her beloved daughter.

I had a sense of the pleasure Mother felt with Angela, because I felt it too. She was becoming a friend. I was no longer alone. I had someone to tell my stories to, someone to share a meal with, someone new. We went out for pizza, for a drink, for meals in the winter-empty restaurants of the Cape.

"Tell me about your village."

"I told you everything."

"I want more — the priest, the *alcalde,* your neighbors, the weather."

"You were in Chiapas. You know very well what is the weather."

But because she was homesick for her pueblo in the mountains, Villaflores, she went into detail. I heard about the scandals, the local heroes, the boy who became a football star, the woman who made the best tamales, the part of the river where the small boys swam, the day the Federales burned the marijuana fields and everyone was high from the drifting smoke, and the priest, Father Ruiz, who had a secret girlfriend and two children. Of villagers who had crossed the border to the United States with the help of coyotes and the cartels, how they were working on farms in California. Angela's trips by bus to the coast, to La Angostura and San Cristóbal.

Telling me these stories, Angela became sad and sentimental, would fall silent, and then, "When I has enough money I will go home."

"And get married and have children," I said, testing her.

She laughed, saying, "That is for someone else."

I posed no threat to her virtue. I knew how to be a friend. I listened, encouraged her, praised her. She helped me with the subjunctive: *Si hablara español mejor, no tendría que ir a clase,* If I spoke Spanish better, I wouldn't have to go to class. *Llámame cuando quieras,* Call me whenever. *Si yo fuera rico,* If I were a rich man . . .

She said, "I don't know what you want from me."

I wanted what any man might want: one night to hear a soft knock on my door, to find Angela outside on the steps, her hair drawn into a brush on the back of her head, her eyes lustrous, a slightly drunken smile on her face, her skin so smooth, in a black cape and red shoes on her small feet — unexpected, nine at night, perhaps — smiling, and as she reached for me her cape falling open, revealing her in lacy underclothes, a short nightgown or lingerie, maybe holding a bottle of wine. Male fantasy, the better for remaining a fantasy.

Angela was not beautiful. I wanted to tell her: I hate great acting, great beauties make me laugh, great meals are ridiculous. Angela had health, she had strength, she was graceful, so she had power. She was loyal and kind and capable, and she was the right size. She was someone you'd trust with your life, or your mother's life.

"What do I want?" I said. "I want you to do what you've been doing — helping my mother."

She was not only resourceful, she was calm, and that had the effect of soothing Mother. I often found Angela kneeling before Mother, massaging her feet, gently working her hands over the sharp bones and stringy sinews, the arthritic joints swollen to lumps.

"For the circulation," Angela said.

"This is Angela," Mother said, stroking Angela's hair.

"Feel them — they are so cold, so stiff. The pressure point in the feet help the whole body." And she would pinch a toe, saying, "This is her shoulder. Go ahead, feel them. So cold."

"I believe you." I could not bear to touch Mother's bony feet.

After a few minutes, Angela would excuse herself. "You stay with Mother. I come back."

On her return to the room, she'd look closely at me, as if to determine what I'd said or done, because she had suggested that I was too abrupt or did not linger. Angela tried to sense the degree of warmth I'd created in the room.

One of those days she found me in the corridor, heading home. She looked around to see whether anyone was listening and then said in a low voice, "Do you tell Mother you love her?"

"Of course. *Claro.*"

Angela stared at me. Did she know I was lying? I said to myself that I'd tell mother I loved her as soon as I could, and it seemed less of a lie.

"Because that is medicine. Love is medicine."

The strange aspect to this was that I was determined to tell Mother I loved her, less to please Mother than to impress Angela and win her approval. I suspected that underlying Angela's question was her belief that if a man could not tell his mother he loved her, and mean it, how could he enjoy a loving relationship with a woman such as Angela herself? There was a point where amateur psychology overlapped with folk wisdom, two related fields of simplicity and obvious superstition. But I craved Angela's good opinion of me, and hoped obscurely for more than that.

The possibility that this friendship and affection might grow into love made me happy. Why does love matter? Because it offers hope, and most of all because it promises a future. There is a tomorrow in loving. Lovers take risks, they make plans, they believe that years from now they will still be in love, and the intensity of love concentrates the mind and gives it health.

Mature love looks beyond sexual desire — someone my age had known that, its pleasures and deceptions. Someone who'd grown up poor like Angela was especially practical in that matter, since her whole life was dedicated to survival — sex was incidental and risky, desire was a distraction. I had now arrived at the insight and wisdom she'd known for years, that love involved trust, that she needed to be secure, with the assurance that I would protect her and her family. In that respect my being much older was an asset. I had achieved the status of a protector. That was why she needed to see me being more loving with Mother. If I proved that I was protective toward this ancient and fragile woman, Angela would look upon me with greater favor, because in her watchfulness, what she wanted more than fine clothes or a car or jewelry was the survival of her family — a lesson we siblings had not learned from Mother. Angela was not selfish in her instinct to preserve and prevail; she was obeying an animal instinct that made her decisive, and resistant to temptation. I now understood her as triumphant in her animal spirit.

And I had been slumbering. Another aspect to love was its vitality. With Missy Gearhart, my failure as a fiancé, love — or what passed for it

— took the form of work. "You have to work on that," she'd say. "We need to work it out." "You need to work on your attitude." It was all work, the job of living, the obligation to health ("I'm working on my glutes," she also said, lying on the floor and kicking). With Angela my effort was joyous, so I looked forward to pleasing her. It was all an awakening.

Mother, too, had been more alive in these winter weeks. "Take me for a ride"— she meant in her wheelchair, around the public rooms of Arcadia. She did not talk about death or dying. She made plans. "There's a concert next week." It was February. "Presidents' Day there's a dinner."

For Mother there was now a tomorrow, a next week, a next year, a next birthday. It was the confidence of being cared for by Angela, of being loved, though I had yet to say those words to Mother.

A memo from Fred in the form of an emailed bulletin threatened to end it all. He had a habit in his retirement of treating us as junior partners. This behavior was a hint of how he'd managed his law firm, and over the years, as the senior child in the family, there had been so many memos. Once they had come as printed letters, folded into an envelope, or single sheets he'd circulated at family meals. This was an email. I thought that with Mother in Arcadia we'd seen the last of these long-winded memos.

"It has come to my attention," this one began, and then I saw it was headed ANGELA and consisted of five numbered paragraphs and various subsections, alphabetized, with brackets and addenda. I scanned it quickly, growing agitated.

"Fred's the most devious one in the family," Floyd used to say, "so naturally he's the one most prone to suspicion. He believes all people are as tricky as he is."

The memo continued, "Angela spends a great deal of time with Mum. She has become conspicuous in this — in Mum's room, wheeling her outside, and has been observed looking in Mum's drawers, where her valuables are kept."

I had wondered whether this issue might be raised when Franny and Rose claimed that Mother was colder toward them, more distant, that Angela's caregiving was interpreted as manipulative.

"There is an unfortunate tradition," Fred went on, "of caregivers insinuating themselves in the lives of their clients and exerting subtle pressure wherein they end up as substantial beneficiaries, often sole beneficiaries."

He portrayed Angela as a wily, desperate, intrusive, greedy functionary ("Even the authorities at Arcadia have become concerned") who had wheedled her way into Mother's affections and was taking advantage of her.

"The status of her visa or green card needs to be looked into," he wrote, then spoke of another — perhaps the worst — of Angela's transgressions: "There are occasions, as I can testify, when Mother fully believes that Angela is her natural daughter."

There was more, and then an ominous conclusion: "I have asked Arcadia to take appropriate action."

I called Angela. It was late afternoon — she'd be on the food cart, taking meals from room to room. No answer.

In my attempt to reply to Fred, I was so frantic that I kept hitting the wrong keys, and so I got into my Jeep and drove the five miles to Fred's house in Yarmouth. A snowfall that morning, turning to sleet and now a sudden freeze, kept me going slowly, my fury building in my impatience.

Fred was in his driveway, bent over a wide-bladed snow shovel, using his good arm to chip ice from the wheel tracks. In his wool hat and overlarge coat and rubber boots, breathing hard, he reminded me of Dad. But then I, too, probably looked like Dad, who in his retirement became a sort of janitor, enjoying menial chores — sanding, painting, shingling, fixing leaks. Fred heard the Jeep, he glanced up, he turned away, and most annoying of all, with lowered head he went on jabbing his shovel against the layers of ice.

"I just got your email."

"Just got it?" He was facing away from me. "I sent it two days ago."

"I don't check my email every day," I said. "Look, you're making a mistake. Angela is good for Mum."

"I've already taken care of it." Still with his back turned to me, chipping the ice with his clumsy shovel.

"I thought this was a matter for discussion." I wanted to punch his head or snatch his silly hat.

"It was. But you didn't respond." He chunked and hacked at the ice, and that he was clumsy in it made him seem more offensive in his rudeness. "Franny and Rose happen to agree with me."

"Agree with what? Jesus, would you mind stopping for a minute and just look at me?"

He turned slowly to face me — unshaven, angry, with hateful eyes. "I know why you're here," he said. "You think you haven't been seen with your friend Angela?"

"What are you talking about?"

"At the pizza place. Elsewhere."

"What sneak told you that?"

"So it's true, ha."

"We spend most of the time talking about Ma."

He affected a derisive laugh. "Ma — whom you obviously haven't seen for two days. Because if you had, you'd know that she has a new nurse. Not Angela, who, as I said, was manipulating Mum."

"She was feeding her, bathing her, massaging her feet."

"And what was in it for her?" Fred had a way of lifting one eyebrow in a querying way that he probably thought clever, but it made him seem like a stage villain. "More to the point, what was in it for you?"

"You think I was in some sort of conspiracy with Angela to defraud Ma?"

He looked at me with a pretense of incredulity, twitching — more acting — and delivered an actor's cliché. "I honestly don't know what to think."

"Ma depended on Angela," I said, my voice hoarse with anger.

He nodded. "It's called elder abuse."

I only now registered that I had been out of the picture. I had not seen Angela for three days — in my buoyant, confident mood I'd been writing my book. The last matter Angela and I had discussed where Mother was concerned was the big question: Had I told Mother I loved her? I'd said yes, meaning that I'd fully intended to, and I'd been intrigued to find out how Mother would react to an unexpected — and unprecedented — declaration of love.

So the removal of Angela as Mother's nurse and caregiver, the banning her from Mother's room, the implication that she was up to no good and that I was a conspirator in the plot — all of this was old news.

Fred had turned his back. I walked around him and, facing him, said, "Why didn't you mention this about Angela before. At the clambake, say?"

"You didn't ask."

"I didn't ask because Ma was happy!" I said as he swiveled, chipping a low shelf of ice with his shovel. I stepped in front of him. "And healthy."

"She's lost some speed on her fastball."

"What does Gilbert think?"

"He's in Fallujah."

"What about Floyd?"

"He's insane."

"Hubby liked Angela," I said, protesting.

"Until he saw you holding her hand at Punchy's Pizza in Marstons Mills."

Darkness had fallen while we stood bickering in the snow and broken ice of Fred's driveway, and the darkness brought a black frost. The puddles of minutes ago now were topped with a thin ice crust; the wet snow had stiffened and crunched underfoot. I wanted to snatch the shovel from Fred and batter him senseless.

"God, I hate this family."

"Step aside, I'm trying to work."

"I'm going to Arcadia. I'll set them straight. You can't take sole charge like this. Ma was depending on her."

"For money."

"Angela is keeping her alive, you fuckwit."

His back was turned again. "They won't let you in. It's too late. They don't let visitors in after seven."

"I'll go tomorrow. You can't stop me."

"I'll call them," he said with a hiss of threat in his voice. "I'll do it now. I won't let you upset Mum. Her birthday is next week. She's counting on it."

"Call them. Do what you like. There's something I have to tell her — nothing to do with you. I'm going tomorrow."

Though his back was still turned, I heard his mocking "Huh," and at the same time I looked up and saw Erma at the window, backlit by a lamp, her hair glowing.

Trying for a dramatic exit, hurrying to my Jeep, I slipped on the ice, and then I had trouble starting the engine, pounding the gas pedal with my foot and flooding the carburetor. When I got the car started, my wheels spun in the snow as I backed up, skidding, and finally I slewed on the slick road, bumping a snowbank.

And there was no tomorrow, only another bulletin from Fred. I read it when I awoke at nine. My fury with Fred had exhausted me, so I'd slept late.

I have just spoken to Arcadia. Mother passed away peacefully this morning. She was found at 7:20 in her favorite chair, the Cape Cod Times open on her lap to the crossword page, the sun coming through the window.

And then two more paragraphs about funeral arrangements, flowers, and setting out the details for the choices of coffin.

58

STRANGERS

S O, Mother's wake, Mother's funeral. We'd pondered them for decades but never spoke the words aloud. We were spared any anxiety, because they were rituals, with all of a ritual's inevitability. The satisfaction of such a ceremony — a cannibal feast, a high mass, a baptism, a burial — is that it has been rehearsed over the years and keeps you from having to think. Showing up is all that is necessary. Spontaneity is not required — indeed, it is discouraged, as a derangement of the sequence of consoling ceremonial moves. We were putting Mother to rest, and in all the emotion and the potential for disorder — howls, tears, the frenzy of loss — we needed to be contained by a ritual's predictable formulas and its steady tempo, going through the motions.

All over the Cape, in this last week of winter, an overnight thaw had melted much of the dirty, pushed-aside snowpack, thinned and shriveled the scaly plates of surface ice, giving onto gummy black soil in places and making everything messier — wet streets and dripping trees — early signs of mud season, exposing the ugliness of sodden earth, soon to be hacked open for a grave.

In this disorder and uncertainty, the rituals of the wake and the funeral, like the insistent protocols in the burial rites of a savage tribe, kept us in line. We were too old, too confused, and too exhausted to think straight. We needed help in this progress of burying Mother.

Because of the weather, the cold, the wind, the spatters of rain, we wore hats.

The onrush like a tidal flow of strangers or people I barely recognized, and the accumulation of my straggling family — Julian and Harry from London, without wives or children but accompanying their mother, my first wife Diana, and her partner Piers, the photographer; my second wife, Heather, and her new husband; and Melissa Gearhart ("Missy," she said, greeting me, as though I might not recognize her, and I almost didn't), recently divorced, the bullet I had dodged, with Madison now married and with a long-haired child of her own, either a boy or a girl, named Sky; and Mona from long ago with our son Charlie. So much for my irregular past, all of them come to pay respects and venerate Mother, and all of them, young and old, grayer, heavier, somber, like strangers.

My past had woken and risen to gather as in one of those maddening, teasing, overpopulated dreams — this, too, every feature of it, was dreamlike, in the sense of being irrational, improbable, cruel, slow-moving, yet set to its own obscure rhythm, unstoppable, nor could I shake it off.

No one said much. What was there to say? "So sorry." "It was painless." "She had a good life." "I'll miss her." "How you doing?"

The awkward sentiments of people who'd hardly known her, or not known her at all, the unconsoling clichés of strangers, who interrupted us in our grieving, as if having been summoned by Mother to make us even more miserable.

"Your mom was the complete package," someone said to me. A cousin? An in-law? Someone's older child? A beefy balding person, in any case, who gave me a clumsy hug.

His remark made me look at Mother — so small and skinny in her oblong box, doll-like, and so changed since I'd last seen her, wearing makeup. She was another stranger here.

We stood near the open casket at close quarters in the receiving line — Fred, Floyd, Hubby, Gilbert, Franny, Rose, and me, greeting relatives whose names I hardly knew, accepting the sighs of sympathy and the chorus of clucking.

In a far corner of the room at this funeral home, Angela stood, her hands clasped, too shy to sit, her face glowing with tenderness, her eyes fixed on the casket, the wisp of Mother lying lengthwise, her bony fingers intertwined on her pink blouse.

In the past, birthdays and weddings we'd regarded as occasions for settling old scores, for teasing remarks and cruel exit lines. *Take that!* But a funeral was different, hushed voices, solemn expressions, no sudden movements; it was a ritual of suppression, of whispers and subdued emotions.

Children, grandchildren, great-grandchildren—a tangle of them. Who were they? Whom did they belong to? What were their names? More strangers, the vassals and outliers of the far-off country known as Mother Land.

"How are you doing, Dad?" Julian asked, hugging me. He was much taller than me, and the hug was a comfort.

"As usual, thinking about *David Copperfield*."

"I love him," Jonty said. He'd been standing near, and now I stared at him in pity. "I took Loris and Jilly to see him in Vegas."

Jonty, once an imp, was middle-aged and leathery. He said he jogged. Benno and Bingo looked dowdy. Fred's kids conferred among themselves. His son Jake had become immensely wealthy, having transitioned from computer programming to creating iPhone apps that variously detected gluten, peanuts, monosodium glutamate, or high-fructose corn syrup in restaurant meals. "You point your phone at the food," he said, and still holding his phone, Jake swiped at it, showing photos of his yacht in the Maldives.

"Remember when you ate the Styrofoam cup?" Hubby said, craning his neck at the photos.

"Montaigne was wrong about death," Floyd said. "He claimed that people who died when they were old were not whole. 'God shows mercy to those from whom he takes away life a little at a time'—an advantage of growing old. You're killing off half a person, or a quarter, he says. No! Ma was all there. She was working out a clue to a crossword at the very end. Is it tactless to ask what the word was? I feel a poem coming on."

For relief, I went over to Angela and hugged her. I was comforted by having her to hold, fitting her body to mine, the vitality in her arms, flesh and blood, the reassurance of her strength. I was more upright next to her.

"She loved you," I said, "like a daughter."

Angela was too moved to speak. She believed in the afterlife: Mother was in a Mexican heaven, with flowers and frilly dresses and mariachi men in floppy sombreros plunking guitars. For Angela, Mother wasn't dead but had simply moved on to her reward, the next level, an eternal fiesta.

"Thanks for coming," I said.

She clutched my hand, warming it, allowing blood to throb through it. And then she let go — a man nearby was staring at me.

"You probably don't remember me," I said. I'd been saying it all day. "I'm Jay."

He was a pink-faced man with a white mustache and white hair, yellowing in parts. He said, "We're from the neighborhood."

"Mother was so sorry to leave the neighborhood. Which house did you live in?"

"No, this neighborhood," he said, in the cranky way of someone being corrected, and he jerked his thumb out the window.

"You knew my mother?"

"No, we . . ." He faltered in annoyance and looked away.

The woman beside him spoke up. "We normally go for a drive down-Cape on Saturdays. But the streets are unsafe with the black ice."

"So you decided instead to come to my mother's wake?"

The woman chewed at me in a hostile way and sighed as a sort of objection, while the mustached man took a plastic inhaler out of his pocket and sucked on it like a stoner with a bong. The other couple stood in wet feet on the carpet, clenching and unclenching their fingers.

"I don't see what the problem is," the man with the inhaler finally said.

Before I could speak, Rose — who'd sidled over to listen — said, "I think it's time for you people to go." She spoke with such ferocity, all four strangers left. Then Rose turned her back on me.

"They're closing the coffin," Fred called out.

We took turns kneeling before Mother's body.

I was last. I formed the three words in my head, then whispered them to Mother's floury face and looked for a reaction. Mother seemed to be smiling — her smile of triumph, one I knew well.

• • •

The funeral mass was another helpful ritual, everyone with a role to play, the same people from the wake and more, the vast unrecognizable extended family. I had always thought of my family as a small angry knot of quarrelers, but this was a crowd with certain features in common, round-shouldered shufflers, close-set eyes, dangling arms, the related citizens of Mother Land.

It had been so long since I'd entered a church I simply followed along, grateful for the ritual. I found no comfort in the prayers, but they helped pass the time—the mutterings, the hand gestures, the blessings, the swinging thurifer, the swirling smoke of the incense. Then from the pews, the sobs and honks of grief, like idiot laughter.

All a waste, I thought, my life in Mother Land, among my fractious family, every one of them in this church venerating Mother's polished sepulcher, containing not just Mother's remains but (as I imagined in my feverish grief) a whole epoch, the ragged fury of jostling bodies and grasping hands and crow-like voices. I couldn't pray it away. I seemed to be sorrowing for Mother, but I was sorrowing for myself. I saw with shame that I'd endured it, or rather, it had poured through me, as Floyd had once described the human body—my meat and plumbing.

But I was still here, more alive for being old. Julian and Harry on either side of me, and nearby, Charlie, on his knees, his head down, praying to the woman who had denounced his birth as shameful. He had entered my life as a mistake, and now was a blessing. We were alive, we were quick, we kept moving, and I contemplated his accidental origin, my hard year, my best year, my expulsion from the family—his, too.

Exile had saved me. Only in my old age and in Mother's ancient lastingness had I understood her as my muse. To tell that story I'd need to build on the bigger story, of my family. I had gone away to make my life, I had returned at Dad's death, and I had stayed for Mother's long decline. And there she lay, in the big box parked in the center aisle.

Learn to forget, people say. Let go. Give it a rest. Don't brood. But that's the worst advice for a writer. It is necessary to remember, even to brood, and writing helps you to remember, and at last to forget. Not to write about Mother, or to falsify or prettify her, was wasteful. To see her clearly, and re-create her on the page, was to give her life and make her matter. Sitting there in church, I felt the surge of survivor's strength that had always vitalized Mother at a funeral. I was up to the task, for my life in Mother Land had been an immense journey, of the sort I'd taken many times and recounted in books, and this had all the aspects of the travel books I had loved from childhood, in the genre of *Wrecked on Cannibal Island.*

Nothing was wasted, and though I'd regretted being summoned back from Mexico for Mother's final years, perhaps that too had been essential, as a rehearsal for another departure, another life.

Angela sat at the back, her head lowered, mourning, and at the end of the service, as we passed her, the seven of us as pallbearers, kicking beside the casket on a rubber-wheeled gurney, I glanced at her tragic eyes. Then I beckoned, and took her hand and guided her, so that Angela joined us, making a symmetrical eight pallbearers, four a side.

The procession of cars in sunshine along the back roads and by snowy fields and bare trees; then the gravesite, more ritual, more prayers, and a shake and spatter of holy water from the gold aspergillum, while we stood, dumb in the trampled snow, the core group of siblings and Angela. Behind us, the cluster of ex-wives, former girlfriends, children, stepchildren, grandchildren, great-grandchildren, nameless and bewildered citizens, from the remotest parts of Mother Land. Up front, next to Mother's casket, a young priest was intoning a prayer and making hand signals over an open holy book, a complete stranger, speaking to God, recommending Mother, invoking her name.

"The ground's too frozen to dig," someone said softly. It might have been Hubby. "Even a backhoe. Even a jackhammer."

"So what'll they do?" I asked.

Someone mumbled, someone gargled, but I could tell — even grunts and mutters are identifiable and familial — they were uttered by my siblings. Our grunts were nothing at all like other people's grunts, or utterances. Floyd was murmuring to a nephew, "Van Gogh said life was probably round."

"Maybe store the casket somewhere?"

Someone sighed a familiar sigh.

"Because if they don't get the hole dug today, what happens?"

The varnished wooden box containing Mother was propped on a pallet, surrounded by flowers, a wreath on top, the young priest still absorbed in his incantations.

"What's with all the questions, Jay?" someone said — it sounded like Rose.

"Just wondering."

"What for?" A harsh accusing whisper. "You writing a book?"

Hubby said in a teasing voice, "Leave this chapter out. Make it a mystery."

Just then a small warm hand found mine and calmed me, and I hung on.

No one spoke again, no need to. Mother was gone, and she'd taken part of us with her.

After decades of tribal warfare — furious, bloody, hurtful, wounding — this funeral gathering was a minor crisis, two days of low-grade anxiety. Finally, it's over.

Like strangers jammed together in an elevator stuck between floors, we hold our breath. At last the confining thing coughs, then starts again and trembles down the shaft, and jolts at the ground floor, the doors slipping open. Released to the fresh air of sudden freedom, we disperse in silence, eight of us, and don't look back.

A wide blade of afternoon sun slants through the cemetery trees, surprises the remnants of eroded snow twisted among the tombstones and turns all of it golden. A warmer wind lifting from the southwest tickles a sweetness from the earth, a foretaste of spring. Another peculiar day.

Villaflores, Chiapas, 2015